authors by registering for the free monthly newsletter at
www.orbitbooks.co.uk

Praise for L.E. Modesitt, Jr.

'Resplendent . . . fantasy with an inventive and expertly
handled scenario, life-sized characters and flawless
plotting'

Kirkus Reviews

'An intriguing fantasy in a fascinating world'

Robert Jordan

'Fascinating! A big, exciting novel of the battle between
good and evil and the path between'

Gordon R. Dickson

'Modesitt has created an exceptionally vivid secondary
world, so concretely visualized as to give the impression
that Modesitt must himself have dwelt there'

L. Sprague de Camp

L·E Modesitt JR

THE ORDER WAR

orbit

www.orbitbooks.co.uk

I

CHAOS-BUILDING

1

Justen watched from the smooth stones of the oldest pier in Nylan as the *Shierra* pulled away and out into the channel. The black iron plate of the deckhouse and single turret glistened in the morning sunlight, and the four-span gun pointed forward like a black staff aimed at chaos.

A thin line of white water flowed aft from the newest warship of the Mighty Ten as she eased out into the Gulf of Candar between the twin breakwaters that dated back to the building of Nylan itself.

The young man in engineers' black brushed a hand through his short and light brown hair before glancing at the three students. 'Watch closely, with just your eyes, after she clears the breakwater.'

'Watch what?' asked the thin, redheaded boy.

'The ship, silly,' answered the stocky girl.

'Why?' questioned Norah, a petite and big-eyed blonde girl.

'Watch,' repeated Justen.

As heat pulsed from the *Shierra*'s funnel, visible only as a wavering of the greenish-blue sky to the west, white streaks seemed to flow back from the bow as the black warship built up speed. Suddenly, both wake and ship vanished, leaving only the heat lines across the western sky.

'What happened?' asked Daskin, the redhead, a hand raised to scratch his thick, curly hair.

'The Brother raised his shields, of course, just like we're going to be taught to do.' The stocky girl, Jyll, did not quite snort her disgust, but flipped her hair away from Daskin.

Justen stepped back to avoid swallowing long, black, loose

tresses. He did not contradict her statement about being taught shielding, but it would be years before any of these three were ready – at least from what he could tell, but that, thankfully, was not his decision.

'Let's go.' He turned uphill, and the three students followed, Norah trailing, her eyes still turning seaward toward the heat lines that were the only trace of the *Shierra*. A light breeze, bearing a remnant of chill from the later winter, ruffled his black overtunic.

As they passed the armory, a lanky, red-haired woman in green emerged.

'Krytella!' Justen waved.

'Justen. I'll walk up to the classroom building, if you're headed that way.' Krytella smiled. 'Do you know if Gunnar's anywhere around?'

'No. He's up at Land's End, studying the Founders' records of the Change.' Justen tried to keep his voice level. Gunnar, always Gunnar, as if his older brother were the great Creslin himself.

'Are there any? Real records, I mean?'

'I suppose there must be. Dorrin certainly left records.' Justen stopped outside of the long and low black stone building that almost seemed part of the grassy hillside.

'But he was an engineer.'

'He also wrote *The Basis of Order*. Most of it, anyway.' Justen gestured at the three students. 'You can get something from the fruit table in the dining hall. Then we'll meet in the corner room.'

'Thank you, Magister Justen,' the three chorused.

'I'm not a magister, just a junior engineer of sorts,' Justen observed, but the three had already trooped off.

'How can you be happy offering beginning order-instruction to spoiled kids?' asked Krytella.

'Why not? Someone has to, and—' Justen stopped, realizing that once again Krytella had compared him, unfavorably, to his older brother. He forced a grin and continued. '—and I'd better catch up with them before they eat all the fruit.'

'Tell Gunnar I need to talk to him.'

'I will, but you'll likely see him before I do.'

'Have fun with your students.'

'Thank you.'

The three had not eaten all the dried fruit, having left at least half of it. In passing the snack table, Justen grabbed several dried pearapple sections and stuffed them in his mouth. He chewed and swallowed quickly. Then he walked down the stairs to the belowground corridor that bisected the sunken indoor garden. The garden separated the dining wing from the classrooms.

The three looked up from their cushions as he closed the door.

'Take out your *Basis of Order*. Let's take a look at the third section of the first part, page fifty – the part about the concentration of order.' Justen waited as they paged through the books that were still too stiff, as if the only time they read was when Justen insisted. 'Would you read it, Norah?'

The wide-eyed blonde cleared her throat. '. . . a staff, or any other object, may be infused with order. If the Balance is maintained, concentrating such order must result in a greater amount of chaos somewhere else. Therefore, the greater the effort to concentrate order within material objects, the greater the amount of free chaos within the world.'

'What does that mean, Daskin?'

'I don't know, Magister.'

'All right. You read the words, the same words.'

'The same words?'

Justen nodded.

'. . . a staff, or any other object . . .' Daskin repeated the words already read aloud by Norah.

'Now, what does it mean?'

Daskin sighed. 'I guess it's something about why the engineers don't put order into everything they build.'

Justen nodded at Jyll.

'Is that why there are only ten of the black iron ships?' she asked.

'How much order goes into building a ship like the *Shierra*?' Justen probed.

'Lots, or you wouldn't have asked,' Norah said, grinning.

'How much iron would it take to build a hundred ships?'

'But iron's stronger, isn't it?' asked Daskin.

'You can grow more oaks and firs, but you can't grow more iron. Once you've taken iron out of the earth, it's

used. Once you remove that iron from the high hills . . .
then what?'

All three looked blankly at the floor.

'What holds Recluce together?'

'Order,' the three muttered.

'What does iron do?'

'Holds order.'

'Fine. What happens if we take all the iron out of the high
hills? Why do you think we try to buy as much iron as we can
from Hamor, or even from Lydiar?'

'Oh . . . That keeps more order in Recluce?'

'Right.' Justen forced a smile. 'Let's look at the question of
limits. Where will you find that, Jyll?'

The stocky girl shrugged.

Justen took a deep breath instead of yelling. He waited before
saying, 'Look toward the end of the opening chapters. All of
you. Tell me when you find something.'

Justen walked from one corner of the room to the other. Had
he and Gunnar been so slow?

The three students continued to page slowly through *The Basis
of Order*.

Finally, Norah raised a hand. 'Is this it?' She cleared her
throat, then began to read slowly: 'If order or chaos be without
limits, then common sense would indicate that each should have
triumphed when the great ones of each discipline have arisen.
Yet neither has so triumphed, despite men and women of power,
intelligence, and ambition. Therefore, the scope of both order
and chaos is in fact limited, and the belief in the balance of forces
demonstrated . . .'

Justen nodded. 'What does it mean?'

'I'm not sure.'

The young engineer looked out the window, across the
ridgeline and northward to the blackstone walls that separated
Nylan from the rest of Recluce. Then he looked downhill and out
across the Eastern Ocean. Maybe Krytella was correct. Someone
had to teach, but was he the right one?

2

'The road has reached the old domain of Westwind.' The older counselor rubbed her forehead for an instant, then dropped her arms onto the ancient black-oak table of the Council Room. The faint sound of surf from the beach below the Black Holding hissed in through the half-open windows on the early spring breeze.

'The road does not concern me so much as the troops that precede it,' suggested the wispy-haired man.

'Ryltar . . . the road is the key to the troops, and to the trade that follows. When that road is finished, it will be the only direct access to Sarronnyn.'

The third counselor pursed her thin lips, then coughed. 'So far, the Sarronnese have lost nearly two thousand troops.'

'The Spidlarians lost twice that, and there the Whites razed three cities, and we did nothing,' responded Ryltar dryly. 'No one can even precisely locate Diev to this day.'

'At the time, we didn't exactly have too much with which to respond.' The older woman, black-haired and broad-shouldered, shook her head.

'You are so good at keeping me honest, Claris.' Ryltar smiled.

'You're rather good at making me sick, Ryltar,' added the younger woman. 'The point is that Fairhaven has taken the next step in implementing Cerryl the Great's master plan for conquering Candar. The question is what we intend to do about it?'

'Ah, yes. The great master plan of which we have heard so much for so many decades. Thank you for reminding me, Jenna.'

'Ryltar, be serious.' Jenna held back a sigh.

'I am being serious. Why don't we face the facts? First, with our ships, even if all of Candar falls to Fairhaven, just how could the White Wizards threaten us? Second, we scarcely have the trained troops to send an army to Sarronnyn, nor could we raise such a force without conscription, and conscription would destroy us more surely than Fairhaven would.' Ryltar turned toward Jenna. 'Just tell me. What is the threat to Recluce? What can Fairhaven really do to us?'

'Destroy our basis of order, or reduce it to the point where our ships can no longer defend us.'

'Oh? Have you been talking to old Gylart again?'

'I don't think that Gylart's age automatically discredits his logic,' interjected Claris. 'Jenna's – or Gylart's – point is valid. The Whites are creating 'domesticated' order to increase their chaos power. Once they take Fairhaven, what is to keep them from taking Hamor? Or for the Hamorians to follow the same example? How would that affect your most profitable trade routes then, Ryltar?'

'We are talking centuries. Besides, I return to my original point. Just what *can* we do?' Ryltar smiled again.

3

'Run up the ensign,' ordered the captain. On the staff above the iron pilothouse fluttered the black ryall on a white background. 'Looks to be a Lydian trader.' Hyntal turned to the two engineers. 'We'll just pull alongside for a mite, Brother Pendak, and you see if you sense anything.'

Pendak nodded.

'Captain! She's turning! Trying to run before the wind.'

'Shields!' snapped the captain. 'Just between us.'

'Shit,' muttered Pendak.

'Want help?' asked Justen.

'Not now.'

Justen sensed the effort Pendak marshaled to create the barrier that blocked the Lydians' view of the *Llyse*.

'Starboard a quarter.'

'Coming starboard a quarter,' echoed the woman at the helm.

The *Llyse* turned downwind, and heavy turbines whined beneath the plated decks, the sound so faint that Justen sensed the increased power rather than heard it. Ahead off the *Llyse's* starboard bow, Justen sensed the Lydian ship, flying only the duke's banner, not the crimson-trimmed white banner of Fairhaven, as it lumbered through the heavy swells. What he and the crew saw off the bow was a black emptiness. What the Lydians saw was an empty sea off their port quarter.

'Course bearing on the Lydian?' asked the captain.

'Steady on the starboard forequarter, Captain. Three cables and closing,' answered Pendak, the ship's Brother.

'Bring her port an eighth. What devil's trick are the Whites up to now?'

Captain Hyntal had never forgotten that his great-great-grandfather had captained the *Black Hammer*. Unfortunately, he had never let anyone else forget it either, reflected Justen.

'Coming port an eighth.' The woman at the helm eased the wheel port to parallel the Lydian's course.

Spray flashed across the deck, and tiny droplets misted into the pilothouse where Justen stood beside Pendak. The older engineer's forehead remained beaded with sweat from the effort of holding the single-edged shield in place.

Hyntal turned toward the gunnery chief. 'Ready, weapons?'

'Turret's ready, Captain. Shells and rockets on standby.'

'Drop the shields, Brother Pendak,' ordered Hyntal. 'Let's see what those devil Whites have added to this stew.'

The Lydian ship appeared off the starboard bow. The carved plate over the unused paddle wheel read *Zemyla*. Pendak wiped his forehead and reached for the water bottle. 'Harder to keep a single-edge shield than a circular one, Justen.'

'I could tell,' Justen whispered back.

Hyntal glared at the engineers but said nothing as the *Llyse* edged up to the trader.

'She's not furling those sails.'

'Put a signal rocket across her bow.'

Flssttt . . . The signal rocket flared in front of the *Zemyla*.

The *Llyse* kept abreast of the trader until a blue-edged white banner floated on the aft jackstaff. Then a second parley flag flapped over the mainmast as the trader shortened sail.

'Grapples.'

'Aye, grapples.'

'Boarding party.'

The stern-faced, black-clad marines mustered on the starboard side, then swarmed onto the merchantman.

'It's your turn, Brothers,' suggested the captain.

'You wanted to see what it's all about, Justen,' Pendak said. The younger engineer followed Pendak up the ladder and onto the gently pitching deck of the *Zemyla*, where the crew had already circled away from the boarders and were clustering either on the poop or near the bowsprit.

The black-clad marines marched the man in the captain's jacket to the foot of the mast. 'They say he's the captain.'

'Have you always been the captain of this ship?' asked Pendak wearily.

'Yes, Master.'

The wrongness of the words twisted at Justen. He looked at Pendak. Pendak looked at the head marine, an intense-appearing young man named Martan. 'Find the first mate.'

Martan and another marine turned, but even before they took a full step, a man jumped from the poop into the sea.

For a time, the marines and the two engineers watched the water below, but no head appeared and Justen could sense no one there.

'Was that the captain?' asked Pendak, turning to the pseudo-captain.

'No, Ser.'

The wrongness still turned in the man's words.

'Find me the second mate.'

'I'm the second.' A burly man stepped up to the marines, his face and forearms tanned and leathery, his hair sun-bleached and his trimmed beard a mixture of blond and white. His words rang true to Justen.

'Is this man a convict?'

'Begging yer pardon, Master . . . but ye'll put us all in a terrible stew if this goes on.'

'Do you want us to sink the ship?' snapped Pendak.

'We'd be fools to want that.'

Justen cleared his throat softly. Pendak looked at him, then nodded.

'Were all of you threatened if you didn't agree to call this man the captain?' asked Justen.

'I wouldn't say as it was a threat exactly.' Sweat appeared on the burly mate's forehead.

'More like you didn't have much choice?'

'I don't know as how I could answer that.' The words choked forth, and perspiration coated the mate's face.

The soaked shirt and red face made Justen's decision. 'That's all.'

'We'll need to look around,' Pendak added. 'Not that we expect we'll find anything.'

'As you wish, Order Masters.'

'You want to take forward?' Pendak pointed toward the bow.

'Fine.' Justen walked forward, and his senses ranged over the ship. Pendak was right. The ship felt orderly, too orderly. Before long, he walked back to the marines, where the older engineer waited. 'Nothing. Baled Sligan and Montgren wool, dried fruits, perfume wood, and some big jugs of oil.'

Pendak shook his head. 'Let's go.' He nodded toward the marines, then turned to the burly second. 'Good sailing, Mate.'

'Thanks be to ye, not that most will, Wizards.' The perspiring man half-saluted.

4

The dull clank of one hammer and yet another laid upon chisels echoed through the chill air of the deep canyon.

A line of bent figures trudged back from the pile of rock that marked the edge of the construction. Each worker passed the deep, straight clefts that separated one foundation block from another, each foundation block a stone cube thirty cubits square.

Behind the laborers stretched the knife-edged raw slashes that marked the great Westhorn Highway. The base of that highway had been formed from the mortared and fitted stones that linked the foundation blocks. Each long section was as straight as a quarrel, a segment of the road that would run from Fairhaven to the Western Sea through Sarronnyn and to Southwind.

A wall of solid stone terminated the western end of the canyon. The trees and soil more than two hundred cubits above had been removed, and the dust and white ash from that removal sifted downward into the chill depths. Workers coughed, squinted, and blinked away the ash and grit. But they kept walking, lugging their baskets of fractured stone from the pile at the end of the canyon back to the unloading station.

Three figures in white – white boots, tunics, and trousers – stood halfway between the unloading platform and the mountain wall that marked the end of the road.

Their breath floated like white steam above the cold stone and over the scattered patches of snow and ice.

Behind them, the stone-master directed the spout to spew the smaller granite chunks into the space between two foundation blocks. The yet-unlined watercourse beside the leading edge of the road held no water, nothing except powdered rock, grainy snow, and scattered ice fragments.

Tweet! Tweet! A whistle split the chill.

'Stand clear! Stand clear!' The warning shrilled from the thin lips of the overseer, a woman in white leathers who also wore a sword and a white, bronze-plated skullcap.

'Close your eyes! Close your eyes!'

The nameless workers huddled behind the movable plank barriers, eyes closed.

Crack! Crackkk!

A flash brighter than the noonday sun, sharper than the closest of lightnings, flared across the stone wall that faced the end of the highway. Rock fifty cubits deep splintered, separated, and slid into a rough pyramid at the base of the canyon. Rock dust mushroomed, adding a powdered white mist to the air, blurring the sharp edges of the canyon walls.

'Head out. Load up,' called the overseer.

Two of the three wizards walked slowly, tiredly, back toward the amber coach that waited where the smooth-finished paving stones ended.

The workers staggered from behind their barricade toward the pile of granite that would be removed for fill, or for reshaping by the stonecutters before the masons came and fitted and mortared the stones together.

'Load up!' came the command again.

The workers' steps carried them once more toward the tumbled rocks, as workers' steps had carried nameless prisoners for centuries on the great highway to the west. Even before the dust had settled, those steps carried them, as so many before them, forward toward the loading rack that other prisoners had slid into place beside the tumbled stones.

'Just the gray stones . . .'

The long line of workers edged forward, men and women bearing identical baskets.

Clink . . . clink . . . Behind them, the stonemasons resumed their work, crafting the flush-fitted gray walls and storm drains that linked the base blocks of the road.

The loading crew began to place the squarish stones into the loading bin, and the first porter eased his basket into the rack.

'Next!'

The workers shuffled forward, their leather boots scraping on sharp-edged stones.

'Next!'

5

'What'll you have, gents?'

Gunnar coughed, cleared his throat, and motioned to Justen.

'Dark beer.' Justen glanced past the serving woman toward the new gas lamps by the door, still unlit in the afternoon light pouring through the half-open windows of the inn.

The woman looked at his black tunic and trousers.

'Dark beer,' he repeated.

'I don't even want to know about your day, Engineer.' The heavy, gray-haired woman shook her head and glanced toward Gunnar.

'Greenberry.' The sandy-haired man's fingers drummed idly on the polished dark oak.

'That's not much better. You like anything to eat? The mutton pie's tasty, and even the chops are good today.'

'No, thank you,' the brothers said, almost in unison.

'Well . . .' murmured the woman, turning toward the kitchen. 'No telling with wizards and engineers . . . just no telling, but what they've done today, who'd really want to know? Dark beer and greenberry . . .'

Justen grinned.

'The beer's not good for you. Why do you drink it? Just to make Father angry, or to annoy me?' Gunnar smiled faintly.

'I suppose that annoying my terribly superior older brother is as good a reason as any. Except that it's not true. I just happen to like the taste. Besides, I am not a great Order Master, a superior Air Wizard such as you. I'm just a lowly engineer who toils in the work-rooms under the scathing eye of Altara.'

'Is she really that bad?'

'No. She pays no attention when you do it right, and she gets hotter than the Little Easthorns the day they were raised when you don't.'

'Justen! Gunnar!' a bright voice interrupted.

Both men looked up as a black-haired young woman paused near their table.

'Oh, Aedelia. How are you?' asked Gunnar. 'How's your brother?'

'His leg's much better, and Mother said to tell you hello when I saw you.'

'What are you doing in Nylan?' asked Justen.

'Father was bringing in some timber for the shipwrights and I was waiting, when I thought I saw you two come in. So I told Father I'd be back in a bit and came to say hello.' Aedelia smiled broadly.

'Could you join us?' Justen motioned to one of the two empty chairs, trying not to be too obvious in his admiration of her endowments.

'I wish I could, but Father's already delivered the timber and it's a long drive back, even with an empty wagon . . . or mostly empty. We did get some fresh fish and a bolt of Austran linen.' Aedelia straightened up. 'I really do have to go.' With a last smile, she was gone.

Clunk . . . clunk . . . The two heavy mugs came down on the table. 'There you be, honored young gents. And that'll be five for the both of you, three for the beer and two for the green stuff.'

Gunnar extended a half-silver. The woman nodded and took the coin.

Justen lifted his mug and took a deep swallow. 'Ah . . . that's good.'

'Do you do that just to annoy me?'

'No. I do it because it tastes good, and it *was* a long day. And because – Leave it at that.' Justen stopped and glanced into the corner, where two white-haired men sat hunched over a Capture board. The game had clearly only just begun, since most of the white and black tokens were still stacked beside the board. He looked back at Gunnar. 'Krytella was looking for you the other day, when you were at Land's End.'

'And you're telling me now?'

'I haven't seen you since then,' Justen pointed out before taking another swig of the dark beer.

'You're drinking that too fast.'

'So? Drink your damned greenberry.'

'Justen . . . I haven't done anything to you, have I? We are brothers, you know.' Gunnar's voice was lower, softer.

'No, it's not you. It's just . . .' Justen shrugged.

'Women problems?'

'I suppose so.' Justen took another swallow from the mug. 'And student problems.'

'I told you that teaching wasn't all that Verdel said it was.'

'You've told me a great deal.'

'Sorry.' Gunnar sipped the greenberry. 'Are you going for a ship's Brother slot?'

'I went out with the *Llyse* the other day—'

'I know.'

'I know you know. You know everything. Just let me talk, all right?'

'Sorry.'

'Anyway, I watched Pendak. He seems pretty good with the shields, and he can tell when someone's not telling the truth. But I don't know. The whole business really bothered me. That poor crew had been manipulated. They didn't even know who the captain was.'

Gunnar nodded. 'Pendak told me about that. He was upset.'

'Why would someone do something like that?' Justen took another swallow of the dark beer.

The blond man shook his head. 'Maybe the White Wizards are trying to provoke us again.'

'Why would they do that? It's never been terribly effective before.'

'People's memories are short.' Gunnar paused. 'What did Pendak do?'

'What could he do? The real captain jumped overboard. And the ship hadn't really done anything.'

'I don't like this,' Gunnar muttered, slowly sipping his greenberry.

'That's what Pendak and Captain Hyntal said. Why would a merchant ship try to get away when we were just on a routine patrol? It doesn't make sense.' Justen took another swallow of the dark beer, licking the remnants off his lips before setting the mug on the table.

'It has to make sense. We just don't know how.' Gunnar looked up. 'There's Krytella.'

'Of course.'

Gunnar frowned, but stood and waved. 'Krytella!'

The redhead smiled broadly and hurried across the room, gracefully stepping around the unoccupied tables. 'I was looking for you.' She leaned forward and kissed Gunnar on the cheek.

'That's what Justen told me. It took a while to wind up the search of the archives.' Gunnar gestured toward one of the empty chairs.

Justen took a last sip of the dark beer and motioned to the serving woman. Gunnar was so damned noble. He hadn't even tried to point out that Justen had waited three days to mention Krytella's inquiry.

'Thank you for remembering, Justen.' Krytella's smile was warm, her pleasure genuine. That Justen knew even with his merely average – for an engineer – order-senses.

'Yes, folks? Would the healer like redberry or greenberry?'

'Redberry,' Krytella answered.

'Another dark beer,' Justen added.

The serving woman raised her eyebrows but only said, 'Coming up – one redberry and a dark beer.'

'You shouldn't—' began Krytella.

'I know. Good engineers and good wizards don't drink alcohol because it's bad for their order-senses.'

'Oh, Justen . . . I didn't mean to be short with you. But I am a healer, and . . .' The redhead shrugged.

Clunk . . . clunk . . . Two more heavy mugs arrived. 'That'll be another five for the two.'

Justen handed over a half-silver.

'Thank you.' Krytella inclined her head, then took a swallow of her redberry.

'Just before you arrived, we were talking about how the White Wizards were playing games with a Lydian ship.' Gunnar sipped from his greenberry as Krytella waited for him to continue. 'They planted some illusions in the crew's minds about who was captain, and then they conditioned the crew to run from the *Llyse.*'

'That doesn't make sense.'

'The real captain jumped overboard and drowned. He never came up.'

'Are you sure?' Krytella set her redberry down.

'I was there,' Justen answered. 'There wasn't any sign of life. I suppose that could have been an illusion, too. But it really doesn't matter, does it? The damage was already done.'

The redhead nodded slowly. 'I see what you mean. Recluce drove a poor captain to suicide. But I still don't see why the White Wizards would bother.'

'It has to have something to do with their effort to take over western Candar.' Justen looked at the mug without lifting it. He really hadn't wanted a second dark beer.

'But what?'

'It doesn't matter,' suggested Gunnar. 'They can't control the sea. There's too much basic order in the oceans.'

'Maybe that's not their objective,' Justen pointed out, all too conscious of how alive and vibrant Krytella seemed, sitting there between them . . . even as she leaned toward Gunnar.

'What other aim would they have?' Krytella took a small sip from her mug.

'If they build distrust of us ... and then if we do commit any forces to Sarronnyn or Suthya, wouldn't the Sarronnese be worrying as much about Recluce as about Fairhaven?'

Krytella looked at the older brother. 'What do you think, Gunnar? Is that possible?'

'It could be.' The blond man shrugged, then grinned. 'But we certainly won't solve that one this afternoon.' He took a deep swallow of the greenberry.

Justen glanced toward the Capture game in the corner. 'Is that old Gylart over there?'

'The Gylart who's Counselor Jenna's uncle? Or the fisherman?' Krytella asked.

'The former counselor.' Justen took a sip of the second beer. It did taste good, he decided.

Gunnar nodded. 'It's the old counselor.'

'He's good at Capture.'

'How can you tell?'

Justen lifted his shoulders and smiled sheepishly. 'He just is.'

'Would you two like to come to dinner?' Krytella smiled. 'I think it's a fish stew, but it smelled good, and there's plenty of it. Mother and Aunt Arline baked pearapple bread, too.'

Justen's stomach growled. 'I think that's my answer.'

'Justen . . .' Gunnar sighed.

'Fine. I need to help them. Just show up after the second evening bell.' Krytella flashed another smile and pushed back her chair.

'Do you have to go?' asked Gunnar.

'If I'm having company, I do.'

Justen watched as the redhead left the public room. Then he took another sip of beer before turning to his brother. 'You lucky bastard.'

'Why?'

Justen shook his head. For all that he could see storms an ocean away, Gunnar was sometimes so dense. Was that why the girls swarmed around him? Justen took another sip of the second beer that he hadn't wanted at first. At least a home-cooked dinner would be better than eating in the engineers' mess.

6

'The Iron Guard has secured the Roof of the World, and Zerchas is studying the remains of the Westwind archives . . .' The tall, older wizard at the speaker's podium coughed.

'Couldn't be much left after ten centuries.' The sotto voce murmur echoed through the momentary silence before the tall wizard continued.

'. . . and has discovered that the Sarronnese garrisons had preserved some of the original manuscripts, Cerryl's name be praised.'

A young, broad-shouldered, clean-shaven and black-haired White Wizard stood just inside the doorway. He pursed his lips and motioned to another young wizard before stepping through the archway and walking down to the row of couches in the antechamber.

The second wizard, round-cheeked and fair-haired, followed.

'Cerryl's name be praised, Cerryl's name be praised! It wants to make me puke, Eldiren. Did you know that Cerryl was a fifth-rate White Wizard, if that? He wasn't fit to carry the great Jeslek's boots.' The young black-haired White Wizard who spoke glanced toward the archway to the Council Chamber. 'Let's walk down to Vislo's.'

'It's scarcely fashionable, Beltar.' Eldiren scuffed a white-leather boot on the granite floor.

'Fine. Then no one fashionable will be there.'

The two young men walked out into the warm spring and the white light of Fairhaven, out into the shadow cast by the Tower. Beltar paused momentarily, then marched across the short, wiry grass of the new Wizards' Square, for all that it was three centuries old. Eldiren scurried to keep up.

'Why are you so upset by old Histen?'

'First, he's playing games with Lydian ships. What good will that do?'

'He's trying to force the Blacks into being seen as tyrants.'

'Has that ever worked before?' snorted Beltar. 'And then all this praise of Cerryl the Great – Cerryl the Great! I can raise the chaos springs from the rock beneath Candar and no one cares. Worse than that, Zerchas and Histen have threatened to turn the Iron Guard and the White Company on me if I try.' Beltar halted at the far side of the square and took several quick breaths. 'Forget Vislo's.'

A young boy sitting on a passing farm wagon pointed toward the white-clad wizards. 'There's one! And another one. Real White Wizards!'

Eldiren raised a hand and waved.

'He waved. He waved!'

'That's it,' muttered Beltar. 'Play to the peasants.'

'Why not? It doesn't hurt, and it certainly costs nothing.'

'You sound like Zerchas and Histen and Renwek.'

Eldiren touched Beltar on the shoulder. 'Sometimes . . . what they say makes sense.'

'Oh?' The black-haired wizard turned and looked back at the glittering White Tower.

'You're bitter because they don't need your powers now. They will.'

'They don't think so.'

'Does it matter what they *think*? Do you really believe that Recluce will stand idly by as we finish the Great Highway through the Westhorns and take over the entire west of Candar?'

'Why not? They didn't do a damned thing after Spidlar or south Kyphros, or the islands.'

'They weren't ruled by the Legend. They also weren't the home of Megaera. Besides, once we take Suthya, Southwind will fall—'

'Suthya! We haven't even attacked Sarronnyn.'

Eldiren shook his head. 'Recluce can't stop us in Sarronnyn. You know that. What's really left after that? Suthya, Southwind, and a bunch of druids in Naclos. No one lives in the Empty Lands or the Stone Hills.'

'No one ever will.'

'When Recluce finally marshals order, then they'll need you. Don't throw it away by giving them any excuses now. That was your idol Jeslek's problem. He forced his power on them, and that made him a target too early. Let Histen and Zerchas be the targets.'

Beltar pursed his lips. 'I don't know.'

'Think about it. You have time. They don't. Anyway, you might as well enjoy Fairhaven now. Look at the Council members. They meet, and then they have to go back to their posts all across Candar.'

'Another one of Cerryl the Great's wonderful ideas. Scatter the able away from Fairhaven.' Beltar scuffed a boot against the curb-stone.

Eldiren shook his head, then waved back to another small boy.

7

The wide porch of the house low on the hill and its location in the older section of Nylan – barely above the armory and practice fields, and overlooking the warehouses that served the port – were the only aspects that confirmed the structure's age. The varnish on the recently refinished red-oak flooring of the porch was clear, and the oil-stain preservative on the wood framing the wide windows was fresh. The black stones of the exterior wall shimmered with calm and order.

'Is this the place?' asked Gunnar, oblivious to the straggly nature of his fine, sandy hair.

Justen grinned. 'We'll find out.' He rapped on the door, then waited.

After the sound of scuffing footsteps, the door opened. 'Oh . . . you must be Krytella's friends. Let's see. The tall one is Gunnar. That's you, young man. And you must be Justen.'

The gray-haired and round-faced woman smiled. 'I'm her Aunt Arline. She's down at the port-master's getting Dagud. He's the assistant port-master, you know.'

'I am very pleased to meet you.' Justen gave a slight bow to Arline.

'We appreciate the invitation. Home-cooked meals are a treat for us,' added Gunnar.

'Do come in. Come in.' Arline stepped back into the front hall-way. 'There's the parlor. Now just have a seat. It won't be a moment, I'm sure, before Krytella is back. And this is Wenda. Her task is to entertain you fine young gentlemen.' Arline continued through the parlor and past the archway into the large kitchen with its long table.

Wenda, whose short red hair cascaded in every direction, stood next to the lamp table on the right side of the window overlooking the harbor, striker in hand. She wore a linen shirt, and faded brown trousers over scarred and scuffed brown boots. 'It's early, but you're company, and that means I can light one lamp.'

The parlor contained a low, padded bench with a back and armrests, three wooden armchairs, a rocking chair, several straight chairs, and two narrow lamp tables. The red light from the setting sun cast a deep, reddish shadow across the room.

'I'm Justen, and this is my brother Gunnar.'

'I know. He's the Storm Wizard. Krytella talks about him when she thinks I'm not listening.'

Justen grinned as Gunnar blushed.

Wenda squeezed the striker twice before the lamp wick caught, and she deftly adjusted the flame to keep it from smoking. She set the striker next to the base of the lamp and plopped into the rocking chair.

Gunnar took one of the armchairs, while Justen sat sideways on the corner of the bench, from where he could see the front porch.

'I like it when Aunt Arline's here and when we have company. Then I don't have to help as much in the kitchen.' Wenda looked straight at Gunnar. 'Can you make storms, big ones?'

Gunnar coughed and shifted his weight in the oak chair. 'There hasn't . . . well, making big storms isn't a very good idea. Lots of people died all over the world when the great Creslin did that.'

'I know. I just wanted to know if you could. Can you?'

'I suppose so . . . if I had to.'

Justen caught sight of two figures and a glint of red hair turning from the walk beside the highway onto the stones that led to the house. 'I think your sister and father are home.'

'She always comes home too soon when we have company. So does Father.' Wenda rocked forward in the chair and stood.

Justen rose, and Gunnar followed his example as Krytella entered the parlor. 'This is my father, Dagud. Father, this is Gunnar, and Justen.' Krytella smiled at both young men. 'Did you meet Wenda, and my mother, Carnela, and Aunt Arline?'

'Not your mother,' Justen responded as he nodded. 'She's been in the kitchen.'

'I see you lit the lamp.' Krytella's eyes pinned Wenda.

'We have company.'

'I made that rule.' Dagud grinned. 'Besides, we don't have company that often.' He looked at the two guests. 'Would you care to wash up?'

'Yes, if you please.'

'Yes.'

Dagud led the way to the alcove off the kitchen, where there was a second sink, clearly added after the original house had been built. He leaned back toward the kitchen. 'How soon before dinner?'

'You can sit down as soon as you wash up,' answered a tall, thin, dark-haired woman standing before the stove.

'Go ahead,' suggested Justen, nodding to Krytella after Dagud had dried his hands.

You are always the gentleman, Justen.'

Justen wished she saw more than that in him, but smiled in return.

'Wenda . . .' called Krytella as the smallest redhead headed toward the table.

'Do I have to?'

'Yes,' chorused Dagud and Krytella.

Wenda washed her hands after Gunnar, then trailed the others to the table.

'You sit there, Justen, and Wenda will be next to you . . .'

Justen followed Krytella's directions, although he wished he were the one sitting beside the healer instead of Gunnar.

Carnela set two baskets of warm bread and a huge tureen of stew on the long, polished-oak table. 'Sit down, for darkness' sake. Things are hot.'

When the two guests had been introduced to Carnela and everyone had been seated, Dagud cleared his throat for silence, then spoke. 'In the spirit of order, and in keeping with the Balance, those of us gathered together this evening dedicate ourselves and our souls to the preservation of order in our lives and thoughts.' Dagud looked up from his plate and smiled, reaching for the ladle in the off-white pottery bowl before him. Steam rose from the stew. 'It's been a long day.' He dipped twice and filled his bowl nearly to the brim, then served Carnela.

In turn, she broke off a chunk of the fresh and crusty bread and laid it beside his bowl before taking a chunk for herself and passing the basket to Krytella. The tureen of stew followed.

Justen found himself swallowing from the aroma of spices, especially those of ryall and pepper, overlaid with something else. When the huge serving tureen arrived, he followed Dagud's example, carefully ladling the thick fish-and-vegetable mixture into his bowl. Then he turned to Krytella's younger sister. 'How much would you like, young lady?'

'My name is Wenda, and I would like it half full.'

'Then you shall have it exactly half full, precisely half full, as only an engineer can ensure.'

'I would hope so.'

Gunnar coughed, and Krytella grinned before speaking. 'Good luck, Justen.'

Justen ladled the stew, extending his order-senses and trying to ensure that the bowl was precisely half full.

'That was pretty good,' conceded Wenda.

Justen smiled.

'You just might be a good engineer,' she teased.

'Wenda. Do you wish to have the remainder of dinner with us?' Carnela glanced at her daughter, and Justen felt the chill.

The littlest redhead turned to Justen, her words earnest. 'I beg your pardon, Magister Justen.'

'Thank you, Wenda.' Justen nodded.

In turn, Carnela nodded at her daughter.

'Might I have some bread, please?' asked Wenda in a small voice.

'Just a moment, dear.'

Justen broke off a chunk from a fresh loaf and offered the basket to Wenda.

'Thank you.'

'You are welcome.'

'The white pitcher is redberry, and the gray one is dark beer,' announced Krytella.

Justen waited until the gray pitcher arrived before filling his mug. Gunnar watched and shook his head minutely. Justen grinned. Krytella frowned momentarily. Justen stopped grinning.

'How is the port business?' asked Gunnar, looking at Dagud.

Justen took a mouthful of the hot stew, followed by a quick swallow of the lukewarm beer. His second spoonful of stew was smaller, and he chewed off a corner of the warm, crusty bread.

'It's slowed down a bit, maybe because of the problems in Sarronnyn. Haven't seen a spring this slow in a mess of years. Only ones with the same number of ships are the Hamorians.'

'All they care about is the gold in their pouches,' sniffed Arline. 'No sense of propriety or decency there.'

'Well, some of ours trade that sharp,' laughed Dagud.

'The good Counselor Ryltar and his family, you be saying?' asked Arline.

'He beats the Hamorians at their own. Fastest on the east-west Hamor route. They say he makes a devilish lot there.' Dagud sipped from his mug.

'What about the Nordlans?' pursued Gunnar. 'Some say they still prefer to trade at Land's End.'

'Aye, some say that, and a few more ships put in there, but that's as much because of the winds from Nordla as because of the port facilities.' Dagud paused to take several mouthfuls of stew and a chunk of bread.

'They say the Council's talking about expanding the old port at Land's End, but that's foolishness, chaos-tinged foolishness at that. You look at the weather records and you'll see that the number of days you can't get in there goes up every decade. It was only two years ago when that Lydian side-wheeler got her back snapped on the breakwater.' Dagud took a noisy slurp of the dark beer.

Justen took a quieter sip, his eyes lighting on Krytella's flashing green eyes and wide, mobile mouth.

'Would you like some more of the stew?' Arline lifted the deep bowl and handed it to Justen.

Justen looked at his empty bowl, grinning sheepishly. 'I guess I would.'

'And have some more bread, too.'

Justen accepted the bread, took a chunk and passed the basket back toward Gunnar, who had also taken a second helping of stew. 'The stew is wonderful. Thank you.' He inclined his head to Carnela.

'It's a real treat,' Gunnar added.

'Is your mother a good cook?' asked Arline. 'She must be. You boys – pardon me, I know you're older than that – you appreciate good food.'

'Actually,' Gunnar ventured, 'our father is the cook, and he's very good.'

'Well, I've heard of that. It's good to know.' Arline took a small chunk of bread from the loaf in the basket.

'What do engineers do, Magister Justen?' asked Wenda in a high voice that squeaked between wide-gapped front teeth. 'You wear black . . . does that mean an engineer is like a magister?'

'Engineers make things for ships.'

'You're too old for me. Do you have any other brothers, younger ones?'

Krytella grinned as Justen shifted his weight in the red-oak chair. 'No. We do have a little sister. Her name is Elisabet.'

'Why isn't she here?'

'She lives in Wandernaught with our parents,' interjected Gunnar.

'If your father cooks, what does your mother do?' asked Wenda politely.

'She's a smith.'

Carnela raised an eyebrow.

'She could have been an engineer,' explained Justen after swallowing more stew, 'but she said she wasn't interested in building ships or living in Nylan.'

'Sensible woman,' offered Arline.

'She has been called that,' Justen said.

Krytella glanced sideways at Gunnar, who continued to watch

Justen. The young engineer looked at the red-haired healer before finishing the last of his stew and turning his eyes to Dagud. 'Do you think trade here in Nylan will pick up?'

'Trade always picks up. Just a matter of time. Could be years. But then, it could be seasons, too. Might take until the nastiness in Sarronnyn's over.'

'What will happen there?' asked Wenda. 'Will the Whites win?'

A silence fell across the table. Arline coughed softly. Justen took a small sip from his mug.

'I don't know that anyone can say, child,' Dagud finally answered. 'That's matter for the Council, I'd guess.'

'It is getting late, and we mustn't keep you out too late,' said Carnela, rising from the table.

Gunnar followed her lead and stood. 'You've been very thoughtful to have us.'

Justen gulped down the last of the beer in his mug and swallowed too rapidly, the liquid hurting his throat as it went down. He stood as quickly as he could. 'Very thoughtful,' he echoed, trying not to cough . . . or to laugh as he saw the glint in Krytella's eyes as she stood.

Carnela and Krytella followed the brothers through the parlor and to the front door.

His hand on the heavy iron of the door handle, Gunnar bowed to Carnela. 'Thank you again for the dinner. I enjoyed it very much.'

Justen looked at Krytella's mother, seeing the same lanky figure and mobile mouth that so resembled her eldest daughter's. 'It was delicious, and I had a very good time.' He glanced back toward the parlor. 'And a delightful dinner companion.'

'I won't tell her that,' replied Krytella. 'It would make her insufferable. More insufferable,' she added. 'I'm glad you could come.'

'So are we,' Gunnar said, taking another step back on the porch.

Justen nodded and followed.

Then the brothers turned and began to walk toward the brotherhood quarters.

'They're a nice family,' mused Gunnar.

'Yes,' agreed Justen. *Especially the older daughter.* He kept pace with his long-legged brother as they passed under the lamp that neither needed to make his way in the dark.

Finally, Justen spoke again. 'Do you think everyone in Recluce is trying to avoid thinking about Sarronnyn?'

'What can we do? We don't have an army. Besides, what can they really do to us?'

'I don't think it's that simple.'

'It probably isn't. That's why people don't want to think about it. It's troublesome and far away. They hope it will stay away. But we wear the black, and they don't want to talk about it.'

'Krytella's a healer.' Justen paused to look toward the harbor, empty in the starlight except for the *Llyse*.

'Healers are different.' Gunnar kept walking.

So is Krytella, thought Justen. He turned back and hurried to catch up with Gunnar, not that he had more to say at the moment.

8

The slight White Wizard inclined his head toward the man seated at the table. 'Were you aware, Ser, that the Sarronnese have sent an envoy to Land's End?'

'Sit down, Renwek. Don't be so formal.' Histen gestured to the seat across the table, then poured wine from the pitcher into the second glass.

Renwek seated himself, nodded to the High Wizard, and took a small sip from the goblet. 'You do not sound terribly worried.'

'At the present time, I doubt that the Black Council will commit any great presence to rescuing Sarronnyn.' Histen sipped his wine and looked toward the half-open Tower window and the pale white glow of Fairhaven in the darkness.

'How can you be sure your . . .'

'My spy . . . my agent? Is that what you mean?'

Renwek nodded. 'How can you be sure that your "gifts" will remain effective?'

'They won't. One can never ensure that aid which is purchased will remain purchased. But these purchases are so recent that it's most unlikely that the Black Council will act hastily on Sarronnyn's request, or that Recluce will provide a great deal of assistance.'

'Are you certain that our . . . "influence" cannot be traced?'

'Gold, so long as we do not touch it, is actually order-based, Renwek. Honest and non-magical corruption does not require the touch of chaos.' Histen took another sip from the goblet. 'And compared to the alternatives, buying even a season's delay in action by Recluce is cheap at the price.'

'Would Recluce have acted in any case?' Renwek set his goblet on the table.

'With the Blacks, one can never be certain.' Histen shrugged.

'What about your . . . recruiting efforts?'

'They go well. The Blacks never should have abandoned their policy of exiling malcontents. They lack our discipline.' Histen laughed. 'You see the irony of that? The mages of order lack discipline in governing themselves, while we masters of chaos champion discipline.'

Renwek looked into the depths of the red wine.

'Heresy, Renwek? Chaos is indeed heresy.' Histen lifted his glass.

9

usten hung the leather apron on one of the pegs and pulled on the ragged exercise shirt. Then he took the battered red-oak staff from where it leaned in the back corner of his narrow, open closet.

'The armory all right?' asked Warin.

'Fine. It's old enough.'

'What does that have to do with anything?' The older engineer pulled on a loose, padded tunic, then lifted a gleaming black staff, bound with recessed iron bands, from his closet.

'Practicing with staffs is good exercise, but it's quaint, like the armory. What good is a staff when you're faced with rockets or shells – or with that fire the White Wizards throw? It's just a relic from the time when anyone who had a different thought was tossed into exile.' Justen twirled the staff close enough to Warin that the older engineer stepped back. Then he thrust the battered red-oak length theatrically toward his closet. 'Take that, you White villain!'

Warin laughed. 'Let's go.'

With an exaggerated shrug, Justen followed him out of the engineering hall and onto the front porch.

'Going to get some exercise?' asked the tall, muscular woman. 'Must be that you don't work hard enough here. We'll let you two take the place of the rolling mill, if you need the work.'

'You need a different kind of workout, Altara honey,' replied Warin.

'I'm willing, Warin, but you'd be in two kinds of trouble. Even if you could walk home, Estil wouldn't leave enough of you to feed the crabs.'

The two apprentices behind the senior engineer laughed.

'You got me there, Altara. Even young Justen's kinder and easier on me.' Warin took three dancing steps down the stone stairs to the stone walkway. A stiff breeze ruffled the wispy blond hair that remained on his head.

'Don't let him fool you, Justen,' called Altara as Justen followed Warin down the stone-paved walk that led to and across the High Road, the grand highway that connected both ends of the island nation.

'Don't let *her* fool *you*,' Warin said, then paused and looked up the long slope. The highway was clear in the spring twilight, no wagons, no horses, just stone blocks still close-fitted after centuries of use. 'She'll be over practicing with us before long.'

Justen suppressed a grin. Almost every day after work, he and Warin sparred while Altara made wise remarks before joining the dozen or so regulars working out with staffs or wands. And almost every day, Warin said that Altara would be following them to exercise. Was all life a long series of repeated words and actions? Shaking his head, Justen twirled the staff, then dropped it against the stone and caught it on the rebound.

'Hard on the staff,' Warin commented.

'But it's fun. After all, it's not as though I'll ever have to use a staff for anything serious.' Justen paused before the open doors of the armory, glancing at the black stone that showed no apparent age for all of the centuries that had passed since Dorrin or one of the other original engineers had ordered and laid it – except that probably the great Dorrin hadn't done much of the stonework himself. He'd doubtless been too busy building the famous *Black Hammer*.

Warin continued into the armory, and Justen hurried his steps to catch up.

'You never know.' Warin stepped onto the open expanse of the practice floor, setting his staff against the wall and beginning a limbering routine.

'Know what?' asked Justen, following the older man's example and swinging his arms to loosen the tightness in his shoulders.

'When you might need that staff, young fellow.'

In the far corner, a group of ships' marines exercised, led by Firbek, a big blond giant with the build of a Feyn River farmer. Justen paused and checked his boot laces, then watched as the marines swarmed up the ropes hung from the high beams.

He snorted, thinking to himself: *It's been years, maybe centuries, since we've had to board anyone's ships in real force.* Then he frowned, recalling his adventure on the *Llyse*, before chuckling as he realized how grumpy and serious his thoughts were. *And what are you doing, Justen, old man? Waving around an oak toothpick that's just as obsolete.*

He continued stretching, grunting as the exercises pulled at muscles tightened by his work at the engineering forge.

'Already you're showing how out of trim you are. You should be easy pickings,' gloated Warin before walking toward the empty northeast corner, farthest from the marines.

Justen picked up his staff and followed. He wiped his hands dry, squared his feet and raised his battered staff, nearly a cubit shorter than the shimmering black wood lifted by Warin.

'How you manage with that little twig, I don't know.' The black staff whistled around.

Justen parried, then slid his staff and countered.

Warin stepped back, off balance, and Justen eased forward, feet balanced. For a time, the thrusts, blocks, and parries alternated.

'Darkness . . . good . . . for a young fellow. Who . . . says it's . . . useless . . .'

'Need . . . the exercise . . .' Justen panted in return, barely managing a parry of Warin's thrust, sliding under the older man's guard and tapping his ribs.

'Ooooo . . . that could have hurt.' Warin straightened and took several deep breaths.

Justen bent forward and gasped for air. As he repositioned himself, his eyes flicked to the open armory door to see Altara enter, alone and carrying both a staff and the hilted wand used for blade practice.

'Ready?' asked Warin.

'All right.'

Warin's staff swept forward, and Justen danced backward, his eyes half on the other side of the armory.

The blond marine had detached himself from his troops and walked over to Altara. 'Altara?' Firbek bowed deeply. 'Would you care to spar?'

'Not with staffs.'

'I'd be honored to use wands.'

At the word 'wands,' Justen glanced toward the center of the armory, then dropped his shoulder and barely managed to deflect Warin's staff.

'Justen? Are you all right?'

'Sorry . . . just wasn't paying attention.'

'We can stop.'

'For a moment . . .' Justen let the end of his staff rest on the clay floor, packed hard by the feet of generations of practicing engineers.

Warin followed Justen's eyes toward the pair in the middle of the armory.

'Wands?' mused Altara. 'I suppose so . . . if you're not out for blood.'

'Would I attempt that against a master engineer?' Firbek smiled broadly.

Justen shook his head. Firbek's words felt wrong.

Warin looked from Justen to the center of the armory. 'They're just sparring.'

'I hope so.' Justen lifted his staff and walked toward the marine and the engineer as their wands crossed, uncrossed, and crossed.

With a sudden thrust-and-slash motion, Firbek's wand brushed past Altara's and slammed into her right shoulder.

Altara dropped her wand, stepping sideways involuntarily.

Firbek's follow-through continued as if he had not been able to halt the motion, and the wand snapped toward Altara's leg.

'Oooo . . .' The engineer glared at Firbek. 'That's enough. I won't be able to lift the arm without hurting, and probably won't walk straight for weeks.'

Justen turned and handed his staff to Warin. 'Hold this.'

Warin opened his mouth, then shut it and nodded. 'Be careful.'

'Nonsense. I'm never careful. That would get me in trouble.' Justen bent and picked up Altara's wand. He inclined his head toward her. 'Might I borrow this?'

'I'd prefer to fight my own battles.'

Justen smiled politely. 'I'm scarcely fighting. You know that I think swords and staffs are totally obsolete, Altara. They're only good for exercise.' He flipped the wand into the air, catching it by the hilt and making a mock thrust, all in the same smooth motion. Almost without stopping, he completed the thrust, then grinned at Firbek and saluted the marine with Altara's wand. 'Here's to you, and to obsolete weapons and traditions, Firbek. A friendly match.'

'Ah, Justen . . . you clown too much. You need a lesson – or three. Even in a friendly match.' The tall marine smiled and lifted his wand, returning the salute with far greater formality than Justen had offered.

The wands crossed. With his greater height and reach, Firbek attempted to keep Justen beyond striking range. Justen stepped inside, pressing the more heavily muscled marine back with the quickness of his wand.

The wands continued to cross, uncross, and slide across each other, Justen's moving ever so slightly faster than Firbek's.

Then, with a burst of speed, Justen stepped completely inside the marine's guard and knocked the wand from his hand, almost casually. 'Got you that time.'

Firbek massaged his hand for a moment, then retrieved his wand. 'Another round?'

'Why not?' Justen offered the semi-mocking salute again, but cut it short as Firbek slashed at him with the oak wand. Instead of pressing the attack as before, Justen concentrated on defense, on weaving a web that Firbek was unable to penetrate.

The wands continued to cross and recross. Sweat beaded on Firbek's brow, and he slashed wildly, leaving his chest exposed. Justen smiled but merely continued to hold the marine at bay, deflecting each thrust or slash. Firbek's slashes became wilder, stronger, until he appeared almost as though he were hacking at Justen.

The smaller man danced aside, letting his wand slide the other's aside or down, or merely avoiding the heavier wand.

'You . . . seem to . . . feel you're pretty . . . good, Engineer . . .'

'I'm all right . . . for an engineer playing . . . with obsolete toys . . .'

Firbek slashed again.

This time, Justen's wand slipped behind the hilt of Firbek's and twisted. The marine tottered, then stumbled and pitched forward.

'I'm so sorry, Firbek.' Justen grinned. 'I need to be going, but perhaps we could have another round at some other time. Just for fun, of course.' He turned and extended the wand to Altara, who frowned. 'My thanks for the loan, Master Engineer.'

'My pleasure, Justen.' Altara's words were low as she accepted the practice wand. 'But you still have to be in the hall tomorrow. We're going to start work on the new heat-exchangers that Gunnar and Blyss designed.'

Justen forced a smile. Gunnar even showed up in the armory, for all that he never deigned to lift a blade or a staff. 'I'll be there.'

He turned, but Firbek had vanished.

'That was . . . interesting, but Estil's probably expecting me by now.' Warin handed Justen the battered red-oak staff.

'I'll walk back with you.'

Outside, the clouds had moved in from the Gulf, and a light, drizzling rain seeped over Nylan. Justen stopped on the stones half-way to the road and wiped his dripping forehead on his sleeve.

'That was dangerous, Justen.' Warin looked back at the armory. 'He is Counselor Ryltar's cousin.'

'What can he do?' Justen shrugged. 'It was just a friendly match. He said so himself.'

'Do you ever take anything in life seriously?'

'Not much. After all, we're not exactly going to get out of it alive.' Justen bounced the staff off the road stones and caught it. 'Might as well try to enjoy things along the way.'

'You have a warped sense of enjoyment.' Warin paused. 'Estil's probably waiting. I'll see you tomorrow. And I'll lay a staff on you yet.'

'Only if you catch me watching a pretty girl.'

'I'll make sure one walks in.'

'Who?'

'I could have Estil stop by.'

'That's not fair.'

'So?' Warin half-waved and began to trot uphill toward the line of houses along the ridgeline south of the black stone wall that marked the edge of Nylan.

Justen twirled the staff, then turned downhill.

10

Jagged-edged, red-sandstone upthrusts formed a circular amphitheater between the gray stone hills to the north and west and the rolling dunes to the south. A narrow strip of browned grass wound eastward from the red sandstone, gradually widening and greening as it neared the great forests.

Within the small, natural-appearing theatre were three women. The three rested upon knee-high stones, smoothed either by nature or by hand into shapes comfortable for sitting. The silver-haired woman in the center rocked slightly, eyes closed.

The red granules within the square formed by the five-cubit-long sandstone border stones shifted, slowly rearranging themselves.

In time, the map appeared, the granules faithfully depicting in miniature the very peaks of the Westhorns themselves. A white line arrowed through the peaks, the whiteness tinged with the dull ugliness of dried blood.

Slowly, white-sparkled granules of sand dotted the tiny peaks and valleys, growing and spreading westward until the entire map glimmered an ugly white.

After a time, the mapmaker in the center released a deep breath and the depiction lost its sharpness as the sands slumped into their natural state. But the whiteness remained.

11

Justen adjusted the lamp wick. Although gas lamps were coming into vogue, the quarters of the Brotherhood still used oil, generally from the carnot nut.

A rapping sounded on his door.

'Yes?'

'It's your big brother.'

'Come on in.'

Gunnar eased into the room, carrying a pitcher. 'I can tell you're getting ready for a big night. I've got some redberry here.'

'I thought you and Turmin were headed back to Land's End.'

'That's tomorrow now. Counselor Ryltar asked Turmin to his house for dinner. He wanted to get Turmin's opinions on the mess in Sarronnyn.' Gunnar set the pitcher on the lamp table. 'You have any mugs?'

'Over on the second shelf.' Justen finished adjusting the lamp's wick. 'Doesn't Ryltar live somewhere near Feyn? Why Turmin? From what I heard, Ryltar isn't exactly fond of the Sarronnese, and Turmin's mother was born in Sarronnyn.'

'Ryltar lives on the ridge just outside the black wall. It's toward Feyn, but not that far.' Gunnar shrugged. 'You know as much as I do. I suppose Turmin will tell me sooner or later. Anyway, I'll have to leave early tomorrow to meet him there, but it's better than playing lap cat at Ryltar's.' Gunnar took the mugs and filled them. 'Let's play Capture.'

Justen grinned. 'Why not?' He walked over to the small bookcase and took the board and the box containing the black and white tokens from the top. 'What are you doing this time?'

'Turmin thinks the weather's still changing, but more slowly.' Gunnar handed a mug to his brother. 'He thinks that there will be signs in the plants on the high hills to the west of Land's End – something about places where the weather is right on the edge.' Gunnar pulled one of the two straight-backed chairs up to the desk.

After setting down his mug, Justen put the board on the desk and the token box beside it. Then he pulled his chair up and sat down while Gunnar divided the white and black tokens.

'White or black?' asked the older brother.

'White this time.'

Gunnar nodded, and Justen set a token in one of the depressions in a rear lattice – the three-token one. Gunnar ignored the lattice and placed his first token in the center point of the main lattice on his side of the board.

Justen dropped a token in the four-point lattice to the rear of Gunnar's.

'You're doing it again.' Gunnar added a second token to his lattice.

Justen put his second token in the three lattice and added the third to complete it.

Gunnar added the third to his main lattice. 'Shouldn't have let me get this far. Now you can't catch me.'

Justen frowned, then set a white stone in the other three lattice behind Gunnar's lattice.

Gunnar added another token, and they continued until Justen had both three and four lattices, and Gunnar had six tokens in one twelve and five in the other.

Gunnar smiled and dropped a black stone into place, followed by five to complete the first, and the bonus that allowed him to complete the second.

Justen shrugged. 'It's yours.'

'You don't want to play it out?'

'Why bother?'

'I still don't understand why you build three or four groupings rather than concentrate your efforts.'

'It seems to make more sense. Nothing in life lets you concentrate on just one thing.' Justen laughed. 'Besides, it's only a game. Life's serious enough.'

Gunnar frowned momentarily, then lifted the pitcher. 'Some more redberry?'

'Certainly. Why not? Another game?'

'Of course.' Gunnar finished pouring the redberry and took a sip from his mug.

12

'Tryessa D'Frewya, the envoy from Sarronnyn,' announced the young man in black who had opened the dark-oak door to the Council Chamber, once the study shared by Creslin and Megaera, the Founders, whose joint portraits framed the wide window behind the table.

The Sarronnese envoy entered and bowed deeply, her emerald silksheen trousers and blouse rustling. 'Honored Council members.' She straightened.

Claris motioned to the table. 'Please have a seat. Would you care for some of the green brandy?'

'I would be delighted. Tradition or not, it is always a treat.' Tryessa slipped into the oak armchair. The young man in black carefully poured the pale green liquid into the crystal goblet beside her, then retreated to his position by the door.

The youngest counselor brushed a strand of red hair off her forehead and took a sip from an identical goblet.

'What brings you to meet with the Council?' asked Ryltar, his casual tone a contrast to the order of his dress and his precisely brushed, thin blond hair.

'Surely you must know, honored Counselor. As we speak, the White Company and its Iron Guard have taken the old domains of Westwind—'

'As you took them in the time of Dorrin,' countered Ryltar lightly.

Claris cleared her throat.

Jenna half-turned. 'I don't think that was the question, Ryltar. Tryessa was attempting to suggest something, I believe. Were you not?'

'I was suggesting that Fairhaven's efforts are a matter of concern.'

'To whom?' inquired Ryltar politely.

Claris raised her eyebrows but did not speak. Jenna turned toward the blond man.

'It is certainly a concern to all of us in western Candar,' Tryessa said. 'Even the Naclans sent us an envoy suggesting that we ask for the aid of mighty Recluce.'

'The reputed druids of Naclos? They actually exist?'

'They have existed for centuries, perhaps even from before the time of the Angels.' Tryessa's voice was wry. 'They produce exquisite woodworking, although it's not carved. Apparently they can persuade the trees to grow in a certain way. I have a bench I inherited. It doesn't age much. It was my great-grandmother's. But I wander. When the druids are interested, it is clearly due to a concern that goes beyond Sarronnyn.'

'You make a strong case for the concerns of western Candar,' admitted Ryltar.

'Ryltar . . .'

'I believe that the envoy has clearly stated the urgency of the matter, Ryltar,' declared Claris coldly.

'Thank you, Counselor. In view of those concerns, the Tyrant would hope that you would recall Sarronnyn's steadfast support of the open-trade policies long espoused by Recluce.'

'The Tyrants have always been fair in matters of trade.' Claris kept her voice level.

'Although it is certainly of mutual benefit,' Ryltar added smoothly.

'The Tyrants of Sarronnyn have been more than scrupulous in dealing with Recluce,' responded Tryessa.

'What would you have us do?' asked Claris. 'You know we do not maintain a standing army large enough to send much in the way of troops. And our ships cannot help you with a conflict in the Westhorns.'

'Not directly, but Fairhaven still must use the oceans.'

'Are you suggesting that we employ our ships to restrain trade to Fairhaven? After all the years of working to ensure fair and open trade on the seas?' inquired Claris.

'The Tyrant understands the difficulty of such a suggestion.'

'What of Suthya and Southwind?' asked Jenna.

'They have sent significant commitments of troops and supplies. But . . .' Tryessa shrugged.

'You doubt that such troops will be adequate?' Ryltar cleared his throat and sipped his brandy.

'The White Wizards have over five thousand troops in the Iron Guard alone.'

'That does make it difficult,' observed Claris. 'Yet you suggest we give up a long-held belief in the freedom of trade. Are there not other options?'

The Sarronnese envoy sipped from the goblet once more before speaking. 'Even some sort of token would help. Perhaps a group of Order Masters, healers, a small squad of warriors – they are the descendants of the Westwind Guards.'

'We see your concerns, and we share many of them. What you ask is difficult, and we must consider—'

'I see.' Tryessa rose, leaving most of her brandy within the glass. 'I see. Then I will retire and allow you to discuss the matter freely. I will be at the old inn. It is one of the few lasting memorials to the commitment to and belief in someone of Sarronnyn. Except, of course, your Black Holding here.'

'You are sharp for one seeking favors.' Ryltar smiled.

'I do not seek favors. I seek justice and perception. I seek those who would look beyond blind devotion to custom to a deeper meaning and belief.' Tryessa returned the smile with one equally false.

'We will indeed discuss this, Envoy Tryessa,' declared Claris as she rose from her chair behind the table. The two other Council members rose with her.

'My thanks to you.' Tryessa bowed and departed.

The three reseated themselves. Claris motioned to the trainee in black. 'You may go, Mryten.'

As the door closed, Ryltar said, 'Rather demanding, your envoy.'

'Rather accurate.' Jenna sipped her brandy. Her lips tightened as she set down the goblet.

'Without principle, we have nothing.' Claris's fingers brushed the stem of the goblet before her.

Jenna glanced through the window at the whitecaps rising far out on the Eastern Ocean. 'If we follow that principle, Fairhaven will take all of Candar . . . and then who will stand between the wizards and us?'

'No one else has ever stood between us. No one ever will. You're both deluding yourselves if you think that's a possibility.' Ryltar looked only at the dark oak before him.

'Then perhaps we should change our devotion to principle and let our use of principle serve us instead of binding us,' snapped Jenna.

'We could take a middle course,' interposed Claris. 'We could ask for volunteers to help Sarronnyn. I think many would wish to help. It is an adventure, and many seek adventures, especially since we no longer need to use exile as a tool.'

'That would be acceptable to me, certainly.' Ryltar smiled. 'Let those who wish to get involved with the White devils do so.'

'That's not enough,' said the youngest Counselor. 'Even those the most interested could not do so without some compensation.'

'I'm sure that if the Tyrant is so concerned, she would provide supplies and a modest stipend,' suggested Ryltar mildly.

'That would seem agreeable to me. Then we could offer this as a first step and wait to see what happens, or if a greater commitment is needed.' Claris's fingers tightened around the goblet's stem.

Finally, Jenna nodded.

13

'You need to study the preface again.' Justen fixed his eyes on Daskin.

'But it's boring. The stuff in the back's more interesting. I can't wait until I can do that.' The boy squirmed on the leather pillow, his eyes finally resting on the polished graystone floor.

'Have you tried any of it?' Justen continued to stare at the student.

Daskin flushed.

'It doesn't work for you, does it?'

'I'm not grown up . . . not full wise, anyhow.'

'Daskin . . .' Justen's voice was soft. 'Not everyone can be an Order Master. And for some, it takes years.'

'You just won't teach me.'

'Don't be silly, Daskin. He's paid to teach you.' Jyll flipped her long black hair back over her shoulders with a practiced gesture.

Norah's fingers continued to rub the smooth gray worry stone, her eyes vacant while her senses focused on the clouds above Nylan.

'If everyone can't be an Order Master, why do we have to learn this stuff? It's boring!' Daskin threw the black-covered book on the floor.

'Now you've done it,' whispered Jyll.

'I don't care! It's stupid. It's boring . . . and I hate it.'

'It's going to rain all day and all night, and maybe tomorrow,' announced Norah, her words and the glint in her eyes proclaiming her mental return to the classroom.

'How come stupid old Norah can find the clouds and I can't?' Tears streaked from Daskin's eyes.

Justen knelt in front of the boy. 'We're all different, Daskin. My brother can find the clouds over Lydiar and play in the winds that flow from the Roof of the World. I can't. I can forge things and work black iron, but every time Gunnar picks up a hammer, we're all afraid he'll smash his fingers. Even Dorrin's brother was a fisherman. And without his brother, Dorrin would never have founded Nylan. We have to do what we can.' The engineer patted the youth's shoulder.

'It's still stupid,' muttered Daskin, but he wiped his face on his sleeve and scooped up the book.

'Read the first part again. I'll see you tomorrow.'

Daskin trudged out the door, lagging behind Jyll, who had hurried out first. Justen slipped his own copy of *The Basis of Order* into the pack he still carried rather than the satchel that some of the older engineers affected.

'It is going to keep raining,' insisted Norah.

Justen smiled ruefully. 'I'm sorry, Norah. I should have paid more attention to you. You're very talented with following the weather, and you should be pleased that you do so well.'

'It might even rain for two days.'

'We'll have to see. You can already do that better than I can.'

'I can?' Norah stood, still rubbing the worry stone.

Justen nodded. 'I'm an engineer, not an Air Wizard. I can make black iron, and rockets, and parts for engines and cannons, though.'

'I like the clouds, especially the misty ones.' Norah bent and picked up her pack. The heavy brown canvas, battered and scuffed and stained, had been new when Justen had begun to teach her a season earlier. 'What are we supposed to read?'

'The preface again.'

'That's fuzzy, like the soft clouds.' Norah shouldered the pack and half-walked, half-skipped, toward the open door. There she stopped and turned. 'Good-bye, Magister Justen.' Then she was gone.

Justen shook his head. Why were all the Air Wizards so . . . he groped for a word, then decided that Norah's term 'fuzzy' fit as well as any. Even Gunnar was fuzzy sometimes, as if he weren't there even when he was. Then again, who could tell where an Air Wizard really was? He snorted, closed his pack and lifted the heavy leather pillows onto the table before picking his dark-gray water-proof from the peg beside the doorway. After closing the door, he walked down the half-dozen steps and along the sunken corridor until he reached the stairs to the west wing.

He took the steps two at a time. The smell of mutton stew oozed from the dining hall that served the older students, many of whom would have been candidates for exile in Dorrin's time.

Before he went outside into the rain, Justen pulled on the dark-gray waterproof but left the hood down. Stepping carefully around the puddles in the road, he walked downhill toward the engineering hall.

The soft, warm rain had plastered his hair to his skull, and he was sweating by the time he climbed the four stone steps to the building. Stopping under the wide porch, he brushed the water from his face with the back of his left hand. Then he stamped his boots and wiped them on the rush mats before stepping into the anteroom that contained the open closets where the engineers left their aprons, gloves, and work clothes.

Justen pulled off his tunic and the good shirt he used for teaching and hung them on the pegs in one of the doorless and narrow closets. Then he took down his leather apron, fastened it on, and stepped through the archway into the hall and walked toward the smaller forge in the right rear corner of the hall. His apprentice, Clerve, was working on bolt blanks.

Justen grinned. He'd hated making bolts. The cutters made threading them easy, but the bolts were still a pain – even when using the metal lathe to true the blanks. Threading the nuts had been worse . . . and still was.

'How soon will you have the new evaporators worked out?' asked Warin, pushing his too-long wispy hair back off his forehead with his forearm.

Justen grinned ruefully. 'When we figure out how to keep the cooling side from corroding the system so badly. They still leak too quickly.' The idea of using seawater evaporators to get continuous fresh water had been used on only the last two black ships, and the Brothers on both ships, including Pendak, were spending more time and order-mastery on holding the evaporators together than on the rest of the power plants, including even the newer turbines.

'Good luck.' Warin turned back to the milling table.

'Thanks.'

Clerve looked up from the anvil toward Justen.

'Yes . . . you can stop working on the bolts for now,' Justen told him. 'Lay out the plans on the board there.' He nodded toward the inclined drafting board set back from the forge, then walked over to his bench, where he checked his tools.

As Clerve laid out the drawings of the flash chamber, Justen checked the hoist and crane that held the flash-chamber assembly, then lowered the circular, black iron structure another two cubits so that the curved base rested less than a cubit above the packed clay floor. He checked the space where the vapor separator would go, using his calipers, locking them and setting them on the full-scale drawing. The actual length between the flange brackets designed to hold the separator was a tenth of a span smaller than the measurements on the parchment sheet. Justen nodded, suspecting that the cold iron had contracted more than calculated, as it usually did. The question lay in calculating the contraction that would take place on the smaller vapor-separation assembly.

Clerve watched as Justen measured again.

'We'll need a half-span thickness in the two-cubit-square plate.' As Clerve started toward the plate storage room behind the hall, Justen added, 'Use a cart. That's four-and-a-half-stone worth of iron.'

'Yes, Ser.'

While he waited for his apprentice to return, Justen added more hard coal to the forge, readjusted the air nozzle with the long iron rod, and pumped the bellows slowly, checking to ensure that the sprinkling can was full. Charcoal would have been easier to use, but Recluce still had insufficient forests for resupplying all its charcoal needs. The compromise was the use of charcoal by the town smiths, while the engineers bought coal from Nordla or Sarronnyn, despite the high shipping costs.

Justen watched the glowing of the coals. At least he didn't have to work on resmelting the plate from the old *Hyel*. In a way, the Mighty Ten were really the Mighty Eleven, with the oldest warship being broken, resmelted, and recycled to provide the materials for the warship under construction.

The cart creaked across the floor; Clerve used a leather harness to pull it easily.

After taking a deep breath, Justen took the calipers and

transferred the measurements to the iron plate. With a light hammer and a chisel, he marked the rough-cut lines. 'There. Swing the crane . . .'

Clerve positioned the forge crane.

'Easy now,' cautioned Justen as the two swung the plate into position over the forge fire.

Then Justen wrestled the special cutting plate into place over the anvil, wiping his forehead with the back of his forearm. The way things were going, finishing the one flash chamber would probably take half a season, not that the engineers were in any hurry. The new *Hyel* was not planned for launching for another four years.

After ensuring that the special hot set was laid by the long anvil, he checked the heat of the iron, watching as the area he had marked turned dull red, then began to lighten slowly. Justen waited until the iron along the cut line was nearly orange-white before he nodded to Clerve. They swung the plate over and lowered it onto the anvil.

Clung . . . clung . . . Justen's hammer strokes were even, steady, splitting the iron along its grain.

'All right.' The engineer and his apprentice used the crane to lift the plate, which they rotated and swung back over the fire. 'Next line is a crosscut.'

'How many heats, do you think?' asked Clerve.

'Two, I hope.'

Once again Justen watched the iron color until he nodded and they positioned the metal on the cutting plate.

'I was wrong. Three,' the engineer added as they replaced the iron over the forge fire.

Two heats later, the oblong shape that would be one side of the base of the vapor separator lay on the cutting plate. Justen used heavy tongs to set it on the brick annealing shelf at the back of the forge, not wanting it to cool too slowly.

Then they readjusted the brackets on the plate, and Justen measured the metal for the second cut.

'Why don't we use something like the bench shears?' asked Clerve.

Justen grinned. 'Forget already?' He swung the metal over the forge fire once more.

Clerve blushed. 'It seems so silly.'

THE ORDER WAR   47

Justen silently watched the iron heat for a time, then nodded. In moments, the orange-white section of the iron rested on the cutting plate and Justen's hammer lifted and fell . . . lifted and fell . . . until they swung the iron back onto the forge.

'The reason for not using shears on engine parts isn't silly. It's a question of what works. You cut the iron with something like that and you twist the fiber too much. We have the same problem with casting iron, or even steel. You need a wrought-iron base for black iron.'

'They say the Nordlans can make a steel that's almost as good as black iron,' ventured Clerve.

'Almost as good isn't always good enough.'

They swung the iron back onto the cutting plate, and Justen took up the hammer again. 'A little better this time. Only two heats.' He set aside the hammer and used the tongs again to set the second iron section next to the first on the forge bricks. 'Let's readjust the brackets. A couple more sections and we won't need the crane.' He wiped his forehead, but did not swing the metal onto the forge.

'I suppose I'm like an old magister, but I need to finish what I was telling you about the shears. After using shears or some sort of wrenching cut, when you try to order the metal into black iron, the order bonds don't match and you have to tear the whole thing apart. That's why it took ten years to build the *Dylyss*.'

Clerve shook his head. 'Just because they used shears?'

'No . . . because they used violence to cut the metal. There's a difference between force and violence.'

'Teaching again, Justen? Here in the engineering hall?' Altara stood behind Clerve, who stepped aside with an averted glance.

Justen blushed.

Altara smiled at Clerve. 'I don't eat apprentices, Clerve. Really, I don't. Nibble perhaps.'

Clerve, in turn, blushed.

'You can take a break.' Justen nodded at the apprentice.

'Are you where you can stop?' asked the master engineer.

Justen nodded. 'It's slow going.'

'Most engineering is.'

The two engineers watched as Clerve trudged toward the side porch, where both a breeze and the water spigot provided cooling and where the apprentices usually gathered.

'Have you thought about joining the engineering group that's going to Sarronnyn?' asked Altara.

'No.' Justen blinked, trying to dislodge a speck of grit from his left eye.

'Do you want to come with us?' asked Altara.

Justen looked at the thin-faced master engineer with the muscular shoulders and dancing green eyes. 'Why are you going? Dorrin couldn't stop the Whites. How do you think you can?'

'Do you want to sit around Nylan for the rest of your life mooning after Krytella while she hunts down Gunnar?' Altara grinned and waited.

'Hunts down? You make her seem like a mountain cat.' Justen felt himself flush again, and not from the heat of the forges.

'I know women, Justen. After all, I am one, you know.'

'You don't let most of us forget it.' He managed a grin.

'That's what I like about you. You can say something like that and it doesn't sound nasty. You almost – almost – make it sound like a compliment. I also enjoyed your little match with Firbek.'

'How's the arm?'

'Still a bit sore.' Altara paused. 'Why didn't you join the marines? You're certainly officer material, and you're the kind that people would follow.'

'You know what I think about hand weapons.'

'I know.' Altara sighed. 'That's one of the few things I think you're wrong about.'

'Why?'

She gestured around the engineering hall. 'We're cheating on Dorrin. We still have only ten ships – except that we don't. We have eleven for purposes of the Balance. And if you – Have you ever compared the size and tonnage of the *Black Hammer*?'

'How could I? I'm not a master engineer with access to the most venerable records.'

'Sorry. Well, take my word for it. The new *Hyel* will displace nearly three times what the original *Black Hammer* did.'

'I don't see Chaos Wizards sprouting all over Candar,' observed Justen.

'No . . . just an Iron Guard with twice the strength of our marines, plus the Whites, both of them overrunning Sarronnyn, and our beloved Council suggesting that volunteers to help the beleaguered Sarronnese would be in order.' Altara shrugged. 'I'd be pleased if you'd think about it.' She smiled politely, though not warmly, as she headed toward Warin and his milling machine.

Justen took a deep breath. Did he really have a choice . . . if he wanted to stay an engineer? He trudged after Clerve to get a drink of water himself, and to reclaim his apprentice.

14

Severa handed over the leather post bag to a young man Justen did not know, apparently old Havvy's replacement as the local post agent. Justen slipped down from the damp leather of the post wagon's seat and stood beside the wagon, trying to use his limited order-senses to remove the moisture from the seat of his trousers. Finally, he shook the rain off his oiled waterproof and lifted his pack out of the wagon bed behind the second seat.

Gunnar was dry – somehow, rain never landed on Weather Wizards, even though none of them ever talked about it. At least Gunnar's pack had a sprinkling of water on the canvas. Gunnar brushed away the droplets before swinging the pack onto his back.

'Thank you.' Justen handed two coppers to Severa.

'My pleasure, young magisters.' The wagon-mistress's face crinkled into a smile. 'I hope you will enjoy your holiday, and give your mother my greetings.'

Justen nodded.

'Perhaps someday you'll be as good a smith as she is.' Severa's smile faded into mere politeness as Gunnar extended his coppers.

'Thank you,' Gunnar said, and inclined his head.

'Just don't take yourself too seriously, Gunnar. You may be the finest Storm Wizard since Creslin, but a good smith's of more use to most than either an engineer or a wizard.'

'Yes, Severa.'

The woman grinned. 'Don't mind me, boys. Been riding wagons too long. Off with you!' She watched as the post youth placed another leather post bag with the half-dozen already in the wagon bed.

Gunnar waved, turned, and started walking.

Justen paused, taking in the town for a moment. Not much changed in Wandernaught. Severa had stopped at the post house, next to The Broken Wheel, a two-story stone-and-timber structure, and the only inn. Old Hernon had died right after Justen had gone to Nylan, and Justen didn't know the couple who ran the inn now, but the facade and sign were the same – even down to the cracked spokes on the broken wagon wheel.

A young woman and a child stood under the small awning outside the coppersmith's, waiting for the gentle rain to stop, and two men wrestled barrels from a wagon into Basta's Dry and Leather Goods.

Justen shifted his pack, stretched his legs, and began to walk on the rain-slicked but level paving stones – west, past the inn, past Seldit's copper shop. He didn't catch up with Gunnar until they were out of town and abreast of Shrezsan's, the house – with its attached barn – sitting next to the stream where the family had woven wool and linen for generations.

Actually, Justen recalled with a smile, Shrezsan had been one of the few girls who had liked him better than she did Gunnar – even if she finally had married Yousal, in the Temple no less.

On the south side of the road rose the gentle, rolling hills that held the groves: cherry, apple, and pearapple. The rain had not quite stripped the flowers from the branches, which still held thin green leaves.

Gunnar slowed and crossed the road, putting a leg up on the low stone wall separating the grass on the road's shoulder from the orchard grounds.

Justen waited, brushing water from his short hair.

'I think I miss the groves the most. Even the pearapples in Land's End aren't the same.' Gunnar stroked his bare chin. 'Wandernaught's a better place than either Nylan or Land's End. It's peaceful.'

'I suppose you'd put a big temple here, and move the Council to Wandernaught.'

Gunnar smiled. 'Why not? Maybe I will.'

Justen swallowed. Did Gunnar really think he was going to be on the Council?

The blond man sighed and turned back to the road. 'Elisabet's already getting worried.'

Justen wondered how Gunnar knew that. Did he feel it?

The two resumed walking. They reached the fork in the road and took the left branch. The timbered, black-stone and slate-tiled house stood on the south side of the road, the smithy behind it in a separate building. Two small groves flanked the buildings. A wiry figure in brown waved from the base of a tree and began to walk toward the house.

'Gunnar! Justen! Mother! They're here.' Elisabet bounced off the wide porch and down the crisply cut stones of the walk. She threw her arms around Justen, squeezed, and released him, then offered Gunnar the same treatment. 'You're here. Right when Mother said you would be.'

'Of course they are. Severa always makes the post house by mid-afternoon.' Cirlin, still wearing her leather apron, had quietly appeared behind her daughter.

'Good to see you,' boomed Horas, his dark hair plastered to his skull. 'I won't give you a hug. I've been out working with the trees, and I'm dirty and soaked.'

Elisabet, sandy-haired and slender, resembling Gunnar, reached for her brothers' hands. 'Let's get out of the rain. I can't push it away for very long.'

Gunnar glanced at his mother and raised his eyebrows.

'I think we've got three of you.' Cirlin's voice was wry. 'I'll be in soon. I need to finish some latches.'

'Do you need any help?' Justen asked.

'I'm not running an engineering hall.' Cirlin laughed. 'Nerla's a good apprentice. It won't take long.'

Justen let his sister lead him up onto the covered porch, where he took off his waterproof.

Elisabet waited for Gunnar to remove his, too, then took both garments and headed for the rear porch that served as a sheltered place for drying coats and laundry.

'Some things don't change. The youngest still gets stuck with the coats.' Justen grinned.

'Not always.'

'Dinner's going to be late,' announced Horas, standing in a corner of the porch and shaking water from the short, oiled-leather jacket he had worn. 'Late, but good.'

'It's always good,' Justen agreed.

'Not always,' retorted Elisabet, sticking her head out through the open doorway from the parlor. 'Not when he makes the fish stew.'

'Fish has a long and honorable tradition, but I'm not fixing that tonight.'

'What are you fixing?' asked Elisabet suspiciously.

'A surprise.'

'I hope it's the spiced-lamb casserole.' Elisabet turned to their father. 'It's chilly. Can I heat up some cider with the spices?'

'So long as you use the striker and not magic,' called Horas. 'And would you start the kindling in the oven, please?'

'Even if that's not funny, Father, I will. I'll make sure to use the striker for both. It might take all evening.' Elisabet squared her shoulders and marched back into the house.

Gunnar raised his eyebrows.

Horas grinned. 'I just teased her about that. I tell her that if she's not careful, I might find out that she's a throwback to Megaera. Not that she's got the slightest flicker of the White about her, at least according to your mother.' He nodded toward the parlor.

His sons followed him inside and he closed the door, then moved to the ceramic heat-stove in the corner, where he used an older striker. 'I can't ward off the chill with all that order-mastery. An old man like me needs his heat on days like today. It's almost like winter hasn't quite gone.'

'Old man? Hardly.' Justen laughed.

'He's setting us up for something, Justen. You need more wood split?'

'Well, it wouldn't hurt if you did some before you left. Of course, I wouldn't ask that as soon as you got here.'

'But he couldn't wait to make sure we know.' Justen seated himself on the padded stool nearest the stove. Unlike Gunnar, for him, the internal order-mastery necessary to raise his body heat to ward off the cold was work. And the heat of the stove was always relaxing.

'Watch the fire for me, Justen, while I start in on dinner?'

Horas closed the heat-stove and eased toward the kitchen.

'I'd be happy to.'

Gunnar settled into the old rocking chair that had been their grandmother's, the one she had rocked in while she told them all the stories about Creslin and Megaera, and even the near-mythic tales about Ryba and the Angels of Darkness and the Demons of Light.

Justen smiled, recalling her words: 'It's real enough if people believe . . . The truth behind the words is what matters, child.'

Elisabet's steps on the polished hardwood floors broke Justen's reverie. His sister carried two steaming mugs.

'Thank you.' Both brothers spoke simultaneously.

'Justen, will you play Capture with me until dinner?' Elisabet looked at the floor.

'Aren't you supposed to help Father?'

Gunnar slid out of the rocking chair. 'I'll go help. Maybe by now, he'll let me in on just how he does it.'

'Gunnar cooks almost as well as Father.' Elisabet brought the board to the low game table and drew up a stool. 'Wait. I forgot my cider.'

While she retrieved her mug and set out the board and the tokens, Justen rose and added several already-split chunks of wood to the fire in the stove. Then he took the small broom and swept the wood dust and splinters into the dustpan and emptied them into the stove before carefully relatching the door.

'White or black?' Elisabet sat with her back to the stove.

'You can have black,' he offered.

'Goody!'

Justen set his token in the right rear three-token lattice.

'Gunnar says not to bite on that.' Elisabet placed her first token on the left point of her main lattice.

Justice dropped a token in the other four-point lattice on Elisabet's side of the board.

Elisabet added a second token on the other point of her lattice.

Justen added his second token in the three lattice and dropped the third to complete it.

Elisabet edged another token into the main lattice, right in the center.

Justen frowned, then set a white stone in the other far-side three lattice.

Elisabet pursed her lips, looking at Justen's completed small lattice, but added another token to her centerpiece. 'One more . . .'

Justen shrugged and sipped the hot cider. 'This tastes good.'

'Thank you.' Elisabet placed another black token.

They alternated placing tokens until Justen had four lattices, all the threes and fours.

Elisabet put the seventh token in her first twelve and grinned, adding five more stones to complete it and then using the bonus to complete the second twelve.

Justen added a token to the nine block, while Elisabet concentrated on the single seven.

Token followed token.

'I've got the four!'

Justen grinned. 'You certainly do.'

Elisabet used the capture bonus to cut off the rear three.

'That fire feels good.' Cirlin stepped into the parlor from the porch.

'I beat Justen! I beat him, Mother!' Elisabet bounced from her stool.

'Aren't you supposed to help your father with dinner?'

'Gunnar said he'd do it. I don't often get to play Capture with Justen or Gunnar anymore. And I beat him!'

'She did,' Justen admitted. 'She plays a lot like Gunnar does. Maybe all Air Wizards play alike.'

'I need to wash up,' Cirlin said.

Justen rose. 'So do I.' He turned to Elisabet. 'Since you won, you may have the honor of putting away the board.'

'But you have to wash up, too, Elisabet.'

'Yes, Mother.'

Cirlin shook her head. Justen eased his stool back into its usual place and followed her into the kitchen.

'Things are looking good,' announced Horas.

Justen sniffed. Aromas of spices and lamb filled his nostrils. 'You didn't just fix that?'

'Darkness, no. It's been simmering all afternoon. It won't be long now.'

Gunnar carried two baskets of bread to the big circular table.

'He's even got the cherry conserve for you, Justen.'

The younger brother walked to the corner pump and sink and began to wash his hands. Cirlin dried hers and motioned to Elisabet.

'Can I help?' Justen asked Gunnar.

'All this goes on the table.'

Justen carried over the pot of conserve and the stack of plates, setting one plate in front of each chair.

'Sit down, everyone,' Horas invited.

'I get to sit between Justen and Gunnar,' Elisabet announced.

When all five had been seated, Horas coughed, then spoke softly, so softly that Justen found himself leaning forward to catch the words: 'Let us not take order so seriously that love and hope are lost, nor so lightly that chaos enters our lives, but live our lives so that each day reflects harmony and joy in living.'

Horas set the casserole in front of Gunnar. 'Help yourself. The dark bread just came out of the oven, specially for the lamb, and there's the conserve, and a jar of pickled pearapples, and don't forget the spice sauce in the pitcher . . .'

After refilling his mug with warm cider, Justen waited for the brown stone casserole to be passed around. He ladled out a large helping for his mother and then one for Elisabet. He took and even larger portion for himself.

'It's a good thing I made plenty,' Horas observed.

'You always make plenty. That's why my forge is never cool.' Cirlin laughed. 'Men householders feel like they have to feed armies, even when only the three of us are here.'

Justen offered the bread to his mother, then to his sister. He inhaled deeply as he broke off a chunk and smelled the heavy warmth of the dark loaf. 'Smells good.'

'No one bakes the dark bread the way he does.' Cirlin dipped a corner of bread into the casserole and lifted it to her lips.

Justen dipped his bread into the thick sauce, letting the spicy warmth, the mixed tang of rosemary and citril and bertil, ease down his throat.

For a time, only the sound of eating rose from the table.

'I can tell that no one was hungry.'

'Not at all.'

'Would you pass the casserole, Elisabet?' asked Gunnar.

'You ate too fast, and you had a whole plateful.'

'I was hungry. I've been working hard. Searching out the weather takes just as much food as smithing or engineering does.'

'I suspect all good work takes energy.' Cirlin lifted the casserole dish and handed it to Gunnar.

'Thank you.'

Justen broke off another chunk of the warm, dark bread and slathered it with cherry conserve.

'Something's bothering you.' Cirlin looked at her younger son.

Gunnar nodded in agreement.

'I'm probably going to have to go to Sarronnyn,' Justen acknowledged.

'You have to go?' The smith raised her eyebrows. 'I thought the Council asked for volunteers.'

'One of the master engineers has suggested that it would do me good.'

'Altara?' mumbled Gunnar.

'Not with your mouth full, son,' suggested Horas,' even if you are a great and mighty Weather Wizard.'

'Of course.' Justen sipped the last of the hot cider and reached for the covered pot.

'I can't say as I'm surprised. We've played too loose with the Balance for too long.' Cirlin coughed and took a mouthful of cider. 'You know that Dorrin warned about that.'

'He did?' Elisabet sat up straight in her chair.

The smith nodded. 'But it doesn't matter. He knew that people wouldn't listen. They never do. That's why I'm glad I'm just a simple smith.'

'Simple?' Justen's eyes darted to the wall and the interlocking black-iron circles that formed an image of the sunrise over the Eastern Ocean.

'When will you leave?' asked his mother.

'That hasn't been decided.'

'I still don't think it's a good idea,' Gunnar said, tugging at his chin.

'Most adventures aren't. I think Justen's saying he doesn't have much choice,' Cirlin said.

Justen chewed another mouthful of the warm, dark bread and cherry conserve, enjoying the taste before answering. 'I don't have to go. No one could make me go, but I don't feel right about saying no. I can't quite say why.'

'What do you think, Gunnar? Not in your heart, but considering your sense of order.' Cirlin held her mug in both callused hands, letting the warm vapor drift across her face.

Gunnar frowned before answering. 'I trust Justen's feelings. I don't like his going to Sarronnyn. The whole business reeks of more than normal chaos.'

'If there's much chaos at all there, that's a problem,' added Horas.

Cirlin lifted her mug and drank slowly before lowering it. 'It could be a problem for everyone in Recluce.'

Silence dropped across the table.

'Can you really catch the rain?' asked Gunnar, turning to Elisabet.

'Yes, I can.' Elisabet laughed. 'But I get tired soon. There's so much rain. I don't know how you do it.'

'I don't, silly little sister. I—'

'I'm not silly.' Elisabet looked at her father. 'Is there another surprise?'

'I can't keep anything a secret, I guess, not with four Order Wizards around this place. I had hoped you might be coming.' Horas grinned at his sons. 'So I baked a couple of cherry-pearapple pies.'

Justen had to smile in return, trying not to think about engineering and Sarronnyn and the chaos that awaited him, looking at the golden-brown crust of the pie Elisabet set before her father.

15

Stones here and there had tumbled from the wall of the ancient causeway, but the structure across the gap from the Roof of the World to the ridgeline leading down toward Suthya and

Sarronnyn remained sound enough that even the heavy steps of the Iron Guard neither shook it nor displaced another stone.

With its gray uniforms, gray banners trimmed in crimson, darkgray boots, dark-hilted weapons in gray scabbards, the Iron Guard of Fairhaven marched northwest down the causeway. Behind the gray assemblage waved the crimson-trimmed white banners of the White Company, crackling in the chill winds that whipped off the snow-covered peaks encircling the high plateau and the rebuilt citadel once called Westwind.

Like a gray-headed white snake, the column wound lower.

In the narrow defile leading to Sarronnyn, behind heaped lines of stone and under blue-and-cream banners, waited groups of women and a few men.

No parley flags were offered or sought as the Fairhaven forces reached the rock-strewn narrow valley, where patches of snow and ice huddled on the north side of each boulder.

The wind howled, and the Iron Guard marched forward.

'Archers! Fire!' A wave of iron-shafted missiles arced into the blue-green sky and dropped into the long column.

'Shields up!' The small iron shields of the gray-clad warriors rose. Men fell, those in gray mostly silent, those in white screaming as the iron shafts burned through them.

A dull rumbling echoed down the valley. A spray of boulders bounced toward the gray figures.

Hsssttt ... hssstttt ... From behind the Guard, firebolts lanced up the rocky walls. White rock dust sprayed down like rain.

Soldiers in gray, white, and blue coughed.

'Archers ...'

'Shields ...'

Hsssttt ...

Soldiers continued to cough and die. Some screamed – either Whites struck with iron arrows, or Sarronnese burned with firebolts when their positions were overrun and they were forced from behind their stone barricades.

The cold wind whipped the fine white rock dust across the valley long after the fires died.

Two White Wizards studied the overrun Sarronnese position.

'They know how to use the stone to block the firebolts.'

'It didn't help them much.' The heavier man glanced at a

charred body with mere blue tatters cloaking the black obscenity that had been a woman. Only the gray blade remained intact, almost untouched.

'Not this time. We still lost two score of the Guard and probably four times that in the lancers and the White archers.' Zerchas looked back east to the high peaks of the Westhorns. 'And we're barely into Sarronnyn.'

'We can replace the lancers and archers.'

'I know. That's not what bothers me.'

'The Guard, isn't it?'

'Of course it's the Guard. If I had my way, the White lancers would lead. They'll be useless if we ever fight a really good Black force – like Westwind was, or like the legion of Southwind. That's when we'll need the Guard. Or if Recluce ever acts. But the Council seems to think that the Guard was developed to safeguard cowardly wizards. Or shirttail relatives in white coats.' Zerchas snorted. 'Bah!'

'What could we do?'

'Bring up a couple of those young, impatient hotheads. Like Derba or – what's the arrogant one's name – Beltar, that's it. Let them use themselves up.'

'I don't know. That . . . what about the chaos reserves?'

'Why did Cerryl insist on them? So we'd have them to use. Besides, Recluce has cheated anyway. Their fleet probably uses five times the order the first fleet did – the ships are three times bigger and almost of all-black iron.'

'Beltar doesn't like you.'

'I don't like him. But he'll come. Just flatter him. Tell him he's indispensable. Young, self-important men always like to feel that way. He'll come.' Zerchas stepped around another pile of charred bodies. 'Send a message to Histen. He's good at that sort of flattery.'

'You think Histen will – He's not overly fond of you, either.'

'Of course he will. Beltar's a danger to him in Fairhaven. Ever since Cerryl, you'll notice that damned few High Wizards leave powerful Whites in Fairhaven. They say that's because concentrating chaos is dangerous.' Zerchas laughed. 'It is, and not just because of the corrosive effect on the city. It's also dangerous to the health of the High Wizard.'

'You're a cynical bastard.'

'So?' The White Wizard leaned into the wind as he walked toward the white-oak coach that flew his banner.

16

Justen looked at the traveling clothes on the bed, wondering if he could get them all in his pack.

Thrap . . .

'Come on in, Gunnar.' It had to be Gunnar. Even Justen could sense the order in the figure out in the hallway.

The sandy-haired wizard stepped into the clutter of the room. 'You're still packing at the last moment, I see.'

'Why do it any earlier than I have to?' Justen shrugged and cleared off the desk chair. 'Have a seat.' He began to fold a heavy pair of work trousers.

Gunnar turned the chair to rest his arms across the back. 'I've been thinking, Justen.'

Justen folded the shirt and stuffed it into the big brown pack. 'Now, where are those—'

'I don't like your going off to Sarronnyn. It doesn't feel right.'

'You want me to back out?' Justen pulled the trousers and shirt back out of the pack. The spare boots had to go in first.

'No. I know you can't do that. I talked to Turmin. He agreed with me. You engineers could benefit from a good Weather Wizard.'

'You're going with us?'

Gunnar shook his head. 'I can't leave that quickly. I'll come with the next group.'

Justen folded the shirt over the toes of the boots, then refolded the trousers. 'What changed your mind? You seemed to think we wouldn't have much effect.'

'I don't know if we will. But you need a Weather Wizard. So I'm coming.'

Justen folded a work shirt into the pack.

Gunnar stood up. 'You've got a lot to do. I'll see you in the morning.' He patted Justen on the shoulder before leaving.

The engineer looked at the mess on the bed, wondering what he would do with it all. Gunnar was right, of course. He should not have waited so long to pack. He shrugged. Weather Wizard, indeed. He swallowed, then picked up the clean underclothes. They would fit in the pack. Somehow.

17

Justen walked up to the tree, old but ungnarled. Its spreading, heavy limbs arched into the green-blue sky, and the ground around the trunk was flat and covered with a carpet of short green grass.

Wondering, he looked down at the grass, for most old trees had roots that visibly twisted into the ground, and grass seldom grew close to those roots. And Recluce had no lorken that old, not as slowly as the black-wooded trees grew.

'Some things are indeed what they seem.' A slender young woman, dressed in brown, appeared beside the tree. Her hair was spun-silver, not the silver of age but a glowing silver, the color shown in the few portraits of the great Creslin.

'Are you Llyse?' he asked, thinking that the weather mage's sister had had spun-silver hair, according to the legends.

'No.' The melody of her voice rang a melancholy silver. 'She died a long time ago. For you.'

'She died for Creslin, I think.' Justen wondered why he was explaining. He swallowed. 'Who are you?'

'You order-wielders always put such stock in names.' She smiled. 'You will know me when the time comes.'

'When will that be?'

'After Sarronnyn, you will find me . . . if you choose the true way. You cannot continue to hold chaos at bay with black iron. Look to the trees.'

Justen glanced at the tree. When he glanced back, the silver-haired woman was gone.

Darkness fell then, and Justen found himself lying on his back.

'Mmmhhh . . .' The words tumbled from his mouth before he sat up in his bed. His packs waited on the desk, looming there in the predawn darkness like two small mountains.

After Sarronnyn? He squinted. The dream had seemed so real: the silver-haired woman, the enormous lorken, the mysterious conversation. *After Sarronnyn. Look to the trees.* What had she meant?

He lay back on the bed, but his eyes remained open as the grayness of dawn seeped into the room. What was the meaning of the dream? Was there any? Or was he just worried about the trip to Sarronnyn?

18

The *Clartham*, almost two hundred cubits of red oak and fir, stretched nearly the length of the western pier, her brightwork glistening in the midday sun. She carried but two masts, and a pair of high funnels rose just forward of where the mizzenmast would be on most ships.

'That's a big ship,' murmured Clerve. An overstuffed pack and a black-leather case bearing his guitar rested by his feet.

'The Hamorians have bigger vessels. It takes something that big or bigger to handle even the Eastern Ocean. The Great Western Ocean's supposed to be wider and rougher, though.' Justen brushed his hair from his forehead, glad of the cool morning breeze as he stood in the bright sunlight.

While he waited for Altara to finish her discussion with the blond Norland cargo-master, he studied the side paddle wheels, protruding another five cubits from the gently rounded midships curve of the trader, forward of the funnels. The paddle wheels necessitated the use of longer, braced gangways to reach the ship's deck, and even a special crane for cargo loading and offloading.

Beside Altara rested three large and heavy-looking crates. In front of the crates waited the other four engineers: Nicos, Berol, Jirrl, and Quentel. On the other side of the engineering group stood Krytella and the two other healers, an older, wide-faced man and a stocky woman. Beside the three were their packs and two small crates.

Justen motioned to Krytella.

'Where's Gunnar?' Krytella mouthed the words to avoid interrupting the discussion between Altara and the cargo-master.

Justen provided an exaggerated shrug. 'He said he would be here,' he mouthed back, trying not to frown. Gunnar was never late; without fail, he planned ahead, even if he didn't always look as if his mind followed his body.

Krytella looked uphill toward the Brotherhood barracks, then back to the pier stones at her feet. Justen admired the planes of her cheeks, the clear, glowing skin.

'How long will it take?' asked Clerve, his Adam's apple bobbing in his thin throat, his straw-colored hair spraying in every direction.

'To reach Rulyarth? From what I've heard, a good ten days. That's if they don't port someplace like Tyrhavven or Spidlaria.'

'That's a long time to be on a ship, isn't it?'

Behind Clerve, the cargo-master grinned even as he listened to Altara.

Justen grinned back. 'It takes three to four times that long on the trip west from Jera to the easternmost point of Hamor. It's even farther if you go that way to Nordla.'

Clerve shook his head and glanced beyond the black stones of the breakwater and out into the nearly flat waters of the Gulf of Candar.

'Those crates of tools?' asked the blond Nordlan officer, his eyes moving from Altara to the wooden boxes.

'They're about seven stones apiece.' Altara looked down at

the Nordlan, a man well above the average height of most from
Recluce.

Justen buried a grin. Altara overtopped the tall Nordlan, and
he suspected that the man was finding it hard to look up to the
older engineer.

'Seven stones?'

'Metal-working tools. You can certainly handle a mere three
crates on this monster. And don't stick them in the bilges where
they'll rust. Then you can put the healers' two small crates on
top of ours.'

'And where, Honored Engineer, would you have me place
them?'

'Never mind.' Altara squatted and picked up one of the crates,
slinging it up onto a broad shoulder. 'I'll just put it where it
belongs. Then you can put the others next to it.'

'Uh . . .'

'Engineers! Get your gear. You, too, Justen, Clerve. Don't
gape like some backhill type from Mattra.'

'We'll follow the engineers.' Ninca, the chief healer, picked up
her pack, as did the wide-faced man. Then she looked at Altara.
'You'll make sure the supplies—'

'I'll make sure,' Altara affirmed.

Krytella bent down for her pack.

Justen stooped and picked up the pair of heavy waterproofed
canvas packs, wondering how he had gotten suckered into
volunteering to stand off Fairhaven and the fearsome Iron
Guard. The strange dream still lingered. Who or what was
the silver-haired woman?

'Let's get moving.' Altara marched toward the gangway.

Justen looked at the cargo-master trailing Altara and grinned.
Even the Nordlans were finding it hard to deny her, and it was
their ship.

'Justen!' Both Justen and Krytella looked up as Gunnar's lanky
figure marched along the pier. He waved a black staff.

'Get on board after your good-byes.' Altara shook her head.
'Clerve . . . follow me.'

The apprentice looked at Justen. Justen nodded, then turned.

After a moment, Ninca inclined her head to Krytella before
following the engineers.

'I'm sorry I'm late,' Gunnar began, 'but Turmin caught me at the dining hall . . . and then Warin stopped by to give me this for you.' Gunnar handed the shining black-iron-and-lorken staff to Justen. 'He said you'd need it, even if you do think personal weapons are obsolete antiques.'

'But . . .' Justen shook his head as he took the staff. Warin? Giving up his prized staff? 'I can't take this.'

'You have to. He said he'd build a black-iron rocket and aim it at me if you didn't. Anyway, that's why I was late.'

'You're here.' Justen grinned at his older brother. 'And I'm sure that whatever Turmin said was important, too.' He shook his head again. 'Warin . . . I can't believe it.'

'What did Turmin say?' asked Krytella.

'He thinks it's important that I take the next ship to Rulyarth.' The sandy-haired wizard shrugged and looked along the pier, where a half-score of port workers and Nordlans loaded boxes and bales into the cargo net of the crane, and lowered his voice. 'He's talked to Gylart, and the old counselor told him something that has Turmin stirred up. Turmin wouldn't tell me what, but he's switched from reluctant agreement with my going to Sarronnyn to something like enthusiasm.'

'How do you feel about it?' Although Justen felt Krytella at his elbow, smelled the soft scent of trilia, and sensed her warmth, he continued to face his older brother.

'Worried, I guess.' Gunnar kept looking straight at Justen. 'But you, younger brother . . . just take care of yourself.'

'At least until you get there?' Justen chuckled.

Gunnar hugged Justen for an instant before releasing him. 'At least that long,' admitted the Black magician before looking at Krytella. 'And you, Healer . . . make sure he takes care of himself.' He smiled quickly.

'I will, Gunnar.' Krytella's eyes flicked to the stones of the pier for a moment. 'And you take care of yourself on your trip.'

Justen swallowed at the not-so-hidden worry in the woman's voice.

'We weather types have a little advantage there, but I'll do what I can to see that your trip isn't too rough.' Gunnar grinned, then added, inclining his head toward the gangway, 'You'd better go.'

Justen glanced toward the ship and saw Altara striding

back down the railed gangway, still trailed by the Nordlan cargo-master. 'I suppose so.'

Gunnar stepped forward and gave Justen another hug, a quick one, which Justen returned. Then the weather mage patted Krytella on the shoulder and stepped back, watching as the two shouldered their packs. Justen held the staff in his left hand.

Altara marched up to the remaining crates. 'Clerve's waiting up there to show you our spaces.' She lifted another crate and turned to the cargo-master. 'Can you or your boys get the last one of ours and the two for the healers and put them all together?'

'We can manage, Engineer. We have loaded the ship a few times.'

'You know . . . you Nordlans didn't invent the steamship.'

'But we're the best long-haul traders in the world, Honorable Engineer.'

'Well said!' Altara grinned, turned, and paused, looking at the three still standing on the pier. 'I said to stop gawking.'

Justen motioned to Krytella, and the healer led the way up the gangway.

Clerve stood just forward of the funnels and waved as he saw Justen. 'Over here, Ser.'

Krytella and Justen followed the apprentice down an open staircase.

'It's a ladder, they say,' explained Clerve.

The Recluce contingent shared three narrow rooms, each with four bunks. The forward bunk room was for Altara and the chief healer, Ninca, and her consort Castin, the broad-faced healer. Justen found himself assigned the bunk over Clerve in the room with Nicos and Quentel. Krytella shared the aft-most cabin with Berol and Jirrl, the two women engineers.

After stuffing his packs into a doorless cubby at the foot of his too-short bunk and laying the black staff to one side, Justen made his way topside, where he joined Krytella at the starboard railing of the *Clartham*, midway between the bowsprit and the paddles. They watched silently as the lines were singled up, then reeled in, and as smoke poured from the funnels and the paddles slowly turned.

The vibration from the heavy iron engines crept through the

timbers of the ship and through Justen's heavy boots. Slowly, slowly, the *Clartham* pulled away from the pier and eased into the channel.

'I wish Gunnar were coming with us instead of traveling later.' Krytella watched the pier from where Gunnar had waved before turning and walking back up the hill, apparently oblivious to Krytella's tears and her eyes focused upon him.

How could Gunnar know the weather hundreds or thousands of kays distant and not see the love in a woman's eyes from less than two cubits away? Justen refrained from shaking his head.

'To begin with, he hadn't planned on coming at all.'

'I know. He decided to come because he worries about you.'

'That doesn't make a lot of sense. I can take care of myself.'

'I'm sure you can.' Krytella sniffed. 'But caring about someone doesn't have to make a lot of sense.'

Justen wanted to bite his tongue. Instead, he said softly, 'You're right. We don't always think of things that way.'

'Excuse me, Justen. I need to find Ninca.' Krytella turned and headed aft.

Justen watched until her green-clad figure disappeared down the ladder. He looked back at the sun hanging over the stone pillars marking the channel and then westward at the gentle swells of the Gulf of Candar.

After he'd turned back and studied the twin funnels, which reached nearly fifty cubits above the deck, Justen eased past two seamen coiling a line and made his way aft to the ladder that led toward the huge steam engine. He climbed down and ducked through a narrow doorway.

The metal boiler walls already panted like a spent dog, even as the *Clartham*'s engineman checked the wedges bracing the iron. The smell of hot oil permeating the space, the muted hissing of the huge pistons, and the low rumble of the gears assaulted Justen.

'Who ye be?' shouted a heavy voice.

'Justen.'

'Ah, you're a Black engineer! We'll have no secrets from ye!' shouted the *Clartham*'s engineman. The wizened gnome grinned at Justen. 'What think ye, Engineer?'

'Impressive.' Justen let his senses drift across the engine and the firebox, recoiling slightly at the high level of chaos and the small margin of safety between the order of the iron and the power it contained. 'You run close to the limits.'

'She'll hold. Captain Verlew says trade goes to the swift, and the *Clartham*'s one of the swiftest, save for your ships, of course. But we're close, leastwise, to your traders. Except for that demon Ryltar – he drives his ships closer to the edge than we do.' The engineman frowned. 'Wouldn't want to run engines for him, Black ship or no. Suppose that's why he holds the east-west Hamor runs.' The engineman checked the gauge and added another wedge.

Justen tried not to wince at the stresses on the boiler. Instead, he nodded and let his senses run over the gears and the shafts to the paddle wheels, much simpler than the turbines of the latest Recluce ships. But without order-strengthened black iron, the Nordlans were limited in what their boilers could handle.

He frowned, recalling a passage from one of Dorrin's old texts, claiming that anything other than low-pressure steam engines would be impossible without using black iron. Yet the *Clartham*'s boiler was certainly not low-pressure, not with a fifty-cubit draft on three funnels.

As the engineman adjusted the steam flow and checked the bearings and lubrication, Justen leaned back against the ladder and continued to study the engine system.

19

The wind cut out of the northeast like a cold knife, slashing across Justen's uncovered face. The morning sun, bright in the green-blue sky, provided light but little heat. Justen flexed his fingers inside his heavy leather gloves, thankful that he had brought both the warm sheepskin coat and the gloves.

Altara stood on the lookout's catwalk, halfway between the bridge and the port lookout's station, one gloved hand on the railing, gesturing with the other as she talked to the blond cargo-master, who occasionally leaned out of the bridge house.

Berol and Nicos hung over the starboard railing, clearly miserable from the twisting and pitching of the trader.

Overhead, the sails billowed, occasionally cracking in the wind, and the engine beneath the deck lay silent, only enough heat in the boiler to allow for a quick firing up.

North of the *Clartham*, a Black ship kept station, having joined the Nordlan trader as she passed north of the Sligan coast. The dark bow of the older Black ship – the *Dorrin* – cut through the chop of the Northern Ocean. White spray cascaded across the bow, occasionally reaching the single gun of the turret.

'Some escort,' observed the Nordlan seaman who recoiled the line he had coiled the afternoon before. 'Looks mean. Glad it's on our side. Leastwise, we won't have any boarding parties from the Whites this trip.'

'Do they do that often?' asked Justen, grabbing the rail to keep from being tossed against the bearded sailor.

'Nah . . . just to remind us that they're the boss. You bow and scrape and they leave you alone.'

'Like you do in Nylan?' Justen kept his face straight.

'Well . . .'

Justen grinned.

'Yeah. We're just traders, and we need to get along.'

'Serren! Stop jawing. Get moving!' The lean female third mate gestured toward the mainmast, where a handful of men and women swarmed upward. 'Looks like a bad squall's moving in.'

The seaman gave a last twist to the rope and eased languidly toward the mast.

Justen turned back to watch the *Dorrin*. Would the first engineer have wanted a ship named after him? Somehow, Justen doubted it.

20

Clerve, Altara, Justen, Berol, and Krytella stood near the bow as the *Clartham*'s paddle wheels carried the trader into Rulyarth.

Once again Justen sensed the thin edge between chaos and order within the heavy iron engine below. He doubted that the ship would make more than a handful of trips before the boiler or the cylinders or the steam lines – or something – blew apart. He wiped his forehead in the still air.

'It's bigger than Nylan or Land's End. A whole bunch bigger.' Clerve pointed toward the four long piers jutting out into the harbor. 'Look at the ships. What's the big one?'

'That's a Hamorian trader.' The lean third mate paused by the Recluce group, a grin creasing her wide mouth. 'Big and sloppy.'

The air over Rulyarth was clear, with the pink stone buildings of the port silhouetted against the blue-green sky.

'It's pretty,' offered Berol. 'They build mostly with stone, don't they?'

Justen sniffed once, then again. The harbor smelled faintly of dead fish and seaweed.

'Everything important's built of stone, and the stone's just like Sarronnyn and the Sarronnese,' offered the third mate. 'Pretty, hard, and backward. They don't do much with steam or engines. That's probably why they're going to lose to Fairhaven.' Standing by Justen's shoulder, she stopped, then nudged him. 'What's a handsome young fellow like you doing here? Just going out to throw your life away against those White devils?'

'The Whites aren't exactly invincible.' Justen flashed a smile, then continued to study the heavy-timbered wharves as the paddle wheels reversed to kill the ship's momentum. The words of the dream – 'after Sarronnyn' – popped into his head. What would happen in Sarronnyn? Could they help the Sarronnese stop the Whites, or would it be a futile effort?

'Maybe not, but a handful of you are going to stop them when the best troops left in Candar aren't succeeding? What a waste.' The third glanced toward the bowsprit, then marched toward a sailor. 'Get that back in shape!' Her arm pointed at an uncoiled line. The seaman's shoulders slumped.

'She's rather sweet on you.' Krytella edged closer to the worn wood of the railing and looked at the gray harbor water churned up by the paddle wheels.

'She also has a tongue sharper than a blade.'

The faintest hint of sulfur and cinders mixed with the odor of dead fish as a gust of wind whipped across the deck. The paddles slowed, and the *Clartham* eased against the rope-covered bumpers of the pier; a strained creaking joined the whistle of the wind and the muffled splashes of the paddle wheels.

'Lines tight! Now!' The third's voice rasped over the background noises like a file across cold iron.

'Her voice is more like a file,' observed Altara from behind Justen.

'Justen has such charm.' Krytella laughed gently, openly. 'Especially with the savage beasts.'

'Thank you.' Justen bowed, then grasped the railing to catch his balance as the ship, after rebounding from the pier, shuddered at the end of the taut mooring lines.

'Double up, and walk her in!'

'Get your gear on deck.' Altara walked toward the ladder below without waiting for an acknowledgment.

The others followed.

In time, the Recluce contingent marched down the gangway to the pier. Justen's pack rested easily on his back, cushioned by wide straps. He carried Warin's black staff in his left hand. Already the staff had begun to feel as though it belonged to him. After stepping onto the pier, he shook his head at the thought – an obsolete staff, his?

An officer in a gold-braided jacket, accompanied by two Sarronnese troopers – all of them in the traditional blue and cream – waited on the weathered planks of the wharf. The officer's eyes darted from Justen's black staff to Altara. Then she bowed slightly to the senior engineer. 'Section Leader Merwha.'

'Altara. I'm the chief engineer of the group. This is Ninca. She is the chief healer.'

The dark-haired and stocky healer nodded curtly.

'Only ten of you?' the officer asked.

'That's seven engineers and three healers.' Altara looked down on the officer. 'Dorrin was only one, and he managed to destroy half of the White forces in Spidlar.'

'He also failed to win.'

'You have a point.' Altara grinned. 'There will also be a Black marine detachment following, as well as a Weather Wizard.'

'How soon?'

Altara shrugged. 'Whenever the next ship from Nylan gets here.'

'Trusting the Legend, let's hope it won't be too long. Now a Weather Wizard, one like the great Creslin – that would be a help.'

Justen shook his head. Trust the Balance to set Gunnar up as the saving hero.

'So when will this great wizard be arriving?'

'When the great winds arrive, of course,' added Justen with a faint grin.

Altara shook her head, half in affirmation.

'Can you all ride?' Merwha gestured toward a stone-and-timber building standing on a rise behind the pier. 'That's where we're headed. The horses are stabled there.'

'One way or another,' responded Altara. 'Some of the engineers, I suspect, haven't had much practice lately.'

'Practice they'll get. It's a seven-day ride to the capital at Sarron. How much cargo did you bring?'

'I'd guess about a wagon's worth. Twenty stone-worth of tools and materials, and—' Altara gestured toward Ninca. 'How much in the way of healing goods and equipment?'

The green-clad healer inclined her head. 'We did not weigh it all, but we have two large crates and two small ones. Certainly less than the twenty stone of the engineers.'

'Sirle, have them bring the wagon here,' ordered Merwha.

The darker of the two Sarronnese troopers turned from the *Clartham* and began to walk shoreward, her steps light on the weathered timbers despite her heavy boots.

Merwha shifted her attention back to Altara. 'Once they have your crates unshipped, the wagon crew can load while we get you mounted and ready to travel.'

'There is one thing,' Altara added. 'According to the agreement, there is a stipend for food . . . and, of course, all iron and charcoal are to be supplied.'

'You sure you're not from Nordla?' asked Merwha. 'I'd rather have it straight before we've ridden six days.'

'The Tyrant suspected you might.' Merwha unstrapped a leather purse and offered it. 'That was for a larger contingent. I trust it will last somewhat longer.'

'We always stick to our agreements.'

Merwha nodded. 'Unlike some.'

'Unlike some,' Altara agreed.

Justen glanced back at the *Clartham* before studying the pier: a long structure anchored on round wooden posts – logs stripped and planed roughly into shape – nearly a cubit across. He tapped his staff on the heavy planks, weathered and gray. The dull thud and vibration of the staff against his hand confirmed the pier's solidity.

At the end of the pier, Trooper Sirle reached the waiting wagon, and with a flick of a whip, the teamster on the seat started the two-horse team toward the *Clartham*.

Only the faintest vibration traveled up through Justen's boots. Even with the heavy wagon rolling out to the ship, the pier felt nearly as solid as if it had been built of stone.

21

'Easy, horse. Easy . . .' Justen patted the beast's neck, taking care not to lean too far forward. According to his limited order-senses, his mount was old, docile, and without even a rudimentary sense of self-identity. Justen's lips twisted. He'd known statues with more awareness, but at least the gray had no interest in contesting who might be master – a contest Justen felt he probably wouldn't win with a more spirited mount such as the one Altara rode.

The chief engineer edged the bay up beside him. 'How are you doing?'

'That depends on how far we have to go.' The junior engineer glanced at the hard-packed clay that ran in a gentle curve roughly south for about a kay before swinging south-west toward what appeared to be a bridge. His eyes flicked to the heavy gray sky. 'I just hope it doesn't rain for a while.'

'I'm no Weather Wizard, but it probably won't rain until later, not until after we're off the road. Merwha says we'll be staying in the inn next to the barracks in that town ahead.'

'What town?' snorted Nicos. 'There's a bridge and a wide spot in the road.'

'It's at least as wide as Turnhill,' quipped Jirrl. 'Maybe even wider, and this place has a river worthy of the name.'

Nicos opened his mouth, closed it, and grinned. 'Fair enough. I suppose I deserved that, even if . . .' He shook his head. 'But Turnhill is a prettier sight, I daresay.'

Clerve, riding behind Nicos on a mare even more swaybacked than Justen's, smiled broadly. Altara urged the bay forward to rejoin the Sarronnese officer.

Justen's smile slipped as he swatted at a large fly that buzzed around his right ear. The fly evaded the motion and headed for the other ear, but Justen's fingers were quicker. 'Got you!' He wiped off his fingers on the gray's shoulder. The horse plodded on.

Another fly buzzed toward him. Justen swatted, but missed.

'Why don't you set a ward?' suggested Krytella, riding up beside him.

'Wards aren't exactly that easy when you're moving. Besides, I'm an engineer, not a mage or a healer.'

'It's not that hard. It didn't take Gunnar very long to learn. Let me show you.' Krytella eased her mount closer to Justen and brushed a stray red hair back off her forehead. 'Just let your senses feel the pattern.'

Justen closed his eyes and tried to block out visual distractions and the conversations of the other riders. Even so, he couldn't help but overhear parts of what was being said.

'. . . not see a lovelier stream than the Eddywash . . . not like this flowing brown bog they call a river . . .'

'. . . Iron Guard and the White lancers . . . isn't much left of Deneris . . .'

Justen wrenched his senses back to the patterns Krytella wove.

'Do you see?' the healer asked.

'Can you do it again?'

As she repeated the gentle order-spinning, Justen tried to mimic her manipulations.

'You almost had it! Try it again.'

Justen tried once more.

'Not quite. I'll do it again.'

After several more demonstrations by the redheaded healer, Justen finally wove a thin order-web around the gray and himself.

'Thank you ever so much, Master Justen.' Clerve swatted at several flies and nearly fell from his swaybacked mount, his hand swinging past the guitar case as he regained his balance.

'I'm sorry.' Justen concentrated, then sighed and wiped the sweat from his forehead as he set a second ward around the apprentice engineer.

'That won't last,' warned Krytella. 'He didn't set it himself.'

'I know, but maybe the flies will bother someone else and forget about Clerve.'

'How did you do that, Justen?' asked the apprentice.

'I followed the healer's instructions. But it won't stay too long, so enjoy it.' Justen pursed his lips. Something about the wards bothered him, not that he could exactly understand why.

'I told you that you could do it.'

Justen grinned.

'You might make a mage or a wizard yet.'

'Hardly.'

'Here comes the bridge. Will we really get to stop?' asked Clerve.

'Of course.' Krytella glanced to her right, where the sun still hung well above the river and the western horizon. 'We might even get to see what we're eating for dinner.'

'It's supper here.' Berol's voice drifted forward above the muffled thuds of hooves on the damp clay of the road.

Less than fifty cubits from the bridge stood a kaystone bearing a single name: Lornth. Merwha reined in until the Recluce contingent closed up, then eased her chestnut forward.

More of the hard pink stones formed the two-span bridge over the River Sarron, now scarcely a hundred cubits wide. The paving blocks that comprised the roadway were hollowed with use. An old man with a broom watched from the far end as the Sarronnese officer led her charges across.

Justen glanced over his shoulder after crossing. The sweeper was back at work. 'I wonder if each bridge has a sweeper.'

'Probably,' said Nicos. 'They're all clean, and that's more than I could say about the ones I saw in Lydiar last year. Most of them filthy and grimy.'

On each side of the road stood single-storied buildings. Each building's walls were smooth-finished, as if plastered, in a pink so pale that it was almost white.

Justen extended his senses to discover that each wall was in fact brick covered with a hard surface. 'How do they finish the walls?' He turned in the saddle toward Nicos.

The other engineer shrugged.

'It's a local cement, I think.' Berol's voice carried over the echo of hooves on the stone pavement of the town street leading toward a square. 'Clay and burned limestone crushed together into a powder. Some of the red clays allow it to dry even underwater. They probably use it for the bridge piers.'

Nicos shrugged; Justen grinned.

The murmur of voices in the central square died away as Merwha led the contingent around to the right. Neither grass nor sculpture graced the square, which was merely an open, stone-paved expanse surrounded by two-and three-storied buildings. Justen saw a chandlery, a cooper's shop, and a dry-goods store – where one of the traditional maroon Sarronnese carpets, showing four-pointed curled stars, hung in the window. A handful of carts stood in a rough rectangle on the stones in the middle of the square. Less than a score of Sarronnese – peddlers and their customers – were scattered about. All remained silent as Merwha led the double line of riders out of the square and down another stone-paved street.

'. . . Black bastards.'

'Hush . . . maybe they'll help . . .'

'. . . don't know who's worse . . .'

Once they had left the square, the murmurs behind increased.

'And they want more of us?' Quentel's voice carried back from near the head of the column.

A small boy darted from an alley, saw the horses and the seven black-clad riders, and dashed back into the shadows.

Merwha reined up before a long timber-and-brick building. 'Your mounts will be stabled here.' She pointed across the street to a two-story building whose facade bore the image of a tilted bowl with liquid flowing out. Under the faded image were the words, *The Overflowing Bowl*, in Temple script. 'You'll stay there tonight. The Tyrant pays for your lodging, but your meals are yours.'

Justen nodded at the almost ritualistic phrases that Merwha had uttered every night.

'We leave at the second morning bell. Tomorrow night, with luck, we'll be in Sarron itself.'

Gingerly, Justen dismounted. His legs did hold him, although the muscles above his knees cramped for a moment.

'Use the end stalls!' Merwha added with a motion toward the section of the stable farthest from the inn.

Justen flicked the reins and walked tiredly toward the end of the stable. The gray lumbered after him.

'It feels good to walk.' Altara fell in beside the younger engineer.

'It will feel better to sit down . . . I think.' Justen turned toward an open stall, leading the gray to the manger and tying the reins. Then he unfastened his pack and the black staff and leaned them against the wall before beginning to loosen the saddle girth.

By the time he had unsaddled, watered, fed, and brushed the placid gray, thrown his gear over his shoulder, picked up the staff, and closed the stall door, most of the others were waiting, except for Nicos and Clerve, who straggled out as he watched.

'Men . . . always bringing up the rear.' Altara smiled after she spoke, then gestured toward the inn. 'Let's go.'

'You'd rather we brought up . . . the front?' asked Justen with a wide smile.

'Justen . . . you might be promising more than you can deliver.'

'It could be fun to see,' added Jirrl.

Even before they reached the sign above the double doors, a young woman in trousers emerged and bowed to Altara. Her eyes flicked from Altara's blade to Justen's black staff. 'You are the travelers from far Recluce?'

'That's one way of putting it,' answered the chief engineer.

'If you would follow me . . .'

'Lead on.' Altara's voice was cheerfully resigned.

'They expect miracles,' muttered Quentel.

'Then we'll have to deliver them,' answered Jirrl.

'Easy enough for you to say, woman,' retorted Nicos. 'Most of us can't charm the iron the way you can. We need hammers.'

Justen grinned. The only things soft about Jirrl were her manners and her voice. Her arms were as hard as the black iron she forged with such apparent ease.

The entry foyer was vacant except for those from Recluce and their guide.

'The five rooms on the second floor are yours. No one else is staying here tonight, but the public room—' she turned and pointed through the archway—' serves some of the officers from the Tyrant's forces. Some others, too. Supper begins at the first bell. That's not long.' She bowed to Altara.

'Thank you.' Altara returned the bow. 'Put your gear in your rooms, and wash up, if you're so minded. Then we'll eat together.'

The narrow stairs creaked, and the dark wood, although recently restained, was worn.

Altara and Krytella took the corner room, while Clerve and Justen ended up in the one that resembled a large pantry and contained just two beds and an open cabinet with three shelves. An empty basin and pitcher stood on the cabinet, and two worn towels were folded beside them.

After testing the beds, Justen tossed his pack on the one that seemed marginally harder and set the staff in the corner. Then he opened the shutters and looked out at the back wall of the barracks, then down at the narrow alley separating the two buildings.

'I'll get the water, Ser,' Clerve offered.

'Thanks.' Justen nodded and sat on the edge of the bed. He really wanted a shower, or even a bath. Neither seemed popular in Candar, although his nose was slowly becoming accustomed to the local variety of odors, most of them vaguely disagreeable.

He stood up and took two steps back to the window, trying not to sneeze at the dust raised when his sleeve brushed the dusty sill. If he sat, his buttocks ached. If he stood, his legs ached.

'Here's the water.' Clerve grinned. 'I brought a bucketfull, too.'

Justen turned and smiled back, reaching for the bucket.

Cold as the water was, he not only washed, but shaved, and felt almost rested by the time he tossed the last of the wash water out the window and descended to meet the others in the foyer.

Even though the first bell had sounded, only two small tables were occupied, one by a Sarronnese officer, the other by a local couple.

Altara studied the public room. 'No large tables. Those two in the corner . . .'

Nicos, Berol, and Jirrl sat with Ninca and her husband Castin at the corner table. Krytella joined the other engineers – Altara, Clerve, Justen, and Quentel – at the next table, set along the wall of rough-hewn pink stone. A fresh-faced serving girl, her flame-red hair braided into a single pigtail that fell between her shoulder blades, stepped up to the table. 'We have dark ale, pale beer . . . some redberry, and red wine.'

'What about food?' asked Altara.

'We have fish stew or burkha. There might be a mutton chop or two still left . . .' She looked toward the kitchen and lowered her voice. 'But the chops are a mite strong, if you know what I mean.'

Justen nodded wryly. Strong mutton chops would have him tasting sheep for days.

Altara pursed her lips. 'What's best – the burkha or the stew?'

'They are both tasty, although our . . . travelers . . . often prefer the stew. The burkha is spicy. They're both three pennies, and so are the drinks, except for the redberry. That's two.'

'Does the fish stew taste like fish?' asked Justen.

The serving girl smiled. 'It is a fish stew, Ser.'

'I'll have the burkha and the dark ale.'

Altara raised an eyebrow, but added, 'The fish stew and the redberry.'

All the others had redberry, and only Castin, in addition to Justen, chose burkha.

'Redheads are rare here,' observed Krytella as the serving girl headed for the kitchen.

'She's got hair more flamed than yours, Healer,' said Jirrl. 'Would you not say so, Justen?'

Justen fingered the battered edge of the table and nodded. He preferred the darker red of Krytella's hair.

In the far corner, the local couple, a gray-haired man and a younger woman, glanced again toward the Recluce tables, then stood abruptly and walked out.

The Sarronnese officer grinned and shook her head before taking a last swallow from her mug and raising it to indicate the need for a refill.

'Dark ale.' The words accompanied the thump as the serving girl set a heavy mug before Justen. 'Redberry the rest of the way around.' She looked at Justen. 'Three for you, Ser, and two for each of the others.'

Justen fumbled in his pouch for a moment before extracting the three coins. The serving girl scooped up the coins in a swift, sweeping movement, then turned and recovered the empty mug from the Sarronnese officer.

After taking a sip of the warm and bitter brew, the junior engineer massaged the muscles above his left knee. They had stopped aching for the moment, at least. For the first days of the trip, he hadn't been sure if they ever would.

'Still sore?' Quentel set his mug – almost completely hidden by his massive hands – back on the table.

'It's getting better.'

'You should have practiced a few other antique skills, like riding,' suggested Altara. 'Do you want to spar after supper?'

'No. I want to rest.'

'I'll spar,' Quentel volunteered.

Altara winced. 'Countering your wand or staff is like hitting an iron bar.'

'I could try,' suggested Krytella.

'I suppose it would be good for me,' Justen admitted.

Altara grinned. 'You and Quentel together. I'll work with the healer.'

'More bruises,' grumped Justen.

'I doubt it,' rumbled Quentel. 'You never stand still long enough.'

'I'm not quite as nimble now.'

'Good!'

Justen groaned.

The serving girl slid a brown stoneware plate in front of Justen, and a second before Altara, sitting to his right, then continued around the tables, dropping the plates quickly. Last, she placed a still-steaming loaf of brown bread in the middle of each table.

Altara looked at her platter and then at Justen's. 'You do have a way with them, don't you?'

Justen looked from his plate to the chipped stoneware before Altara, from the heaping stack of browned meat covered with a white sauce to the two slices before the senior engineer. A stack of green leaves rested next to Justen's meat, compared to three small leaves on Altara's plate.

'He certainly does.' Krytella glanced at her platter, nearly a mirror of Altara's. Both women shook their head.

Justen speared a small section of the meat, sliced it in two and stuffed half in his mouth. He grabbed for the ale and took a quick swallow.

'I see you're enjoying the burkha.' A hint of laughter pervaded Altara's words. 'Try the bread, if it's too hot.'

Justen took another swallow from the mug, followed with a mouthful of warm bread. Then, still chewing, he held the empty mug aloft to catch the serving girl's eye. 'Bread helps . . . didn't realize it was *that* hot,' he mumbled.

'There are lots of things we often don't realize,' added Ninca. The older healer leaned toward Altara from the adjoining table and asked the chief engineer, 'Do you know what sort of quarters we'll have in Sarron?'

'I've been assured that they're more than adequate.' Altara's tone was dry. 'And there's plenty of clean water, Merwha told me. They think we have some sort of obsession with washing.'

'We do,' laughed Quentel.

The serving girl took Justen's empty mug, flipping her braid by his face as she left to get a refill.

Justen shook his head. The ones he didn't want wanted him, and the one he wanted didn't even seem to acknowledge that he was anything other than Gunnar's younger brother. And, of course, Gunnar wasn't interested in Krytella except as a friend, just as Krytella wasn't more than friendly to Justen himself. *Is life always so perverse? Or is it that people always want what they can't have?* He looked at the remaining chunks of meat and carved off a thinner slice, slipping it into his mouth carefully. His forehead still perspired, but he was beginning to enjoy the taste: a strange mixture of sweetness, nuttiness, and fire.

He ate another piece of burkha, nodding as the serving girl replaced his empty mug with a full one. Even the leaves in the burkha didn't taste too bad.

'I think he actually likes that stuff, Krytella,' said Altara.

'Hot breath won't help you in sparring,' added Quentel.

Justen thought about Krytella's adoring looks at his absent brother Gunnar and took another slice of burkha. Sparring might be a relief of sorts.

22

Justen reined up the gray and looked uphill at the south wall of the smithy. Beside the wall ran an antique millrace. Was it still serviceable, or merely an ancient miller's dream?

A jagged line of white planks contrasted with the weathered boards that comprised the majority of the smithy's wall. He glanced toward the sprawling house, then at the outbuildings. All bore similar patterns of rebuilding, including a scattering of fresh red tiles on the house roof that stood out from the faded, almost rose color of the older tiles.

'Rather hasty repairs.'

'Ser?' asked Clerve.

Beyond the smithy was a single new building, low and long, a repetition of the Sarronnese barracks they had been quartered near for almost every night of their trip. The entire holding lay close to two kays below the outer wall to Sarron proper and stood by itself in the middle of hillside meadows that sloped up toward the pink granite of the city. Justen nodded. The Tyrant might accept help, but the Blacks of Recluce would be quartered outside the city.

'This is your . . . area, Chief Engineer,' announced Merwha.

'Safely outside Sarron, I see.' Altara's tone was dry.

'The people of Recluce are known for their desire for privacy.'

'Far be it from us to disabuse that notion.' Altara nudged her mount toward the smithy.

Justen and Clerve followed, with the Sarronnese officers trailing.

After dismounting and tying her mount, Altara slid open the wide door to the smithy. Her eyes swept around the twin forges. Although the smithy had been recently cleaned and the hard-packed clay floor was swept bare, Justen could sense bits of metal buried deep in the clay. Both of the great bellows showed new leather and bright metalwork.

'Not used in years, then cleaned up in a hurry.' The chief engineer snorted. 'Still, it'll do for a start. We'll need another forge, probably.' She turned to Nicos. 'Let's get everything unloaded. We've got work to do – lots of it, from what we've seen already.' She paused. 'Justen, you and Clerve take care of the tools. Get them out and put together some racks and what have you.'

Justen nodded.

The chief engineer turned to Quentel. 'Can you unload the wagon and get the crates in there for Justen to organize?'

Justen looked toward the healers and watched Castin unstrap a large bag, which he lifted single-handedly. Justen frowned, then grinned as he realized that the bag held flower petals for the chickens that Castin insisted he would be raising.

Clerve sighed. His fingers strayed across the leather guitar case.

'It's not that bad.' Justen grinned. 'Do you want to sweep out the old farmhouse?'

'I'll help with the tools, Ser.'

23

Justen tapped on the flatter, trying to smooth the plate on the anvil. He wished Clerve would get back with the charcoal. Working with a striker was far easier than working alone to fuller the plates into the thin sheets necessary for the rocket casings.

Toward the back of the smithy, Altara and Quentel wrestled with the big wheel they were attempting to install as part of a makeshift hammer mill. Justen took a deep breath. Having a hammer mill might help in the rough fullering. But without the use of a blast furnace, the hammer mill would be essentially cold-forming, even with the power from the small millrace, and almost as tedious as hot fullering.

Berol and Jirrl were alternating use of the small lathe, truing the rocket heads and waiting for Justen and Nicos to form more casings. Then they would slip the flush-riveted casings over the molding frame and true and smooth the outsides to reduce the chaos created by the air when the rocket was fired.

Justen lifted the hammer and repositioned the flatter. Maybe the hammer mill would help.

Hoofbeats drummed into the smithy between the strokes of the hammer, and some of the red dust of Sarronnyn seemed to precede the Sarronnese messenger. She strode into the smithy, glanced around at the engineers, then drew herself up. 'I seek Chief Engineer Altara.'

Altara set aside the tongs and wiped her forehead. 'Yes?'

'You are . . . the chief engineer?'

'None other. We're working. Engineers' work is dirty work. What would you like?'

'Ah . . . Ser . . . Section Leader Merwha would like to inform you that the detachment of Recluce marines and the Weather

Wizard will be here shortly. They have just turned off the river road onto the Tyrant's Highway.'

Altara nodded. 'Thank you.'

The messenger waited.

'Thank you,' Altara repeated. 'I can't do much until they actually get here. Convey our thanks and respects to Section Leader Merwha.'

Justen grinned as the messenger looked at the packed clay floor, then saluted and departed.

'No wonder they can't win a war . . . always interested in announcements . . .' mumbled Nicos from the adjoining forge.

'That goes for all of you. You can greet them when they get here.'

Justen lifted the hammer again . . . and again.

Even after the clopping of hooves and two blasts from a trumpet, Justen continued to hammer out the last casing section until it needed another heat. Then he set aside the hammer and wiped his dripping forehead on his ragged upper sleeve.

'You don't believe much in formalities and ritual, do you?' asked Quentel.

Justen jumped, so silently had the big engineer slipped up beside him.

'Wish I could get that kind of jump on you in sparring,' Quentel joked.

'You did well enough.' Justen fingered the still-healing bruise on his shoulder.

Quentel laughed. 'I have half a dozen. For a man who says that personal weapons are obsolete, Master Justen, you do rather well. Darkness help us if you took them seriously.'

'But I do.' Justen shrugged. 'I have to, since everyone else does.' He blotted his face on his sleeve. 'Shall we go greet the new arrivals?'

The two were the last to leave the smithy.

Krytella was already talking to Gunnar.

'. . . Sarronnese . . . don't even understand how much astra adds to the effect of boiling water . . . and . . .'

'Justen!' Gunnar looked over the healer's head toward his brother. 'You look like you've been sweating up a good storm.'

'We've been busy. How was your trip? Not that you'd let it get too rough.'

'Turmin insisted that I not meddle with the weather unless the ship was threatened.' Gunnar shrugged. 'It was fine, so I enjoyed the sunshine.'

'Our crossing was too chill to enjoy any warmth.' Justen gave his brother a wry smile. 'How was the ride from Rulyarth?'

'Horses are horses. I'm sore.'

'So was I. It passes.' A figure in marine blacks caught Justen's eye, leading a horse toward the stables at the end of the recently built barracks. Justen studied the marine for a moment before turning back to Gunnar.

'Why's Firbek here?'

'He's a marine, and this is the first real fight in centuries.' Gunnar glanced toward the barracks, where the marines continued to unload. 'I also understand that the good Counselor Ryltar prevailed upon Firbek.'

'But why?'

'I thought you knew,' interjected Krytella. 'Firbek and Ryltar are cousins. He wanted Firbek to be here so he could get a firsthand report he could trust. Ryltar's not at all in favor of anyone from Recluce being here. People say there was quite an argument in the Council.'

'Hmmm . . .' Justen pursed his lips.

'Well, Council politics aren't going to get this beast curried and watered.' Gunnar laughed.

'I'll help,' offered Krytella.

'I suppose I'd better get back to the forge.' Justen took a deep breath. 'I'll talk to you at dinner – supper, I guess they call it here.' He watched for a moment as Gunnar and Krytella led the the bay toward the stables. He cleared his throat and headed back into the smithy.

24

Thankful for the high clouds that reduced the midday heat from oppressive to merely uncomfortable, Justen crossed the yard from the smithy to the old house that quartered the healers and held the makeshift dining room – public room for both the marines and the engineers.

Cheeep . . . eeeep . . . eeeppp . . .

On the north side of the house was the small pen that had held the chicks. Now half-grown and half-feathered, they pecked in the claylike soil between their feedings. One came up with a fragment of a dried flower petal, cheeping with success.

'How long do you think before we can have some fowl?' asked Clerve.

Justen glanced at the parti-colored birds. 'A while yet, I'd say.'

'I'm getting tired of potato soup and noodles and dried beef.'

Justen nodded, then wiped his forehead. Clouds or no clouds, it was still hot, and much hotter than on Recluce. His eyes flicked toward the garden, flourishing despite the heavy, clayey soil. He clumped up the steps onto the porch and toward the open door, stepping aside as one of the younger marines left, shaking water from his hands.

'Good luck, Engineers. More noodles and spiced beef, if you can call it beef.'

The engineer nodded politely at the marine. Castin's cooking wasn't nearly so bad as the marine said, but Justen suspected that some of the judgment lay in the marine's assignment to clean-up duty. The marines always ate first, since, even with two long trestle tables crammed into the room, it wasn't really big enough for the score of marines alone, let alone the engineers and healers.

Most of the engineers and the others had already seated themselves by the time Justen and Clerve entered. With the heat from the hearth that Castin had converted to a makeshift stove, and with the inevitable burning grease, the ends of the two long trestle tables nearest the kitchen remained empty. Justen suspected that in winter, the ends by the drafty windows would be empty, not that any of the engineers really anticipated being in Sarronnyn through the winter – one way or the other.

'Well, if it isn't Justen.'

Justen tried to keep from blushing, but failed. It wasn't his fault if there were always more things to do than he had time for. He seated himself next to Jirrl and across the table from Gunnar and Krytella. Clerve sat on his left.

Eyes turned toward Castin as he set a large bowl of noodles on the end of each table.

'Noodles again?' asked Berol.

'They're egg noodles. They're good for you. My hens are laying now.'

'They're still noodles,' said Nicos.

'I know, I know,' expounded Castin. 'It's only noodles and seasoned beef. But the noodles are much better than you'll find in Sarron—'

'That's not saying much, Master Cook.' Quentel's voice was gruff, but his eyes smiled.

Castin shrugged and turned back toward his kitchen, returning almost immediately with two more bowls filled with a steaming brown gravy in which swam small chunks of meat.

Justen poured the lukewarm water into his mug, wishing for a dark beer, or even for redberry. Still, the water cut through some of the dust.

In his last trip, Castin brought back two large baskets filled with fresh-baked bread and sat down at the end of the table, next to Ninca.

'Are you sure this stuff is beef and not seaweed? And how do we know your noodles are real noodles and not some strange form of quilla beaten into the shape of noodles?' Nicos mock-glared at the dark-haired and broad-faced older healer.

'No engineer has ever had to eat cactus roots at my table.' Castin paused, frowning. 'Still, it *is* an idea . . .'

Gunnar guffawed.

'How about those chickens?' asked Clerve.

'Those are not chickens, young man. They are the most delicate of fowl, with a tenderness you will not believe.'

'I'll believe it when I get to eat one,' cracked Nicos.

'Could we just let Master Castin eat?' Altara's voice was acerbic. 'Or would you like to help grind some quilla roots into noodles? Or would you rather run the kitchen for Firbek and the marines?'

'Not me, thank you,' muttered Clerve, his voice barely loud enough for Justen to hear.

'Castin does very well, and he's awfully good-hearted to put up with all this.' Jirrl reached for the noodles and served herself before passing them to Krytella.

The healer served Gunnar and took a smaller portion for herself before handing the bowl to Justen.

'Noodles again?' asked Berol, sliding onto the bench beside Clerve.

'Of course. But they're egg noodles, not just plain noodles.' Justen filled the chipped crockery plate before him and grinned at the big woman. 'Actually, his sauces are splendid. With those sauces, even quilla would taste good.' He handed the bowl to Clerve.

Krytella doled out a small amount of the sauce and raised her eyebrows. 'I believe you also like burhka, and . . . ah . . . spice . . .'

Gunnar swallowed hard, then coughed. 'It's a good thing she's a healer, Brother.'

'Now what did you do, Justen?' asked Berol.

'Nothing. I just said that Castin makes good sauces.'

'Are you sure you didn't say that you liked things saucy?'

Justen felt himself flush. Was all the teasing because of that tavern girl in Lornth?

'He must have a guilty conscience, Krytella. Look at him.' Berol slapped the table.

Justen finally gave an exaggerated shrug and turned to Clerve. 'This is what you have to look forward to.'

'Only if you like it spicy and saucy.'

Justen claimed the bowl with the meat and sauce and ladled a liberal amount across the pile of noodles.

'He does like the sauce.'

'Don't all men?'

'Even wizards . . . I'll bet,' added Jirrl.

Justen grinned as he watched Gunnar flush.

Clerve ladled only a small portion of the sauce, but fished out several chunks of beef.

'At least the younger men are more . . . choosy about their sauce.'

Justen and Gunnar began to laugh.

25

'So. The Tyrant has agreed to provide lodgings, supplies, and compensation for those whom Recluce sends to oppose us?' Histen laughed harshly.

'It would seem that is the case.' Renwek looked back toward the draped arches that led to the empty Council Chamber.

'And how many have been sent?'

'Only a few handfuls have volunteered, most of them engineers and healers. Just one young Storm Wizard.'

'Just one young Storm Wizard? Enlighten me, Renwek. Was there not just one young Black Storm Wizard in the time of Jenred the Traitor?' Histen's lips turned at the corners as he waited for an answer.

'Ah . . . yes, High Wizard. But this one does not seem so great as Creslin.'

'Creslin could not stop Fairhaven in Candar itself for all his power, and I doubt he could do so even today. Clearly, Recluce does not wish to offend Sarronnyn. Just as clearly, they do not intend to make a great commitment. Still, it is a good idea to be wary when Storm Wizards are involved.' Histen shook his head. 'I had a message from Zerchas.'

'And what does the honorable Zerchas want?'

'He suggests that some of the stronger and more vocal young

hotheads – like Derba and Beltar – be dispatched to help in taking Sarronnyn.'

'Is he that honorable? Or does he have something else in mind?'

'Probably, but he's also being careful. He worries about casualties to the Iron Guard.'

'What about the lancers?'

Histen's eyes narrowed. 'Zerchas is absolutely correct. The Iron Guard is the key to our success, especially if those engineers from Recluce forge a great deal of black iron.'

'But the lancers routed the rebels in Kyphros . . .'

Histen sighed, once and loudly. 'Renwek, please consider your words before uttering them. Others may not have my patience.' He half-turned, then looked back. 'Find out exactly what Derba and Beltar have been doing lately. Let me know. I will be in the Tower this evening.'

Renwek bowed.

The High Wizard turned and walked toward the Tower.

26

Justen set aside the hammer as he saw Gunnar standing just inside the smithy. He wiped his forehead on his sleeve and waited for his brother to step closer.

'What are you working on?' Gunnar asked.

'Part of a launching frame. Firbek thinks that the rockets will be very useful against the Iron Guard.' Justen stretched out his fingers, then ran them idly over the smooth wood of the hammer's haft, his eyes drifting to the adjoining forge, where Clerve was helping Nicos. The apprentice lifted the hammer and struck. Justen smiled faintly and focused on his brother.

'Maybe.' Gunnar ran his thumb along his jaw. 'Maybe. Do you want to go into Sarron?'

'When?' Justen wiped the dampness from his forehead again

and glanced toward the rear of the smithy, where Altara had just straightened up from readjusting and leveling the shaft bearings for the still-unfinished hammer mill. 'We've got a lot to do.'

'Later . . . right after you finish.'

Both men paused as Clerve delivered a series of blows to the metal on Nicos's anvil. Justen wrinkled his nose to forestall a sneeze from the combined odors of metal, soot, and hot oil.

'That'll be a while.'

'It certainly will be.' Altara had walked in behind Gunnar. 'He'll be on that section of the frame until the shadows have dropped on those pink walls. And he's going to have to go with you on with that Sarronnese detachment the day after tomorrow. So here you are, cutting into productive—'

Gunnar looked apologetic. 'I didn't mean . . .' He paused. 'But he would be helpful—'

'You two.' Altara shook her head. 'All right. He can leave – this time – when that cross brace is welded and the brackets are set. That's still going to be a while.'

'Thank you.' Gunnar inclined his head.

'Why do you . . .' Altara paused. 'It's not as though you're exactly a drinker, young wizard. Did Justen put you up to this?'

'Not this time.' Gunnar closed his lips tightly for a moment, as if holding a grin.

'What are you up to that you need Justen?'

'I just want to get a feel for Sarron. If I go alone . . .' The blond man shrugged.

'I don't know as that's a good notion, going into Sarron itself, since it's more than a little clear that the Sarronnese are not overly fond of our getting too close. Still, I couldn't keep you here, Gunnar, if I wanted to, and maybe the two of you together will get into less trouble.'

'How about three?' asked Justen, looking toward the corner of the barracks building where the green banner flew. 'Besides, having a lady with us—'

'You want to take the young healer, strip away all our talent?'

'It's a good idea,' added Gunnar. 'This is one of the last bastions of the Legend.'

'Fine. Assuming that Krytella wants to accompany you two

young scoundrels. Just let Justen get on with his work for now.'

Gunnar nodded, bowed, and left.

Altara pursed her lips, then blotted her brow, leaving a damp streak of soot. She frowned and rubbed the smudge off with the back of one heavily muscled and lightly tanned forearm.

'When I look at you two . . .' she shook her head '. . . I just feel trouble. Not the ordinary kind of trouble. Something different.' The chief engineer coughed. 'Then, maybe it's this place.'

Justen nodded and swung the pieces of the cross brace back into the forge.

'But you do good welds, and your casings don't need much polishing, Bertol tells me.' Altara looked straight at the young engineer. 'Don't let that go to your head. You're still not that good at really fine work, like turbine blades.'

'Yes, Chief Engineer.' Justen grinned. 'Do you want to help me with the . . . fine work?'

'Justen, your work there probably isn't that fine.' Her lips quirked before she turned toward Nicos and Clerve. The apprentice set down his hammer as the chief engineer approached and passed him.

When the metal sections in the forge began to glow even brighter than the cherry red needed for fullering, Justen let his perceptions wash over the metal, waiting until the temperature eased slightly higher. Then he swung both pieces into position and completed the scarfing before the metal cooled. Following that, he slipped the sections back into the forge. After watching and adjusting the sections through another reheating, waiting as the iron reached even higher temperatures, he replaced them on the anvil and with three even strokes of the hammer, completed the first weld.

The sun was still above the horizon, if only by a few hands, when at last he left the smithy, washed, and changed.

Gunnar and Krytella sat on stools on the narrow porch of the old farmhouse that the healers – and Gunnar – shared. The engineers, Justen reflected, had the dubious privilege of smaller, if newer, cubicles in the roughly constructed barracks provided by the Tyrant. In the rain, all the rooms smelled of the stable at the north end.

'Sorry,' Justen offered as he stopped at the bottom step. 'The braces took longer. Most iron work does, I think.'

'No matter. Got your weekly pay?' asked Gunnar.

'All five pennies' worth? That won't go far. The Tyrant is so generous . . .'

'We're supposed to be helping them, not behaving like mercenaries for hire.' Krytella stood and adjusted her belt, the green tunic, and the knife. She also carried a short staff, half the length of the black one Justen had left in his room.

'I sometimes think help means different things to different people.' Gunnar climbed off the stool, which rocked on the warped and uneven planks until he put out a hand to steady it.

'It's a long walk.' Justen's eyes flicked from the dusty road up the hill toward the granite walls of Sarron, shaded even more toward the pink by the late-afternoon sun.

'It's better to leave the horses here, and you could use the exercise, anyway.' Gunnar headed toward the road.

'You haven't been hammering heavy iron all day.'

'I rode out past the Klynstatt Marshes and spent half the day grubbing through the ironwood forests.'

'Would you two stop trying to convince each other that you had the harder day?' Krytella stopped at the edge of the road to let a horse cart pass.

'Men . . . they're all the same.' The driver, a flaxen-haired older woman, grinned at the healer, then flicked the reins, and the cart full of rushes wobbled past the three, the left axle squealing so painfully that Justen winced at the lack of order in even that simple mechanical device.

'You can sense disorder in machines as well as healers do in people.' Gunnar pulled at his chin as he resumed his long strides uphill.

'At times.' Justen shrugged his shoulders, trying to relieve some of their tightness.

By the time the three reached the stone causeway leading to the walls, they were damp from the effort and the humid air.

The sentry studied the two men in black and the woman in green. 'Recluse types? From down there?' He gestured down the long incline toward the Recluse enclave, whose roofs just peeked above a grassy hill.

'Yes.' Gunnar smiled politely. 'We've never been in a city this large and prosperous.'

The woman in stark, dark-blue leathers ignored Gunnar and turned toward the healer. 'Where are you bound?'

Krytella swallowed and then grinned. 'To the market. The boys have never seen a real market. Then for a good dinner. Is there anyplace you'd recommend?'

'Any of the taverns off the traders' square are pretty good . . . except for the Brass Bull. I wouldn't take two nice young fellows there.'

'The square? Is that just off—'

'Take the main way until you get to the Guard barracks. The traders' square is just past there to the left.' The sentry stepped back and motioned them on. 'Take care of those two, lady. We don't want trouble here.' She nodded to Krytella as the three passed.

'I'm beginning to understand why Creslin didn't think much about the idea of coming to Sarronnyn.' Justen grinned.

'Or why he worried about being tied up with a redhead?' asked Gunnar.

Krytella blushed.

Even late in the afternoon, the avenue toward the main square was half-filled. They eased past a wagon full of tanned hides that were being unloaded into a large building. Justen wrinkled his nose at the acrid smell that seeped from the wagon bed.

'They must have used it for more than tanned leather,' Gunnar observed.

Justen let his perceptions touch the wood. 'It feels similar to some quenches, except with an edge.'

Krytella and Gunnar exchanged a quick glance that Justen ignored as the three stepped into the market square, still nearly filled with vendors despite the nearness of twilight.

'Carpets . . . carpets from the best midland wool . . .'

'Blades . . . the best blades this side of Hamor . . .'

'See the best carpets in Sarron . . . soft as a baby's cheek . . . stronger than spun brass.'

'Spices . . . fresh spices. Get your astra here . . . fresher than the Blacks' best . . .'

At the last boast, Krytella paused and turned toward the hawker, her eyebrows raised for a moment. The woman who stood before a small, dark-wood cart with nearly a dozen cloth bags spread out on the sale board fell silent.

'All the way from Hamor, and they're fresher than from Recluce?' probed Krytella.

'They are fresh . . . lady.'

Krytella smiled faintly, then nodded first toward Gunnar, then toward Justen. She began to walk toward the far side of the square, toward a narrow, gray building that topped the two beside it by a handful of cubits.

Justen held back a frown, but turned and followed the other two.

'Look at that lady . . . two hunks like that!'

'Like the blond one . . .'

'No . . . the darker one's got a nicer ass. The blond's a little thin.'

Justen glanced sideways at Gunnar, grinning, but his brother's thoughts were off somewhere, certainly not focusing on the local conversation.

'A little thin? He makes your Friedner look like an underweight calf. Bet you wouldn't turn him out of your bed, Cerla. Of course, the dark one's definitely something . . .'

Justen felt himself flushing and turned to catch Krytella's eyes. The healer was also flushing.

'They're rather . . . direct here.' Justen caught sight of a tasteful inn board displaying a silver shield rimmed in black. 'There's an inn, and it's not the Brass Bull.'

The Silver Shield's public room, despite a faint smokiness that recalled burned grease, had unshuttered windows and a faint breeze that Justen appreciated on a close afternoon. Most of the tables were empty, and the three sat in the corner at a circular table that offered each of them a view of the doorway.

Gunnar gestured to a serving boy, thin and younger than most apprentices on Recluce. 'Could we have some drinks?'

The serving boy ignored Gunnar and turned to Krytella. 'Yes, my lady?'

Krytella grinned at Gunnar, then looked to the youth. 'What do you offer?'

'We have red wine, dark beer, lager, and redberry.' The youth's voice almost squeaked. He cleared his throat and waited.

Krytella nodded toward Gunnar, then toward Justen.

'I'd like a dark beer,' Justen said, trying not to grin.

'I'll have a redberry,' Gunnar said.

The youth looked to Krytella, then finally asked, 'Your wish, lady?'

'A redberry.'

The youth looked from her to the two men, raising an eyebrow.

'Two redberries and a dark beer,' Krytella told him.

'Thank you.' The youth hurried toward the back room, his slippered feet whispering on the worn and wide-plank floors.

Two white-haired women sat at a table along one wall with a game board between them, nursing mugs of something. Justen glanced toward the pair, trying to determine the game, which seemed to employ red and black counters.

'Are you finding out anything?' Krytella lowered her voice.

'Besides too much chaos for a home of the Legend?' Gunnar's voice was equally low. 'No.'

Justen licked his lips and tried to let his thoughts go blank, to let his perceptions pick up a sense of what might be happening in Sarron.

Near the door, a single woman, dressed in the blue leathers that indicated a soldier in service to the Tyrant, sipped from a chipped, gray-crockery mug. Her gray-and-black hair was cropped short, and a white scar crossed her left cheekbone. Two empty mugs stood on the corner of the table.

As his perceptions drifted past the older soldier, Justen caught a sense of regret, almost of emptiness, but the emptiness was honest, close to ordered sadness.

Justen could catch hints of something out in the square, like a faint but unseen white mist that tugged at the corners of buildings and drifted along the gutters and peered from the covered sewers.

'Your beer, Ser.' The serving boy set a mug before Krytella.

'That's for my friend.' She nodded toward Justen, who sat up with a twitch at the thump of the mugs on the table.

The youth smiled politely and set one redberry before the healer, and the other before Gunnar. 'That will be a silver and four, Ser.' The beer stayed put.

'A silver and four?'

'With the White devils coming through the mountains, there's been some hoarding. They say they burn anyone who's a Legend-holder.'

Justen handed Krytella a half-silver, as did Gunnar. The healer handed the server three half-silvers. 'The extra is yours.'

'My pleasure, lady.' He blinked long, sooty eyelashes at the healer. 'My pleasure.'

Justen watched as the boy minced back toward the kitchen.

'Don't glare, Justen, dear. It's not becoming.' Krytella's voice was pitched loud enough to carry to the other corner table, where two round-faced traders – one in gray, the other in brown – gestured at each other across a tray of glittering stones. Both women paused for an instant and studied the three from Recluce. Then the one in brown flashed a quick smile to Krytella before turning back to her dickering.

'Was that totally necessary?' Justen didn't know whether to grin or be annoyed.

'Absolutely.' Krytella winked, then looked at Gunnar.

'There's too much chaos under the surface here, but I haven't been able to really link it to any one place.' The Air Wizard lifted his mug to his lips and sipped. 'There's also a lot of fear.'

Krytella slid the beer in front of Justen, who decided to say nothing about his own, obviously far weaker, attempts to track the underlying chaos. Instead, he took a long swallow from the mug and listened to the low-voiced conversation.

'You think the Whites already have the city?' Krytella asked.

Gunnar shook his head. 'The traces aren't that strong. But if they get here, I don't think there will be much resistance.'

'Why not?'

Justen could have answered that easily enough, but he took another sip of the dark beer, more bitter with its hints of chaos than it should have been, and an illustration of the answer.

'Order, especially, needs a focus. If you start bribing or removing the people around whom order would build . . .' Gunnar shrugged.

Justen nodded. Gunnar had explained even more clearly than he could have.

Krytella paused and took another sip of redberry. The three sat silent for a time, occasionally sipping from their mugs.

'Would you like anything else?' The serving boy batted the long, sooty eyelashes at Krytella.

The blatant nature of the come-on twisted Justen's stomach, especially when he realized that the youth was not chaos-driven, at least not beyond the normal desires of young men.

'I should think not, thank you.' Krytella offered a smile, patently false, but the youth batted his eyelashes back in return before bowing and departing.

'This place *is* different,' admitted Gunnar.

'I can see why Creslin didn't want to come here,' added Justen, trying not to grin as he baited the healer.

'If that's the way you feel, well . . .' mused Krytella' . . . I think it makes me glad we're helping the Legend.'

'Are we?' Gunnar asked.

The soldier at the father table set her third mug on the corner of the table, then stood and walked with exaggerated care toward the open doorway to the square. The serving boy reclaimed the mugs and the coin that rested beside them.

'I would hope so.' Krytella lowered her voice. 'The Sarronnese haven't been able to slow the Whites, and that's why they asked for Firbek and the marines to join them on the north road that leads to Middlevale. I wanted to go with you and Justen, but Ninca said someone has to stay.'

'I wasn't exactly given much choice.' Justen's voice was wry. 'And no one can tell me exactly what I'm supposed to do, except to try to figure out some way to help. Gunnar here can at least use the winds to spy out where the Whites are, or to bring in a fog or something.'

'I'm sure you'll do just fine, Justen. Dorrin was very successful at that,' Krytella reassured him.

'That was centuries ago. Who knows how successful he really was?'

'You sound somewhat skeptical, Brother.'

'I'm always skeptical of legends and tales of long-dead heroes.'

The scraping of a chair interrupted the low-voiced conversation as the two traders rose from their table and left. Justen glanced around the near-empty public room, vacant now except for them – and the long-lashed serving boy, who waited by the doorway to the back room. 'Everyone else has left.'

'I'm done,' Krytella said. 'I hope your feelings about Sarron were worth the overpriced redberry.'

'Probably not.' Gunnar swallowed the last of his drink.

'The beer wasn't bad,' Justen added. 'Bitter, but not bad.'

'How you can drink that . . .' muttered Gunnar.

The healer shook her head but said nothing, ignoring even the last flirtatious smile and batted eyelashes from the serving boy.

Only a handful of hawkers remained in the square outside the Silver Shield, and even those were packing their wares into cases or packs as the three headed back toward the main gate – except for the carpet merchants, who had rolled their wares into long, heavy tubes. Although the tannery wagon had long since left, Justen could still smell a lingering odor of solvents and manure as they passed the barred door of the leather shop.

The gate guards scarcely looked at the three leaving Sarron and walking down the causeway behind an empty farm wagon pulled by a single swaybacked chestnut.

Gunnar jumped aside to avoid a steaming pile of just-delivered dung. 'It doesn't pay to follow horses too closely.'

'Not on foot, anyway.' Justen shivered as once again he felt the miasma of chaos that seemed to lurk beyond the pale pink granite walls of Sarron, like a too-early winter fog seeping out of the Westhorns and across the unharvested green of the land.

'Are you cold? You aren't sick, are you?' asked Krytella.

'I will be if you'll take care of me.' He forced a semi-lecherous grin, then let it drop away as he caught the worried expression on his brother's face.

The sound of a single horse echoed through the twilight, and the three glanced downhill toward the rider in black who swung past the farm wagon.

'Healer!' Firbek reined up. 'The chief engineer needs you. One of the engineers got an arm caught in the mill.'

Something about the marine bothered Justen, even though he could sense that the man told the truth.

'Give me a ride.'

Krytella took the marine's hand and swung up behind the saddle with a quick boost from Gunnar. The two brothers watched as the heavy-laden horse headed back downhill.

'Where are the other two healers?' asked Justen, brushing

away an unseen mosquito. He swatted again, too distracted to try to set up a ward against the hungry insects.

'They were requested to visit the Tyrant. Apparently her daughter, the heir, had some difficulty that Ninca thought they could help. In the interests of harmony and goodwill, the chief engineer agreed.' Gunnar motioned toward the enclave. 'We probably ought to get back.'

Justen nodded, and they began to walk more quickly downhill.

'You felt it, too, didn't you?' asked Gunnar.

'What?'

'Firbek. He doesn't feel quite right. It's not chaos, but it's . . . something.'

'I've always felt that way about Firbek.' Justen laughed harshly.

'You may have a reason. Still . . .' Gunnar shrugged. 'We'll have to watch him when we head into the Westhorns.'

The brothers kept walking.

27

Justen rubbed the muscles above his right knee, then his left. Finally, he slipped one foot out of the stirrup, flexing it and trying to reduce the cramping. Even with all the riding he'd done lately, he wondered if he'd ever get used to horses.

He glanced down the sloping hill to the right, where the stream that eventually fed into the River Sarron wound its way through the rocky foothills of southeast Sarronnyn. To his left rose the Westhorns, their heights still glittering in the summer air with ice that even the Great Change had not been able to erase. Sarron itself lay nearly five days behind.

How had he gotten into this mess? His limited experience on horseback had certainly not prepared him for so many days in the saddle. The gray plodded around another narrow turn in the road. And why was he here? With Quentel's right arm shattered and useless for seasons, if not forever, why was he riding with armed soldiers who certainly knew far more about the business of slaughter than he could ever pick up in watching a fight or two?

A chill breeze whipped down the canyon and ripped at his jacket. He shook his head.

'Cold, isn't it?' asked Yonada, the black-haired officer who rode up beside him.

Justen turned and shifted his weight in the saddle. 'It's not the chill. It's the riding.' His gloved fingers brushed the black staff in the lance holder, feeling the warmth of order even through the leather and even as his head throbbed at the evasion he had voiced. Somehow, the evasions and the little deceptions bothered him more than they used to. Was it because of the closeness of the Whites?

'You get accustomed to it.'

The carts behind Justen creaked. He turned in the saddle, swaying somewhat, to make sure that the rockets and the launching frame remained securely lashed in place.

Yonada followed his look, licked her lips. 'I can't believe you can ride so close to all that powder.'

'You are.' Justen grinned.

'Only because you are, Engineer. How can you be sure that some White Wizard won't touch it off?'

'I can't. But not one of them has been able to touch powder held in black iron since Dorrin came up with the idea centuries ago.' Justen looked forward to the beginning of the column, where Gunnar rode beside Dyessa, the angular force leader, who reminded Justen of a handful of iron rods not quite fully welded together.

Just before the two disappeared around the switchback, Dyessa smiled at Gunnar in response to whatever he had said.

Justen shook his head.

'That wizard, he must be something.' Yonada flicked the reins gently. 'Dyessa almost never smiles.'

'Oh, he is.'

'You know him?' The black-haired Sarronnese officer laughed. 'I suppose that's a stupid question. You're both from Recluce.'

'Recluce isn't that small. It takes a solid six days to ride from one end of the island to the other. That's almost as far as from Rulyarth to the Tyrant's palace in Sarron. There are lots of people I don't know. But the wizard's my brother, Gunnar.'

'Younger?'

'Older,' corrected Justen with a wry smile. 'Air Wizards always tend to look younger. Why, I don't know.'

Yonada's horse edged closer to his, and Justen studied the road as they neared the switchback around which the others had disappeared. To the right of the road, the stream had cut a channel only a handful of cubits wide. Just beyond the switchback, the water dropped into a narrow gorge of dark, reddish rock almost thirty cubits deep. The canyon narrowed until the road was barely wide enough for but a single cart – hemmed in on the left by a sheer ledge that rose nearly a hundred cubits and by the gorge on the right. Beyond the gorge and the rushing water was another sheer wall rising to a greenish-blue sky, partly obscured by hazy white clouds.

Even at midday, the road was shadowed and cool, although Justen occasionally felt a gust of warmer and moister summer air probing the depths of the canyon from somewhere.

'We're almost there,' the Sarronnese offered.

'Where?'

'Middlevale.' Yonada took a deep breath. 'This could be—' She broke off in mid-sentence.

Justen caught a hint of raw fear behind the words. What was it about the Whites that so bothered the Sarronnese? The fact that the Sarronnese viewed the invasion as a White crusade against the Legend?

Beyond the switchback turn, the road narrowed even more, then opened onto a small valley with steep walls of reddish rock. Middlevale was hilly, perhaps two kays long, filled with rocky, shrubcovered hillocks and scrub oak. A small inn, with but two chimneys and a single story, hunkered just off the dusty road between two larger hillocks not more than half a kay from Justen. From a stripped sapling between the hut that served as a stable and the inn itself flew the blue ensign of Sarronnyn.

Justen pursed his lips and turned to Yonada. 'I don't understand why you didn't defend the eastern gap there.' He pointed to the far end of the valley and to the narrow defile from which the White forces would presumably emerge.

'We tried that idea when we were forced out of Westwind. But the Chaos Wizard just loosened the rocks in the narrow canyons – and Derla's whole force was smashed. The Whites can't do that on open ground.'

'If they drop rocks, doesn't that block the way for them later?'

'They just blow up the rocks. It takes a while and slows them down, but they can do it. We can't.'

Justen nodded. He hadn't fully considered all the things that a Chaos Wizard could do in mountain warfare.

Two riders galloped across the valley, raising thick dust that hung behind them like a red fog. Justen squinted to make out what was happening as the scouts reined in near the middle of the Sarronnese forces, foot levies in two roughly parallel lines perpendicular to the road, reinforced in the center by the horse troopers. On each flank were additional cavalry, carefully positioned behind copses of scraggly trees.

'Over there!' Firbek stretched in his stirrups and pointed toward a taller hillock in the midst of the Sarronnese forces. 'We need to set up there. Get that cart moving!'

The marine ranker on the cart snapped the traces, and the cart groaned past the inn and toward the hillock pointed out by Firbek.

A thin, bearded man – broom in hand – and a gray-haired woman watched silently from the doorway of the inn.

'Why don't they leave? There's going to be a fight here.' Justen looked back toward the center of the Sarronnese troops, where Gunnar, Dyessa, and the bulk of the reinforcements had joined up.

'I don't know. Everyone was told to leave. Where there's a battle, the Whites burn everything to ashes.'

The battle ensign dipped twice, and three short blasts from a trumpet followed.

'Strike two! Strike two!' Yonada stood in the stirrups and gestured. 'Form up.' She lowered her voice and turned to Justen, pointing to the hillock where Firbek stood amid the brush and red rocks. 'I'll see you there later.'

Justen watched as Yonada's squads peeled away. He rode alone toward the marines, feeling almost useless . . . and some-how vaguely regretful that the friendly Yonada was gone. And he wondered why he was riding into a battle for no really good reason – just to observe? His fingers brushed the black staff, and he smiled faintly at the warmth of the order residing there.

What was he supposed to discover? A new weapon, as if he were some second Dorrin? And who knew whether any of the stories about the great Dorrin were really true? Justen hardly felt comparable to the venerated ancient smith. At least Gunnar could ride the breezes and tell the Sarronnese leaders where the enemy forces were.

Justen tried to send his perceptions out beyond the valley, but he could sense nothing past a few hundred cubits. He nudged the gray, who did not move until he knocked his booted heels into her flanks. Then she ambled toward the hillock where Firbek wrestled the rocket launching rack off the cart. Justen dug his heels into her flanks again, and she lurched into a trot, forcing him to grab the edge of the saddle and hope his staff didn't bounce out of the lance holder.

Great engineers didn't have to hold onto saddles, did they? Justen hung on until the gray slowed down to a walk at the beginning of the hill's upslope. He reined in near the top and looked eastward.

What seemed like a stream of white-coated figures issued from the defile at the far end of Middlevale and poured into the flat plain.

The Sarronnese trumpet sounded again, and the foot soldiers dropped to a kneeling position behind hastily heaped piles of earth and sand, holding long pikes ready to lift.

The blue cavalry dropped blindfolds over their mounts' eyes.

The White forces marched forward several hundred kays, then halted – out of bow range.

Hssttt!

A firebolt flared from amid the white banners waving behind a cluster of head-high, pink-gray boulders to the right of the east entrance to Middlevale.

The gray under Justen whimpered and sidestepped, and the engineer urged her partly back down the hillock, where he dismounted and tied her to the same scrub oak as Firbek's mount. Then he scrambled back up the rocket emplacement.

Another firebolt flashed from the area of the white banners, dropping just short of the front line of the Sarronnese. Even before it had hissed into a blackened spot on the sandy earth, another fireball arced into the Sarronnese lines.

A scream echoed across Middlevale.

A heavy roll of drums thundered from the east end of the valley, and the White foot and lancers began to move forward as another fireball smashed into the left side of the thin Sarronnese line.

'Rockets ready!' snapped Firbek.

Justen frowned. The Whites were well beyond the normal range of the ship-to-ship rockets. He edged up to Firbek. 'The rockets aren't accurate at that distance.'

'Strike the first!' ordered Firbek, not even looking at Justen.

Whhstt! After heading straight from the small launcher, the rocket neared the White lines, then curved to the right, past the soldiers in gray, and exploded in a gout of flame against a boulder.

'Another one!' snapped Firbek.

The two marines lifted another rocket into the black iron tube.

'It's too far,' Justen said.

'We can't get any closer.' Firbek turned toward the woman marine with the striker. 'Strike it.'

Whhssttt!

The second rocket flared straight toward the Iron Guard, then twisted upward, exploding in a shower of iron fragments and flame.

The White lancers rode forward at an even pace, carrying white-bronze lances with tips that glistened with fire. Justen scanned the lines, noting that the Whites outnumbered the Sarronnese almost two to one.

Another roll of drums, and the White lancers charged.

A staccato trumpet command warbled from the Sarronnese side, and the pikes came up, except at the far left flank.

The lancers peeled away from the pikes, all but those directly in front of the marine position, where nearly a full squad angled through and began cutting the pike-holders down from behind. The left flank began to crumple.

'There. Lower the launcher!' Firbek jabbed toward the White lancers.

Hhhsttt! The firebolt exploded in front of the launcher, and one of the marines flared into a charred pillar, toppling forward on the crest of the hill.

Ignoring the sickly odor of burnt meat, Justen grabbed the lefthand wheel on the launcher and began to crank while the woman marine slipped another rocket into place.

'Strike it!'

Justen released his hold on the wheel and concentrated, trying to sense the air around the rocket, but the missile curved into the stony ground and cartwheeled into a fir, turning the tree into an instant torch.

Hhhssttt! A firebolt flared from the higher stretch of road on the far side of the valley and washed across the leading row of the Sarronnese to the left of the gap in the line so quickly that none of the four even screamed as they turned into dark ash.

'Do something, Engineer!' bellowed Firbek.

'Cover!' ordered Dyessa.

The Sarronnese scattered for boulders, for low, rocky rises in the uneven valley floor, even for the few tree trunks.

The Iron Guard horse formed up into strike squads at the far end of the canyon.

Justen glanced around, searching for Gunnar, but his brother was nowhere to be seen.

'Another rocket!' demanded Firbek.

Justen and the remaining marine adjusted the launching frame, then dropped behind it as a firebolt washed harmlessly over the black iron.

As soon as the flame subsided, Justen lowered the launcher until it was pointing directly at the nearest lancers, then forced himself into a semblance of detached calmness. This time, he concentrated on the rocket itself, trying to add a touch more order to the casing, a sense of smoothness, a sense of direction. He continued to pour order into the metal even as the marine touched off the fuse.

Crrrummpp! The fourth rocket exploded where it had been aimed – right in the midst of the lead squad of the White lancers – casting black iron shards into dozens of bodies. The White lancers, even those barely touched by the shrapnel, flared into points of flame.

A wave of whiteness flowed back from the destruction and

swept around Justen. He staggered and put a hand out to the launcher frame to steady himself.

'You all right?' the marine asked.

Justen forced a nod against the internal chaos and straightened up.

Of the entire White lancer squad, only a single figure remained, and it wheeled its mount and galloped back toward the swelling lines of soldiers in dark gray: the Iron Guard, waiting like a storm on the horizon of the Eastern Ocean. Even on the left flank, the White lancers had peeled away, although Justen had not seen why.

For a long moment, the battlefield seemed frozen, motionless.

Then another set of drum-rolls rumbled from the east, and the white-clad foot began to march forward, away from the Iron Guard, almost like breakers preceding a wave.

'Another rocket!' ordered Firbek.

Justen again smoothed the flows and forces around the rocket and then watched as a whole section of White forces flashed into flame with the missile's explosion. But the white-clad wave continued onward, rolling toward them even as Justen struggled to remain upright against the white backlash.

'Strike!'

Whhhssttt . . .

'. . . strike . . .'

'Whhssttt . . .

'Strike . . . strike . . .'

How long the marine lit off rockets and Justen smoothed their path to destruction and chaos, the engineer was unsure, only that the pattern ended.

'Ser! We have only a handful of rockets left.'

Justen studied the valley, noting the greasy black splotches across the entire eastern end and the seemingly endless lines of white and gray troops marshaled below the red rocks.

The sun hung barely above the western lip of the canyon valley. Had that much time passed?

A double drum-roll rumbled into the late afternoon, and now the gray-clad Iron Guard foot marched forward toward the concentrated knot of Sarronnese foot, backed with the remaining archers and perhaps two squads of cavalry.

The Sarronnese held only the two central hillocks and the ground between.

'Why don't they go around?' Justen asked no one in particular. 'We couldn't stop them now.'

'Once they start to fight, Engineer, they leave no survivors.'

Justen's stomach tightened. All he was supposed to have done was to watch and learn. Instead, he had been killing, and he was just about to be killed.

'Might as well try the rest of the rockets.' Firbek's voice was hoarse.

Justen helped depress the launcher once more and waited for the woman to squeeze the striker. And Justen again smoothed the flows and forces around the rocket. The black iron missile flared into the advancing Iron Guards. A handful fell like leaden dummies or disjointed marionettes, but there were no flares and explosions – not as with the White lancers.

And still more troops seemed to pour from the defile in the eastern end of Middlevale.

Justen glanced to his left and right. More than half of the Sarronnese forces seemed to be down, burned to ashes, or missing.

'Strike another one!' Firbek demanded.

Justen concentrated once more on supplying order to the rocket. And once more another set of Iron Guards toppled as they strode toward the scattered Sarronnese forces. But the Iron Guards advanced as slowly and steadily as the tide.

Three more firebolts flared from the line of boulders just beyond the eastern entrance to Middlevale. Two dashed themselves against stony hillocks. Screams followed the third, which had struck two mounted troopers on the edge of the command post where Dyessa and Gunnar remained, still mounted. A scraggly fir began to burn.

'Get that light-fired rocket in the launcher!' Firbek glanced toward the white banners at the end of the valley. 'Aim it toward those white banners.'

The woman marine slipped the rocket into place and looked up, striker in hand. 'You like to help us, Ser?'

Firbek scowled, but he walked over to the remaining case of rockets.

The marine ranker squeezed the striker.

Justen belatedly focused his attention on the rocket, enough so that it wobbled only slightly before plowing through a line of foot soldiers under a crimson-fringed gray banner. Another wave of whiteness flowing back from the destruction swept around Justen, and he put out a hand to the launcher frame to steady himself.

'You all right, Engineer?' The woman marine looked at him.

'Sort of.'

Firbek levered out another rocket.

'Shouldn't we save a few?' asked Justen.

'For what? Wait, and they'll all be at our necks. Will be anyway before long, unless the wizard pulls out a miracle.' Firbek slid the rocket into the tube.

A heavy drum-roll sounded, and a wave of dark-gray mounted troops swept forward, riding through the foot in dark gray to take the charge.

A woman in Sarrónnese blue scrambled up the hill toward them.

'The commander wants another barrage on the Iron Guards.' The messenger conveyed the order to Firbek calmly.

'We're almost out of rockets. We'll fire until we're done.'

'I will so inform her.' The messenger hurried back downhill, ducking calmly as another firebolt flared past her.

'Strike!'

Whssttt . . .

'Strike . . .'

'*Whsstt . . .*'

'That's it, Ser. That was the last rocket.'

Justen slumped against the hot metal of the launcher frame, not sure which was worst – the dizziness, the nausea, or the splitting headache. He straightened and staggered back down toward the gray, where he grasped for his black staff.

'We needed more rockets, Engineer. I asked for more.'

Justen touched the black staff before speaking. 'We made what we could, Firbek. They're darkness-hard to forge.'

'Hard to forge? Is it easier to die?' After glancing toward the Iron Guards headed uphill, Firbek unsheathed his sword.

Justen gripped his staff.

A rumble of thunder – thunder, not drums – echoed across

Middlevale, and a chill sense of blackness followed. Justen scrambled back toward the launcher and stared.

Like a black tower, Gunnar stood on a low hillock to the right of the one where Firbek, Justen, and the marines had labored with the rockets.

A second dull rumble filled the sky, and the thin clouds overhead seemed to thicken even as Justen watched. A third, longer, rumble echoed through the skies, and darkness fell like an early twilight as cold gusts of wind whipped across the burned battle plain.

Even the Iron Guard slowed, and the white banners at the east end of Middlevale seemed to droop, despite the wind.

Rain began to fall, first with scattered droplets, then more heavily, like a flight of cold arrows, and finally, as the afternoon skipped abruptly to late twilight, in sheets that flayed like whips.

Justen clutched his staff and staggered toward the gray, untying his own reins and Firbek's. He thrust the marine officer's reins at him, then mounted the gray and spurred her toward the other hillock, where Gunnar still stood like a short, dark tower.

Unable to see more than a few cubits beyond the gray's mane, Justen used his order-senses to guide him toward Gunnar's profligate squandering of order, lowering his head against the rush of wind and water.

Were the Whites having as much trouble as he was? Did it matter? He spurred the gray across the space between the hills and up the slope.

'Get back!' ordered Gunnar, his voice cutting through the tumult like lightning. 'Get everyone out of here!' He struggled into the saddle of the bay.

'But they'll drown in the gorge if you've called rain!' yelled Dyessa over the whistling of the wind.

Justen eased the gray closer to where Gunnar wobbled in his saddle.

'They won't. But they'll die here for certain.' Gunnar steadied himself, grasping the edge of the saddle.

Dyessa gestured to the woman with the trumpet. Three short double blasts sounded against the storm. The ensign swirled and dipped three times.

'Again! Keep it up!' Dyessa spurred her mount toward the bottom of the hill.

Justen forced a sense of order into the black staff, then extended it to Gunnar, who shook his head.

'Touch it!'

Gunnar shook his head again.

'Damn it! Don't be so frigging proud! You need it, and we need you to get out of here! Touch it!'

Gunnar reached toward the staff, and Justen thrust it against his brother's palm. The Air Wizard straightened even as Justen could sense his thoughts departing. Justen eased the gray next to the bay and began guiding his brother's mount toward the inn, toward the west end of the narrow valley, vaguely aware that the single remaining marine rode the rocket cart not more than a score of cubits ahead and that Firbek held the harness of the cart horse. He tried to ignore the shaking in his knees, not certain whether it was exhaustion or fear, or some of each.

The thunder rolled like massive drums beating through his skull, and the rain raised welts across his unprotected face, but Justen kept both horses moving, ignoring Dyessa as she chivied her troops in their retreat.

The wind whistled, the thunder drummed, and Justen rode slowly past the bare roof beams of the inn, its thatch torn loose by the force of the storm.

Behind him, the trumpet wavered.

The rain pounded through his black jacket as if he were barebacked, and with each step, the gray slowed as red mud began to form.

Before him, the sheer red rocks loomed like a wall. He edged the horses to his left and through the narrow gap. Once inside the canyon, the force of the wind and rain dropped, although the volume of the deluge did not abate.

Perhaps a dozen Sarronnese foot straggled down and around the switchback, just behind Firbek and the empty rocket cart.

The dull rumbling of the thunder echoed over Middlevale and down into the canyon. To Justen's left, the narrow cascade had become a rushing torrent, rising to within a handful of cubits below the road. How long would it continue to rise?

'That should do it for the storm.' Gunnar straightened in the saddle, looking over his shoulder.

Justen followed his brother's eyes, catching sight of the Sarronnese commander as she guided her chestnut around and through the retreating forces until she caught up with Gunnar and Justen.

'Now what? The storm won't hold them long.' Dyessa shouted to make herself heard above the wind and rain.

'Is everyone out of the valley?'

'Those that are alive.'

Gunnar lifted his shoulders and let them drop, then closed his eyes.

Justen reached over to keep his brother from falling.

A ripping, rushing, and drumming sound rose over the rain, and the sky grew darker. Even from the depths of the canyon, Justen could see the whirling black tower that swept upward.

'Light!'

Even Dyessa's face paled as she gazed back.

The roaring increased, as if the stone walls were being beaten like drums.

Thuunnk . . . unnkk . . . uinnkk . . .

A series of impacts rocked the roadbed itself, but the roaring dropped to a whisper, and the sky began to lighten. The rain kept falling, subsiding to a normal heavy downpour.

Gunnar slumped across the neck of his mount.

'You!' snapped Dyessa. 'The Recluce marine!'

Both Firbek and the woman marine turned.

'Hold there.' The Sarronnese commander jabbed toward the unconscious Storm Wizard. 'Get him on the cart. He can't ride.'

Dyessa watched as Justen and Firbek carried Gunnar onto the cart.

As he covered Gunnar with the Air Wizard's own waterproof and stepped back to remount the gray, Justen glanced to the gorge, where the water level had suddenly dropped back toward its earlier level.

'What happened?' Dyessa asked.

'I need to ride back a little. I think Gunnar dammed the valley.'

'Good. The damned Whites can't handle water.'

'What if the dam gives before we get out?'

Dyessa glanced back up the canyon, toward the unseen wall of stone and rubble behind her. 'It had better not.'

Justen had already turned. He let the gray pick her way through the last of the Sarronnese stragglers trudging downhill through the mud and rain. By the time he reached the straight section of the canyon below the switchback, he could sense the mass of stone and brush that Gunnar's whirlwind had thrown into the stream and gorge. Still, he rode almost to the switchback.

Dark water oozed through the gaps in the stones and cascaded from dozens of points into the gorge, half-filling it in its rush toward the distant River Sarron.

Justen forced his abused order-senses to enfold the storm-built barrier Gunnar had created. After studying the barrier for a time, he shook his head. His brother wasn't a bad engineer for a Storm Wizard. He wiped yet more water out of his face and turned the gray back down the canyon. Cold rivulets ran down inside his blacks, chilling him through and through. Even the inside of his boots felt soaked.

Dyessa was still waiting, but Firbek and the rocket cart – and Gunnar – were out of sight farther down the canyon, the creaking of the cart masked by the dull swishing of the continuing rain.

The Sarronnese leader looked at Justen. 'Will whatever he did hold?'

Justen wiped more rain from his face, a useless task, and shook himself. 'Forever . . . or until there's a drought and several Chaos Wizards.' Seeing the doubtful look on Dyessa's face, he added, 'There's a lake building up in Middlevale, or what was Middlevale. That much water carries a lot of order. A good Chaos Wizard or two could blast away the stones there, except for the order of the water. The lake has to be drained or dried up before wizards can do much. And they won't be doing anything until this rain ends, and I think that's not going to be for a long time – days anyway – and then if any of them survived, which I doubt many did.'

'Good. We can reinforce Zerlana somewhere.' Dyessa touched the reins and raised her voice. 'Let's get moving.'

Before she could start, Justen lifted his hand. 'Wait. Have you seen Yonada?'

'She fell in the first attack, Engineer. She bought you wizards the time to save the rest of us.'

Justen swallowed. *Yonada gone? Just like that?*

'I don't think I'll ever understand you wizards.' Dyessa shook her head. 'You devise black weapons that destroy whole squads and call storms that turn valleys into lakes and drown entire armies, and then you're surprised that someone dies.'

Justen dumbly flicked the reins. He needed to find Gunnar . . . at least.

Dyessa picked her way ahead, encouraging, organizing, as the remnants of two forces shambled back toward Sarron. Clutching the black staff, Justen rode slowly to catch up with his brother, hoping he could do something, but scarcely knowing what.

28

A jolt rocked the cart as it rumbled off the even pavement of the pink stone bridge and onto the packed clay ruts of the road. Gunnar moaned, but did not open his eyes. From his saddle on the still-placid gray, Justen lifted his left hand, reaching out instinctively, but the cart settled back into its faintly swaying roll and Gunnar lapsed back into a deeper sleep.

Even from where he rode beside the cart, Justen could sense the depletion of the order-forces within his brother. He glanced up at the marine in black riding near the front of the column beside Dyessa. Firbek rode with his knees, both hands gesturing. From the movements, Justen suspected he was explaining once again the limited range and shortcomings of the ships' rockets.

Justen snorted. Part of the problem was Firbek's lack of guts. When a weapon's accuracy was limited by range, you either moved up to get in range or you let the enemy get close enough to use it. Firbek had done neither. He'd just fired rockets almost for the sake of firing them, and had forced Justen to squander his limited abilities on getting a handful to go somewhere close to where they had been aimed. And that had meant Gunnar had damned near killed himself calling a huge storm.

So . . . now . . . while Firbek was explaining away his short-comings, Justen was worrying about his brother, laying the black staff next to him when he could, and hoping the proximity of that order would help Gunnar.

Ahead, the clay road leading from what had been Middlevale merged with the main road to Sarron. Soon they would be traveling the last section of the road that had brought Justen from Rulyarth to Sarron, since Middlevale was north and east of Sarron.

Dyessa rode past, headed toward the rear of the column, her eyes ignoring the marine driving the cart and the uncon-scious man under the worn, blue wool blanket. Justen's eyes followed her as she circled the short column and headed back to its head.

As Dyessa completed the circuit, the column turned onto the main road. Justen looked to the northwest, back along the route toward Lornth, but the river town was lost beyond the rolling hills.

Gunnar moaned again, and Justen tried to reach out, not only physically, but with his order-senses . . . only to find the same gentle barrier that had blocked him ever since the fight. How could one call the mess at Middlevale a battle?

After wiping his forehead, Justen shifted his weight in the saddle again and tried to ignore Firbek's continuing conversation with the Sarronnese commander. The rocket cart creaked, Gunnar occasionally moaned, and the gray carried Justen toward Sarron.

Well before the column trudged up the final section of the road, a single figure in green galloped downhill on a bay mare, pausing but momentarily beside Firbek and Dyessa. Krytella reined up next to the cart, dismounted, and without speaking, handed the bay's reins to Justen.

Only after she had spent some time with Gunnar, infusing enough order into the restless Air Wizard that her face had paled even under the afternoon clouds, did she slip off the still-moving cart, reclaim the reins, and remount. Her voice was cold. 'You let him do this . . . why did you let him? He's your brother.'

'I did what I could. I did give him some order before he called the storm, but once he collapsed, I really couldn't reach him.' Justen wiped his forehead again. Since summer had come to Sarronnyn, it seemed like all he did was sweat. 'I tried.'

Krytella frowned. 'You transferred a little order. How, I don't know.' Her eyes flicked back to the unconscious figure.

'I tried using the staff.' Justen cleared his throat, wondering if the clouds rolling in from the east were the result of Gunnar's storms and if they would bring more rain. 'He'll be all right, won't he?'

'He'll live. Whether he'll see or think is another question.'

'Like Creslin?'

'I don't know. I just don't know.'

Dyessa eased her mount up beside Krytella's bay. 'Greetings, Healer.'

Justen glanced past her to see that Firbek had remained near the head of the column.

'Greetings.'

The Sarronnese commander gestured vaguely toward the rocket cart. 'I hope he will recover.'

'So do I.' Krytella paused, then the words burst out as if she could no longer hold them. 'What good were all Gunnar's efforts? They clearly weren't enough to win the battle, were they?' Krytella's eyes flashed across the bedraggled column, perhaps a third of its original strength.

'No, Healer. It was just the only time we happened to have stopped the White devils in more than a season.' Dyessa looked down from her mount. 'Victories against the Whites are not exactly cheap. I thought that you of Recluce understood that. This one only cost me two-thirds of my forces – and to stop just a small body of the White devils.'

Krytella's eyes turned to the still figure on the rocket cart. 'Do you really care?'

'Healer, I am glad that your Air Wizard will survive. He and the engineer saved us. They more than deserve . . . our gratitude.' Dyessa took a deep breath. 'Whether that gratitude will mean much in the seasons ahead, I question, given our inability to hold the White devils back.'

'I . . . was too hasty . . .'

'No.' The dark-haired commander smiled sadly. 'You are probably correct. But we all do what we must.'

Krytella and Justen watched as Dyessa guided her mount back

toward the front of the riders. The column turned eastward onto the last uphill stretch toward Sarron.

The clouds thickened, and low rumbles of thunder punctuated the growing gloom.

'He really did it . . .' murmured the healer.

As the raindrops began to fall, Justen eased the gray closer to the bay on which Krytella rode, her eyes focused somewhere beyond the road.

'Krytella . . . you have to show me something.'

'What?'

'How to transfer order-force from me to someone . . .'

'That's a healer's—'

'I tried, and I couldn't do it. And Gunnar almost died.'

Krytella looked steadily at Justen. 'As much as you're jealous of Gunnar, you love him, don't you?'

Justen looked at the ground. 'He needed help, and I couldn't give it.'

'Oh, Justen . . .' The healer's hand brushed Justen's for a moment, so gently that he could not be sure that it had happened, but a warmth flowed from her to him. 'That's how it feels.'

Justen tried to ignore her closeness and to concentrate on the order-patterns. Pushing aside her warmth and sweet scent, he focused his thoughts. Ignoring the might-have-beens, he let his senses grasp the flow of order. He owed Gunnar that, if not much more.

29

The thunder outside the smithy was deep enough to be heard over the clanging of metal and the slow pounding of the hammer mill, tended carefully by Quentel, whose left arm was bound in a splint of wood and canvas.

Justen lifted the hammer, touching the iron arrowhead on the forge. He frowned. Too bad the engineers couldn't cast black iron, or that the Sarronnese smiths couldn't forge black iron, either. Like everything, black iron had its limits. Since it couldn't be cast, that meant, at least so far, that the Blacks hadn't been able to make more than a handful of black iron guns – just those on the Mighty Ten – and since the Whites could touch off cammabark or powder held in regular iron, albeit with difficulty, anyone who wasn't a White or on a Black ship risked having cannon blow up on them.

Probably the Iron Guard could use long guns or cannon, even if the regular White troops and wizards couldn't. But that limitation wouldn't help the Sarronnese much. The engineers had made a few muskets for hunting, but they weren't feasible for war. Making a musket by hand out of black iron took too much time and effort. Arrowheads were another story.

Justen took a deep breath, reflecting that the idea for arrowheads had been his, and pulled the next sheet of iron from the forge. Four quick taps with the hot set and the first rough shape was ready. Then he scarfed the base and reheated the iron to welding temperature before tapping the holed rod stock to the base. He followed with another tap to the hot set and a reforming on the special mandrel that sat in the hardie hole.

'You'd think you'd been doing that all your life,' observed Nicos, stopping for a moment on his way back from outside. The older engineer wiped sweat from his face. 'This place is hotter than Recluce was even before Creslin fixed it. I can sure see why he never wanted to come here.'

Justen nodded, recalling his trip to the Silver Shield in Sarron. 'I can think of several reasons.'

'Do you think the arrowheads will work?'

'They'll work. I just hope the Sarronnese understand how well.'

'They're in trouble. You'd think they'd use whatever works.'

'Maybe . . .' Justen cleared his throat, trying to swallow the taste of charcoal and metal. He reached for the pitcher and took a swallow of the lukewarm water.

'With the true Legend-holders, you never know.' Nicos flashed a smile and turned toward the hammer mill.

Justen resumed forging. After he had a dozen of the rough-cut arrowheads, he nodded to Clerve, who began the tedious job of filing and grinding them before Justen used the last touch of heat and order to turn them into black iron. Then the striker would use the smooth wheel on the grindstone for a final polish.

While Clerve filed and rough-ground, Justen finished another dozen forms, then began the careful ordering of those completed by Clerve.

By midday, each man was soaked from the heat of the forge and the hot, damp air that seemed to well out of the ground. But Justen had more than three dozen of the special arrowheads ready.

'That's enough for now.' He wiped his forehead and placed the hammer on his bench.

At the rear and newest forge, Altara set aside her tongs and walked over to where Justen banked the edge of his coals.

'How are you doing?'

Justen nodded toward the last half-dozen gleaming black shapes on the hearth. 'Around two score this morning. That's not enough for even a few moments of battle.'

'Dyessa wants to try them first, and Firbek thinks you ought to go with the next detachment.'

'I'm no marine.' Justen squinted at the salty sweat that had run into his left eye. He blotted it away and then walked out under the side eave of the smithy, scarcely cooler than the forge area, so still was the midsummer air.

The chief engineer followed. 'I'd like your opinion on whether we should make more arrowheads. Firbek wants more rockets.'

With a snort, Justen scooped a handful of water out of the bucket set on the small table and splashed it across his face. Altara waited.

'We'd get better results with the arrowheads,' he said at last.

'I won't get that answer from Firbek, especially if you don't go with Dyessa.'

'So . . . I have to go because Firbek loves the rockets?' The young engineer sank onto the rough bench, letting his eyes rest on the road, where two heavy-laden wagons rumbled downhill, headed eastward from Sarron. Farther downhill, another wagon also lumbered eastward. Justen shook his head.

'I could ask Clerve to go. And Krytella has suggested that the Sarronnese could use a healer,' Altara told him.

'No. I'll go. Clerve would just get himself killed. I can at least duck.'

'You don't think I should let the healer go?'

'No. The way the Whites fight, there aren't many wounded.'

'I got that impression.' Altara caught Justen's eyes. 'Thank you.'

'When does Dyessa leave?'

'Sometime within the eight-day, probably before the end days.' Altara paused. 'Why do you look so glum? You seem to forget that you were successful in stopping the White thrust through the northern pass.'

'I suppose.' Justen snorted softly. 'We were successful – if that's what you call losing three-quarters of the Sarronnese forces, half of our black iron equipment, and almost killing the one real wizard we have.'

'Justen, you're too hard on yourself.'

Justen stood. 'I'm going for some cold water and to check on Gunnar. The healers are getting some supplies from the river wharf.'

'You'll keep working on the arrowheads?'

Justen smiled and shrugged. 'I still think they'll be more useful than Firbek's rockets.'

As Altara watched, Justen stepped off the worn planks of the side porch and onto the red clay that separated the smithy from the old house. First he made his way to the pump behind the dwelling, where he rinsed one of the buckets thoroughly, even adding a touch of order to it to ensure that the water would remain pure, before half-filling it. Then he carried the bucket back to the front porch. When he stepped up to the door of the old house and looked back toward the smithy, Altara was no longer on the side porch, but had apparently returned to work.

He climbed the stairs almost on tiptoe, setting each foot down as quietly as possible. When one stair creaked, he froze for an instant, then continued. He slipped into the small garret room where Gunnar dozed. Pausing briefly, he studied his brother's open, unguarded face.

As quietly as he could, Justen used the small bucket to fill the pitcher on the stand beside the sleeping man and then slipped onto the stool beside the bed. Even as he watched his brother, the openness vanished and Gunnar's jaw tightened. A half-mumble escaped the nearly closed mouth. Gunnar's body shuddered and half-turned on the pallet.

Justen felt a sense of whiteness, of chaos held at bay. He remained sitting, wishing for the black staff, but forcing himself to remain calm. Then he recalled what old Dembek had taught him – about the depth and the order of the Eastern Ocean, about the solid grain of the iron – and slowly let the order settle around him. Reaching out gently, as Krytella had demonstrated, his fingers brushed his brother's forehead. Then, even more slowly, he let that concentrated order seep from his fingertips.

'. . . mmphh . . .' The tension oozed from Gunnar's face, and his breathing deepened slightly. The flickering of his eyelids slowed, but did not stop.

Justen waited for a time, leaving his perceptions extended, seeking a return of that fragment of chaos, but the unseen dark calm of order remained.

In time, the engineer retreated down the narrow stairs as quietly as he had come, blotting the dampness from his eyes and face, trying not to swing the bucket into the walls, and keeping his booted feet to the outside edge of the risers to reduce the creaking of the ancient steps.

30

Although Justen could sense the storms building to the west of Sarron, the air in the smithy remained hot, damp, and still, and the hammer mill's monotonous and continuous beat had given him another headache.

He coughed, set down the hammer for a moment, and watched as Clerve used the grindstone to polish and smooth the finished black iron arrowheads. After a deep breath, he eased the iron stock into the forge and waited for the metal to heat. Then he reclaimed his hammer and started in again on the next set of the deadly arrow-heads. Arrowheads and more arrowheads – he was even dreaming about the damned things.

'I think you have enough arrowheads to prove how good they are,' suggested Altara.

'I'm not so much interested in proof as in protection.'

'After the last battle, I can understand that.'

'I thought you might. Gunnar really did most of it, and he's in no shape to go anywhere.' Justen let go of the hammer and wiggled his fingers. After a while, even forging out the roughed-out arrowheads cramped his hands. 'Some of them escaped. Firbek wasn't exactly pleased.' His nose itched from the soot and dust in the air, but he managed to stifle a sneeze.

'I know.' Dark circles framed the chief engineer's gray eyes. 'He keeps complaining about the rockets. He also said that he lost two mules and a launcher because of the flash flood. He seems to have forgotten how that flood saved his life.' She paused for a moment as the hammering from the other anvils seemed to crest.

'Nothing's right for Firbek. Gunnar stopped the Whites almost by himself, and paid for it. Firbek's already forgotten that we had to bring Gunnar back on the rocket cart. I suppose Firbek bitched about that, too. A misuse of good ordnance equipment . . .' Justen wiped his forehead and glanced at the adjoining forge, where Berol and Jirrl worked on the rocket heads.

'He's a little more understanding than that,' Altara cracked a faint smile.

'Not much. Gunnar was blind for the first day or so. He's still dizzy.'

'Krytella says his sight is fine now.'

'Next time it will be worse. At least that's usually the way it goes.' Justen sighed. 'I'm beginning to understand why Dorrin invented order-forging.'

'Firbek's convinced that the rockets are the only thing that will stop the Whites' Iron Guard.'

'Rockets are fine against ships at close range, but they're not all that good against troops,' observed Justen.

'You apparently managed.' Altara's eyes narrowed. 'Firbek said that you did something. He's kept insisting that you go on the next campaign.'

'I'm so popular. You want me to go. Firbek wants me to go. But he didn't ask me.'

'He won't. He doesn't want a favor. He believes in orders. It was enough for him to ask if there were any way to make the rockets more accurate.'

Justen snorted. 'We can't make the casings that accurate, and the ones with fins aren't much better.' He cleared his throat. 'Cannon are much more accurate. Why can't we make a cannon, put it on a big wagon rather than on a ship? I know . . . we can't cast the cannon out of black iron, but we could make the shells like rockets with the powder inside.'

'In the first place, it's called a carriage, not a wagon, and it takes a lot of work to build gun carriages right. But we could do that,' admitted Altara. 'That's not the problem. Where do you put the powder so that their wizards can't touch it off? Rockets have all their powder inside black iron.'

'Put the powder in black iron magazines in cloth bags or something until the moment you put it in the gun. The White Wizards couldn't find it and touch it off that quickly.'

'And how do you transport the magazines, especially in the rains? How many would it take for even a single cannon? Besides, you need to work on the arrowheads. You just can't do everything at once.'

'I know. I'll have another three score done before I finish tonight.'

'You expect the marines or the Sarronnese to have them attached and fletched overnight? You are leaving in the morning, you know.'

'Fine.' Justen sighed. 'They'll work whenever they're fletched.' He pulled the iron from the forge and picked up his hammer.

Altara stepped back, a sad smile on her face.

Justen set the cherry-red iron on the anvil and lifted his hammer.

Clerve continued to file the burrs off the roughed-out forms. Around them, the chorus of metal on metal continued.

After he had finished another half-score rough forms, Justen paused as a black-clad figure walked through the front entrance. Still holding the iron in the forge, he looked over as Firbek approached. 'Greetings, Oh hallowed and heroic marine leader.'

Firbek offered a bright smile. 'Greetings, exalted toiler in metal and fire. We look forward to seeing you early tomorrow.'

'And I, you.' Justen forced a smile.

The marine offered a smile equally forced before he turned and walked past the second forge to the corner where another shaft had been added to the main millshaft. There Altara and Nicos were wrestling with the small lathe, which had seized up.

Justen took a deep breath, trying to calm down. He didn't want to hit the arrowhead too hard. Why did Firbek set him off? Why had Firbek always set him off? The engineer took another deep breath, then gestured to Clerve. 'I'll be back in a moment.' He walked quickly out of the smithy to the side porch.

The water bucket was empty. With a harsh laugh he picked it up and walked through the sultry air toward the pump. After getting the water running with the hand pump, he splashed his grimy face until it felt clean and momentarily cooler. Then he filled the bucket and headed back to the smithy, past the garden, where the beans were already knee-high and blooming.

Justen glanced back to see a taller blond figure walking slowly from the house. Gunnar gestured toward the bench, and Justen nodded, setting the nearly full bucket on the rough stand, and waited for his brother.

'How are you? Sit down, for darkness' sake,' he greeted Gunnar.

'I think that answers your question.' The corners of Gunnar's mouth turned up momentarily. 'At least I can see, and I can walk a dozen cubits without feeling like I'm going to fall over.' He settled slowly onto one end of the bench.

Justen took the other end.

'How are you doing?' asked Gunnar.

'All right – except that I have to go on that expedition against the Whites.'

'That's tomorrow, isn't it?'

'Of course.' Justen shook his head. 'I've been thinking, Gunnar.'

'Dangerous occupation for an engineer.'

Justen ignored the comment. 'You know that order-forces can't use gunpowder, not without the danger of some White Wizard setting it off. Why can't we return the favor?'

'You want to handle chaos?'

'That's not what I meant. If you create a storm – like Creslin did – it results in destruction. Isn't there some other way to create the same effect?'

'You'd better stick to engineering, Justen.' Gunnar shook his head, then winced. 'Darkness . . . can't even shake my head without getting frigging dizzy.'

'If you and Creslin can create destruction through the use of order—'

'Darkness!' Gunnar winced again. 'I don't know. Maybe there is some way. Go ahead and figure it out, but you could end up like me . . . or like Creslin. It's demon-damned scary to wake up blind, and so dizzy you can't even move.'

Justen wiped out a cup and half-filled it, then extended the cup to his brother. 'Here.'

'Thanks.' Gunnar sipped the water slowly. 'We've got a big problem here.'

'I think I'm beginning to realize that.'

'I've watched the Whites' Iron Guard. What if they do the same thing with ships?'

Justen wrinkled his forehead, then nodded. 'You mean that we wouldn't be the only ones relying on the basic order of the ocean. How would that change anything?'

Gunnar set the cup on the bench between them. 'There's no reason the Iron Guard couldn't develop their own Blacks.'

'But wouldn't that just repeat what happened in the time of Creslin?'

'Maybe. How many Creslins are there? Would you want to bet Recluce's future on it?'

Justen grinned wryly. 'I wouldn't. But why the great conversion? You didn't seem to think the Whites were such a big threat.'

'I suppose that's because I understand what I did.' Gunnar looked at the planks between his boots.

Justen waited.

'I called up one of the biggest storms since Creslin. And what happened? Maybe . . . just maybe . . . I destroyed a thousand troops, and it didn't even really slow down the Whites, or not much. Without you, I probably would have died—'

'That's not—'

'It is, younger brother, and we both know it.' Gunnar paused. 'I was stupid, and I could do it better now. And I could probably focus a storm on a really big army, or on a fleet. But there's no one else who can or would try, and I clearly can't do that sort of thing very often.' He shrugged.

'So you're saying that . . . eventually . . . Recluce will lose?'

'It wouldn't ever come to that, but it wouldn't matter, would it, once Fairhaven took over Hamor, and Nordla, and Austra? Not that any of that will happen in our lifetime.'

'So what are we supposed to do?'

Gunnar looked straight at Justen, suppressing another wince. 'Whatever happens on this expedition tomorrow, get your ass back here. You're worth more alive than if you throw yourself away on a battle that won't mean much over the long run.'

'It might not be that simple.'

'It never is.' Gunnar sighed. 'It never is.'

31

'Come on, old lady.' Justen patted the gray's neck, letting a trickle of order flow from his fingertips. So far, the canyon remained comfortably cool, but it was far short of even mid-morning.

Wheeee . . . ah . . .

'I know. I know. You don't like this fighting business either.' The engineer studied the canyon. Like most of the canyons that contained roads through the Westhorns, it had been sculpted by running water, or the running water had found it the easiest path toward the Northern Ocean.

'You really don't have to talk to your horse, Engineer,' observed Firbek, turning back in his saddle. The marine rode beside the cart horse.

A woman marine named Deryn flicked the reins to encourage her mount to keep up with Firbek as the column wound uphill toward yet another vale in the Westhorns, where Dyessa hoped to be able to reinforce Commander Zerlana before the White forces arrived.

'The horse doesn't talk back,' Justen said with a laugh.

'You haven't said enough for her to answer,' cracked Firbek.

'Well put,' Justen conceded, patting the gray again.

The road turned sharply where the stream had struck a wall of solid granite. Justen noted the narrow gap and the relatively less steep and boulder-studded slope. The water flowed over a wide granite shelf in a mere half-cubit depth – and the streambed itself was less than two cubits below the roadbed. The engineer smiled. Maybe it wouldn't take magic to build a lake. Then he frowned. Why was he thinking about how to stop the Whites if the Sarronnese had to retreat?

Because he was worried. Dyessa was grim, not even talking to Firbek. The Sarronnese troops acted as though they were being sent to a slaughterhouse, and not even Gunnar had been able to give a real victory to Dyessa at Middlevale. Darkness, his brother still had trouble standing up for long periods.

Justen shifted his weight in the saddle, still uncomfortably hard, but said nothing as he followed the column up the road by the stream, occasionally glimpsing above the canyon walls the ice-covered spires of the Westhorns.

Yee-ah . . . A black vulcrow flapped from a dead fir limb and laboriously climbed out of the canyon, heading eastward.

Was that a normal vulcrow, or one of those possessed by a White Wizard? Justen touched the black staff.

Innumerable turns later, the column marched into a circular valley, one with gentle slopes but with the same rocky hillocks that had characterized Middlevale. This time, the Sarronnese were dug in less than a half kay from the western entrance. Berms of earth and rock protected cavalry mounts, while the Sarronnese foot had erected what looked like a stone wall in the form of a semicircle.

White banners – along with green, gold, and crimson – waved at the far end of the valley.

A rider in blue leathers trotted up to Firbek. 'The commander suggests that the hill to the left, there, offers the best command of the approach to our lines. Follow me, if you would.'

Justen grinned. The messenger clearly conveyed Zerlana's suggestion as an order.

'Thank you.' Firbek's voice was cool and polite. He turned to Deryn, then to Fesek, the other marine who rode beside him.

'Follow the messenger.' He looked at Justen. 'Are you coming, Engineer?'

'How could I not?'

'Indeed. How could you not?'

Justen tapped his heels into the gray's flanks. The horse whinnied and fell in behind the cart. The engineer dismounted halfway up the hillock and tied the mount to a scrub oak before climbing up to the hilltop, where the marines were setting up the rocket launcher. He left the black staff in the lance holder beside the saddle.

'Let's get those rockets ready.' Firbek remained mounted while Deryn and Fesek adjusted the launcher. Then Fesek stacked the rockets next to the launcher while Deryn tightened the brackets.

Justen shrugged, then began to lug boulders so as to form a low wall. After positioning nearly a dozen of the huge stones, he looked up. Firbek had dismounted and tied his horse downhill next to Justen's gray, where both mounts attempted to browse on the scattered clumps of grass that sprouted from the rocky soil.

A light breeze blew out of the east, carrying fine dust and the faint odor of horses . . . and perhaps, thought Justen, fear.

'Ready?' asked Firbek.

'Yes, Ser.'

'How about you, Engineer?'

'As ready as I suppose I'll ever be.'

A heavy drum-roll rumbled like thunder across the valley, and a wave of White lancers, hundreds of mounted soldiers, charged toward the Sarronnese lines. Behind them, methodically marched the foot levies under the green-and-gold banners.

Hssttt . . . The first firebolt slammed into the hillside on which flew the blue banner of Sarronnyn, turning several scrub oaks into charcoal.

Hssttt . . . Another firebolt hit higher on the hill, but merely scoured lichen off the stones from behind which Zerlana and her small staff watched the battlefield.

Hssttt . . . The next firebolt arced down behind the stones, but the absence of screams reassured Justen . . . somewhat.

The gray banners of the Iron Guard remained well to the rear as the White lancers galloped across the valley. Not until the lancers were less than two hundred cubits from the stone wall was there any sound from the Sarronnese. A trumpet, clear and crisp, sounded two sharp notes, then repeated them.

The first flight of arrows arced out from behind the heaped stone-and-earth walls sheltering the front lines of the Sarronnese.

Justen held his breath as the black iron-tipped arrows sleeted downward onto the White lancers charging across the valley floor.

Crump . . . crump . . .

Openmouthed, the engineer watched as each of the White lancers struck by a black iron-tipped arrow exploded in flame.

A faint and ragged cheer rose from the Sarronnese lines even as another flight of the iron-tipped arrows arced into the already hazy morning sky. The arrows fell like fireballs among the lancers. Riderless horses, some of them burning, screamed. The light wind carried the acrid odor of burning hair and charred flesh to Justen. He shook off a sudden dizziness and waited.

Hssttt . . . hssttt . . . hssttt . . . Three quick firebolts burned across the valley and splashed against the earthworks. One too-curious soldier screamed as she flared into an instant torch.

Justen swallowed hard.

'Let's get those rockets ready.' Firbek glared at Deryn and Fesek. 'We'll hold until the Iron Guard marches, unless the regulars get too close.'

A handful of the White lancers straggled back toward the east end of the valley, followed by empty-saddled mounts.

For a time, an uneasy quiet, broken only by the whisper of the wind and the faint muttering of the Sarronnese troops, held the west end of the valley.

Then, from the eastern side, the drum-rolls rumbled forth, and another set of lancers changed toward the Sarronnese, passing through the foot soldiers. Once the second wave of lancers passed, the foot moved forward, using brush and hills for cover, steadily moving toward the Sarronnese.

Hssttt . . .

Hssttt . . .

The firebolts dropped onto the earthworks with little effect, except for creating a briefly burning bush.

In response, another flight of arrows dropped into the lancers, with yet more explosions and burning bodies. Justen swallowed, both at the destruction wrought by the black iron and the realization that few of the special arrows remained. Another wave of dizziness struck him, and he shook his head again.

This time, the remaining lancers circled back, regrouped, and joined by a third group of fresh cavalry, charged the Sarronnese once more.

Although the arrows still fell among the lancers, some of those hit continued to ride forward. Others fell, but they fell like ordinary men, and the weight of the charge, the sheer numbers of more than five hundred remaining lancers, pushed at the thin line of blue-coated Sarronnese.

The bodies of white-clad men and their horses piled into a line less than a hundred cubits from the shallow Sarronnese earthworks.

The heavy drum rolled, and the lancers peeled away to reveal the Fairhaven foot, carrying light, white shields, almost upon the Sarronnese lines and marching forward. Behind them, White archers appeared, and a flight of white shafts arced toward the Sarronnese.

'Now!' snapped Firbek.

Click . . .

Justen flattened himself just before the rocket passed through where he had been standing. He shivered on the ground, not really understanding why he'd had enough sense to drop out of the way, or had he been dodging from the arrows?

'I told you to be careful!' Firbek's massive hand slammed into Deryn, throwing her to the ground, where she lay cradling her arm.

The big marine turned the launcher and nodded at Fesek, who clicked the striker to light off the first rocket.

Justen climbed to his feet, trying to brush away the dirt and a glob of manure that had stuck to his tunic. Sweat oozed from his forehead as he thought about how close to him the rocket had come. He turned toward the Fairhaven forces.

The black iron missile plowed into the ground to the left of the center of the green-bannered forces. A low, growling sound accompanied the White advance, part murmurs, part yells, part the sound of booted feet on hard ground as the foot-sloggers stormed over the bodies and charged toward the thin blue line behind the low stones.

Another wave of white arrows flew, and Justen dropped

behind his stone wall. Deryn scrabbled awkwardly behind the cart.

Standing behind the black iron frame, Firbek racheted up the launcher and nodded. Fesek struck the fuse, and this time, Justen tried to order the initial airflow. The combined effort succeeded, and the rocket slammed through the center of the White foot, creating a fireball and strewing charred bodies for a dozen cubits.

Another ragged cheer rose from the Sarronnese even as the wave of destruction rocked Justen. He steadied himself on the topmost rock of the wall he had built, fighting the nausea and dizziness created by the havoc. He glanced over at Deryn, who was trying to fasten some sort of makeshift splint on her forearm; he sensed not anger, but sadness in her.

Arrows fell on both sides, slashing into white-clad and blue-clad forms alike. Justen dropped onto his knees; so he could see the field without presenting a target for some archer.

'Another.' Firbek lifted the rocket into the launcher.

The second rocket widened the hole in the White center. Justen leaned against the stones and groaned.

Hhsstt . . . The answering firebolt fell short, almost charring some of the White foot.

'Another. The White Wizard's getting tired.'

'Again . . .'

Somehow, the engineer infused some order into each launch, trying to stay out of view of the White archers, fighting the recoil of chaos and dizziness.

'Hold.'

The remaining handful of the Fairhaven assault forces, those under the green banner of Certis, crept back behind makeshift barricades of bodies and brush and stones. For a time, a low sighing swept the valley, composed of the wind and the moans and cries of the wounded and dying.

Then a heavy drum-roll thundered from the west, and a wave of troops under the crimson banner started forward.

Once more the White archers lifted their bows, as did the Sarronnese, and the late morning sky was filled with death.

Hhstt . . . hssttt . . .

'We need to stop them! Strike it!' Right after the rocket left, Firbek was lifting another into place in the launcher.

After a deep breath, Justen added a touch of order, enough so that the rocket hit just left of the center of the new assault.

Hsssttt . . . This time, the wizard's firebolt splashed in front of the launcher.

Firbek cranked up the launcher. 'There. He's on that low hill. Strike!'

The second rocket splashed flame before the White Wizard, who dropped from sight. Firbek readjusted the launcher. 'Strike!'

Firbek changed the launcher angle, and the rocket seared the hilltop where the wizard had stood.

'Again.'

'Strike again . . .'

Somehow, the engineer infused some order into each launch, trying to stay out of view of the White archers.

Despite the rockets, the White foot reached the Sarronnese line, and the clash of metal joined the smell of charred bodies, the odor of burning rocket powder, and the screams and moans of soldiers and horses. Sarronnese archers loosed shafts at ranges so close that at times, one shaft transfixed two Fairhaven troops.

. . . *hssttt* . . . *hsstt* . . .

The firebolts alternated between the Sarronnese and the Recluce positions, but Firbek and Justen now concentrated on the White foot troops.

'Strike!'

Then the three men in black stood in a lull as the shattered White foot fell back even as another set of heavy drum-rolls started and the gray banners were lifted and dipped.

Three short double blasts sounded over the isolated shouts, the screams, and the hissing of the occasional firebolt. The ensign swirled and dipped three times.

'That's the fall-back order!' yelled Fesek.

'We've still got rockets!' Firbek protested.

Justen pointed to the comparative handful of blue-clad Sarronnese. 'Zerlana doesn't have much in the way of troops left. And they're calling in the Iron Guard.'

Firbek stared for a moment, then dropped his hands.

Justen yanked the marine's arm and pulled him to the ground.

'Dumb bastard—'

Hhhssttt . . . hsstt. Nearly a score of arrows followed the firebolt above Justen's head.

'We're the target!'

'Let's get moving!' Justen crouched behind the launcher, pulling the brace pins while Fesek and Justen carted the dozen and a half remaining rockets, wrapped in a canvas, to the mule. Then they placed the launcher on the cart. Deryn pulled the fuses one-handedly and put them in a leather bag strapped next to the canvas on the mule.

Justen nodded at the safety precaution, then mounted the gray.

A firebolt flared around the mule, which tottered forward three steps before collapsing.

Arrows arched over the hilltop.

'Keep moving!' ordered Firbek.

'You move!' Justen flung himself off the gray and tried to remove the canvas from the dead mule. As if he were moving through deep snow, he untied the rockets, one by one, until he could lift the canvas off and then get it over the gray's back.

Hssttt . . .

He re-tied one rocket, then another . . .

. . . hsssttt . . .

. . . and another . . .

White arrows flew by his shoulder.

. . . and another . . .

. . . hssttt . . .

With a sigh more like a sob, the engineer grabbed the gray's reins and began to run, using the hillock as shelter from the direct attack of the White Wizard.

Behind him, the drum-rolls mounted. Beside him trotted three blue-clad soldiers. Ahead, he could barely make out the cart and the two marines riding into the canyon between two lines of archers and troops waiting to cover the retreat, if necessary.

Another wave of arrows dropped around them. One slammed into the woman beside Justen, pinning her arm to the dirt. Justen reached down and absently snapped the arrow, then lifted her onto the gray, right on top of the rockets, even as he pulled out the shaft and handed her a scrap of canvas.

'Bind it with this.'

The soldier looked at him blankly.

'Wrap it if you want to live!' he ordered, flicking the reins to keep the gray moving.

'Tough little bastard . . .' muttered the soldier to his left.

Tough? Justen hadn't even lifted a blade or his staff, and he felt like chopped meat. The ground seemed to sway underfoot, and his head ached as if it had been beaten with a truncheon. He coughed and kept walking until he, the gray, and the wounded soldier were in the canyon.

There, since the bedraggled column was still moving, he kept walking, leading the gray.

'Engineer!'

Justen looked up at the sound of the voice. A Sarronnese officer whom he did not know was leading a riderless horse, a dapple.

'Mount up!'

Mechanically, he climbed into the empty saddle, still holding the gray's reins.

'Thanks . . . fellow. But I'll walk with mine.' The wounded soldier slipped off the gray, shivering as her fingers touched the black iron. She trudged slowly downhill.

Justen eased the dapple around them, still leading the gray. Making his way down the canyon, his head cleared slightly and after a time, he looked back at the winding column.

What could he do to stop the Whites? It would not be that long before they wiped out the wounded, took their arms and supplies, and looted the dead.

What Gunnar could do with wizardry, perhaps he could accomplish with order-mastery and the powder in the rockets, since his senses indicated that the Whites were not immediately upon the heels of the remaining Sarronnese.

On the way in, he had studied at least a handful of places in the narrow canyon where a rough dam might be erected, especially the place where the stream had turned abruptly at the granite face – if he recalled the spot correctly.

Less than half a kay into the canyon, Justen paused at a narrowing in the walls and studied the first outcropping. A frown followed as he noted the depth of the pooled water below. While the deep water stored order, it was also likely to swallow the amount of rock that might be forced loose.

As he rode, he discovered that either he had caught up with the marines or they had slowed to wait for him. They rode on silently.

Once Justen reached the narrow granite wall that he recalled, he guided the dapple and the gray off the road and onto the narrow streambank, where he studied the canyon walls again. What he had in mind still seemed possible.

'Why are you stopping, Engineer?' Firbek circled back.

'I'm going to build a dam.'

'With what? Magic?'

'Hardly. The rockets, for one thing.'

'I need those rockets.' Firbek put his hand on his blade. Farther downhill, Deryn had reined up the cart. Beside her, Fesek sat on his mount. Both looked impassively over the intermittent flow of soldiers, most of them wounded, at Justen and Firbek.

'So do I.' Justen smiled, and his fingers closed around the black staff. 'And I saved them. I also helped forge them.'

Firbek glanced from Deryn, still cradling her shattered left arm, to the gray and the canvas holding the rockets. Then he laughed. 'Fine! Do what you will.' He looked at Deryn. 'It's his decision.'

Justen watched for a moment as the three turned their mounts and the cart back onto the dusty mountain road to follow the Justen forces back down to the foothills and the river. Then he tied the horses to a scrubby root protruding from the loose rock. If he used the tree . . .

'Engineer . . . what are you doing?' Zerlana, surrounded by a half-squad of heavily armed cavalry, reined up beside him. 'We'll need those rockets on the plains.'

'Begging your pardon, Commander. They will do more good here.'

'Would you explain?'

Justen shrugged, then pointed to the boulder-strewn slope to the right of the road. 'Most of those stones are fairly loose.'

'We all know that. Every spring we have to clear the road.

But the White Wizards will just blast apart those few boulders you can bring down here.'

'Not if I can get enough of them in the streambed.'

The commander studied the road. 'You can't raise the stream more than three cubits, I'd guess. How would that help?'

'Would you want to bring your forces through three cubits of icy water?'

'Can you do this?'

'I don't know.' Justen shrugged. 'It's worth a try. If it works, they'll have to use the road that leads from their highway, and that goes to Cerlyn, which puts the Whites a lot farther from Sarron.'

'And if it doesn't?'

'You lose some rockets and one engineer – at most.'

'How much help could you use?'

'Three people. Any more would just get in the way.'

Zerlana rode downhill toward a group of light horse that had reined up just at the turn when she had stopped next to Justen.

The engineer stood by the dapple, absently stroking the gelding's neck, while his perceptions ranged across the sides of the canyon, seeking out weaknesses in the rock and the thin soil cover.

Before he had finished sensing the rock and soil faults, three mounted soldiers rode up, two in blue leathers, one in gray.

'The commander said you needed help.' The hard-faced blonde with a razor-thin, blood-edged cut along the right side of her jaw reined her chestnut in, almost on top of Justen. 'What are you doing?'

'Blowing up the hillside to make a dam once our people get downstream.'

'Our people?' asked the brunette. The woman in gray said nothing.

'Anyone I fight for is my people.' Justen held in a sigh.

'How long will this take?' asked the hard-faced blonde.

'Most of the afternoon.'

'That's too long. The Whites will be here before you're done.'

Justen shook his head. 'Hardly. They haven't left the battle-field. They've got some cleaning up to do.'

The brunette snorted. 'Didn't like those black arrows, they didn't. Wish we'd had more.'

'When the commander reports to the chief engineer, there will be more forged.'

'Not enough.'

'That's what we're here for. This buys more time to forge weapons and gather troops,' Justen reminded the three. 'What I need from you are boulders from up there that look and feel not too steady, like they might move with a huge push. We need some way to mark them . . .'

'Here's some white cloth. It'll last for a while, anyhow.' The blonde's laugh was nearly a cackle.

Justen nodded. 'While you're doing that, I'll be moving the rockets into place.'

He thrust a small iron pry-bar, taken from the canvas that held the rockets, into his belt, then unloaded four rockets from the gray. Using the tree root, he levered himself onto the lower ledge, from where he scrambled onto the sparsely grassy rocky incline. Cubit by cubit, he struggled up as far as he could go.

'This one looks like it might move, Ser,' offered the brunette.

Justen put a hand on the boulder, a time-smoothed monolith that protruded from the hillside, letting his senses surround the granite. He shook his head. 'This is still attached to the ridge below. Let's try that one over there.'

'It's not as big.'

'They have to be able to move.'

After three tries, Justen found two boulders that seemed to fit his needs. After using the pry-bar to gouge out a long hole on the up-slope side of the larger boulder, he placed two rockets inside and gently tamped in the sandy soil as well as he could, leaving only the twisted fuses exposed.

'Get up behind that rock! All of you!'

He used the striker, then scrambled for cover, slipping and scraping the side of his face as he clawed his way behind the ridge rock that the brunette had thought would move.

Crummppp . . . uumpp . . .

Sand exploded from the boulder, and the stone rocked, then settled.

'Darkness . . .' Justen eased over to the boulder, ignoring the blood on his cheek, and touched the granite, then shoved. The blonde's shoulder joined his, and the boulder groaned forward

. . . and began bouncing downhill, carrying several smaller rocks and some sand with it.

The next boulder also took two rockets, but it fell onto the road itself, although one of the smaller rocks tumbled into the stream.

By the time he had returned for more rockets and carted them up the steep slope, falling only twice and scraping his face once again, Justen's blacks were soaked from his waist up. A quick look at the sky confirmed that the hazy clouds remained in place.

More rocks, more holes, and more rockets resulted in a growing pile of stone in the narrow gap where the canyon turned.

After splashing their faces clean, the four sat by the stream to rest. Shortly, Justen stood.

'Let's get the horses around the bend. Then we'll muscle these rocks into some sense of order.'

'This is worse than fighting. You can only die there. Here, you get tortured.' The blonde shook her head.

Justen shrugged. 'It hurts me, too.'

The replacement mount – more heavily muscled than the gray – a pulley, the three soldiers, and Justen managed to wrestle the larger boulders into a line across the narrow point in the canyon before the sharp bend. With the stones in its bed, the stream had risen enough that it lapped at the edge of the road.

'Now we'll drop some more stones. Smaller ones.'

The three exchanged looks. The blonde shrugged. So did the woman in gray.

After a moment, the brunette grinned. 'All right, Engineer. We'll help you drop more stones.'

When there were only four rockets left and the sun had dropped well below the canyon rim, Justen straightened up. 'Let's go down and finish.'

The four waded through calf-deep water before they could climb over the makeshift berm, or dam. The three climbed onto perches above the road, since water was flowing across the roadbed.

'Shit. No wonder no one ever took Recluce . . . takes too much friggin' work.'

'Better than listening to Dyessa or Zerlana bitch about . . .'

'Dyessa . . . miss her. Good sort for a field leader.'

Justen looked toward the three, but they said nothing.

'Miss her? What happened?'

'Demon-damned wizard got her, I think, there at the last charge.'

The engineer pursed his lips, then swallowed to moisten his dry throat. Dyessa herself had been right. Why was he so surprised that individuals died?

Finally, he stood and walked back to the low berm, where he stopped and studied the bank above the stream. Then he unstrapped the launcher and carried it to a flat spot, settling it carefully in the heel-deep water. He adjusted it, aiming it right above the stream.

'Why are you doing this now? Why didn't you start with this?' The blonde in the blood-smeared and tattered blue leathers coughed after she spoke.

'You need the bigger rocks to hold the smaller fragments and dirt.' Justen touched the striker, extending his perceptions to smooth the flow of air across the rocket.

Whssttt . . . crummpp . . .

With the second rocket, a solid wall of rocks, sand, soil, even roots, fell into the stream, turning the clear water reddish-brown. Almost instantly, the water began to seep onto the road.

Justen carted the launcher down below the dam and aimed the next rocket toward the bulge overhanging the road. Although a considerable mass fell with that rocket, he used the last one to bring down more material.

Then he strapped the launcher onto the dapple and stood panting, his blacks soaked with water and sweat, his face scraped and bloody. He grinned.

'You look like crap, Engineer. Why are you smiling?' Even as she questioned, the trooper in gray grinned. Then she mounted.

Justen struggled into the saddle, patting the gray on the neck. 'That's a girl. Just get old Daddy Justen back to Sarron.'

'. . . tough little bastard . . .'

'. . . sort of like him . . .'

Justen looked back at the low dam, sending his senses into the rocks and earth and the few limbs. It wasn't as massive or as solid as Gunnar's work, but it would hold, at least for a year or two, and that would be enough time to force the White armies onto the southernmost route, the one through Cerlyn.

32

The two White Wizards walked up the hill. The boot heel of the shorter touched a dark object in the dust. He jumped slightly at the hissing sound.

'Another one of those black iron arrows?' asked the larger and stockier man.

'The darkness-damned things are everywhere.'

'Tell me about it. You don't have to send a dispatch to Histen asking for another two thousand lancers.'

'They didn't . . . not that many, did they?'

'Jehan, I'd guess they had about score forty of those black arrowheads. Do you want to guess how many they'll have forged by the time we get to Sarronnyn by the southern route?' Zerchas took a deep breath as he reached the hilltop, where he turned west and studied the low water blocking the western exit from the valley.

'The Iron Guard could take this road.'

Zerchas looked mildly at Jehan, who in turn looked at the cart tracks in the ground.

'Can you tap the chaos springs?'

'Me?' Zerchas snorted. 'Maybe the late, great Jeslek could have, but that Black engineer's dam is founded in cold running water laid over solid granite. Send Histen another message and get one of those hotheads, like Beltar, out here. Let him deal with the order recoil. I'd rather not, thank you.'

'You think there could be that much of a problem?'

'Do you want to try it, O great Jehan?'

'Ah . . . I think not.'

'Then don't ask me to.' Zerchas's eyes went vacant for a time.

Jehan glanced downhill at the coach and the detachment of White lancers that surrounded it, then toward the slowly spreading lake, and finally back toward the eastern end of the valley, where the gray banners were being furled and the tents struck. He moistened his lips.

Zerchas cleared his throat. 'That dam's not all that well built. Once we get into Sarronnyn, a small team could drain it easily from the other side. If the water had settled some, and if we had the materials, we could send a boat down there now.'

'We don't—'

'I know. We'll just have to take the longer route. The road's better anyway.'

'Everything's taking longer. The way things are going, we'll be at winter's doorstep before we even reach Sarron.' Jehan spat downhill, his spittle hissing as it struck a fragment of black iron.

'I doubt that. The Sarronnese have lost nearly half of their army already.'

'They'll draw more levies.'

'Sarronnyn has never been that well equipped for war. The whole idea of the Legend is against war.'

'What about Westwind, or Southwind?'

'One's long dead, and the other's dying.' After taking a last look at the shallow water, Zerchas turned and began to walk downhill. 'Let's go. You need to get that message off to Histen. Ask for Beltar by name.'

'As you wish.'

33

Four figures rode up the incline from the river road to Sarron, slightly behind the main mounted body of the returning Sarronnese force, but well ahead of the foot soldiers. Unlike most travelers in recent days, they came from the south. As on most summer days in Sarronnyn, high hazy clouds covered the sky, barely decreasing the burning of the white yellow sun, but giving a more greenish cast to the sky.

Justen wanted to wipe the sweat off his face as he reined up outside the Recluce enclave and tugged on the reins of the dapple to bring the horse to a halt beside his gray. The scratches and bruises had left his forehead tender. With the back of his forearm, he gently, very gently, blotted the dampness away, ignoring the itching of the scrape across his right temple.

He turned in the saddle to face the Sarronnese troopers. 'Thank you.'

'None of the soft masculine stuff, Engineer. Wish there were more like you around.' The blond inclined her head. 'We'll see you again.'

'I trust that it is not too soon.' Justen offered a wry smile.

'We'd hope the same in some ways, no offense to you, Engineer. Not that we would mind seeing you.' The soldier in gray glanced back toward the southeast. 'We won't be fortunate in that way. I'd like a couple of quivers of those black arrowheads before we see those White devils again.'

The Sarronnese troopers nodded one after the other.

'We'll do what we can.' Justen watched for a moment as the three turned their horses back to rejoin the remnants of the Sarronnese cavalry.

Then he rode toward the end of the barracks that held the stable, leading the dapple and giving a half nod at the sound of metal on metal and the dull thuds of the hammer mill. The smell of oil and quench water tickled his nose. Two of Castin's chickens scuttled from the door to the stable as he reined up and dismounted.

After unloading and stabling the dapple, he led the gray into the last empty stall. Then he walked across to the pump, where he got a bucket of water to wash off the worst of the grime. The second bucket was for the horses, and he lugged it back across the sunbaked clay. He poured half into one stable bucket and half into the other, providing a bucket for each horse.

After letting the mounts drink, he curried the dapple quickly and had begun to unsaddle the gray when he heard steps. Altara stood outside the stall.

'I just got back.' He unbuckled the girth.

'I saw. Firbek said you were using good rockets for what he called light-fired foolishness.'

Justen pulled the girth clear of the buckle and straightened up. 'I used them to build a dam with. So I guess that was foolishness.'

'What did Zerlana say?'

'I don't know. I never talked to her afterward. She was too busy.'

'Justen, sometimes . . . sometimes you're as bad as your brother. You two . . . you just do something important and never tell anyone.' Altara shook her head. 'It's a good thing no one's worried about trade routes right now.'

'I suppose so. That really hadn't crossed my mind.'

'How soon can you get back to work on the arrowheads? Zerlana sent a messenger – she said the black iron arrowheads turned all the White lancers they struck into fireballs. She wants as many as we can deliver.'

'I told you they'd work.' Justen stepped out of the stall and into the light.

'Darkness . . . what happened to you?' Altara glanced toward the dwelling across the dusty yard. 'You need a healer, at least to check out all those scrapes. How did you manage to get all cut up like that?'

'I was wrestling with a mountain. That's what happened when I used the rest of the rockets – they were ones I'd saved, by the way – to build the demon-damned lake. This one's not as deep as the one Gunnar built, but it should make the middle pass road almost impassible for the Whites.' Justen racked the blanket and the saddle, and picked up the curry brush.

'Firbek said you'd never do it.'

'He's welcome to go swim in it.' The young engineer stepped back into the stall and began to curry the gray, who whickered and sidestepped.

'Easy, lady.' He stroked her, and she settled down.

Altara squinted and peered over the stall at the horse. 'Is that the same gray?'

'Same one.' Justen forced himself to keep brushing. Darkness knew, the poor beast deserved it.

'It doesn't look the same. She looks less swaybacked . . . younger somehow.'

'Probably just decent treatment and enough food.' Justen set down the brush.

'I don't know. I wonder if you couldn't have been a healer. Krytella says you actually helped heal Gunnar.'

'He's my brother.'

'I'm going to get Ninca to look at your face.' Altara shook her head as she left the stable area.

Justen kept brushing; the gray whickered once more.

'I know. I know. Summer's not even close to being over, and it's going to get hotter.' Even before he finished speaking, the gray slurped water across his boots. 'Thank you, too.'

The gray whickered again, and Justen studied the animal. Was it possible that he had infused enough order, inadvertently that the horse was healthier? He shrugged. It was certainly possible, but a little order was small enough repayment for the gray's having lugged him all over Sarronnyn.

He set aside the brush and rummaged through the nearly empty barrel of oat cakes before coming up with some morsels for both horses. The gray whickered and nuzzled his arm; the dapple merely ate.

Justen closed the stalls, shouldered his pack, and trudged through the afternoon heat and the dust raised by his boots toward his room in the barracks. He realized that he needed to get something to eat. Had anyone left anything from the noon meal?

'Justen! Ninca needs to look at that face of yours.' Altara waved from the side porch of the smithy.

The young engineer turned toward the two women. Altara stood aside as Justen climbed the steps to the porch.

Even before he slumped onto the bench, the older healer was peering at his face. He could sense the light tendrils of order touching his scrapes and scabs.

'You kept it fairly clean. That I can see. There's no chaos anywhere, almost as though I'd done it myself. Just keep the dirt out of the scrapes. You won't look very pretty for a while, young engineer, but I've seen worse. After you wash at night, and make sure you do, put a little of this ointment on the cuts and scrapes.'

'Thank you.' Justen took the ointment in the small box. He also intended to keep up with his own order-ministering.

Ninca gave him a wry grin before she turned to Altara. 'Might as well take another look at that big engineer's arm, since I'm here.' She frowned. 'Seems like the Sarronnese never heard of real healing. Someone in the Tyrant's court always is wanting healing. And Krytella's always getting badgered by some woman or another in the streets.'

'Not enough food.' Altara's voice was matter-of-fact as she looked straight at Justen. 'We do need more arrowheads . . .'

'I know. I need to put this away and get something to eat.' He pointed to the battered leather pack.

'Castin might have put something by,' Ninca observed.

'I'll see you later,' Altara told him.

Justen watched the two women enter the smithy, then stood and lifted his pack.

'Wait a moment,' said Gunnar. Justen's brother stood in the smithy doorway through which Altara and Ninca had just passed. 'You might as well sit back down.' Gunnar gestured to the other end of the bench with his left hand. In his right hand was a covered basket. 'Altara isn't going to force you to pick up your hammer or whatever at this very moment.'

Justen's eyes flicked toward the smithy, then to his pack. 'Actually, I was going to put this in my room and try to find something to eat.'

'I thought you might be hungry when I saw you coming.' Gunnar set the basket on the bench. 'There's some sliced chicken, brown bread, cheese, and a pearapple there. I didn't bring anything to drink, but here's a cup, and the water in the pitcher's cold.' The Storm Wizard seated himself crosswise on the bench, one leg on either side.

'The water's never cold,' protested Justen. But he set the pack down.

'It is now.'

Justen sat and poured some water into the cup Gunnar had produced. He sipped. 'You're right. How did you do it? Some sort of storm wizardry?'

Gunnar nodded, a faint smile on his face, a smile that faded as Justen watched. He wrinkled his brow.

'Using order still hurts, doesn't it?' Justen asked, stuffing a chunk of chicken in his mouth and beginning to chew.

'It depends. I can use the winds to scout with, and that doesn't hurt. Trying to move . . . to arrange things, even the air, still can be a bit . . . difficult.'

'Doesn't quite . . . hurt like . . . the demons of light,' mumbled the younger brother through his mouthful of chicken and the chunk of still-warm brown bread he had added to the somewhat dry fowl.

'More like a cut across the skull, or a headache. But it's getting better.' Gunnar paused and watched Justen wolf down several more mouthfuls before he spoke again. 'You're not quite as white as one of the healers' bandages.'

'Was hungry. Not that much food left . . . on . . . the way back.' Justen looked at the remainder of the loaf. 'Castin is baking small loaves these days. And the taste is bitter.'

'He says we don't notice the difference, whether they're big or small. We eat everything anyway.' Gunnar sobered. 'There's not much food left anywhere. The grain is from the bottom of the granaries. It gets a touch of mold – the good kind that helps fight chaos – but it does taste bitter.'

'It's not winter. Why are the granaries so low?'

Gunnar looked at Justen. 'That's just it. Sarronnyn gets its fruit from the upland groves, and they bloom late. The grains haven't headed yet.'

'So . . . in mid to late summer is when the food stocks are lowest. From the long look on your face, I'd assume that Fairhaven has tried to cut off trade with Sarronnyn.'

'That's really not the problem. It's the people. Sarronnyn produces plenty. It always has. But if you were a farmer out there—' Gunnar gestured to the west '—would you want to sell much if you worried about the winter and whether the Whites would fire your fields the way they did in the south Kyphros or Spidlar?'

'Everyone's hoarding.' Justen swallowed and reached for the water.

'Right. And that means something else.'

Justen gulped half a cup of cold water and used his belt knife to slice off a chunk of the hard, yellow brick cheese. He waited for Gunnar to continue.

'It means that the Sarronnese have already lost hope.'

Justen nodded, chewing the tangy cheese that seemed to coat his teeth. He took another sip of the cool water. Even with

Gunnar's wizardry, the water didn't stay cold in the heat of summer.

'You're worried,' Justen finally said.

'Yes, younger brother. I'm worried. Even with your engineering of the dam, it won't be more than another three to four eight-days before the Whites are almost to Sarron.'

'That's time to make a lot of black arrowheads.'

'They don't work any better than regular arrows on the Iron Guard, and the Whites are moving all their Iron Guard forces onto their wizards' road.'

Justen pursed his lips. 'Maybe Firbek was right. Maybe we need more rockets.'

'Maybe.'

The two brothers sat silent on the bench, looking to the south, looking through the heat waves that rose from the river road.

34

'Come in.'

The broad-shouldered White Wizard stepped into the tower room.

The thinner man in white studied a glass upon a seemingly antique white-oak table for a time before turning.

'You requested my presence?' Beltar bowed deeply to the High Wizard.

'I did.' Histen gestured to the glass, and a group of buildings appeared in the midst of the swirling white mists. 'A small detachment of engineers from Recluce has arrived in Sarronnyn.' Histen gestured again, and the image in the glass vanished. 'Already, they have been rather effective in slowing down the advance of both the White Company and the Iron Guard.'

Beltar waited.

'They also brought a descendant . . . of Creslin.'

The younger wizard raised his eyebrows.

'He turned Middlevale into a rather deep lake. Unfortunately, a detachment of the Iron Guard happened to be there at the time.'

'No other forces?'

'The others are more . . . shall we say . . . replaceable. Perhaps two score returned, and we anticipate that for some time, the northern route will be blocked.'

'It does sound like quite a deep lake indeed.' Beltar pursed his lips. 'What else?'

'Is that not enough?'

Beltar smiled politely. 'A single lake would not be that great an impediment to the redoubtable Zerchas.'

'Actually, there were two lakes. The second was created just on the middle road. It is shallower.'

'But enough to keep the White forces off the road, no doubt.'

'A minor impediment, I am sure.'

'Certainly,' agreed Beltar with yet another smile. He waited.

'Ah . . . you see,' temporized Histen. 'The other thing is that the engineers are providing weapons.'

'Like their rockets?'

Histen frowned. 'They have begun, just begun, to forge black iron arrowheads.'

Beltar nodded slowly. 'I presume the casualties among the White lancers were rather heavy.'

'We lost nearly four hundred before they ran out of arrows.'

'And you don't want the situation to get out of hand?'

'Ah . . . yes. The Iron Guards are being sent their cannon.'

'So the rumor is true . . . that cannon were cast by the Lydians.' Beltar bowed. 'Clearly, you have thought matters out in great detail, High Wizard. How may one such as I be of service?'

The High Wizard fingered the gold amulet that hung around his neck. 'You have suggested that . . . the more effective aspects of the renowned Jeslek's approach . . . might be suitable.' The High Wizard paused.

Beltar continued to wait.

'Have you not?'

'I believe I have made some comments to the effect that much of import that Jeslek accomplished has been perhaps overlooked.'

'You at least have less arrogance than your idol. We believe that someone of your abilities would be useful in countering this Storm Wizard, and perhaps also in offsetting those arrowheads and black iron rockets their engineers have forged for the Sarronnese.'

'In short, you want me, and the newly developed cannons, to destroy the engineers and the Storm Wizard before the world realizes the vulnerabilities of our forces?'

'Let us say that a expeditious victory in Sarronnyn would be to everyone's advantage.'

'I appreciate your faith, and I am at your disposal.' Beltar bowed.

35

After securing the black staff in the lance holder, Justen swung into the gray's saddle and rode across the dry clay and scattered clumps of grass in the yard until he reached the half-dozen marines. One of the chickens clucked from a perch on the lower railing of the rickety fence around the healers' garden. Absently, Justen wondered why, wherever healers went, they had gardens, or nurtured the gardens of others.

Firbek's eyes flicked over the cart and its marine driver, then settled on Justen. 'Ready, Engineer?'

'Whenever you are.' Justen nodded and lifted the reins. The gray sidestepped, then carried him up beside the marine officer.

'Where is this spring, or whatever it is?'

'According to the directions from Merwha—'

'Merwha?' Firbek interrupted.

'She's the Sarronnese officer assigned to help with our supplies. According to her, we take the back road, the one that skirts the east side of the city, until it forks, and then we take the right fork for about five kays, maybe six. About halfway up that road, we'll run into the yellow branch – that's what they call it. Smells like brimstone. The brimstone comes from the springs . . .'

'I have the idea.' Firbek turned his head toward the marines. 'Head out. Uphill to the second fork.'

Justen let the gray keep pace with the bigger man as Firbek led the group onto the main road heading toward Sarron itself.

A blue-painted coach, leather bags strapped to the roof, rolled past Justen on its way downhill to the river road. The coachman held the well-oiled reins of the two matched bays. Beside him sat a guard dressed in blue-and-cream livery, holding a cocked crossbow.

'A copper . . . just a copper, noble Sers.' A boy in a ragged loin-cloth held out his hand to Firbek. One leg, bent and twisted, dragged in the dust as he limped downhill, away from the city. 'Just a copper . . . a poor copper.'

Firbek ignored the beggar, edging his horse into the center of the highway. Justen slipped a copper from his purse and flipped it to the boy.

They had ridden less than fifty rods uphill before they had to edge to the side of the road again, this time because an empty farm wagon was drawing past a small cart piled high with household goods, and drawn by a small donkey. A white-haired woman and a white-bearded man walked beside the donkey. Neither looked up at the mounted soldiers from Recluce, or even at the farm wagon as it rattled by.

Justen brushed his fingers across the black wood of the staff, then swallowed.

'Make way . . . make way!' shouted the tall woman riding at the head of nearly a dozen mounted guards. Behind the guards, rolling downhill from Sarron, rumbled two wagons, each covered with canvas bound over loads that reached a good four cubits above the heads of the teamsters. Six horses strained to pull each wagon, and the heavy wheels powdered the dirt scattered across the stone slabs of the roadway leading into Sarron.

Creaakkk . . .

Justen followed Firbek and the rest of the squad off of the granite paving and onto the shoulder, eyeing the curve in the heavy timbers of the wagon bed.

'Damn!' muttered the redheaded marine driving the cart as it rattled and bounced through deep ruts on the shoulder.

Because he wondered exactly what lay under the canvas,

Justen reached out with his order-senses to touch the passing
wagons. Fabric – heavy, woven fabric, bound in rolls – rested
under the canvas. Fabric? Rugs? The Sarronnese were known
for their rugs, and rugs were certainly heavy. But the wagons
bore enough rugs to fill a small warehouse.

Justen frowned.

'What are they carrying, Engineer?' asked the woman marine
behind Justen.

'Rugs.' His voice was distant as he pondered the significance
of the wagon-loads of rugs, and of the second dozen guards who
followed the wagons.

'The weaseling merchants are abandoning Sarron,' snapped
Firbek. 'They beg for our help, but they won't even stay in their
own city.'

'We haven't exactly been all that successful in stopping them.'
Justen's voice was dry.

'Turn at the fork!' Firbek pointed to the side road on the right,
which branched off to the southeast just before the main road
widened into the causeway that entered Sarron.

The narrow, packed-clay road followed the pink granite outer
walls of the city, roughly a kay from the outermost stones.

'No moat,' offered Firbek after they had covered another
kay.

'Not that much water here, I suspect.' Justen frowned as he
looked up and recognized the stone arches of the main aqueduct.
'No . . . that's not it. Probably the heat.'

'What's the heat got to do with it?'

'You put water in a moat someplace that's this hot and it gets
all stagnant, scummy, green. You get lots of mosquitoes, flies,
bugs. Lots of diseases.'

'Hmm . . .' Firbek pursed his lips. 'Walls aren't high enough.
No more than fifteen or twenty cubits. I don't think the gates
would hold off a ram for long, either.'

'Probably not,' Justen returned. 'It's been more than a thousand years, maybe longer, since anyone threatened Sarron.' He
brushed away a fly once, then again, before concentrating and
setting a gentle ward against the insects, thankful that he'd at
least picked up that art from Krytella.

'Can't forget that the Whites think a long ways ahead. Not
these Sarronnese. Ha! Rug merchants, all of them.'

Justen rode on without responding, occasionally looking back at the city walls as they receded, occasionally wincing as the cart wheels squeaked. The right-hand fork in the road appeared not more than two kays beyond the east side of the walls.

In time, still before midday, the faint odor of brimstone began to drift from the water beside the road, a stream beside which grew no large trees, for all of the age of the stone fences.

'Smells like rotten eggs.' The marine driving the cart screwed up her nose.

'Eggs smell better,' answered a rider behind Justen. The comments seemed to loosen tongues that had been silent.

'. . . what's this stuff for . . .'

'. . . the engineers use it . . . rockets . . .'

'. . . smells so bad. Sure it's not chaos-touched?'

They rode another kay and more before they reached the stone walls of the healers' enclave. The red-oak gates had been swung open and chained in place.

Inside the walls there was an open, paved courtyard, almost free of the smell of brimstone. To the right was a stone-walled but thatched building that appeared to be a stable, while a garden with sculpted trees stretched from the courtyard to a long, low building with a red-tiled roof.

Justen dismounted and tied his gray to the hitching rail that doubled as a fence between the stone-paved courtyard and the garden. A light breeze carried a slight hint of brimstone across the grass and ruffled the long-stemmed blue flowers that bordered the courtyard's paving stones.

A figure in a green tunic and trousers walked from the tile-roofed building and down the stone walk that split the garden. Justen looked up to Firbek.

'We'll be happy to wait here,' the marine said.

Justen walked toward the green-clad woman. At an angle to his right, between the stable and the main building, he could see the drying pans filled with the orange-yellow of brimstone. He halted several paces from the gray-haired healer.

'You must be the engineer from Recluce. I am Marilla, healer leader of Gyphros.' She bowed to him.

Justen returned the bow, noting the deep, dark circles around the woman's eyes. 'As the Tyrant may have informed you, we have come for some brimstone.'

'We wish it were otherwise.'

'So do I,' confessed Justen.

'It is already bagged, Ser.' The woman pointed down the path to Justen's right. 'The bags are stacked just beyond the far corner of the stable, this side of the drying pans. I regret that there is no cart path, but each of the bags holds only about a half-stone of brimstone. We also bagged what little nitre we had. There are five bags of that.'

'How many bags of brimstone?'

'Four score.' An apologetic look crossed the healer's face. 'We did keep what we thought absolutely necessary for healing, just a stone or so.'

'That's more than we could have asked.' Justen bowed again. 'And bagged, no less.'

'We had an outpost at Middlevale, Engineer. The Whites killed all score and five, even though they offered no resistance. We all have sewed for the past eight-day.' The healer's face hardened. 'Though you do not follow the Legend in the way we do, you have come when few have. Direct your weapons well toward the legions of accursed light.'

'We will do what we can.' Justen looked toward the pile of what he had thought stones, then back toward the cart. 'May I have the marines load the brimstone?'

'Of course. Afterward, we will have laid out bread and meat and cheese on the table under the tree there.' Again, the healer looked apologetic. 'We have only redberry and water.'

Justen smiled. 'That will be more than adequate. And I thank you.'

'No thanks are necessary.' The healer turned.

Justen walked back to the marines.

'What was all that about?' Firbek, still mounted, glared down at Justen.

'The brimstone is all bagged, about four score half-stone bags. There are five bags of nitre as well.' Justen coughed, then continued. 'After your troops load the cart, the healers will be laying out a full meal on the outdoor table next to where the brimstone bags are stacked.'

'Four score?' asked Firbek, a frown crossing his face.

'Four score,' repeated Justen. He repressed a smile as he

watched the words about the food pass among the mounted marines.

'All right. Follow the engineer! And no slacking if you want to enjoy that meal!'

Justen patted the gray on the shoulder and glanced toward the healer, who watched from the corner of the garden as the marines carried the bagged brimstone from the enclave and as three other healers, two men and a woman, carried out large platters that they set on the table, followed by pitchers and crockery mugs.

After watching the last bag of brimstone as it was loaded and tied in place, Justen gave the gray a pat and started toward the table. He was as hungry as the marines.

'Ser?' The older healer nodded toward the gray.

'Yes?'

'Is that staff yours?'

'Ah . . . well, yes. It was a gift, but it is mine.'

'You are far more than an engineer, young man. But do not place too much trust in the staff.'

Justen flushed.

The healer smiled. 'I know your book says that—'

'My book?'

'The one by your patron – *The Basis of Order*. Our bodies may live in the hills, but that does not mean our minds do.' The older woman gestured toward the table, where the marines had begun to eat. 'You need to eat also. But remember that a staff is to be used, not leaned upon.'

Justen tried not to shake his head. First, Firbek and his displeasure at the amount of brimstone, and now this? He'd have to talk to Gunnar. He definitely would.

36

Justen leaned back and let the cool evening breeze – coming out of the east and off the Westhorns – blow over him. On the other end of the porch, Clerve struggled with a battered guitar and an old song.

> . . . *down by the seashore, where the waters foam white,*
> *Hang your head over; hear the wind's flight.*
> *The east wind loves sunshine,*
> *And the west wind loves night.*
> *The north blows alone, dear,*
> *And I fear the light.*
> *You've taken my heart, dear,*
> *Beyond the winds' night.*
> *The fires you have kindled*
> *Last longer than light.*

> . . . *last longer than light, dear, when the waters foam white;*
> *Hang your head over; hear the wind's flight.*
> *The fires you have kindled*
> *Will last out my night* . . .

Justen listened to the words that dated back to the founding of Recluce. He did not look toward the steps where Gunnar and Krytella sat and talked in low voices. Although they were close enough that he could have called the words on the breeze with his senses, he did not. The cool breeze ruffled his hair, hair that had gotten too long.

'How about something a little more cheerful?'

The whispered request carried even against the rustling of the breeze, and Clerve resettled himself on the stool brought outside for the night.

> . . . *sing a song of gold coins,*
> *A pack filled up with songbirds,*
> *A minstrel lusting after love,*
> *And yelling out some loving words* . . .

'That's better. Got anything about the White devils? Or these fancy Legend holders?'

Justen grinned at Quentel's flat tones.

'You know, if it weren't for the Legend . . .' began Berol.

'I know,' rumbled Quentel. 'I wouldn't be here hammering out rockets for the Tyrant.'

'It would be better if we had more of them.' Firbek's cool tones rode over Clerve's strumming.

Justen turned to see Firbek. Somehow, the big marine had slipped onto the corner of the porch almost silently. The young engineer frowned, unseen in the darkness, at the sense of wrongness in Firbek's words.

'We're forging too late into the night already. We don't need any more accidents.' Altara's voice was as cold as Firbek's.

'Can't we just enjoy the music?' asked Castin. 'Let this poor old cook who's been cooped up in a kitchen hotter than your forges just enjoy the young fellow's playing.'

'By all means. By all means.' Firbek sauntered down the steps and across the darkened yard, barely missing the garden fence as he headed back toward the marine barracks.

'. . . always spoiling things.'

'Sing another one, boy!' commanded Castin.

Clerve's fingers crossed the strings, and his clear voice brought the others into silence.

> *I watched my love sail out to sea,*
> *His hand was deft; he waved to me.*
> *But then the waters foamed white and free*
> *Just as my love turned false to me.*
>
> *Oh, love is wild, and love is bold,*
> *The fairest flower when e'er it is new,*
> *But love grows old, and waxes cold*
> *And fades away like morning dew . . .*

'Just like the young, always moaning about how sad love is.' Castin slipped an arm around Ninca's waist. The head healer pretended to ignore his gesture, but Justen caught the sense of her smile, even in the darkness.

'One more, and then . . .'

'And then what?'

'Never mind . . .'

Even as Clerve touched the strings again, Quentel slipped into the darkness, followed shortly by Altara.

If I'd held scores of flowers,
or laid within my lady's bowers . . .
If I'd held reigning powers,
or struck down the sunset's towers . . .

As the last silvered notes died away, Castin and Ninca rose, then Berol and Jirrl.

Krytella stretched and stood. 'Clerve sings well. I enjoyed listening. But I'm tired, and tomorrow I have to go check on the Sub-Tyrant's daughters. Again,' the healer added with a mock groan.

'Tribulations of being a good healer.' Gunnar chuckled, his right hand on the railing of the porch steps.

'It was a nice night.' Justen stretched and stepped toward Krytella.

'Good night, Gunnar . . . Justen.' The healer stepped around Justen, who watched as she slipped inside. He swallowed, wishing the words had really been for him. He turned as Clerve approached. 'Thank you. You sing well.'

'Thank you, Master Justen.' Clerve nodded as he eased down the steps and headed toward the end of the barracks, where the engineers had their rooms. Gunnar and Justen stood alone on the steps.

'There won't be that many more good nights.' Gunnar glanced toward the south. 'The Whites have fought clear of the Westhorns and have reached the upper river road.'

'The Tyrant hasn't said anything.' Justen coughed.

'Have you seen all the levies marching in? Or all the people fleeing?'

'You make it sound like the Tyrant is staking everything on Sarron. It's still a seven-day ride, for darkness' sake, to Rulyarth.'

'Their belief in the Legend isn't so strong as it once was.' Gunnar shrugged. 'And everyone fears the terrors of the Whites. If Sarron falls, so will Sarronnyn.'

Justen shivered at the cold certainly in his brother's voice.

If Sarron falls, so will Sarronnyn. He heard the words again and again, long after he had climbed onto his pallet, until, sometime in the early hours, he drifted into a troubled sleep.

37

Justen set aside the finished black iron arrowhead, the last for the morning. After Gunnar's report to Altara, the engineers were alternating between forging rockets and arrowheads, working even later into the evening as the blue-clad messengers galloped up the river road with continuing reports of the White advance.

Firbek insisted that only the rockets could hold back the Iron Guard. Justen pursed his lips. Was the Iron Guard that formidable? So far, all he had seen were the standard White forces. Was the Iron Guard being saved for confrontations with order – for an invasion of Recluce, perhaps?

The engineer took a deep breath. Speculations and guesses would not forge anything. 'Get something to drink. Then we'll go back to the rockets.'

Clerve wiped his forehead again, nodded, and set aside the hammer.

Justen watched the younger man walk toward the side porch, then followed. He needed a drink and fresh air as much as the striker did. He lifted the empty pitcher that sat on his bench.

Nicos shifted the iron in his forge and looked up as Justen passed. 'How are you doing?'

'Another score or so of the arrowheads. The rockets take me more time.'

'They take everyone more time. They're a light-fired pain in the ass.' The wiry engineer glanced past the hammer mill. 'Quentel's none too happy about handling all that powder, even in black iron boxes in the root cellar.'

'I wouldn't be, either.'

'And Firbek.' Nicos snickered. 'He bitched like the demons when Altara told him that the marines would have to help load the powder in the rockets.'

'Firbek's always bitching, especially behind someone's back. I don't like the man all that much, but I couldn't say why.' Justen shrugged and lifted the pitcher.

'Can't like everyone. Just so he does his work.' Nicos turned the iron again. 'This – coming to Sarronnyn – seemed like a good idea at the time. Now it's not looking quite so good.'

'I know.'

Nicos swung the iron onto the anvil, and Justen walked out of the smithy and onto the covered porch. In the hot, still air, Clerve sat crumpled like a damp cloth on the bench, his clothes dark with sweat. Justen looked down at his own clothes, even damper than the younger man's.

Finally, in the silence, Justen picked up the bucket and the pitcher and stepped out into the late summer sun, wondering when, if ever, the Sarronnese summer would turn into autumn and the seemingly endless heat would stop. He trudged across the dust toward the pump. Three chickens gazed at him silently from the shade on the north side of the old house.

'Too hot to cheep. That's hot.' He filled the bucket and trudged back to the porch, where he filled a mug for Clerve.

'Thanks, Justen. I don't see how you do it. You just keep going.'

'Practice.' Justen frowned as belatedly he forced himself to order-spell the water, both in the bucket and in Clerve's mug. At least, after badgering Krytella for almost an eight-day, he had learned how to order-spell against water disease. Of course it didn't help if he didn't remember to use what he had learned. Justen glanced at Clerve. He hoped that the one gulp the striker had taken wouldn't hurt him.

The engineer wiped his forehead on his sleeve before pouring a mug for himself and forcing himself to sip, rather than gulp, the lukewarm water.

Finally, he picked up the pitcher and looked at his striker. 'Come on. We need to get back to work on rocket casings.'

Clerve sat up. 'Will the rockets really do any good? Aren't the Whites still advancing?'

'I don't know. But they'll do more good than if we did nothing.'

The two walked back into the smithy, where the hammers clanged and the hammer mill thumped.

Justen set the full pitcher on the bench, then took up the sheet iron. Clerve worked the bellows while Justen eased the metal into the forge and watched it slowly change color.

In time, out came the cherry-red iron.

Clerve lifted the hammer . . . let it fall, and raised it again . . . let it fall, and raised it again. Every so often, he paused and wiped his forehead.

In between the hammer strokes, Justen adjusted the iron on the anvil, watching the worked metal get thinner and thinner.

When Clerve paused, Justen wiped the sweat off his forehead on his upper sleeve. He took the calipers and measured, then nodded at Clerve and returned the metal to the forge. After reheating the iron, this time Justen took the smaller hammer and the flatter. Following a last set of taps, he stepped back and let the metal cool, nodding at Clerve.

The younger man powdered the chalk line, then set the template against the metal. A quick set of snaps, and the rocket-casing outline appeared in white on the parchment-thin metal.

With the heavy bench shears, they slowly cut out the casing. The distortion created by cutting the casing did not impair the rocket's function much, not when compared to such precise forgings as turbine blades or pump components. Justen laid the flat iron on the hearth and took a deep swallow from the pitcher of water.

Would the rockets help? What about the cannons that Gunnar said were being moved along the river road? How could the rockets help against them? Wasn't there *some* way?

With a deep breath, Justen brought one side of the casing into the forge to heat it before punching the rivet holes and bending the metal into its final cylindrical shape. Later, somehow, he needed to think about the cannon and powder. Later. Somehow.

38

Justen eased less than a thimbleful of the ground powder onto the hearth of the forge before stoppering the flask and setting it on the iron plate on the workbench. Then he took a pine splinter from the shavings box and thrust it into the coals, blowing faintly until the wood flared into flame and he could withdraw the splinter.

At full arm's length, he thrust the flaming tip into the powder, closing his eyes and concentrating with his senses as the powder flared. After opening his eyes, Justen set the glowing splinter on the hearth, pursing his lips.

Once again he poured a minute amount of the powder onto the hearth and restoppered the flask. Again he closed his eyes and concentrated. This time, the powder remained powder.

With a sigh, he picked up the pine splinter and thrust it back into the coals until it again flamed. Then he carefully touched off the powder, his eyes closed and senses extended. The brimstone-infused smoke residue curled up from the plate.

Kkkchewww . . . Justen rubbed his nose, which continued to itch. He frowned and set aside the splinter as he reached for the powder flask. *Kkkccheww* . . .

After a series of sneezes, he rubbed his nose again, then poured a fingertip of powder on the iron once more. He concentrated, trying to replicate the patterns. Nothing happened.

With another deep breath, he recovered the splinter and lit it, then thrust the flame into the tiny pile of powder, trying to hold in his mind the combinations of joinings that led to the chaos of destruction.

The order-patterns failed again. Justen frowned. The patterns existed. He just had to create the proper ones. What did a fire need? Something to burn . . . and air. A fully damped fire or stove or hearth didn't work well. Was there a link to the air? Or did he need to create one?

He reached for the powder once more . . . and concentrated . . . and reached for the powder . . . and concentrated.

His eyes burned and his legs ached when . . . *Whhsstt!* The brightness burned through his closed eyelids, and the smithy seemed to lurch under him for just an instant.

Dumbly, he looked at the iron. Not a trace of powder remained. Nor was there any smoke. He poured out another dribble of powder and tried to replicate the patterns.

Whhssttt . . . The brightness burned at him, and the smithy lurched around him, even though his feet remained planted on the ground.

Justen shook his head. Did he really want to use the patterns? His brain seemed to almost whirl inside his skull. After taking a deep breath, he brushed off the iron and turned toward the door.

The stars shone coldly as Justen stepped into the early autumn evening. The acrid smoke, not of powder but of a distant fire, burned in his nostrils, carried northward along the river, foreshadowing the White advance. His tunic ruffled in the cool breeze, and he turned to the door, which he slid closed as gently as he could. Despite his efforts, the squeaking was loud enough to silence the night insects for a moment.

'Justen? What in the demon's hell were you doing?' Gunnar stood in the darkness not ten steps away.

'The impossible.'

Gunnar sniffed and looked toward the empty powder flask in Justen's hand. 'I should have guessed. Do you know what that felt like?'

'Felt like?' Justen took another deep breath.

'That's what woke me. It felt like you'd twisted order into chaos.'

'Not exactly. You build two small order-patterns, and when you link them . . . well, they create their own chaos.'

'Order *creating* chaos? That's impossible!'

'It doesn't work quite that way.' Justen tried to explain. 'It's more like there's too much order for the structure, and because it can't be held together, the expansion creates chaos – sort of like when you heat water to steam.'

Gunnar nodded in the darkness, a gesture that would have been invisible to anyone but a wizard – or an engineer. 'Trust an engineer . . .'

'You don't sound pleased.'

'I'm not sure that I am. I think there's far more to what you've done than you realize.' The older brother brushed his hair off his forehead and stood silent in the darkness.

Justen waited.

'You've linked building and destroying, order and chaos.' Gunnar laughed nervously. 'There have never been any Gray Wizards because no one has figured out how to bridge order and chaos. You have managed to turn order into chaos. But Gray magic has to work both ways. Can you turn chaos into order?'

'I don't think I'd even want to try – not even to preserve the Legend.'

They both looked to the east, uphill at the dark walls. Only a scattering of torches or candles wavering through windows lit the city.

'Good. It might not be enough, even so,' said Gunnar wryly. 'Now can you let me get some sleep, without any more twisting order out of its fabric?'

'It wasn't like that.'

'It felt like that.'

'All right.' Justen sighed. 'I'll see you in the morning.'

'No, you won't. I'm riding south to see if I can spy out the scope of the White advance. The Tyrant wants more details on those cannons, or long guns. I should be back by evening.'

'Well, as you said earlier, make sure you get your ass back in one piece.'

'Right.' Gunnar laughed, then clasped Justen briefly. 'Good night, except that it's more like good morning.'

For a moment, Justen watched his brother walk toward the old dwelling. Then he turned back to the barracks and his small room.

39

Justen paused outside the smithy door, looking up at the gray clouds, feeling the faint breeze at his back, a breeze that actually promised to cool the smithy. Perhaps fall would arrive after all.

He turned back to look at the road. For the past few days, the rumbling of wagon wheels and the clopping of hooves had filled every lull in the noisier work of the smithy. The traffic on the main road remained almost continuous. Carts and coaches rolled north to Rulyarth; troops and supplies straggled into Sarron before being dispatched to the fortified earthworks southeast of the city. Less fortunate souls limped down the road, northward toward the ocean.

Justen shook his head and entered the smithy. As he did, he felt as though someone were looking over his shoulder and into the shop. He looked back, but no one was there.

'Well, make yourself useful.' Standing at the second forge with Nicos, Altara set down her hammer and punch. 'These all need to be riveted.'

Justen studied the square, black iron frames, his eyes going from the completed frames on the racks to the dark sections of wood. Then he walked over to the benches and picked up a piece of wood, then another, examining the three stacks, each of a different shape.

Beyond the wood stood the kegs of nails and spikes.

The young engineer looked back over his shoulder again. Still, no one had come through the front door of the smithy. 'Have you seen Gunnar?' he asked.

'He's on the hills west of Klynstatt, using the winds to spy out where the damned wizards are putting their troops, especially the Iron Guards.' Altara cleared her throat. 'We need to get these done. We have to get them in place before the Whites get too close.'

Justen nodded. 'I'm surprised that Firbek isn't complaining that we still don't have enough rockets.' He glanced through the open doorway and into the yard, where the marines were working with the new adjustable launcher. 'Has Firbek said anything about . . .' He let the words trail away.

'About your order-smoothing the rockets when they're launched?' Altara snorted. 'He's decided he likes me better than you, and you know how much he likes me. He asked if I'd help with the rockets if the Whites reach the marsh defenses.'

'If? More like when.'

'I share your optimism.' The chief engineer shrugged. 'I said I would. Nicos will handle the mines. You can back up whoever needs it – or follow whatever mischief you have in mind for the Whites.'

Justen looked sharply at the older engineer.

'Gunnar said you ought to be free. He didn't say why. I don't argue with Weather Wizards. And no one is about to question either your courage or your enterprise.' Altara cleared her throat and looked at him. 'But you still need to help rivet those casings now.'

Justen hung up his tunic and walked to the forge. He looked at the mine casings again. In the press of survival, was serving order much different from serving chaos? Both seemed bent on inventing better means of destruction.

After repacking the charcoal and pumping the great bellows until the fire glowed nearly white-hot, he picked up the tongs and swung the first section of casing into the forge, letting it heat until it reached cherry red and he could punch out the rivet holes.

On the road outside, the wagons rumbled and the blue-clad troops marched. And women and men and their children walked northward.

Justen swung the iron from the forge and set it on the anvil. Then he lifted his hammer and punch.

40

The Sarronnese forces and their earthworks formed an arc just below the top of the hillside. To the right were the Klynstatt Marshes, and beyond them ran the River Sarron. To the left, the northeast, were the ironwood forests, where the darkness under the gnarled branches was filled with heavy, twisted roots and dank pot-holes. The odor of stagnant water and the thin, warbling cry of the needle lizards occasionally drifted southward.

Threads of black smoke rose in the southeast, marking the passage of the White horde that had drawn itself up at the far end of the Klynstatt valley. Between the White forces and the Sarronnese, the trade road ran like a brown cable tying two weights together.

Behind Justen, the old stone watchtower on the hilltop flew the blue ensign with the eagle: the battle flag of Sarronnyn. Justen stood on the right-side edge of the earthworks and studied the road, not only with his eyes, but with his senses.

Perhaps two kays away, partly shielded by a low rise not even steep enough to be called a hill, the White forces had formed up under their assorted banners: the crimson of Hydlen, the purple of Gallos, the green of Certis, the gold of Kyphros, and, of course, the crimson-edged white of Fairhaven and the crimson-trimmed gray of the Iron Guard.

Justen glanced back toward the stone watchtower that Zerlana had taken for her command station. Krytella and the healers waited behind a low earth berm to the left of the tower. Farther to the north-west, perhaps four kays across the plateau, lay Sarron itself, with only browning fields separating the city from the oncoming battle and its outcome.

A steady wind from the east, chill from the ever-present ice of the Westhorns, flapped the few blue banners of the Sarronnese

and the green-and-black flag of the single detachment from
Southwind, hard-faced women all, from the youngest trooper
to the grizzled commandant.

Heavy gray clouds imparted a sense of impending doom.
Despite the cool breeze, Justen wiped his forehead. Was that
sense of doom made even stronger by the odor of burned fields
and houses? Or did it reflect merely his own inexperience? His
fingers gripped the wood of the black staff, suddenly slippery in
his hands.

A low, thudding drum-roll issued from the chaos forces and
echoed down the valley toward the defenders.

Thurumm . . . thurumm . . . In a staccato rhythm, the
hoofbeats of the White lancers' mounts rumbled down from
their emplacement on the far side of the valley. Behind the
lancers waited the troops of Gallos and Certis, as well as those
of the Iron Guard. Over a berm on the opposing hillside flew a
single white banner. The chill from that small berm drew Justen's
attention even as he dropped behind the earthworks.

The White lancers neared the foot of the hill held by the
Sarronnese and drew up on the higher ground above the marsh
to Justen's right – just out of easy bow range and just short of
the buried mines under both the transplanted hillside grass and
the road.

A single firebolt flashed from the area of the white banner
and flared toward the Sarronnese hillside, spreading until it
impacted. Several thin lines of greasy black smoke spiraled
skyward, but no screams followed the flame.

The ground shook. In a line behind the watchtower, the
blue-clad riders stood by their blindfolded mounts and
waited.

Justen nodded. So far, Zerlana had anticipated the wizards'
tactics.

A semi-hush fell across the hillside; Justen waited.

Thwuppp! A circular section of hillside between two trenches
erupted.

'Long guns!'

'They've got cannons!' Clerve glanced at Justen.

'Gunnar thought they did.' Justen rubbed his forehead. 'That
makes sense. We've got rockets.' He studied the area.

'But they can't forge black iron,' protested the apprentice.

'So . . . the Iron Guard can use plain iron or bronze, and we still can't use chaos to fire their powder,' snapped Justen.

Thwuppp! Screams followed the second shell.

Thwuppp!

Justen located the emplacement; three guns behind a low hill to the left of the main body of the White forces.

Thwupp!

'Try the rockets!' Firbek bellowed, his voice harsh.

Justen sensed rather than heard the flint and steel of a striker and the *whoosh* of a naval rocket. He also could feel Altara's order-touch on the missile. The smoking exhaust and the patch of fire on the front of the hill shielding the guns confirmed the rocket's target.

A second rocket followed the first, with as little success.

Thwupp! Another section of trenching exploded and strewed timber, earth, and bodies across the hillside.

Justen extended his senses toward the guns until his head ached, but he could not reach them.

Thwupp! More churned earth and bodies appeared on the hillside.

'Keep down!' Justen scrambled away from Clerve and along the trenching to his left, holding the black staff in his left hand as he scrambled around kneeling archers.

'Watch it! Oh . . . sorry, Ser.'

But Justen was past the archers' squad leader, and the other archers moved out of his way. By the time he reached the end of the trench, he was already breathing heavily.

Nearly half a kay of open hillside grasses, no more than knee-high, separated the trenches from the scrub oak and thornberries on the edge of the ironwood forests.

'Do you want to do this?'

No one answered him. He took several deep breaths, grasped the staff more tightly.

Thwupp!

Even before the vibration from the impact of the incoming shell had stopped, Justen levered himself out of the trench and ran for the forest, hoping he was out of bow range, hoping the Whites would think a cannon shot wasted on a single man.

'Who's that?' a voice bellowed from behind the dust raised by the Whites' shelling.

Justen ignored the voice and kept running, thinking as he did that he was forgetting something important.

Thwuppp!

His breath ragged, Justen finally skidded behind a scrub oak, his feet nearly sliding out from under him on the rough ground. So far, the Whites seemed content to wait out the Sarronnese forces.

Another set of rockets splattered against the front of the hill protecting the White cannon.

Justen shook his head, wondering why Firbek didn't try to loft the rockets over the hill. But how could one gauge the trajectory? Still, it wouldn't do much good to fire directly at the hill.

Justen took another breath and headed downhill, his perceptions extended. He hoped there weren't too many White scouts or archers out.

Less than three hundred kays downhill, the engineer paused as he sensed the White archer just inside the deeper forest. Flattening himself under another scrub oak, he caught his breath. He still couldn't feel the cannons; he could only hear the continuing shelling and the intermittent screams.

The Sarronnese were in trouble. If they charged, the White Wizards would fry them with firebolts. And if they stayed in the trenches, eventually the shells would destroy them. If they retreated, all too many would be cut down by the greater numbers of mounted White lancers or the Iron Guard.

And Justen was trying to sneak past an archer, feeling helpless the whole time, just to get close enough to the cannons to see if he could duplicate his trick with the powder.

He began to crawl through the grass, trying to ignore the jabbing of the rocks and the difficulty of carrying his staff. After less than thirty cubits, he paused under another scrub oak.

Thwupp! Upslope, the shells continued to fall.

Think, he told himself. *What about a shield like the ones used on the Black ships? Could I hold it together without falling on my face while walking half-blind through the brush and rough terrain?*

He took another breath.

Whssst! An arrow flew overhead.

Justen ducked, still trying to concentrate on weaving the light-shield around himself.

Thwupp! Yet another shell struck the hillside behind him.

Slowly, he wove the shield until his eyes saw nothing but blackness. His mental senses provided only a rough image of the ground and the low trees around him.

'Damned Black Wizard! He's gone.'

'Shoot anyway.'

'Where?'

Justen edged downhill gingerly until his perceptions lost the first archers – and picked up a second pair. He took a deep breath and continued on toward the gun emplacement. Behind him, the shells fell.

A faint rustling, the sound of boots, seemed to come from the ironwood forest, but his senses seemed confused far beyond the point where the heavy trees began.

He kept moving downhill.

Thwupp!

'There's a Black scout on the flank somewhere! Aim for those bushes! There!'

Justen flattened himself as arrows flew in his general direction, then scrambled up and hurried more quickly downhill. Even the grass seemed to grab at his boots.

'He's closer. Try there!'

Justen scrambled into a depression that might have been a dry streambed and struggled downhill.

'Lost him . . . for light's sake.' The voice from the forest was more distant, and Justen hoped he stayed clear of the White Wizard who seemed to be tracking him.

The gun emplacement was still hundreds of cubits away when he found he could actually sense it, but his vision was so scattered that he pushed onward in his darkness, finally halting short of the hill shielding the cannons, as much afraid of Firbek's useless rockets as of the arrows and cannons of the Whites.

Justen's legs shook as he settled into the grass and began to concentrate on the powder in the White's plain iron shells. Would his effort work? It had to.

He rubbed his forehead and took a deep breath, concentrating on creating the special order of powder and air . . .

Crummpp . . . crummppp . . . crummppp. The waves of

successive explosions and fire welled over the hilltop, burning away the grasses even on the top of the side nearest Justen. That twisting, wrenching, yet somehow unseen, collision of order and chaos screamed like a runaway steam boiler through his skull, and he crashed face-forward on the grasses and dirt.

41

The ground rumbled, and a huge gout of flame exploded into the sky.

One of the three White Wizards standing behind the makeshift berm that commanded the Fairhaven forces staggered, then crumpled into a heap. The other two exchanged glances.

'Darkness-damned Blacks!' Zerchas peered toward the roiling flames where the cannon of the Iron Guard had stood moments before. 'How . . . what . . . Did you feel that twisting?'

Beltar wiped his forehead. 'I . . . never felt anything like that. It was like a flash of order turned into chaos.'

'Every White in Candar felt it,' snapped Zerchas. 'You're the high-powered Chaos Master. What was it?'

'I don't know.'

The stockier wizard scuffed a white-leather boot in the dirt. 'I think you'd better find out.'

Beltar glanced across the valley, watching puffs of flame as an occasional black iron arrowhead found a White lancer. 'It can't happen again right now.'

'Are you sure about that?'

'Yes. Besides, whatever that Black did required powder, and there isn't any more.'

'There certainly isn't. There aren't any more cannon, either.'

'Ummm . . .' Eldiren struggled into a sitting position.

'Well?' Zerchas looked at the slight wizard on the ground. 'Do you know what happened?'

'Ummm . . .' Eldiren moistened his lips. 'Any water?'

Beltar extended his water bottle, and Eldiren swallowed.

'Never mind. We've gotten half their forces already.' Zerchas turned to the messenger in white. 'Tell Jekla to have the Fifth and Third begin their assault. The Fifth and Third. Do you have that?'

'Yes, Ser. Marshal Jekla is to have the Fifth and Third begin their assault.'

Beltar glanced at Zerchas. 'You still want me to hold back?'

'What point is there in your throwing fire against earthworks?'

'I could topple the city.'

'Fine ... but that would just make the Sarronnese more desperate and cost us more troops. Magic doesn't win battles,' Zerchas snorted. 'Troops do.'

'How about Jehan? He's using magic to help the Iron Guard turn the flank.'

'The Guard will win the battle, not the magic.' Zerchas turned and walked toward the hillcrest where the marshals awaited him.

Eldiren looked at Beltar. Beltar shrugged. They both watched as the purple banners sallied toward the earthworks of the Sarronnese.

42

The smell of smoke and brimstone, and burning grasses, and charred bodies, seared Justen's nostrils and throat. Still lying on the grass, he coughed, holding back a retching sensation.

Crump ... A last, smaller, explosion rumbled behind the hill.

Slowly, the engineer rolled into a sitting position. He rubbed his throbbing forehead. Now all he had to do was to get back to his own side of the field. He reknit his light-shield and began the walk northward.

Past the confusion and screams from the White side, he made

it halfway up the long slope holding the Sarronnese forces, using the shallow but dry streambed for cover from wizardly scans. Then he had to stop. His unseeing eyes burned, and the pulsing within his head threatened to split his skull.

The same rustling and muffled thudding he had heard on the way down still appeared to be coming from the ironwood forest. He frowned. Could the Whites be sending troops through the iron-woods? How? The thorn-trunked trees shredded leather like flower petals, and in places there was hardly room for a single man, let alone for any real number of troops, to squeeze through the briars and the thorns.

As he listened, the sound seemed to fade. He shook his head and continued uphill, not releasing his shields until he was well inside the trenches.

'Ser . . . where'd you come from?'

'The cannons,' Justen answered without thinking, still rubbing his forehead.

'You did that?' The archers' squad leader jabbed a thumb toward the blackened hillside where the cannons had been. Only smoke twisted up from behind the hill.

Justen shrugged and edged back to where Clerve waited.

'Where did you go?' the apprentice asked.

'I tried a trick with the cannons.' Justen sat down on the damp clay of the trench's floor.

'That was you?' Clerve looked to the engineer. 'The whole order-fabric shivered, like a sour copper note.'

'Thanks. That's all I need to hear.'

'A drum-roll rumbled across the valley.

'Justen! The Whites are charging. Right toward us!'

'They won't get here, not yet.' Still, Justen levered himself to his knees and peered over the heavy timber brace at the slope below.

A line of purple-clad levies surged uphill toward the lower front line of the trenches where the Sarronnese pikes and halberds waited.

Cruump! The lower hillside and road erupted. Even the timbered clay wall before Justen and Clerve buckled, and the concussion threw them against the rear wall.

Justen staggerd up and peered through seared eyes downhill. The sundered earth had flowed uphill and buried the first line of defenders within their earthworks. Another wave of whiteness from the devastation struck him, and he slumped to the bottom of the trench under his own darkness, darkness propelled with a white agony that slammed at his skull.

How long it was before he climbed out of the white agony, Justen did not know, only that his fingers were clutched around a heavy timber.

'Mother of light!' screamed a soldier from the revetment below, a trench above the one that had become a tomb.

Justen squinted his eyes against the pain of the wounded soldiers. Their agony pounded against his senses. His upper arm throbbed. A wooden splinter had ripped through his jacket and tunic. He looked at it dumbly as behind his timbered wall, he struggled against the pain searing through his skull. How had Dorrin stood it?

He swallowed and touched the wooden fragment in his arm gingerly, swallowing with relief at the knowledge that the wound was superficial. Despite the burning in his eyes and the hammering in his skull, he worked out the wood, then glanced at the other side of the trench, where Clerve lay sprawled facedown in the clay. The white hammers beat through his skull so heavily that he could barely concentrate or see beyond a few feet.

In the lull that followed the destruction, Justen bent down and touched Clerve, sensing the ragged breathing, and offered a small touch of order to the striker. The younger man's breathing steadied, and strangely, the throbbing in Justen's skull subsided to a duller ache, so regular that it took him a moment to realize that another drum-roll had begun.

He peered downhill to see a wave of troops, both crimson and purple, marching forward.

A flight of black-tipped arrows cascaded into the ranks of the White forces, and puffs of flame flared intermittently. Justen nodded to himself. Not all the White forces were chaos-tinged, probably not even the majority save for the White lancers, who drew directly on chaos.

A low moan caught his attention, and he knelt beside Clerve. 'Ohhh . . .'

Justen offered Clerve a sip of water as the apprentice pulled himself into a sitting position.

'Hurts . . .' mumbled Clerve as he swallowed.

Justen touched the heavy red wetness soaking the side and back of the other's sleeve. How had he missed the bleeding? The engineer looked around the debris of the half-collapsed trench, but could find nothing to bind the wound with. He glanced past the timbers.

A wave of yelling and the intermittent sounds of steel on steel echoed uphill as the Fairhaven troops crashed over the first line and poured into the trenchworks, splitting to follow the trenches to the higher emplacements.

The banners continued to push uphill, reaching halfway to the higher defenses. Arrows – not many, but enough – flew from the trenches beneath the watchtower toward the first ranks, trying to slow the advance.

Justen gnawed on his lower lip as he edged toward Clerve. '. . . got to move.'

The apprentice squinted, his eyes rolling, before he toppled backwards. The blood kept welling from his arm and shoulder. Justen lifted the youth in his arms and staggered upright. He glanced back. The banners following the troops neared the trenches despite the handfuls of arrows that rained down upon the Whites' uphill charge.

Justen ignored the words of the soldiers he passed as he struggled through the trench that angled uphill, all the time half-wondering how he could have overlooked Clerve's wound.

Bent under the youth's weight, he trudged through the damp, clinging clay in the trench bottom, determined to reach the healers. How long it took, he did not know, only that his head pounded again by the time he laid Clerve on an empty pallet.

'Ugghhh . . .' A trooper on an adjoining pallet retched.

'This one looks like a pincushion.' A cool voice drifted in from out of his sight.

'There's Justen! That's Clerve.'

At the sound of Krytella's voice, Justen tried to turn his head, but the effort was so great that blackness clouded his vision. He steadied himself.

'Can you—'

But the healer had already begun to strip away ruined fabric. Justen slowly walked back toward the crest of the hill. His feet carried him without thought.

To the left of the watchtower stood Altara, beside the left

rocket launcher. The blankness in her eyes showed that her senses were elsewhere, upon the rockets, upon the struggling forces halfway up the hill.

Two trumpet blasts blurted from the watchtower, followed by two more.

Whhhsttt!

'Lower. Crank it down a notch,' ordered Firbek.

One of the marines loaded a rocket, while a second adjusted the launching frame. At the left launcher, another set of marines replicated the actions.

'Strike!'

Whhsttt! Whssstt!

Justen's eyes followed the smoke of the black projectiles, watching as two fiery impacts scattered Certan and Gallosian levies across the hillside.

'Load and strike!'

Whhhsttt! Whhssstt!

Another impact, and another recoil of whiteness and death drove Justen back a step, almost into the unmoving Altara. He looked down to see that the chief engineer had locked one hand around an earthwork brace so firmly that both hand and arm had bleached into an unhealthy whiteness.

He winced at the pain that spilled from her and stepped back another pace.

'Darkness . . .'

His eyes turned to the long slope below, then toward the righthand slope, between the marsh and the edge of the earthworks, where the Sarronnese cavalry charged into the flank of the White forces, driving them down and back.

Three quick trumpet blasts followed, and the blue horse wheeled and retreated, but not before a pair of firebolts turned half a dozen riders and their mounts into charred heaps.

Then the arrows flew – regular arrows, Justen noted absently – and even more of the Gallosians fell.

Justen retreated another few paces and leaned against the cool stones of the tower.

A young man darted up to him and handed him a chunk of cheese. 'The lady healer said for you to eat this.' He was gone before Justen could open his mouth.

Whhhssttt!

Another rocket roared down the hillside, followed by another.

The engineer sat on the damp clay and took a bite of the cheese, glancing toward the marines and the launchers.

'Hold it!' Altara broke from her concentration.

'Why?' asked Firbek.

'We're hitting more of our troops than theirs. Besides, they're pulling back. Wait . . . for either the Iron Guard or the White lancers.'

'Stand down.' Firbek's voice was dull.

Justen mechanically ate the cheese, then sipped lukewarm water from the bottle he had forgotten was on his hip. The worst of the pounding in his head lifted. Almost a hush had fallen across the heat of midday.

Altara came over and sat down beside him. 'Might as well rest while we can. They'll be back. Outside of the rockets, we don't have much left.'

Justen offered her the water bottle.

The chief engineer took a swallow and handed it back. 'Thanks. What did you do to the cannon – or do I really want to know? It felt like you were playing with chaos, but you sure don't show any signs of it.'

'I figured out how to combine order and powder to make chaos.' Justen took a deep breath. 'Is it always this way?'

'What way? You've been in more of this than I have.' Altara gave a wry smile.

'So . . . disorganized. I don't mean the fighting . . . but things happen, and I can't seem to put the pieces together. Clerve was wounded, and I just gave him water and looked at him for a while. Somehow, at first I didn't even see he was hurt. How does anyone keep track of what's happening?'

'Most people don't, I'd bet.' Altara glanced across at the marines, all but Firbek sitting behind the low timbers that braced the back of the hillcrest berm. 'Firbek just kept firing those rockets.'

A deep drum-roll echoed.

'Shit. That sounds like the White lancers.' Altara struggled to her feet.

The drum-rolls continued, answered in turn by four short blasts from the Sarronnese signal trumpets.

As in the previous battles, the White lancers rode forward

at an even pace. The tips of their white-bronze lances glittered with cold fire. Forming out of bow range, they were almost five deep.

'Ready!' ordered Firbek.

'Hold it,' snapped Altara. 'Wait until they're closer. Aim for the flat just where the slope begins. They'll have to slow there, and they'll probably bunch up.'

Another roll of drums, and the White lancers charged.

'Ready!'

A staccato trumpet command warbled from the Sarronnese watchtower, and the remaining pikes lifted on the left side of the third line of trenches. The lower trenches were vacant, nearly leveled by the fighting, the firebolts, the cannon impact, and the earlier mines.

Whhsstt! The first rocket arced over the lancers and flared on the hillside behind the White cavalry.

'There . . . on the flat. Lower the launcher!' Firbek jabbed toward the White lancers.

Whhssttt . . . whhsttt! Two more rockets flared off the hillcrest. One exploded harmlessly in midair, far short of the lancers. The second gouted flame across the right end of the charge, and dirty white ashes drifted out among the cattails and swamp grass of the marsh.

Another trumpet blast, and black-tipped arrows began to strike the White lancers as well.

'Strike!'

Whhsttt! Whsstt!

'Strike!'

Whhhsttt!

The screams of men and horses echoed from the Fairhaven side of the field for the first time in the day. Yet the lancers pounded onward, past the flat and to the edge of the Sarronnese trenches – and around them, using the thin wedge of ground between the end of the earthworks and the slope to the marsh as a turning point before riding down the pike-holders from behind.

'Aim at the trench edge! There!' snapped Justen, knowing that Altara was caught with her senses order-smoothing the rockets.

'Strike!' Firbek ignored the engineer.

Justen tapped the marine on the shoulder. 'Aim at the trench edge! There!'

Firbek glared but shouted to the marines, 'Uphill! A touch to the right. At the end of the trenches.'

Whhhsttt . . . whsssttt . . .

The first rocket charred a patch of cattails in the marsh. The second rocket, aimed with a touch of order supplied by Justen, exploded on point: amid a clump of White lancers turning the flank of the Sarronnese forces.

Hssttt! A lone fireball arced over the earthworks and flared across the right launcher.

'Eeee . . .' The marine aiming the launcher fell forward, burning.

Justen swallowed hard, trying not to retch at the odor of charred meat.

While he fought to control his churning stomach, another marine took the left-hand wheel on the launcher and read-justed the crank. The woman marine slipped another rocket into place.

'Strike it!'

Whhsttt! The rocket exploded in midair.

Whhsttt!

So did the next rocket. Justen frowned. Had the Whites discovered a way to explode powder in black iron?

The heavy roll of drums increased, and the levies from Hydlen and Lydiar began to march forward, following the path of the White lancers.

'Strike!'

Altara continued to concentrate on the rockets.

Whhhsttt!

Despite the huge gaps in the ranks of the lancers – fully two-thirds of them had been killed, fired, or downed – the remainder hacked their way uphill, seemingly ignorant of the damage created by black iron arrowheads and rockets. Behind them, stolidly marched the White levies, their small shields held high against the iron arrows.

The Fairhaven strategy was working, Justen realized. In trying to hold off the lancers, the Sarronnese had failed to target the levies, and now those levies were more than halfway up the hill.

Yet . . . still the crimson-and-gray banners had not moved. *Why has the Iron Guard not been pressed into the fight? And why are there so few firebolts from the White Wizards?* Justen glanced from one end of the field to the other.

Whhhsttt!

Another drum-roll echoed across the valley. Now the gold-and-green banners began to move forward. *How many troops do the damned Whites have?*

'Strike!'

Whhsttt!

Still . . . the rockets went off, although now half of them were exploding in midair rather than where they were aimed.

Justen's head ached, and he did not understand how Altara remained standing.

Hsssttt!

Justen ducked as another wizardly firebolt arced past, splattering on the antique stones of the watchtower. His eyes drifted back to the lower right-hand side of the field, where the Whites surged upward. Below them, it appeared as though the marsh had solidified. Realizing that the dark masses were bodies, Justen forced himself to swallow the bile in his throat. Everywhere he looked there were bodies: burned bodies, ashes, bodies with arrows through them, bodies coated in dull red.

Another drum-roll rumbled across the hillcrest. Justen shivered, then turned. The sound had come from the northeast, from the direction of the ironwood forests.

Not five hundred cubits to the north, formed up at the edge of the ironwoods, were hundreds of dark-clad troops.

'Darkness!' Justen swore. The banners on the field below had been decoys. He should have trusted his feelings!

Another drum-roll and the Iron Guard began to march forward. Arrows arced from behind them toward the Sarronnese. Justen dropped in back of a timber brace, now wondering what he could do.

Suddenly, a familiar figure appeared beside the watchtower. Justen shivered as he felt the webs of order building around Gunnar. He could sense his brother's call to the great winds and the storms from the Roof of the World.

A cold, whining, whistling wind whipped out of the southeast and across the hillside. The Sarronnese battle ensign flapped wildly.

Behind Justen, Firbek continued to direct the rockets against

the remnants of the White lancers, apparently oblivious to the
threat from the ironwood forest.

'Strike!'

Whhhsttt!

Justen glanced back toward Gunnar and the oncoming Iron
Guard, and he shivered as the wind continued to rise and the
sky darkened.

Gunnar stood apart from the tower, like an ancient tree rooted
in time.

Scattered ice pellets began to rattle against the stones of the
tower. Dark clouds roiled into the once-clear sky, and a rumble
of heavy thunder rolled across the valley as the storm swept
down upon the White forces.

The drum-rolls faltered for an instant.

Hhhssttt! Another firebolt flared – this time from behind the
Iron Guard – and splatted against the watchtower.

Justen, fighting his headache and feeling of despair, struggled
to throw an order-shield around Gunnar.

Hhhsstt! The next firebolt angled wide of the Storm Wizard.

Justen kept concentrating, clinging to the heavy timber for
support as he poured his strength into creating the barrier that
would protect Gunnar while his brother called the storms.

'Form up down there!'

Justen frowned at the words as another figure – massively built
and in blacks – turned from the rocket emplacements and walked
swiftly past Justen and across the ridge through the wind toward
the Black Weather Wizard.

Justen frowned. Then he stood. 'Gunnar!'

Locked into the winds, Gunnar remained rooted. Justen began
to run toward his brother, wishing for his staff, but it was buried
in the hillside collapse. He pulled out his belt knife, realizing that
he would not reach Gunnar before Firbek did.

'Firbek!'

The big marine lifted his blade.

The winds whistled, and the ice fell, pounding, slowing the
advance of the Iron Guard to less than a crawl.

Justen twisted the shield between the marine and Gunnar.
Firbek paused, and Justen lunged forward, plunging the knife
into Firbek's right shoulder. The marine dropped his own blade,
but his left hand slammed Justen to the ground, causing Justen to

release his knife as well as his order-shield. Then Justen grabbed the blade that Firbek had dropped.

Firbek's open palm slammed across Gunnar's unprotected face just as Justen swung the blade up. Firbek jumped back, but Gunnar staggered, then toppled onto the trampled brown grass.

Justen walked toward the marine. Firbek backed away, circling around toward the vacant rocket emplacements. Justen advanced, wondering if Firbek had dismissed the marines or if they had fled when they had seen the Iron Guard. Then he saw the black-clad figures, now bearing blades, circled around the Sarronnese force leader.

The winds subsided, and the ice pellets became less frequent.

'Choose, Engineer! Me . . . or your brother.' Firbek pointed toward the oncoming Iron Guard.

Justen could sense both of the oncoming White forces. Blue-clad figures began to scurry over the top of the hill, hastening back toward a Sarron that seemed impossibly distant.

Justen angled toward the nearest rocket launcher, Firbek's blade still in his hand, nearly tripping on the still form of Altara. His eyes on Firbek, Justen bent down. The chief engineer was unconscious but breathing, and he offered her the slightest touch of order before straightening.

'So . . . what are you going to do, Firbek?' Justen tried to turn the wheeled frame of the rocket launcher toward the advancing gray-clad forms. 'Join the Iron Guard?'

The big marine used both arms to turn the second launcher toward Justen. 'It's not a bad idea. At least Fairhaven isn't filled with hypocrites.'

'You really believe that?'

'Look at the Mighty Ten! They could destroy anything on the ocean, and the Council just builds each ship bigger than the last but insists that we can't help anyone. We've got shitty rockets when we need shells.'

'This isn't the time for philosophy. Why don't you turn that downhill before the lancers get here?'

'For what?' The striker in Firbek's hand flicked.

Justen, ignoring his searing headache, threw a light-shield around himself and stepped aside.

Whhhsttt!

Justen jerked sideways, then turned toward Firbek again.

Firbek touched the striker to the second rocket and yanked the launcher around, toward the engineer he could not see.

Whhsstt! The rocket flared past Justen, who was now running.

Justen swung the sword, at the last moment turning it so that the flat of the blade slammed against Firbek's head.

The marine dropped.

'Aaaeee . . .'

A searing whiteness blinded Justen for a long moment. He shook his head to clear it. His mouth dropped open as he looked to the left of the watchtower and saw Sarronnese troops dashing past the burning command tent, now no more than drifting ashes.

After barely glancing at the unconscious marine, Justen sprinted toward the blazing tent beneath the stone watchtower. Stopped by the heat – hotter, seemingly, than a forge – he glanced around. Gunnar tottered up beside him.

'Do something!' Justen yelled. 'Call a storm . . . anything!' The ends of his hair crinkled as he moved toward the flames.

'Don't you feel it?' Gunnar shook his head sadly.

Justen opened his mouth, then shut it. The tent contained only bodies. 'That bastard . . .'

'Who?' Gunnar squinted.

Hhhsstt! A firebolt splashed across the ancient stones of the tower. Justen staggered, then turned back toward the rocket launchers. He had taken only three steps before the first crimson banner – and more than two-score lancers – surged over the hilltop. He looked over toward the ironwood forests, only to see the Iron Guard less than two hundred cubits from the tower, marching in tight array.

He glanced back toward the spot where the remaining marines had gathered and saw Altara's tall figure, blade in hand. The black-clad marines and the remaining Sarronnese guards were marching swiftly back toward Sarron, their shields held high against arrows.

'Shield yourself!' shouted Gunnar. 'They're all around us. Get back to Sarron!'

As Justen watched, his brother disappeared from sight, although Justen could sense the bending of the light.

Hhhsttt! Another firebolt flared past, so close that Justen could feel the heat.

Justen gripped the blade he had taken from Firbek more tightly, whirling toward the squad of Sarronnese beneath the watchtower. Circled around the tall, blond woman, the Sarronnese backed away from the White forces, almost running toward the road to escape the pincer-like movement of the lancers and the Iron Guard.

Hhhsttt! Hhssttt! Two firebolts flared past Justen.

'Aeeeiii . . .' One Sarronnese trooper choked out a scream before falling in a charred heap. Four others just fell silently.

Feeling as though he walked through heavy, sticky mud, Justen turned toward Sarron and tried to knit the light back around himself. Even the darkness wavered.

Trapped! If he didn't shield himself, the archers or the Guard would get him. If he did, he wouldn't have enough strength left to escape the White forces.

He ground his teeth against the throbbing in his head, the watery feeling in his legs, and took a step, then another. Downhill . . . toward the marsh. Toward water, the one thing that the damned White Wizards couldn't incinerate or twist. Toward water, far closer than the all-too-distant walls of Sarron.

He took another step . . . and held the light-shield . . . and another . . . and held the light-shield . . .

His head pounded. When the pounding occasionally stopped, fire seared across his skull. But he struggled on downhill, knowing he dared not fall. The White Wizards seared their battlefields clean of all bodies, dead or not.

Another step, and another . . . until the steepness of the slope leveled into a softer footing. Softer between the bodies, at least.

At the edge of the marsh, he stopped, surrounded by death. Out in the deeper water, in the late afternoon, a single frog croaked, and Justen could occasionally hear the buzz of flies and the drone of mosquitoes over the sound of marching feet and the hissing of firebolts.

The way north was too steep. In his darkness, he edged southward, slowly, the mud sucking at his boots. He stepped around and over the bodies that seemed endless.

At some point, he released the light-shield, too tired to hold it, and looked back. He swallowed, realizing that he had traveled less than two kays and that the systematic looting and weapons recovery of the Whites continued. No one looked his way, or perhaps no one cared. He staggered southwest, away from the battle, away from the Whites, and away from Sarron.

At last there were no more bodies – only marsh and mud and mosquitoes and flies and dampness and stenches he could not identify.

After the real darkness of twilight fell, he climbed onto higher ground, eventually falling asleep behind a stone wall, not far from a road whose destination he did not know.

43

'Justen! Where's Justen?' The voice rasped from Gunnar's raw throat.

'We don't know.' Altara glanced again to the south, but the columns of smoke were too far away to be seen.

'Damn! Can't even move my head.' Gunnar's voice died away, and his eyes closed slowly as though he were fighting sleep itself. Lying on the marines' rocket cart, now empty of weapons, he looked more dead than alive. The bloody marine lying next to him moaned as the cart lurched around the corner and down toward the compound where those of Recluce had prepared to defend Sarron.

Still walking quickly to keep up with the cart, the chief engineer placed a cold cloth on the magician's forehead, then pulled herself onto her mount.

'No healers?' asked Deryn, her arm still encased in leather braces.

'No. They're . . . dead.'

'Damn Whites. Why'd they fire on the healers?'

Altara shrugged. 'Why does chaos do anything?'

'I can't believe it about Firbek.'

'He likes fighting,' added a third voice. 'I expect he'll do rather well in the Iron Guard.'

'We're leaving,' announced Altara. 'As soon as we can.'

'Leaving?'

'Leaving. We've got a Storm Wizard who's damn-near died. Almost half of our engineers and all of our healers are dead or missing. And Sarron will fall in days, if not sooner.' She glanced back over her shoulder at the pink granite walls. 'So much for the Legend.'

The ground trembled underfoot.

44

In the gray before dawn, Justen sat on the edge of the stone wall, slowly chewing the handful of overripe redberries he had picked from a late-bearing bush and listening to the twitter of insects and the whisper of the breeze from the north. With the wind came the faint odor of ashes.

The trees were turning, not golden or red, but a muddy brown. Was that because the trees of Sarronnyn were different, or because of the influx of chaos?

The engineer shook his head wryly. The Whites had done nothing to the trees. How easy it was to think of everything in personal terms. The trees and the stones would endure whether order or chaos triumphed in Sarronnyn.

He swallowed the last of the berries. After having slept poorly and breakfasted on a few handfuls of berries, he was still tired and hungry. He had no pack, no staff, no knife, a blade without a scabbard, the clothes on his back, perhaps three golds and a few silvers, and a handful of copper pennies. He also had no mount, and most of the White forces stood between him and Sarron.

At least, after the redberries, he could stand up without feeling like he would fall over. One thing was clear enough. He was not about to get anywhere, especially around the Whites and back to

Sarron – or to Rulyarth – on foot. With a deep breath, he looked around. To the southeast, not much more than a kay away, stood a small cot with two outbuildings. The lack of smoke from the chimney and the overall stillness indicated that the holding was probably deserted.

Justen turned to the southwest, but the Klynstatt Marsh continued to straddle the River Sarron for another two to three kays. The swamp was the main reason why most boat travel stopped just above Sarron itself. While it was highly unlikely that anyone would follow him through the marsh, he was doubtful that they would have to, since the large water lizards were not known for their finicky appetites.

He climbed up onto the stones, carefully balancing himself by holding on to a scrub oak that grew beside the half-tumbled wall, and looked back to the north. A low pall of smoke, or fog, hung over the northern end of the marsh. Even as far away as he was, he could sense the White forces to the east of the river and the marsh, presumably preparing for the assault on Sarron itself.

He jumped down from the wall and crossed the twenty cubits of browning grass that separated him from the deserted road. When he reached the strip of clay, he studied the ground for tracks, but there were only a handful, all headed to the south, away from the battlefield.

There would be no mounts to the south, just refugees. Justen turned north, prepared to cast a light-shield around himself at any moment, his ears and senses alert for White outriders or travelers.

Only the sound of the insects, the occasional *terwhit* of an unseen bird, and the rustling of the marsh grass beyond the road and across the wall to his left broke the quiet of the early morning.

Justen had covered nearly two kays when the winding road seemed to sway underfoot and he stumbled. After recovering his balance, he stopped, putting his hand to his forehead. Was he weaker than he thought? He lifted his hand, looked at it, and concentrated. The road swayed under him again. He glanced northward and caught sight of an oak, the higher branches wavering as if blown by the wind. But the air remained quiet, almost heavy in its stillness.

The ground continued to tremble as Justen hurried to the next hillcrest, where he could gain a better view of the approaches to Sarron.

As he paused on the crest, he pursed his lips – so visible was the focus of chaos emanating from the old watchtower that had been Zerlana's command post. Even though he could not see Sarron, he had no doubt about what was happening there.

Should he continue? He smiled wryly. The more chaos, the more chance he had of finding a stray mount unattended – or at least of being undetected. Besides, he had no desire to cross most of Candar on foot, not if he could find a way around the Whites and rejoin whatever remained of the engineers.

Justen quickened his steps slightly, heading northward.

45

In the early light, Beltar glanced at the two blue-clad bodies outside the watchtower. The dark-haired sergeant's eyes were open, sightless. The other corpse lay facedown. Neither captive had revealed much about the Recluce engineers. Beltar raised a hand, and a hint of flame flickered around the bodies. Only white powder remained, drifting away on the wind.

'Much neater that way,' he muttered.

The shortest wizard frowned, scuffing a white-leather boot across the fire-hardened clay. 'Don't waste your strength.'

The third wizard rubbed his chin, eyes flicking from Eldiren to Beltar and back again.

'I'm not exactly a weakling, Eldiren.' Beltar looked to the other wizard. 'What do you think, Jehan?'

'I doubt few have your powers, Beltar.' Jehan's tone was dry. 'Except perhaps Zerchas, and he always points out that wizardry has its limits.'

Beltar snorted and stepped through the open archway. He climbed the two-score steps of the watchtower. From the open battlements, the entire city of Saron was visible to the

northwest, its pink towers glowing in the early morning light.
The watchtower from where the three wizards surveyed Sarron
cast a long shadow like an arrow toward the city. A faint cloud
of brown smoke rose above the city, and early as it was, a line
of figures stretched from the gate downhill toward the River
Sarron.

'What do you plan?' asked Jehan.

'To bring Sarron down, of course.' Beltar's mouth smiled, but
his eyes did not reflect the smile.

Beltar turned and, eyes closed, stood motionless on the stones.
A faint white haze shimmered around him.

Jehan swallowed, looked at Eldiren. Eldiren shrugged and
looked toward the northwest and the city.

The ground shivered, once, twice. A faint wave rolled through
it, lifting the beaten grass and the ripped clay of the battlefield in
a swell, then the fields beyond, before momentarily disappearing
from sight on the downhill slope that dropped away from the
old tower.

The tower itself rocked with the beginning of another swell,
and Jehan put out a hand to the battlement to steady himself.
Eldiren glanced from Jehan to Beltar to the fields in the low
valley that separated the tower from Sarron. The first series of
swells crossed the green expanse.

Another set of shudders rolled from the tower, the swells
seemingly growing in height as their distance from the White
Wizards increased. The handful of horses held by the lancers
below whinnied. Several skittered, as though they wanted to
escape their holders.

'Hold, damn you . . .'

'. . . blindfold them . . .'

'Should have thought of that earlier . . .'

With yet another shudder, the land heaved again. One stone
dropped from the tower to the ground, and a horse reared,
its whinny almost a scream. A dull rumbling echoed from the
ground beneath. To the northwest, the towers of Sarronnyn
swayed. Faint cracks echoed back toward the wizards, barely
audible above the scuffling of the horses, the whinnies, and the
low curses of the lancers just beyond the tower.

With an even louder crack, sharp as a whip, a corner split
from one of the distant towers. The section hung motionless

for an instant before swaying out slowly and dropping down beyond Sarron's city walls. A gout of dust marked the impact.

Beltar shifted his weight silently, and another set of tremblors raced through the ground toward Sarron.

The city walls wavered, rocking slowly back and forth, until more white-pink stones began to tumble.

Jehan swallowed again. Eldiren wore a grim smile. Beltar's face was expressionless, but sweat collected on his forehead above his still-closed eyes.

With each successive tremble, more stones toppled from the towers and walls, some of them crashing downhill toward the River Sarron, but most into the city. Thin plumes of smoke began to rise from behind the now-jagged walls. Soon the plumes were thicker, darker, and joined by columns of white smoke, until a heavy pall spilled over walls and city.

Another loose stone dropped from the watchtower, and Jehan glanced from the gap in the crenelation to Sarron itself even as an entire section of the city wall collapsed like a waterfall of stone and a huge gout of dust billowed skyward.

The smoke over Sarron grew even heavier, blurring the lines of the battered walls, and the figures on the main road scurried like ants from a disrupted hill toward the river. The sound of distant shrieks, screams, and wails blended into a low, moaning buzz.

The sun had climbed well clear of the horizon before Beltar reopened his eyes and looked out upon the distant smoldering pile of rubble – rubble that still shivered with aftershocks, rubble that was crowned too often with tongues of flame. Greasy black smoke mingled with white smoke to pour into the sky, and flames licked at the horizon.

'Did you leave anyone?' whispered Eldiren.

Beltar turned. 'Perhaps. Those away from the buildings and walls.'

'Why didn't you do that in the battle?' asked Jehan.

Beltar turned and made a sweeping gesture over the ash-covered and churned earth of the hillside to the south of the tower. 'It's almost impossible to destroy a braced earthwork.'

'But you could have sneaked around through the forest and destroyed the city. Their army would have surrendered,' pointed out Eldiren.

'Then we would have had thousands of angry armed men

and women who had absolutely nothing to lose. Because they rejected our terms, we could destroy the city. That's accepted by people. Destroying cities without fighting battles isn't . . . at least not until you've fought more than a few.'

'But that's crazy.' Eldiren shook his head.

'No. That's war.' Beltar started down the stairs as hazy clouds began to gather around the smoking ruins of Sarron.

A faint smile crossing his lips, Jehan nodded before following the other two down the narrow steps of the watchtower.

46

Just around the bend in the road, past a copse of scrubby willows, stood something alive. Justen extended his senses, smiling as he caught the feeling of a horse. He frowned, trying to discern whether a rider also rested nearby, but he could sense nothing.

Carefully, he drew his cloak of light around himself and eased as silently as he could along the road . . . stopping, listening, and easing forward . . . stopping, listening, and easing forward . . . until he passed the willows.

When he was convinced that only the horse waited, he dropped the shield and looked. A chestnut gelding stood beside the road, grazing the short grass that grew on the side away from the marsh. Justen grinned, thinking about his already-sore feet, and eased toward the horse. He paused as he saw the dark stains across the saddle, on the blanket and the chestnut's mane.

The gelding whinnied. Justen took another step and stopped. The chestnut whuffed and sidestepped away from the road and into the stubbled grainfield, backing away from the hedgerow that seemed to start with the scrubby willows.

'Easy, fellow. Easy . . . now.' The engineer stepped forward.

For a moment, the gelding just watched. Then he lifted his head and sidestepped again.

'Easy . . .' Justen took a small step. So did the gelding. Justen tried again, but the wary chestnut continued to back away.

Finally, Justen reached out with a sense of order to reassure the skittish horse.

Wheee . . . eeee! Almost as if Justen had burned him, the big gelding wheeled and galloped away across the stubble, puffs of dust rising as his hooves struck the ground.

Idiot! Of course you scared him. He's a White mount. The engineer frowned. *Will I have that trouble with any mount?* He shook his head. Not all the Whites had been equally chaos-tinged, and with the numbers who had been killed and wounded, there had to be some available mounts somewhere . . . didn't there?

Two twisting turns in the road later, he encountered another mount, but the sense of Whiteness was so strong that the engineer just sighed and trudged onward, wondering if the Whites would have totally leveled Sarron before he could even get five kays down the road.

Justen paused and looked to the marsh and back to the road. The trail that skirted the marsh – the one he had taken the evening before – could not have been more than three kays long, yet the road twisted and turned so much like a lizard that its length was closer to twice the length of the trail. He took another deep breath as he sensed another horse.

A small bay mare grazed near the road, on the marsh side. Justen frowned as he saw the blood-streaked saddle. Pausing behind a scrub oak, he listened, but save for the distant vibrations of wagons and troops, he could hear nothing. Then he stepped forward.

The saddle pad was gray. Justen extended his senses, but there was no sign of chaos beyond a faint lingering hint of Whiteness, as if someone tinged with disorder had paused and departed. Nor could he sense anyone else near the horse.

Slowly, the engineer inched forward. The mare looked up for a moment. Justen paused. The mare whickered but did not move. She continued to regard Justen.

In the grass, between the road and the wall, lay a dark-gray bundle.

Justen frowned, then eased over to the wall, where he sat down for a moment.

'You all alone, now, lady?' he asked conversationally, looking toward the gray bundle that could only have been the mare's rider. He touched the figure with his order-senses, but the trooper was dead . . . and had been dead for a time, possibly since the battle of the day before.

Unlike the other horse, the mare did not skitter at the pulse of order, although Justen had not directed it at her. Still, her steadiness was a good sign. He continued to sit on the wall.

'You're the faithful kind, not like those others. You're waiting for your rider to get up. But I don't think it's going to happen.'

The mare whickered again.

Justen slid to the adjoining stone, nearer to the mare and her dead rider.

'I wish you'd think about letting me get closer.' He eased across two more stones, so close now that his mud-smeared boots almost touched the outstretched hand of the dead Iron Guard.

Slowly, Justen leaned forward and half turned over the body. Despite the short black hair and the dullness of the dead face, the woman had been attractive . . . and young. Somehow, the broad, muscular shoulders and dark hair reminded him of Altara. The dead Iron Guard could have been the chief engineer's sister. A black-tipped arrow was still clutched in her left hand, and her right shoulder and chest were caked with blood.

Justen forced his hands to be steady as he laid her on her back. He closed his eyes for a moment, thinking about black iron arrow-heads – and of how proud he had been of their effectiveness and his craftsmanship.

Whuuuff . . . The mare nudged his shoulder.

'All right, I'll do what I can. But I'm going to tie you up so you don't run away.'

He tied the mare to a sapling that grew at an angle from the wall, then searched the pack and saddlebags, but found nothing there that resembled a shovel.

You're a damned fool. He straightened the woman's body and dragged it into a depression on the other side of the wall. He took from the trooper only her purse, containing five golds and a silver, her belt knife, which he placed in his own sheath, and her empty scabbard. Firbek's blade stuck out of the Iron Guard's smaller scabbard, but a too-small scabbard was better than none. Then he wrapped the dead Iron Guard in the ground tarp that had been rolled behind her saddle. He rerolled the blanket and replaced it behind the saddle.

You're still a sentimental fool. He began to pile stones over her covered form, looking up the road every time he set a stone in place. By the time the cairn was completed, he was drenched and shaking.

Then he looked helplessly at the water bottle stowed behind the saddle and laughed. The ration bag was empty except for a small, dried chunk of cheese and three battered biscuits. He attempted not to gulp them all down at once, but to chew them slowly between sips of the water.

'Best meal in days,' he told the mare as he untied her and eased into the saddle.

After turning the bay north, toward the smoking heap that had been Sarron, he glanced back, but his eyes blurred as the image of a younger Altara clutching a black-tipped arrow came to mind.

'Let's go, lady.'

The mare sidestepped, then continued northward at an easy walk.

At the next stream, Justen stopped and let the mare drink. He refilled the water bottle at the same time and peeled a few last redberries from a small bush beside the stream. He was still hungry and shaky.

After remounting, he glanced toward the northeast. The smoke billowing into the sky was thick and gray.

Less than a kay beyond the stream, the road curved downhill and then up and to the right. Justen reined up, then looked at the patches of ashes on the backside of the hill and at the lumps of metal. He had almost reached the battlefield without realizing it. On the far side of the depression lay the churned earth of the Sarronnese defenses, now blanketed in heavy gray ash.

Just beyond the curve in the road that led to the flat between the two hills, he could sense a wave of Whiteness, almost as though a barrier stretched across the road, a barrier that extended from the ironwood forests far to his right and almost to the marsh.

Scores of mounted troops held the road ahead – clearly a rear guard for the massive White forces that marched toward Sarron itself. Justen frowned.

What chance did he have, even if he could maintain a shield for the next five to ten kays, of passing through the Whites' surveillance undetected? He sat on the mare, stroking her neck, considering his options.

Realistically, he'd have the demon of light's own time trying to get through the next few kays, with at least one Chaos Wizard scanning the narrow space between the marsh and the forests, and probably part of the forests as well. Even if he did get through, then what? Sarron was a pile of smoking rubble, and the engineers and Gunnar were either dead or on their way to Rulyarth. But he would have known, somehow, if Gunnar were dead.

But if he didn't try, he'd have to circle so far south and west that he might never catch up with the fleeing Sarronnese – or with the remaining engineers and Recluce marines.

Pushing that thought from his mind, he eased the light-shield around himself and the mare and stroked the mount on the neck even more reassuringly. 'Now . . . it'll be dark, but Papa Justen wants to go home.'

Whheee . . .

He stroked her neck, projecting what reassurance he could as the mare stepped delicately forward.

The ugliness of the White troops mounted as he urged the mare around the curve in the road, guiding her onto the shoulder, where he hoped the puffs of dust from her hooves would not be quite so obvious.

Straining, Justen could hear a few of the troopers' muttered words.

'. . . waiting here . . .'

'. . . no damned loot . . . no women . . .'

'. . . Girta got all the luck.'

'. . . call being around Zerchas luck . . .'

The area on the marsh side of the road, less than ten cubits wide before it sloped steeply downhill, was empty of mounted troops.

Justen tried to breathe easily, quietly.

'Order! Archers!'

With the snapped command, the White lancers fell silent. Justen tried to pull up the mare.

Wheee . . .

'There! See the puffs of dust. There's a Black spy!'

Through the unseen reddish-white fire, Justen could sense the presence of a White Wizard – not a terribly strong one, but the man didn't need strength with as many troops as he had. The engineer wheeled the horse away and nudged her down the road, flattening himself against her back.

'Archers! Release in volley. Volley one!'

Thunngg . . . unngg . . . unnggg . . .

'Where, damn it?'

'What—'

'Horse high! Horse high!' snapped the wizard.

The engineer edged the horse as far to the edge of the drop-off as he dared, urging her back, away from the soldiers.

Thunngg . . . unnggg . . . unnnggg . . .

He could sense the arrows flying overhead, and more toward the center of the road, as he rode sightlessly around the curve and out of the line of fire.

'Hold! We don't know what tricks he's up to! Remember those traps in Spidlar! Hold . . .'

Justen took a deep breath when he finally let the horse drop into a fast walk and lowered the light-shield. He'd just been lucky that the Whites were afraid of an ambush.

After checking the empty road behind him, he turned in the saddle and looked downhill toward the River Sarron. Beyond the marsh to the south, there might be a bridge or a place to ford. While his knowledge of Sarronnyn's geography was sketchy, he did know that the town of Clynya offered a crossing. He shook his head. Clynya was more than three days' ride.

He studied the wave of unseen whiteness behind him once more, hoping that none of the rear guard were about to ride after him. He studied the winding road ahead, a way that would take well past mid-morning to even get past the marsh and to the point where the road ran along the river again.

The mare whickered, and he patted her neck. 'Easy . . . easy. We've got a long way to go.' He just hoped it wasn't too long.

He swallowed as he realized that they would be riding past the cairn of the dead Iron Guard again. He took a deep breath as the image of a laughing, dark-haired woman settled in his mind for a moment.

Order-tipped arrows? Wonderful craftsmanship?

He patted the mare and kept riding.

47

Justen wiped his forehead on his sleeve, then gave the mare another pat. To his right, the river twisted and turned through the bottom-land, while thickets rose out of the adjacent backwaters. On the western side of the River Sarron were stubbled fields interspersed with rock-walled meadows turning brown, where even some few scattered flocks of sheep still browsed, as if their shepherds knew that the cold running water protected them.

Should he try to find a ford? Justen looked down to the river, which spanned nearly a hundred cubits. Despite the lack of rain, the center of the muddy flow still churned ominously. The light breeze carried a half-leafy, half-musty, smell of autumn up from the river.

The engineer glanced toward the west, where the sun hung mid-way between the zenith and the smoke-smudged horizon. Then he sighed and took a swallow from the water bottle.

The rocky slopes above the road held several small meadows and stone trellises bearing vines. The grapes had been stripped, and the few houses he had seen were shuttered tightly. He'd found a few berries, and even a pearapple tree with enough fruit not only to eat, but to store in the otherwise empty saddlebags. Though he was not ravenous, some solid bread and hard cheese would have been welcome.

'Let's go, lady.' He patted the mare again and lurched slightly in the saddle as she started uphill.

How long they had ridden before he saw the thinnest of smoke plumes from the holding chimney, he did not know, only that the sun hung lower in the afternoon sky.

'Should we try to buy something?' he asked the mare. Receiving no answer, he turned her off the road and up the cart path toward the low, stone and thatched-roof dwelling. Even as he watched, the thin line of smoke seemed to get thinner, but he could still smell the faintest hint of burning wood.

A stone wall, broken by a single open gate, surrounded both the house and what appeared to be a thatched barn. From somewhere behind the wall, Justen could hear the sound of a saw.

'Father!' called a sharp and high voice.

'Hullo, the house,' Justen called as cheerfully as he could, reining up perhaps twenty cubits short of the gate.

'Just stay right where you are, fellow!' A thin-faced man appeared behind the wall, standing on something that raised him so that his chest and the longbow he held were clearly visible.

'I was hoping to buy a few provisions.'

'Got nothing for sale.' The man kept the bow centered on Justen's chest.

'I can pay. I'll even leave the coin in plain sight.'

'Don't want none of your coin.'

'I'm not a White – I'm an engineer from Recluce—'

'Don't tell me. You're riding a horse with a gray saddle cloth. Means as you're either a White scout or a deserter, or worse. If I could be certain you're a no-good, you'd be dead now. Sides . . . even if you be from the devil isle, what's the difference? Fighting over our corpses, that's all.' He raised the bow fractionally.

Justen frowned, then drew the cloak of light around himself and the mare, nudging her sideways quickly and flattening himself against her neck.

Thunnn . . .

The arrow passed over his head, close enough that he could feel the wind of its passage.

'You bastard wizard! You get close, and I'll still get you!' The man had nocked another arrow. 'I can see your tracks in the dust. You can't hide everything with your tricks. Now get out of here! I got plenty of arrows, and I might miss – but I might not.'

Shaking his head behind the light-shield, Justen used his perceptions to help him turn the mare.

'Just keep going! We don't need your kind here. You come back, and I'll chase you to the Stone Hills.'

Justen kept himself as low in the saddle as possible as he

guided the mare down the drive and back onto the road. Once beyond the bow's range, he released the shield and found himself shaking.

'They're not exactly too friendly. Chase us all the way to the Stone Hills? It's hot, and it doesn't sound like a friendly place.'

The mare whickered, once, softly.

'You don't want another rider spitted with an arrow.' Before all the words were out of his mouth, the image of the dead, dark-haired Guard appeared in his mind. Had she even seen the archer who killed her? Maybe it hadn't been one of his arrows. He shook his head. It had been his idea, and that meant all the arrows were his.

The mare's former rider hadn't been touched with chaos, but in the end, that hadn't mattered. She had died, and so had thousands of Sarronnese. So had Clerve and Krytella. Justen's eyes blurred, as did the visions of the redhead and the dark-haired Guard.

He rode, not really seeing, for a time.

While there were other holdings, those few he could finally see from the road were silent, closed, and seemed almost hostile. So after climbing and descending three more hills, he spotted a pearapple not too far from the road with a few fruits left. He picked them, and some late berries growing by a narrow stream. He ate one pearapple and the berries, washed them down with stream water – order-spelled for safety – and hoped his system would not rebel against all the fruit. As he ate, he brushed aside a whining mosquito and some flies. The mare grazed quietly.

Finally, he stood and shook himself.

'Time to get moving . . . again.'

The mare slowly raised her head, brown-tipped grass disappearing into her mouth.

They continued southward on the road, the only road, which followed the river until they reached a slightly higher hill. At the hillcrest, Justen paused as he studied the river valley below and the small town on the west bank. He had reached the point where the river forked into its upstream branches. Rather than attempt a massive span across the Sarron below the junction, the Sarronnese had built two bridges, one across each fork. From what Justen could see, the western river fork was nearly twice the size of the fork before him. The town, whose name

Justen could not recall, lay on the western side of the western branch.

Again, the houses and barns scattered across the hillsides through which he rode remained shuttered tight or empty, or both, while he could see smoke and movement on the far side of the River Sarron.

After studying the scene below for a time, he urged the mare forward and down toward the bridges. Perhaps he could finally get across the river and turn back toward Sarron and Rulyarth.

As the road flattened, he passed a series of buildings that appeared to be an inn, but the sign had been removed from the posts by the road, and even the stable door had been boarded shut. Recent and heavy-rutted tracks led from the closed inn toward the bridge ahead.

After glancing back at the inn, Justen continued toward the bridge on the raised roadway that overlooked lower, swampy ground.

Yee-ahhhh . . . A vulcrow cawed from a bare-limbed tree, then flapped back in the direction of Sarron.

Justen reined up at the edge of the stone bridge. The center section of the span, which had obviously been of timber, had been removed, leaving a gap of roughly ten cubits. The locals had clearly not spent much effort on blocking the eastern bridge, but he suspected that the western bridge would be different.

The water beneath the bridge seemed almost shallow enough to ford. Justen nodded and looked back at the gap between the sections of stone pavement. The opening was almost narrow enough for him to clear it himself. Did he really want to try jumping the horse? Could he manage to hang on? Or would it be better to try the river?

'You up to a short jump, lady?' He patted the mare, but she did not answer. He sighed and guided her back to the clay approach to the bridge. Then he studied at the span. The gap looked wider than before.

'Darkness screw it!' he snapped. 'Let's go!' He nudged the bay into a canter, then a gallop. Her hooves clattered on the stone, and she jumped – even before Justen had urged her – and landed cleanly on the other side.

Justen bounced in the saddle, grabbing her mane with one

hand and the saddle with the other, leaning over so far that his head almost scraped one of the bridge abutments. His stomach churned, and he was breathing hard by the time the mount slowed to a walk and he managed to get himself straightened in the saddle. His ribs hurt where he had apparently bounced into the hilt of Firbek's too-big sword.

The clay of the road was lined with deep wagon ruts, probably those of the wagons carrying the bridge timbers. The ruts ran past the narrower road that headed southeast into the dry and rolling hills.

Justen rode up to the larger bridge and noted the kaystone: Rohrn. As he suspected, all three center sections, except for the stone piers, had been timbered, and had been removed. Did the people of Rohrn really think the lack of a bridge would stop the Whites?

He grinned. Given the depth of the river, it would certainly slow them down. Then he shook his head as he turned the mare back. How was he ever going to get across? On the side where he rode, there wasn't even a trail paralleling the western branch of the river. Probably the smaller road he had just passed would turn or join another trail that would wind back to the river. Probably . . . but trying to get out of Sarronnyn was proving harder than he had thought. But then, everything was proving harder than he had thought.

He turned the mare back toward the last crossroads, glancing to the west, where the sun had half-dropped behind the horizon. To the right of the road was a narrow, recently plowed field that paralleled the river and stretched several hundred cubits westward to the top of a low rise. A split-rail fence separated the field from the road, and another marked the far end of the field. Because of the gentle rise, Justen could not see the ground beyond the farther fence, only a regular line of trees.

He still needed to find a place to camp – and to find something more to eat, and some grazing for the mare. To stay too close to Rohrn, with its dismantled bridge, probably wasn't very wise.

Justen flicked the reins and looked toward the crossroads.

Then he paused and turned in the saddle. There ought to be another road somewhere, but he hadn't seen it, not unless he'd overlooked something. But after two different sets of archers having fired at him, and without a decent meal, he wasn't thinking all that clearly.

Finally, he urged the mare onto the road heading yet farther from Rohrn, from Sarron, and from Rulyarth. He took a deep breath and patted the mare again.

This time, she *whuffed* back at him.

48

The more slender of the two figures in white winced as he studied the mists swirling through the flat glass on the table. The candle illuminating the glass flickered as he leaned forward and attempted to make out the dim figures within the mist.

'Darkness,' muttered Beltar. 'What's that?'

'A woman and a tree. A sending of some sort, except that it's order-based, and yet it's not. It feels like it's from the southwest.'

'From Naclos? The druids? I don't like that.'

'Like what?' interrupted a rougher voice. Zerchas stepped into the tent. 'I felt someone playing with a screeing glass.'

Behind him followed Jehan, his face carefully blank.

'There's some sort of order-projection coming out of Naclos,' Eldiren observed mildly.

'Out of Naclos? We've never been able to see into Naclos.' Zerchas turned his head and spat out into the darkness, then gestured. A white flame flared where his spit had landed.

'That's rather . . . excessively cautious.' Beltar's voice was cool, polite.

'Superstitious, you mean? Some superstitions have reasons behind them, young Beltar.' Zerchas laughed harshly. 'Now what's this nonsense about the druids?' He peered toward the glass and the dark tree.

Jehan's eyes followed those of Zerchas.

Abruptly, the image vanished.

Eldiren swayed on his stool, putting a hand to his brow. His face appeared pale in the flickering light.

Beltar and Zerchas exchanged glances, although behind them, unnoticed, Jehan staggered for a moment and straightened, recomposing himself.

'The druids? That much order?' blurted the burly White Wizard. 'But why?'

'It has to be connected with that engineer – the one who did the black arrowheads and made that second dam.' Eldiren mumbled the words.

'Didn't he leave with the others?'

'He's not on the river road to Rulyarth. There were only five engineers in that group.' Beltar put a hand on Eldiren's shoulder. 'Let go of the glass,' he added in a lower tone.

'He could have been dressed as a marine. He's the one that the Recluce marine – Firbek's his name, I think – says is good with weapons,' suggested Jehan.

'Firbek looked at them all in the glass.' Eldiren nodded at the glass, now only a mirror resting upon a table.

'Then find him and be done with it, if he's so important.' Zerchas's lips turned into a sneer. 'Surely your powers are up to handling a mere engineer! Either capture him or kill him. Then you won't have to worry about the Naclans.'

Beltar seated himself before the blank glass, frowning momentarily as the white mists appeared again. Slowly, an image formed, that of a man sitting by a stone wall.

Then the mists swirled over the image, and the glass blanked. 'What—'

'He threw up a barrier. I don't think he's just an engineer.' Beltar closed his eyes and massaged them gently.

Eldiren's eyes met with Jehan's, and Jehan gave the minutest of headshakes.

'Where is he?' asked Zerchas.

'He's not that far away,' answered Beltar. 'Somewhere on the road toward Clynya.'

'Oh . . . leave him alone. What can one engineer do?' asked Zerchas, again spitting through the flap of the tent and incinerating the residue even before it could strike the ground. 'Even if he were a second-rate Black, he couldn't do much.'

'Show-off . . .' mumbled Eldiren.

Jehan winced.

'On second thought,' Zerchas added, 'perhaps this engineer could be a threat. Eldiren, you can take the Second and Third lancers and find him.'

'Ah . . . we haven't really sent any forces as far as Clynya.' Beltar stood up from the stool.

'We have now. Eldiren, you can take the Fifth, what's left of them, as well. There aren't any holdings toward Clynya anyway – only orchards and sheep. Just head up the River Sarron past Rohrn to Clynya. You probably can't cross until you reach Clynya in any case. That way, you can ensure everything is secure there while Beltar and I begin the march toward Rulyarth.' Zerchas smiled. 'Jehan will take your place here with Beltar.'

'The Black could always hide in the Stone Hills,' suggested Eldiren.

'Even an engineer from Recluce couldn't be that naive.' Zerchas snorted. 'Once you've taken this renegade engineer, you can march down the south branch of the Jeryna River. Take your time. We'll meet you in Jerans . . . when we can.'

'That's asking a lot.' Eldiren swallowed.

'I'm sure you'll manage. But I wouldn't take any powder.' Zerchas bowed, and added before turning and departing, 'Good evening.'

Jehan looked at Eldiren and shrugged behind Zerchas's back.

'Come on, Jehan. You're not staying here . . . yet.'

Jehan turned and followed the older wizard.

For a moment, the two remaining White Wizards stood silently. Only a few voices penetrated the tent from the camp beyond, those and the faint chirping of insects and the intermittent croaking of a frog.

'Beltar . . .' Eldiren rubbed his forehead. 'Those are all units that are short because of that engineer. I doubt if there are five score left. And the hill Sarronnese don't exactly like outsiders.'

'I know.'

'Can't you do something?'

The broad-shouldered White Wizard shrugged. 'What? Zerchas still commands. That's why he's dumping Jehan on me – to make sure I'm a good boy.'

Eldiren pursed his lips and looked at Beltar. Beltar met his glance. After a moment, Eldiren's shoulders slumped and he walked into the darkness.

Left alone in the tent, Beltar took another deep breath.

49

Justen put his arm out to the tree, encircled by a carpet of short green grass. The bark of the lorken was deep-ridged and nearly as black as the wood he would find beneath. Yet he had seen no lorken so massive this far in his ride from Sarron, not that he had been allowed much time to ponder trees.

'You have had little enough time to find this tree.' The slender young woman with the silver hair, still dressed in brown, appeared beside the dark and massive trunk.

'Is this another dream?' he asked.

'No. Not if you consider dreams as the fragments of sleeping thoughts poorly perceived, and even more poorly recalled.' Her voice rang a sad silver.

'But who are you?' Justen tried to step forward and found he could not.

'You will find my name in Naclos. That is where you must go, if you would find yourself.' Her face was somber. 'You have not, you know. Unless you find yourself, you are fated to . . .' She paused. 'But that I cannot say. Only that you will never rest. For you have created chaos from order, and that will twist your very being unless you come to the Balance.'

Justen pondered for a moment.

The rustling of steps, the crackling of a branch, and the low whisper of the wind woke the engineer. He quietly eased into a sitting position next to the stone wall, his senses and his eyes searching the darkness around him.

He squinted as a light that was not a light began to glow in the air less than three cubits away. As he watched, the face of a dark-haired man peered at him from the glowing white mists.

Recalling, all too belatedly, his screen training, Justen forced himself to concentrate and to weave the starlight around him, hoping to hide himself from both physical and magical searchers.

For a time, for what seemed a long time, he sat in his dark cocoon until he was certain that the White Wizard had lost his vision. By then, whoever or whatever had prowled the road had also vanished. When he released the shield, only to the darkness of night, he began to shiver. The shivers continued despite the warm fall air, even when he wrapped his cloak around himself to add to the warmth of the blanket.

The blanket failed to add much warmth, and he shivered through the night, so tired that he shivered through the dawn and did not stagger up until the sun had not only cleared the horizon, but the tops of the scrubby trees on the eastern hills.

Standing in the morning light that gave little warmth, he was so chill that he half-expected his breath to steam. He stretched gingerly, letting his senses and eyes search the area, but he could sense only of a handful of birds, some assorted small rodents, and the mare.

He washed in the stream that was little more than a trickle, but the best water he had been able to find, and drank, wincing at the metallic taste. His incipient beard itched, and he wished he had a razor, but that luxury had been lost along the way as well.

After fishing a battered pearapple from the saddlebags, he slowly ate, hoping that the fruit would not be too acid on his empty stomach. As he finished the pearapple and washed his hands clean of the sticky juice, heavy wings beat through the morning.

Ye-ahhhh. At the sound of the vulcrow, he turned toward the half-dead willow, a good fifty cubits up the streamlet, where the bird had alighted. Something about the vulcrow's arrival bothered him, and he extended his senses, but only until they touched that vague whiteness that confirmed his fears. The distant White Wizard was linked in some way to the bird.

Ye-ahhh. The vulcrow flapped into the sky toward the south.

'Almost as if he were looking for us,' mumbled Justen. And why had the bird headed south?

He groomed the mare quickly with the curry brush he had

found in the left saddlebag and dropped the saddle blanket into place, wishing that it were not dark gray on both sides and that the red stripe did not show through. Then he hefted the saddle onto the mare. With only a single whicker, she let him.

After rolling the blanket and slipping it into place behind the saddle, he mounted, looking around for the vulcrow, but the black bird was nowhere in sight . . . yet.

He let the mare take an easy pace as he continued to study the road for signs of a turnoff for Clynya, or for a way to turn west and get back to the river. He wished that he had followed the river, but he'd been reluctant to ride across others' fields, harvested and plowed under or not, and his earlier encounter with the holder and his bow had disabused him of any notion of impartiality on the part of the locals. His black garments seemed as unpopular as those of the Whites or the Iron Guard.

Turning in the saddle, Justen looked to the west, but he could not even make out the line of trees that marked the western fork of the river. To his east, he could see – barely – a few trees that might be following the smaller tributary to the Sarron.

Why wasn't there a road closer to Clynya? What had he over-looked?

Yee-ah . . . yee-ah . . . From a pile of stone that marked a field corner another hundred kays ahead, the dark vulcrow called.

Justen moistened his lips. Only another few kays and he would turn west, road or no road.

50

'How can we catch him, Ser Wizard?' The force leader of the White lancers nodded politely at Eldiren.

'It shouldn't be that hard. He's not awake yet, and may not be for a while.' The White Wizard glanced to the still-graying eastern horizon. 'He doesn't seem to have much food, and he's not yet aware that we're following him. He's also not taking the quickest route. He missed the first turn to Clynya—'

'How could he do that? He's a wizard, too.'

Eldiren laughed.

The officer stepped away from the mare.

'He didn't expect trickery from the locals. They plowed over the road, built a fence, and even planted some bushes.'

'But how—'

'When you can use the vulcrows and see things from the air, it's obvious that when a road starts in the middle of a hillside, something's thing's been done.' Eldiren handed the officer a sheet of parchment. 'Take your fastest half-squad and lead them along the route marked. You have to get to the crossroads, marked with the red cross there, before he does.' Unlike Zerchas and Beltar, Eldiren climbed into the saddle of a white mare, not into a coach, before continuing. 'All you have to do is take the shorter road, the one he didn't take, and hurry. Just wait at the crossroads until we join you or until you get a message. If the engineer comes, capture him, of course. That's all you have to do.'

'All? Capture an engineer wizard with a half-squad? We still have to make up a day's travel.'

'No. If you get there first, he'll turn away. He won't come to you.'

'But two days' travel in one?'

'Less than that, really. I'm sure you'll manage.' Eldiren waited for the officer to mount, looking pointedly at the other's horse. 'I doubt that anyone is going to stop us, at least not until we reach Clynya and try to cross the river there, and that will be a while, perhaps longer, and the political situation may have changed.'

'Begging your pardon, Ser Wizard, but you sound as though you'd rather chase this engineer, even to the Stone Hills, than go to Clynya.'

'Our task, according to the great Wizard Zerchas, is to track down this engineer, if possible.' Eldiren grinned briefly. 'Now get your squad and get moving.'

'Yes, Ser.'

'Unless you'd rather go with Zerchas . . .'

'We'll be moving right out, Ser.' The officer swung quickly into his saddle.

51

Justen pulled up at what looked to be a footpath – or less. He still had not seen a road back to the river, or toward Clynya, and he had traveled another three kays, more than he had promised himself. But the road he was traveling, from what he could tell, had curved until it now ran almost due south, separating ever more widely from the river with each step the bay mare took.

'Shall we take it?'

Since the mare waited for his decision, he turned her onto the path that began between two fields. The dusty path ran alongside a stone wall that traversed a gentle slope for several hundred cubits. Every fifty cubits or so, Justen had to guide the mare to the left or duck or push the yellow scrub-oak leaves and branches out of his face.

'More like a dog's way,' he muttered as a branch rebounded and scraped the side of his face.

The wall turned back toward Rohrn just over the top of the hill, and so did the path. Justen reined up. From what he could see, the path ran parallel to the road for several hundred cubits, then angled again toward the river, but not in nearly so direct a line as the section he had just covered. He shrugged. Somehow . . . somehow, he had this feeling that no matter which way he went, getting to Clynya wasn't going to be easy.

Yee-ahhh. The same white-tinged vulcrow sat on a bare limb of a dead pearapple not more than two dozen cubits away, almost at eye level with Justen.

The engineer took a deep breath, looked away from the dark bird and studied the path. The dusty track *looked* like it turned back toward where he thought the river ran.

Yee-ahhh.

'All right. Any way is better than sitting here.' He paused. What about the White Wizard? And what about the dream?

Why was the wizard sending his familiar after Justen? Should he think about Naclos? Naclos was somewhere to the south, either over the spur of the Westhorns or across the Stone Hills – and the Stone Hills were just about the driest and hottest spot in Candar. Had the dream been merely a dream?

He flicked the reins. 'Let's find the river and try to get across.'

Yee-ahh. The vulcrow flapped into the midday sky, a black blot against the high gray clouds that promised neither rain nor sun.

The mare carried him downhill and eventually to a branch in the path, where again he reined up. The right-hand branch seemed to head back toward Rohrn. Where the left went, who knew, except that it seemed to flank the side of the stubbled grainfields that had appeared behind the sheep meadows and to run toward a jumble of small buildings perhaps a half-kay ahead.

With an exasperated sigh, Justen guided the mare onto the left-hand path.

His stomach growled. Too bad there had not been more food in the saddlebags. Why not? Had the Iron Guard gone into the battle hungry? Or had she been so new to fighting that she had not learned the need to carry her own supplies? Was she any different than poor Clerve, who hadn't wanted to fight at all? Justen shook his head, and his eyes burned again.

'Got to keep moving . . .' he mumbled to the mare, trying to make out the buildings on the low hummock ahead, and finally wiping his eyes and swallowing. His stomach growled again, and the mare whickered plaintively.

'All right.' Justen laughed at the incongruity of it all – his stomach growling and the mare whickering as on a path that might not go anywhere, he tried to reach an unseen river while being watched by an unseen White Wizard and an unseen dream druid.' All right. Let's see if we can get some food.'

As he neared the hovel – not even a house – he let his senses drift out in front of him. A single person hid behind the rough stone walls of the well between the hovel and the ramshackle structure that probably served as a barn. Even from more than a hundred cubits away, Justen could sense the pain and the fear.

With a deep breath, he slowly rode forward into the yard,

studying the dusty tracks indicating that animals had been gathered and herded away at least several days earlier.

What looked like a heap of rags beside the well moved.

'Are you all right?' asked Justen.

'Fine. Priest ye be . . . asking a question . . . be that stupid . . .'

Justen strained to catch the sharply spoken words, the first he had heard in the old and lower-Temple tongue. After dismounting, he looked for a place to tether the mare.

'Rahmra . . . too worried . . . about his old bones to come. Sent a young fellow instead.' The heap of rags revealed itself to be a gray-thatched woman who looked sightlessly at Justen.

Justen frowned and wondered how to answer the woman. What was she doing by the well, and what should he do?

'You . . . be of the Temple?'

'Yes, but from a farther domain, lady,' he finally answered. His senses had confirmed that the woman had broken her leg. 'How did you hurt the leg?' he asked.

'Be the first sensible words you said. And maybe a healer? To help old Lurles.'

Justen tied the mare to the post on the far side of the well and looked over the stones. A frayed rope end moved in the slight fall breeze. 'I know a little. You slipped when the rope broke?'

'Slipped. That idiot Birsen undermined the step, forgetting his wife's mother . . . forgetting, I say, sure and he didn't forget. Hoped the Whites or his trickery would get me. You aren't one of them, be you?'

Justen chuckled. 'No. There's a White Wizard who's been following me, but he must be a good way behind.' *I hope*, he added mentally. 'Let's see what we can do for you, first.'

Lurles tried to straighten herself on the tilted stone that had once been a step, but the wave of pain that swept from her almost forced Justen to stop. 'Oh . . . ummm . . .'

'Easy . . .' His fingers brushed across the rags – almost clean, he was surprised to find – and across the leathery, sun-darkened legs. 'It's broken.'

'Course it's broken. No other way I'd be left here. But I can't walk with the flocks, and Firla has to carry Hyra.'

'All right. Let me carry you to your . . . pallet.'

'I got a bed. Maybe not fancy, but it's a bed, and it's mine own.'

Justen grinned. He liked the old woman. Then the grin faded. As old as she looked, he doubted she was as old as his own mother, and Cirlin certainly didn't look old and withered. Light as she was, Justen had no difficulty in lifting her and carrying her back to the hovel.

'Long time since I got swept away by a young, strong fellow. Almost worth it.' Her harsh laugh betrayed the pain. 'Mine's the one with the headboard, in the corner.'

The hovel contained one long room, with a cooking hearth at one end and two beds – one in each of the corners at the end opposite the hearth – two tables, four stools, and three rough wooden chests along the back wall. On the smaller table were still stacked buckets, several pitchers, and various cooking implements.

Justen laid the woman on the bed, then studied the leg, both with his senses and his eyes. Should he try? How could he not? 'I think I can set it.'

'Set what?'

'Put the bones so that they will heal right.'

'Then stop jawing about it and do it. Just like you Temple types . . . and you men. Talk and talk.'

'It will hurt.'

'Can't hurt worse'n having Firla did. Almost died then.'

Justen took a deep breath. What else could he do? If he didn't set and try to splint the leg, she'd probably die, or never walk straight again.

It took him three tries and three waves of white-hot agony before he managed to get the bone ends back together. The last try dropped the woman into unconsciousness, and Justen almost crashed into the floor himself.

When he could stand, he looked about for something he could use to bind the leg in position. With a last check around the hovel, he half-walked, half-staggered, out to the old barn, where he tried to avoid the worst of the manure and ignore the stench. A single hen, apparently overlooked by the holders, clucked at him from a back rafter.

He found no rope, but took three stakes and an old hide that seemed sound enough to be cut into thongs.

Lurles was still quiet when he returned. One of the stakes was too long. He managed to break it and whittle the end

smooth. He cut a series of thongs and started to arrange the
stakes around her leg, then frowned. He couldn't splint the leg,
not without lifting it. And he needed more support around the
break. Again he searched through the hovel, until he found what
looked to be an old cutting board. After cutting half the hide into
an oblong, he put the hide on the board and eased both under
the leg beneath the break. Then he wrapped the hide around the
leg, placed the stakes, and began to bind the stakes as tightly as
his senses indicated was safe. When he was finished, he let a
little order trickle from him into her leg, focusing on the ends
of the bone.

'Ooo . . .'

'Just be quiet. The worst is over.'

'Didn't hurt as bad as Firla.'

'I'm glad.' Justen shook his head. If the pain she'd suffered
from his inept bone-setting was less than that of childbearing,
he didn't want to be around any birthings anytime soon. 'I need
to find something you can use to get around with – in a while.
You shouldn't move that leg right away.'

'Lying here, I'll starve.'

'Not immediately.'

'Birsen got a second staff. It's under their bed.'

Justen retrieved the heavy staff and set it beside her bed. 'It's
on the floor.'

Her hand groped from the low bed until her fingers identified
the wood. Then: 'Thirsty.'

'I'll see what I can do about retrieving the bucket and rope.'

'Spare rope's in the third chest.'

Justen opened the chest and found a short coil of hemp rope,
two wooden mallets, and a saw blade wrapped in oiled rags.
After taking the rope and closing the chest, he turned. 'I'll be
back in a while. I need to fix the bucket and water my horse.'

'Not going anyplace.'

'Please don't.'

Outside, a faint drizzle had begun to fall. He looked to the
north at the thickening clouds. Only early afternoon, and he
had rain to contend with. He didn't even have an oilcloth or
a tarp. He swallowed as he recalled burying the trooper in the
ground tarp. No . . . she deserved that little. He shook his head
and peered over into the well.

Whhheee . . . eeeee . . .

'I know, lady. You're thirsty and hungry,' Justen told the mare.

The well was shallow, not more than eight cubits deep, and the frayed rope had caught on something almost within reach.

By holding on to the one sound well post, Justen managed to stretch himself far enough inside the stones to grab the rope. He frowned as he studied the end of the rope. It had not frayed, but had been cut almost all the way through. To keep the Whites from getting water – or to try to harm the old woman?

Justen decided he didn't like Birsen. After cutting another four cubits of rope, he tied it to the existing well rope. He untied the short upper piece and thrust it into his belt before lowering the bucket, lifting it, and setting the water on the stone well wall. He let his senses drift across the water, order-spelling the slightly murky liquid. He could feel the dizziness with the order-spell, and he realized how hungry he was getting.

Still . . . the first bucket went into the small trough, and he untied the mare and retied her where she could drink. The second bucket he left on the stones, realizing that he had not brought anything out with which to carry water back inside.

'Forgot a water bucket,' he explained, stopping to replace the rope he had not used. He also pulled out the loose rope and set it on the corner of the big table.

'Not real practical, you Temple fellows.'

'No.' Justen laughed, took both pitchers off the smaller table, and went back to the well. He returned shortly with two full pitchers of pure and cold water.

First, he helped ease the older woman into a sitting position, propped up against the old headboard. Then he went back to the serving table and poured some of the water into a battered crockery mug that he carried to Lurles.

'Here.'

She groped until she had the mug, then drank greedily.

Justen pulled up a stool and sat down to rest his unsteady legs before pouring a drink for himself. The water helped enough that his immediate dizziness receded.

'We need to get you something to eat.'

'And ye, too, I suppose, young fellow?'

'If we're being honest, lady – me, too. I'm no angel, able to live on tall peaks without sustenance.'

'Bah . . . load of manure. Not the Legend bit about men, but about women being so pure. People who have blades use them. Could be man or woman. Makes no difference. Except men are nastier.'

'Food,' suggested Justen.

A silence stretched out between them.

'You be no Temple priest, be you?'

'No. I'm not. And I'm not a healer, either. I know something about it, and if you can stay off that leg . . . much . . . for a while, it should heal straight.'

'Must be a Black devil . . . stead of a White one.'

'Yes, if you want to put it that way,' Justen admitted. 'I am from Recluce.'

'Why ye bother with old Lurles?'

'I needed food, and you needed help.' Justen silently damned himself for being honest with the old blind woman, but somehow it was important to him, if to no one else, not to deceive her.

'You could have left me.'

'Not after I knew you were hurt.'

'Why do you need food?'

'I was separated from my brother in the fighting, and I was trying to get to the river where I could cross, but the bridges were gone at Rohrn. I was hoping I could get across near here, but I missed the river road somehow.'

'Wizardry, most likely. There be a three-way fork at Rohrn – the two bridges and the road 'long the river. But there be no fords till the bridge at Clynya. It's a deep gorge most places there. You take the by path from here, and it climbs and climbs, not that it be so noticeable . . . only when you be tired.'

Justen mechanically refilled her mug and offered it back to her.

'There's bread and cheese in the hole by the serving table.'

'Are you sure?'

'You smell like an honest fellow. You talk like an honest fellow, and you act like one. I be wrong before, and be wrong again. That be life.' She laughed, and despite the blackened and missing teeth, Justen could see that once she must have been a pretty girl. He swallowed, set the pitcher down, and walked to the serving table.

Several old loaves of bread remained in the hole, as well as two large blocks of hard yellow cheese, each wrapped in wax. One had been opened and roughly resealed. He took that lump and one loaf, replacing the stone before straightening.

'How many slices of cheese and bread would you like?'

'My, and being served cheese in my own bed by a young fellow yet . . .' Another laugh followed. 'One thick one.'

Justen sliced three slices of each – all of them thick – and set them on a wooden platter that he carried back to the corner. After easing one slab of cheese onto a thick slice of bread, he took the mug from Lurles and placed the bread and cheese in her fingers. He eased back onto the stool.

'Strong fingers – like a smith's. You be a smith?'

'Yes. I work with the forge.'

'Good. Never be knowing a bad smith.' Lurles' words came between mouthfuls.

The bread and cheese tasted far better than any meal Justen could remember – at least any recent one.

'You fixed the well rope so I can get water?'

'You shouldn't . . .' he mumbled through another mouthful of bread and cheese.

'Bother. You be a Black smith, and you can't be staying here. Not if you want to live. This stuff ye put on my leg – how long do I keep it there?'

'I'd guess four to five eight-days. But it will be a season before it's really healed.'

'Bother that.'

'Stay off it as much as you can or it will break again.' Justen swallowed the last of the second slab of bread and cheese, amazed that he had eaten it all so quickly.

'You men . . .' Lurles reached outward, and Justen refilled the mug and handed it to her. She drained the mug and bent down to set it on the floor.

'You sound as though you believe in the Legend.'

'Bother the Legend. Look at Birsen.'

Justen cleared his throat. Finally, he added, 'The rope at the well didn't break . . .'

'The bucket dropped into the water. I heard that.'

'The rope was cut almost all the way through. I brought back the top piece.' He walked over to the table and reclaimed the rope, bringing it to the older woman and placing it in her hands. He watched as her deft fingers explored the hemp.

'Have to do something about that boy.'

'Boy?'

'Birsen. Just a big, selfish boy.' Lurles levered herself around slightly in the bed, wincing at the movement. 'Told Firla he was too good-looking. So was Tomaz. Be ye good-looking, young fellow?'

'Ah ... I never thought about it. My brother was the good-looking one.'

'Men ... sure and you thought it. You be plenty fair, an' my word on it.' Lurles grinned. 'Now ... I be fine, and best ye be going afore those White devils catch up to ye.'

'How ... but what about you?'

'You be not able to take me, be ye? If you fill the water buckets, I be able to rest here.' She laughed. 'No White devils trouble themselves with folk this poor.'

'I'll take care of the water.'

'And take the other block of cheese and a loaf.'

'You need it.'

'And you be not in need? Healing my leg and tending me, worthless as I be, be worth something, my fine young Black fellow.'

Justen shrugged and grinned as he picked up the two small water pitchers and headed out through the rain. The mare whinnied as he hauled up the well bucket.

'I know. You're probably hungry, too.'

Back inside, he wiped the rain off his face and hair, then set the pitchers down. 'The water's on the table. Do you need anything else?'

'Nay.' She paused. 'There be a smidgeon of grain in a small cask behind the post in the near corner of the barn. For your horse.'

'If it wouldn't be too much a loss, a little would help.'

'Young fellow ... I can't recall ye to Firla knowing not your name.'

'Justen. It's Justen.'

'Then be off with ye. You spent enough time with a old woman.'

Justen touched her forehead lightly, offering a small flow of order, hoping it would help.

'You sure no Temple priest ye be?'

'No Temple priest. Just a lost smith of sorts.'

'Get the bread and cheese, and the grain, and be off with ye now.'

Justen took the remainder of the cheese that he had already cut – about half the size of the block that remained – and one loaf, leaving two. He swallowed as he took a last look at Lurles from the door.

'I be fine. Off with ye!'

He closed the door quietly and firmly and went to look for the grain for the mare. The rain had dropped off to a fine, drizzling mist.

52

The path, as Lurles had predicted, turned and twisted on a gentle slope, so gentle that Justen was surprised when he looked back over his shoulder that he could see the eastern fork of the River Sarron winding southeast, away from Rohrn. The slight curve of the hill blocked his view of Rohrn and the junction of the rivers.

Justen searched for the hovel, but could see only a thatched roof. He hoped that Lurles would be all right. He took a deep breath and turned, just in time to duck under an overhanging branch as the path wound back toward the south.

Had this been a mistake? Probably, but as far as he had gone, wouldn't it be even worse to try to retrace his steps?

Still, the ride was somehow oppressive.

The few hovels and the one larger holding he had passed were shuttered and still, although he had the feeling that the larger holding had not been abandoned, but fortified, and he had ridden around it.

The dreams bothered him, especially the second one with the same woman, and the same clarity, and the same message – of sorts. The first one had been about the trees, the second about Naclos. Who knew much about Naclos, except that it was the home of the druids, who supposedly had something to do with trees? Sometimes wonderful cargoes of wood came from Diehl, the one port in Naclos, and sometimes people talked about the druids. But no one knew very much about them . . . yet he was having dreams about a beautiful druid.

Yee-ahh. A vulcrow called from a pile of weed-tangled stones heaped in a corner of a meadow that had once, perhaps, been tilled.

Justen frowned. Was it the same bird? He let his perceptions drift toward the dark feathers, then stopped. Either the White Wizard had more than one familiar, or it was the same vulcrow.

His stomach tightened. Were the Whites after him specifically? Why? Had they discovered he was the one who had touched off the cannons and built the black iron arrows? If not, why were they following him? Or could it be due to his ill-advised attempt to sneak past them?

He twisted in the saddle, but could see no travelers on that small section of the road he had left in the morning. Although the clouds blocked the sun, he could sense that it was well past mid-afternoon, and he was still wandering through the gentle hills trying to find the road to Clynya.

Would he ever get there?

The path forked again, and he turned the mare westward, in the direction he thought might lead to the river. He glanced back over his shoulder, shivering at the quiet, and at the chill damp of the fall air.

53

'He stopped for a while outside of Rohrn. I lost him in the rain, but he's still not that close to the Clynya road.' Eldiren gave the reins a little flick to encourage his mount to continue at a fast walk.

'Do you think that Yurka will catch him?' The sub-officer's voice was low, deferential.

'The way things are going, Yurka will probably reach the crossroads before he does. The path the engineer's taking is actually longer and slower than either main road.' Eldiren laughed. 'That's why Fairhaven builds roads. That's why the Blacks' own great Creslin insisted on highways on Recluce . . . and this poor engineer hasn't learned the lesson yet.'

'What are you going to do with him?'

'Yurka? Nothing. He won't catch the engineer.'

'He won't? I mean the engineer, Ser.'

'The engineer will sense Yurka and his troops and head back along the crossroad he got too impatient to wait for and should have taken.' The White Wizard shook his head. 'We may even have to slow down.'

Eldiren ignored the puzzled expression on the other's face and continued. 'You know, if we catch this engineer, we'll have to mount an assault on Clynya. I am quite certain that the bridge there will be highly fortified. They might even destroy it.'

The sub-officer swallowed.

'Of course, if this chase to catch the engineer takes too much time and is hard on the mounts, we'll probably have to retrace our steps, say, to Rohrn, or perhaps back down the Sarronnese road.'

'But the Wizard Zerchas will . . .'

'That's true. The Wizard Zerchas would . . .' Eldiren pursed his lips and smiled gently.

54

Justen squinted in the twilight, trying to make his way through both mist and dim light to find, if possible, the elusive road to Clynya.

The mare whuffled, as if to tell him she was tired of paths and narrow lanes winding nowhere.

Justen took a deep breath, wishing he could send his senses on the wind the way Gunnar did. Unfortunately, his talents did not lie in that direction, and the farthest he could sense things without using his eyes was several hundred cubits in any direction.

A faint metallic sound echoed through the dampness. Justen tightened the reins and brought the mare to a stop under an oak that had barely half its foliage. As he strained to sense the source of the sound, a yellow leaf fluttered down and landed on the back of his wrist. He shook it off.

Ahead was a stone wall nearly eight cubits high that stretched at least two hundred cubits across the hilltop. In the watchtower on the corner were two men, one armed with a crossbow. Justen continued to listen, trying to pick up the murmurs.

'. . . some deserters from the Tyrant's force seen around Rohrn . . . trying to get across the river.'

'. . . wish 'em luck!'

'. . . thinks the Whites will be coming this way . . . lancers, maybe.'

Just his luck! Justen had stumbled onto an estate, or the fortress retreat of a local official who maintained his own forces. He pursed his lips, listening for a time longer. Another yellow leaf fluttered down, past the mare's right eye. She flicked her ears and shook her head. Justen patted her neck and whispered, 'Easy . . . easy there, lady.'

'. . . think they'll attack . . .'

'Sometime. Not now. Only five . . . six score . . . not enough to take us . . .'

'. . . about a wizard . . .'

'. . . walls . . . back to Jera . . . right on the rock below.'

'Hope so . . .'

'Wish Bildar . . . get here . . .'

Justen patted the mare's neck again and eased her around and back down the path toward the last fork. While he was positive that the river road did not lie far beyond the holding, he did not intend to try to sneak past any holding that could stand off six-score White lancers, especially since the mist could lift at any time and it wasn't even dark yet.

He did not breathe easily until they had retreated almost half a kay, back to the last fork in the trail. As he sat in the saddle, he yawned. Why was he so tired?

Grinning momentarily, he shook his head. Besides a lack of food, a lack of good sleep, constant worry, the effort to heal an old woman – not to mention the physical beating taken in the battle for Sarron – he had no real reason to be tired.

Shrugging, he urged the mare down the left-hand trail. It was more like a path and seemed to parallel the unseen road rather than join it. As he rode through the growing darkness, he watched the grounds to his right, with their neat and squared stone walls, well-kept rail fences, far better tended than most of the lands he had passed. Most probably they belonged to whoever held the walled keep he was avoiding.

Not until the meandering path had carried him and the mare back into the ragged and rocky sheep meadows and sagging walls and fences did Justen even consider stopping, despite his near-constant yawns and sore muscles. A few bites of the cheese and a chunk from the stale bread while he rode had helped relieve his headache and the worst of the soreness, but not the yawns.

Finally, the path turned slightly toward the west – at least Justen felt that it was turning toward the west – and resumed a gentle climb over several hills. Justen had lost exact count, trying as he was to remain awake and being only half-alert, when the path dipped and then turned to run almost due south, alongside a depression between the hills.

A hint of order, of unseen order, tugged at Justen, and he reined up, shaking his head. He looked downhill, but his eyes had trouble focusing, although from the dimness below, he could hear a gurgling stream, apparently beneath a small grove of pine trees. He squinted and tried to use his senses. So far as he could feel, there was a cleared area under the trees, and neither animals nor people around. The cleared part of the almost tiny valley sandwiched between the two hills seemed to carry a sense of calm.

Justen studied the hillside. One part of the slope downward was almost clear of bushes and trees, but his eyes seemed to skitter away from the trees. Using mainly his senses, the engineer guided the mare through the gaps and under the tall trees. After he dismounted, his knees almost buckled when his feet touched the pine-carpeted ground.

'Ooooo . . .'

Whuufff . . .

'Thank you also, lady.'

The mare tugged at the reins, pulling Justen toward the stream, which ran over large pebbles and between boulders and larger rocks.

'Not that way, idiot. You'll get your hooves stuck there. Here.'

While the mare drank, Justen studied the setting. No more than a half-dozen tall pines formed almost a circle, covering the center area with spreading branches. The brook appeared from behind a tangle of thorn bushes and redberries, ran through the clearing, and vanished downstream into an equally rambling mass of vegetation.

Justen pursed his lips and called on his senses again, studying the area, finally shaking his head. Beyond a vague sense of some underlying order, almost permeating the rocks and the pines, he could find nothing. Clearly, years in the past, the miniature valley had been created for some orderly purpose, but of that purpose, nothing remained. At least nothing that he could sense.

After he watered the mare, he continued to walk around the cleared space, but he could find no sign that anyone had stopped or camped there recently. Finally, he unsaddled the mare and tethered her to a pine branch, with enough leeway that she could browse on the thick grass beyond the trees and in the narrow space before the tangled vegetation sprouted.

After that, using his senses, since it had grown almost pitch dark, he fumbled out his rations and began to eat, propped up against the trunk of a pine, listening to the gentle gurgle of the stream and the whispering of the pine limbs in the evening breeze.

Dinner, although it was supper in Sarronnyn, he recalled, was one of the pearapples, some cheese, and a chunk of bread, accompanied with liberal amounts of cool water from the stream. While the water had seemed clean enough, he had still taken the precaution of order-spelling it. Who knew what sheep fields it had seen?

The heavy needles and the blanket provided the softest bed he had felt in days, or had it been seasons? Although the grove appeared and felt safe, he set a simple ward – the only kind he knew – to wake him if anything large ventured nearby. Then he pulled the blanket around himself and collapsed.

Waking up was difficult, and his feet felt sluggish. Somehow, he was no longer in the grove, and he had been running after the mare, who kept dancing away from him, just out of reach. On the far hill-top, Gunnar marched northward, ignoring him even as he shouted his brother's name.

Yee-ah . . . ! The black vulcrow swooped from out of the sky, and Justen threw up an arm to ward off the bird.

Hhsstt! Hssstt! Two firebolts seared past him, one so close that his hair singed.

He looked over his shoulder. A squad of white-clad riders pounded across the side of the hill. He began to sprint toward the mare.

Just as his fingers closed around the reins, he stumbled . . . and looked down at a body in dark clothes.

'Krytella!' He reached down. The red hair turned darker and shorter, and his fingers clutched at rotting cloth as with a shudder, he dropped the dead Iron Guard, whose liquid flesh flowed into the ground.

He woke with a jolt, wiping the sweat from his forehead. Had it been just a dream? For a moment, it had seemed so real. Or was the White Wizard after him again?

Shivering in the chill, damp air, he let his senses touch the calm around him, reaching out to make sure that nothing lurked in the darkness beyond the grove, but all he could sense was the faint, underlying sense of order. He sensed neither chaos nor dread.

He fumbled for the water bottle he had set beside the tree trunk and swallowed several small mouthfuls of the cool liquid. What had the dream meant, if anything? He certainly knew that both Krytella and the Guard were dead. Was his mind trying to tell him that he couldn't catch Gunnar? Or that, for all the calm around him, the White Wizard and his familiar still stalked him? He closed the water bottle and set it back against the bark of the trunk. Then he pulled the blanket around his shoulders again and leaned back.

In time, his heart stopped pounding and his eyes closed.

Above him, the pine branches swished in the wind.

55

With the gray of dawn, Justen was up – first, currying the mare as she cropped the thick grass beyond the fir-needle carpet where Justen had slept, then watering her, and finally, washing himself in the stream. Those duties completed, he breakfasted on the next-to-last pearapple, two handfuls of almost-dry berries that he was able to retrieve from the thickets without getting scratched into shreds, and bread and cheese. He refilled the water bottle and stretched.

Whheee . . . eeee.

'You're even ready to go?' He lifted the gray saddle blanket into place, then the saddle. The mare stood patiently as he fumbled with the girth and cinch. After checking the saddle, he rolled up the blanket and tied it behind the saddle. He stretched again and looked into the bright blue-green sky.

On the slope beyond the stream, a raft of yellow leaves swirled off a squat oak in the gusting wind that seemed to mix warm and cold air as it ruffled Justen's dark hair. He used his fingers to brush the leaves off his forehead. 'Getting too long.' He touched the itchy stubble on his chin and shook his head.

Whheee . . . eeee . . .

'We're going.' Justen checked his limited gear and climbed into the saddle. The mare sidestepped twice before settling down.

'Feeling frisky, lady?' He patted her neck.

The warmth of the sun was more than welcome when he rode out of the trees and back up to the narrow path.

Justen glanced back at the grove and blinked once. Despite the order embodied by the small area, his eyes wanted to skip over the space, particularly the pines, just as they had the night before.

'Definitely strange,' he muttered. What was there about the trees? Or was he still so tired that he was imagining things? Except that despite the unsettling dream, he did not feel tired, certainly not nearly so tired as the day before.

The path continued almost due south, over at least a handful of rolling hills, before angling back to the west. The brown-grassed meadows were longer, as if not so heavily grazed, and fewer cultivated fields graced either hills or valleys. Since leaving the grove where he had slept, Justen had seen no trees except for a few scrub-like bushes, and but a single hovel, with only a rickety barn. That hovel, like all those save Lurles', had been shuttered tight and abandoned.

In the still, morning air, the twittering of insects seemed subdued, and only a few birds flew, landing to scrabble in the stubbled grainfields.

After bearing west once more and crossing two more low hills, the path widened into a trail, or narrow road. Justen reined up just below the second hillcrest when he saw the small orchard below and to the left of the road. Half a kay away on the almost-flat ground stood less than a score of nearly bare-limbed trees, surrounded by a low, tumbled stone wall. Two sod-walled buildings, as dilapidated as the wall, sagged toward each other to the west of the orchard. Between the buildings was a heap of stone that looked to be a rock-walled well.

Glancing down at the road, Justen thought he saw a mass of hoofprints beneath a thin coating of dust. He nodded. Of course. All the sheep or goats, or whatever, had been herded westward, perhaps over the bridge at Clynya. Was that bridge still standing, or had the Sarronnese destroyed it, too? Was he ever going to get back to Rulyarth – or to Recluce?

The sun and the still air had warmed the high plains as though it were a summer day, and he wiped his forehead. Then he took a deep breath and studied the road again, but he could see no recent tracks, although he was well aware that he was no tracker. Slowly, he followed the road toward the apparently abandoned orchard.

Once he reached the wall, he stopped, studying the trees, thinking they might be olive trees. As he followed the road closer to the buildings, he sent his perceptions ahead, nodding in relief as he discovered the structures were empty.

He looked at the almost-empty saddlebags, then at the buildings. Finally, with a look down the dusty road to ensure that no one was coming, he turned off and rode along the short lane to the two soddies.

'Hullo!'

Only silence greeted his hail, not that he had expected a response.

Dismounting by the well, he was pleased to find a battered bucket and a rope. In a few moments, he had lifted a bucketful of water, order-spelled it, and refilled his water bottle, drinking a mouthful and splashing the road dust off his face. Then, since there was no trough, he refilled the bucket and set it out for the mare. She slurped noisily.

Justen studied the buildings. The one to the right of the well looked like it had been a dwelling and not repaired in years. The door on the windowless second building was newer, and fastened with an iron latch. A set of recent wagon ruts ran from beside the second sod building back toward the lane and presumably out to the road.

Again, Justen looked to the road before walking over to lift the latch and open the door. A trace of brine drifted to him as he peered inside at the empty timber racks. Not quite empty, he realized. Beneath one rack stood the recently shattered remnants of a large barrel.

With another look around, Justen slipped into the building and walked over to the barrel. The top had been removed, and small, round objects littered the floor: olives. He peered into the bottom of the barrel to discover several handfuls or more of the fruit. After reaching down and pulling out a damp olive, he nibbled at it. Beneath the saltiness of the brine that had been used to cure it, the olive was certainly edible, if still somewhat bland.

The olive growers had been in a hurry to pack up their wares, since they had taken what they could easily retrieve and left the rest.

Since there was nothing in which to store the remaining olives, Justen walked back to the mare and unstrapped one of the saddle-bags, the empty one, and carried it back into the warehouse, where, leaning headfirst into the barrel and avoiding the sharp points of the two broken staves, he began retrieving the still-damp fruit, eating some of the olives in the process and trying not to break his teeth on the pits.

He finally straightened and saw that the bag was more than half full. He started to leave the storeroom, then shook his head. Even though the olives, had he left them there, would have spoiled, he couldn't just take them. Finally, he laid two coppers on the rack.

When he stepped back into the yard, the mare whickered, then moved toward a clump of grass and began to graze. Justen set the saddlebag on the well coping and lowered the bucket again, this time to wash his hands of the salty residue. After rinsing them, he dried them on his trousers.

He looked at the saddlebag. He had not been able to use all of the abandoned olives, since some had begun to spoil already. Finally, he shrugged and began to concentrate, hoping he could add enough order to the fruit to at least retard spoilage.

A hint of dizziness passed over him, and he sat down on the stones next to the bag to rest.

'For a mere engineer, you're not doing that badly.'

Yee-ahhh.

Justen straightened with a jump.

The vulcrow perched on a dead olive branch, its head cocked to the side, almost as if studying the engineer.

Whheeee . . . eeee.

'I know. We're in trouble, lady.' He looked toward the road, but saw no one. Then he stood, lifted the saddlebag, and walked over to the mare to refasten the leather bag in place. He took a few more olives and popped one in his mouth before remounting.

Yee-ahhh . . . yee-ah. The vulcrow was still calling from the olive tree.

Justen flicked the reins, and the mare carried him out to the road. The air remained hot and still.

In less than two kays, the road turned south again. Justen had opened his tunic as much as possible. Sweat oozed from his entire body, and the sun had not even reached its zenith in the blue-green sky.

The grass stretching out from the road was shorter, browner, and sparser now, with patches of sand and rock between clumps. The rock walls had vanished after he left the olive orchard behind, and no streams graced the flat plateau he rode across. Only the heavy wagon tracks over sheep prints indicated use of the road.

After unstoppering the water bottle, he took a deep swallow.

Another kay ahead, he could see a few low bushes in a line almost perpendicular to the road he traveled, and above them, the air seemed to waver, like the mirage of a lake. Justen looked over to the west, but the plain seemed unchanging as he rode toward the illusion, which receded, and the bushes, which did not.

The bushes marked the junction with another road, wider, and marked intermittently with stones. The new road also had animal and wagon tracks, all of them headed toward Clynya, Justen hoped.

'Maybe this time, we'll actually get there.'

Justen drank more of the water, then touched the mare's neck, trying to sense how she was doing in the heat. So far, she seemed strong.

Although the sun continued to shine through a cloudless sky, a faint breath of air puffed out of the west as Justen rode toward the river road. The few scattered hovels were, like the others he had seen, abandoned.

Justen frowned. Were all the Sarronnese petrified of the Whites? Why? Despite their dislike of the Legend-holders, the Whites generally fired or destroyed only the cities of those who refused them. Then Justen grinned wryly. By their belief in the Legend, most Sarronnese probably had to refuse the Whites.

Still . . . wasn't there any way to stop the Whites? He shook his head, absently patted the mare, and continued to ride.

Toward midday, he began to look for another hovel, without people and with a well, as much for the mare as for himself.

Unbidden, the image of the dead Iron Guard appeared in his thoughts again, clutching the damned black iron arrowhead. He pursed his lips and squinted in the bright light, trying to determine whether the lump on the plain ahead meant available water.

The lump turned out to be another sod-walled hovel. Although it had a well, the water in it was almost brackish, and Justen was so dizzy after order-spelling the salt from two buckets that he sat on the sandy hot ground eating warm olives and sipping from his refilled water bottle while the mare drank.

Before he left the hovel and the well, even though he felt full, he drank more water and topped off his bottle.

Toward mid-afternoon, the grass began to thicken once more, and the suggestion of rolling hills began to appear, along with a few trees, and stone pillars to mark the corners of grazing lands. He passed three houses that stood almost in a group; while shuttered, they were substantial and seemed well tended. He took advantage of their vacant status to water the mare and refill his bottle, since in the flatness of the land, he had found no streams.

Then he began to see more grainfields, with still more dwellings, again shuttered, although he had the feeling that some of them were occupied.

Even later, the ground began to slope downward. He passed another side road, the first one in a while that was more than a path; it was almost as wide as the road he traveled, but it headed due south, not exactly what he had in mind. It also bore wagon tracks. Justen nodded and urged the mare toward the river. A slight breeze blew out of the west, bearing a hint of dampness and the odor of something like hay.

As he crossed the crest of another hill, Justen peered toward a hazy line of trees pasted on the horizon. Undoubtedly, they marked the river. He glanced toward a bare-limbed tree beside the road and swallowed as he saw the vulcrow again, staring . . . waiting.

Yee-ahh . . . yee-ah. The bird flapped away over a field as the mare carried Justen steadily westward. He wiped his forehead again. While he could feel a faint breeze, the late afternoon sun still beat down on the road – and on him.

By the time Justen reached the top of the next hill, he could

make out puffs of dust ahead, if slightly to his right, between
the infrequently spaced trees that apparently followed the river.
His stomach tightened. A horse train that long meant troopers,
perhaps a score of them, and any troopers in this part of
Sarronnyn could only be White lancers or Iron Guards. That
they were already almost in front of him meant that they would
reach the crossroads before he did.

While he could not see the White Wizard's vulcrow, he had
no doubt that the bird lurked somewhere nearby.

He reined up. What would they do once they reached the
crossroads? Would they head on toward Clynya or turn toward
him? Were they really after him?

He pursed his lips, thinking, absently stroking the mare's
neck. He was too tired and not strong enough to hold a
light-shield for long, yet it was almost another two kays to
the crossroads. Finally, he pulled the mare over next to a scrub
oak and dismounted. If the troops headed his way, he could just
wait, use the light-shield, and let them pass. If they continued
on to Clynya, he could follow at a discrete distance.

He smiled and unstoppered his water bottle. Then he retrieved
some olives, which he ate with a chunk of the bread and a slice of
the cheese, saving some for the next day, although of the bread,
there was little more than the end crust left.

His smile faded as the sun touched the horizon and the White
troops began to camp at the crossroads.

Yee-ah . . . yee-ahh. This time, the vulcrow circled overhead.

Justen swallowed. If he had any doubts . . .

He studied the flat road he had covered. Where could he go
now? Could he wait? If he retraced his path, he was bound to
run into the White Wizard's forces. Yet he was no match for a
score of White lancers, and the gentle slope to the crossroads was
so open that he couldn't cross the fields without being seen, and
his senses were not sharp enough to trust on fields he had never
seen. One hole, and the mare would break a leg. And the Whites
were already warned to fire above any dust puffs. He swallowed,
wondering if he could just wait until full night.

Yee-ahhhh . . .

He turned again to look back along the road he had taken.

Beyond the second hill, he could see more dust.

'Darkness!'

Yee-ahhhh . . . yee-ahh.

Justen tiredly remounted the mare and turned away from the crossroads. There had been a side road two hills back. Because the Whites might get there first, assuming that the second dust cloud represented more Whites – and from its size, a larger group – he would have to chance the open fields.

Restraining his impulse to have the mare trot or canter, he rode back down the gentle slope they had just climbed, his eyes studying the terrain to his right, to the south, trying to memorize it.

Then, at the bottom of the hill, he drew the light-shield around himself and the mare and turned south across the open grasslands, hoping his memory would not play him false.

56

Eldiren frowned.

'What happened, Ser Wizard?'

'He disappeared. One of those cowardly Black tricks. But it won't help him now. We've got position on him.'

'I beg your pardon, Ser?'

Eldiren shook his head.

The officer just shrugged apologetically, apprehensively.

Eldiren sighed. 'It's simple. He knows that the others hold the crossroads, and he's an engineer, not a mage. So he will either try to circle around them and get on the river road on the other side of our forces, or he will try to get to that side road up ahead.'

'But . . . from what you said, he's more than a kay from it. We're just a few hundred cubits.'

'He'll cut across the fields, but he's going to have to do that half-blind, and that will slow him down. Take another score – say the Fourth. Ride past the crossroads and just keep going until you get to the fork in the road on this side of the river. You'll know it. After the roads join, it's only a couple hundred cubits to the big drawbridge that crosses the Sarron into Clynya. The bridge will be up, of course. Just hold the fork as close to the bridge as is safe and wait for us. Forage as necessary.'

'What about the engineer?'

'If you hold the fork, he can't cross the river. He'll have to travel into the wilds for another day, maybe longer . . . but once you go past him and get on the river road, he won't head that way. And we'll be right behind him. If you see dust puffs, you know what to do with the arrows.' Eldiren smiled.

The officer shivered.

57

Justen blotted the sweat from his face wondering how he and the mare had kept going. He was tired, and so was she. Every time he tried to get to the river, it seemed as though more White troops had arrived. He had no energy left with which to shield himself from the damned vulcrow, and the sun never stopped beating all day long. His exposed skin was bright red, and his face burned night and day. His own salty sweat was like acid on his cheeks, and even his skin under the short beard itched and burned. Again, he wished for a razor. Some men used knives to shave, but he wasn't up to that, especially without some form of soap or oil. He rubbed his aching forehead again, trying to forget the pain in his legs.

So why did he keep going?

The dust that he knew was rising from the road behind him partly answered that question. A score or more of White Lancers and a White Wizard chasing him were certainly good reasons to keep riding.

Overhead, the vulcrow circled, keeping his location pointed out to the White Wizard. Yet it was almost a game, a deadly one, as if the White Wizard were holding back. By sleeping less and riding longer for the past two days, Justen had managed to keep ahead of the Whites. But each day, he awoke from a troubled sleep with less energy left, and no quick or easy way to replenish his supply of now-exhausted bread and cheese. The few shuttered homesteads and hovels in the parched southern grasslands were not abandoned, but filled with armed and fearful souls.

He was almost out of olives, and only brackish water that he had order-spelled had kept them going. At least there was still grass – browned but chewable – for the mare.

At the top of another of the dry and endless hills, Justen turned, taking a deep breath. The Whites were closing in again, and it was but a bit past midday.

He turned again, noting the fork in the road ahead. The left-hand fork was narrower and headed straight for the dull, gray hills. He could see one stone wall off the left road. The main road swung westward and looked flat and empty.

Justen took the left fork. In the hills, there might at least be somewhere to hide.

Less than half a kay southward into the hills, on the slope above the road, stood a long stone building, roofed in weathered clay tiles. Justen turned the mare up the lane.

Whheeee . . . eeee.

'I know. It's steeper, but we need the water.'

As he rode into the yard, a figure dashed for the door of the dwelling. The door clunked shut with a thud, and a bar dropped into place. By the well lay a bucket filled with water. Justen grinned. He rode the mare to the door of the dwelling.

'If I could trouble you,' he said loudly, 'I'd appreciate taking some of that water, and if you had any traveling provisions to spare, I'd leave some coin for you.'

No one answered.

'All right. I'll just be taking the water, and I'll leave some coppers by the well.'

Justen leaned forward in the saddle, taking his weight off his sore thighs and cramping muscles, before half-climbing, half-falling, out of the saddle. He steadied himself by grasping the edge of the saddle.

Finally, he dipped a finger in the water and tasted it – slightly brackish, but not enough as to require the order-spelling that he wasn't even sure he could carry off in his present condition.

There was a circular trough by the well, and he poured some of the water into it for the mare, who immediately began to drink.

'Easy . . . easy, lady.'

Then he drank some of the remainder and splashed the rest across his face and neck, both to cool himself and to remove the dust and grit. Remembering his promise, he took two coppers from his purse and set them on the coping. Then he lowered the bucket into the shallow well and brought it up. After retrieving his water bottle, he began to fill it.

'Get out of here! Go on!'

Justen looked up to the doorway of the dwelling, where a woman had an antique crossbow trained on him. Her dark hair, shot with gray, flared away from her narrow face as she concentrated on her aim.

'I'm leaving,' Justen protested. 'The coppers are right there.'

'That's the only reason you're not dead.'

Justen capped the water bottle and replaced it in the saddle holder. Then he forced himself to take another deep swallow of water from the bucket. 'You might be careful. There are a couple score Whites on the road behind me.'

'I'll be careful enough. But bother your Whites . . . you brought them, you deserter. Let them chase you into the Stone Hills, for all the good it will do you.'

'I'm not a deserter. I'm a Black engineer.'

'You're all one and the same. Now get on that poor horse and get out of here.'

'The Stone Hills?' asked Justen, pouring some of the water in the bucket into the now-empty trough. He could tell that the mare needed more, and the water was warm enough that she wasn't cramping.

'Maybe you're not quite so bad . . . it doesn't matter. Just like the Roof of the World is the coldest spot in Candar, the Stone Hills are the driest. And that's the only place this road leads to . . . except for the old copper mines, but they're long worked out.' Her face hardened. 'Soon as your horse finishes that, you be gone.'

'Could I buy a loaf of bread or something?'

'Your coin's not worth it.' She raised the crossbow.

'Thank you.' Justen half-climbed, half-dragged, himself onto the mare, half-fearing a bolt in the back. But the bolt did not come as he rode back downhill and turned toward the Stone Hills. Perhaps the Whites would not follow past the copper mines.

With a glance over his shoulder at the dust cloud that was less than two kays behind, he laughed harshly.

58

'Sending Beltar to Sarronnyn was a masterstroke, Histen.'

'No, sending gold to Recluce was better. Without that marine turning on the Storm Wizard, we could have lost another army.' Histen stepped away from the screening glass upon the white-oak table.

'What happens when the Storm Wizard recovers?' Renwek absently adjusted his red-leather belt.

'Nothing. He's on the way back to Recluce, it appears, with the remaining engineers. Except for the one that Beltar claims is wandering loose in Sarronnyn.'

'That doesn't sound good.'

'Actually, it is rather good, because Zerchas and Beltar are arguing about what to do. And young Derba, who's more of a hothead than Beltar, doesn't want to cause trouble until he knows who will win.'

'What about Jehan?'

'I worry about poor Jehan. He thinks too much. So does Eldiren. Of course, you do, too, Renwek.' The High Wizard cracked a smile as he walked to the window. After glancing at the cold autumn rain and rubbing his forehead, he eased the window closed. 'There are times I wish we had a Weather Wizard.'

Renwek coughed nervously. 'Won't that Weather Wizard reveal your . . . influence?'

'My bribery, you mean? What is there to reveal? The only

person the wizard could know about has joined the Iron Guard.' Histen poured two glasses of the red wine. 'It is going rather well.'

'Not that well. We have lost a small army and almost half of another.'

'We have Sarron, and we'll have all of Sarronnyn before long – those parts that Beltar doesn't reduce to rubble. Besides, losses like that will keep Zerchas humble.'

'Zerchas is rather cunning.' Renwek pursed his lips. 'But then . . . Beltar is stronger than Zerchas. If he takes on Zerchas, he might—'

'He might replace Zerchas? Of course he will. Not all of Zerchas's scheming will work. Jehan's too smart to do Zerchas's treachery, and Zerchas knows it. More important, Jehan will somehow avoid crossing Beltar.'

'You think you know them all, don't you?'

'That's the real part of being High Wizard. Any young fool with power can incinerate his rivals.'

'And what will you do when Beltar climbs the Tower like Jeslek did?'

'If he does get that far . . . hmmm.' Histen paused. 'Like Sterol, I would offer him the amulet. Unlike Sterol, I would not scheme, but offer my full support before leaving for Lydiar . . . just about as fast as I could manage.'

'That is not exactly the height of honor.'

'There is a great difference between breaking one's word – which I have not done – and waiting around to be incinerated by someone who doesn't understand the difference. Beltar won't chase after me. Derba would, the arrogant idiot.' Histen drained the glass. 'In the meantime, send another shipment to Recluce.'

'But why? You don't need—'

'Renwek . . . always pay your traitors well, even after their treachery. If no one finds out, they'll be grateful, and you might need them again. If someone does find out, it draws attention to the gold and not to the giver.' The High Wizard laughed. 'In this case, the gold probably wasn't necessary. I'm sure he was only following his own inclinations. But guaranteeing his inclinations was cheap.'

Renwek nodded, but pursed his lips.

59

Justen slowed the mare to a halt, trying to sense what was bothering him. Overhead, the sun still blazed with the heat of summer, hotter with each step the mare carried him into the Stone Hills. Was he even in the Stone Hills?

He glanced up the road, still wide enough for heavy wagons, if crumbling at the edges. Where were the copper mines – abandoned or otherwise?

Yee-ahhh . . . yee-ahhh.

The vulcrow landed on the limb of a weathered gray cactus over-looking the road, stared at him for a moment, then flapped back into the cloudless sky.

A dull pounding, almost like the roll of drums, startled Justen, and he looked over his shoulder. A line of White lancers, less than a kay away, had spurred their horses into a canter toward him. Even as he looked, they seemed to close the gap to several hundred cubits.

Justen turned and glanced around. The road ran above the dry watercourse between two low hills. A few clumps of brown grass, scattered cacti, sand, and rock covered the hillside. The hot wind threw grit at his blistered and raw face.

To the right, about two hundred cubits ahead, was a road cut into the hillside, and after the cut, what had been the main road narrowed to little more than a trail.

The mines? Justen nudged the mare with his boots. Tired as she was, she began to trot. The engineer glanced back again. The hard-riding lancers were close enough that several had lifted their blades.

Justen turned his attention to the road. Should he take the narrow trail or the mine road?

He decided on the mine road and urged the mare toward the road cut. 'Come on, lady.' The effort was probably useless, but

with a White Wizard so close and looking for him, and with no
vegetation or cover, even light-shielding wouldn't be enough.

Yee-ahhh . . . yeahhhh. The vulcrow swooped in front of
Justen, one wing almost grazing his face.

Wheeee . . . eee. The mare skittered and nearly fell. Justen
grabbed her mane to stay in the saddle as she stopped just
below the road cut.

Yee-ahhh.

Justen flicked the reins. 'Please . . . lady.'

Thunnggg . . . hissttt. The arrow flew past his ear.

'Shit . . .' he muttered, realizing that it had come from in front
of him. He flattened himself against the mare, simultaneously
trying to cast a light-shield around them both.

Thunnnkk . . .

Whheeeee . . . The mare screamed, and Justen winced at the
pain that her cry carried.

'Got the first horse, leastwise. That fellow won't make it far
without a mount.'

'Get the damned bird!'

Thunnkkk!

As the mare slumped to the ground, Justen felt his way clear,
grabbing the half-full water bottle and the blanket from their
holders and trying to sense his way off the road.

The lancers charged toward the fallen mare, who must have
reappeared from nowhere, thought Justen, as he struggled away
from the mine-road cut.

Thunggg . . . thungg . . .

'Ambush!'

'. . . 'ware the arrows! Watch out!'

'Call the wizard!'

As the lancers regrouped, Justen slowly limped toward the narrow trail that he could feel rather than see. The vulcrow flapped
in the road, an arrow through one wing, and a single lancer lay
in the dust. Justen did not look back as he struggled uphill.

He doubted that the few Sarronnese hill folk, tough as they
might be, would stop the lancers for long.

Hhssttt! A firebolt splashed on the uphill side of the road
behind Justen.

He continued to walk blindly and steadily away from
Sarronnyn, away from any water he knew about, and away from

the White Wizard, his feet upon a quickly narrowing trail. The trail did not so much halt as merge with the now-dry watercourse that climbed gently between the two browning hills.

Justen reached the top and stepped behind the husk of a dried cactus before releasing the light-shield.

Below, the lancers had dropped back beyond bow range, and waited.

One of the Sarronnese archers, almost indistinguishable from the brown and muted red of the land, nocked another arrow and let it fly.

Hhhsttt! The firebolt tracked back the arrow's path.

'Aeeeiii . . .' The screaming archer flamed for a moment, then toppled into a charred heap.

Another archer lofted an arrow toward the lancers, this time without leaving the rocky cover.

Hssst! The firebolt flared harmlessly against red sandstone.

Justen nodded and slipped downhill and out of sight. Since he had seen only one vulcrow, it might be a while before the White Wizard could bring another one after him. He hoped so.

Farther downhill, he stopped and took a deep swallow from the water bottle, then threaded the loops through his belt. After loosening the strap on the blanket roll, he slung it over his shoulder and let the blanket swing under his arm.

He looked at the gray hills ahead. He hoped there were a lot of cacti, because he was headed for Naclos, like it or not. He had no illusions. Most likely, he'd die on the way. But Naclos offered a chance, and he had no doubt that surviving in the hill country of Sarronnyn for any length of time was impossible for him. Perhaps he could struggle through the Stone Hills to the green lands of Naclos. Perhaps there was something to the dream, the vision of the silver-haired druid. Perhaps.

He snorted and kept walking, his eyes peeled for any vegetation that might harbor either water or nourishment.

60

The two silver-haired women – the age of the older distinguishable from that of the younger only by the darkness behind her pupils and the barely visible fine lines radiating from the corners of those too-wise eyes – stood on opposite sides of the sand table. Neither spoke.

The older woman concentrated, and a replica of the Stone Hills appeared in miniature in the sand.

The younger woman, her hair falling but to her shoulders, concentrated in turn. Sweat beaded on her forehead. Her lips tightened, and her eyes closed, but her hands remained by her side, seemingly relaxed.

A faint smile creased the lips of the older woman as she watched the other's efforts.

In time, a small portion of the bas-relief map churned momentarily, and a small spike of sand appeared on the northern edge. The woman with the shorter hair smiled broadly for a moment. 'He's there.'

The other nodded, sadly, and raised her eyebrows. 'He is strong, but is he strong enough?'

'I think so,' answered the younger, 'but we never know. Not until . . .'

'Yes . . . only a handful ever endure the Stone Hills for more than a few days. Are you sure you want to go?'

'Yes,' answered the younger. 'My sending, my duty.'

The older woman released a deep breath, and the sharpness of the relief map subsided into vague and rounded contours. 'Your duty . . . it may be long.'

'You regretted yours? I have always enjoyed his songs.'

The older woman's faint smile faded. 'He has lost much. So do we all. And the times apart are hard, especially if you must share him.'

'That will not be so.'

'As the Angels will.'

The younger woman nodded, and her fingers brushed the other's before she turned to begin gathering what she needed for the trip ahead. She had little time to waste, not if he were already in the heat of the Stone Hills.

61

Eldiren glanced across the half-dozen charred heaps that had once been living beings. 'Those five were Sarronnese hill-fighters.' He pointed to the figure stretched closest to the mine road. 'That was the Black engineer.'

'Weren't we supposed to capture him?' ventured the lancer sub-officer.

'I doubt that Beltar and Zerchas will be that unhappy to learn that he is dead,' said Eldiren dryly. 'Not after he dragged us almost into the Stone Hills. He nearly made it – we couldn't have followed far into the hills.' The White Wizard laughed. 'Though I doubt he would have lasted long out there, either. Still . . . would you want him around to make more of those cursed arrowheads?'

Three of the closest lancers shook their heads vigorously.

'Was he the one who touched off the cannons?' asked the sub-officer, nervously glancing at the ramshackle and weathered timbers of the mine buildings on the flat behind the White Wizard.

'Most probably,' admitted Eldiren, raising his hands.

Hhhssttt! The white fire played over the four bodies closest to the mine structures until they were white ash.

The White Wizard turned toward the mine buildings, and fire splashed across the structures. For a moment, the wizard watched. 'That should get rid of this pesthole.'

Then he turned to the remaining body and nodded. 'He led us

quite a chase. May their good ones all die so young.' His hands
lifted again, and the white fire incinerated the corpse. Only a few
white ashes and a dark splotch on the sandy ground remained.

'Let's go.'

'Yes, Ser.' The sub-officer turned to the half-score of lancers.
'Mount up and head back. We'll water at that stead again.'

The White Wizard turned his mount back toward the hills and
saluted. Then he wheeled the white horse after the lancers.

62

Justen missed the mare, and not just because his feet were sore.
She had given him her best, and had probably done the same for
the dead Iron Guard. And what had been her reward? Death, by
an arrow meant for him.

He trudged along in the thin shadow of the gully, trying to
keep heading south while staying out of the direct sun.

Looking back, he could see dark smoke circling into the sky, a
sign that the Whites had fired the old mine buildings. That would
give him more time. He shook his head. More time for what?

The Whites wouldn't chase him any farther. Not without a
road, or any possible water for a score of lancers and their
mounts. And especially because they probably doubted that he
could survive the Stone Hills.

Justen's eyes flicked from stone to stone along the dry
depression. Everything looked shriveled, even the cacti, and
the only sounds were those of his raspy breathing and his feet
crunching on the hard and sandy soil.

The first hill was gentle enough, but the sunlight on the far
side struck him like a firebolt. He squinted out at the dryness and
the gray stone before him. Somewhere to the south lay Naclos,
somewhere beyond the hills – as if he could ever get there with
only a half-full water bottle and no real skills for enduring in a
stone desert.

One thing was clear, very clear. He couldn't travel during the heat of the day. He needed a cool spot where he could rest. His eyes darted down the hillside, looking for something sheltered, and hopefully uninhabited by anything that would regard him as dinner.

From what little he knew, none of the bigger mountain cats lived in the hotter regions, and the killer lizards needed more water than the Stone Hills provided. But snakes and spike rats could be dangerous enough.

He took the slope one easy step at a time, squinting against the light, until he reached another low point between what seemed endless hills. Instead of climbing yet another rise, he followed the depression to the east, toward the westernmost spur of the Westhorns – well beyond his vision. But the Stone Hills widened the farther south they flowed.

He trudged for nearly a kay until he found a large boulder with two grayish lumps tucked under the eastern side. Each wrinkled lump was the size of a small bucket and bore hard brown spines. Justen nodded and looked at the overhang provided by the boulder. Then he took out the blade he had lugged across Sarronnyn and poked around, trying to scrape away the loose sand and to see what else might be in the cool shade. A reddish insect scuttled out, and Justen stamped on it and scuffed it away into the full sunlight. He scraped some more, down to a mixture of hard red clay and sand-stone. Nothing else appeared. He unrolled the blanket and used some rocks to hold one edge of it in place on the rim of the boulder, forming a rough awning.

After that, he studied one of the gray cacti. Finally, he used the long blade to cut a slice from one side. A sticky substance clung to the blade.

Sitting down under the boulder and behind his blanket awning, he took a deep breath and studied the slice of cactus, first with his eyes and then with his order-senses.

The sticky, saplike substance held water, and his senses indicated that he could probably lick or eat the gooey stuff. He touched his tongue to the grey pulp.

'Oooo . . .' The pulp was more tart than an unripe pearapple, and more bitter than fresh-harvested brown seaweed. Justen took a tiny nibble and sat down to wait and see how his empty stomach reacted.

If he were to get across the Stone Hills, he was going to need more water and more food, and there was no one out here to bring it to him.

He half-dozed, half-dreamed, until he could feel the air begin to turn cooler. Then he slipped out from his awning, to realize that the sun had almost set, with an orange glow coming from the west. The air was still warmer than in Nylan in mid-summer, if far cooler than it had been at midday.

He looked at the cactus, then sliced off a larger chunk this time, forcing himself to take a mouthful. It tasted like sawdust mixed with rotten seaweed, but he gagged perhaps half of the bite down. He decided not to eat more for the moment and began to roll up the blanket.

A faint chittering began to echo along the depression, indicating that at least some insects existed. With a small swallow from the almost depleted water bottle, Justen began to walk southward again, trying to avoid climbing when possible, and looking for anything that might resemble food or water.

He saw several of the gray cacti, but decided against trying any more until his stomach decided whether they were as edible as his senses insisted they were.

A brown-gray rodent skittered from a crevice in a rock, then dropped back out of sight as Justen's boots crunched in the sand. The slightest hint of air brushed across his still sun-blistered face, and he took a deeper breath.

Maybe . . .

63

. . . and maybe not.

Justen tried to move, knowing that the heat of yet another day had nearly passed, but his eyes would not open. His fingers explored the puffiness, and he gently worked the gunk away.

Three days of eating various types of cactus hadn't killed him, but his face was bloated, and he felt dizzy most of the time.

He'd hoped to follow the dry streambed until he could sense water under the sand, but the water was either not there or too deep to sense. As one eye and then the other opened under swollen eyelids in the light of late afternoon, he tried to moisten his lips, but both tongue and lips were dry. There just wasn't enough water, and he'd had to tighten his belt so much that his trousers would have flapped loosely around his waist and legs had there been any real wind.

His back was sore, and he didn't want to think about the blisters on his feet, or on his face. Instead, he rolled forward onto his knees and managed to rise. He rattled the water bottle – still empty – then replaced the blade and scabbard on his belt. The blade was useful for cutting the cactus sections to begin with because with it, he could avoid the long thorns, but both his knife and blade had acquired sticky edges that no amount of wiping seemed able to remove.

He rolled the blanket as tightly as he could and strapped it into place, then started downstream, or at least downhill. The curves in the sand indicated that at one time there had been water in the dry streambed. Besides, downstream was roughly southward, roughly toward Naclos, although Justen could see no end to the stony slopes and valleys.

His eyes opened more as he walked, and he watched for the type of cactus that was greener rather than gray, the one that had more water and was, of course, rarer. But neither green cactus nor obvious stream or pothole appeared in the ever-dimming nightfall.

He kept trudging, trying every so often to find some sense of water, some hint that the Stone Hills were not so dry as he had heard they were. By now, he could identify the rustle of the spike rats, and the hiss-click of the red insects with the nasty-looking tails. Even a spike rat would be tasty, but the rodents never got close enough for either his blade or a stone.

The dry sand was everywhere – in his boots, in his festering blisters, in his ears – and where it didn't itch, it burned. He stopped to slice a corner off of a gray cactus, the only one he could find, with barely any moisture in the pulp. He chewed as he walked on under the stars.

He finally slumped against a boulder in the middle of the river that probably hadn't held water since before the founding of Recluce and let his feet rest, looking over at a dark patch on a slab of rock beside the dry wash.

He let his senses drift to the rock, then straightened and lurched over to the rock, feeling the dark moss. Moss? He pulled the knife from the sheath, then stopped, letting his senses, shaky as they were, probe the softness beneath the darkness that would have been green in the light.

He uncapped the water bottle and put the top in his purse. Then, carefully, his fingers trembling, he began to cut away the top layer of moss, clearing it from the edges of the narrow fissure. He began to dig inside, and dampness touched his fingers. He bent over and licked the stone, oblivious to the muddy and mossy taste. Then he edged the knife in deeper, and a thin stream of water began to trickle out. He bent down and began to lap in up, certain that it would be gone in instants. He kept lapping, until the fullness of his stomach told him that he could hold no more.

Then he put the bottle against the stone, but the flow oozed past the top. He twisted the knife blade deeper, and the scraping echoed across the sandy stream bottom. But a thin line of water spurted ever so slightly away from the stone, enough that he could press the water container against the edge of the stone and listen to the water trickle inside.

His fingers were shaking when the bottle was full and capped, and he filled his mouth again, and again. Not wanting the water to escape, he pushed some of the moss back into the fissure, reducing the thin stream back to an oozing flow.

Then he searched for a place to rest, to let the water help his body renew itself.

Three times during the night, he drank as much as he could hold.

In the dull gray before dawn, he sat up, his blanket drawn around him. How long should he stay by the dribbling water? How long would it last?

He walked back to the rock for another drink, unplugging

the moss, but only a slightly increased oozing greeted his efforts, and his senses could not penetrate the rock far enough to see if more water lay deeper and beyond the reach of the knife.

'Have to find more . . . somewhere . . .' he mumbled to a spike rat, which vanished behind a hump of sand.

After rolling the blanket and shaking the sand from his boots, he lapped at the thin, oozing line of moisture from the rock, trying to get the last driblets. Then he loosened his belt a trace and started back down the streambed, roughly southward, to see how far he could get before the sun turned the sand and rock back into an oven.

The little water cache in the rock had bought him some time, and his step was firmer, his head clearer, although his guts felt heavy. He walked on the exposed rock floor of the wash where possible, since the soft sand dragged at his boots.

As the sun climbed, turning from orange to white in the everclear, blue-green sky, even the faint rustle of scattered insects vanished and the heat and stillness grew.

64

The dark-haired engineer paced along the heavy-timbered wharf, glancing back at the puffs of white smoke floating into the sky from the stacks of the *Pride of Brista*. Her eyes flicked down the pier toward the warehouses, past the two Hamorian traders and the sleek lines of the powered schooner that had no nameplate and bore black rigging and canvas – a smuggler if any vessel deserved the name.

Wagons continued to roll up to all four ships, disgorging goods.

''Ware the wagon! 'Ware the wagon!'

Altara moved back out of the path of the carter, then stepped farther aside as two women, dressed in dark-blue leathers and carrying blades, escorted their consorts and three children along the rough timbers. Behind the family came three handcarts, heaped cubits high with bales and bags. And behind the carts followed three hard-faced guards, each woman bearing double blades and a pack.

One of the guards nodded to Altara, and the engineer returned the nod, her eyes flicking back toward the head of the pier.

Puffs of smoke rose from the tall stacks of the two-hundred-fifty-cubit-long Hamorian steamer: *Empress Dafrille*. Altara frowned at the order-tensions radiating from the boilers, then sighed as she saw Gunnar's blond and gangling figure striding down the pier. She stepped aside for another wagon, this one laden with rolls of Sarronnese carpets destined for one of the Hamorian ships.

'. . . loose the sling!'

'. . . bound for Atla in Hamor . . .'

Altara peered over the bustle of people and cargo toward Gunnar and waved.

The weather mage waved in return and kept walking, disappearing for a moment behind another wagon, this one filled with wooden crates.

Gunnar shook his head as he approached.

'Not any trace of him?' asked Altara.

'No. He's alive. I think I'd know if he weren't. But wherever he is, it's a long way from here.' Gunnar hopped on a bollard to avoid a careening hand truck loaded with three crates, then dropped back to the pier beside Altara.

'You took long enough.' She glanced toward the *Pride of Brista*, where two sailors on the pier were beginning to help single up the lines. 'We need to hurry.'

'I climbed the bluff over there. I thought the height might help. Besides, we're not leaving until later.' Gunnar dodged as a heavyset woman rolled an empty handcart back toward the head of the pier.

'The port-master is clearing the piers so two more steamers can berth. Everyone's being pressed to load more quickly.' Altara threaded her way along the edge of the pier, not looking back to see if Gunnar followed.

'Everyone's given up.'

'Wouldn't you? The Tyrant's dead; the heir's a sickly fifteen-year-old, and there's no real army left. Sarron's a pile of rubble, and the Whites are three days from Rulyarth.' Altara snorted. 'You'll notice we're not staying, either.'

'Some help we were.' Gunnar stopped short of the gangway of *The Pride of Brista* as a hefty stevedore rolled an empty hand truck down.

'We couldn't do it alone. You and Justen wiped out about an entire army between you. What else did you expect to do?'

Gunnar shrugged helplessly.

'You two Blacks, get on board. We're lifting the gangway,' called the second from the deck.

Altara and Gunnar exchanged glances. Altara nodded at Gunnar, and the sandy-haired man stepped onto the plank. The engineer followed.

65

With a last deep breath, Justen halted at the top of the stony rise. He chewed slowly on the chunk of green cactus, gently brushed aside a flake of dried skin from his blistered face, and eased himself onto a lighter-colored stone that seemed flat. The too-big blade in the two-small scabbard banged against rock and his bruised leg.

'Ooooo . . .' Even now, in the early morning, the stone had picked up enough sunlight to be uncomfortable. He turned his head and looked back to the north. Heat wavered off the gray stones that covered the rows and rows of hills, each hill like the one behind it. Then he studied the hills before him. Was the faint line on the horizon the high forest of Naclos . . . or another mirage?

He blinked, wiping his forehead. The ground seemed to shiver, and he sat on the hot stone and took the water bottle from his belt, swallowing about half of the remainder and studying the bottle before replacing it in his belt. How much longer could he could keep finding water?

Some of the dizziness abated. In time, he stood and eased down-hill, placing each booted foot carefully on the loose rock, looking for an overhang or a shady spot before the full heat of midday, or, equally important, for one of the small, green tub cacti and the moisture it would contain, or for another pocket of rock water, or a small sinkhole.

According to his all-too-rough calculations and his own sense of direction, the high forests of Naclos were still days away. All that lay behind him or ahead of him was stone, the endless gray stone of the Stone Hills, a dry ocean of rock.

'Ocean of rock, ocean of stone . . . can't drink either one.' He laughed hoarsely, then continued to slog along the partly shaded dry washes that headed roughly southward, his eyes and senses alert for water or for the few edible cactus fruits.

One foot . . . and then the other . . . one foot . . . and then the other . . . while overhead, the white-orange sun blazed through the clear blue-green sky. One foot . . . and then the other . . .

66

'The Whites have taken both Rulyarth and the harbor. Suthya is surrounded on all sides.' Claris rubbed her forehead for an instant, then sipped from the black glass goblet on the Council table.

The roar of surf from the beach below the Black Holding provided a background for the cold drizzle that fell beyond the closed windows. Only two of the oil lamps in the wall sconces were lit.

'You can see why I felt that any significant commitment of resources to the Tyrant was premature at best.' Ryltar brushed back a wispy lock of brown hair.

'Ryltar . . .' The third counselor coughed, then moistened her thin lips. 'Our handful of volunteers cost the Whites dearly. Perhaps more would have saved the Sarronnese.'

'Jenna, dear, have we learned nothing in the centuries since the Founders? The great Creslin himself could save only those who were willing to save themselves, and that was with all his power. The Sarronnese were not willing to fight, not the way Southwind would, or even Suthya.' Ryltar lifted his goblet, then set it down without drinking.

'And now Suthya and Southwind stand alone, each separated by a Sarronnyn held by the White devils. Not exactly promising, you must admit.' The black-haired and broad-shouldered older woman shook her head, then took another sip from the goblet.

'Let's be honest, ladies. Where would we have gotten enough troops to have made a difference in Sarronnyn? Without leaving Recluce itself defenseless? All told, we have . . . what? Score forty marines? Another score twenty students with some skill at arms? We have not exactly pursued the art of land warfare.' Ryltar smiled.

'Why it is that your reasoning always leaves me queasy, Ryltar?' Jenna glanced outside as a flash of lightning overpowered the glow of the oil lamps. 'Perhaps it's because you have been the one who has continually opposed increasing the number of marines. Or increasing the iron-ore shipments from Hamor.'

Ryltar shrugged. 'I don't deny it. One must pay for such expansions, and I have always opposed increasing tax levies.'

'Let's not get into that this evening,' suggested Claris. 'The point is that Fairhaven has taken another step in its master plan for conquering Candar. The question is what we intend to do about it?'

'Ah, yes. The great master plan.' Ryltar smirked.

'Ryltar . . .' Jenna sighed.

'We still have to face the facts. First, our ships will stop Fairhaven from ever being a threat to us, even if all of Candar falls. Second, as we just discussed, we scarcely have the trained troops to make much of an impression. And where would we send them? To Suthya, already surrounded? To Southwind – which Fairhaven may wait years to attack, if it ever does?' Ryltar turned in the dark wooden armchair and stared at the oil lamp beside the painting of the silver-haired man that hung on the inside wall overlooking the table. 'What can Fairhaven really do to us?'

'Destroy our basis of order—'

'Jenna,' interjected Claris, 'we've discussed this time after time, and you won't change Ryltar's mind tonight or any other night. Do you have any specific ideas?'

'Fine. Just – Oh, never mind.' Jenna paused. 'At least the engineers could forge a huge supply of those black iron arrowheads and we could send those to the Suthyans.'

'How would we pay for them, and for the iron?' countered Ryltar.

'I suspect, given their effectiveness, the Suthyans would willingly pay for such weapons,' added Claris dryly. 'That's a good idea.'

'I don't like it. We're not supposed to become arms merchants to the world.'

'We're not. And, as you like to point out in regard to armies, we couldn't ever build that kind of force ... but we could send a few thousand arrows.' Jenna smiled sweetly.

'I don't like it, but . . .' Ryltar smiled grimly '. . . it's far better than sending our people to die. We did lose more than half of those "volunteers," you know.'

'I know. Including your nephew, if you consider what he did a loss.'

'Jenna . . .'

'I beg your pardon, Ryltar.'

'I accept your apology, fellow Counselor.'

Another flash of lightning from the storm on the Eastern Ocean flared through the Council Room, and the windows rattled with the thunder that followed.

'I think that's enough for tonight,' suggested Claris. 'I'll talk to Altara and Nirrod later in the eight-day about the arrows.'

Ryltar stood, nodded, and departed silently.

Jenna gathered several documents and slipped them into a leather folder.

'You were hard on Ryltar.' Claris glanced from the windows to the younger woman.

'He's hard to take. Doesn't he understand?' Jenna shook her head. 'Sometimes I think we never should have stopped the practice of exile. The whole idea of the trial posed by dangergeld makes sense. Some people just can't understand what we have and stand for without seeing the alternatives.'

'It would take a danger greater than any we have faced to get people to agree to that.'

'That's why there's a Council,' snapped Jenna. 'To make the unpopular decisions that have to be made.'

'Jenna . . .'

But the youngest counselor had already taken her folder and stalked out.

67

When he finished anchoring the blanket in place, Justen eased into the shade and scraped away the hotter sand until he reached the cooler rock and clay. After checking for insects and spike rats, he unfastened his belt and laid the blade aside, then pulled off his boots, ignoring the blisters on his feet. Keeping chaos from the open sores was not a problem, but he had no real strength with which to heal them.

Finally, he turned and leaned his back against the stone before opening the quarter-full water bottle. He drank half, saving the rest for when he started out again at twilight, and carefully recapped the bottle.

His eyes had scarcely closed when he saw the tree again.

Once more, Justen put his arm out to the lorken, except that now the black-barked trunk was surrounded not by a carpet of short green grass, but by sand that burned with the heat of the sun. He tried to step forward, but the sand burned through the soles of his boots.

'Keep trying to find this tree, and it will find you.' The slender young woman with the silver hair, still dressed in brown, and still barefoot, appeared in the heat beside the dark and massive trunk that radiated coolness and order.

He tried to speak, but his tongue was so dry that he could not.

'The path to finding the tree, and to finding yourself, will be yet more difficult.' Her voice chimed with the sad and muted silver he recalled from the last dream.

'More difficult . . .' Justen mumbled through thick lips. 'More difficult?'

'The order that is truth is colder than the Roof of the World in winter, drier than the Stone Hills, and farther than Naclos for a White mage.'

The tree and the woman faded, but the hot sun flared, and Justen woke with a start to find that something had shaken a corner of his blanket awning loose and that the heat of the sun fell on his uncovered forearm with the force of red-hot iron.

He eased to his feet and crawled outside his makeshift awning to reset the rock that had held one corner of the blanket in place. His bare feet burned before he managed to get back behind his shelter.

Even when he finally drifted off into another period of uneasy dozing, his feet still felt hot and his eyes gritty, but no more images of trees or of the silver-haired woman came to him.

As the slightly cooler air of twilight fluttered the blanket that served as his awning and sunshade in the afternoon, Justen leaned forward, trying to moisten his lips with a too-dry tongue. Once more, with his inability to find enough water, his eyes felt gritty and swollen, and they burned as he forced them open.

He fumbled for the water bottle, then concentrated to steady his hands as he drank the last from it.

After shaking the sand from his boots, he eased them on and stood up, glancing to the west. From the orange glare, he could tell that the sun was close to setting.

Next, he shook the blanket clear of the boulder. His hands

trembled again when he rolled it up. The first time he tried to slip it into the leather loops and strap, he fumbled, and it unrolled onto the sand.

'Darkness . . .' He coughed and tried to swallow, but his throat was so swollen that he would have choked had there been any moisture in his mouth to swallow.

Finally, he had the blanket rolled up, and he began plodding southward again, along another dry gully.

Even before the orange of sunset had faded, he stumbled and fell on his knees. A sharp-edged stone cut through his trousers and bruised and gashed his right knee, which began to throb dully.

Slowly, he picked himself up, looking for a cactus or some sign of water. Seeing neither, he kept walking.

Scritttch . . .

At the sound of the spike rat, his eyes slowly focused on the low boulder where the rodent had been, but his feet continued to move. Then the toe of his left boot caught, and he felt himself falling forward.

For a long time he lay on the hard, rocky ground.

Scrittchh . . . scrittch . . .

Something tugged at his trousers. Finally, he rolled on his side in time to see the spike rat skitter out of sight behind a rounded stone.

A little later, as twilight faded into darkness, he gathered enough strength to sit up, and finally to stand.

'Got . . . find . . . water.'

He stood in the midst of water, cool water flowing through the Stone Hills, yet he could not open his mouth and drink. All he could do was to put one foot in front of the other.

Then he could no longer do even that, and he slumped beside a rock.

'. . . how it ends?' Had he spoken the words, or thought them? Did it matter?

Still, the wondrous water flowed through the hills, the water he could not touch or drink, though he watched it and sat amidst its swirls and dancing spray.

'Gunnar . . . Krytella . . .'

The dead Iron Guard rode the bay mare through the shallows toward him, but the torrent carried rider and horse away. A black lorken began to grow from the middle of the streambed, and its blackness oozed over him.

68

The tall man tossed one stone, then another, out across the sand and into the waters of the Gulf of Candar. He picked up a small, flat stone, dropped it, and walked down to the water's edge, where in a thin line of white, the Gulf nibbled at the white sands of Recluce.

His eyes took in the heavy gray clouds, foretelling winter, that churned across the offshore waters toward him. Then he shook his head and began to walk southward, back toward Nylan. His booted feet kicked sand as heavy steps carried him down the narrow beach under the cliffs and toward the wider expanse of sand that in turn led to the breakwater of the harbor.

As he neared the breakwater, a figure in black joined him.

'Are you all right?' asked Altara.

'I'm fine.'

'That's why you're prowling the beaches all the time? That's why you were talking to Turmin about whether Blacks could scry?'

'I'm fine.'

'You're worried. He's your brother, wherever he is out there.' The chief engineer nodded toward the waters of the Gulf of Candar.

'At least you say "is."'

'I think you'd know.'

'He's in trouble, Altara, and I don't even know where he is. I should have stayed with him.'

'You didn't know.'

'He saved me from Firbek. If he hadn't—'

'He'll be all right. He is a survivor, Gunnar.' Altara laid a hand on the wizard's forearm for a moment.

'Not many survive what he's undergoing, I think.'

'It's that bad?'

'Worse, probably.' Gunnar looked out toward the storms, the twilight, and thought of the long winter ahead. 'Worse.'

II

ORDER-MENDING

69

Justen woke shivering in the dark. How could he shiver in the heat of the Stone Hills? Had he just imagined the water? What had happened to all the water? And to the Iron Guard? As he turned his head, a line of fire burned from his eyes to his neck, and he shuddered.

'Do not move yet,' a husky and musical voice told him. 'You are still very ill.' The words were like high Temple, but somehow different – more lilting, more like a song.

'Where . . .' Justen's voice was so dry that the single croaked word was all he could manage.

'Hush. Please drink this.'

Liquid dribbled onto his lips, and he licked it away, then took several small sips of the bitter-tasting drink. After a moment, his unseen rescuer placed the bottle against his lips. He drank some more.

The heat of the air that flowed across his face told him that he was still somewhere warm, if not hot, but he could not see. Had he gone blind? Or was he in the demons' hell for his misuse of order?

He tried to reach his face, his eyes, but his arms would not move.

'Your eyes will heal. They are only swollen.' Again, the musical voice.

As if the struggle had exhausted him, he sank back, and the blackness welled over him again, just like the shade of the lorken he had never seen, save in dreams.

When he woke once more, it was cooler, darker even through his swollen eyelids. His body still felt like every cubit had been beaten and then left in the sun to rot.

Wordlessly, the bitter liquid was offered, and wordlessly, he drank.

The third time he woke, he could swallow more easily, but his eyes still felt puffy, and he did not try to open them, although his hand crept across his cheek to a filmy substance that covered his eyes and most of his nose.

An involuntary shudder sent another wave of white fire from his eyes to his neck.

'Please do not try to move quite yet.'

'My eyes . . .' Justen rasped.

'They will heal, but you must rest. Please drink some more.'

Justen slowly drank the proffered bitter liquid, feeling stronger as it seemed to flow through his body. Or was someone infusing order into his limbs?

Again, he slept.

When he woke, the air was hot with the heat of midday, and his eyes remained locked in blackness. Had he but dreamed of drinking and of the musical voice? Was he still lying against the rock in the middle of the Stone Hills?

He licked his lips; the swelling seemed almost gone, and when he swallowed, his throat did not bind with dryness. Remembering the pain when he had tried to move his head earlier, he let his fingers touch his face lightly, brushing what felt like scabs across his cheek and a bandage across his eyes.

'You feel better.' The musical words were not a question.

'Yes.' Justen swallowed.

'Can you hold this and drink?'

Justen took the water bottle, which felt like his own, and managed to drink from it with only a bit of the liquid drooling out the side of his mouth.

'Drink as much as you can. It helps the healing.'

When his stomach protested and even before he could speak, cool fingers lifted the bottle from his hands.

'Who are you?' he asked. 'Where are we?'

'You may call me Dayala. We are in the Stone Hills.'

Justen frowned at the lilt to her voice, the tone that seemed somehow familiar, yet totally unknown. He moved his head ever so slightly, realizing that it was on a pillow and that he lay on some sort of mat.

'How . . . where did you find water?'

'I brought some, but you would have been able to find it in time. Do you wish to sit up?'

'Yes.'

The faint breeze ruffled his hair, and the sound of gently flapping fabric passed him, confirming his suspicions that he lay within some sort of tent. The arms that helped him, though smooth, were as firm and strong as any engineer's or smith's. As he leaned back against whatever supported the pillow, he asked, 'You are a woman?'

'You scarcely needed to ask that.'

'I can't see.'

'Do you need to?'

Justen flushed, then reached out with his perception. Woman . . . yes, but a deep blackness surrounded her, like a well of order. He shivered. Never had he felt anyone with that much order or certainty. And yet, that order seemed to hold within it . . . something. Chaos? He shivered again.

'You . . . must be from Naclos.'

A faint sense of laughter swept over him.

'It may seem funny to you . . .' Then Justen had to grin, even though the gesture hurt the corners of his mouth. He had been rescued, and he was irritated because she was amused?

'Would you like some travel bread?'

The sudden moisture in his mouth answered before he did. 'Yes, please.'

'I can see that you are recovering your manners, although you have not troubled yourself to let me know who you are.'

Justen felt himself flushing. 'I am sorry. I'm Justen, and I'm an engineer, a very junior one, from Recluce.'

'Thank you. You need to eat.' Dayala placed a chunk of bread in his hands, her smooth fingers barely touching his skin.

Justen chewed a small corner off the chunk of bread, which had a moist, thick texture tinged with the taste of nuts. Even chewing was an effort, but slowly he finished the bread and found the water bottle in his hands. He drank.

'Tomorrow . . . if you improve . . . we will continue our travel.'

'Where are we going?' Justen forced the question out before yawning.

'To Rybatta.'

'Rybatta?' He yawned again.

'That is . . . my home. You will be welcome there.'

Lying against the pillow, Justen half-shrugged, cutting the gesture short as his shoulders protested. His eyes closed.

70

Justen woke to the sound of the tent flapping overhead in a soft breeze, discovering that Dayala – or someone – had covered him with a soft blanket. For the first time, he realized that all of his clothes, except for his drawers, had been removed. He stretched gingerly, relieved that nothing cracked or sent sharp spines of pain through his body. Then he cautiously inched into a sitting position, his back against the pillow.

From the flapping of the tent, and the cooler air that flowed across his face, and from the grayness that seeped through the bandage across his eyes, he sensed that it was sometime around dawn. He kept the blanket, softer than any he had ever felt, around him, wondering where his clothes were, or if they had been ruined beyond repair by his trek through the sand and the Stone Hills.

He let his perceptions flow around him and discovered the water bottle. He reached out, fumbled a bit in uncapping it but eased it to his mouth and took a deep swallow of the liquid: water, mixed with something bitter. As he recapped the bottle, he heard steps.

'You are awake. I was getting your garments. Repairing them was, shall we say, a challenge.' Dayala set a pile of clothing by his hand. 'You should be able to travel some today.'

'I'll have trouble without being able to see.'

'After you get dressed, we'll take off the bandage.' She turned, and her steps receded.

Justen shrugged. He ought to be able to dress without seeing.

After reaching for his shirt, he discovered he had the tunic. Then he had the shirt halfway on before realizing it was inside out. Eventually, he managed to get himself together and to struggle into his boots.

Breathing heavily, he lurched out from the tent, almost knocking over a side pole.

'It might be wise to take the binding off your eyes now. You ought to sit down.' Dayala guided him to a boulder, warm even in the early light, where he sat as she loosened the knot that held the strips in place around his head and across his eyes.

Justen's still-swollen fingers fumbled with the cloth, and he squinted under the bandage at the distant light of the Stone Hills. Even before he had eased the last strip off his face, his eyes watered and he closed them, not daring to open them.

But finally, when his eyes had adjusted to the worst of the glare, he blinked once, then twice, and peeped at the sand at his feet. His boots looked almost new, as did his trousers.

Dayala stood by his elbow, but he did not look in her direction for a time; he was still squinting. Finally, he turned his head toward her.

The woman's face appeared haloed in light, and she wore what seemed to be a light-brown shirt and trousers, with a dark, woven belt.

Justen blinked, squinting again. 'Can't really see you . . .' He looked more closely at her shimmering, shoulder-length silver hair. He blinked and swallowed again. Then he closed his eyes for a moment, rubbing his fingers together, letting his perceptions inch toward her.

He shook his head, She seemed to consist of a pillar of absolute blackness – yet there was something else, almost like chained chaos, beneath that darkness, strong and absolute as it seemed to be. His perception of her chilled him so much that he shivered. Finally, he opened his eyes to a slit and glanced toward her, taking a long, deep breath.

'It wasn't a dream, was it?'

Dayala shook her head slowly. 'Why do you find it so hard to believe that I am real?'

'I'm not used to dreams coming to life.'

She grinned and shook her head, as if what he had said were childishly amusing. Justen tightened his lips. His stomach growled.

'You need to eat.'

The engineer grinned helplessly, betrayed by his body. 'What about you?'

'I ate already.' She bustled through a pack until she brought out a block of cheese and a half-loaf of bread and handed him both. After struggling with the cheese, he reached to his belt but discovered he had no knife. With a greater effort, he finally broke off a chunk of the cheese. While he had struggled with the cheese, Dayala had retrieved the water bottle, and she set it down wordlessly, still capped, by his feet. He alternated the cheese and bread, but his stomach filled after only a few mouthfuls.

'You have not eaten much in a long time.'

Justen looked down at the long, loose end of his belt. 'A long time.'

'I will pack up now. We should begin to travel while it is still cool.'

Justen's eyes glanced at Dayala's bare feet. 'Boots?'

'Oh, no. They would separate me too much.'

She walked over to the tent, leaving Justen to sip from the water bottle, and slipped the cords that held the side poles. With quick, deft movements, she had the tent on the ground before he had finished and recapped the bottle.

'Wait a moment,' he said.

Dayala paused, looking up at him from a kneeling position.

'You rescued me. You sent those dreams to me. You knew exactly where I was. Not that I didn't need rescuing, and not . . .' he swallowed '. . . that you're not lovely, but I'd really like to know . . .' He shrugged.

Dayala turned and sat crosslegged on the folded tent. 'The Ancient One found you in the dreams of the Angels. This does not happen often, and a sending must be matched to . . . a suitable person. So the Ancient One summoned those who might be . . . suited.' The druid moistened her lips. 'She helped me with the sendings. We did not know if you would come to Naclos.'

'What if I had not?'

Dayala looked down at the ground. 'In some seasons' time, I would have had to come for you.'

Justen pondered. Finally, he asked, 'Did you make me come to the Stone Hills?'

'No! We do not compel . . . not ever.'

'But how did you find me?'

'One of the ancients helped me.'

'But why?'

'The Balance has a use for you. I do not know what it is, only that you . . . are special.'

'So are sacrifices, I understand.'

She blanched as if he had struck her.

'I'm sorry.' He felt as though he had been the one struck. He shook his head. 'I'm sorry. It just seems that everyone but me knows what's going on and everyone is pushing me all over the world.'

A shadow dimmed the intense green eyes. 'I know that you are of great import, of more import than I will ever be. That is hard—'

'Me? A junior engineer?' Justen laughed.

'The power is not in the name, but in the actions, and in the ability to act. Have your actions not already changed the world?'

The image of the dead Iron Guard, still clutching the black-tipped arrow, came to mind, and he shivered. 'I hadn't thought of it that way.'

'The ancients do.'

Justen shook his head. Was this real, or was he still dreaming, and dying?

As he sat there, Dayala slipped from her sitting position.

'I can help you roll up your tent,' Justen pointed out, deciding that since he felt alive, he might as well act that way.

'I am used to doing it alone.' Dayala smiled. 'If you would hold this while I slip the cords around it?'

Justen kept the tent fabric, somehow pleated to stay in its shape, compressed until Dayala had tied the cords. Then he rose. 'Where does it go?'

'You're still weaker than you think.'

'Fine. We can carry it together.' He picked up one end of the tent, now tied into a bundle less than four cubits long but almost a cubit and a half thick.

Dayala picked up the other end easily.

As they walked past the boulders to the still-shaded gully where the horses waited, Justen's fingers rubbed at the fabric.

For the size of the tent, the bundle was light. 'What is the tent made from?'

'A kind of . . . silk.' Dayala laughed as she spoke. 'This goes on the brown stallion at the end.'

Justen swallowed as he looked at three horses. None wore bridles, or even hackamores, and none bore a saddle. Instead, they wore soft, woven harnesses. The two mares were already loaded with thin packs. One carried several jugs. He stepped up beside the stallion, who turned his head to watch as Justen eased the tent over the harness. He found the cords and began to fasten one side.

'Not too tight. Just enough that it won't shift.'

'Ah . . . how are we traveling?' Justen asked.

'The same as they are. The same way you got here. On our feet.' She began to dig in one of the packs, finally lifting out an object that she unfolded and handed to Justen. 'Here. This should help you with the sun.'

Justen took the soft hat, apparently woven from some sort of grass, and eased it onto his still-sore head. Light as the hat was, his scalp did not protest, and his eyes stopped watering quite so much.

'Thank you. This helps.' Justen adjusted the hat. 'But I don't understand. You have horses. And you're barefoot. How can you walk through . . . this?' Was he still dreaming?

'The horses have agreed to help me.' Dayala's voice was matter-of-fact, as though she stated an obvious truth. 'And I hope you will be all right in your boots. They seem so confining.' The woman shivered.

'I hope Rybatta isn't too far.' *Am I saying this*, Justen asked himself, *while just assuming that I can walk to some town I've never heard of with a woman I only met in my dreams?* He shook his head, but the dryness of the Stone Hills and the dull soreness of his feet added to the sense of reality.

'An eight-day or so, I would say, although we will move faster as you get stronger.'

Justen didn't know whether he hoped his healing were fast or slow as Dayala marched out over the hot sand and rocky ground as if her bare feet were shod in the best of leather boots.

They had wound around two wide curves between hills and Justen's steps were slowing when Dayala paused. Her eyes narrowed, even more than required by the endless sun. Justen stopped, as did the horses.

Finally, Dayala pulled a small shovel from the roan's load and walked toward the shaded side of the hill, stopping near a dry and sandy patch. She lifted the shovel and forced it into the sand, almost as if it were an effort.

Justen walked over. 'Would it be easier if I did the digging?'

'Yes. You and the horses will need water, but . . . even here . . .'

Justen ignored the unfinished sentence and began to dig. After four shovelfuls, he was sweating. Four more, and he paused to catch his breath. He looked at the sand in the bottom of the hole, suddenly damp. He resumed digging. After perhaps another five or six shovelfuls, he stopped.

The bottom of the hole had begun to fill with relatively clear water, and Dayala slipped a shallow pan with a tapered end into the hole.

Justen watched as she used the pan to fill the two large jugs carried by the mare, and then filled both their water bottles. Something – like a pulse of order-tinged green – passed between her and the horses. Then she stood aside and let the horses drink, and the depression kept refilling.

'Now we will not have to stop until later.'

Justen cautiously sipped the water, but it tasted only faintly sandy, and his order-senses told him that it carried nothing chaotic. He took another swallow before capping the bottle and replacing it in his belt holder.

The stallion neighed, and the horses moved away from the water. Even as Justen watched, the last of the liquid sank back into the sand. He swallowed, squinted, and turned to follow Dayala as she marched southward.

71

'You requested my presence?' Beltar bowed at the entrance to the room that had been the port governor's office.

Zerchas continued to study the lower part of Rulyarth below the bluff, the part that contained the now empty harbor.

'I did. We've rested enough. Go meet your friend, what's-his-name, in Clynya, or however close he got while chasing that Black engineer.' Zerchas drank the red wine straight from the bottle. 'Go the inland route. I want you to take Berlitos, and we'll both—'

'That seems a bit roundabout,' offered Beltar. 'Just let Eldiren deal with Clynya. If I take Bornt and follow the river to Berlitos, that will leave Clynya and Rohrn cut off. I can swing up to Clynya if Eldiren has problems. Neither Clynya nor Rohrn's that big. Or do you plan to take Bornt?'

'I like your idea better.' Zerchas grinned.' After all, if they don't submit, why . . . you can treat them as you did Sarron. I'd rather leave Jera intact; it's a pretty town, and the port's not bad. Later on, you and your friend can clean up the little places. You have a certain style. The locals already are calling you "The White Butcher."' Zerchas laughed. 'By comparison, I seem almost friendly.'

Beltar remained silent.

'You know, young Beltar,' offered Zerchas, 'the problem with using force is that everyone expects it from you, and when you don't use it, they think you've lost either your powers or your will. You can't make – and keep – the amulet on power alone.' Zerchas shook his head. 'You don't understand. You won't until it's too late. Go on, destroy whatever you want to, but leave Jera alone.'

'I assure you that I will destroy only as much as is necessary, and no more.' Beltar bowed deeply. 'I assume that the remainder of the lancers and the Certan and Gallosian levies are for this campaign.'

'You're very perceptive, young Beltar.'

'And Jehan? Will he be accompanying me?'

'I think not. I have a few other . . . tasks for Jehan. He doesn't need more corruption.'

'I see.' Beltar bowed again before leaving.

Zerchas thought about the younger wizard for a long time, his forehead knotted. 'They never understand,' he murmured. Then he took another deep swallow of the red wine. 'Bah. Turning already . . .'

72

Scrrittch . . . scrittchhh . . .

Justen's eyes opened at the sound of the spike rat. For a moment, he stared into the darkness before his eyes completely adjusted. At least his night vision had returned.

By the time he could see clearly, both the sound and the spike rat had disappeared, but he did not feel immediately sleepy, perhaps because his feet still ached.

The only nearby sounds were the faint swish of a night breeze across the sands of the Stone Hills, still warm even in the quiet toward dawn, and the even fainter whisper of Dayala's breathing.

His eyes turned toward the woman, who lay uncovered on a woven mat, barefooted and bare-headed, wearing the same trousers and shirt, which never seemed to get dirty. Her lips were parted slightly, and the silver hair swirled around her broad shoulders.

Was she beautiful? Not exactly, at least not in the sense that Krytella had been, for Dayala's face was too open, almost blank-looking in sleep, especially with much of the life supplied by her intense green eyes, now locked behind her eyelids. Her

chin was almost elfin, but without the high cheekbones that
Justen felt should have gone with such a chin. Yet, there was
. . . something . . . about her.

He shook his head. Maybe it was just kindness he was
responding to.

She twitched slightly and mumbled, a frown crossing her
forehead.

'. . . my sending . . .'

Justen waited, but she lapsed into a deeper sleep. Before long,
he did also.

Dayala woke before he did. That was obvious from the water,
travel bread, and cheese waiting for him.

'You need to eat first.'

'Not quite.' He smiled crookedly and padded out of the tent,
watching where he put his bare feet and wincing with almost
every step until he stepped behind a low boulder. His chin itched
with the scraggly beard he was growing, and he missed the razor
as much as he did the knife.

When he returned, Dayala was eating a chunk of the bread.
He sat down and brushed the sand from the bottom of his feet
and picked a small pebble out from under the crook of his big
toe. It had felt much larger. Then he looked at his left wrist, at
a thin scab less than a span long, somehow more than a scratch,
yet straight and clean. He shook his head. How had he done that?
He frowned, shrugged, then sipped from the water bottle before
breaking off a hunk of cheese.

'Wish I had my knife . . .'

Dayala looked at the ground, a faint flush rising into her
face.

'What did you—' Justen began.

'It's in the pack on the brown mare. I brought it. I'm sorry
about the sword, but I just . . . just couldn't.'

Justen stopped, still holding the cheese in his hand. 'Couldn't
what?'

'You see . . .' The Naclan looked down again. 'The knife is a
tool, and we even have some knives. I did use yours, as I had
to. But the sword isn't. I mean . . . that's not what it's designed
for, and I couldn't. When you took the shovel, I thought you
understood.'

Justen looked at the cheese and then at the silver-haired

woman. Those impossibly deep green eyes met his. For a moment, neither spoke. Then his stomach growled, and Dayala smiled. He shrugged. 'First things first.'

After the cheese, he chewed a piece of the travel bread, still nutty and moist. When he had sipped some of the water, he caught her eyes with his. 'About the swords and knives?'

'We don't fight, not that way. Swords sever things from their roots. Shovels do sometimes – only it's not as bad here.'

'How do you fight?'

'You will have to see. It's more a matter of . . . restraint and Balance.'

Justen chewed and swallowed another mouthful of cheese and bread, wondering as he did so if anything in Naclos were straightforward. Instead of talking, he just ate, somewhat more than the day before.

'The Balance is important to us, perhaps more so than to . . . others,' Dayala said, then sipped from her own water bottle. 'Balance cannot be forced, not over time.'

'Why did you call me? That's what it was, wasn't it? You wanted me to come to Naclos. Did you have anything to do with that White Wizard chasing me?'

'No.' Dayala shivered. 'You are . . . unbalanced, but they are . . .' She shivered again.

'Evil?' Justen pursued.

'That is your word, and it has some . . . accuracy.'

'What would be more accurate?'

'Unable to be Balanced . . .' Dayala left the words hanging, as if she were unsatisfied but lacked any way to explain.

Justen sighed, then looked toward his boots. 'If men were made to walk this far, why didn't the Angels give us hooves?' He rubbed the arch and then the ball of his left foot. 'Feels good . . .' He repeated the process with his right foot before shaking his boots to remove any sand or insects that might have gathered.

'Would you really want hooves?' Dayala's eyebrows arched. 'The Demons of Light had hooves, they say.' She paused before adding, 'You do sleep without those boots. That's a good sign.'

'Why?'

'Any good Naclan needs to be in touch with the land.'

'But I'm not a Naclan.'

'You will be before you leave.' She grinned, but the expression faded into a sad smile.

Justen tried not to shake his head. No matter what questions he asked, every answer created even more questions, and he was still tired, too tired to try to straighten them all out. He pulled on his second boot, stood, then bent to recover the thick, woven sleep mat, which he shook out, rolled, and tied with the braided cords.

73

Justen put one booted foot in front of the other. His feet felt like wrought-iron lumps, or cast lead, and it was only a bit before mid-day. His eyes ran over the hillside, catching a few patches of brown grass, and he frowned. Were the hills not as steep? Could they actually be getting out of the damned Stone Hills?

They walked around another curve in the endless valleys between hills, the dull clumping of the horses' unshod feet the loudest sound in the heat of the day. The hill before Justen looked just like all the others, maybe steeper, and heat waves shimmered off the dull brown rocks.

'We must climb. The valley goes too far north from here.'

Justen could not quite hold the groan.

'Do you need to stop?'

'Not yet.'

Although they had stopped and set up the tent for the midday period every day for the last three days, that was because of his weaknesses, not Dayala's. Barefooted or not, she could walk longer and faster than he could, perhaps than he ever would.

'Are you sure?'

'I'm sure.'

Dayala's long legs stretched as she angled up the hill. Justen grimly dug his boots into the sandy soil.

Whheeee . . . eeee. The stallion trotted past Justen as if to chide him for being so slow.

'. . . only got two legs, thank you . . .' he mumbled.

The stallion's head turned for a moment before the horse continued after Dayala. The bay mare also trotted past Justen's slow steps.

He looked back at the roan, but the trailing mare's steps were almost delicate, and she continued to follow him.

'At least not all the horses are out to prove a point . . .'

He continued to slog up the hill.

Dayala and the two horses waited at the top. She stretched a hand toward the south, where, beyond a mere dozen lines of undulating gray stone rises, a faint line of darkness appeared. 'We don't have far to go before we reach the grasslands. Tonight or tomorrow.'

Justen looked at the hills and then at Dayala. 'Late tomorrow.'

'Perhaps. You are still not feeling well?'

'I'm . . . fine,' Justen snapped between gasps. He uncapped the water bottle and took a deep swallow. The water helped. Then he took the light hat off and fanned his face.

As he cooled off and caught his breath, Dayala poured water from one of the jugs into the flat pan and held it for the stallion to drink. She did the same for the mares, then repacked the pan.

'We'll follow that one, more to the west, to begin with. There's a spring just before the grasslands.'

Justen picked up one leaden foot and then another, half-walking, half-sliding down the slope toward the distant line of green.

Dayala walked beside him, breathing easily.

74

Up close, the grasslands were not so verdant as they had appeared from the hillside, existing more as discrete clumps of wiry grass only a few spans high.

Justen kicked at one of the clumps, then stopped and turned to Dayala. 'That bothers you, doesn't it?'

She nodded.

'Because it serves no purpose?'

She did not answer, but he knew that was the reason. What he didn't know was how he had known that his action bothered her. He hadn't even been looking at her.

The rolling hills were easier walking, or his legs were getting stronger, or both. By midday of the first morning on the grasslands, the Stone Hills had vanished behind the northern horizon, even when Justen stopped and looked back from the top of each rolling hill. Dayala had not looked back, but forward.

At the top of another low rise, he paused and took a drink from the water bottle and munched on the travel bread, which seemed endless. 'How much of this did you bring?'

'Three-score loaves. We could live on it alone, but the cheese adds variety.' The Naclan brushed the fine silver hair off her forehead. 'Most men like variety.' Her tone was matter-of-fact.

Justen nodded, then capped the water bottle.

'Does anyone live here?'

'A few people like the grasslands. They have wagons and follow the grass. I did not see any of them on my way to find you.'

Justen pursed his lips. 'You haven't explained how you found me, and why. You know, you haven't really explained anything much . . . just that the ancients helped you.'

'You helped also.' She smiled. 'You have a strong . . . presence, even when weakened.'

'You druids must be rather sensitive.'

'Not compared to the ancients.'

'Ancients . . . you keep talking about the ancients. Who are they? Are they druids?'

'Druids? You talk about druids, and I have said little, assuming it was another word for those of Naclos. But . . .' She shrugged questioningly, even as she continued her steady pace up the gentle slope.

Absently, Justen noted that the grass clumps now grew closer together, almost touching. 'Druids are people who love the trees. Supposedly, all druids are attractive women, and each has a . . . ah . . . special tree.'

'Why is that tree special?'

'If it dies . . .' Justen was reluctant to finish the sentence.

'. . . the druid dies.' Dayala stopped and glanced back in the general direction of the Stone Hills, looking for the stallion and the mares. The horses no longer traveled close to them. 'You will find ancients and others in Naclos, and we all find the trees to be of value, especially as part of the great forest. There are even small parts of the great forest left in Sarronnyn, though few recognize them. And there are many males you would call druids.' She grinned. 'In time, some will think you are a druid.' The grin faded. 'And some of us are tied, the ancients most of all, but not to trees.'

'The ancients? You still haven't explained—'

'You will have to meet them. They are part of your Legend, but which part, you must decide. But we will do no deciding if we do not keep walking.' As the three horses left off their distant grazing and galloped toward her, Dayala turned and walked along the low ridgeline.

Justen took a deep breath, somehow feeling hurt, or that she had been hurt, but not knowing why. He hurried after her, almost running. 'I'm sorry. I didn't mean . . . but you know everything, and I don't know anything . . . except that a lovely woman rescued me and wants me to walk across all of Candar.'

'Not all of Candar, not even all of Naclos. Just to Rybatta.' She tossed her head, and the cascade of silver rang like bells in his head. What was happening? Had she cast some sort of spell?

A smile, almost shy, crossed her face. 'We don't do magic

here. It is far too dangerous, especially near the great forest.'

The horses swept uphill, running free, and Justen watched, just watched, marveling at their grace.

'You are a druid at heart, Justen . . . and I am glad of that. You feel what I feel when I watch the horses.'

'We haven't seen any other horses.'

'No. Most of them live in the Empty Lands. The grasses are lusher there, and deeper.'

'How deep?'

She bent and drew an imaginary line at knee height. 'Of course, they must worry about the steppe cats, and sometimes grass snakes.'

'The Empty Lands?' Justen replaced the water bottle.

'They are like the High Steppes of Jerans, but no one lives there save the horse people and the wanderers. There is little open water and few streams.'

The dark-haired man took a deep breath. 'How can there be lush grass and no open water?'

'The grass has deep roots, and the rains are plentiful, but the soil is sandy in most places. Once it was a forest, before the coming of the . . . old ones, who cut the trees and made it a desert. The ancients turned it back into grassland, and each year, the trees move farther west, and . . .' she shrugged as she walked '. . . someday the forests will return.'

Justen matched steps with her for a time, an easier task on the downhill because his legs were a shade longer than hers, before continuing. 'What about the grass snakes?'

'They eat the rodents, mostly, but some can kill a foal or a child.'

His eyes traversed the ankle-high grass in the gentle valley below. 'How big do they get?'

'As big as they can, of course. The wanderers claim the king of snakes is twenty cubits long and nearly a cubit in girth.'

Justen shuddered at the thought of a snake that large, then glanced sideways.

'Since I have never seen the king of snakes, I could not say.' Dayala's face remained open as she continued. 'I have seen a large snakeskin, very large . . .' She waited.

'How large?' Justen finally asked.

'Oh, about two cubits long.'

Justen began to laugh. When he didn't laugh, he shook his head. And he had thought she had no sense of humor. Finally, he gasped. 'Someday . . . someday . . .'

'I am sure of that.' She grinned.

His feet were lighter as they crossed more hills, and as the sun, no longer the blazing ball it had been over the Stone Hills but still warm, shone through the near-cloudless sky.

The horses sometimes galloped off, circling, prancing, but always returning. At times, Dayala and Justen stopped, rested on a rise, and ate or drank.

As the sun neared the southwest horizon, Dayala pointed to the valley below, where a clear pool of greenish water lay between two smaller hills. 'I had hoped we could reach this. I would like to bathe, to splash in the water.'

'You bathe, swim, a lot in Rybatta?'

'We all like the trees and the water.' She looked to the east, toward the grazing horses, and the bay mare lifted her head and trotted toward them.

Justen could feel the brief pulse of order and wondered if he could duplicate it.

The horses whuffled to a halt on the grassy slope overlooking the pond, and Dayala began to unload the stallion. Justen began with the roan.

'Easy, lady . . .'

The roan whuffled.

'She says she is a mare, not a lady.'

'What do I call her?'

'Threealla is as close as you could say it,' Dayala said cheerfully, trilling the name.

'All right, Threealla. How was I to know? I'll get this off in a moment. Then you can drink or roll in the grass—'

Whhheee . . . eeee . . .

Justen shrugged. Why was he talking to a mare?

He shrugged again. Why not? He'd always talked to horses, except that this one understood . . . or Dayala could understand the mare. He unstrapped the last of the bags and set them on the grass. In the time it had taken him to unload the roan, Dayala had unloaded both the stallion and the bay mare.

He watched as the horses trotted to the far end of the pond, near the rushes that marked a small, marshy area.

'Our clothes need washing, and so do we. We come first.' Dayala slipped off the shirt even as Justen watched. She wore nothing underneath.

He swallowed.

'Did you not want to bathe?' She glanced at him quizzically.

'Ah . . . yes . . .' He looked down and pulled off his tunic, then balanced on one leg to pull off one boot. He repeated the process with the other foot.

Dayala giggled.

Justen refused to look up. He yanked off his shirt, trousers, and drawers, folded them roughly and dropped them on the grass.

'You looked just like a grouchy old crane perched on one leg.'

Justen looked up at Dayala and swallowed, feeling almost unable to breathe as his eyes fell across her: the bronzed skin, small breasts, silver hair, and the deep-green eyes that sparkled with a light of their own. Helplessly, he looked down, seeing his own paler skin and a body that seemed covered with too much dark hair, a body too angular, too thin, for all the breadth in his shoulders. His eyes finally returned to Dayala, focusing on the sole blemish he could see, a faint white line across the inside of her left wrist. He still was breathing too quickly.

She smiled. 'I see I please you.'

Justen gulped. 'Yes . . .'

'You also please me, and that is good, but you need to go in the water.'

Justen did not need to look down to know that. He flushed, then realized that Dayala had also blushed.

Whheee . . . eeee. From the end of the pond, the stallion pawed the grass momentarily.

Justen grinned and dashed into the water. Dayala followed, almost drawing abreast of him as his feet, then his legs, slowed in the resistance of the water. Then he plunged forward, surfacing in the waist-deep pool.

'Oooo . . . it's cold!'

'You complain too much.' Dayala leaned back, letting her hair float on the surface, her shoulders just barely underwater.

Justen looked away, toward the horses grazing on the grass

above the pool; then he paddled toward the small marsh at the far end, where reeds grew. He looked down as he paddled, but only greenish sand floored the pond, and a lone fish, smaller than his foot, flicked away through the clear water.

'The marsh is the heart of the pond.' Dayala had slid through the water like an otter, and eased along beside him. 'If you try, you can feel it.'

Unsure about trying his perceptions of order and chaos while awkwardly paddling along, Justen nodded and followed her suggestion, ignoring the warm Blackness she represented beside him and concentrating on the marsh.

The reeds were thin, narrow spears of Blackness, and patches of White chaos nestled in the mud around them. Tiny black specks flitted through the water between the reeds. Some shelled creature tugged at chaos – a lump of something else dead – yet all the pieces seemed woven together, and the Black and the White seemed bound in a green web.

Justen stopped paddling, started to sink and swallowed a mouthful of water as his toes touched the sand below. He pushed himself into the air and blew out the water.

Dayala, too, almost swallowed a mouthful of water as she laughed. 'You looked . . . so funny . . . can't stop paddling . . . stay afloat . . .'

Justen spit out more of the clean-tasting water, remembering to paddle. 'I'm not much in the water.'

'You do well.' Her smile was warm. Then she dived and flashed underwater.

Justen paddled slowly back to where he could stand, letting the water seep into him, enjoying the coolness as if trying to make up for all the days of heat.

After a time, he reclaimed his clothes, leaving his belt and purse with his boots. As he picked up the garments, Dayala, still dripping, handed him a piece of something green.

'Soap root.'

After washing their clothes, they pitched the tent and hung their clothes over cords strung from the tent posts. Justen tried not to look in Dayala's direction, though he could feel her eyes upon him occasionally.

The horses stayed near the pond but close to the marshy end, where their snickers, whuffles, and neighs echoed off the water.

As darkness fell, softer sounds rose from the marsh, punctuated by an intermittent croak.

In the cool night air, Justen and Dayala sat on the grass, wrapped in the silky blankets, munching on travel bread and sipping clear pond water.

'You are beautiful . . .' His voice was low.

'No,' she responded with an amused tone, 'you find my body beautiful.'

He blushed, glad that the sudden color was not visible in the star-light.

'And I find your body beautiful. That is hopeful.'

He tried not to picture her diving, sporting in the water, sleek and graceful like some water animal. Finally, he took a long sip of water and leaned his head back, looking into the deep purple and the points of light overhead. 'I wonder where Heaven is . . .'

'They say we cannot see Heaven from here, that it was lost forever.'

'Someday maybe we could find it.'

'They say that the Demons of Light destroyed it.'

'We'll have to build a new one, then.'

'Are all engineers builders?'

'Mostly. I'm not that good an engineer . . .' he broke off, then finished '. . . except in destruction.' His words caught in his throat. 'I didn't realize how much that bothered me.'

Her hand touched his briefly, fleetingly, and the warmth crept up his arm. So he just sat and watched the dark silver of the pond and listened to the night. With the faint buzzing from the marsh, Justen frowned as he realized that there were no mosquitoes.

'That is because they sense you could ward them off.'

'Huh?'

'The mosquitoes . . . they sense your power.'

'Must be different mosquitoes. Or Naclos is different, very different.'

'Naclos is different.'

With that, Justen could agree.

They sat quietly for a time. Justen fell silent and his eyelids grew heavy. Finally, he stood and eased his way into the tent, and after wrapping himself in the quilt, he slept.

Dayala slept an arm's length away, yet somehow he could

sense her presence as if she were next to him, and once his hand
reached out in sleep to touch her . . . and touched nothing.

75

Above Justen, the hills seemed to curve away, as though he
stood at the edge of an invisible circle.

They walked up the hillside until they came to a path in the
grass, marked only by a slight depression that wound up and
around the hillside from the right.

'That's the way we'll take to Rybatta tomorrow.' Dayala
nodded toward the path.

Justen glanced back toward the west, where the sun almost
touched the rolling grassy hills, but he said nothing. It had to
be near mid-winter by now, yet the trees were green. Was the
great forest this far south?

'It will be slower for the first day, until we can leave the tent
and the jugs at Merthe.'

'The horses?'

'Oh, no. It wouldn't be fair to them, not in the great forest.
We're nearly at the edge of the great forest. Can't you feel it?'
Dragging him by the hand, Dayala almost skipped up the last
few cubits to the top of the hill, dodging around a few saplings
and scrub bushes that Justen did not recognize.

They halted by two long, flat boulders – worn smooth by
generations of observers, perhaps?

Justen noted a depression in the grass, almost a path, heading
at an angle down toward the great forest. 'Wouldn't it be easier
to take that path?'

'That path is for later. Right now, it will take you nowhere.'

'It looks like it heads toward Merthe.'

Dayala shrugged. 'If you wish, tomorrow we can follow it,
but it ends not far into the forest. With each generation, it goes
farther.'

'Oh.' Justen looked at the almost-path, then shook his head.

Dayala sat down and studied the great forest, green with a golden tinge cast by the setting sun. Justen surveyed the solid roof of greenery that stretched out below the hill and was almost on a level plane for as far as he could see.

'Sometimes I come here and just watch the great forest for days.'

Justen opened his mouth, then shut it. Days? Yet Dayala didn't seem the type to exaggerate.

'Not days, perhaps not even a day.' Dayala laughed. 'But the forest makes you lose track of time. That's one of the trials, but it's perfectly safe to look at.'

Trials? For a moment, Justen stood at the edge of an unseen chasm. He shook his head again.

'We can rest here for a moment. Later, we'll set up the tent in the meadow back there. It's below the crest on the grassland side. The horses won't be here for a while.' Dayala shifted her weight on the rock with a smile. 'It's good to get back. The Stone Hills are fun, and it's always good to walk the grasslands. The Balance there is so simple.'

Every time he felt that he was about to understand Dayala, she referred to something else that hinted at more he did not know.

Why was the Balance simpler in the grasslands than in the great forest? Justen let his senses pass over the subtle mixture of green that began a hundred cubits below the boulder where he sat in the sunset. His feet still ached at the end of the day. From the corner of his eye he saw Dayala's bare feet dangling over the rock next to his booted ones. He shook his head.

What he didn't know . . . So simple? He frowned, letting his perceptions fall toward the golden green of the great forest.

Mixtures of order and chaos, their patterns intertwining, caught his attention, and he dropped into them. There – an upwelling of pure black, somehow brilliant green simultaneously, twisted around a fountain of white tinged with green . . . and . . . there . . . a gentle pulsing of two smaller order-beats against a flatter, rounder kind of chaos, except . . . how could chaos have any order or form?

Had there ever been such a mixture and intertwining of order and chaos? Justen let himself drift along the lines of power toward a small fountain of blackness that somehow seemed to geyser deep into the rocks below Naclos, almost like a fast-growing tree penetrating all else beneath the forest.

Underneath, a torrent of white boiled around the base of the black fountain.

A cool thread of green beckoned to him, but he felt as though he almost understood the patterns being woven . . .

A line of white lashed from nowhere, and needles like knives burned through him. Another, thicker band of white began to twine around him, even as the thinner white line slashed at him again. A band of black ripped at him, and he tried to wrench free, but another line of white, tinged with red, slashed, and his soul and his face burned.

The cool thread of green tugged, beckoned . . .

'Dayala?'

'Justen . . .'

His thoughts merged with that green, but the lashes continued, black, white, black and white, fading slowly as he and Dayala dragged their perceptions from the great forest.

'Paradise has its thorns,' he gasped. He released his grip on Dayala's hands, his eyes widening as he saw the burns, the ripped sleeves and trousers, and the blisters crossing Dayala's face in a zig-zag pattern. His eyes flashed toward the forest, but the green canopy was silent. 'What . . . happened to you?'

'Hush . . .' She extended the water bottle.

His head ached as if it had been caught in a smith's iron vise. But his tears were for the blisters and burns on her body. He struggled up and put his hands on her shoulders, where neither shirt nor body suffered. 'You . . . have some first.'

She drank, then said after handing him the bottle, 'You're too strong, too much of a temptation for the forest.'

As he drank, he saw, for the first time, that his sleeves were in tatters and that red burns and weals crisscrossed the flesh beneath. His face and forehead burned, much as they had in the Stone Hills.

'We need to go down.'

He followed her to the hillcrest and down to the clearing where the three horses waited. The stallion pawed the ground. The bay nibbled on a low, green plant, not much higher than the half-cubit-high grass around it.

'I know, Threealla. You had to wait for us slow humans.' Justen walked up to the roan.

Whheeee . . . eee. The roan tossed her head.

Justen shook his in response, stopping short as darts of fire shot down his neck and arms. Dayala turned away and leaned against the stallion's flank for a moment.

He took a deep breath, and silently they unloaded the horses.

'This will help.' Dayala extracted a small, oiled package from one of the bags and stepped up to Justen, a cream on her fingertips.

He stood still as she brushed the cream across the blisters on his face. Almost immediately, the worst of the stinging began to abate into a duller pain.

When she had finished, he took the package and brushed the cream, as gently as he could, across her face.

'Thank you,' she said.

He swallowed. How could she thank him when his carelessness, his failure to understand her warning, had harmed her?

'I did not explain well.'

Justen shook his head. 'I did not listen well.' His stomach growled.

A quick smile crossed her face. 'I hear your stomach. We should eat.'

'I'll get some water. The stream below?' he asked.

'That is safe . . . even for you.' The faint smile remained for a moment longer.

When Justen returned with one of the large jugs filled with clear and cool water, the horses stood watching as Dayala finished anchoring the tent in place.

He looked at the horses. 'They're waiting.'

'Of course.'

Justen understood, but how did one thank a horse? Finally, he bent his head and concentrated on expressing his appreciation through his perceptions, through a somehow warm pulse of order.

Wheeee . . . The roan tossed her head, then lowered it and turned, followed by the bay. The stallion pawed the grassy ground once . . . and was gone.

'That was gentle. You will make a good druid.' Dayala sat

cross-legged on one of the sleeping mats set in front of the tent and motioned for Justen to sit on the other. Two clear cups sat empty between them.

As he sat down, she offered him a half-loaf of the travel bread. He poured water into the cups, noting that the blisters on her face had begun to lose their angry red color. His stomach growled again.

Dayala smiled. 'Best you eat. Undergoing a trial makes you hungry.'

'Do all druids have to face that? Will the whole trip through the great forest be like that?'

'Oh, no.' Dayala mumbled the words through a mouthful of crumbs. 'If you do not seek order or chaos, nothing will happen. It is the seeking that offers the invitation. If you remain within yourself . . .'

Justen nodded. Clearly, using order – or chaos – as an aide to perceiving or traveling would be fraught with great danger. He frowned. 'But what if a jungle cat—'

'If it attacks you, then it is a form of chaos, and you may respond accordingly. If you attack it, the forest perceives you as chaos.'

'Not much hunting, huh?'

'No.'

Justen ate several more mouthfuls before speaking. 'But cats have to eat? What can they attack?'

'Anything that is smaller or cannot escape. The whistling pigs, or the hares, sometimes a fawn.'

'That seems disorderly. Strength seems to rule, not order.'

Dayala licked her lips and drank from the clear cup.

'I'm still confused,' Justen told her. 'What you seem to be saying is that any first action, by order or by chaos, meets a reaction, but that those who are strong enough can get away with it.'

Dayala nodded.

'Why wouldn't the forest strike back at the cat?'

'It does not use pure order or pure chaos.'

'Oh. But if I respond to a physical attack, you're saying that my response transforms the purely physical into a question of order and chaos?'

'No. You . . . any druid transforms the physical into a question of order-chaos Balance.'

Justen swallowed.

'That is why the great forest struck at you. Nature resists any attempt to separate its . . . Balance . . . into two levels of being. What you see and feel, and what you feel beyond that . . .'

Pondering, Justen munched through two more bites of the nutty and filling travel bread.

'So . . . separating order from the world that creates it is a form of violence?'

Dayala nodded. 'Separating chaos, while easier, is also violent . . . and evil.'

'Wait a moment. You're saying that separating either order or chaos from the . . . everyday . . . world is evil.'

The druid paused to finish another sip of water. 'It is hard to explain. If you strengthen order in a tree, that is not evil, because a tree grows to strengthen order. Nor is it evil to allow chaos to exist, but to create order separate from the tree or to place chaos where it would not occur . . .'

Justen put his hands to his head, but let them fall away as they brushed his blisters. 'Then . . . why the trial? I mean, if you're not supposed to—'

'It is not that easy.' Dayala looked toward the faint gray remnants of twilight to the west. 'We dug in the desert to find water. That did violence to the ground, but dying when water was there and when the digging created only a little chaos would have created more chaos. That is not quite right . . . but . . .'

Justen took a deep breath. 'So the trial is to—'

'To show that you are strong enough to use order wisely. If you cannot resist the forest, then . . .' She shrugged, and Justen received a feeling of sadness and worry.

After a time of staring into the twilight, he asked, 'How does one resist the forest? How did you resist it?'

'It was difficult. I bound chaos in order and walked through the fountains of each. Every person has a different way . . . those who return.' She looked down. 'I am tired, and we must carry much tomorrow, as far as Merthe.'

Later, with the silky quilt drawn up to his chest, Justen lay back on the sleeping mat, staring at the tent fabric overhead. 'Was that what you meant when you said that magic was dangerous in the great forest?'

'All unbalanced use of order or white force is dangerous. It is much more dangerous in the great forest.' Dayala shifted her weight, and Justen could almost feel the pain in her arms.

'I still don't understand why you got burned and cut. You said it wasn't dangerous. Didn't you already pass your trial?'

Dayala was silent, so silent that Justen sat up, wincing at the pain in his arms as he levered himself about to look at her.

She winced as he did, although she had not moved, and tears streamed down her face, silver to Justen's night sight, silver in the darkness.

'Oh, darkness.' His eyes burned, and he looked down at the scar on his wrist, the scar that matched the one on hers, and both scars seemed to flame with a matching blackness. 'Darkness . . .' And ever so gently, he placed his fingers against hers.

Their tears continued to flow long after Justen laid his mat beside hers so that their fingers would remain linked, long after the low sounds of the great forest echoed gently over the hilltop.

76

Eldiren concentrated on the screeing glass, but despite the sweat on his forehead, he could not break through the white, swirling mists that covered the glass.

'One of those places . . .' he muttered as he released his hold. The glass shimmered with the blankness of a mirror. He cleared his throat.

'It's all those trees,' Beltar said, gesturing toward the ancient forest in the valley below the White camp. 'Isn't that why no one can ever look into Naclos?'

'That's what they say.' Eldiren patted his still-damp forehead with a square of folded cloth. 'When are we supposed to link up with Zerchas?'

'After we take Berlitos.'

'How are we going to do that?' asked Eldiren. 'I can't even

see most of their troops because of the order in the trees. Trying to attack would cost us whatever troops we have left. Can't you shake it down?'

Beltar shook his head.

'The trees?' Eldiren prompted.

'I don't know, but I can't tap enough of the chaos-flows in the ground. All I get are little tremors. There's a lot of old order here.'

'Still, you're not doing badly. We hold Clynya and Bornt – only that little place, what's-its-name, up on the first branch of the Sarron—'

'Rohrn,' supplied Beltar. 'Forget it. That one will have to wait. We need to get through without losing any more troops. Clynya wasn't exactly a pushover. If you hadn't managed to circle back through the hills and start those fires—'

The herald entered the white-walled tent.

Beltar looked up. 'Yes?'

'The Sarronnese refuse any terms, Ser.'

'Oh?'

'They were most arrogant, Ser.' Sweat streamed down the man's face, and his blue cap, held at his waist in both hands, was dark with dampness. 'They . . . they said that Berlitos had never surrendered, not even to the greatest Tyrant in history, and that they weren't about to surrender now.'

'Idiots!' snapped Beltar.

The herald waited.

'No, they won't surrender. Of course they won't. Honor and all that crap!' Beltar paced across the tent, then back.

The herald glanced toward Eldiren.

'So now what?' Beltar asked.

Eldiren gestured toward the herald.

'Oh.' Beltar nodded. 'You may go.'

'Thank you. Thank you, Ser.' The herald fled.

'You seem to have them all terrified, Beltar.'

'I wish the order-damned Sarronnese were terrified instead. But no. It's like they have to force me to use my powers.'

'You just said you couldn't do that here,' pointed out Eldiren.

'I said I couldn't shake down the damned city, and they probably know that.' The White Wizard fingered his chin. 'You were saying something, or I was. Fires, that was it.

I wonder what Berlitos is built of. There's not much stone around here.'

'You'd burn it?'

'Why not? It's better than losing an army. Jera is the only city I *have* to save.' Beltar smiled. 'They can use all these damned trees to rebuild it . . . if there are enough of them left. Besides, the storms won't hold off that much longer.'

'Burn it?' asked Eldiren again.

'Why not? I seem to be condemned to use force. So I might as well. Right now, Zerchas wants results. I'll get him his results.' Beltar walked to the entrance to the tent and looked down at the forest city of Berlitos. 'I'll get him his order-damned results.'

Eldiren looked at the blank glass and then at Beltar's back. He pursed his lips, but did not wipe the sudden return of sweat to his forehead.

77

The road was wide enough for a single wagon, not that Justen had seen any wagons since they had entered the great forest not much past dawn. He had seen handcarts, pulled by men or women, large, smooth-skinned buffaloes carrying bags or barrels attached to padded harnesses and following druids who used no apparent direct control, and nearly a score of people walking from one place to another under the green arches of the towering, brown-trunked trees.

Beneath the monolithic trees that rose more than a hundred cubits into the air grew shorter trees and bushes, each almost as if placed, never touching any other. Some were squatty, dark-trunked lorken, others oaks that seemed never destined to reach the heights of those Justen had known in the highlands beyond Wandernaught as a child, heights he had thought soaring until seeing the great forest of Naclos. The forest canopy turned the road and all beneath it into a green-lighted temple, almost demanding worship.

Without the sun bearing down on him, Justen had tucked the woven cap into his belt. His head felt less sweaty without the cap, but the covering had clearly helped him across the Stone Hills and the grasslands.

As they walked deeper into the great forest, Justen found himself speaking in whispers. 'How much farther to Merthe?'

'A while. It is not even mid-morning.'

He shifted the heavy packs on his shoulder, glad he was neither a pack animal nor a soldier, not usually, and looked down the road, momentarily empty except for them.

The dark-splotched form of a forest cat almost as tall as Justen's waist slipped across the road a hundred cubits ahead of them, vanishing silently into the undergrowth. Justen felt for the knife at his belt, not that a knife would have done much good against such a monster. 'Are you sure we're safe?'

'As long as you don't start order-probing again.'

'But what would stop—'

'You are with me.'

Justen swallowed, momentarily feeling like a stupid child, wanting to say childishly, 'Yes, Mother.' Instead, he tried to receive some form of order-impressions – rather than trying to send or investigate. He had already learned the dangers there, as the soreness on his face and arms reminded him.

The road followed, as it gradually descended, a stream that grew slowly wider and slowly noisier. On each side grew bushes and occasional flowers. He paused to study a purple trumpet bearing a stamen that seemed to flow like golden notes from the bell of the floral instrument. The purple flower had its own space, like every plant, no matter how narrow, no matter how frail.

As he turned toward Dayala, who had stopped during his examination, Justen marveled at the unseen gardener who maintained the trees, even the flowers that peered from scattered beds, and the road – or roads. 'Who takes care of all this?'

'The great forest takes care of itself. As it should be.'

As it should be? Justen did not voice the question as he strained to keep up with Dayala. The road followed the river, and they passed a few more souls, all adults and all walking with that determined stride that he had come to associate with Dayala.

'Everyone walks.' He shrugged his shoulders in an attempt to relieve some of the growing soreness from the heavy pack.

'Except when we take the river. How else would it be?'

How else could it be if the Naclans did not use animals for riding or pulling carts?

It was near midday when the road turned and before them, a stone bridge crossed the stream. When they stepped onto the span, Justen saw on the other side of the stream a small dwelling, almost entirely shaded by trees, and beyond the smooth, dark walls, sunlight fell on the lower trees and the grass – grass he had not seen since they had entered the great forest.

In the kay-wide circular space that appeared to be Merthe, there were none of the monolithic forest giants, but only a scattering of shorter trees, most set right against the low houses. More than two-score dwellings or other low buildings sat on curving, stone-paved lanes.

A silver-haired man carrying a large covered basket nodded at Justen and Dayala as they took their last steps off the bridge and walked onto the sun-splashed road leading into the town.

'Pleasant-looking place.'

A faint breeze flowed from the great forest into Merthe, ruffling Justen's hair from behind. He pushed the locks back off his forehead, aware that they were all too long, but glad that he no longer had to wear the woven cap.

'Why should it not be?'

With no answer for that, Justen glanced toward the second dwelling they passed, where two children played a hopping game. The older girl nodded solemnly as they went by, while the younger waved cheerfully.

Behind the house was a garden with neat rows and staked plants that grew as tall as Justen's shoulders. The leaves in the garden were still green.

'Does it never frost here?'

'Seldom.'

'So the plants grow year around?'

'Most of them do.'

Justen was pondering this as he saw a pair of cows chewing on the lush grass behind another dwelling, the animals apparently unstaked and unfenced. He shrugged his shoulders, trying to release the stiffness and soreness from carrying a pack far heavier than he had lugged before.

Dayala walked toward a low building, with three oaks square against each side wall. 'This is where we will leave the traveling equipment.'

An archway, not a door proper, offered entrance to the shop. As they stepped inside, Justen glanced at the curtains that had been tied back, but no door lay behind them. He tried not to frown, but why was there no door? Were there no thieves? Even though Recluce had few thieves, if any, the dwellings and shops had doors.

'Dayala! You found him! I'm so glad for you.'

Justen raised his eyebrows as a squarish young woman bounded out from behind a small loom on a table in the rear of the building.

'Justen,' Dayala gestured toward the woman, 'this is Lyntha.'

'I am honored.' Justen bowed slightly.

'No. I am honored. So few ever make it to Merthe, or to the northern reaches of the great forest.' Lyntha grinned.

Dayala slipped out of her pack with an ease Justen admired, an example he followed far less gracefully, if with more relief.

'Here is the tent . . . and it is ordered . . . and the water jugs . . .'

The engineer rubbed his shoulders as he watched Dayala unload items from the two packs. Some went on the nearly empty flat wooden table, while others, such as the big water containers, Lyntha carried into a back room.

'We'll put the other things away. You were weaving . . .'

'My sister will be having a son, and she will need a comfort quilt for him.'

'She has waited a long time.'

'Not so long as you!' Lyntha laughed.

Dayala flushed, so briefly that Justen almost missed the flash of color. 'Some of us are just luckier than others.'

Even as Lyntha returned to the loom, Dayala began to place items on the racks around the room. Justen fingered the wood on a staff, tightly grained and smooth lorken, almost glossy to the touch.

'What about the travel bread?' he wondered aloud.

'That will be used for the cows and chickens.' Dayala carried some of the sealed waxed containers back into the rear section of the building, and Justen followed with the remainder.

When the packs were empty and placed on racks, Dayala turned to him. 'It would be fitting if you would consider leaving your water bottle . . .' She inclined her head toward the wooden rack that contained only the bottle she had placed there and one other.

Justen unfastened the bottle and leather strapholders from his belt. 'What about the water? There's still some inside.'

'Lyntha?' Dayala gestured. 'Justen forgot to empty this bottle. Could you take care of it?'

'Just leave it on the end of the rack. He's not the first, and he won't be the last. Why, last eight-day, old Fyhthrem not only left a pack here full, but she had olffmoss in it. What a mess that was. She apologized and later brought by some dried pearapple flakes in wax for the travel food. But it happens. A little water, that's nothing.'

Justen set the bottle and straps on the end of the rack, glancing back at Dayala. She nodded and walked toward the table where the stocky, silver-haired woman was operating a small hand loom.

'We must go.'

'You'll be back before long.'

'Of course. At the proper time.'

Justen bowed to Lyntha. The woman flushed briefly but returned the bow with a nod. Then he followed Dayala back into the warmth of the sun, loosening his tunic as they crossed what passed for a central square on their way toward another low building, also without any signs or indications of its function.

Inside another doorless room, they stood amid a half-dozen chairs and tables, all empty, when a silver-haired youth, barely to Justen's shoulder, stepped into the room.

'Dayala!' He grinned at the silver-haired woman. 'Mother said you'd—' He turned and bowed to Justen without finishing the sentence.

Justen returned the bow.

'You're as eager as ever, Yunkin.' Dayala shook her head.

'Someday I'll be just like you.'

'I hope not!' Dayala laughed and looked around the room.

'You should sit at the corner table there. It's the coolest, and I'll get you something to drink.'

They sat down, with Yunkin hovering at their elbows as they pulled up their chairs. 'What would you like to drink?' The silver-haired boy looked from Justen to Dayala even before he finished the question. 'Is he the order-mage from beyond the Stone Hills, young ancient?'

'Yes. This is Justen. He was born in Recluce.' Dayala flushed.

'Welcome to Merthe, Ser.'

'What do you have to drink?'

'Redberry, greenberry, light ale, and dark beer.'

'The dark beer, please.'

'And you, lady?' Yunkin attempted a more formal tone.

'The light ale.'

'Mother . . . I mean . . . we have . . .' the boy grinned, then forced himself back into a more composed demeanor '. . . cheese and bregan.'

'That would be fine,' Justen said. *Anything but travel bread. Anything.*

Dayala nodded, and after the boy had scurried through the archway toward the kitchen, she raised her eyebrows. 'Anything else?'

Justen looked at the smooth, wooden surface of the table, unable to detect the joins in the wood. Finally, he asked, 'What did he mean when he called you a young ancient?'

'It is a term of respect. He was being polite. I . . . am not close to being an ancient.'

The youth scurried back, the dark brown of the beer and the gold of the ale clear through the thin crystal of the tall glasses he carried.

Justen waited for Dayala to drink, then took a slow sip of the beer. Both the tang and the smooth power of the brew made him glad his first sip had been small. His body was now unused to any sort of spirits. 'This is good.'

'You are one of the few from Recluce who drinks beer, are you not?'

'I suspect I'm the only engineer who does.'

'That is good.'

'The others don't think so, especially my brother.' Justen swallowed, wondering how Gunnar was, wondering if the others had reached Recluce safely. But they must have made the journey safely. He would have felt something surely had Gunnar been injured. Or would he?

'They look only at the surface of the Balance.' She sipped from her glass more slowly than Justen.

Before he could respond, Yunkin had arrived with two wide platters, one of which he slid in front of Dayala and the other before Justen.

Justen took a deep breath, inhaling the fruity-nutty aroma of the pastry and the tang of the cool cheese. He had forgotten that cheese could be anything but warm, somewhat off-tasting, and mushy.

'You look hungry.'

'I am hungry.' Before he had realized it, he had finished both the cheese and the pastry, as well as most of the beer, without saying a word to Dayala.

The boy appeared with a pitcher, half-filling the crystal goblet before Justen. As Yunkin walked back to the kitchen, Justen frowned.

'You seem disturbed,' Dayala observed.

'How did he know I only wanted that much?'

'He did not. He just felt the Balance. Do you want more?'

'No.' Justen sipped the cool and smooth dark beer. 'No.' But he still frowned. Again, he felt as though he had missed something he should have understood.

He held his empty glass silently until Dayala finished. She had said nothing further, and he had not felt like asking any more questions that would make him feel stupid or child-ish.

'We should go. Rybatta is still a distance from here.'

Justen frowned, realizing they had not seen Yunkin's mother, and that something else had seemed odd. 'Don't we owe them something?'

'Of course. I'll send Duvalla some greenberry preserves or some juice. You're a smith, aren't you? Yual . . . needs to meet you, and I know he would let you use his forge. Not many can handle that, so anything decorative of iron would be welcome and appreciated.' Dayala stretched her legs and shifted her weight on the wooden chair.

'But . . . how can you make things work like that?'

'Justen, do you remember how the great forest felt? How can it not work?'

'I'm a child in some ways, remember? Please stop being quite so condescending and cryptic. Tell me as though I were the stupidest and slowest child.' That was certainly how he felt.

'It's the Balance. If you do not repay voluntarily, then others will respond to that imbalance.'

'You mean . . . if I didn't repay them in some way, a neighbor or someone would remind me?'

'Only if you were a near-child.'

'Near-child?'

'One who has not passed his trial.'

Justen took a deep breath. 'All right, what is the trial? Plain and simple.'

Dayala's green eyes fixed on him. 'That is when you become an adult, a druid. That is when you walk the great forest with your mind, alone, without help.'

Justen shivered. 'Like I tried to do the other night?'

Dayala nodded.

'And all druids do . . .'

'People can leave Naclos, and some do. Those who stay must pass the trial.'

Justen blotted his suddenly damp forehead. 'So, assuming I passed my trial and I didn't repay a service, what would happen?'

She shrugged. 'It does not happen often. Most of us, even forgetful ones, are reminded.'

'But if I didn't . . .'

'I could not say. A forest cat, perhaps a white-mouthed snake . . . the great forest has its ways.'

Justen shivered as though once again he stood on the edge of an enormous chasm. 'You don't get much choice.'

'Why should we? Is it orderly that people should be allowed to cheat others or to eat more than they contribute?'

'But a productive person—'

'No. The great forest understands, and so do we. A sick man repays when he can. So does a nursing mother. You *know* in your heart what is right, do you not?'

'Not all people do.'

'All those who live in Naclos do.'

The cool certainty of Dayala's words chilled Justen even more. He lifted the beautiful beer glass, studied the curves, and set it down.

A system of unforgiving, absolute justice? What had he gotten himself into?

'You are disturbed.' Her fingers reached out and touched his arm. 'That is good, a sign of your good heart. The forest protects those of good heart.'

'I wouldn't have known.'

'I do not doubt you would follow the Balance even so.'

Justen was not so certain of that, but he fingered the beer glass without speaking.

78

'This is my dwelling.' Dayala gestured to the wooden cottage in the clearing ahead. She shifted the pack on her back, which contained some bread and cheese from the market in Rybatta, the modesty of which she had apologized for three times since leaving the center of the town.

In the dimness of the twilight, Justen peered at the low structure, seemingly set between four massive oaks. The oaks were lower than the soaring monoliths that reared into the sky. Then he swallowed, realizing that they actually formed the living corner posts of the cottage.

How many houses had he looked at in Naclos without being consciously aware that they were part of the trees? What else had he looked at and not seen? He glanced sidelong at the silver-haired druid.

'It's . . . orderly.' Behind a narrow lawn to the rear of the house rose a number of low trees, almost resembling hundreds of bushes, that extended several hundred cubits back toward the great forest itself. 'What are all the trees? Or are they bushes?'

'They're what I do.'

Justen forced a laugh, pulled at his beard, uncertain as to how to proceed, before asking, 'And what is it that do you, mysterious druid?'

'I work in wood.'

'You're a carpenter?'

Dayala shook her head. 'No . . . I work with the Balance. I could not handle cutting tools.' Her hand held back one of the entry curtains.

Fingering his beard again and feeling the itchy skin beneath, Justen wished she did. Where would he find a razor?

'Yual makes such things. Perhaps he could help.'

After inclining his head in embarrassed acknowledgement, Justen stepped through the entry and into a large main room. The walls were of smooth-paneled wood without visible seams, and the hardwood floor matched the walls and ceiling. Two long wooden benches formed a right angle in the far corner of the room. One archway showed a kitchen containing a compact stove of clay and iron. Justen looked at the stove, set in an alcove, and nodded, noting that the tree had grown, or been grown, to leave a space for the stove and the brick chimney behind it.

A bathing room contained a tiled and freestanding tub, but a built-in jakes. Justen glanced at Dayala, then nodded. Certainly, trees could use such . . . waste products.

He peered into the guest room, containing little more than a stool, a closed chest, and a wide bed on which lay a pillow and a folded blanket of the same warm and silky material that had covered him most nights on the journey to Rybatta – except that the blanket on the bed was black, as was the pillowcase. A woven rug, patterned in triangles, covered half of the smooth wooden floor. On the wooden chair was laid a set of brown trousers and a shirt, both looking to be his size. The garments made it clear where he was sleeping.

'I thought you might need some clothes.'

'Obviously, you were convinced that I would make it across the Stone Hills.'

'Hope can often make it so.'

Justen looked down at his ragged shirt, and then at hers. 'I trust you left some for yourself as well.'

'I do not need quite so much in the way of covering, but I am sufficiently provided.'

'You are indeed well provided.' Justen attempted a leer.

Dayala stifled a yawn. 'If you would like to wash up, the well is out back, and so are the buckets. I will prepare some food.'

'The bread and cheese are fine. You're tired.'

'I am tired.' Dayala smiled. 'And bread and cheese and some fruit are what we are going to eat.'

Justen grinned back and went to carry water.

79

Justen sat on the gray boulder, letting his bare feet dangle in the cool water.

Whhnnn . . .

Idly, he brushed away the tiger mosquito, then raised the faintest of order-shields to guide away the hungry female, and any other insects that might decide to nibble on him.

'You've gotten much . . . better.' Dayala's hand rested beside his on the stone. Her warm fingers glided over his wrist for an instant.

'More delicate, you mean?' Justen grinned and turned his foot, kicking a small jet of water at her.

'Delicate? I think not. Gentle, perhaps, but it will be years before your touch is . . .'

'Refined?' Justen stretched. 'Why did the mosquitoes out in the grasslands not bother me, and why do these still nibble?'

'Because the grasslands are still.'

'Oh. Here there is too much power of too many different kinds?'

'Something like that.'

'I'm hungry.' He yawned.

'No . . . you're not. Listen to your body. Does it really need food?' Dayala gave him a broad smile.

Justen felt the blood rising into his face and looked over at the white edges of the stream, where the fast-flowing water broke around the rocks. Then he looked back at Dayala. Her eyes dropped.

'You're blushing.' He grinned. 'You're . . . blushing.' He twisted and slid off the rock onto the pine-needle carpet. He held out a hand.

Dayala's fingers closed around his as she flipped clear of the stone and jumped down beside him.

'Not bad for an ancient druid.'

'I'm a very young druid. Very young. Otherwise . . .' She disengaged her hand and smoothed her hair back.

'Otherwise?'

'I would not be here.'

Justen frowned, realizing that while her words were true, more than a little had been left unsaid. 'Only young druids travel after strangers in the Stone Hills?'

'This is true.'

'But . . . why you? You never have really answered that question.'

Dayala looked down at the grassy patch on which she stood. 'Let us walk back.'

Justen followed her through the woods, which seemed nearly parklike. When they reached the gently curving road that would lead them into Rybatta and out again to the cottage that lay on the far side, he leaned closer to her. 'You were going to tell me . . .'

'This is a story that you must tell yourself in time, as you come to truly know Naclos and those of us who dwell here. But I will tell you another story.'

Justen frowned, then took a deep breath and listened.

'Once a young girl asked her mother what her life would be like. Would she have lovers, or just one special lover? Or would she serve the Angels, and listen to the giant trees, and to the voices under the ground, and to the winds that cross all Candar and whisper their secrets to those who can hear? How long would be it be before she would know these things?

'Her mother smiled but said nothing, and the girl asked again. What will my life be like? How will I know? But her mother said nothing. And the girl began to cry. She wept as only a child can weep, with great sobs. When she stopped weeping, her mother brought her an unripe Juraba nut. The green ones are so hard that they can be opened only with a sword or a sledge or a great, heavy mill. And her mother told her that her life was like the Juraba nut.' Dayala stopped speaking and nodded to a thin older man who carried a basket of green pearapples.

The man nodded with a slight smile as he passed.

'And?' asked Justen.

'That is the story.'

Justen pursed his lips and thought. 'Your story seems to say that if you attempt to force an answer before it is ripe, you will destroy it, just like you would destroy that green nut.'

Dayala nodded.

'The question is . . . how does a stranger, or a near-child who has never seen a Juraba nut, know when the nut is ripe?'

'The shell splits, and you can see the inner husk and the nut pod for yourself.'

'Wonderful. Was that mother your mother?'

'Of course. That is how I know the story.'

'Have you seen the ripe nut?'

'No more than you have, dear man.'

Justen shivered at the warmth in the words 'dear man' and the admission they contained. Ahead lay a narrow footbridge at the juncture of two paths. Beyond the bridge, the giant monoliths thinned and the cleared area that was Rybatta proper began.

'Hello, young angels.' A small, silver-haired girl cradling a basket filled with waxed packages of cheese and a waxed honeycomb nodded politely, stepping aside to let them cross the narrow span.

'Harmony be with you, Krysera.' Dayala smiled.

Justen nodded, and Krysera returned the nod solemnly.

After they were out of earshot, Justen asked, 'So now I'm a young angel? Just what does that mean?'

'It's a term of respect. She isn't quite sure of what to call you. Because you live here with me and not in the strangers' house, you're not a stranger. You radiate order and power. So you must be a young angel.' Dayala shrugged as if the conclusion were obvious.

'Strangers' house?'

'If we had a real stranger, he or she would stay with Yual or Hersa. She is the copper-worker. Diehl has a large strangers' house, what you would call an inn. When we travel, we stay in guest houses.'

'So why am I not a stranger?'

Dayala touched his arm, the spot where only a faint scar remained. **You are not a stranger. Not now . . . not ever.**

The force of the words, felt in his mind, staggered him, and he stumbled. Dayala's hand steadied him for a moment, but her fingers almost seared his skin. He glanced sidelong at her and saw the dampness on her cheeks, and his eyes burned.

What was happening? To him? To her?

They had walked another hundred cubits when Dayala finally spoke again. 'Let us go to the river pier.'

'Any reason?'

'I need to speak with . . . Frysa about how many boxes she will need.'

They passed the small market stall with the neatly stacked pearapples, the closed barrels of grains. Down the open but narrow steps in the cooler cellar were the cheeses and the riper fruits. Dayala waved to Serga, the shopkeeper, and the rotund man waved back.

'Boxes? Your boxes? What does she need them for?'

'To trade. We do trade for some things, like copper, and your woolens from Recluce, although we do not need many warm garments, and mostly the wool is used for other things.'

'So you provide boxes for trade as a way of repaying the great forest and the others in Naclos?'

'Exactly.' Dayala laughed softly. 'You see! You do understand.'

'Sometimes.'

Only a single boat was tied at the stone pier, and it was empty.

Dayala led Justen past the pier and to a small, round building formed by a single tree – not an oak, but a species with which Justen was unfamiliar. Inside, on a stool sat a woman, also silver-haired and green-eyed, but deeply tanned. As she rose, she reminded Justen of Dayala, although he could not say why.

'Justen, this is Frysa.'

Justen bowed. 'I am honored.' And he felt that he was, just as he felt that Dayala had not fully explained who Frysa was.

'You have a handsome soul.'

Justen flushed, and he glanced at Dayala. She also had colored.

'He is modest, and that is to the good, for both of you.'

Dayala nodded before speaking. 'I forgot to ask how many boxes you will need.'

'A half-score would be enough for now. You will have more time . . . later.'

Justen looked out absently at the river, smooth and nearly a hundred cubits wide between the tree-lined banks, and at the single boat. Smooth as the water was, paddling upstream would be difficult.

'How do you find Naclos?' asked Frysa.

'Seemingly peaceful, and very unsettling.'

'He's honest, too.'

Justen tried not to blush again, and failed.

'Already, except for your hair, you look more like us, inside at least, than those of Recluce.'

Justen shrugged, unsure of how to react. 'I cannot see that deeply into myself. So I must accept your observation.'

Frysa reached out, and her fingers brushed his bare wrist. 'Remember to trust yourself.' She looked at Dayala. 'You must be going. Thank you. You have been very fortunate. Even so, it will be difficult for both of you.' She turned to Justen. 'She is not so strong as you, though it seems otherwise now.'

Without looking, Justen could feel Dayala blushing.

The two women embraced, and as they parted, Justen bowed again. 'It was good to meet you, and I wish you well.'

'He is also generous.'

'Yes.' *Generous of soul, and knows not why . . .*

Justen swallowed at Dayala's unspoken words, wondering if the stray thoughts that passed between them would only grow stronger, wondering . . . He shivered.

In silence, they walked back past the single boat.

'How do the boats get upstream? I don't see how they could paddle all that distance.'

'Sometimes we can get the river people – the otters – to pull them, but only if the boats carry no people. The otters will pull light cargoes.'

'So anyone who goes downriver by boat must walk back, or paddle themselves?'

'Yes. But it's not that bad if you can sense the currents.'

Again, silence dropped between them as they passed the guest house on the square and the small dry-goods store that held linens and the fine, spider-silk cloth.

'Frysa's a relative?' Justen asked.

'Yes.'

'Your older sister?'

Dayala shook her head with an amused smile.

Justen shook his. 'Your mother? Doesn't anyone get old here?'

'Of course. Just more slowly. Aging is a form of chaos, and it can be balanced.'

'Your mother, of course. How stupid of me.' He shook his head. 'Why didn't you tell me?'

'I wanted her to see you as you are. You are honest and open.' **And that is rare . . .**

Justen's eyes threatened to water at the damning honesty of her unspoken words. What was happening to him?

'The great forest insists that you recognize yourself, and that is very difficult.'

'Difficult . . .' He laughed harshly.

They had passed the long rows of bean plants at the edge of Rybatta proper before Justen spoke again. 'How do you make your boxes? By growing them on those bushes? I know. It's more complicated than that, but is that the idea?'

Dayala nodded.

'It's work?'

She nodded again.

He shook his head as they walked up the curving path to her house. 'All this takes some getting used to.'

'I understand.' Dayala stopped in the middle of the main room, dropping her hands.

For a long time, Justen looked at her, at the silver hair, the green eyes, and the dark, open orderliness within that screamed out a terrible honesty. Then he eased his arms around her, and her arms went around his waist. Their lips brushed. **Want you . . . coming to love you . . .** Justen blushed at the boldness of his thoughts.

For a moment, Dayala's lips pressed his, and she squeezed him to her before easing back and holding him almost at arms' length.

She was breathing heavily. 'The nut . . . isn't quite . . . ripe.' Then she wrenched out of his arms and ran into her room. So hard . . . unfair. Angels never said . . . love you. Not right yet. Don't know . . . how long . . .

Justen staggered under the emotional barrage of words, as warm as summer and as pointed as arrows. He finally sank onto a stool.

As quickly as he learned one thing, he learned more that he didn't know.

80

The center of Berlitos stood on the top of a low hill that swelled out of the forest, a forest filled with trees still gray in the winter cool. The Temple to the Angels – polished amber wood – rested beside a three-story structure. Even in the center of the hilltop city, a few gray-green trees blurred the outline of the low buildings.

Beltar stood on the hastily erected log platform and cleared his throat. A light but steady wind blew from behind him out of the northeast and toward the city.

Standing at Beltar's shoulder, Eldiren glanced nervously toward the hill city and back at the relative handful of troops that flanked the platform, less than score fifteen in all. And Zerchas wanted them to take most of western Sarronnyn?

'Ready, Eldiren?' asked Beltar.

'For what? You're doing the work.'

'You can help,' snapped Beltar.

The slight White Wizard shrugged.

Shortly, a firebolt slashed into a house more than a kay away, and the thatched roof began to burn. A second bolt arced into a closer structure in the valley below the hill, and a third flared farther and dropped onto the polished wood of the Temple. White smoke, followed by a black smudge, rose.

A heavy bell tolled once, then again, and again, the leaden echoes ringing through the gray morning.

Beltar grinned and wiped his forehead. 'We seem to have gotten them a little stirred up.'

Eldiren frowned and concentrated. A small, whitish firebolt spilled against the bottom of the hillside. No smoke followed the impact.

A second large blast of flame plowed into the Temple, and another into the tall structure beside it. Tongues of flame licked at the wood.

Flames began to spread from the thatched house, now engulfed in flame at the base of the hill.

'Ser! There are troops headed this way!'

Beltar looked at Eldiren. 'You take care of them. You don't have any range, anyway.' Then he looked at Yurka, now the lancer commander. 'Form up in front of the platform.'

'Yes, Ser.'

Another firebolt arced across the sky, landing on the right side of the hill, where more smoke began to twist into the sky.

Eldiren glanced at Yurka. 'Get the archers ready – those we have. Before long, someone's going to be marching up that road, such as it is.'

'Yes, Ser.' Yurka eased his mount back toward the north side of the hill. 'Kulsen! Get your squads up here.'

Eldiren concentrated, and another fireball arced toward the thatched houses below the center of the city. Shortly, another roof burst into flame. The White Wizard smiled grimly.

Beside him, Beltar lifted an enormous sphere of fire into the sky, then let it fall like a meteor on the structure beside the Temple, where flames splashed in all directions.

'See that?' Beltar grinned. 'So I'm not as great as any Tyrant? Let them say that now!'

Another firebolt followed.

From the narrow road down toward the valley between the Whites and the outskirts of Berlitos, a thin, wavering trumpet sounded.

A wedge of soldiers in iron-plated leather corselets and wearing blue sashes marched along the muddy road toward the White forces. Before them came a single youth with a faded blue banner.

'Archers!' called Yurka.

'First rank, release!' Kulsen's voice was harsh, and a thin rain of arrows dropped into the Sarronnese soldiers. A handful staggered and two fell, but the Sarronnese pressed uphill.

Another flight of shafts dropped into the Sarronnese, followed by two fireballs in succession. A blue-sashed soldier flared into a pyre of flame and greasy black smoke.

'Second rank!'

Another scattering of arrows slected to the southwest.

'Lancers!' snapped Eldiren. 'Third and Fifth!' He wiped his forehead with the back of his sleeve. Another fireball blasted into the advancing infantry.

The two-score lancers charged the Sarronnese behind a third flight of arrows and two more firebolts.

Two larger fireballs dropped into the center of Berlitos. By now, flames – fanned by the growing wind from the northeast – were everywhere in the center of the city.

Less than a score of Sarronnese infantry remained – none with halberds or pikes – as the White lancers swept through the Sarronnese and re-formed for a return sweep.

'Poor bastards,' muttered Yurka. 'Just out here without any idea of why or how.'

'Like us,' said Eldiren curtly, almost under his breath. He winced, but another fireball flared into the Sarronnese. Three broke and ran, only to be cut down immediately by the returning lancers. Then only two of the Sarronnese foot troops remained standing. One lancer clutched his arm; the others seemed unscathed.

The last two Sarronnese turned and ran.

'Let them go,' said Yurka wearily. 'There will be more.' His mustaches flared in the wind that had become almost a gale.

'I don't think so,' said Beltar. 'Look.'

Eldiren and Yurka turned to the west, where a wall of flame swept up the hillside to meet the flames that crowned what had been Berlitos. Eldiren dropped his arms.

Crack! Eldiren turned. A lightning bolt forked out of a dark sky, and a patter of rain slapped against the timbers of the platform.

'The rain may save them,' offered Kulsen, even as he unstrung his bow and put the strings into a waxed pouch. He turned to the score of archers. 'Save your strings, then reclaim your shafts – those that you can.'

The older archers had already begun to protect their bows.

Eldiren turned back toward the city as the rain began to fall steadily, watching the flames rise in the wind, seemingly undamped.

'Wouldn't surrender to us? The next copper-bit town will.' Beltar looked toward Eldiren.

'I am certain they will, Beltar.' The slight White Wizard slowly sat down on the edge of the platform, letting his legs dangle in the air, taking ragged breaths as though he had completed a footrace.

'I'm no mere Tyrant. They'd better learn that.'

Eldiren nodded silently.

The rain continued to fall, and soon a cloud of steam began to rise from the charred ruins of the city. Then soot began to fall with the raindrops.

The White lancers drew cloaks over their armor and rode under the trees at the edge of the clearing to escape the worst of the slashing rain.

For a time, Eldiren sat on the edge of the platform. Finally, he heaved himself erect, climbed down, and walked through the muddy ground to his horse. He mounted slowly as the rain began to let up.

Once in the saddle, Eldiren took a crimson cloth and wiped the dampness off his uncovered head. The cloth came away gray and sooty.

'Let's go!' snapped Beltar. 'There's nothing left here – or there won't be.'

'Form up.' Yurka's voice was expressionless as Beltar headed for his coach.

Eldiren guided his mount up beside the lancer officer.

Yurka looked at the White Wizard for a long moment. 'This isn't war.'

'Yes, it is,' answered Eldiren tiredly. 'War is slaughter, and Beltar is very effective at it.'

'The light save us all.'

The two rode silently beside the column that represented the remains of the Third lancers. They continued westward, circling the ash heap that had been a town.

As the column neared a crossroads, a woman stood, her ripped blouse streaked with ashes. She began to run, barefooted, lifting a kitchen knife. Yurka, drawing his sabre, reined up the chestnut.

'Bastards! White bastards!' She lifted the knife even higher and turned toward the apparently unarmed Eldiren.

The White Wizard urged his mount sideways, but the woman lunged forward. Eldiren gasped but managed a short blast of flame at the woman.

The charred figure shivered, then pitched forward in the mud just short of Eldiren. The wizard swayed in the saddle, holding on to his mount's mane for a time.

'You all right, Ser?' asked Yurka.

'I'm all right.' Eldiren's voice was flat.

'I'm sorry about that madwoman. I should have stopped her.'

Eldiren shook his head. 'I should have avoided her.'

'She would have tried to use that knife on someone.'

'I suppose I would have, too. Wouldn't you?'

Yurka nodded. 'That's the way it is.'

'Yes. It is.'

Behind them, the coach rolled around the dead woman, and the archers split their files to avoid the corpse. The rain continued to fall.

Eldiren did not look back. He only swayed in the saddle and listened to the creaking of the coach and the occasional crack of the coachman's lash.

The low sounds of the lancers' conversations blended with the fading hiss of steam and with the soft pattering of the scattered rain showers.

After a while, Eldiren wiped the soot off his brow with his hand and then wiped his hand on the grimy cloth tied to his saddle, bright crimson not long before. No matter how often he wiped his forehead, his hands came away dirty. There was soot everywhere, even with the ruins of Berlitos a dozen kays behind them, and the spring rains seemed to come down gray as well.

'I am no mere Tyrant,' Beltar had proclaimed. No one would accord him that title, not now.

Despite the faint sunlight between the clouds, Eldiren shivered.

Behind the thin White Wizard, Beltar's coach creaked as the four-horse team pulled it along the muddy road leading to Jera.

81

'Yual needs to meet you. He is waiting for you. Besides, I have work to do, and so do you.' Dayala took Justen by the arm and walked with him out to the road. 'You remember the directions?'

'Over two bridges and past the splintered oak. Then take the uphill lane to the clearing.' Justen grinned. 'Is it safe? I mean, for a near-child like me to wander around alone?'

'As long as you don't order-probe all over Naclos. Besides, not much happens around Yual.'

'I get the feeling that you very much want me to meet him.'

'I do.'

'Why?'

'Because.' Dayala grinned. 'You need to work with your hands, not just with your mind. I see you twitch, and your body needs that work.'

'All right, most excellent druid. I bow to your knowledge.' His fingers brushed hers, and their eyes locked for a moment. Impossibly deep were those green eyes, and for a timeless moment, Justen could neither move nor speak.

'Justen . . .' . . . need to go . . .

He shook himself like a wet water cat. 'I'm going. It's off to Yual's I go.'

He could feel Dayala's eyes on his back until he had walked around the first curve in the road and out of her sight.

Yual's holding sat on a low hill. Around the hill grew none of the monoliths. Gray, thick clouds scudded above the forest, and a heavy rain pelted onto the hillside and against the two buildings crouched there. The house and the smithy were the first structures Justen had seen within the great forest that were not grown by some tree or another.

Justen shrugged and walked out from the high canopy into the rain and up the stone-paved lane toward the smithy.

Like every door in Naclos, the door to the smithy was open, and Justen stepped inside. There he waited until the silver-haired man reached a stopping point and set the rough-forged blade on the forge shelf to anneal. Then Justen stepped forward.

'You must be Justen.' The smith's eyes were not green, surprisingly, but a clear brown that seemed just as piercing as the green eyes of the other Naclans. He smiled broadly. 'Dayala said you would be here, and I was hoping that you would come. My forge is yours.'

'You're too kind.' The younger engineer bowed.

'I am not kind at all. I am hopeful. So few in Naclos pursue smithing, and it has been more than many years since an outside smith has come this deep into the great forest.'

'I bring no tools . . .'

'I have a few extra ones, and you may borrow as necessary to forge what you need.'

Justen glanced around, from the ubiquitous anvil to a second, smaller anvil, at the great bellows, albeit curved differently, and at the hammers and tongs, racked neatly in two stands.

From the forge came the gentle heat of charcoal.

'Charcoal?'

'Even in the great forest, trees die.'

'And iron?'

'There is enough in the bogs.' Yual gave a wry smile. 'Those of us in Naclos use little iron compared to Sarronnyn.'

'Or especially to Recluce.'

'That is a concern to the Balance.' Yual gestured to the forge. 'If you do not mind . . .'

'Please go ahead.'

'You certainly can examine my poor work, and when I finish, we can see how I might help.' The smith took a small pair of tongs and swung the blade blank into the forge fire.

Justen picked up a hammer, running his fingers across the smooth grain and the curves, nothing how it was shaped to the smith's hand. Finally, he set it down. 'Beautiful tools.'

'Ah . . . I am a toolmaker. You are a smith. The fire . . . it beats out from you like the forge of the gods.' Yual retrieved the red-hot iron and slipped it onto the anvil, using precise and even strokes with a mid-weight hammer to draw the blade thinner.

On a table at the back lay some of Yual's finished work. Justen studied it: a set of knives, a warren, a stone-cutting hammer and matching chisels, some large and hooked needles. There were no tools for shaping wood, nor for farming. For gardening, but not for farming. And no razors.

What should he forge? Justen frowned. He owed gifts to many already, from the gear shop in Merthe to the guest house there, and certainly to Dayala, and now to the smith. Still, he should be able to forge his own razor.

He fingered a small section of what looked to be bar stock, except that it was softer iron, and squarer. He paused, realizing that Yual must partly smelt his own iron. His estimation of the 'toolmaker' rose another notch.

What could he forge for gifts? Perhaps some decorative items, except for the gear shop; for that shop he had already decided on a pair of fire-strikers. Even druids had lamps – and stoves, if only for things like breads – and travelers often needed fires. The flints might be a problem, but he could ask Yual about that before he started. If there were no flints, perhaps he could make a travel lantern.

For Duvalla, he could forge a decorative nutcracker, and for Dayala, he had an idea . . . if he could but execute it.

While Yual worked, Justen found a drawing board and a stick of charcoal. He began to sketch, rough-figuring what he had in mind to make after the razor, and remembering that bog iron was probably scarce.

'A smith who thinks before he lifts iron.' Yual laughed, standing over Justen, who had not even noticed the other's approach.

'Oh . . .'

'I am doubly honored that you share both your thoughts and your trust.'

'I'm the one who is honored.' Justen's words were fact, for he was neither particularly special nor trusting.

'How can I help you?' Yual asked.

'If I could borrow some flame from the forge and pay you in some way for the use of iron and tools . . . all I have is some poor skill. I could use whatever anvil you do not need.'

'You see my iron. What works for you is yours. I had planned to use the large anvil for some tools . . .'

'The small anvil would be fine.'

Yual nodded.

'And should you need it, I can work the bellows on the bigger pieces.'

'That would help,' admitted the older man. 'I have an extra leather apron.'

After pulling off the brown shirt that Dayala had provided, Justen tied the apron in place.

Yual had returned to the forge and the large anvil by the time Justen had found the small length of iron he needed, the smaller hammers and punches.

In time, the forge rang with two hammers.

Later, after suggesting that they eat, Yual set bread and a basket of fruit on the table, then a pitcher. 'This is dark beer, but I have water.'

'The dark beer is fine.' Justen wiped his forehead. Both his hands and arms were tired. It had been too long since he had worked the iron, and his strokes were neither as sure as he would have liked nor as clean. He took a deep breath, then sipped the beer, enjoying the not-quite-cool liquid and looking down the grassy hill to the point where the great forest resumed.

'It's pleasant here.'

Yual swallowed a mouthful of beer. 'Some find it too . . . removed from the forest.'

'Do all Naclans have to be that close to the forest?'

'I don't.' Yual laughed. 'My daughter sometimes travels far from the forest, but her mother gets unsettled if too long away from the trees. We're all different, just as all of you are.' The smith snapped an end off the bread and offered the loaf to Justen.

'Thank you.'

'You keep the iron as soft as you can, I saw, until the last steps, and you always work with the grain. That's the way I do, but not the way the Sarronnese forge.'

'They can't work order into the metal. So it doesn't matter, I suspect, but I don't want it to get brittle. That's the advantage of black iron over steel. There's more flexibility. That's why our boilers can take more pressure than those of the Hamorians.' Justen chewed off a mouthful of bread from the end that he held.

'Delicate work with that double hinge on the nutcracker.'

Justen nodded. 'Stronger, though. The flutes aren't what I wanted, exactly, but I'm out of practice.' He took another sip of the smooth, dark beer. 'May I come back?'

'Of course. So long as you stay in Rybatta, you are welcome.' The words were warm, but Yual gave the faintest of frowns, as if to ask why Justen would ask such a strange question. At least that was the impression Justen received.

'I owe a lot of people, and perhaps I can show you something. I'll try, anyway.'

'I am sure you will.' Yual refilled Justen's mug, then pulled a green apple from the basket and began to eat it.

Justen took a firm pearapple, thinking about the work still to do.

The sun had touched the lower trees before Justen had racked the tools and swept the smithy. Then he walked quickly through the twilight, carrying only the razor, wrapped in a heavy, leaflike husk that Yual had supplied.

Dayala's house was quiet, dark in the dimness of late twilight, when Justen stepped inside.

'Dayala?'

As his eyes adjusted to the dimness, he saw a figure slumped on the short couch in the main room: Dayala. He stepped forward quietly, listening to the gentle breathing that was almost, but not quite, the faintest of snores.

Had she eaten anything?

'Oh . . .' **Think too loud . . .**

'I'm sorry. I not exactly used to controlling how loudly I think.'

The druid slowly sat up.

'Are you all right?' Justen asked.

'I am tired. It is hard to work with the small trees, and I did promise some boxes . . .'

'I know.' Justen stepped around her and into the small kitchen. He took his belt knife and sliced several slabs of bread from the loaf that remained and rummaged in the low cupboard for some cheese. 'I think there's a ripe pearapple on the tree. I'll be right back.'

There were two, and he brought them both in after washing them in a bucket of water drawn from the well.

Dayala was still rubbing her eyes when he set the platter on the table and lit the small lamp with his striker. There was some juice in a pitcher, and he set the pitcher and two mugs on the table. Then he half-filled her mug.

'Thank you.' She yawned again, easing her chair up to the table.

'What did you do today . . . exactly?'

'I finished only one box. It's on the low table there. It's not very good. I tried to rush too much.' She sipped the juice. 'How did you find Yual?'

'He was very friendly. I need to go back. Smithing is slow work, especially when you're out of practice.'

'Going back would be best, I think. I also have much to do.'

Justen looked toward the low table. 'Could I look at the box?'

'If you remember that it is far from my best work.'

Justen lifted the oval box of smooth-finished blond wood with a wide grain. The top slipped off easily. There were no signs of joins or glue, as if the box were a seamless whole. 'This is beautiful.' He gently replaced it and sat down on the chair across the table from her.

'Please . . . it is not my best.'

Justen swallowed. 'Your best must be . . .' He could not finish the sentence, for he had no appropriate word.

'You are . . .' . . . **too kind** . . .

'No. One seldom sees such crafting.'

Without speaking more, the druid slowly ate a single slab of bread and one chunk of cheese. Then she sipped more juice, and yawned – once, twice.

Justen tried not to yawn, but his mouth opened almost as wide as hers.

'We are both tired.' Dayala pushed her mug away.

'It has been a long day,' Justen admitted. Still, he was puzzled, since Dayala had admitted that she did not handle edged tools.

She was exhausted, clearly, and her work was beautiful. But how did she do it?

They put back the bread and cheese and staggered to their respective beds.

'Good night.'

Justen was not certain whether he had spoken or Dayala had, but sleep crept over him before he could decide.

82

'You must learn from watching . . . and listening.' Dayala's fingers tightened around his, then loosened but did not break away. 'He is almost as ancient as some of the old ones, and his songs teach much.'

'Young lovers . . . I see you hiding there on the bench.'

Justen frowned, for the voice was youthful and strong. The silver-haired man with the guitar in his hands, sitting by the small fountain that sprang from nowhere, looked no older than Justen himself.

Justen extended the faintest of order-probes toward the man while looking at Dayala, until he could sense her guarded approval.

'I was young once. Enjoy it.' The laugh was friendly, warm, and so was the sense of order that Justen received, but an order that contained a hint of . . . something bound within it.

Dayala touched his arm as the singer's fingers touched the strings. Sitting on the bench grown from the dark lorken, Justen watched and listened. The silver-haired man's fingers glided across the strings, and the golden notes floated into the twilight, each one soothing even as it chilled, warming as it cooled.

The druid's hand rested coolly in Justen's, and they listened, and wept.

. . . down by the seashore, where the waters foam white,
Hang your head over; hear the wind's flight.
The east wind loves sunshine,
And the west wind loves night.
The north blows alone, dear,
And I fear the light.
You've taken my heart, dear,
Beyond the winds' night.
The fires you have kindled
Last longer than light.

. . . last longer than light, dear, when the waters foam white;
Hang your head over; hear the wind's flight.
The fires you have kindled
Will last out my night.
Soon I will die, dear,
On the mountain's cold height.
The steel wind blows truth, dear,
Beyond my blade's might.

. . . beyond my blade's might, dear, where the waters foam white;
Hang your head over; hear the wind's flight.
I told you the truth, dear,
Right from the start.
I wanted your love, dear
With all of my heart.

Sometimes you hurt me,
And sometimes we fought,
But now that you've left me,
My life's been for naught.

My life's been for naught, dear, when the waters foam white;
So hang your head over, and hear the wind's flight.
So hang your head over, and hear the wind's flight.

Justen was the one who hung his head, tears still caught in the corners of his eyes at the terrible longing held in the golden notes.

'Perhaps you recall this one. I apologize if the accent is not quite right, but it has been a long time,' the singer said.

Dayala cleared her throat softly.

'You do remind me, a bit, of her, young lady. What is your name?'

'Dayala.'

'A lovely name.' The singer turned cold, green eyes upon Justen. 'Remember what you have heard here when you leave Naclos, fellow. Leaving is hard, but being left is harder. I know. I have done both.'

'Who . . . are you? I ought to know, I feel.' Justen shrugged helplessly. 'I'm always grasping, as though I were on the edge of things.'

'Names do not mean that much, not after all this time. Once I was called Werlynn, and once I had children.' The man lifted the guitar. 'It was hard to leave. Everyone thought I died on the journey. It was better that way. For them, at least.'

Dayala nodded.

'Do you recall this song?' The long fingers caressed the strings.

> Ask not the song to be sung,
> Or the bell to be rung,
> Or if my tale is done.
> The answer is all – and none.
> The answer is all – and none.
>
> Oh, white was the color of my love,
> As bright and white as a dove,
> And white was he, as fair as she,
> Who sundered my love from me.
>
> Ask not the tale to be done,
> The rhyme to be rung,
> Or if the sun has sung.
> The answer is all – and none.
> The answer is all – and none.
>
> Oh, black was the color of my sight,
> As dark and black as the night,
> And dark was I, as dark as sky,
> Whose lightning bared the lie.
>
> Ask not the bell to be rung,
> Or the song to be sung,

Or if my tale is done.
The answer is all – and none.
The answer is all – and none.

They sat on the bench for a long time after the silver-haired singer had gone, holding hands tightly, holding shoulders tightly, holding souls tightly.

83

Justen set the iron blossom on the table, turning it so the light from the window would strike it until sunset.

Then he laid the other items on the eating table: two nut-crackers, the strikers, the scrolled trivets, and two travel lanterns that could carry either the inset lamps or candles.

Even with Yual's help and the softer-wrought bog iron, he had spent, on and off, most of the spring and early summer creating the pieces – those and the design for the small water turbine in which Yual had been so interested.

Justen peered out into the garden, where Dayala still walked among the low bushes that seemed more like trees. His hand fingered his once-again smooth chin, not that Dayala had seemed to note the difference, but he felt better clean-shaven. She had offered him a small vial of some sort of soapy oil that had reduced the number of cuts he suffered at the hands of his own craftsmanship.

After pacing around the room, reorganizing his efforts once again, he glanced back at the iron trilia, the thin steel petals bending just so. But Dayala remained out in the garden, and the sun had begun to drop below the unseen horizon.

Finally, Justen slipped out through the front archway and quietly walked into the garden. He paused by the first tree, looking down at the fist-sized closed pod that seemed larger than when he had studied it several days earlier.

Dayala stood well to the back of the garden, her fingers intertwined with one of the bush-trees, oblivious to Justen as he approached.

Watching with his senses as well as his eyes, Justen swallowed as he felt the slow transfer of order from the druid to the tree. Then he stepped back and eased his way to the front of the garden, shaking his head. Why had he not quite seen? If trees could be made to grow houses, certainly they could grow boxes, and who knew what else?

Was Naclos always to be this way, where he took what was said in one fashion while it was meant in another? Where Dayala thought he understood, and he thought she understood?

He paced across the short, open space before the house, back and forth, back and forth, as the twilight dropped across the house and garden.

'Justen . . . you didn't tell me you were home.' Dayala stood by the oak that formed the corner post of the house. She held something in her hand. 'I wanted to show you something.'

Although she smiled, Justen could sense her exhaustion.

'You're tired. You're trying to do too much in the garden.' And this time, he knew what he meant when he spoke. Anyone who could walk him nearly to death across the Stone Hills and yet was too tired to eat after working the trees was definitely spending too much energy on her work.

'Please?' She held up a box.

He stepped forward, and she extended the nearly oblong object.

His fingers closed on it and he shivered, feeling the smoothness, the order, and the absolute serenity the box embodied. Then he looked at the fine grain, at the design of hammer and anvil on the lid. 'It's . . . beautiful.' **More than beautiful . . .**

'I did it for you.'

His eyes burned, and he looked down.

'Justen.'

His raised his eyes to meet hers.

'You cannot learn everything at once. And we both need something to eat, I think.'

He nodded and followed her inside, still marveling at the box, at the finish and the grain and the design. How had she managed to grow the hammer and anvil?

'Oh . . .' he blurted. 'There's something for you on the table.'

Dayala was already bending over the iron trilia. 'Justen, it's gorgeous! It looks so real.'

He shook his head, knowing that his poor work with iron could scarcely compare to the real artistry that she had shone.

'And these . . . for Duvalla and the others. They will be so pleased. But the flower—'

He watched as tears streamed down her face.

'But . . . it's nothing compared to this.' He held up the box she had given him.'

'No. My poor box is nothing.' . . . *nothing at all* . . .

He set the box on the table next to the iron trilia, and their hands touched.

'Don't you see?' she sobbed. 'It is easy to make the trees grow into patterns. They want to help. But cold iron? It fights all the way, and to think that you made something so beautiful from metal. You put the fire that is within you in that, and it will never die.'

'Don't you see . . .' he answered, his voice breaking '. . . the trilia is only cold iron, nothing like your art.' . . . *nothing at all* . . .

'But it is you, *you!*' Her fingers tightened around his.

Through blurry eyes, he saw her and understood – finally, he thought – that the gift was the self and the sacrifice, not the object. And yet the object created from soul had beauty – because it was created from the soul?

For a time, they stood by the table, eyes and hands locked.

Then Dayala laughed softly. 'We still need to eat.'

He nodded, and his eyes fell on the box for a moment, while hers turned to the iron trilia. He set the box beside the blossom and lifted the other gifts one by one to the small side table while she brought out some fruit and a loaf of bread.

84

Dayala set the berry bread on the oval breadboard, sliding the loaf into place with a long wooden paddle. The table lamp flickered with the breeze created by her movements.

'I don't know if I can eat any more.' Justen took a deep breath. 'It smells good.' His hands cupped the mug that remained half-full of dark beer.

'I learned it from her.' Dayala inclined her head toward Frysa.

'Mothers always get the blame.' Frysa's eyes twinkled for a moment. 'Even when they're praised.'

'Unless fathers do,' Justen added. 'My father has always been the cook. Gunnar took after him in that respect. I can do a little.'

'Gunnar?' asked Frysa.

'My older brother. He's an Air Wizard.'

'He still seeks you,' murmured Dayala. 'That is what one of the ancients told me.'

Justen swallowed. Gunnar, still searching?

'He knows you are well.'

'He's probably worried, though.'

'It must be nice to have a brother.'

'I have a younger sister, too. Her name is Elisabet. She's a Weather Wizard also, or she will be.'

'We have few children here,' Frysa answered slowly. 'Not all stay, but the great forest can support only so many.'

Justen nodded. People would have to exist in the order-chaos Balance as well. 'Are there too many people in other lands?'

Frysa and Dayala looked at each other, then back at Justen. Finally, Frysa spoke. 'There is always a Balance. Here, we know that Balance, but we would not be so foolish as to declare what that Balance might be elsewhere.' Her eyes flicked toward the iron trilia that sat on the side table. 'I could not come close to such artistry. Nor could most Naclans. So how should we presume?'

Justen sipped just enough beer to wet his throat. 'So you suspect that there are too many people in at least some places, but you believe it is up to those who live in such places to reach their own decisions – or to fight with the Balance on their own?'

'One can scarcely fight the Balance.' Dayala's lips quirked after she responded.

'I understand. They must reach their own terms with the Balance, but if they fail to do so . . .' He shrugged, then pursed his lips. 'Is that why I am here? To allow an outsider a chance to right the mess beyond Naclos?'

'You were bound to try, whether we helped or not. You are a Shaper,' said Frysa flatly.

'You try to help those who are going to try, and you always have, haven't you?'

'When we could. Many have refused our knowledge.'

Dayala took a small swallow from her mug and watched the conversation between her mother and Justen.

Justen took another deep breath. 'We met this singer – Werlynn. You helped him?'

'No. He went out to help you with his songs and his son. It was very hard on him, and he still is not . . . quite reconciled . . .'

'His son?'

'He had a daughter who was killed when quite young, and his son was blind for most of his life. They both died young . . . young for druids, anyway.' Frysa smiled sadly. 'He blames himself.' She pushed back her chair. 'I must go. Tomorrow I am going downriver to Diehl, and I will need to be alert for the river currents.'

Justen and Dayala stood as Frysa did and walked with her toward the front archway, where Dayala drew back the hangings to let her mother pass into the soft, late-summer night.

A faint chirping and the croak of a frog echoed in the darkness as the older silver-haired woman, her hair almost glowing in the purple darkness, slipped away toward the center of Rybatta.

Dayala closed the hangings.

After returning to the table, Justen looked down at the uneaten berry bread. 'It smells so good, but I just couldn't. I'll have some in the morning.'

'You understand your body best.'

'I suppose.' Justen paused, then swallowed. 'I'm almost afraid to ask.' He paused again before speaking. 'I've met your mother twice now, but . . .'

'My father?'

Justen nodded, his heart dropping.

Instead, Dayala laughed. 'I should have told you. I'm sorry. You've already met him. But I didn't want . . .' She shook her head. 'Some things are different here.'

Justen's thoughts whirled. What man reminded him of Dayala? Where? Then he nodded and asked slowly, 'Yual?'

'Of course. That is why . . .' I can bear the flame . . .

'But . . . why don't they live together?'

'Sometimes they do. But Yual likes the more open spaces, and sometimes he travels the Empty Lands, or the grasslands. He went to Sarronnyn several times before I was born.'

'And your mother is more tied to the great forest. Yual told me that, except that he didn't say it was your mother – just that it was his daughter's mother.' Justen shook his head. 'You all think I see more than I do. And I still don't have the answers I feel I need.'

'I could take you to see Syodra. She has a talent with the sands, and that was how I found you.' Dayala squeezed his fingers. 'It would be easier . . .'

'Easier?'

'The sands at the edge of the Stone Hills are sometimes clearer, but,' Dayala shrugged, 'they are not always . . . cooperative. For what you seek, the forest sands could help.'

'Anything would help, I think.' Justen squeezed her fingers, his breath somehow constricted by her closeness and his desire. 'Is this nut ripe yet?'

He could feel the sadness in her.

'No . . . not yet.'

'What does it take to ripen it?' He tried to keep his tone light, knowing that he was scarcely deceiving her.

'A trial. Your trial.'

He nodded, not exactly surprised. How could she dare to love fully someone who could not stand up to the great forest on his own?

'It's not that. You have to understand – to feel – before you are ready.'

He understood all too well. Dayala, like it or not, loved him, and she did not want to push him before he was ready. But if he waited, would he ever be ready? It was already late summer, almost fall, and the cold winds would be blowing across the Gulf and chilling Recluce before long, while the first snows had already begun to fall on the Westhorns.

'Could we see Syodra soon?'

'Tomorrow.'

85

'Syodra, this is Justen. Can you help him?'

The older druid had silver hair longer than Dayala's, but the same green eyes, although her tunic and trousers were of a silvered brown. She stood beside a raised bed of sand that was enclosed within the roots of a lorken tree.

'I can show him what the sands say. He will have to find his own meanings.' Syodra smiled politely and inclined her head.

'I will leave you two. The sands work better without confusion.' Dayala touched Justen's hand and started down the path.

'What are your questions? Think deeply about them as you ask.' Syodra dipped her hands into the colorless sands held by the lorken roots.

'People call me a Shaper. All I want to do is to stop the spread of unbalanced chaos that is Fairhaven. How am I going to do that?'

The sands quivered and colored, and Justen watched as there appeared an image of darkness spreading across a white tower, blotting it out. Then the sands churned and the space turned a brilliant white.

'Darkness covering Fairhaven, replaced by light. What does that mean?'

Syodra remained silent, and Justen nodded to himself. 'My meanings, I know.'

He wet his lips, then asked, 'I'm supposed to be myself in order to succeed in this trial. How can I be that?'

The second image was clearer, that of Justen clasping a bloody sword and a skeleton to himself and bowing his head.

'That seems rather far-fetched, but there must be a truth there . . . somehow,' Justen said wearily. 'What would you show me?'

Syodra inclined her head and glanced toward the colored sands, which boiled on the table, then came to rest with an image of a red-haired woman dressed in black. Beside the picture was a flag bearing a crossed rose and blade.

'Are you saying that you're responsible somehow for Megaera becoming a founder of Recluce?'

The sands churned again, less violently, and the image of two broken black bracelets replaced the image of the banner.

Justen shook his head. 'I don't understand that one. I suppose it really doesn't matter. I'll either understand it or . . .' He shrugged. 'Why is it that I can't quite grasp things?'

The sands boiled again, and a single pillar of black appeared, separated by a low wall from a pillar of white. A chain of green led from the white pillar to the black, except that the links from each pillar ended in a sundered link lying on the smooth stones of the wall.

'Anything else?' The image of his clasping the bloody sword and the skeleton echoed in his thoughts, and he shivered.

'No. You have seen enough.' The silver-haired woman smiled sadly, then pointed toward the pathway.

Justen inclined his head, bowed slightly, and backed up several steps. He turned and eased past the huge black oak. In the root that had been grown into the shape of a bench, overlooking the natural pond, sat Dayala.

'Did you find what you wished?'

At the combination of huskiness and music in the druid's voice, Justen sighed and slowly sank onto the seat beside her.

'Not exactly. It's like everything else I find in Naclos. Everyone is so helpful, but half the time I don't understand the answers, at least not until later.'

Instead of looking at her, Justen idly reached for a long stem of grass. He shivered again at the image of the sword and skeleton.

Dayala's hand touched his.

'Sorry,' he apologized. 'I forget.'

'If you had real need of it,' she began.

'I know. I'm nervous. I keep thinking that if I knew more . . . but I never will. Not that much more. Can you tell me any more about the trial?'

Dayala shrugged nervously. 'You know more than most. You almost went through the trial the first time you met the great forest. That makes it both harder and easier. You know more, and you have more reason to fear. And you should not fear. You are strong enough, if you trust in yourself.'

'So when do I undertake this trial?'

'Whenever you wish. We will have to go back to Merthe.'

'Can we start tomorrow?'

Dayala nodded.

86

Justen sat on the edge of one of the narrow beds, looking across the darkness to Dayala, who unfolded the thin blanket provided by the guest house.

Somewhere he could hear Duvalla singing softly, and the warm odor of fresh-baked bread wafted through the half-open window. A few voices, only a few, for even the center of Merthe was far quieter than the edge of Rybatta, drifted to his ears, but he could not make out the words.

'There have to be some rules for this.' Justen's voice bore an exasperated tone. 'Otherwise, I could just go up on the overlook and say "Hullo, great forest" and walk away.'

'If the great forest accepted the trial, it would not be that simple. And if it did not, then it would not be a trial. But there are rules. You must enter the great forest on the path that leads downhill from the black rocks. You must always stay on that path until you reach the end, or until you can go no farther, and then you must return by the path to the road to Merthe.' Dayala took a deep breath, then added, 'I am bidden to tell you one other choice.'

'Bidden?'

'You must choose between the safe and the glorious. Those are the only choices open to you.'

'The safe and the glorious? What does that mean?'

Dayala looked at the floor.

Finally, Justen spoke again. 'When is the trial over?'

'When you set foot on the road to Merthe.'

'Proof of the will and the way, I guess.' Justen nodded, then frowned, shifting his weight on the narrow sleeping pallet. 'Dayala, you make it sound so simple, but nothing is that simple.'

'Simple does not mean easy. It is simple to walk across the Stone Hills to Naclos, but was it easy?'

'Why me? Why did you risk your life to get me? Why did you risk it again when I got tangled in the great forest?'

She looked down and did not speak.

Justen waited, sitting on the pallet, drumming his finger on the wooden frame.

'Justen, you see and you do not see. Would I tie my life to yours and then unnecessarily endanger you?' . . . **do love you** . . .

Justen saw tears in her eyes, and he could feel the combined sadness and frustration they represented. His own eyes burned. 'But why? Why did you tie us together?' He could barely choke out the words. 'You didn't have to . . . to rescue me.'

'Because you are a Shaper. What you . . . learn if you survive the trial, will let you . . . change the world . . . and no Shaper, the Angels decreed . . . can go unfettered.' Her words were more sobs than coherent phrases by the last syllable.

A cold chill settled over Justen, colder than the winds off the Northern Ocean.

87

Justen walked alone, wearing brown trousers, brown shirt, and his old black boots. He and Dayala had walked from Rybatta back through Viela to Merthe, where she waited. Now he walked toward the edge of the great forest, toward the overlook, trying not to think too much of what awaited him there above the great forest. Trying not to think of the druid who had held him like a lover, but who was not a lover, not yet. Trying not to think too deeply.

And he had once thought of Naclos as almost a park, where trees and animals and druids lived in peaceful harmony!

He stopped where the path split, one fork heading out into the grasslands, the other uphill through the low brush to the overlook. Then he turned and started uphill, wondering how many others had made the same choice and how many had headed into the grasslands as wanderers, forever exiled from the land of their birth.

Just before the hillcrest, in the clearing where they had spent that night more than who knew how many eight-days before, he took a last look toward the grasslands – out toward the Stone Hills, where everything had seemed so simple. Then he climbed the last few cubits and looked down on the forest.

There are two ways . . . the safe and the glorious . . . the safe and the glorious . . . the safe and the glorious.

Justen swallowed, then shook his head. Darkness damned if he would creep. Not for the Whites of Fairhaven or for the intertwined order and chaos of the great forest of Naclos.

The sun touched the western horizon, and Justen took another deep breath. He'd taken too many breaths, and not enough thought.

He frowned. The form of the trial was his, so long as he came to terms with the forest, so long as he walked the forest in full order and in body.

But there was no stipulation on how he accomplished that challenge. He grinned and pursed his lips, bracing his back against the smooth, dark stones, dark with order . . . and with blood.

He shook his head nervously, then looked across the great forest and into the golden dust of twilight.

He broadcast his challenge to the great forest.

I am! Here I am!

No . . . oh, be careful, Justen . . .

Even from afar, he could feel the clear, thin thoughts from Dayala, and he barely had time to push a vague sense of reassurance back toward her before the first lash of white spiked out of the twilight toward him.

He imagined himself as a stolid black iron anvil, a basic force of order, and the lash shattered on him, white blobs of chaos burning in the air around him . . . burning, yet not burning.

Before that first lash had shattered against his presence, two other, thinner, webs – one of white and one of black – circled around him, spinning tighter as if to crush the basic order within him. His breathing became labored, shallow.

Justen let himself become iron, white-hot iron just below the point of burning, radiating heat . . .

The twin spirals began to radiate heat back at him. Without moving his mouth, Justen grinned and let his iron core accept their heat, take it all, just as heat-greedy iron would always take that heat. Making that heat his, he took the first step down the path. The two pulses shriveled under his iron will, hard like the hands of the sometime-smith he was, even before he reached the lower bushes at the edge of the great forest.

I am Justen! I am me!

Crack . . .

A heavy branch thundered through the canopy above him, dropping almost at his feet and blocking the path.

Justen paused, then released the heat he had received from the second attack. The bark of the fallen branch smoldered, then flared, and he burned through the heavy wood as a blade would cut through a stick of cheese.

He set his left foot inside the forest, and his right. Sweat poured from his forehead, and dark shadows rose in the light he cast.

Cracckkk ...

Justen burned away the second trunk-sized limb before it reached him, and stepped deeper into the green gloom.

With each cubit, the path grew fainter, harder to discern, as if it were fading away with each step, but Justen put one foot, and then another on that disappearing path.

Another burst of power flared in the depths of the forest, and an enormous forest cat charged toward Justen, who flinched. The cat's teeth – each tooth larger than a belt knife – glinted like silver blades, and the extended claws dripped blood.

Justen concentrated on bending light, on bending force around himself, and the cat vanished.

A figure in dark gray stepped forward out of the shadows, holding a short shaft. Justen slowed, but the soldier with the shadowed face carried no blade, no shield, only the short length of oak barely a finger's thickness.

The souless eyes of the Iron Guard looked through Justen as she extended the order-tipped arrow. *You are of chaos, as surely as I am ... for death is chaos, and you have created death, not just by your own hand, but by the hands of hundreds ...*

He shivered, then looked through the figure with his order-senses, but only the tiniest pulses of energy appeared behind the image.

Take it ... it is yours, great Master of Chaos.

Master of Chaos? Never! He put up a hand as if to push the arrow away, knowing that the image had to be some gambit of the great forest's.

Take it ...

The Iron Guard hurled the arrow at his outstretched hand, and fire shot through his left arm as if a knife point had ripped open his arm from wrist to shoulder.

It is yours, Master of Chaos, returned to you ...

Justen squinted, trying to see beyond the image, but nothing stood there, and his eyes watered as he walked past the Iron Guard, his arm almost leaden with the pain.

A red-haired woman stood beside the path, beckoning, smiling ... except that her face was half-charred and the bones of her cheeks and forehead protruded from split and blackened flesh. Ashes clothed her.

Come with me, Justen. You loved me . . . and I suffered this because of your love . . .

No! Justen gritted his teeth. *I did not cause that suffering. Firbek did! You never loved me! You loved Gunnar.*

Her arms reached for him, and Justen threw up more shields, but a finger, impossibly long, reached out and seized his good right arm, and her nails burned into his forearm like white-hot iron spikes from his own forge. His flesh sizzled, and the stench of it filled his nostrils.

You loved me, and your love has killed me.

Justen trudged forward, his arms hanging limply, into the darker shadows that lay in his path.

A black-haired woman in blue leathers wheeled her horse, then halted the beast, steam rising from its nostrils, across the path. She pointed the shortsword at Justen's breast.

Come . . . great Bearer of Destruction. Join us.

Behind her, Justen could sense the rising hordes of the dead, could feel the white-cloaked figures. He stopped.

Join us . . .

Blood dripped from one arm, while the other bore four blackened spots, burned through shirt and skin and flesh, spots aching with the pain beyond pain.

Join us . . .

He looked dully at the horse soldier. What was he missing? His head throbbed. He could not lift his arms.

Join us . . . Great Deceiver . . . believer in your creed of order alone . . . order alone . . .

The sword touched his chest, burning away his shirt. Smoke rose into his nostrils.

Join us. You cannot escape.

Cannot escape . . . Cannot escape. The words rang through his ears and head . . . *cannot escape.*

Then Justen laughed and grasped the blade, ignoring the slashes across his palms. 'No! You join me. I accept you! You are my chaos, my evil. You are me!'

A dull wailing rose and fell . . . rose and fell . . . and Justen released the shields that had blocked him from the great forest and that had turned himself against himself.

He lay on the path, and before him growled the forest cat, not impossibly large but extraordinarily real – and less than ten cubits away.

Slowly, he staggered up, his slashed palms burning with sandy grit, his arms barely able to help him rise. He glanced at his left arm and the open gash that ran from wrist to elbow, and at the four charred depressions in his right forearm. He swallowed.

The cat growled.

'Go home, cat. I don't want to play anymore.'

He squinted. In the darkness, the path seemed to tilt before his eyes. He straightened and put one foot in front of the other.

'No light-damned forest is going to—'

The cat growled once more.

His teeth clenched tightly, Justen stared at the cat.

The cat's tail twitched, and one paw lifted.

'I won't . . . won't, won't!' Justen howled, and howling, drew together the patterns he had used but twice before, knowing now that he needed neither powder nor cannons, but only order and will, order and will . . . *order and will!*

Whsstttt . . .

The ground trembled, the forest monoliths swayed, and a single line of light flared from Justen's hand, passing over the giant cat and leaving no sign of the animal, no burned ashes, no screams. A pathway burned straight ahead for as far as Justen could see.

The echo of his order-chaos shift reverberated in his brain as if two mirrors reflected the sun back and forth down an endless corridor, a corridor stretching simultaneously deep into the earth and up into the heavens. And all along that corridor, the ancient Angels wept, and Ryba – she of the swift ships of Heaven – held her head, and the Demons of Light smiled before they drowned in the darkness of brilliant order.

And somewhere, a forest cat slunk off to lick its paws, to sleep away its terrible nightmare of an ancient Angel.

Justen coughed, then staggered forward, concentrating on one step at a time. He took a step and a deep breath, a step and a breath, a step and a breath . . .

How long it took, he did not know, save that when the grayness of dawn lightened the forest, he stepped onto the road to Merthe.

Dayala stood there, white-faced, red-eyed, scars on her arms
and across her face, blood oozing from her hands.

'That bad . . . ?'

He took a last step onto the road, and his knees crumpled.

Her arms were strong and gentle – like a lover's – as she lay
down with him and their tears and blood mingled and fell on
the dust.

88

'Zerchas was right, you know.' Beltar sipped a glass of wine
and glanced at the surf beyond the breakwater. 'Jera is too pretty
a place to destroy.'

Eldiren silently lifted his goblet in assent.

'We'll probably have to head back to Rulyarth soon, if this
mud ever clears from the roads. It's hard to believe we've been
here all summer, nearly half a year.'

'Sometimes . . . until we lose more troops taking some for-
saken crossroads that decides the war's not over. You don't see
that here in Jera.'

'War is ugly, Eldiren. Enjoy the benefits while you can. At
least you don't have to worry about Jehan slinking around and
reporting to Zerchas every time you take a piss.' Beltar took a
healthy swallow from his goblet.

'Jehan's not that bad. He probably doesn't have much choice.'

'With Zerchas, probably not. But I still have to worry about
him. Once we get on the road, it won't be so bad.' He lifted the
goblet again. 'They say the roads will freeze several eight-days
before the snows fall, if they fall at all.'

'Snows? It's barely harvest time.'

'The winter comes earlier here. We'll have to start prepara-
tions for the attack on Suthya . . . if we want to begin right after
the spring thaw.'

'They won't surrender?'

'Zerchas says not. The Suthyans want to haggle over every-thing. I think they'll knuckle under once the armies begin to chew up their countryside.'

'Like Sarronnyn? The Sarronnese still haven't knuckled under. They never will. They hate us.'

'Never say never, Eldiren.'

Eldiren toyed with the empty wine glass, holding it up and catching the light of one of the wall lamps in the clear crystal.

'They say you can scree in a good crystal goblet.' Beltar laughed. 'Ever tried it?'

'No, I cannot say that I have.' Eldiren glanced toward the half-empty bottle of red wine.

'See if you can look into Naclos. Maybe it would be easier with the goblet.'

'Naclos?'

'Try to find out what happened to that engineer.'

'He died.'

'Eldiren. Someone who twists order into chaos isn't going to get fried by one of your firebolts. Zerchas may think so . . . but we know better. Don't we?' Beltar smiled. 'Why don't you try to find him in Naclos? For me . . . rather than for Zerchas.'

'Beltar . . .'

'You don't have to explain. No one wants to commit suicide to make Zerchas happy. Light knows, I wouldn't. But try to scree for that engineer. I feel uneasy, like he just might be up to something.'

Eldiren set the goblet on the table before him, took a deep breath, concentrated, and looked at the mists forming in the space between the thin layers of crystal. The center of the goblet momentarily reflected the dark circles beneath his sunken and deep-set eyes.

The serving girl – daughter of the villa's former owner – turned and looked openmouthed at the twisting pillars of white and black that writhed in the mists of the goblet.

A soundless shriek split the twilight, and the goblet shattered, strewing glass fragments over the table. Eldiren pitched forward onto the table, and blood oozed across the linen. The serving girl sank into a heap in the doorway.

Beltar shook his head groggily before picking a glass splinter out of his cheek. 'Darkness . . .' He lifted Eldiren's face off the table linen, picked out the glass fragments, and then blotted the cuts with a cloth soaked in the wine.

After that, the White Wizard struggled to lay the younger man on the couch against the wall, where Eldiren breathed slowly, as if stunned by a blow to the head.

Beltar looked at his empty wine glass, then at the still half-full bottle. He shook his head and instead, reached for the last chunk of the now-stale bread left in the basket.

He did not have to wait long before the hooves clattered on the stones outside.

'Where is that mangy, lying excuse of a wizard?' Zerchas stepped over the still-prostrate body lying in the doorway. His eyes flicked from the glass and blood on the table to the unconscious man on the couch.

'Dead? That engineer's so dead that his latest feat has shattered every screeing glass in Candar. Engineer? He's no more an engineer than . . . Eldiren is a White Wizard.' Zerchas turned toward Eldiren. 'Too bad he's stunned, but it's easier this way. Lie to me, would he?'

Beltar stood. 'You didn't give him much choice, Zerchas. You really wanted me to protest, didn't you? So you could have an excuse to be rid of both of us.'

The serving girl shook her head, her eyes widening as she watched the two wizards.

'Words. All you do is talk.' Zerchas lifted his hands, and a line of white stars flashed toward Beltar.

White flame gouted from Beltar, meeting the crackling, spark-ling line of reddish-white stars in front of Zerchas. White ashes began to drop from nowhere onto the floor as the white flames pressed the stars closer and closer to Zerchas.

The walls shivered, and the rest of the goblets shattered.

The serving girl's mouth opened to scream, but her cry was soundless as she pressed her body against the wall.

For a moment, the white flame curled away from Zerchas, and the white star-points arrowed toward Beltar, but again, they shriveled into ashes as a wall of flame filled the doorway. Then only two piles of ashes remained in the doorway. One had been a White Wizard, the other a girl.

Beltar grinned widely, before his legs buckled under him.

89

The tall blond man stood on the black cliffs overlooking the Gulf of Candar, just inside the black walls that marched across the grass to mark the separation between Nylan and the rest of Candar.

He stood as he had often stood over the course of the past year, eyes closed, senses spread to the wind, searching. The knee-high tips of the browning grass brushed against his black trousers. He stood in the darkness of mid-evening, responding to a sense of . . .? What he had felt he did not know, only that he had sensed something and that he needed to respond.

From the west, the steel torrents of the high winds that scoured the Roof of the World rushed across southern Candar and dipped low across the waters between the island continent and the White-dominated bulk of Candar.

A thin shaft of twisted black and white seemed to lance into the heavens, and a roll of unseen thunder buffeted his skull.

The scream of agony – twisted black and white – staggered Gunnar, and unprepared for the violence of the sensation, he stumbled, tripping over a small boulder. His arms waved in an attempt to catch his balance, but his leg scraped the boulder and he plunged forward.

Slowly, he picked himself up, wiping away the blood from the cut on his forehead and wincing at the stinging in his leg. He could feel the bruise forming on his calf. But he smiled. 'Justen . . .'

Justen was alive, of that he was certain. That scream had been of agony and triumph. Justen was alive. But where? That was another question.

He limped along the path beside the dark stone wall. Perhaps Turmin had felt the twisting and turning of order and chaos and would know from whence it had come. Perhaps not. But Justen was alive.

90

Justen watched as Dayala walked back from her trees toward the front of the house. He smiled. **Lovely druid . . .**

She lifted her head and returned the smile. **Handsome druid . . .**

'I am a druid?'

'Anyone who undergoes your kind of trial is a druid.' Her eyes flickered to the white lines on her forearms. A gust of wind ruffled her hair, and she shivered, not entirely from the chill.

'Sorry,' he murmured, leaning forward and brushing her cheek with his lips. 'I never meant . . .'

'I know. And the great forest helps one heal.'

'No. You helped us heal.'

She shook her head. 'I knew how, but you had the strength for us both.'

Justen shrugged. 'Then show me.' He grinned.

Dayala touched his hands. 'You should know, but I will show you what you already know.'

'I'm waiting.' He grinned again.

'Look at yourself,' instructed Dayala.

Justen looked down, seeing brown cloth and the soft brown boots that were not leather.

'With your mind, your senses.' Dayala laughed softly.

Justen followed her instructions, somehow scanning his own body, seeing the linkages between muscle and bone, the tiniest bits of white-flecked chaos within himself, as within all living things, and the flow of order holding chaos at bay for now . . . until he was old and gray.

'See how you are. Now, watch this.'

Her senses enfolded his left arm, and he watched as the tiny flecks of chaos somehow *twisted*. They remained, but instead of being free-flowing, they were locked into order.

'You try on your other arm. You do not destroy chaos, but lock it into order so that it cannot escape.'

Justen struggled to replicate what Dayala had shown him. For all the ease with which she had locked the chaos behind order, he failed.

He tried again, scanning his body, seeing the small changes in the cascading order that flowed from point to point, from fingernails to fingers to arms. He shook his head.

She watched as he tried again . . . and again. The fourth time, he managed the *twist*, but not the lock. He looked at the patterns on his left arm, and tried once more.

By the time he matched her efforts, he was soaked with sweat. '. . . think you're in better shape than I am.'

She raised her eyebrows. 'You haven't finished.' Then she grinned.

Justen swallowed and tried extending the effect across the rest of his body. The sun had set by the time he finished.

'It is harder to do on yourself, but that is what is important.' Especially for me . . . and for you.

Justen nodded, understanding why, knowing that druids had only one consort – ever – for how could one go through the agony of merging souls more than once?

'Now you can meet the Ancient One, for she will not meet with anyone who has not faced the great forest and become a true druid.'

Justen studied himself again. On the outside, he looked no different . . . did he?

'People may say you look younger. Then again, they may not. You are younger than most who find the way from outside.'

Justen's thoughts were still on the ancient. 'Who is this Ancient One?'

'The one who can help you understand what you must do.'

Justen could not help but sense the sadness behind her words, and he turned and held her in the twilight, not wanting to question, only wanting to grasp the moment as her lips fell upon his.

L. E. MODESITT, JR.

91

Dayala pointed. 'There is the grove.'

'Why now?' **Just as we have truly found each other . . .**

'When the Ancient One knows, she knows. And because it is already late.'

Justen glanced toward the sky, unseen above the high forest canopy, reflecting that it was not even mid-morning. *Late for Candar; late for you; late for me. Gunnar always claimed that I was always late.* The sometime-engineer, sometime-druid, took a deep breath and squeezed Dayala's hand before letting go.

'I will be waiting,' she told him.

Although he had sensed that she would be waiting, her words were welcome reassurance, and he smiled.

In the middle of the grove, a single black lorken grew, twisted with age, yet no higher than Justen, and a silver-haired woman, garbed in pure silver, stood beside the tree.

At first glance, she looked scarcely older than Dayala, but Justen could sense the age behind the smooth skin, and he understood that youthfulness was a product of the lesson he had just learned from Dayala.

He inclined his head. 'I am here, Ancient One.'

'You have questions, young druid.'

'I would ask how the great evil done by the Masters of Chaos may be righted.'

'Why do you say that the actions of the Masters of Chaos are evil? Chaos is chaos, and order is order. Can you ask chaos to be order, and order to be chaos?' The woman's words were calm, measured, as if she stated the most obvious of facts.

'But . . .' protested Justen '. . . is there no meaning to order? Is there no purpose to life? Why do so many struggle to put order in their lives? Even under your Legend, the ancient Angels fled Heaven.'

'Your questions ask for the meaning of life, as if the ancient Angels had written the answers in stone as a riddle for those who came after to find and unravel. Neither the world nor the Angels have a purpose. The world exists. It needs no meaning. Men and women need purposes.'

'But what about order and chaos? They exist,' said Justen.

'Indeed they exist, as does the world. But thinking beings are the ones who ascribe values to order and chaos. Why does a person do anything?'

'Because he, or she, wants to.' Justen frowned. 'Or has to.'

'And if that person refuses?'

'Someone could use force.'

'Can that person move the muscles of his or her body?'

'You're saying that every person chooses to act. That's cruel. What if children, or a family, will starve or be tortured?'

'That is still a choice.'

'Are there are no higher values? Is there is no difference between a person who serves good and one who serves evil? Or between a person who is coerced into unwise acts and one who does them willingly?'

'Of course there is a difference. But not to the world – only to thinking beings.'

Justen paused. 'Then if the world does not care, why should not a person do whatever is pleasing? For what purpose should anyone try to do good deeds? The world does not care.'

'Either selfishness or selflessness will destroy a person. If a soul is too selfish, thinking only of personal ends and desires, and should she live long enough, none will support her and many will try to tear her down. To survive, one must become so strong and so heartless that neither love nor affection could or would desire to reach such a person. And in the end, such a being is no longer a person, but a soulless machine like the engines on your black ships.

'A person who is too selfless is blown hither and yon in the gusts of others' needs, for there are always more needs than even the most charitable of humans can address. Should a person be strong enough to address the most worthy and pressing of needs, then she will either bleed to death from the demands upon her or lose all warmth in a mechanical quest to fulfill the world's needs. Then she becomes so selfless that she, too, is no more than a selfish soul in the quest of selflessness.

'Thus, a person who would live a meaningful life must always struggle between selfishness and selflessness, always questioning. When she gives up the struggle, she allows others to determine the meaning of her life. She may not even be aware that she has relinquished the struggle, for those others may indeed represent a belief in something she finds better and higher, and she will follow their simple rules with great relief. They may be the rules of the Angels, the Demons of Light, the Black Brotherhood, or the White Council. Yet we have observed that most humans who give up that struggle question why life has no meaning, especially when troubles befall them.' The thin lips turned slightly at the corners.

'You're not terribly cheerful. Your philosophy doesn't offer a great deal of comfort.'

'You did not ask for comfort. You asked for wisdom. Wisdom is seldom comforting, because much of what humans find comforting is nothing more than illusion.'

For a time, Justen looked past the ancient but unlined face. Finally, he swallowed. 'Is it good for the Chaos Masters to control all Candar?'

'You are placing values on such actions. When you ask such a question, you have already decided that for the Chaos Masters to absolutely control Candar is bad. But do you ask whether it is good for the Order Masters to control absolutely Recluce and the oceans around Recluce?'

'Then are you saying that such control is an illusion? When I have seen cities fall and soldiers die?'

The woman shook her head. 'The illusion is that control by either is good. Under the Balance, total domination by order or by chaos can only lead to death of one kind or death of another.'

'You mean that we should allow chaos into our lives?'

'That, too, is an illusion. Chaos exists in all lives. So does order.'

Justen sighed. 'What are you telling me? That what I seek is an illusion? That it is meaningless to seek order?'

'I said no such thing, young druid.'

'I'm not a druid.'

'You are a druid. Whether you accept that remains to be seen.'
She smiled. 'You wish to halt what you see as evil in the spread
of chaos from Fairhaven. So do we. Such a great deed is not
possible unless the Balance is considered. Have you asked what
makes such chaos possible?'

'Often.' Justen shrugged.

'And?'

Justen shrugged again.

'Can chaos be created?' asked the ancient Angel.

'I don't think so.'

'You are correct. In some places, order must spring from
chaos. Here, chaos must spring from order.'

'So what must be done to reduce the power of chaos?'

'That is up to you. You know how, but you must find the
will and the way.' The ancient Angel smiled. 'That began with
the trial.'

'How?'

'You could have left Naclos as a child, remembering nothing,
or you can leave as a adult, remembering all, and possessing the
knowledge and commitment to do what must be done.'

'Why couldn't I have just left?'

'You are still barely beyond being a child. You have difficulty
accepting faith . . . so I will use the tool necessary for children.
Try to leave. Go! Walk away from me.'

Justen started to turn, but his legs would not move. Concentrating his will within himself, he lifted one leg . . . but he could
not turn and set it down heavily.

His eyes saw the darkness, and the chaos, within the ancient
orbs of the Angel, but even as the realization of that antique
madness clawed at his thoughts, he stood rooted, unmoving.

'That is why you will leave as a knowing adult. That is why
you faced the trial of the forest . . . and risked losing all memories
of Naclos. And Dayala risked losing her life for you. You might
remember that as well.'

The pressure around him relaxed, and Justen held back a
shudder.

'You know what must be done.'

Justen nodded slowly.

'Dayala will help you prepare. There is no other way.'

Justen looked into the power of the Angel's eyes and saw again the deep wells, one of white, one of black, each tinged with green. The depth of that power made Gunnar's control of the storms look like a child's game, his own recent understandings like a fumbler's beginnings at Capture.

'Do you understand?'

'Not everything, but enough, I hope.'

'So do we.'

'Why me?'

'We cannot save you, nor can one people save another. Salvation must always come from the soul and the self; it can never be forced . . . as you will discover.

'You must find the way and the will, and your journey began with the trial. That was only the first. There will be more and greater ones, in Recluce and beyond. Tomorrow, or the next day, you and Dayala will begin the trip to Diehl. That is the next step on your journey. Remember, too, that there are always two ways – the safe and the glorious, and for the glorious, there is a far higher price.'

Justen glanced away from the deep eyes, suddenly unable to focus on the brilliance of that combination of order and chaos. He studied the dark tree by her shoulder, and when his eyes refocused, she was gone.

He walked slowly from the grove, his feet heavy, feeling that somehow they were already on the road to Diehl.

92

The boat glided downstream with only occasional guidance from Dayala. Justen sat on the midships seat, watching the light play over her face as she kept the craft in the center of the unseen currents.

'Did the ancient tell you why we had to come to Diehl?'

'How else will you return to Recluce?'

'I don't want to leave you.'

'We have talked of this before. You cannot leave Recluce, if that is what you truly choose, without first returning. If you choose to return, I will be here. I will always be here for you.'

Always . . .

Justen swallowed at the poignancy of the shared thought and reached out to grasp her free hand, the one not on the mounted oar that served as sweep and tiller.

In silence they passed a grassy stretch on the west bank, where a single house, grown by two oaks, sat in a small clearing.

A girl on her knees in a garden patch waved, and Justen waved back.

'How much farther to Diehl?'

'At least another half-day.'

He squeezed Dayala's fingers again.

As the boat left the clearing and the house behind, Justen let his senses drift beneath the surface of the water, catching the flashes of light that were the fish, or a bottom-feeding turtle, and, nearer to the bush-cloaked banks, an occasional otter.

'It's a lot more pleasant than walking.'

'Even boating has its drawbacks.' Dayala eased the craft toward the eastern bank to center it back in the main current.

'Walking through the Stone Hills doesn't?'

A hard pulse of reddish white glimmered deep beneath the dark surface off to the right of the boat.

'Oh . . .' murmured Dayala.

'Oh?' Justen sat up straighter.

The water exploded into a white froth, and the boat rocked as a pair of jaws as long as Justen himself ripped into the air, followed by a massive gray-green body covered with mossy scales. When the huge water lizard dropped back into the water, the second wave nearly capsized the boat, soaking both Justen and Dayala even as they had to brace themselves to keep from being thrown into the water.

Justen grabbed for the sword he had long since left in the Stone Hills, then snatched the spare oar, knowing it would not do much good against the jaws he had seen.

Two eyes as big as water bottles fixed on the boat and its occupants, and an aura of chaos and hatred oozed over the river like a clammy rain. The water lizard, easily twice the length of the boat, churned toward them.

Remembering his ordeal at the edge of the great forest, Justen reached again for order and will, bending them toward the giant reptile.

Whhssstttt . . .

A line of white light flared from the lizard toward him. The water roiled, the boat pitched, and Justen raised his hand, a hand that seemed to move impossibly slowly, to send a single line of darkness back along the white line until it passed through the giant lizard.

But the white light swept over Justen, and his head seemed to split into fragments even as the echo of his order-chaos shift reverberated in his brain and as the two mirrors within him reflected the sun back and forth down an endless corridor, a corridor stretching simultaneously deep into the earth and up into the heavens.

Then the darkness struck him into the bottom of the violently rocking boat.

The sun was low when Justen felt a soft hand on his aching forehead and cool air across his burning cheeks. 'Oh . . .'

The boat rocked gently and he shivered, feeling chilled by the breeze that swept across his damp shirt. He opened his eyes and coughed. The deep gouges on the planks confirmed that the river lizard had not been imaginary. He shuddered again, wondering if he would ever be able to accept the strangeness of Naclos, where everything seemed so peaceful on the surface – just like the river itself.

His head turned, searching for Dayala, feeling that she were somehow absent, not there to his mind.

'I'm here. Someone has to guide the boat, at least some of the time.'

Justen tied to lever himself up, but his legs refused to move. 'My legs . . .' He looked at them, unable to see any wounds. He called on his order-senses, using the pattern that Dayala had taught him, but he could sense nothing, as if he were suddenly order-blind. 'I can't see. I mean . . .'

'It's all right. It's just a mind bruise, and it will pass.'

'Mind bruise?'

'That's how the water lizards stun their prey. You have to maintain a barrier, a shield.'

'For how long? Days? Seasons?' Justen shivered again, not

just from the cold, although the late afternoon sun should have warmed him. His head still ached.

Dayala had slipped behind him and wrapped herself around him, her warmth lifting the chill. 'Just for a while. It never lasts more than a day. You might have a headache for longer.'

He blinked, then rubbed his eyes, gratefully accepting her warmth. 'Every time I think I've learned something about this place, I run into another nasty surprise.'

'You do have a habit of attracting them. I haven't seen a water lizard that big in a long time.'

'Why me?'

'Because you are a living fountain of order, and order in that quantity draws chaos, dear man.' She slipped back to the rear of the boat and reclaimed the tiller.

'You mean this will happen to me all the time?' Justen groaned.

'No. It won't even happen after a while in Naclos.'

'Oh? Pardon me if I sound skeptical. What happened to our giant friend?'

'The lizard? The turtles and the carp are having a feast.'

'Thank you.'

'I didn't do anything. I'm not sure I could have. You stunned it, and it drowned.'

Justen took a deep breath. His legs were beginning to tingle. Probably a good sign, he supposed.

Dayala eased the tiller, and the boat lurched. 'We don't mind the ones that get as big as cats . . . but that one was older than Diehl, I think.' She shivered.

So did Justen, recalling the chaos light emanating from the lizard, a force stronger than that of any mere wizard. And he had thought that Naclos was so peaceful.

'Your dangers are more obvious.'

Justen rubbed his forehead, then realized that Dayala was repeating his gesture. 'Oh . . . my headache or yours?'

'Some of each, I think. You'll know in a while.'

Justen took another deep breath and looked at the dark water.

'We won't make Diehl tonight,' Dayala said.

'Somehow, I figured that out.'

Dayala laughed, and Justen reached out for her free hand.

93

Dayala guided the boat around the last turn in the river and toward the the single long pier in the harbor. Except for an uncrewed fishing boat, the pier was empty, though it was long enough for at least two oceangoing ships.

Standing in the prow, Justen held the line in one hand, waiting until Dayala's deft motion with the sweep propelled the flat-bottomed boat close enough to the pier for him to scramble up. The pier smelled of seaweed and barnacles and long use.

After he had climbed up the slimy wooden ladder and tied the boat at the shoreward end of the pier, Justen reached down and took the packs Dayala handed him. Then he extended his hand for her. When she came onto the pier, his lips brushed her cheek. As he straightened, his hand rubbed his forehead.

'Your head still aches?'

'It comes, and it goes,' Justen admitted. 'Less now.'

Her eyes focused on him for a moment.

'That feels better. Thank you.'

'I do not like headaches, either.'

Justen laughed and swung his pack onto his back.

Behind the long pier, of stone and timber, was the port-master's single-story office, of smoothed and polished wood, roofed with clay slates. A chandlery, identified by a sign bearing crossed candles circled with rope, stood at the corner of two streets behind the port-master's office.

A brisk breeze whipped off the bay and across the pier, lifting sand and grit past the couple's legs as they walked toward the chandlery.

'Where are we going?'

'To Murina's. Her guest house is on the other side of Diehl, the side closest to the great forest.'

Justen nodded.

Two traders in purple trousers and gold tunics stood under the overhanging eaves shading the front of the chandlery. The man had a grizzled beard, while the woman's hair was shorter than Justen's, although her face was lined and she bore the white shadows of chaos and age within her.

'Another damned-handsome druid,' muttered the woman. 'Never saw such standoffish men. Shame.'

'The women are beautiful creatures, too,' added the bearded trader. 'But you can keep them both. I'd rather not be turned into a tree, thank you.' He laughed.

So outsiders saw them both as a druids? Did he really look that way, or was it his brown clothing?

They walked past a tavern, proclaimed by a sign bearing a silver bowl and an unfamiliar cooking odor that filled Justen's nostrils. Heavy, almost rancid. Yet the smell was familiar. He frowned. Grilled lamb? But he had never thought of lamb as a heavy odor.

He pursed his lips, recalling that he had eaten no meat since he had come to Naclos. Nuts, cheeses, even eggs of various sorts, but not meat.

At the next corner, Dayala took a right-forking road that seem to angle away from the harbor. Justen followed, still drawing in the feel of the town, trying to explain to himself why it felt different from Rybatta and Merthe, or from any of the others in Naclos.

He glanced at a row of brick shops – the middle one shuttered against the strong afternoon sunlight – and then at the houses beyond the shops; they were more like those of Kyphros; heavy-walled and blank-faced, presumably arranged around a central garden courtyard.

Diehl seemed orderly enough, and there was no sign of chaos whatsoever in the area. So what bothered him about the place?

He rubbed his chin and looked sideways at Dayala. Did she feel the same way?

'Yes. You should know that.'

He should? Then he nodded, grinned, and shook his head. Part of the uneasiness he felt was not his at all, but hers, and he was still having trouble getting used to their overlapping feelings.

Shallow – that was the word that described Diehl. Shallow.

The orderliness of the town – compared to the Balance between order and chaos that existed in the great forest – seemed without any real foundation. Would Recluce seem that way, too? He pulled at his chin, then readjusted his pack. Much of the weight in the pack consisted of small items such as the box Dayala had made for him, destined for Recluce, and included a smaller box that Dayala had insisted he take for Gunnar as well as several others to give as he saw fit. Certainly, one would be for Altara.

Unlike Rybatta, Diehl was compact, with the houses almost crowded together – until they suddenly reached the edge of the town.

Justen looked back. They had scarcely come a full kay, yet not two hundred cubits ahead, the first line of the giant trees began.

Nestled almost beneath those trees stood Murina's guest-house, at the edge of the great forest that began just to the northeast of Diehl proper. The guest-house, as all proper-guest-houses, suspected Justen, was grown from the oaks that formed each wall.

He had not realized that he was holding his breath until he released it. Then he laughed, sensing that part of his relief was Dayala's as well.

They almost skipped up the stone-flagged path to the front archway, where Dayala jingled the bells that hung on a woven strap.

'Coming . . .'

Murina, like virtually all druids, had silver hair, but like Yual, her eyes were brown rather than green. Unlike Dayala, she was tiny, coming barely to Justen's shoulder.

'Dayala . . . it has been a time.'

'It has. This is Justen.'

Justen bowed. 'I am pleased.'

Murina laughed. 'Not so pleased as I am to see you. I like Dayala, and it is clear that you are special to her.'

Justen flushed, surprised at the directness, then flushed again as he felt Dayala's reaction.

'May you always feel so.' The guest-house keeper laughed softly once more. 'Please come in. Shersha will show you to your room while I finish my baking, if you do not mind.

Then perhaps you will join me for some juice on the terrace.'

Dayala and Justen nodded.

A tiny and solemn-faced girl stood in the hallway inside, beyond the archway.

'Shersha, you remember Dayala? This is Justen.' Murina gestured toward him, and Shersha inclined her head. 'They will have the big room above the terrace, the one with the window on the garden.'

'That's the best,' Shersha affirmed. Then she turned and led them around a corner, up a wide staircase with low steps and to a hallway with another archway.

'I hope you will like it.' The girl's voice was shy.

Justen stepped through the hangings in the archway. Although modest, the room had a window overlooking the rear garden. There was but one bed, double-sized. He looked at the bed and then at Dayala. He could feel her blush even before he saw the color rise to her cheeks. 'We like it,' Justen choked, trying not to laugh.

'Thank you, Shersha. Tell Murina that it is perfect.'

'We are glad that you are pleased.' Shersha inclined her head and turned to go.

'It is perfect,' Justen echoed. 'I hope we will be able to stay for a while.'

'Mother would be pleased.'

From the archway, they watched the clear-eyed girl skip down the hallway. Justen lowered the hangings and slipped his arms around Dayala.

Her lips found his, and they moved toward the wide bed.

94

Late afternoon had come before Justen and Dayala rose and washed and dressed and descended to the terrace, where Shersha

escorted them to a table with four chairs, then returned with
three large brown mugs.

Murina pulled a chair up to the table and looked at Justen.
'Much has been said about you. I can see why.' She grinned.

Justen blushed.

'You're modest. I understand why Dayala likes you, and that
is good.'

Justen felt once again that as much had not been said as said,
but he answered politely, 'I still feel somewhat like a child here.
But compared to all of you, I am. So I suppose that's to be
expected.'

'Not exactly a child, is he?' Murina raised her eyebrows and
glanced at Dayala.

'No. He knows more than he thinks he does ... and more
than either I or the ancients expected.' Her hand crept under
the table and squeezed Justen's.

'And less, I suspect,' Justen added wryly, his eyes following the
flight of a brilliant green bird, with a black head and a yellow
beak, that swooped past the corner of the terrace and lit on the
edge of the kitchen roof below.

'I see my friend has arrived.'

'He comes often?' asked Justen.

'Every day before twilight. He sings a song or two and waits
for a reward.'

'And you reward him?'

'Shersha usually does. I think he really sings for her, but I like
his songs.'

The green bird cocked his head, then dipped it twice, as if
bowing to the audience, and began to sing – a short series of
notes somewhere between silvered bells and the golden-strung
notes of the singer called Werlynn. Justen listened and felt almost
disappointed when the two short songs were done.

Shersha appeared on the terrace and tossed some berries
toward the songbird, who caught one on the wing and then
returned within moments to scoop the others off the terrace stones.

'Can you tell us what has happened in Sarronnyn?' asked
Justen.

'The traders say that the Whites of Fairhaven hold all of
Sarronnyn and that come spring, they will attack Suthya.'

'That would leave just Southwind and Naclos.'

'They will never come here.'

Justen nodded. 'What about Southwind?'

'Southwind could fall. We could do nothing outside of the great forest.'

'That's something I still don't quite understand.'

'Most peoples have rejected the Legend and the truth behind it.' Murina shrugged. 'Do we have armies? How could we help?'

'Yet no one here fears Fairhaven.'

'What is there to fear? Their wizards are so unbalanced that any attempt to use chaos in the great forest would destroy them.' The guest-house holder smiled at Justen. 'The same would be true of your Order Wizards.'

'I found that out.'

Shersha carried out a long loaf flanked with a line of cut cheese and several pearapples. She set the platter in the middle of the table.

Justen raised his eyebrows at the evidence of the knife.

'Some of us can use knives,' said Murina with a smile.

'Just those of you with brown eyes?'

'It helps, but Trughal is a green-eyed smith.'

Dayala shook her head with a half-smile, then reached for a slice of cheese.

'Sit down, child.' Murina gestured to Shersha, who promptly perched on the fourth chair and reached for a pearapple.

After finishing the piece of cheese and breaking off a corner of the loaf, Dayala turned to Justen. 'Tomorrow you should talk to the traders, and I will talk to Diera. She is the . . . port-master.'

'Diera knows everything,' volunteered Shersha.

'Not quite everything,' corrected Murina with a smile.

Justen took a large chunk of the warm bread. 'I suppose I should try to find out what else is happening in the world. Not that I expect things to have changed very much.'

'They never do,' said Murina. 'But enjoy the bread. Warm bread is better than cold gossip.'

Dayala nodded, and Justen took another mouthful of the warm and crusty bread.

95

'There's no point in attacking this late in the year.' Beltar glanced out the window of the coach. 'Let some time pass, and let the Suthyans feel some pressure. Anyway, before we deal with Suthya, we need to convince the Sarronnese that we're not White devils.'

Eldiren shifted his weight on the padded cushion and rubbed his forehead, massaging the thin white scar above his right eyebrow. 'The Sarronnese will be as bad as the Spidlarians. Worse, much worse.'

'Anyone can be convinced . . . somehow.'

'Like you convinced Zerchas, perhaps,' responded Eldiren dryly.

'Well, yes. If all else fails.'

'Aeee . . .' A dull thump followed the cry, and the coach slowed.

Beltar yanked open the door in time to see a mounted figure spurring his horse up the long, sloping hillside. The coach driver's body slumped limply against the roof of the coach, an arrow through his chest. The guard beside the driver struggled with the reins.

Two squads of White lancers raced up the hill in pursuit of the attacker, but the attacker seemed to be widening the gap.

As the guard wrestled the coach to a halt, Eldiren looked at Beltar. 'I think we have a great deal of convincing yet to do.'

'Bah! They'll learn.'

Eldiren's eyes followed the White lancers, who had continued to fall behind the single rider. 'When we can't even catch one man?'

'You should talk.' Beltar lifted his arms. A huge fireball arced from the White Wizard across the hillside, landing on the fleeing rider. Fire splayed in all directions, and smaller fireballs bounced downhill. One struck the leading lancer. A quick scream, and two pyres of greasy smoke dotted the hillside, each one consisting of both horse and rider.

Beltar grinned.

'Was that really necessary?' asked Eldiren.

'I couldn't let him get away with it.'

Eldiren looked back toward the charred lancer and mount, and at the greasy smoke swirling into the gray sky. 'I'm sure our lancers understand that you couldn't let him get away with it.'

'Stop carping. You couldn't have done anything.'

'You are so right, Beltar. Unlike some, I do know my limitations.'

The stocky White Wizard glanced away from Eldiren and at the guard. 'Get him down, and let the healer look at him.'

'He's dead, Ser.'

'Then get another driver. We still have to get to Rulyarth.'

'Yes, Ser.'

Eldiren refrained from the smallest of headshakes.

96

'Justen, tomorrow a Bristan trader will dock here at Diehl. The ship will take you home to Recluce.'

'Recluce isn't home. Not now.'

Her smile was sad. 'You cannot say that until you return there. And if you do not, it will always be home. Home must be relinquished at the hearth, not at the ends of the earth.'

She lifted a leather bag and set it on the bed. 'These are for you.'

'What does the bag have to do with the trader? Or my leaving?'

Dayala eased the stones onto the coverlet.

'Why, Dayala? These are worth a fortune . . . anywhere.'

'The ancient said that you would need them on your quest.'

'Is that just another way to bribe me to leave?'

'That is unfair, Justen. She has no need to bribe.'

'To make me feel better?'

'I do not think she values you that cheaply.'

'Then why?'

'Because you are powerful, more powerful than you know. You will twist anything to do what you think is correct. These will help make that twisting easier on everyone else.'

Justen's face took on a puzzled expression.

'I still do not understand all that you do,' Dayala went on, 'but you make things from the parts of the earth, from the metals and other substances. If you must build everything yourself, you will twist more than if you can buy parts or metal.'

Justen paced around the table, trying to grasp the meaning behind Dayala's words. 'If I make things myself, it creates more . . . disorder . . . more chaos?'

'Of course.' Dayala smiled as if what she said were so obvious as not even to be a question.

He shook his head.

'Justen, think of it this way. If you buy your iron from Yual, he has already made it in the most orderly manner. While you have greater skill with the forge, you do not have his skill in extracting the iron, and you will disrupt the earth and the forest more in making your iron . . .'

'I understand.' Justen smiled wearily. 'But the ancient gives me too much credit.'

'Not enough, I think. And there is another reason, a selfish one.' Dayala slipped the stones back into the bag.

'Oh?'

'Having such resources may keep you from being too delayed in what you must do.'

'You want me to come back?' He shook his head, feeling the pain she felt. 'Sorry . . . stupid question. But why can't you come with me?'

Her lips tightened.

'I don't want to leave,' he protested.

'You cannot stay. Not now.'

'Will I ever be allowed to stay? I'm not a druid. Isn't this just a kind way of forcing me to leave?'

'Kind?' her voice broke.

Justen watched as the tears flowed, as her entire fabric of order shivered somehow, not losing itself, but ... suffering. Then his arms were around her.

'How can she do this?' Justen's eyes burned. 'She's no Ryba ... no Angel. There isn't a drop of warmth or kindness—'

'Order is not kind, nor is the Balance ... and you are a druid.'

He swallowed, recalling the ancient Angel's words: '*You did not ask for comfort. You asked for wisdom.*' Yes, he had asked for wisdom. He had asked what had to be done to reknit the world into one fabric. He had not asked to be separated from the one being ...

'We have the hope of a long life, Justen. But would you be happy living it if all Candar were under the White Wizards and all the oceans under the hand of the Black Mages?'

'No.'

Dayala smiled sadly, then spoke into his silence. 'Tomorrow you will just walk down to the dock. Diera will tell the captain it is our wish that you be transported to Recluce. The Bristans stop at Nylan on most of their trips, anyway.' Dayala looked toward the harbor, avoiding Justen's eyes. 'We also have a cargo of lorken, which will be worth far more to them in their trade at Recluce.'

Justen nodded. From what he had heard, most woodworkers outside of Recluce preferred not to use lorken, despite its strength, its deep, black color, and its tight grain.

'We have tonight.' He took her hand.

'We have tonight.' Her fingers grasped his hungrily.

97

The black trousers and shirt felt strange to him as he walked hand in hand with Dayala down to the stone pier in the harbor.

'You have the stones?'

Justen nodded.

'Try to save some of them for as long as you can. I cannot tell you why, but my feelings say that you will need them.' Dayala squeezed his hand.

'I trust your feelings.'

'Then trust them enough to know that you will return.'

He squeezed her hand back, and they walked to the end of the pier, where the sole ship was moored. Justen could sense that the engine was cold, but the crew moved across the scrubbed decks with a sense of purpose.

The Bristan ensign – the sun above an ice floe – flew at the jack-staff, and emblazoned on the upper part of the ship's stem in gilt letters was the name *Nyessa*. The railings were recently varnished, and the brasswork glittered.

They stopped opposite the plank to the ship, and Justen gave Dayala a last embrace, a last kiss, a long sharing of salty lips and tears. Their fingers lingered for an instant after the kiss, until Justen finally stepped away and shifted the pack on his back. Then he walked up the gangway.

'You the honored passenger?' asked the squat man in the green jacket.

'Justen.' The druid-engineer inclined his head. 'I understand that the port-master arranged my passage.'

'Bikelat, second mate,' replied the officer. 'Oh, she arranged it all right. Captain Gaffni'd take you to Hamor for the cargo she transferred.' The officer glanced from Justen to Dayala, who remained on the pier, and back to Justen. 'Don't know what you did, and don't know as I'd want to.' He paused. 'Need to stand back, Ser. We were just waiting for you.'

As Justen stepped aside and then moved along the rail, from where he looked down at Dayala, the officer called, 'Forward sheet up! Let's go!'

Two hefty sailors, a man and a woman, cranked up the gangplank while canvas billowed out overhead.

'Lines away!'

Justen locked eyes with Dayala, and for a moment, they seemed together.

'Wouldn't be leaving a lady like that, fellow.' The second shook his head as he came up beside Justen.

'Not exactly my choice, either.' Justen's throat was thick as he watched the green water widen between them. **Good-bye . . . love . . .**

Her fingers touched her lips. **I am . . . with you always . . .**

'You're one of them, aren't you? You're talking to her . . .' The second stepped back.

Justen forced a rueful smile. 'I was born and raised on Recluce, trained as an engineer.'

'Darkness save . . . someone,' muttered the officer. 'Glad they like the captain.'

Justen frowned as the man walked away toward the poop deck, where the captain supervised the piloting out of the bay. Then he watched the pier until Dayala was less than a spot on a finger of stone.

Not until after the *Nyessa* cleared the twin hills and the channel between did smoke begin to stream from the funnels. Shortly thereafter, the heavy engines began to turn the paddles and the Bristan trader chugged northeast across an almost glassy sea.

Justen climbed to the poop and stood by the fantail, still glancing back, still sensing the twined strand of . . . something . . . that led back to Naclos. Was this what made him a druid – that he loved and was bound to one? Or was it something deeper? Or was he a druid at all?

Finally, he turned to study the sea ahead, its swells beginning to grow choppy as a breeze freshened out of the southwest.

98

Justen kept one hand on the poop railing as the *Nyessa* plowed into a wave that buried the bowsprit. Green water gushed down the deck, and spray flared close to where Justen stood. In the early morning light, despite the noise of the wave, the ship seemed quieter.

Of course, Justen nodded to himself. The paddles were silent, and the steam engine was cold. While the wind held, the captain didn't need to burn the coal.

'Always get a good wind coming out of Diehl,' observed the second, pausing beside Justen for a moment, his long blond hair slicked back by wind and spray. 'Most times, anyway.' He glanced at the blacks Justen wore. 'Don't see how . . . you a druid and one of those mage types. Didn't know anyone could be both.'

'I'm not sure you can. I started out as an engineer . . . smith type. Somehow I ended up in Naclos to avoid the Whites in Sarronnyn.'

'Talk about going from the flame to the forge.' The second whistled. 'Bet Wesser would like to get you looking at his engines! You know engines?'

Justen nodded. 'Most types.' How long had it been since he had dealt with steam and turbines and screws and shafts and condensers? Though more than a year, he still thought of himself as an engineer. But was he? Could someone who had sensed the great forest and who remained tied to a druid – perhaps was a druid – be an engineer?

As he thought of Dayala, her warmth, her quiet depth, a wave of sadness poured across him. He pursed his lips. He suffered two exiles of sorts: one from Recluce, one from Naclos. Yet he was scarcely cheered to return to Nylan, except to see Gunnar, Elisabet, and his family. What could he tell Altara, or the Council? That their pursuit of order was almost as wrong to the ancients as Fairhaven's pursuit of chaos?

Who would believe him? Yet how could he lie?

His stomach growled.

The edge of another wave spilled across the forecastle, and below on the damp deck, two sailors re-coiled lines, ignoring the thin sheet of water, while another surefootedly clambered up the mainmast. Across the poop deck, another sailor, a heavy-shouldered woman, took a hammer to a metal pin on a winch crank.

Justen's stomach growled again. He straightened and headed for the crew's mess, located under the bridge, where it took up a space not much bigger than two of the cabins like the one Justen shared with the third mate. Two short tables were bolted to the floor, as were the backless benches. The grooves in the table held racks containing deep baskets.

Breakfast was dried fruit – pearapples and peaches – biscuits, and tea that slopped from a metal pitcher with each lurch of the *Nyessa*. Justen sat in one corner, where he could wedge himself between the bench and the bulkhead.

Two sailors sat at the other table, and the third mate lurched into the mess and sat across from Justen. 'Rough weather seems to suit you, Ser Justen.'

'It's not too bad, not so long as I'm careful how I walk.' Justen shrugged and poured tea into one of the battered gray mugs. After trying to crunch a biscuits and feeling the hard wedge slice at his gums, he dunked the biscuit in his tea mug.

'See that you found the only way to eat cook's biscuits. Bloodied my gums on them more than once,' observed the third officer cheerfully.

The two sailors eased quietly out of the mess, but the woman nodded behind the third's back and shook her head sadly.

'Wonderful day. Clear, breezy. Makes a man glad to be upon the sea.'

Justen nodded and reached for a pearapple. It tasted smoky and salty, but he ate it anyway, reflecting that it was far tastier than gray cactus.

'Captain's got us running right before the wind. Master of using the wind, the old man is.' The words spewed out with fragments of biscuit.

Justen smiled faintly and took another sip of tea.

III

THE ORDER-CHAOS
WAR

99

The sandy-haired wizard dashed through the doors of the engineering hall, looking from right to left and back until he spied the tall, dark-haired engineer. 'Altara! He's safe. He's on his way into port.'

The chief engineer set down the calipers. 'You can finish that, Nurta.' She walked around the tool forge and toward Gunnar. 'How soon?'

'I think it's the ship off the channel. I think.'

'I'll meet you there.' Altara nodded at Gunnar. 'Go on. He is your brother.'

Gunnar dashed back through the hall and out into the bright summer sun, settling into a quick walk down the hillside as he judged that the Bristan ship – the ice-floe ensign made that clear – had not yet passed the outer breakwater.

There was something odd about Justen, that he could tell even from a distance – some sort of fine order-thread that seemed to stretch back toward Candar. He grinned. But then, there had always been something odd about Justen.

Gunnar walked more quickly, knowing that he would be on the pier before the ship arrived.

100

Justen squinted into the sun, watching the pier. The *Nyessa*'s paddles backstroked and slowed the trader to less than a crawl as it sidewalked up to the vacant space between two heavy bollards. Docked closer inshore on the pier was a two-masted, black-hulled schooner with a single side-wheel and a thin funnel. A light wind out of the west added to the fall's mid-morning chill.

After glancing at the pack by his legs to ensure it was still there, Justen studied the pier, where a half-score dockworkers were engaged in unloading the schooner, and where a handful of men and women stood clearly waiting for the *Nyessa*.

A tall, sandy-haired man and a dark-haired woman – each in blacks – stood apart from the waiting docking crew.

Justen waved, and they waved back, although he wondered how Gunnar had known his brother had returned.

The first officer stopped beside Justen. 'Ser, your share of the cargo will be deposited with the port-master's bank under your name.' She unfolded the parchment sheet. 'Is this correct?'

Justen scanned the document, trying not to swallow at the unexpected share accorded him: half of the lorken's estimated value. It would run to nearly a hundred golds. Finally, he nodded. 'When will the funds be available?'

'Well, Ser. This is really an estimate, based on previous cargoes, but the debts have to be settled before we out-port again.'

'I see.'

'The druids are very precise, Ser. No one who cheats them ever gets another cargo.' The first laughed softly. 'Herko found that out the hard way. We'd rather not. So if you have any questions, please . . . please talk to me or the captain.'

'I'd like a copy of the final invoice left with the account, if you don't mind.'

'No, Ser. We would provide it anyway. That way, there's no confusion. Now, if you would excuse me . . .'

'Oh, yes. Go right ahead.' Justen watched as the lines went to the pier workers, and the crew began to winch the *Nyessa* into place. Finally, he slipped his pack onto his back and edged over to where two husky crew members were lowering the gangplank.

Altara and Gunnar were waiting as he stepped off onto the stones still damp from the rain of the night before. Gunnar wrapped his arms around him, and Justen hung on to his brother for a moment. Then they separated.

'How did you find this ship?' demanded Altara. 'What have you been doing?'

'Where have you been? How did you get here? I was worried when we got separated in Sarron.' Gunnar's questions spun at Justen more quickly than a whirling turbine blade.

Justen held up his hand, half-laughing, even as his eyes watered at the concern and love radiating from his brother. Was this something else he hadn't seen before? 'Stop,' he choked out. 'I can't answer everything at once.'

'Why not?' Altara grinned as she spoke.

Around them, dockworkers and sailors doubled up the lines to the *Nyessa*, and several horse-drawn wagons creaked down the pier past the schooner and toward the Bristan trader.

'I'm hungry,' Justen confessed. 'Houlart's is open early, isn't it?'

'Still thinking about food?'

'Anything's better than cactus.'

'Houlart's is open,' Altara responded, 'but whether anything that's available this early is more edible than cactus is another question.'

Justen readjusted his pack, and the three walked along the pier toward Nylan.

'How long did the crossing take?' asked Gunnar.

'Five days. But the captain used sail as much as he could.'

'Five days? Where did you come from? You didn't come from Armat or Southwind then?'

'No. From Diehl.'

'Naclos? You must have crossed all of Candar, or did you ship around Southwind?' Gunnar dodged around a porter trundling a handcart.

'I've seen a great deal of Naclos, especially the Stone Hills and the northern grasslands.'

'Elisabet has been worried, you know.'

'I really . . .' Justen sighed. 'I should have sent a message, but . . . so much happened, and I didn't know how to. No,' he corrected himself, finding that he did not want to misrepresent the situation. 'Naclos was so strange that sometimes it seemed unreal, and I just didn't think about what else was happening or who might be worried. I knew I had to come back, but in a way, I really found it hard.' He shook his head.

Neither Gunnar nor Altara spoke as they turned off the pier and went down the road past the port-master's and toward the shops behind the harbor front. A shadow passed across the three, cast by a small and fast-moving cloud.

Justen tried not to frown as the same feelings that he had first felt in Diehl – except stronger now – swept over him. All the buildings, solid black stone, somehow seemed lopsided, as if they were tilting toward him and about to fall. He blinked several times, trying to rein in his sense of order-chaos imbalance.

'Are you glad to be back?' Altara asked.

'I don't know. It's good to see you both – really good. And I want to go to Wandernaught and see everyone.'

Altara and Gunnar looked at each other, but again did not speak.

'There's a lot to do,' Justen continued after a moment. 'It seems like . . . I don't know.'

'What have you been doing?'

'Surviving. A lot of things.' Justen pointed to the sign of the black waterspout that marked Houlart's. 'I don't want to start until I can tell you the whole story at once . . . not in pieces.'

The public room was empty, not surprisingly for mid-morning in Nylan. As he walked past the first tables, Justen glanced at the Capture board lying on the empty corner table, wondering if he would play Gunnar any differently now. He set his pack between his chair and the wall, and as he dropped into the wooden armchair, he half-shrugged, realizing that he had no real desire to play Capture.

Altara waved to the serving woman in the corner, a small woman in a blue cap who scurried over to the three.

'There's still sausage and eggs and fried white seaweed,' began the woman.

'Do you have any bread, heavy conserves, and beer?' asked Justen. 'And some white cheese?'

'He hasn't changed much,' whispered Altara to Gunnar.

'Might as we could manage that, Ser. And you?' asked the server, turning to Altara.

'Just greenberry.'

'I'll have some of that bread, and greenberry,' Gunnar said.

The serving woman nodded and turned, and Justen moved his chair slightly, looking down at his pack.

'The ship?' asked Altara.

'Why not let him begin at the beginning?'

Justen watched as the serving woman brought his mug of beer and set it on the dark wood table with a thump.

'Be a moment for the bread, Ser, and the greenberries.'

Justen took a small sip of the dark beer. It tasted more bitter than he remembered, but then he took a healthy swallow. 'All right . . .' He held up a hand before the questions began again. 'I'll tell you the main points. First, I was so tired by the end of the battle in Sarron that I couldn't hold the shields long, and I was on the wrong side of the hill, with all those wizards between us. Before I figured out what had happened, I couldn't get back. So I thought I'd go upriver, try to find a horse and cross the Sarron and double back . . .'

Between sips, Justen detailed his travels in Sarronnyn, outlining the problems with the White Wizard who had kept chasing him and telling how he never could get to a ford on the river. Then he began on the dreams.

The serving woman set two mugs of greenberry on the table and left as quickly as she had come.

'You had these dreams before you left Recluce?' asked Gunnar.

'One. But I thought it was just a normal dream. Then, when I ended up trying to cross the Stone Hills . . .'

The bread, the white cheese, and the cherry conserve arrived. Justen began to eat, interspersing words with food.

'But you said the Sarronnese hill raiders killed your horse.'

'I crossed the Stone Hills on foot. For the first part, I was alone. I had trouble finding water, and when I tried the gray cactus, it made me sick. The green ones weren't too bad. But I just couldn't find enough water. It was a good thing Dayala found me.'

'Dayala?'

'She's a druid . . .'

'From the look on his face, Gunnar, she must be something.'

'How did she find you? She just went into the Stone Hills and found you? Why?' Gunnar pursued.

Justen finished a mouthful of bread and cheese, silently reflecting that the cheese seemed heavy, and thicker than he recalled. 'She was the one who sent the dreams, and she used the sands to find me. It took a while for me to heal. I wasn't in very good shape, and of course we had to walk back to Rybatta, which is where she lives. The druids don't ride animals, but the animals will carry loads for them – usually.' Justen described the slow trip back, but omitted his initial encounter with the great forest. When he reached the point where he was describing Dayala's work, he lugged his pack onto his lap.

'You two don't believe half of what I'm saying. Poor Justen's lost it all. He's out of his mind. Here.' He handed the first box to Gunnar and the smaller, dark-grained one to Altara.

Gunnar swallowed, and Justen could sense his brother's awe and order-probing of the box.

Altara just looked . . . and looked . . . before speaking. 'There aren't any joints.'

'No. She grows them.' Justen grinned. 'After all, she is a druid.' Then his face grew somber. 'It's not as simple as that. It really takes work. She was more tired after a day of working the trees than I was after a day of smithing.'

'I thought the druids didn't work metal.'

'So did I, but her father is a smith. Uses bog iron, but he lives a bit away from the others. Only a few of the druids are comfortable with things like blades and knives.'

'What—'

'Hold it,' Justen interposed. 'I've talked and talked. Now, it's your turn.'

'But you didn't finish—'

'I'll finish later. What happened after the battle in Sarron? I felt the White Wizard shake down the city, but after that, I was too much on the run.'

'The Sarronnese, except for the people in Berlitos, pretty much just gave up after the Tyrant died.' Altara paused to take a swallow of greenberry. 'We managed to get back to Rulyarth. That was a mess. People were bribing . . . killing . . . anything to get out of Sarronnyn. A bunch went into Suthya, but no one thinks the Suthyans can hold out for long. We got passage back on *The Pride of Brista* – deck passage, and it rained the whole way. Two of the marines died from wounds and chill. That's what happens without healers.'

'What happened to Firbek?'

'Last time I saw him, he was turning over our launchers to the

Iron Guard. According to the Sarronnese troopers who escaped and came here last spring, he led a detachment in the sack of Rulyarth.' Altara's voice was cold. 'Gunnar was surprised. He thought you'd killed him.'

Justen shook his head. 'I stabbed him, but he slugged Gunnar and got away. Then all the lancers charged over the hill, and he turned the rockets . . . on the healers.'

Altara exchanged glances with Gunnar. 'Gunnar thought the White Wizard did that.'

'No. It was Firbek. It was partly my fault. He was trying to get me, but the rockets went past me and into the healers' area.' Justen looked at the table. 'Clerve, Krytella – none of them knew what happened. I'd still kill that bastard if I got half a chance.' He waved to the serving woman. 'Another round of drinks.' He looked at Gunnar. 'Can you pay for this? I'll be able to repay you in a day or two.'

'Don't worry about it.' Gunnar touched his shoulder. 'I'm just glad you're back.'

'After you got home . . .' prompted Justen.

'The Council talked to us, one by one.' Gunnar pushed the empty mugs to the center of the table as the serving woman deposited three more and collected the empties. 'Turmin asked me a lot about how chaos felt up close.'

'And everyone pretends that nothing happened.' Altara snorted. 'Except that Ryltar pushed through an increase in the tax levy on local merchants to beef up the marines in case they're needed on the merchant fleet.'

'Why not tariffs?' asked Justen.

'Because higher tariffs cut trade,' snapped Altara. 'Taxes here come out of our pockets. Where else can we go for food or goods? Oh, and traders were exempted, of course.'

Justen sipped the second beer. Somehow, taxes seemed as unreal in Recluce as Dayala's box-making had at first seemed in Naclos. 'It sounds like nothing's changed since before we left for Sarronnyn, except that next spring, the same thing will happen in Suthya.'

'No, it won't, because the Council won't even send volunteers next time. They'll just wring their hands,' Altara said.

'Is that so bad?' asked Gunnar. 'We weren't exactly all that effective.'

'No. You and Justen only cost them two armies and delayed them almost a year. But everyone's convinced that we can do nothing.' Altara looked at the mug. 'I'm almost ready to start drinking beer – or brandy.'

Justen shivered, thinking about Krytella, Clerve, and the dead Iron Guard. 'There's too much order and too much chaos . . .' he mumbled.

'Too much order and too much chaos?' asked Gunnar

Justen shrugged. 'Something one of the older druids said. I'm still thinking about it.' A twinge and a flash of light flared in his skull. 'I'm thinking a lot about it.'

Altara and Gunnar exchanged glances again.

'You never did say how you got from Rybatta to Diehl and home, or why it took so long,' prompted Gunnar.

'I took a boat downriver, but a lot happened before I did . . .' Justen began to describe Rybatta and the cooperative aspects of Naclos.

Altara let out her breath slowly as he began to speak, and Gunnar leaned back slightly in his chair.

Again, he tried to avoid discussing the coercive nature of the great forest, his trial, and his ties to Dayala. He also did not mention his feelings of order imbalance.

In some ways, it was going to be lonely in Recluce, Justen thought, lonely indeed.

101

Justen opened the door. Nothing had changed.

The oil lamp still stood on the corner of the desk; there was not even a speck of dust on the bronze or the glass of the mantle. Only the narrow bed was different, with the coverlet and sheet neatly folded at the foot rather than in place on the pallet itself.

After closing the door and setting his pack on the bed, Justen walked to the window and eased open the inside shutters and then the window, so that the fall breeze whispered into the still air of the past.

He opened the pack and took out the remaining half-dozen boxes, each wrapped in the soft, husklike leaves that protected them, and set each box, still-wrapped, on the side of the desk. His fingers tingled as they brushed the smooth grain of the last box where the leaf had not quite covered the wood; the grain spoke of silver-hair, long fingers, and green eyes.

For a time, Justen stood over the desk, eyes closed. Then he took a deep breath and turned to his personal toiletries: the razor he had forged at Yual's, some soap from Rybatta, a soft cloth for his face, a small, bronze-framed mirror.

He shook out the brown trousers and tunic, softer cloth than the blacks he wore again, and hung them on the pegs in the wardrobe. The pack went into the bottom of the wardrobe, leaving space for boots, assuming that he got another pair of black ones.

After closing the doors of the tall cabinet, he went to the small bookcase and lifted the Capture board and the box containing the black and white tokens. Then he set the board down and studied the box, all too aware of the joints in the wood, all too aware that even the finest craftsmanship seemed somehow like violence, as though the woods had been forced together. He set the box down and shook his head. If Naclos had seemed so unreal, why was he seeing everything differently here?

His eyes turned to the stones of the outer wall, but they seemed set in order. Was it that the wood had been shaped with edges? Was he getting to be like Dayala, unhappy with edged tools? Or was he merely more perceptive now?

With a last look around the room, he turned and opened the door to begin the short walk to the engineering hall and the work that, presumably, awaited him.

The slight depression in the center of the stone steps leading down to the main floor and the street again reminded him of the generations of young engineers who had lived in these quarters, and he could almost sense the men and women of the past looking over his shoulder, their order-stern countenances fixed in time.

Shaking his head, he stepped into the cool, bright afternoon and turned downhill.

An empty horse-drawn wagon clattered past on the street.

Justen frowned at the sight of the driver seated on the wagon rather than walking beside the horse. He blinked and took a deep breath.

Halfway down the hill, he paused opposite the classroom building that had always seemed to form a part of the hillside, but now it seemed to stand out rather than blend. A handful of students had gathered around a stone bench by the statue of Dorrin, chattering like rare birds. For several moments, he stood and watched before turning and continuing down to the engineering hall.

He paused at the bottom step, looking up at the shadowed porch and sensing the ordered masses of metal within the walls, more solid and hulking than he had ever recognized. With another deep breath, he took the low steps and entered the hall, stopping just before the workroom floor.

A young woman whom he did not know worked the forge and occupied the space he had once called his own, and her strokes on the anvil were clean and sure – as were all the strokes of all the engineers.

The dull grinding of the gear-cutters echoed in his ears as he watched.

'Justen? What are you doing here?' The dark-haired chief engineer walked toward him.

He shrugged. 'I am an engineer, I guess.'

'We've gotten along without you for a time, Justen.' Altara laughed. 'And from what Gunnar says, at least your sister would like to see you. So, I expect, will the Council, once they find out you've returned.'

He had wanted to see his family. So what was he doing in the engineering hall? Justen's eyes darted from one mass of heavy iron to another, from anvil to iron casing to fine-drawn turbine blade.

'If they want to see you, I'll ride up to Wandernaught and fetch you. If not, you can come back here in a few days. And don't worry. You'll get paid; such as it is.'

Justen smiled guiltily with the realization that he was far wealthier than he had ever expected to be. The smile faded as he recalled the reason for that wealth.

'You'll have to bring a mount, or I'll take the post coach,' he added.

'I'm sure that the Brotherhood or the Council could spring for a mount if they need to see you. Now . . . go on and tell your family that you're safe and in one piece.'

'Thank you.' Justen slowly turned. Why was he so slow? Of course his parents and Elisabet wanted to see him, and he wanted to see them. So why hadn't it really crossed his mind? Why had he just followed his old habit patterns?

He slowly walked down the steps to the street, his fingers idly stroking his chin.

102

'Well . . . we're almost there.' Severa tightened the reins slightly, and the post wagon slowed as it neared the post house. The Broken Wheel, the two-story stone-and-timber inn, looked almost the same as the last time Justen had been home, except that the cracked wagon spokes on the sign were now a darker brown. A man not much older than Justen, paint pot in hand, waved at Severa. She waved back.

'Who's that?' asked Justen, grabbing the edge of the seat as Severa levered the wagon brake and the wagon lurched to a halt.

'Rildr. He's old Hernon's nephew. They're slowly fixing the old place up. It wasn't terribly run down, but you either fix inns up or they fall apart.'

'I think that's pretty much true of everything.' Justen handed her the two coppers, slipped off the leather seat and reached into the wagon bed for his pack. He looked up at the high, thin clouds that cooled the afternoon without providing rain.

Severa put the coins in her purse, then lifted one of the leather post bags out and onto the stone walk beside the post house just as the young postal worker came scurrying out. 'I'm sorry, Severa. I didn't hear you.'

'If I woke the demons, Lorn, you still wouldn't hear me.'

Severa grinned at the young man, who looked sheepishly at the paving stones underfoot.

Justen shouldered his pack and lifted his hand to Severa. 'Thank you.'

'I enjoyed the company, Justen. Give my best to your mother.'

'I will.' Justen turned and began to walk westward along the main street, past the coppersmith's, and then past Basta's Dry and Leather Goods.

Another wagon stood outside Seldit's, where the cooper and the driver were lifting a large barrel up alongside three others in the wagon bed.

'Good afternoon, Seldit,' Justen said pleasantly as he passed.

'Justen! We . . . no one . . . when did you get back?'

'Yesterday . . . that's when I got to Nylan.' Justen stopped.

'Your dad will be glad to see you.' The heavy-armed cooper coughed. 'Your mom and sister, too.'

'I'll be glad to see them.' Justen grinned. 'Don't let me keep you. I'll be around for a few days, I think.'

'Just goes to show . . .' Seldit shook his head and glanced at the driver. 'Engineers and wizards . . . never tell . . .'

'That's right.' Justen forced another grin. 'You never can. Just like bad coppers, we keep coming back.'

'Off with you. You're still a young scamp . . . sort of.'

Justen waved and turned. Seldit, at least, was the same, even if Wandernaught felt somehow shallower, just as Diehl, and even Nylan, had – although Nylan was the most solid of the three. Yet, it was the most imbalanced, nearly drowning in a surfeit of order.

After he passed the house where Shrezsan had once lived, he came to a smaller structure, one that seemed so new that it was almost not there, where a blond young woman and a child were working in a small garden plot. So, Justen reflected with a smile, Shrezsan and Yousal had moved next to her parents' house, to be close enough to carry on the family wool-and-linen business. Neither Shrezsan nor the child looked up as he strode past and toward the hills that held the cherry and pearapple groves.

Once beyond the first set of groves, its trees certainly as solid as any in Naclos, Justen began to look westward for a sight of the house. When he passed the last cherry grove, the familiar blackstone and slate-tiled house he neared looked no different. It, like Nylan, felt more solid. Was that because of those who lived there? Or because it had stood for longer than many? Justen could see his father's wiry figure on a ladder at the far end of the grove, picking apples. Elisabet's slender figure stood at the base of the ladder, handing up a basket.

She turned toward Justen and dropped the basket, breaking into a pell-mell dash toward her brother. 'Justen! Justen! Father! He's back! He's back!'

The violence of Elisabet's hug almost knocked Justen into the low stone wall by the roadside.

'I knew! I knew you were coming!' She buried her face in his shoulder.

Absently, Justen realized that she was nearly as tall as he was, that she was no longer a gawky girl, but a young woman. He hugged her. 'I'm glad I came.'

Horas had followed his daughter more deliberately, and he stood at the edge of the road, waiting. Justen disentangled himself from his sister's hold and gave his father a hug.

'You've changed,' were Horas's first words. 'A lot.'

'Yes. It's been a long year.'

'He's still Justen,' said Elisabet.

'You might say that he's more Justen than ever.' Horas's words were tinged with warmth and irony.

'Where's Mother?'

'She's at Nerla's, helping her lay out her own smithy. She said she'd be back by mid-afternoon. She wasn't – she said – going to do all the hard work for a former apprentice.'

The three laughed at Horas's mimicry of Cirlin.

'Of course, now she'll have to find another apprentice, unless . . .' Horas looked speculatively at Justen.

'Who knows?' Justen shrugged.

'I think the apples can wait a bit. Let's go have something to drink. There's even some ale left, and—'

'There's a dark cake, with real molasses!' exclaimed Elisabet.

'Will Gunnar be coming?' asked Horas.

'I think so, but not for a day or two. He had to finish something with Turmin, and he said that you ought to have me to yourselves for a bit. I think he was afraid I'd gotten better at Capture.' Justen offered a quick smile.

'Have you?' asked his sister.

'No. I haven't played since I left Sarron, and that was a year ago. Anyway, I don't think I'm any better.'

Horas turned, and his two children followed him up the stone walk toward the covered porch. He waited by the door to the house as Elisabet and Justen stepped onto the porch. 'Redberry and ale, right?'

'Right.'

'Right.' Inside, Elisabet plopped on the stool by Justen's knee and looked at her brother. 'What happened?'

Justen laughed. 'Wait until Father comes back. I'm sure he'll want to hear as well, and I don't want to tell the same story twice.'

'Then you'll want to wait until Mother comes, and I'll have to help with dinner, and then I'll never get to hear it all.'

'You'll get to hear it all.' Justen ruffled her short-cut sandy hair. 'You cut your hair.'

'Long hair gets in the way, and besides, I don't want to be just a brood mare, and that's what all the girls with long hair are.'

'Strong words, young woman.' Horas extended the taller mug to Justen.

'True words!' Elisabet lifted one of the two shorter mugs from the battered wooden tray. 'Lydya is already saying how many children she'll have!'

Justen and his father exchanged quick smiles.

'And don't smile like that. I know what I want.'

'That I believe.' Justen took a slow sip of the ale, holding it in his mouth for a moment. He was glad to find that his father's brew was as smooth as any in Naclos, and he let the ale trickle down his dry throat.

'Well, I think your mother is at the turn,' said Horas. 'So we'll wait to hear your story until she gets here.'

'I told you so.' Elisabet looked at Justen.

'In the meanwhile, we can tell you what has happened here.'

'Not much,' suggested Elisabet.

'I've added some seedlings to both groves, and I suppose you saw Shrezsan's and Yousal's house.'

Justen nodded.

'They're redoing The Broken Wheel, and Niteral has taken over old Kaylert's spread. He says that it's just to get it ready for Huntal – that's the boy who went to Temple school with Gunnar. He and Mara have two girls, and they didn't like the fishing life of her family. So they moved back to the guest house at Niteral's, but it's really too small—'

'Fishing . . . ugh,' interposed Elisabet.

'Some people have to fish.'

'Orchards are better.'

'Not if you don't have an Order Wizard in the family or if you don't like bugs,' observed Horas.

Elisabet stood and dashed off the porch and down the walk to greet Cirlin. 'Justen's home! He's back!'

Horas and Justen looked at each other.

'Still half girl,' Justen said.

'Not for long, I think.'

Justen stood and gave his mother a bear hug as she stepped onto the covered porch.

'What a welcome surprise! But then, Gunnar was always convinced that you'd be back.'

'He knew more than I did.'

Horas disappeared into the house for a moment, reappearing with another ale about the time that Justen and his mother disengaged themselves and Cirlin sat down in the narrow rocking chair in the corner.

'All right. I want to hear everything,' announced Elisabet. 'I've waited and waited.'

'I think Justen's hungry. Perhaps we should wait until after dinner . . .'

Justen caught the twinkle in Horas's eyes.

'Father! You . . . you're just teasing.'

Cirlin shook her head. 'Sometimes you're too eager, daughter.'

'Maybe so, but Justen promised I could hear it all.'

Justen patted her on the shoulder. 'You'll hear everything that everyone else hears.' He took a deep swallow of the welcome ale before beginning. 'I'm sure Gunnar's told you all about what happened in Sarron until the final battle. I'll start there . . .'

The sun was touching the tops of the low hills behind the apple and pearapple groves when Justen finished his abbreviated tale of his travels across Candar. '. . . and when the ship pulled up at the pier in Nylan, there were Gunnar and Altara, waiting for me.'

Belatedly, he remembered and reached for his pack, digging out the three of Dayala's boxes he had set aside for them. He handed the first to Elisabet. 'Dayala sent these.' Then he handed one to Horas and one to Cirlin.

'This is beautiful! It's mine? Really mine?'

Justen nodded. 'It's yours, Elisabet.'

Horas studied the woven grains in the box he held, then set the box gently on the table beside him. Cirlin set hers beside Horas's box.

'She is quite accomplished, isn't she?'

'Yes.'

'And she rescued you from the Stone Hills, and made sure you got home safely? We owe her a great deal, don't we?' Horas's voice was low.

Justen swallowed. 'Not so much as you think. We are all caught in the designs of the Angels.'

'You love her, don't you?'

'Yes.'

'But she's a druid!' protested Elisabet.

So am I, thought Justen, but he did not speak the words immediately.

'She's a druid, and you're from Recluce!' Elisabet looked from Justen to her parents. 'You're not a druid. You can't leave us.'

'I am a druid. Now.'

Horas nodded, as did Cirlin.

'You aren't staying, are you?' asked Horas.

'Of course he is. He just got here,' insisted Elisabet. 'He'll change his mind. He has to.'

'I'll be here for at least a few days. Altara says that the Council may want to see me.'

'I'm sure that they will.' Cirlin took a long pull from the tall mug. 'That time comes for all of us, though. Are you going back to Naclos?'

'I don't understand.' Elisabet looked from one parent to the other. 'He was almost killed in Candar, and you both seem to think that he's going straight back.'

'Not straight, I think. Is it just the druid?' asked Horas.

'She can't have bewitched Justen. Tell me she hasn't, Justen.'

'No. I'll have to go to Fairhaven.'

Elisabet's eyes grew wider. 'None of this makes any sense. Can you all explain what you are talking about?'

'Look at me, Elisabet. Look at me with your order-senses.'

For a moment, Elisabet stared at her brother, then looked away. She shivered and stared down at the floor.

'Now, lass, tell me what you saw,' requested Horas.

'He . . . his order . . . there's no chaos that's not tied up. Gunnar, even, has flecks of . . . loose chaos. Justen doesn't.' Elisabet stumbled through the words and finally looked up. 'It's something . . .' She swallowed without finishing the sentence. 'You meant it. The druids did something. Why?'

'Yes, I meant it. But they didn't do anything. It's something I had to do. And it's about . . . everything.' Justen knew how pretentious the words sounded, but that didn't make them any less true. He hurried on. 'I'm not going there for a while. I have a lot to do here.'

'Good!' exclaimed Elisabet.

'I can't say I'm displeased either,' added Cirlin.

'Since we've disposed of that, how about some dinner?' asked Horas.

The growling in Justen's stomach provided his answer, and he grinned.

'Justen!' cried Elisabet in mock outrage.

He shrugged and then grinned as his father turned toward the kitchen. But his eyes burned, and he looked out at the all-too-familiar and all-too-strange apple trees that were lined up in the growing gloom of twilight.

103

'I'm sorry I had to cut short your time with your family. The Council was very insistent—'

'Altara . . .' Justen cut off the chief engineer's apology, at least the fifth he had heard on the three-day ride from Wandernaught.

'You didn't cut it short, and we'll stop there on the way back. So don't worry.'

'But I do. They haven't seen you in more than a year.'

Justen took a deep breath, thinking about what lay ahead after his meeting the Council. Going back to Candar wasn't going to be easy, but he did not see much choice, not when so much of the vaunted order of Recluce seemed so shallow . . . so one-sided.

'You haven't told me everything.'

'No.'

'What happened to the carefree Justen, the one who called weapons obsolete?'

'I still don't carry them, you'll notice.' He tried to ease a light note into his voice.

'Then was a game. Now you mean it.' Altara pointed to the black structures on the bluff ahead to the right. 'There's the Black Holding.'

The five black buildings seemed rooted into the heavy rock that underlay most of Recluce, and yet, to Justen, they seemed somehow unbalanced, straight as they stood, as if they were about to tip sideways. He squinted and shook his head, but the feeling did not pass as they rode closer. He almost felt as though the ancient order embodied in the stones were about to fall on him.

He took a deep breath as he reined up outside the small and ancient stable. As he dismounted, he patted the horse on the neck, and the stallion whinnied gently.

'You've come a long way from that young engineer who could barely sit on a gray nag.' Altara laughed as she slipped off her bay gelding and handed the reins to the young man in black who had stood waiting as they rode up.

Justen handed his reins to a young woman, and the stallion whickered and sidestepped. Justen looked at the horse, sending the faintest pulse of order toward the high-spirited animal, and added, 'Take it easy, fellow.'

The stallion whinnied and steadied. The young aide's eyes widened and she moved back, even though Justen gave her a reassuring smile. He stepped across a shallow puddle held in the worn hollows of the ancient stones. The rain had not fallen as far south as Alberth, where they had stayed the night before.

'Which way?' Justen inclined his head toward the walkway to the right.

'This way.' Altara motioned to the left way, which circled the stable and took them on the south side of the holding, next to a raised terrace. The path ran between an ancient oak tree and the terrace. Before them, the Eastern Ocean glimmered silver in the morning light of summer.

'Do you think the Council is really interested in where I've been?' Justen took the steps up onto the terrace and crossed to the closed, dark-pine door.

'Of course not. You're the only engineer or mage to have been beyond the port of Diehl in probably five generations. You're one of the few people known to have survived the Stone Hills, and you're the one whose design of ordered black arrowheads cost the Whites nearly an entire army. Why would they be interested in poor little Justen?' Altara grinned.

'I thought I'd ask.'

'If you have to play dumb, don't play it quite that dumb.'

Justen returned her grin and rapped on the door, which opened even as he lowered his hand. A woman in marine blacks and wearing the double shortswords of ancient and fallen Westwind waited.

'Justen, from the engineers. I'm here to . . .' He looked at Altara.

'We're responding to Counselor Jenna's request. I'm Chief Engineer Altara.'

'Welcome to the Black Holding.' The marine smiled politely, 'Do come in.' She stepped back and gestured toward a room beyond the small foyer. 'If you would like to sit down, I believe that the counselors will be ready for you shortly.'

The foyer walls were plain, just as Justen had remembered them from the one time his tutor had shown him the holding years earlier. Clearly, the Founders had not been interested in decoration, and their successors had left the holding as plain, as drab, as it was originally.

The waiting room held nearly a dozen black-oak chairs and a low table, but all the chairs were empty. Altara took one by the window, where she could see a corner of the Eastern Ocean.

Justen walked to the single bookcase, containing a score or more of volumes. His eyes ranged over the untitled black covers.

388   L. E. MODESITT, JR.

'Are you going to sit down?'

'We've been riding for five whole days. I'm not much better as a horseman than I was a year ago.'

'It's been more than a year, and you're a lot better.'

'Not much, but you're right. It seems a lot longer.'

'You're a lot older.'

'Crossing the Stone Hills does that.' Justen laughed. 'I could use a dark ale now.'

'You still drink that stuff?'

'Why not? It tastes good.'

'But you're more ordered now. You remind me more of your brother, or of Turmin.'

'I like beer.'

Clearing her throat softly, the marine stood by the door to the Council Chamber. 'Engineers, the Counselors will see you now.'

Justen followed Altara into the dark-paneled room, his eyes flicking to the portraits that flanked the windows – Megaera and Creslin, the Founders – and back to the three figures who stood behind the Council table.

In the center was an older, dark-haired woman, flanked on the right by a man with brown wispy hair, and on the left by a redheaded woman who seemed close to Altara's age.

The older woman nodded. 'I'm Claris. I appreciate your coming, Engineers. This is Ryltar . . . and Jenna.'

The redhead acknowledged her name with a slight inclination of her head. Ryltar nodded abruptly.

'Please sit down.'

Justen took the right-hand chair, a comfortable but worn blackoak wooden armchair across from the redhead. Altara sat across from Claris.

'The chief engineer has told us of how you got to Sarron and of what happened there – the outcome of the battle – but we don't know what happened to you after the battle.'

'Where should I start? After Firbek tried to turn the rockets on us?'

'We're familiar with that,' Ryltar said sharply. 'Why didn't you fall back with the others? How did you get separated?'

'The Whites came up the hill so quickly, and I didn't have a mount. I also didn't have much strength left at that point. So I pulled a light-shield around myself . . .'

Ryltar nodded for him to continue, and Justen detailed the way he had tried to get back across the River Sarron and how each attempt had pushed him farther into Sarronnyn, until he was south of Clynya.

'Why did you try to cross the Stone Hills?' asked Claris, the older counselor.

'I didn't have much choice,' Justen began wryly. 'There were several-score lancers and at least one White Wizard chasing me, and I couldn't seem to avoid the damned vulcrow . . .' He went on to describe how at every attempt to reach the bridge at Clynya he was almost herded southward and eastward to avoid capture. '. . . and in the end, there didn't seem to be much of a choice.'

'Were the druids . . . helpful? I mean, how did they receive you?' asked the younger red-haired counselor.

Justen frowned. 'It's hard to explain. They rescued me from the Stone Hills. I didn't make it quite all the way across—'

'Just how far did you make it, young man?' interrupted the wispy-haired counselor.

'By the end, I wasn't in much shape to measure, Ser. If my memory is correct, I lasted somewhere between ten and twelve days before I fell.'

'And you had no special help?'

'It sounds stupid, I know. I walked into the Stone Hills with a blanket, the clothes on my back, and a water bottle. At the time, it seemed a great deal more reasonable than it does now. I suppose being chased by a White Wizard can do that to your reason.' Justen smiled briefly, noting the cool look from the older counselor toward Ryltar.

'You lasted twelve days on one bottle of water, and you're not even a mage?'

'Ryltar—'

'Jenna, I'm just trying to see if our engineer is what he says he is.'

'No,' Justen said. 'One kind of cactus – the green one – has water in the pulp. So do the gray ones, but they made me sick sometimes. Twice I found little pockets of water in the rocks. I do have some order-sense. I couldn't been an engineer if I didn't.'

'So you lasted for twelve days on what water you found?'

'It might have been ten . . . could have been fourteen. I wasn't thinking very clearly by then.'

'And what happened?'

'I fell and couldn't get up.' Justen shrugged.

Beside him, Altara grinned at his flat statement.

'And?' pushed Ryltar.

'When I woke up, someone had found me and was trying to get me to drink. It was one of the Naclans.'

'One of the druids?'

Justen nodded.

'So – just like that – they rescued you, fed you, and carried you back to Diehl and then sent you home to Recluce, healthy and healed?' Ryltar snorted.

Justen took a deep breath, paused, and instead of responding, extended his order-senses to touch Ryltar. A slight frown creased his forehead; it was not exactly chaos, he sensed, but . . . something. A disorder that verged on—

'You seem somewhat displeased, Justen,' said Claris.

'No . . .' Justen tried to gather himself.

'Could you explain what happened in Naclos?' asked Jenna gently.

'Well, we walked back. They don't ride horses there. The horses will carry packs for them, but the druids say they have a bargain with them.'

'You walked to Diehl?' Ryltar's voice rose again. 'Across half of Candar . . . after barely surviving the Stone Hills?'

'Ryltar . . .'

'. . . asking us to swallow a lot . . .'

'You might be able to swallow if you talked less and listened more,' snapped Jenna.

'Jenna,' temporized Claris.

Justen took another deep breath. 'First, I didn't go anywhere for days after they found me. Then we walked only a handful of kays a day. We walked to a place called Rybatta. It's on the river, and later we took a boat downriver to Diehl. It did take me a while to recover.'

'. . . should hope so.'

'What can you tell us about the Naclans?'

'They believe in a version of the Legend, I'd say, although they never quite explained it. They live in harmony with all

living things . . . don't take life, even of plants, without reason
. . . appear to be long-lived . . .'

Throughout the explanation, the skepticism on Ryltar's face
became more pronounced.

Finally, Claris held up a hand. 'You seem rather dissatisfied,
Ryltar.'

'I am. How can we believe any of this?'

'I don't sense any chaos. Do you?'

'How could we tell? We need an expert.' Ryltar snorted
again.

'Is that why you have Turmin waiting?' asked Jenna.

Ryltar flushed.

'Justen, with all that is happening, and with what happened
to his nephew, you can understand Counselor Ryltar's concerns
that somehow you are now tied up, perhaps unwittingly, with
Fairhaven?' Claris's voice was gentle.

'I understand the counselor's concerns.' Justen grinned. 'I take
it you want the honored Turmin to check out my degree of . . .
orderliness? I don't have any problem with that.' Turmin might,
reflected Justen, with a turn to his lips.

'You seem amused.' Ryltar had gestured to the marine by
the door.

'I am. I think that Turmin will find me very . . . orderly.
The druids wouldn't have allowed me anywhere near Diehl if
I hadn't been.'

Ryltar's lip curled as Turmin entered the chamber.

Justen stood, nodding to the black mage, as did the others.

'Would you?' Claris nodded at Ryltar.

'Justen, here, has apparently spent almost two seasons in
Naclos, and has recently returned. I appear to be the only one
concerned that he may not be what he seems.'

'That is perfectly understandable with your . . . responsibil-
ities.' Turmin nodded to the counselor.

A faint flush colored Ryltar's neck, and Justen suppressed a
grin. Turmin wasn't anyone's tool.

The mage turned to Justen. 'Do you mind, Ser?'

Justen caught the frown that crossed both Claris and Ryltar's
face even before he answered. 'No, Ser.'

Turmin smiled as he extended his order-perceptions, and
Justen could sense something – but it was far fainter than

the black mist that had surrounded Dayala, and especially the ancient Angel.

The mage frowned briefly, then nodded. After a few moments, he turned to the three counselors behind the table. 'Begging your pardon, counselors, but this young fellow shows more basic order than anyone on Recluce. Even being around him would make your average White squirm.'

'Could this be a trick of some sort?' pursued Ryltar.

'Counselor, again begging your pardon, but you're far closer to the Whites than he is. I don't know of any way to counterfeit order. Do you?'

'Thank you, Turmin,' Claris proffered. 'We appreciate your help.'

'Any time, counselors.' Turmin nodded curtly, bowed to Justen slightly, and with his back to the three counselors, winked.

Jenna covered her mouth, and the faint smile.

'We have a few more questions,' added Claris as the door shut behind Turmin. 'Do you think that the Naclans will fight the Whites?'

Justen took another deep breath. The morning was going to be long. 'So far as I know, they have not fought in any recent time, but I would question whether Fairhaven would wish to invade Naclos. The forests are almost impassible, except for hidden trails. The Stone Hills could not be crossed by an army, and the country produces little that the Whites could use.'

'How do they intend to escape the effect of chaos?'

Justen took a sip of water before considering his answer. How indeed? 'They believe that the forces of the Balance will eventually right the situation . . .' *Helped by one engineer named Justen, I suspect.*

The questions continued, and so did his answers, all of them truthful, all of them as complete as he knew how to make them, and all of them misleading to a Council that could not understand that too much order represented as much of a threat as did too much chaos.

104

After shifting his weight in the saddle, Justen wiped his forehead, although the summer heat was far less oppressive than that of the Stone Hills in the late fall. Absently, he wondered how anything survived there in the summer. With the thought of the Stone Hills, an image of Dayala's face floated into his mind. Should he write? How would he get a letter delivered? And what could he say in words? **Oh . . . Dayala. Miss you . . .**

A faint shadow crossed the road as a puffy white cloud briefly covered the sun.

Had he sensed some warmth in return, or was he merely feeling what he hoped to feel? Justen's stomach growled, and the stallion's hooves clicked on the stones of the High Road, that memorial to the great Creslin. 'Do you think that tavern's open yet?'

Altara had remained silent since they left the stable at the Black Holding. Now she cleared her throat before speaking and glanced out toward the sheep meadows to the west of the road; each meadow was lush with the hardy grass that grew only in Recluce, each separated from the next by the low, dark stone walls. 'The tavern – I suppose so.'

A farm wagon rolled toward them, filled with neatly stacked baskets of potatoes headed for the harbor at Land's End. 'Good day, Magister, Magistra.' The woman in the driver's seat nodded as she spoke.

'Good day.'

'Good day.'

When the wagon was well past, Altara looked at Justen for a time, her green eyes focused intently, before speaking. 'You've changed. Not in any way that's obvious.'

'I suspect that being chased across half of Arronnyn by a White Wizard and nearly dying in the Stone Hills might have had some effect.'

'It's rather more than that, young Justen, except that you're not nearly so young anymore.' Altara looked southward along the stone-paved High Road before continuing. 'You certainly had Counselor Ryltar upset.'

'There's something about him . . .' Justen's hand idly stroked the stallion's neck.

'You're surely not intimating that one of our great and mighty counselors might be less than perfectly orderly?'

'Turmin did.' Justen laughed. 'But I wonder how you'd ever prove anything like that. Or if it's even the case.'

'You look too deeply, Justen. What about simple corruption? Someone from Ryltar's family has been on the Council for the last two generations.'

'I can't believe someone could buy a Council seat without people finding out.'

'Of course not. But if the great trading family of Nylan supports and contributes to the funding of the Council . . .'

'Oh . . .' Justen nodded. Still, Ryltar didn't feel right. Corruption? Who would pay Ryltar for what? And why?

'What will the Council do about Suthya?' Justen patted the stallion on the neck again.

'Not a thing. Berlitos is nothing but cinders, and after the fall of Sarron and the firing of Berlitos, the Council doesn't seem willing to act. Besides, the Whites haven't made a move.'

'So the Council will do nothing? I wonder if someone has paid Ryltar to stop any action.'

'Justen . . . that's a serious charge.'

'I'm not charging, just wondering. Besides, how would you find out? Profits on trading shipments are hard to track.'

'Whatever . . .' Altara shook her head. 'I don't think you'd have to pay Ryltar. He's never wanted involvement with Candar.'

'Idiots . . .' muttered Justen.

'I agree. But why do you think so?'

'The Whites will consolidate their hold on Sarronnyn and send out their secret wizards and undermine the people's faith in order, and Suthya will fall just as Sarronnyn did.'

'You want to go back to Candar to stop them?'

Justen smiled faintly, but did not answer.

'Darkness. You're really thinking about it, aren't you?'

'Do you think the tavern's open?' Justen gestured toward the hamlet they approached.

'If your stomach can stand it, the public house in Extina is better, and it's not quite midday, anyway.' Altara forced a chuckle. 'And the dark ale is supposed to be among the best.'

'I could use a mug of good dark ale.' He patted the stallion's neck once more, hoping the ale would not be too bitter with the aftertaste he had never noticed until he had tasted the ale of Naclos. 'I definitely could.'

105

'Good night, son.' Horas waved vaguely as he headed down the hall to bed.

Justen closed the door and glanced at the lamp in the wall sconce. Did he need it, really? He walked over and gently blew it out to save oil. Then he pulled off his boots and piled up the pillows against the wall before he settled onto the bed.

Justen put his arms behind his head and stretched his feet out on the bed he had slept in for so many years before he had gone to Nylan to become an engineer. Now what was he? Part engineer, part druid, part healer, part who knew what?

As he heard the wind gust through the yellowing leaves of the trees outside, he frowned, recalling Gunnar's long-ago words: *You have managed to turn order into chaos. But gray magic has to work both ways. Can you turn chaos into order?*

Was working with chaos totally wrong – if the goal was order? He shivered. How many people had destroyed themselves in that way? But what if he held the chaos within blocks of order – just as the healing that Dayala had taught him held chaos twisted and locked in order inside his body?

False lead? Magistra Gerra had once mentioned that false lead linked order and chaos, but that false lead was dangerous. Even the yellow-powdered deposits that contained it

were hard to find, and harder to break down into the metal
itself.

Thrap . . .

He smiled, sensing Elisabet on the other side of the door.

'Come on in, Elisabet.'

'It's dark.'

'You don't need a light. No wizard does. Just look.'

'Oh, Justen. You spoil everything.'

'Just because I know you can see without much light?'

'Justen . . .'

'Does Mother know you're up?'

'She won't mind. Neither would Father.' Elisabet plopped
onto the corner of the bed, and Justen moved his feet aside.
'Tell me about Dayala. What's she like?'

'Why do you want to know?' Justen grinned in the darkness.

'Justen, you're in love with this druid, and I'm not supposed
to be curious? Does she have a tree, like in the old tales?'

'Hardly. Most of the druids live in the great forest of Naclos
and don't like to leave it, but not all of them are like that.
Dayala's father is a smith who traveled to Sarronnyn several
times in years past. And their houses are really made out of
trees. She works with smaller trees to make the boxes.'

'You told me that already. What does she look like?'

'Well, she's almost as tall as I am, and she has silver hair
and green eyes. And a very dry sense of humor that's hard to
describe. At first, it was a little hard to understand her, because
the Naclans speak the original Temple tongue—'

'Does she look like that picture of Llyse that's in the old
armory?'

'Hmmm.' Justen tried to remember the picture that Elisabet
mentioned, the one that showed the great Creslin's sister in
battle gear. 'Her hair isn't as curly as Llyse's, and her shoulders
are broader, I think. Oh, and she doesn't wear boots or
shoes. That's so she can keep in touch with everything around
her.'

'Does she wear clothes?'

'Elisabet.' Justen mock-chided his sister.

'She must have something that attracts you.'

'She wears clothes – trousers and a shirt, usually. A silvery
brown color.'

'Is she a good lover?'

Justen tried not to choke.

'Well, is she?'

'Elisabet, I think that's between Dayala and me.'

'She's a good lover. How smart is she?'

'A lot smarter than I am about some things.'

'Oh, dear.' Elisabet drew her knees up to her chin. Finally, she asked, 'How long are you going to stay?'

'A few more days, maybe less. At some point, I should be going back to Nylan.'

'I meant, when are you going back to Candar?'

Justen shrugged. 'I don't know. It won't be soon. There's too much to do. I don't even really know how I'm going to do what needs to be done.'

'Good. I hope it takes a long time. Why doesn't Dayala come here?'

'We talked about that. Until I finish my . . . task, I won't be going back there, either.'

'Justen, you don't sound very happy about this task.'

'I'm not. It has to be done, but I'm not happy about it.'

'Why do you have to do it?'

'Have you noticed anyone else besides Altara, Gunnar, or me very concerned about what Fairhaven is doing? Concerned enough to do anything except to ignore the Whites?'

'Father says that everyone thinks Recluce will be safe even if they take over all of Candar.'

'For a while, probably.'

'Then why—'

'I made order-tipped arrows, Elisabet. They killed a lot of innocent people. Sometimes I still have nightmares about them. That's the problem with evil. Chaos isn't necessarily evil, but the Whites are evil because they want to impose their ways on others through force. But the only way to fight evil is with force, and that makes the ones who fight it almost as bad as the evil ones. I don't want the whole world becoming evil – those who are evil and those who must become evil to stop them.'

Elisabet remained silent.

'If you let evil grow, then it takes more force to stop it, and that means even greater evil in the world. That's what's wrong with the Council's view.'

Elisabet crept up the bed and put her arms around Justen. 'You're very brave.'

'No, I can't say that. I'm angry. I'm angry, and I hate the Angels and the Whites for putting me in this position. If I don't do something, I'm a coward, and if I do, I become like the Whites, doing evil in the name of some ideal.'

His sister hugged him again.

Finally, he shrugged. 'I suppose that's life.'

'You're different. You're more serious.'

Justen forced a short laugh. 'That's life, too.'

106

Justen sat on the chair backwards, his loosely crossed arms resting on the curved back as he faced Gunnar. 'What are you doing right now?'

'Listening to you.' Gunnar leaned back on the narrow bed, his head resting against the paneled wall of the Brotherhood's quarters for senior wizards. The outer walls of Justen's room were only of dressed stone.

Justen sighed. 'I mean, for Turmin, for the Brotherhood.'

'Mostly scouting the high winds, trying to follow what's happening in Suthya. Also, following the wind patterns for the fleet, letting the ships know what to expect, where there are likely to be storms. The usual.'

'There's something wrong with that Counselor – Ryltar, I mean. It's not chaos, but he just doesn't feel right.' Justen pulled at his chin. 'I wish I knew what he's been up to. Could you find out?'

'You want me to spy on a Counselor?'

'It was just a thought.' Justen shrugged. 'It's probably too tedious.'

'You know, I always used to fall for that.' Gunnar sat up. 'You'd tell me I couldn't do something, and I'd have to prove I could.'

Justen grinned.

'All right. I'll spend a little time at it. Just a little, though.'

'That's all I could ask.' Justen sipped from the glass of now-warm dark beer.

'I still can't believe you can drink that stuff and be as orderly as Turmin says you are.' Gunnar frowned.

'The druids have a saying about deeper order.'

'Right. What about this lady ... this Dayala? You always avoid talking about her.'

'You're right. I do.' Justen took a last sip from the mug and set it aside. 'She's hard to describe.'

'Well ... what does she do, beside sitting around being a druid?'

'She makes things out of wood. She grows them, like that box I gave you.'

'Grows them? That's a little much, even for a druid.'

'I thought so, too, but ... it's really hard to explain unless you've been there. On the surface, everything seems so orderly, and it is. But they make each druid balance order and chaos on a deeper level.'

'Make?'

'They have a trial. You either undertake the trial and survive, or you leave.'

'You ... did their trial?'

Justen nodded, then added, 'I almost didn't make it. Sarronnyn was like a child's game in some ways. Not that you couldn't die in either place.'

Gunnar looked at Justen for a long time, and Justen could feel the order-probing. Finally, Gunnar shook his head. 'This Dayala ... was she the reason? Why you did the trial, I mean?'

'Partly. But I still felt I had to. I can't tell you exactly why, except that I felt something was wrong in Recluce. Maybe that was because of Firbek.'

'There can be bad apples in the best orchard.'

'But they shouldn't be put where they can spoil an entire barrel, should they?' Justen shifted his weight on the hard wood of the chair seat.

'What are you getting at, dear brother?'

'Why was Firbek the one leading the marines? I don't believe in coincidences as a rule.'

'You think . . .' Gunnar paused before continuing. 'Is that why you want to know about Ryltar? Because he's Firbek's cousin?'

'Call it curiosity.'

'Curiosity, my foot.'

'Even the White Wizards don't do things without reason.'

'What are you saying?' Gunnar scratched the back of his neck.

'Why are there so few White Wizards in Fairhaven? In a way, why has Fairhaven been even more successful since Cerryl the Great dispersed the great White Wizards to the capitals and the troop stations around Candar?'

'It might be because of the Iron Guard as well.'

'I'm sure that's part of it, but the concentration of chaos is as dangerous to them as it seems to us, perhaps more so.'

'What are you getting at?' asked Gunnar. 'You dance all over the place. This all started when I asked you about Dayala. Or maybe when . . . I don't know. You bring up so many things that I lose track.' Gunnar sighed. 'Oh, well, what do you mean about concentrating chaos?'

'I'm going to force them to concentrate all their chaos in one spot, and make sure that they do.'

'Just how will do you that? Send them a message begging them to do what you say they haven't done in centuries?'

Justen grinned as he stood up. 'You know, that might actually work.'

Gunnar rose from the narrow bed. 'You leaving?'

'I've got to work in the hall in the morning.'

'You never did tell me about your druid.'

'You're right. I didn't.' Justen grinned and headed for the door, opening it and turning back to face Gunnar.

The older brother sighed. 'Next time?'

Justen lifted his shoulders in an exaggerated shrug and grinned again.

107

After wiping the sweat off his forehead, Justen walked out through the engineering hall and onto the side porch. A brisk, cold breeze blew out of the west, and his breath steamed in the late afternoon. The cold air helped him regain his Balance. Sometimes now, he almost felt suffocated in the hall in the presence of so much ordered metal, yet paradoxically, he was even better than before at ordering iron.

He took a deep breath, and he cooled quickly in the cold air, but he stood in the weak light and looked toward the sun, hanging low over the Gulf of Candar.

Dayala . . . are you looking into the twilight, or brooding over your boxes and trees? How long will it be?

He caught a hint of warmth . . . of something. But was it merely his own longing, his own desires reflected within himself?

After taking another deep breath and a swallow from the water pitcher, he returned to the hall, not to his forge but to the raised platform at the rear, where Altara sat at a drawing board.

He waited until she finally looked up from the schematics. 'Yes, Justen?'

'I need to work late. Do you mind?'

Altara raised her eyebrows. 'You're ahead of schedule. You must have learned something in Naclos. Your work is better than when you left. I was thinking of letting you take over more of Fitzl's work. He's considering moving to the wagonworks in Alberth.'

'I need to work on some things.'

'Such as?'

'A model for a land engine.'

'Turmin said it couldn't be done. Too much chaos without the stabilizing order of the ocean.'

'I have an idea.'

Altara mock-winced. 'The most deadly words for an engineer. "I have an idea." So did Dorrin, and look at what a mess that caused.'

'I'm no Dorrin. I certainly couldn't figure out something like *The Basis of Order*. What harm would making a model do?'

'If I recall,' began the chief engineer with a grin, 'he started with a model, too.'

Justen spread his hands.

'I might, just might, consider it,' she relented.

'Oh?'

'If you would consider occasionally sparring with those of us less fortunate in our martial talents.'

'That's blackmail.'

'It certainly is.'

'All right. I stand blackmailed.'

'We'll see you after work tomorrow. Tonight,' concluded Altara with a broad smile, 'you can start on your model. After, of course, you finish what you were working on for the recovery pumps.'

'Of course, honored Chief Engineer.'

'Will changing the impellers solve the problem?'

'I'll have to see. I have a new design that might work.'

Altara nodded, and Justen knew that the conversation was at an end. He nodded in return and walked back to his forge, looking automatically for Clerve. His chest tightened.

Clerve – and for the year or so you worked for me, I never knew until the end that you could sing, or told you how much I appreciated it when I heard your songs. Was life always like that? Never saying what should be said until it was too late?

Justen pulled at his chin with his left hand and looked toward the forge. The problem with the recovery pumps for the new *Hyel* was simple enough. The rates of condensation and collection weren't uniform, and the impellers tended to break when they switched from air or froth to more solid condensate.

Probably the best way to straighten things out would be to overhaul the condensation system, but the problem had been given to him as a pump problem. He sighed and looked at the rough templates for the new impeller blades.

A varying-speed pump would be another answer, but that

made the system much more complex, which certainly wasn't a good idea, not with too much of it already running at the order-chaos limits.

He frowned, his thoughts drifting toward the land engine, and whether a full water jacket around the condenser would even out the pump's flow.

Finally, he shook his head and stepped toward the forge. One step at a time, and the current step was to rough-forge the redesigned impeller blades to see how well they worked. Then he'd have to grind and polish them before annealing and ordering them and locking them into the black iron ring that was the heart of the pump.

He slid the iron into the forge, glancing around the busy hall, listening to the cacophony of hammers, grinders, mills, and cutters that overrode the lower hum of voices.

108

Justen wiped the dust off the battered staff – still in his cubby from well over a year before, when he had left Recluce for the oh-so-heroic expedition to help Sarronnyn. He snorted as he hung up the leather apron.

'I can't believe it. You're actually going to spar with us – with the obsolete weapons.' Warin had deepened his voice almost into the bass range as he picked up a new, black iron-bound staff.

'I actually am.' Justen looked embarrassed. 'I'm sorry about your staff. I really am. But it got buried when the Whites' cannons targeted us, and I know you liked it. I wanted to bring it back.'

'Don't worry about it.' The balding older engineer touched Justen's shoulder. 'I know you would have if you could. Did it help?'

Justen nodded, thinking not of the battles, or of the order

embodied in the staff, but of the concern with which it had been given. 'Yes. Sometimes . . . a lot.'

'That's good. Maybe this afternoon you'll be so out of shape that you won't have a chance.' Warin tapped his staff on the stone tile floor. 'Come on.'

'I'm coming, and I probably won't have. I haven't picked up a staff since I lost yours on the battlefield.'

Justen followed the older engineer out to the near-empty highway across from the ancient armory.

Warin glanced up the long slope, but the highway was clear in the fall twilight. The close-fitted stone blocks remained solidly in place after centuries of use. 'Altara's probably over there practicing already.'

Justen shook his head. Why had Altara insisted on his resuming his old habits of sparring? Trying to see if action would return him to a shadow of his former devil-may-care attitude? Did she think that repeated words and actions could re-create the past? He twirled the staff, then dropped it against the stone and caught it on the rebound. But he had to jump to catch it, and he almost dropped it.

'You're out of practice.'

'So it seems.'

Warin paused before the half-open main doors of the armory, looking back to see if anyone had followed them, then marched into the black stone building that showed no apparent age, for all of the centuries that had passed since the original engineers had built it.

Justen eased out onto the open expanse of the practice floor. He placed his old staff against the wall and began to stretch, feeling tightness and the continuing awareness of the imbalance between order and chaos, an awareness that was becoming easier to handle, although it had not faded. He continued to stretch, glad that his muscles were not nearly as tight as he had feared. How much had Dayala's reordering of his body changed him? He swung his arms to loosen the tightness in his shoulders.

'You don't look that out of shape.' Warin eyed Justen.

'Appearances can be deceiving.'

In the far corner, several other engineers, with Altara at their center, were also exercising. In the near corner was less than a squad of marines.

'Where are the rest of the marines?'

'Some of them moved to the new armory. Don't know why, but it happened after Gerol took over. I suppose they didn't want to associate with mere engineers,' panted Warin from a knee squat. 'Those are Martan's squad. He's Hyntal's young cousin.'

'Hyntal – the captain of the *Llyse?*'

'Do you know any other Hyntals?'

'Hyntal the cooper; Hyntal the silversmith in Alberth.'

'Don't be so patronizing, Justen. We all know you can do the impossible and know the unknowable. Just give us credit for doing what we do and know.'

'I'm sorry.' Justen looked at Warin. 'I really didn't mean to sound that way.'

'It still bothers people, you know,' added a new voice. 'You about ready to show us how out of trim you are?' Altara swung a long staff as she crossed the floor.

'As ready as I'll ever be, I suppose.' Justen wiped his hands on his exercise trousers and picked up his staff. Then he squared his feet and lifted his old and battered staff, more than a cubit shorter than the black length held by Altara.

'You still using that little thing?' Altara brought the black staff whistling around.

Justen slid her staff off his and countered.

Altara stepped back, feet balanced, and brought her staff back in a half-parry. Justen eased forward, ducking the longer staff. The blocks, counters, thrusts, blocks, and parries alternated.

'You haven't . . . slowed . . . down.'

'Don't . . . know . . . why,' Justen puffed, barely managing to slip Altara's thrust and avoid a *thwack* to his ribs. 'That would . . . have . . . hurt.'

Altara eased back and took several deep breaths.

Justen took a deep breath himself before repositioning his feet and waiting for the next attack. Idly, he tried to touch the flow of order and chaos, both within himself and around him.

Altara started forward, and Justen let his body react to the order-balance and watched as his staff flickered and twisted.

'Darkness. What was that?' Altara looked at her staff, which lay on the exercise floor.

'Are you all right?' Justen asked.

'Fine. Didn't even touch my hands.' Altara picked up her staff and looked at Justen. 'Again?'

Justen reached for the sense of order once more, but he had to dance aside twice, awkwardly, before finally slipping into the patterns required. Within instants of his feeling the under rhythm of order-chaos, Altara's staff was flipped from her hands and crashed into the near wall.

'Some defense.' The chief engineer shook her head. 'Your attacks aren't as sharp . . . but I don't think anyone could touch you now.'

'I don't know. You almost got me twice.'

'You seemed to be struggling, like you were trying to find something, but when you found it, I couldn't get close.'

'Guess it was something I picked up in Naclos.' Justen shrugged.

Altara looked intently at him. 'I don't think you just picked it up somehow.'

'Maybe not.' Justen managed a half-smile.

'I think I'll try Warin for a round, if you don't mind.' She inclined her head to the balding engineer.

'My pleasure, Chief Engineer,' said Warin. 'But be kind. I'm not his mightiness, Justen. And he said that he was out of practice.'

'Then let us hope he never gets into practice.' Altara bowed and waited for Warin.

Justen watched, wondering, as their staffs interlinked and whirled. Even more now than before, the staff and weapon play seemed like a game. A game where one could get hurt, but a game. He pursed his lips, then took a deep breath.

'How did you do that?'

Justen turned to face the marine who stood beside him. 'Do what? Sorry, I don't think we've met. I'm Justen.'

'I know. Everyone, I think, knows who you are, if not by sight, at least by reputation.' The black-haired and square-faced marine grinned. 'I'm Martan. I was watching your work with the staff. It has to be technique. You're not in specially good condition, and Altara is, and you made her almost look silly.'

Justen looked at the packed clay underfoot.

'I was curious, that's all,' added the marine.

'I don't know . . . exactly. It's a combination of my old training and of order-sensing, of matching actions to the flow of order and chaos.'

'Chaos?'

Justen gave an embarrassed shrug. 'Whether or not anyone wants to admit it, there's chaos everywhere. Even our bodies have some chaos inside. So there are always flows.'

'Hmmm. I don't know how practical that is for someone who's not a mage.' Martan grinned again.

Justen looked sheepish. 'Probably not very, except that there's not much difference between really good training and what I did.'

'Do you ever think you'll go back and fight the Whites?'

Justen pursed his lips, not wanting to lie or to admit what he had in mind.

'If you need some marines, Ser, let me know.' Martan laughed. 'But I can keep a secret . . . except from Hyntal. He can find out anything.' He looked toward Warin and Altara, who had stepped away from each other for a break. 'It was good to meet you.' He inclined his head and trotted back toward his squad.

Justen frowned for a moment. Was it that obvious that he was thinking about returning to Candar?

109

'You know, Jenna. I've done a little checking on that young engineer.'

'I'm sure you have, Ryltar. Darkness forbid that anyone be termed more orderly than you.'

'Jenna, I believe you are being somewhat unduly hard on a fellow counselor,' interposed Claris. 'What did you find out, Ryltar?'

'He brought back a cargo of lorken from Diehl on that Bristan ship. Half of the sale price went to him. There was no credit to be paid back.'

'You're the trader, Ryltar. Please explain the subtleties to us.' Jenna brushed a strand of red hair off her forehead.

'This young engineer is lost in Candar. He supposedly travels the Stone Hills on foot, walks through Naclos untouched, and loses everything but the clothes on his back – even his horse and his blade. Yet he arrives in Nylan with some well-made clothes and half-owner of an unmortgaged and valuable cargo that nets him more than a hundred golds.' Ryltar spread his hands. 'Does not this seem rather odd, to say the least?'

'You can't be accusing him of chaos-corruption, I hope,' said the oldest counselor, 'unless you're willing to accuse Turmin of lying, or of incompetence.'

Ryltar shook his head. 'I have another question. What scheming are the Naclans doing? Is this a plot to get us to protect them after Suthya falls?'

'Oh, you admit that Suthya will fall?'

'Why not? The Whites will attack either before the snows or first thing in the spring after the thaw. It's clear that we cannot stop them, and Southwind cannot spare the resources now.'

'So, you feel that the druids have somehow influenced this young engineer?'

'Do you have a better explanation?'

'No. But that does not mean there isn't one.'

'I intend to keep watching our young friend.'

'By all means, Ryltar. By all means.'

110

Justen picked up the miniature gear train, then looked at the pieces of the model lying on the workbench. He set the gear train down.

He just couldn't make all the components, not without taking years; in that, the druids and Dayala had been right. And he supposed he could have others make the wheels, perhaps even the chassis he needed. But why did he need the land engine? Because, like Dorrin, he wanted to prove it could be achieved? That was a lousy reason in these days.

Besides, that didn't feel right. It had more to do with bringing a lot of order to Fairhaven. But even an ordered land engine wouldn't be enough, would it?

Oh, Dayala . . . I've gotten myself into a mess. What a mess.

There was no answer, not that he expected one. But at times, he thought he could feel a distant glimmer of warmth.

So what else did he need besides the land engine?

He shook his head. Engineering on the basis of intuition was light-fired hell. Anyway, after he finished the model of the power train, he needed to break down the design to see what he absolutely had to build, what he could do by modifying salvage, and what he could buy.

With a deep breath, he looked at the forge and eased a slip of iron into the coals.

A tall figure slipped inside the hall and walked toward the single forge in use.

'Justen?'

Justen looked up. 'Oh, Gunnar. How did you know I was here?'

'Where else would you be? You're not in your room, and you're not in Wandernaught. Your druid is an ocean away, and you're obsessed with something. This was a good bet.' The Air Wizard glanced at the model. 'This your land engine?'

'That's it. Such as it is.'

'You don't sound terribly happy about it. Was Turmin right?'

Justen frowned momentarily. 'In a way, but it doesn't matter.' He used the tool tongs to ease the slip of iron from the forge and set it on the bricks.

Gunnar pulled up a stained and battered stool and sat down. 'Why not?'

'Well, I don't think I could build a land engine that would run by itself the way one of the Mighty Ten does, but that wasn't what I had in mind anyway. I just wanted one to run from somewhere in eastern Candar to Fairhaven – as sort of a threat to persuade the White Wizards to get together.'

'If you can do it, what's the problem?'

'How would that induce the Whites to congregate?'

'If you managed to get through all the forces they'd send to stop you . . . you'll have to arm it, you know?'

'I hadn't thought about that, but you're right. That will mean it has to be bigger and heavier.'

'With more order, I'd guess, just to hold it together,' added Gunnar.

'Naturally.' Justen pulled at his chin.

'Couldn't you make something that just concentrated or radiated order? Black iron does that in a way, but you have to be close to feel it. What about whatever it was you did with the powder? Couldn't you do something like that?'

'I couldn't keep exploding powder the whole way to Fairhaven.'

'I'm sure you'll figure something out.'

'Since you're here . . .' Justen pursed his lips. 'Have you found out anything about the good Counselor Ryltar?'

'Well . . .'

'I'd appreciate it if you would. I'm getting word that he's expressed more than a passing interest in me.'

'All right. I still don't know what you want.'

'You'll know when you see it. I trust your judgment, brother dear.'

'I appreciate your trust . . . I think.' Gunnar lifted his shoulders. 'I really came by for another reason. I wondered if you wanted to go home at the end of the next eight-day.'

Justen frowned momentarily, then smiled. 'Why not? Sure.'

'Good thought, Brother. You can't brood too much.' Gunnar stood. 'Talk to you later.'

Justen slipped the iron back into the forge. He still had to work out the power-train design.

111

The wispy-haired trader walked up the gangway and onto the dark-hulled schooner berthed at the end of the pier. 'Hullooo . . .'

A light breeze from nowhere wafted around him as a figure, barely revealed in the lamps hung by the head of the gangway, stepped forward. The two lamps flickered, even though the flames were shielded by the smoked-glass mantles.

'Master Ryltar. We'd expected ye earlier.'

'I was delayed. You'd indicated some particular . . . gems.'

'Fire-eyes. From Hamor.'

'Not exactly through the emperor's trading house, I gather.'

The two men walked forward on the deck, and the light breeze shifted past them in the cool fall air.

'Chill night. Even a little wind makes it colder,' offered the smuggler. 'Just a score. Half seconds, half firsts.'

'I'd have to see them.'

'There's a glim here.' The smuggler's striker scratched, and he adjusted the wick of the small lantern on the hatch cover. Then he removed a cloth-covered case from his shirt and set it beside the lantern, easing back the cover.

'Fair quality, if they hold up in daylight,' Ryltar observed.

'Better than fair.'

'A trace.'

'More than a trace.'

'I'll grant a shade better than fair.' Ryltar paused, then added, 'Fifty golds for the lot.'

'Ha. No backwoods lout. You'll not see these again for less than a hundred.'

'Seventy's the best I can do. It will take years to sell these without destroying the market.'

'Eighty, then.'

'Seventy-five, if they look as good in the morning light.'

'We sail by mid-morning.'

'I'll be back with the coin before then.'

The case disappeared, and the lantern flickered. The two men walked silently back midships to the gangway.

'Good night, Master Ryltar.'

'Good night.'

Behind the corner of the harbormaster's building, Gunnar wiped his steaming forehead, glad for the cool air. That Ryltar was involved with Hamorian smugglers wasn't exactly wonderful news . . . but he doubted that simple smuggling was all that Justen had in mind. And if Ryltar routinely dealt with smugglers, might he deal as well with others even less . . . orderly?

The weather mage wiped his forehead again, then turned and walked slowly up the hill toward his room.

112

With short, heavy tongs, Justen eased the old and cracked pump shaft into the de-ordering forge at the rear of the engineering hall. This was an older forge, tucked behind the rolling mill and the gear cutters, both unused for the time. He looked toward the front, but he could see only a corner of the hall past the unused mill. In the limited space within view, he could see Quentel and Berol worked on the lathe.

Justen used the foot treadle to pump more air through the bellows and into the forge. He hated de-ordering black iron, because it was a single-handed job, and because it meant heating the iron to the white-hot burning point, which was even hotter than necessary for welding. When iron got that hot, even black iron, anything could go wrong. Yet the Brotherhood couldn't afford to tie up too much order in scrap metal, nor to waste the iron.

Justen frowned. Why couldn't he adapt the ordering process

that Dayala had shown him and turn it into a de-ordering process? Since the black iron was artificially ordered, and the idea wasn't to create chaos, something like that ought to work.

He took a deep breath and concentrated on the iron, trying to nudge the order bonds back out of place. The iron in the de-ordering forge continued to heat, but nothing happened to the long and cracked pump shaft as the one end started to turn cherry red.

Justen tried again, and felt a dull *clunk* in his mind. A cracking sound followed the mental *clunk*, and Justen blinked. His tongs held only about a third of the former pump shaft. Two other pieces of dull iron lay on the bed of cold gray ashes that had been a forge fire. All three pieces of de-ordered iron were cold – that he could tell.

He shook his head, letting his order senses scan the iron and the forge. The fragments were no longer black iron, and the forge fire was stone cold, as if it had burned out days earlier.

Justen eased the iron left in the tongs onto the fire brick shelf, set the tongs aside, and placed his hand near the iron rod that had been part of a pump shaft. No heat. Were his thoughts and senses deceiving him? He looked around and finally peeled a silver of wood from the bench, then set the tip of the sliver against the iron. Nothing. He repeated the process with the forge fire ashes, and with the other fragments. All were cold.

He pulled at his chin. What had happened?

'Now what have you done?' Altara stood at his shoulder. 'This forge was raging hot when I passed here a bit ago.'

'I don't know exactly. I was just trying to de-order the black iron without using so much heat.'

'Well . . .' Altara surveyed the forge, looking at the cold ashes. Then she stepped forward and passed her hand through what should have been a wall of heat. 'You managed the de-ordering far quicker than I've ever seen it done, but how did you manage to chill an entire forge in moments?'

'It was an idea, but it didn't quite work out the way I thought it would.' Justen pursed his lips.

'Why do I suspect this sort of thing with you?' Altara gave a gentle half-laugh. 'Even when you come up with the most deadly weapons, like those order-tipped arrows, something else, like those White cannons, shows up to counter them.'

'It's the Balance, I think.'

'Dorrin talked about it, but I don't know that everyone took him that seriously.'

'They should have,' Justen blurted.

'Why do I think you know more than you're saying?'

The junior engineer looked at the forge again, his forehead knitting, before returning his eyes to Altara.

'I've been thinking about our sparring match the other day.'

'Yes?' Justen said warily, his eyes flicking back to the cold ashes of the forge.

'So has someone else.'

'Warin?'

'Hardly,' laughed the dark-haired woman. 'Warin *knows* you couldn't do anything evil. Unfortunately, doing good can often be more disruptive than doing evil. Look at our great predecessor, Dorrin. Anyway, it appears that one of the engineers mentioned your skill to someone, and that someone mentioned it to another someone, and, lo and behold, one Yersol, junior factor in the noted establishment of Ryltar and Weldon and cousin of old Weldon himself, stopped me the other day to inquire about the "change' in your sparring. Then Hyntal asked me the same thing. Apparently, his cousin Martan had watched also, except young Martan wants to go on your next "adventure,' and Hyntal wanted to put in a good word for the young fellow. Adventures? You're barely back, and the word is out that you're going on adventures?'

'I doubt that Martan told anyone but Hyntal.' Justen shook his head as he considered the other aspects. 'Ryltar put Yersol up to it.'

'Of course. You are well on the way to proving that you are totally and utterly order-mad – whatever that meaningless term means. I really think that you need some time off to rest from your ordeal.'

'Time off? Are you telling me I'm crazy?' Justen tried to keep his voice level as he studied the older engineer.

'No. You're probably saner than any of us. But cold sanity isn't recommended in the land of the mad.' Altara's face was somber. 'You could do almost anything on your mother's forge that you could do here, couldn't you?'

'Not some of the delicate work, and there's no way I could do gears.'

'I'm sure that there must be some old gears that the Brotherhood has no use for, or some scrap you could pick up for a few silvers.'

Justen nodded, finally understanding. 'I suppose so . . . and the rest would do me good. Ryltar also wouldn't have to cast aspersions on all the engineers, would he?'

Altara nodded.

'You're worried? Really worried?'

'Wouldn't you be? He's one of three Counselors, and mostly the Council does what he wants, at least so far as the engineers and Candar go. He's already suggested that you're a druid spy.'

'So . . . if you've been told, and do nothing . . . ?'

'Exactly.'

'Darkness,' muttered Justen. 'Can't you do something?'

'Do you have any idea? We're not the White Wizards of Candar. Or even if we did have that kind of power, how would one assassinate a counselor without the tracks being traced right back to those with the most reason?'

'So I'm on my own?'

'Justen . . . you've been on your own since before we went to Sarronnyn. The rest of us just didn't know it.'

The junior engineer took a deep breath.

'I also think you'll have more time and freedom to do what you need to do. The word is out that you have enough coins so that you don't need much. But the Brotherhood will pay half your stipend because you are on a rest cure. Ryltar will appreciate that touch, and it's the best I can do. Except I know we have a great deal of 'scrap' – a great deal, and some of it just can't be easily de-ordered.' Altara smiled broadly.

Justen looked at the cold ashes of the forge. 'I don't think there's an easy way to de-order anything.'

The chief engineer shrugged. 'If there is, let us know. We'll be pleased to lend you a wagon to carry some of that scrap to Wandernaught for your experiments. After all, if we could find a cheaper way . . . Ryltar would have to be pleased.'

'Yes, he would.' Justen tried not to sigh. Despite Actara's offers of under-the-table help, he had the feeling that what had seemed merely difficult in Naclos was getting closer to being almost impossible.

'I'll make sure the word gets to the Council about your rest cure.'

'Thanks.'

113

Justen looked around the room before opening the wardrobe and pulling out his pack and setting it on the end of the bed, right above the single wooden crate that would hold his personal items.

After opening his pack, he put the pair of new boots in first. He really hadn't had a chance to break them in, and his old spare boots had long since been lost in Sarronnyn. Then he folded the brown shirt and the trousers he had not worn since returning to Nylan and slipped them inside.

Thrap!

'Come on in, Gunnar.'

'I just heard. I came as soon as I could,' gasped Gunnar. His forehead was damp with sweat.

'It's not that bad – not that you had to run all the way.' Justen forced a laugh.

'You're being forced out of the Brotherhood! That's not bad?'

'It's not the Brotherhood. I'm taking a rest cure. I would have had to leave sooner or later.' Justen picked up the razor he had forged in Naclos and wrapped it in an old work shirt before sliding it into the side of his pack. 'This way, I get a little more time. Sit down.' He gestured toward the chair. 'There's even some redberry in the pitcher.'

'But why? And why now?'

'Counselor Ryltar is trying to use me either to discredit Altara and the Brotherhood or to get them to discredit themselves by standing behind me.' Justen folded the last pair of underdrawers and stuffed them into the top of his pack.

'Is this the order-madness idea?'

'That's what Altara led me to believe. She's worried about Ryltar. Did you find out anything?'

'You were right, Justen. He's not chaos-corrupted – not yet. But he is corrupt. He's taking smuggled gems from Hamor, and probably counterfeiting the seal of the Imperial inspectors.'

'You saw this?'

'Last night on the *Versalla*. She left port a bit ago. Ryltar offered some eighty golds for what looked to be a lot more in gems – fire-eyes.'

'That doesn't surprise me. What does surprise me is that the Council puts up with it.' Justen leaned over and picked up the Capture board, setting it on the bed beside the filled pack. 'Don't want to put that on the bottom . . .' he muttered as he opened the small drawer in the desk, almost dropping it as the long-ago violence with which it had been formed burned his fingers. He grasped the wood more firmly for an instant and lifted out the leather case that contained his drafting kit.

'Coin,' offered Gunnar. 'What sustains the Council, and the Brotherhood, are the trade levies and contributions of the traders. Some of the traders, like Ryltar's family, make significant contributions to the Council coffers. Those contributions keep the levies lower, and in turn, that keeps the smaller merchants happy with the Council.'

'I see. So that's why Ryltar's on the Council, and why the Council is reluctant to cross him?' Justen picked up the box Dayala had given him, felt the warm tingling in his fingers, and momentarily looked out into the chill gray beyond the window.

'It's never that simple.'

'Probably not.' Justen reordered his pack, looking for something soft in which to wrap the box, though it was probably tougher than it looked – like Dayala herself.

'What are you going to do?'

'Go quietly order-mad at home. Altara says that no one will be very interested . . . not in the beginning anyway.'

'Buying time. For what?' Gunnar looked directly at Justen. 'There's a lot you still haven't explained. Just what were you doing that caused Altara, out of the blue, to give you a rest cure? And what do you intend to do in Wandernaught? I can't believe that you'll be content to just take up smithing with Mother or cultivating apple orchards with Father.'

'I think some original smithing will do me good.'

Gunnar theatrically put both hands on his forehead, then thrust his arms toward the plastered ceiling and rolled his eyes. 'Oh, darkness save us. Is it thy will that the Temple of Order endure such profanity in the name of sanctity, or is it such sanctity in the name of profanity, or—'

'Enough!' Justen shook his head, trying not to laugh.

The Air Wizard bounded onto the chair and thrust his right arm toward the window. 'Light! Let there be light! From disordered light, let there come ordered darkness that will shine into the souls of women and – the Angels of – what is it? – ah, yes, the Angels of Naclos forbid – even into the dark and dreary souls of benighted men . . .'

Justen shook with silent laughter at Gunnar's antics.

'. . . but let us also not forget the beneficent Council of Recluce. Include them, too, in the warm and ordered darkness, lest they see the world as it is and not as they wish it to be, unless, of course, there is a profit in seeing true. For which, in that case, let them find the means to charge those in light for the privilege of seeing what they have already seen . . .'

Gunnar dropped off the chair, coughed, and downed the remainder of the redberry – right from the pitcher. 'I can't do it as well as you used to . . . but it's all horseshit. The druids want something. The ancient Angels want something. The Whites want something. The Council wants something. And every last one of them thinks they have a lantern that shines truth only for them. And, yes, none of them want to listen to the lowly engineer, Justen, who just might have discovered something.' Gunnar coughed again. 'Of course, the even lowlier and more insignificant wizard, Gunnar, has yet to discover what that something the less-insignificant Justen has discovered, even though he uses his poor talents to skulk around ships and spy on esteemed members of the Council. Even though the insignificant Gunnar has yet to receive the confidence of the showered-with-order-and-mystic-knowledge Justen . . .'

'All right . . .' Justen sighed. 'Sit down.'

'I hear and obey, most insignificant engineer, recalling that I am even less significant than thee.' Gunnar dropped into the chair.

'You want a straight and honest answer. Fine. Any more order, such as represented by adding bigger and more highly ordered warships to the Mighty Ten, can be balanced only by greater chaos. Any more order, such as represented by the development of an ordered Iron Guard, can result only in greater chaos. More order on our earth, despite all the theories of all the mages, means more chaos, and more chaos means greater and greater power to Fairhaven. The greater Recluce's success, the greater Fairhaven's, and the greater the misery in Candar.' Justen's eyes were like black ice as he fixed them on Gunnar.

'Shit. I had a feeling . . .' Gunnar shook his head. 'I did have to ask, didn't I? And you intend to do something about it, I presume?'

Justen nodded. 'Except that de-ordering something leaves a bigger mess than not having ordered it in the first place. That's why Altara got upset. I de-ordered some black iron without heating it first. It de-ordered and sucked all the heat out of the entire forge.'

'So you're going to turn all of Recluce into cold ashes or ice to save Candar?' Gunnar licked his lips.

'Hardly. I'm not that altruistic. I'm working on something to take to Fairhaven – a land engine.'

'And you expect them to let you do this?'

'No. I'll have to deceive people here on Recluce and use force to get to Fairhaven once I land in Candar.'

'My brother, the lying, altruistic crusader who finally tells the truth, if not the details.' Gunnar grinned. 'This makes more sense. Count me in.'

This time, Justen shook his head. 'What?'

'Count me in.' Gunnar's face hardened. 'I wasn't exactly indifferent to Krytella, you know. Or maybe you didn't. And I'd known Ninca and Castin for a long time. And you, you love this druid, darkness knows why, but it shows, and you won't

even think about returning to her, not until you do what you've
set out to do.'

Justen swallowed, then reached forward, bent down, and
hugged Gunnar. After a moment, he straightened. 'Want to
help take a load of scrap to Wandernaught?'

'Sure. I'll take a good scrap anytime.'

'Even if you can't lift an edged weapon?'

Gunnar grinned, and Justen grinned back.

114

Cirlin stepped out from the smithy while Justen and Gunnar
were still easing the blocks under the wagon wheels. The mist
that was not quite a drizzle flowed around both men and off the
oiled canvas that covered the wagon bed.

'Justen, what on earth have you got there?' asked Cirlin.

'Iron . . . old parts, gear assemblies, engineering stuff.' Justen
straightened and wiped the dampness off his forehead, a dampness mostly from sweat. 'We'll need to unload this somewhere,
maybe in the shed.'

'You'll need to unload the shed before you do. Your father
has it filled with more lengths and sizes of wood than three
generations would need.'

'Well, we could use the wood to build another shed . . .'

'With no two pieces the same size? Leastwise, you'd be giving
him a reason to think about what to do with the wood.'

'What about the horses?' asked Gunnar.

'Where's Elisabet?' asked Justen nearly simultaneously.

'There's room for both in the end stall,' answered the smith.
'Your sister is at Magistra Mieri's for her lessons. You two do
what you have to here, and I'll finish Hruson's harness. Then
we'll have hot cider or ale or whatever.'

'We'll unload later, after we talk to Father about where to
put it all.'

'Fine.' Cirlin turned back toward the smithy. 'Let me finish, and you can tell me the rest then.'

Justen and Gunnar began loosening the harnesses, each working on one horse. After stabling the team, they walked through the increasingly heavy and cold rain toward the house.

'Justen . . . this is cold, and it feels like it could turn to snow.'

'You don't know?'

'It's right on the edge, and I haven't paid much attention. With all your talk about creating chaos every time we put more order into the world, I'm not exactly encouraged to influence the weather.'

'A little bit won't matter. I know . . . it's hypocritical, but I'm already into deception. So what's a little hypocrisy?'

'You're also into sarcasm and bitterness, neither of which is particularly good.'

'You're right on that. We also don't have anyplace to put all this iron.' Justen gestured at the wagon as they passed it and turned onto the path to the house.

'Fine.' Gunnar's face went blank, and he stood in the cold rain, the droplets no longer going around him but falling upon him for a moment, until Justen guided him away, waiting for Gunnar's senses to return.

After some time, Gunnar staggered and took a deep breath. 'It'll still snow at Land's End, but from mid-Recluce south, it will be rain.'

'Thank you.'

Horas had four mugs of hot cider and a platter of shortbread squares on the dining-area table by the time they had taken off their waterproofs and damp boots.

'Your mother should be in shortly.'

'Good,' mumbled Justen, sipping the hot liquid.

Gunnar eased into a chair, then reached for his mug as Justen set down his mug and seated himself.

'I take it that Gunnar was "adjusting" the weather?'

'Moving the snow a little north. Not much, only a little,' admitted the Weather Wizard.

'That's just to give us some time. We need somewhere to put my supplies,' added Justen.

'Must be a lot of iron in that wagon,' observed Horas, lifting his mug and letting the steam curl around his face. 'It should fit in the shed, I'd think. Need to be doing something with that wood, anyway. Your mother's been saying I've collected it for too long.'

'I might need some of it,' Justen said. 'Wood's lighter than iron, and stronger, stone for stone.'

'You're welcome to it.'

The outside door closed, and Cirlin stepped into the kitchen. 'I thought it was going to snow, but it's raining. That your doing, Gunnar?'

'Yes.'

'Well, I can't say as I'm ready for snow, as long as the rain doesn't freeze.' The smith eased into a chair and took the fourth mug.

'It won't. It would melt before long, anyway. It's too early in the winter for freezing.' Gunnar reached for one of the shortbread squares.

'We didn't expect to see either of you for a time yet.' Horas set his mug on the table.

Gunnar looked toward Justen.

'I need everyone's help, I think,' Justen answered.

'That's a rare admission, Justen.' Cirlin leaned back in the chair. 'What sort of help?'

'I need to build a land engine.'

'A land engine?'

'A small ship that travels on wheels. Just on the roads, though.'

The smith pursed her lips. 'That would seem like a large order for a small smithy, even with an engineer such as you.'

'It's not so bad as that. Altara will let me use some old parts and some spare plating, and I've figured out how to convert a steam pump.'

'How will you get them here . . . and what is the purpose of all this?'

'The first wagonload is what I brought.' Justen shrugged. 'And the purpose is to build something that will stop the White Wizards.'

Horas rubbed his forehead. 'I know you two are talented young men, even extraordinarily talented, but you're going to try to build something in our little smithy that will defeat the

White Wizards, when something like eight of you could not do this with the support of the Tyrant of Sarronnyn?'

'It does sound stupid.' Justen laughed once, almost harshly. 'But I think I can do it.'

'Why here?'

Justen looked at the polished stone tiles of the floor. 'The Council would oppose it.'

'Then they'll come here and stop you.'

'Hardly . . . they think I'm mad, that my stay in Naclos has somehow disordered me. That's why I'm here. They're paying me a half-stipend in order for me to take a rest cure at home.'

'Mad?' Cirlin smiled wryly. 'Exasperating, romantic, imaginative . . . still a bit of a scamp. But not mad.'

'Neither the engineers nor the Council know what to do. Even Turmin says there's not a trace of chaos or disorder around me. In fact, he says I'm the most ordered man he's ever studied. They've coined a new term for it – I'm "order-mad." I'm playing on that. I've started to work on ideas for a new type of order-machine to bring true order to Candar, and I really want most of the Council to dismiss what I'm doing. I can't lie about it . . . so the next best thing is for them to ignore me.'

'I suppose I can see that.' Cirlin frowned. 'But won't some people be suspicious?'

'Probably. I think Counselor Ryltar already is. But that's because he's not quite right . . . somehow. Gunnar's looking into him.'

'If it's on the winds, Gunnar will find it.'

'That's what I thought.'

'Justen's right, I think,' added Gunnar. 'Ryltar's involved with smugglers, and a few other things that I haven't traced yet.'

'And if he's corrupt?' asked Horas. 'What does that change?'

Justen frowned.

'If he has been on the Council for these several years, do you not think that they feel the same things you do? And since he is still there . . .' Horas raised his eyebrows.

'They aren't likely to do much even if there is proof of corruption?' asked Justen.

'I'm just a holder and a tree farmer.' Horas shrugged. 'But since when have even the Councils of Recluce acted on charges of corruption when it is not in their interest to do so? Has not

Ryltar advocated staying out of war in Candar? Who would call him corrupt for that?'

'I see your point,' conceded Justen. 'If he's smart enough to be on the Council, even if Gunnar discovers that he's corrupt, how could we prove it, and who would listen to a young engineer who's order-mad and his brother, the Air Wizard?'

'You want me to stop looking?'

'No. I still need to know the truth.'

'I think Justen's right, Gunnar,' added Cirlin. 'You have to know what is true and what is not, even if no one else does.'

'Great.' Gunnar looked into his mug.

'How about dinner?' suggested Horas. 'Elisabet should be home before much longer.'

115

'So . . . you're not going back to Fairhaven for the winter? You're actually staying here in Rulyarth. How incredibly dutiful.' Eldiren blew on his hands. 'You can freeze, together with Jehan and me.'

'Oh, stop it. You know it's not dutiful in the slightest. If I'm in Fairhaven, that gives Histen the chance to accuse me of neglecting my duties. Also, like it or not, troop morale is not favorably affected by commanders who enjoy warm weather and luxury while the fighters don't.' Beltar looked out through the mansion's glazed windows at the fast-falling thick flakes of snow.

'You're actually trying to become a well-loved commander?' asked Eldiren.

At the other side of the table, Jehan's eyes darted from Eldiren to Beltar.

'What are my options? Be relieved or be less respected? No, thank you. Besides, unlike previous commanders, I intend to be ready to move with the thaw. Perhaps before, and that takes work now.'

'A great deal,' offered Jehan slowly. 'It might be prudent, though.'

'How?' asked Eldiren.

'We need more supplies, and they need fewer supplies. We do have some winter troops.' Beltar nodded to Jehan, as if thanking him.

'You're going to harass them in winter. That's not exactly charitable,' suggested Eldiren, a touch of irony in his voice.

'I never said I was charitable. I intend to bring Suthya down quickly and with as few casualties to us as possible.' Beltar gestured at the snow outside. 'We'll have the winter troops train the others in groups – just enough to keep them from fighting and drinking too much, and I'll let it be known that any section of levies or lancers that has too many fights will be rotated into extra training.'

'What kind of training?'

'Taking Suthyan border towns and farms with stores – that sort of thing.'

Eldiren shivered. 'I suppose we'll accompany these . . . expeditions?'

'Of course.'

'Cheer up, Eldiren,' offered Jehan. 'You could have to stay here and listen to complaining troops, and have to execute this trooper or that for torturing some local wench.'

'Is that still happening?' snapped Beltar.

'Not since you turned the last lancer into a candle in the square,' said Jehan. 'But some of them will be back at it once you leave.'

'No, they won't. I'll fry every trooper in any squad that lets it happen,' declared Beltar.

'You can't say that.' Jehan sighed. 'Then the locals will trump up something, and you'll either have to fry an innocent squad or back down and look stupid. Either way, you'll lose.'

Beltar looked from one to the other. 'Then what do you suggest?'

'Don't do anything,' said Jehan. 'Anything that happens will be hushed up because they know you'll fry them if you find out. A local woman or two will disappear. That's the best you can hope for.'

Beltar took a deep breath.

'Power just doesn't solve every problem,' added Eldiren.

'You can make up the training-rotation schedule, Eldiren.' Beltar gave the thin-faced wizard a crooked smile.

Eldiren shrugged. As Beltar stood and turned to depart, Jehan shook his head.

116

Justen studied the plans laid out on the bench, each corner of the drawings weighted down by stones. He glanced from the parts spread on the clean-swept smithy floor to the plans and back again.

'How do you intend to get the power to the wheels?' Cirlin looked at the axle parts, then at the model on the crude workbench.

'Warin helped me with that.' Justen riffled through the stack of papers before he came to the sheet he wanted. 'See this?'

Cirlin looked over her son's shoulder. 'It looks like a box in the middle of the axle.'

'It is, sort of. That's where the drive shaft, just like the propeller shaft, joints the axle. But it lets each wheel be driven at a different rate when the land engine turns.'

The smith glanced toward the iron sections and odd-shaped parts stacked in the racks that Justen had built in the far corner of the smithy. 'Will all of that go into this machine?'

'Most of the stuff here. The other parts I'm supposed to use for material or de-order and ship back to Altara.'

'How are you going to pay for all of this?'

'You want pay? That's fair. How much?' Justen grinned at his mother.

'That's not what I meant, and you know it.'

'I know. But I should pay. If you help me, you can't do other things.'

'You could help me, too, you know. You're a good smith in your own right.'

'I will. But I can pay. The druids gave me a half-interest in a cargo of lorken and sent me off with some "trinkets." That's what they called them.'

'Trinkets?'

'Gems – all kinds. Dayala said that I'd need them, one way or another. So far, I haven't had to cash in any.'

'Why are the druids so willing to support you? That seems a little odd. Charity from strangers needs looking at.'

'It's in their interests. They think the buildup of order in Recluce and the buildup of chaos in Fairhaven should be stopped.'

'Why not just stop chaos?'

'That was where I started. But they showed me more about how order and chaos are related, and I don't think you can stop chaos without reducing order.'

'That's a terrible thought, son.'

'I suppose so, but it makes sense.'

'Why do you believe them?'

Justen did not answer momentarily as he used calipers to measure the diameter of one of the possible axle shafts. 'The Whites' Iron Guard. Why else would a bunch of White Wizards build up order within their own domains unless it benefited them?'

'That doesn't mean—'

'I know. The Iron Guard can stand up to things that the White lancers can't. Why, I can't tell you. On the surface, it's probably not logical, but it feels right.'

Cirlin laughed. 'I'll accept that sooner than logic, Justen.'

Justen set the calipers on the bench. 'This one is flawed on the inside. I'll need to check some others in the shed.'

'Don't track in too much mud.'

Justen shook his head and smiled as he started through the cold, light rain once again – rain that promised to become snow by night.

117

The burly sailor in the officer's jacket walked up the stone-paved wharf of Nylan through light flakes of snow that would not stick to the stones or slate roofs. A brush of wind tossed a few flakes into his face, and he wiped away the dampness with a gray rag that might once have been white. At the end of the wharf, he turned to the right, toward the trading houses set on the lower part of the hillside.

The block-lettered sign above the doorway of the third building proclaimed 'Ryltar and Weldon.' Beneath the name in smaller letters, in both Temple and Hamorian, were the words, 'Factors for the Eastern Ocean.'

He moved under the overhang and opened the door, stepping inside and closing it behind him.

'Might I help you?' A young clerk dressed in brown stood up.

'Captain Pesseiti for Master Ryltar.'

'A moment, Ser.'

Pesseiti shifted his weight from one foot to the other. His eyes traveled from the plain table where the clerk had been sitting through the half-open doorway and into the corner office, then back to the bookcase, filled with what appeared to be ledgers.

'Please go in, Ser.'

The ship's master nodded and walked past the clerk into the office.

Ryltar stood to greet him. 'What can I do for you, Captain?'

'The *Tylera* is berthed at the end of the big pier.' Pesseiti extended a rolled parchment toward the factor. 'I've got the transport for the Ruziosis' woolens – the black and the tan.'

Ryltar unrolled the parchment and read through the neatly lettered contract. His fingers brushed over the seal at the end. 'Seems in line. How do you intend to pay?'

The *Tylera's* captain extended a flat but thick envelope.

'Looks like a warrant on the Imperial Treasury of Hamor.'

'Aye, and it is. How else would old Kylen do it?'

'How indeed,' murmured Ryltar as he slipped the folded document from the envelope and scanned it. 'This time, he even remembered to include the conversion fee.'

'Your woolens are the best.'

'At least among the best.'

'How soon can we ship?'

'The woolens are baled, but they'll need to be properly packed. Mid-afternoon for the first load. Day's end for the rest.'

'Could be better, but could be a lot worse.' Pesseiti nodded, then reached toward his belt. He laid a heavy leather bag on the table. 'This is the bonus payment for the last consignment.'

Ryltar's eyebrows lifted as a draft ruffled the papers on his desk. 'Oh . . . ?'

'For those special cargoes out of Sarronnyn . . . if you know what I mean. The customer was extraordinarily pleased.' Pesseiti straightened and tipped his cap. 'Best I be going, Master Ryltar. We'll be ready to load by mid-afternoon, rain or no rain.'

'We'll have the woolens there, under oilcloth if necessary.'

'Good.' Pesseiti nodded and left.

Ryltar picked up the bag slowly, hefting it gingerly and shaking his head. He wiped his forehead, which was damp, despite the faint breeze and the coolness of the room.

In the tavern two doors down, Gunnar wiped his own sweating forehead. *Gold . . . and Ryltar was surprised. But not too surprised.* He swallowed the last of the redberry in his mug and left four coppers on the table before slipping out into the snow showers.

118

Creaakkk . . . The sound of a heavy wagon echoed into the shed where Justen sorted old iron and black iron parts, looking for a yet smaller gear set. He straightened, wondering if the wagon were that of Cirlin's ironwright or of someone else's, and eased the shed door open, almost welcoming the cold air on his face. The black-bodied wagon, pulled by two large chestnuts, had entered the yard by the time Justen stepped out into the cold. On one wagon side-panel was the symbol of the black hammer outlined in white. Justen looked again at the black-bodied wagon and the two figures on the front seat.

'Altara! Warin!'

The balding smith flashed Justen a grin before dropping from the wagon seat. 'Get out here, you lazy engineer, and help us unload. It's your stuff, after all.'

By the time Justen had crossed the short space between the yard and the shed, Altara had climbed down from the wagon and Warin was already unfastening the tailgate.

'I didn't expect you,' Justen admitted. 'Why did you come?' Then he grinned. 'But I do have some de-ordered iron you can take back.'

'That would help.' Altara set the wagon brake.

Warin tied the horses to the stone post.

'You know, Justen, I still don't know why I'm doing this. We're running behind on the *Hyel* as it is, and here I am almost smuggling you parts and equipment.' Altara brushed a short lock of hair off her forehead.

'Because,' suggested the younger engineer, 'you know that something has to be done about Fairhaven, and this is one way of easing your conscience. Especially since the Council continues to do nothing.'

'You should have been a wizard, not an engineer.'

'He is both, I think.' Warin grinned at Altara. 'At least after his adventures in Naclos – whatever they were. You notice that somehow we never quite get all the answers when we ask him about Naclos and the druids, except that there's clearly a very special druid mixed up in all this.'

'Ah, yes, the one called Dayala.'

Justen felt himself flushing. 'I'd better help unload this. I really do appreciate it.'

'See! There he goes again.' Warin grinned.

'Well . . . you don't exactly talk much about Estil,' countered Justen as he struggled to hoist a box containing a matched gear set.

'I think he's in love, really in love.' Warin grunted as he followed Justen toward the smithy with a second box. His breath was a cloud in the cold winter air.

'You think?' Altar eased a section of thin plate onto a dolly she had unloaded and wheeled it slowly along the path after the others.

'Either that or he's spoiling for a fight.' Warin paused. 'Justen, I almost forgot. I ran into Martan the other night, and he asked me to tell you that he was ready any time you are. He's even dumber than I am, to want to spar with you.'

Justen frowned momentarily. Martan wasn't reminding Justen about sparring. Then he asked, 'Can you stay for dinner?'

'For your father's cooking? That might be one reason we came.'

Cirlin joined the unloading brigade, and the four carried in the supplies Altara had brought, including gear sets, shaft blanks, and a small condenser. Justen noticed several more sheets of thin plate yet to be taken to the shed.

'Why the plate?'

'With your skills, you could turn it into black iron armor, but anything that travels roads has to be light.' Altara grunted as she eased the plate onto the dolly. The dolly's wheels sank slightly into the hard-frozen ground.

'You should be designing this machine.'

'I just might look at your designs. You're the demon's best on application, Justen, but design . . . I don't know.'

'I like you, too.'

'Estil still thinks you're imagining that druid, Justen,' Warin interjected. 'She says no one real could turn your head that much.'

'Tell her,' grunted Justen as he helped Altara ease the plate against the heavy beams on the side wall of the smithy, 'that she could have if you hadn't tied her up first.'

'Lusting after another's man's woman . . . why, Justen, I do believe you actually show a human side.'

Cirlin laughed. So did Altara and, finally, Warin.

'I presume,' added Horas's voice from the smithy door as the laughter died, 'that we will be having company for dinner.'

'We certainly will, and for the evening as well,' added Cirlin.

'We wouldn't—'

'Where would you stay? At the Broken Wheel, where you'd freeze? Nonsense!' snapped Horas.

Altara and Warin exchanged glances.

'We're not that hard to persuade,' said the chief engineer.

'Besides,' added Warin, 'I might be able to find out more about this mysterious druid.'

'Good luck,' said Cirlin. 'I'm his mother, and beside the fact that she's wonderful, beautiful, green-eyed, silver-haired, and saved him from many fates worse than death, I know almost nothing. Oh, and yes, she somehow coaxes trees into producing beautiful boxes and other wooden items.' The smith looked at Altara, who returned the smile.

'It's going to be an interesting evening,' ventured Justen.

'Stop jabbering,' suggested Altara, 'and we'll get this junk in sooner. Also, where's this supposed de-ordered iron? You did mention it, you know.'

'In that bin in the corner. There.' Justen pointed.

Warin walked over and looked down. 'Darkness . . . he really did it, Altara. Those are turbine rings, but they're only soft iron now.'

Altara followed Warin's eyes, and her fingers caressed the iron. 'You could make a business out of this.'

Justen shrugged. 'Call it return for value . . . in a way.'

'It would take three eight-days to undo that with a forge, and I'll bet it didn't take you that long.'

'No.' Justen did not volunteer that the bin contained only an afternoon's worth of effort or that the shed had turned into an ice house, with heavy sheets of ice across everything.

'Good. Then I can report honestly that we're saving time and labor by sending you junk. Now let's get this stuff out to the wagon.'

Even before they had finished stacking the incoming parts and scrap and reloading the wagon, Elisabet was waving from the kitchen door.

'We still need to stable the horses.'

'Altara, go talk to Elisabet. We'll do the horses.'

The chief engineer shrugged and walked through the late afternoon light toward the house while Justen and Warin unharnessed the two draft horses and led them into the stable.

'The brushes are on the shelf there.'

'Altara said you never learned to ride, really, until you went to Sarronnyn. So how did that happen, since you grew up with horses and a stable?' Warin wiped horse hair off his face with his free hand as he finished one of the chestnuts.

'We had horse teams, not riding horses. I could care for a horse. I just couldn't ride well. Are you about done?'

'More than done. It's cold here.'

'It's not that bad.'

'I grew up in Nylan. It's lower and warmer than in mid-Recluce.' Warin watched as Justen poured several scoops of grain into the manger.

'You took long enough,' said Elisabet when the two engineers walked into the kitchen and took the two last places at the big table.

'Hot cider, ale, or redberry?' asked Horas.

'Hot cider.'

'Ale.'

'Ale?' Warin shivered.

'How he can be so ordered and drink ale and dark beer?' asked Altara.

'It's just superficial order.' Justen laughed.

'How can order be superficial?'

'Don't get him started,' warned Cirlin.

'What about the druid, then?' asked Warin.

'Dayala?' Elisabet smiled broadly. 'She's a druid who doesn't have a tree – not one that she lives in anyway, except that her house is sort of grown out of trees, and she always goes barefoot, even in the desert, but she wears clothes.'

'Is that all?' asked Warin plaintively. 'A real druid who doesn't live in a tree? Why does she go barefoot?'

'She is a druid,' answered Justen dryly. 'And she did manage to outwalk me and my boots across the Stone Hills and the grasslands. I never did manage walking barefoot through the great forest or the grasslands, let alone the Stone Hills.'

'Do they use iron?' asked Altara.

'Of course,' answered Justen. 'Some of them do have problems with edged things like blades, and even with knives. But some of us do, too. I understand that Dorrin couldn't deal with blades.'

'I want to hear about the silver-haired druids,' protested Warin, grinning sideways at Elisabet.

'Well . . .' began Justen's sister.

'Elisabet . . .'

'You're no fun, Justen. You tell them, or I will.'

'I know I'm no fun. Wait a moment.' Justen took a sip of the dark ale.

'Here's some fresh-baked bread and cheese!' announced Horas, setting a long platter on the table. 'Ought to hold you until dinner's ready.'

'Don't get this in the engineering hall, do you?' asked Warin, looking at Altara.

'Don't get that at home, do you?' countered the chief engineer.

'No, but he gets a few other things . . .' suggested Justen.

'You should talk, from what I've heard about your druid. And from that cow-eyed look you get when you think about her and you think no one's looking.'

Altara coughed, trying not to choke on her hot cider, shaking her head at the same time.

'What can I say?' Justen laughed. 'What can I say?'

'Probably nothing,' suggested Cirlin. 'Try the bread before it gets cold. And try not to look too cow-eyed.'

'What's cow-eyed?' asked Elisabet.

Altara choked again, then managed to swallow her cider.

119

'I'm still concerned about that engineer – the order-mad one.' Ryltar leaned forward across the black-oak table.

'Order-mad? That's an odd choice of words.' Claris coughed, then sipped from her mug before setting it back on the ceramic coaster bearing a replica of the seal of Recluce. 'What do you mean?'

'Yes, Ryltar, please enlighten us.' Jenna's fingers cupped her mug lightly, almost as if caressing the smooth black finish.

'Well . . . Turmin said that this engineer, this Justen, is clearly the most highly ordered man he has observed. Perhaps too highly ordered. I understand that he is convinced that he must build some sort of land engine that travels the roads the way our ships travel the seas.'

'That might seem impractical, but scarcely mad.' Claris pursed her lips before continuing. 'Everyone thought Dorrin was mad, but we'd scarcely be here if he hadn't built the *Black Hammer*.'

'You don't think that running chaos along our roads, particularly the High Road, is not mad?'

'He isn't doing that, is he?'

'He will be.'

'Ryltar . . . don't you notice a little inconsistency in your arguments?' Jenna's mild tones barely rose above the rain that pelted against the windows. 'You tell us not to worry about Fairhaven, because they're not yet invading someplace, but we're supposed to worry about an excessively ordered engineer who has done far less than Fairhaven has. I'm frankly a great deal more concerned about the increased levies that were marched across the Westhorns and into Sarronnyn before the snows. Now it seems that each eight-day we receive reports of yet another town or hamlet falling to the Whites – and this has been during the winter. The ice has cut off Suthya from sea trade, and the Whites surround the Suthyans. By the spring thaw, only Armat, Devalonia, and a few coastal towns will remain in Suthyan hands.' Jenna looked at her short and square-cut fingernails, then laid her hands on the table.

'Most of Suthya's people are on the coast, and most of their troops are safe,' pointed out Ryltar in a reasonable tone.

'That's true enough, Ryltar,' countered Jenna, 'except that this winter campaign means that the Suthyans will have no territory left to shield them from immediate attack after the thaw, and not enough time to bring in supplies or mercenaries, or anything much by sea.'

'The wizards are fighting among themselves.' Ryltar smiled crookedly.

'One power-hungry wizard destroyed another, and the stronger one has shown himself far more able and dangerous. Suthya will fall even before summer.'

'I still must ask the same question, dear colleagues. What on earth can we possibly do about it?' Ryltar steepled his fingers and waited for a response. 'What, honestly, can we do? We cannot even get ships to Suthya at the moment.'

Jenna and Claris exchanged glances.

120

The cold and late winter rain, interspersed with occasional fat flakes of snow, plastered Justen's hair against his skull. He hefted the rock hammer and tapped around the stone, looking for traces of the heavy yellowish powder that when order-sorted, became grayish false lead. Order-sorting the heavy stuff was harder work than forging black iron. Wizards who handled too much of it for too long, Justen knew, died, but he felt that his control of the order-chaos balance within his own body would help protect him.

Even the powder emitted unseen flashes of chaos, like white embers, and the small traces of false lead seemed like black isles holding chaos; it was almost a miniature replica of the way the great forest of Naclos had felt. Somehow, finding the yellowed, powdery stuff was easier in the rain, even rain mixed with snow, perhaps because the falling water blanked out the more distant chaotic impulses.

Justen lifted the hammer again, wishing he were back in Naclos with Dayala, water lizards, forest cats, Stone Hills, and all. What was she doing? Immersing herself in her work, visiting her parents and friends, worrying about him? He shook his head. Dayala couldn't afford to pine away after him, and the sooner he got on with his work, the sooner he could sort out the mess and head back to Naclos. But what would he do there? Be a smith?

He shrugged. There were worse things, far worse things.

He shivered as cold water seeped down his neck. At that moment, he even would have settled for being back in his mother's smithy in Wandernaught. He lifted the hammer again, moving across the rocky pile.

After a time, he sat down on a stone to rest his legs after the hard work he had done. As he sat there on the north side of the small slag pile, he gently rubbed a bruise on his calf, trying to send an extra touch of order into the injury, and absently wondered what he was doing foraging around the iron mines of Recluce when his land steamer still needed so much more work.

'Simple . . .' he mumbled as he stood and followed his senses through the small piles of rocky wastes that had yet to be broken and turned back into hillsides and forests. 'Trying to trigger an order-chaos collapse, that's all.'

He picked up the hammer and tapped it against another stone, then slid the flap of the oiled-leather gathering bag underneath the stone.

121

After lighting both lamps, Justen eased the powder into the forge and began to pump the great bellows, his senses attuned to the granules that would become false lead. As the heat built up in the powder that he hoped to turn into metal, he could more easily sense the chaos locked in order within the tiny specks.

Thrap . . . thrap . . .

Justen looked toward the door, but kept pumping.

Thrap . . . thrap . . . thrap!

The engineer eased the powder out of the flame and turned toward the smithy door.

A dark and squarish figure in black waited.

'Master Turmin . . . please come in.'

The mage stepped inside the smithy. 'I hope that I'm not too late.'

'Too late?'

'How much false lead have you made?'

Justen swallowed. 'How did you know? I haven't told anyone.'

'We mages have our ways.' A crooked smile crossed the older man's face. 'Not magic. I heard that you were frequenting the slag piles by the old iron mines. When a wizard does that . . .' He shrugged.

'I'm not a wizard like you and Gunnar.'

'No . . . you're potentially far greater, and consequently far more dangerous.' Turmin cocked his head, his eyes straying toward the forge. 'Heating and order-sorting the powder, I presume?'

'I thought it would work.'

'Oh, it will work, all right. And about a season after you've finished with the third or fourth batch, you'll probably die of the wasting sickness. In your case, you're more ordered. You might even make six or seven batches.'

Justen swallowed hard.

'Can we get something to drink? I rode straight from Alberth.'

The younger man nodded. 'Let me bank the forge. Will leaving the powder here hurt anyone?'

'Probably not, if you get rid of it tomorrow. If it's been heated only slightly, you can scatter it into the ocean.'

Justen banked his mother's forge, but left the powder on the brick shelf to cool. Then he blew out the lamps.

Turmin followed him back to the empty kitchen.

Justen extended an arm to one of the wooden chairs, then asked, 'Beer or greenberry?'

'Greenberry. I'm not so ordered as you. Besides, I meant it when I said I was thirsty.'

Justen frowned. 'What about your mount? I forgot—'

'Your sister was kind enough to water Vaegera. I told her I was meeting you on wizardly matters. She also insisted on feeding the mount.'

'Elisabet . . .' Justen shook his head and walked from the kitchen and into the dim adjoining parlor, where a sandy-haired girl leaned forward, cupping her ear to listen.

Elisabet stood up as he entered. 'All right,' she said. 'You caught me. Will you tell me about it later?'

Justen grinned and nodded. 'What I can.'

'Promise?'

'Promise.'

By the time Justen returned to the kitchen and retrieved the pitchers from the cooler, his sister had disappeared. He walked back to the table, juggling two mugs and two pitchers.

After setting down the beer, he filled a mug with greenberry and extended it to the older mage.

'Thank you.' Turmin swallowed the entire drink in two gulps.

Justen smiled and refilled the mug, then poured a half mug of the dark beer for himself. He sat on a stool across from Turmin and waited for the other to speak.

'Justen, I can only talk from the books, the ones locked away in the Temple, because there's no one alive today who can do what Dorrin and Creslin did and wrote about. You know, in their later years, each compiled some remarkable insights. Dorrin's work created *The Basis of Order*, you know?'

'So I've been told.'

'Well . . . once Gunnar told me about your explosive powder trick, I knew it wouldn't be long before you were up to something. I just didn't know what. And I'm certainly in no position to judge your motives, but I would rather have you know the dangers beforehand. False lead has been around for at least two hundred years, perhaps longer. Dorrin mentions it. When you put enough of it together, you get enormous heat, almost raw chaos; yet, in small doses, it's as ordered as any metal, although it doesn't even appear in nature in its pure form.' Turmin took another sip from the mug, and Justen waited.

'The problem is that it also sends out little bursts of chaos—'

'The white flashes?'

'You can see them?'

Justen nodded.

'That's something. Anyway, we don't know why exactly, but if you put a bird, for example, especially a delicate cage bird, near false lead, after a while it wastes away. So have the few wizards who worked with it for any length of time.'

Justen waited. The mage was silent. In the darkness beyond the single lamp on the porch, a lone frog croaked from the small pond downhill from the smithy.

'And?' Justen finally asked.

'That's it. I'll answer any questions you have.'

'Why did you tell me all this?'

'I'm fond of Gunnar, and I think you have a lot to offer.'

Justen pondered the wording. 'That doesn't sound like you're overly fond of me.'

'Whatever you're going to do, it's likely to be terrible. I'm not exceedingly fond of the doers of terrible deeds.'

'Then why didn't you just let me kill myself with the false lead?'

'Probably Gunnar would have died, too.'

'What else?'

'Did you meet an Angel?'

Justen shook his head at the unexpected question, then sipped from the mug before answering. 'She was called an Angel, but I'm not sure she was. She was a druid, and very old.'

'Just as you will be one day, if you survive this madness.'

Turmin eased out of his wooden armchair and refilled his mug before settling back.

'You're not exactly answering directly,' Justen observed tartly.

'I suppose not. It's hard to be direct when you deal with great power.'

'Great power?'

'You have exceedingly great powers, young Justen. I may be old, but I would like to remain hale and healthy for what years remain to me.'

Justen sighed.

'What did you intend to do with the false lead?'

'I thought I had a way to combine it with order so as to destroy chaos.'

'With greater chaos, of course?' Turmin's tone was dry.

'Probably.'

'Would that have done anyone any good?'

'Maybe not. But something has to be done about Fairhaven.'

'Ah, yes . . . the White brethren.'

'We've ignored them, and they've perverted order to serve chaos, and they will take over all of Candar.'

'All of Candar?'

'All right . . . not Naclos.' Justen sighed.

So did Turmin.

'I have a suggestion, young Justen. If you intend to use order to destroy chaos . . . use order, not chaos bound in order. It's a great deal safer for all of us, including you.'

'How?'

'How indeed? Have you seen light through an angled piece of crystal?'

'You get a rainbow.'

'That's a form of order, is it not?'

Justen looked down at the nearly empty mug. 'I suppose so.'

'You've seen the lens experiment, haven't you?'

'The one where one of the magisters lights a fire with a glass? Yes.'

'Doesn't that show that light has power?'

'I think you're reaching, Ser.'

Turmin laughed softly. 'I probably am, Justen. I probably am. Still . . . I know, and now you know, that trying to use false

lead will probably kill you before you can do what you feel you
need to do.'

'Nothing's ever simple, is it?'

'No.' The older mage stood. 'I have a long ride ahead
of me.'

'You could stay here. You're more than welcome.'

'Your courtesy is appreciated, but I have obligations in the
morning.'

'You'll be riding most of the night . . .'

'Sometimes that comes with the responsibilites of being a
mage, Justen. Your turn will come, if it hasn't already.' Turmin
reached down, lifted the mug, and drained the last of the
greenberry.

'At least let me pack a few things for you to eat.'

'That would be welcome, I confess.'

Later, Justen listened as the mare trotted away into the night,
the sound of her hooves echoing over the whisper of the breeze.
He turned back to the forge. Tomorrow he would have to scatter
the powder into the Eastern Ocean. The sea would spread it far
enough.

And then he would have to look at crystals – crystals
and light.

122

'What are you doing?' Eldiren glanced from Beltar to Jehan.

They faced the walls of Armat, across the low valley split by
the River Arma as it flowed in a curve from below the hill where
the White forces massed, across the plain, and down through the
upriver gates. The gates were actually more like towers, with
spiked chains that spanned the river.

With decent siege engines or more cannon, neither the towers nor the city walls would have been a problem. But the
damned Black engineer's destruction almost two years earlier

of a decade's worth of cannon work had yet to be more than partially replaced, especially since smiths favorable to the White viewpoint who could also work iron were not exactly plentiful.

'Doing the Suthyans a favor.' Beltar smiled crookedly. 'I'm going to clean up their dirty river. And their dirty harbor.'

Eldiren scratched his head.

Jehan looked speculatively at Beltar. 'Something to do with the river, and the chaos springs?'

Beltar grinned. Eldiren frowned.

'What are those down there?' Beltar pointed to the four buildings on the hillside below, and to the road that linked them to the main highway to Armat.

'The inn and the hot springs,' answered Eldiren. 'But you made everyone leave.'

'Exactly.' Beltar grinned.

Eldiren's mouth opened. 'You wouldn't—'

'Try me. It's a lot cheaper than losing soldiers.'

The thin White Wizard glanced to the River Arma again.

'It will take some effort, but I can get the river to boil, maybe even for an eight-day.' Beltar shrugged. 'If that doesn't work—'

'You really don't like using troops, do you?'

'But I do. They had plenty to do on the march from Rulyarth.'

'Only skirmishes.'

'So? If the enemy won't fight more than skirmishes, is that my fault? We have conducted a military campaign, and they have retreated. My troops don't want to die trying to storm stone walls. Do you, Eldiren?'

Eldiren shook his head.

'How about you, Jehan?'

'Of course not. Neither do most of the troops, the lancers especially.'

Beltar closed his eyes and began to concentrate.

Shortly, the ground rumbled and brimstone fumes seeped from the buildings below. Troops began to wet scarves against the smell. In time, yellow waters boiled out of the springs and poured across the less than hundred cubits into the River Arma.

Fog, then steam, rose from the river by the time Beltar slumped against the portable table. '. . . take a while . . .' he gasped.

Across the river, a handful of peasants poured from huts and began to walk uphill, away from the steam. Some tried to drive sheep, oxen, and other livestock.

'They won't forget,' murmured Jehan.

'I hope not,' snapped Beltar.

The ground rumbled again as a gout of yellow steam and water erupted from the springs and geysered toward the river.

Eldiren wiped his forehead, wrinkling his nose against the stench. He coughed, half-gagging. 'Are we . . . supposed to survive this?'

Jehan turned his horse back uphill, and Eldiren followed.

So did Beltar, with a grim smile. 'Who says power doesn't work?'

'It works,' answered Jehan absently. 'But what happens when it doesn't? Every time you succeed, you make it less likely that you will survive failure.'

'No White Wizard survives failure anyway,' countered Beltar.

Eldiren let his mount trail the other two, his eyes on the steaming water flowing downstream toward Armat, his nose and guts trying to ignore the stench of boiled refuse.

123

'How did he take it?' asked Gunnar.

'He got rid of the powder, and that's mostly what counts.' Turmin looked out from the terrace to the flat silver of the Eastern Ocean. 'False lead is nasty stuff. Nasty, nasty, nasty stuff.' He shivered.

'But how did you persuade him? Justen doesn't let go of things easily.' The younger wizard shook his shoulders, as if to loosen them.

'I told him to fight chaos with total order, not chaos bound in order. And I pointed out that crystals can order light.'

'Light as a weapon against chaos? Ordered light? I mean, it

ought to work, I suppose. That was Dorrin's theory . . . but no one has ever made it work.'

'I didn't tell him that.'

'That wasn't exactly fair,' protested Gunnar.

'What he was planning would have been a lot worse.'

'Maybe . . . but what if he does make it work?'

'No one has in two hundred years.'

'No one was Justen.'

'It will still be better than false-lead explosives.'

'I hope so. I do hope so.'

'So do we all.'

124

Justen glanced at the cloudless sky of late spring, then carried the odd-shaped frame from the shed out to the stone walk that led from the front porch to the road.

After setting the frame in place on the stone slab in the walk and the square of plain iron beneath it, he tilted the lens in the frame until the light fell in a point on the square of iron. The concentrated sunlight was easily absorbed by the iron, just as magic or chaos would have been.

He waited for some time, but the iron changed not at all. Finally, he edged a splinter of wood into the light. Shortly, it began to char, then flared into a brief flame. During the process, Justen concentrated not on the wood, but on the flow of light, sensing the strands as they passed through the lens.

Could he weave more light into the lens? Not like a shield, where the light was woven away from the object, but in a way that the light would be knit together? He frowned and reached out with his senses to touch that light, as strong as iron and as delicate as spider silk, to weave it into a tighter pattern that flowed through the lens.

As the sweat beaded on his forehead, he could sense the heat on the iron and see the faint, reddish glow.

He tried to widen the web his mind wove, and shadows fell around him as though a cloud had grown to cover the sky.

A single point of light flared on the iron, and a few sparks showered off the plate fragment.

'Justen!' Elisabet shouted.

He shook his head. The shadows vanished, and he stood again in full sunlight, sweat dripping from his entire body. He looked toward the porch, from where Elisabet looked back at him.

She walked down the steps and along the graveled path until she reached him. 'I'm sorry. I spoiled it, didn't I?'

Reaching out, he squeezed her shoulder. 'I can do it again. It works. I know that now.'

'It felt weird, Justen.' Elisabet shivered. 'Then I looked at you, and you were standing in the shadows but there weren't any clouds. And then the metal caught fire. It was on fire, wasn't it?'

'Something like that.'

At the sound of another set of steps, Justen glanced over Elisabet's shoulder toward the smithy. Cirlin, her leather apron still in place, walked briskly along the path toward them. Justen waited.

'Trying to forge without coal or charcoal?'

'Not exactly. I was just trying something out.'

'I'm no wizard, son, but whatever you did—' she shook her head' – it felt like you'd shaken the ground or something.'

Justen looked down at the lens in its frame, then at the fingertip hole in the iron plate.

Cirlin followed his eyes. 'Neat, like a punch. But you didn't do it that way, did you?'

'No. I tried something with sunlight. It worked fairly well. At least I think it did. The iron was actually burning.'

'You burned iron with the sun?'

'I'll have to do more than that if I want this to work.'

'Land engines and iron-burning lenses – darkness knows if I want to see what else you'll come up with.'

Justen almost missed the glint in her eyes, then chuckled.

Cirlin shook her head ruefully before she headed back to the smithy.

125

The tall, redheaded wizard climbed the stairs, a loosely rolled scroll in his hands, a tight smile fixed on his lips.

'Derba, what do you have there?' The slightly stooped figure of Renwek stepped forward on the landing outside the High Wizard's chamber.

'A scroll for the High Wizard.' Derba bowed. 'From Wizard Commander Beltar. That's how he is styling himself.'

'Wizard Commander now,' mused Renwek. 'Even Zerchas was not quite that presumptuous.'

Derba waited.

'Might I see that?'

'But of course. You are the advisor to the High Wizard.' The younger White Wizard offered a too-deep bow as he offered the scroll.

Renwek unrolled the parchment and began to read. Then he closed it. 'Perhaps you should come with me.'

'I would not presume—'

'You already have, since it is clear that you read it first.' Renwek turned and rapped on the door.

'Yes?'

'I have a scroll from Wizard Commander Beltar.'

'Wizard Commander Beltar?' There was a pause. 'Come on in, Renwek.'

'Derba is with me, Ser.'

'Well, bring him in.'

The two stepped into the tower room.

'Beltar is on his way back, with a few picked squads of the Iron Guard and the White lancers.' Renwek bowed to the High Wizard.

'I had no doubt that he would be, not after he persuaded the Suthyan Traders' Council to submit.' Histen snorted softly, his breath steaming in the chill of the spring morning that poured through the open window.

'Persuade is not exactly the word I would have employed, Ser,' Renwek offered.

'Bah! He did not shake Armat to the ground, did he, the way he leveled Sarron. Nor did he burn it as he did Berlitos. What happened to our friend the firebrand?'

'I'm afraid he has begun to learn something about politics and statecraft, Ser. He did boil the river and the harbor and a few hundred souls before suggesting to the traders that he could boil them as well.' Renwek handed the rolled parchment to Histen. 'He took the liberty of sending copies of this to a few people.'

Derba kept a polite smile on his face.

'What does it say?' Histen demanded.

'Nothing.'

A faint frown crossed Derba's forehead, and Histen looked at the younger wizard. 'Perhaps you could tell us what it says, Derba.'

'Uh . . . I would not presume . . .'

'What does it really say? If you've taken the liberty of reading it, and you have or Renwek wouldn't have brought you in, you ought to decide what it means.' Histen's words were soft.

'Go ahead,' suggested Renwek.

'Well, Ser . . . there are many fine words, but not much in the way of meaning. I would guess that there might be a veiled suggestion that when the time comes, he will be more than happy to lift the heavy yoke of duty from your aching shoulders.' Derba smiled nervously.

'Just as you had hoped to do, young fellow?' asked Histen. 'And don't tell me you wouldn't presume. Never mind. Don't answer that. You'll either lie or make a fool of yourself.' Histen turned to Renwek. 'What do you think?'

'Derba has the idea very clearly. Beltar only wishes to serve the Council and to ensure your long and healthy life.' Renwek smiled blandly.

'Ah . . . only to preserve me from the heavy yoke of duty that weighs me down so grievously. Perhaps it is time to retire to Lydiar for my well-deserved rest.' Histen snorted again, softly.

'Ser?' asked Derba involuntarily.

'Lydiar is long settled, unlikely to face revolts and the need for heavily armed troops, and close enough to return to Fairhaven within a handful of days. Besides, Flyrd would be more than happy to return to Fairhaven and take your quarters, Renwek.'

'My quarters?'

'You really don't think you want to serve Beltar, do you?'

'Ah . . . no. I should think not.'

'Then perhaps we should make ready.'

'As you wish, Ser.'

Derba glanced from one older wizard to the other.

Histen smiled at the younger wizard. 'You, Derba, should make ready to help Beltar when the time comes to lift the heavy yoke from his shoulders. After all, is not such altruism and service the highest ideal to which all young wizards aspire?' His laugh rang off-key.

126

Squinting against the unseasonably hot spring sun and sweating from the heat, although a hot spring midday in Nylan was nowhere near as hot as the winter middays in the Stone Hills, Justen stepped up around the corner and under the covered porch.

He paused before the small sign proclaiming 'Hoslid – Trader.' According to Gunnar, Hoslid was as honest as any, or as dishonest, and owed less than most to Ryltar. Justen wanted to avoid Ryltar's firm and Ryltar's scrutiny. So, with a cough, he cleared his throat and walked into the building behind the main traders' square.

The whole idea of building a balloon was ridiculous, but how else could he get the lens high enough that he could gather enough sunlight and focus it where he needed? There weren't any real peaks near Fairhaven. And what fabric was strong enough and light enough?

Justen paused inside the door, letting his eyes adjust to the comparative gloom and the squat figure in brown who lumbered toward him.

'I am Hoslid. How may I help you?'

'I'd like to obtain a thousand squares of Naclan silk blanket cloth.'

'You want what?' Hoslid asked.

'I want a thousand square cubits of thin silk blanket fabric from Naclos.'

'What's that? Never heard of it.' The trader scowled.

Justen frowned, glad he had brought the small cloth Dayala had slipped into his box, but reluctant to part with it. Finally, he took out the piece. 'This.'

Hoslid fingered it and nodded. 'The silksheen. It comes from Naclos.'

'That's what I said.'

'It is very costly.'

'How costly?'

'It is a copper a square cubit. And I would need a deposit. Ten golds.'

'No more than five golds, and that would be for two thousand squares.'

'Seven for two thousand.'

'Six and five.'

'Done.'

'And a receipt.'

'But of course.' Hoslid offered a broad grin.

'When can you deliver it?'

'Five or six eight-days.'

'That's good.' Justen lifted his purse and waited.

Hoslid turned and lumbered toward the empty table in the corner. Justen followed and watched as the trader inked out a contract. Then he read it and changed Hoslid's written deposit of seven golds back to six and a half golds, getting Hoslid to initial the changes before Justen counted out the coins.

'You bargain hard,' the trader said.

'Not hard, just fair.'

'You don't bargain fair, and we don't trade.' Hoslid grinned again.

Justen smiled and looked at the trader, then gathered his own order about him, projecting even greater solidity than he felt.

Hoslid stepped back. 'You're a wizard? You didn't say.'

Justen smiled. 'Does it matter? You got your deposit, and you know you can't cheat me.'

'I would not think of it.' A faint sheen of perspiration coated the trader's forehead.

'Good.' Justen smiled broadly as he rolled up the contract.

127

'Histen! Where in darkness are you?' Beltar pushed back the white-oak door and marched into the topmost quarters in the White tower, the rooms reserved since before the time of Cerryl the Great for the High Wizard.

The stocky White Wizard studied the room. A wide bed stood in the alcove to his left. A white blanket and a set of sheets were neatly folded on the mattress next to a white embroidered coverlet, also folded with the seal of the High Wizard showing.

The screening table contained a blank glass, and the desk next to the empty bookcases contained only a piece of parchment, weighted down by a set of golden links attached to an ancient amulet.

'He's gone.' Beltar turned to Eldiren, who stood in the doorway, Jehan behind him.

'Histen? I am not surprised.' Jehan's voice was calm.

Beltar walked to the desk, lifted the amulet and set it aside, his fingers caressing the links for a moment before he picked up the parchment and began to read aloud. '. . . in the interests of my health, I am hereby relinquishing the amulet of the High Wizard to my successor, Beltar, subject of course to the vote of the White Council. I will be attempting to regain a portion of my former vigor by undertaking less-taxing duties in Lydiar, as wizard to the duke . . .'

He set the parchment back on the desk.

'He felt that a peaceful transfer of power was for the best. That's clear,' observed Eldiren with a faint smile.

'Either that, or he feels that such a transfer will be only temporary,' suggested Beltar.

'Did you notice the way Derba watched as you came in?' asked Jehan.

'I can't say that I did. I was looking for Histen. What about it?'

'Derba's almost as powerful as you are,' pointed out Eldiren.

'Does it matter?'

Eldiren and Jehan exchanged glances.

Beltar glanced around the tower rooms, vacant now except for the basic furnishings, before answering his own question. 'That might be why Histen left. He just might be waiting to let us destroy each other. Histen's shrewder than I am, and he has a lot more experience.'

'At times, Beltar, experience defers to raw power,' added Jehan.

'Perhaps, but that means I always have to maintain that power, as you keep pointing out.'

'Very true.' Jehan's voice was even, almost disinterested.

'And very difficult,' said Eldiren.

'You two are such comfort.' Beltar shook his head and looked at the amulet again before turning back toward the stairs. 'We'll need to convene the Council.'

'Of course.'

128

Justen rolled the uncompleted land engine out of the smithy, the iron bars and oak-framed sides barely clearing the wide door, although the door was fully open. At first glance in the early summer sun, the land engine's framework looked like a haphazard assembly of iron rods, oak struts, and bars, all set amid four iron-tired wheels. The circular, heavy lifting rings in front of the driver and behind the space where the third seat would be rose above the rest of the frame – but not above the squat boiler and funnel that dominated the rear of the machine.

'Ugghhh . . .' Justen strained to push the engine the last few cubits out of the smithy as the front wheels rolled up the slightest of inclines. Despite his grunting, the wheels turned easily enough. Justen's lips twisted at the thought, considering that he had used marine shaft bearings designed for far greater weight and stress. The drive systems were overengineered, and that meant he was going to have to really work on keeping the armor lightweight.

'Good work on the wheels.' Cirlin stood watching from behind Justen, and even Horas had turned from the garden to look. 'They don't bind at all, and the axles are solid – no bowing, even with all that weight.'

'It's ugly-looking,' ventured Elisabet.

'It's not done yet.' Justen slipped a chunk of wood behind one wheel, then straightened. He walked to the other rear wheel and eased a second block in place before heading to the well with a bucket.

Elisabet shook garden dirt from her hands and crossed the yard to the engine. She walked around the framework, her fingers occasionally brushing a rod or a strut. 'It feels solid. It just doesn't look solid.'

Justen returned with the first bucket of water, which he slowly poured into the machine's reservoir. Then he walked back to the pump. With a last look at the land engine, Cirlin slipped back into the smithy.

Across the yard, Horas returned his attention to a row of beans.

'That's going to take a lot of water.' Elisabet peered at the reservoir and then at the bucket Justen carried.

'Not that much,' answered Justen, filling the second bucket. 'It's a ship system, and most of the water is recovered. It would have been lighter without the condenser, and I had to keep the pressure higher . . . well, a lot higher, because I can't use a seawater cooling system.'

He carried the second bucket back to the engine and poured

it into the reservoir. Then he pointed. 'There are spaces for the air to come in, and when the engine's moving, the air goes past all those tubes. That helps to cool the condensate.'

'That's why you want Gunnar to help, isn't it?' asked Elisabet.

'Huh?'

'I'm not stupid, Justen. I'm your sister, remember? This engine can't go that fast. If you want this cooling to work, you need a lot of air, and Gunnar's an Air Wizard. I could even do that. Can I come?'

'No.'

'I didn't think so. It's going to be dangerous, isn't it?' Elisabet continued to study the spaces around the condenser-radiator. 'I'll bet this gets really hot.'

'It does. Not too hot, I hope.' Justen clamped the reservoir cap shut and walked around the smithy to the coal bin, returning with full scuttle. After several trips into the shed and the smithy for shavings, he touched the striker to the small pile in the firebox, waited for the flame, and began to feed in coal.

Horas gestured to his daughter, and Elisabet finally drifted back to the garden and her weeding, while Justen built up the fire and used both the few gauges and his own senses to measure the system's performance.

Wheeee . . .

For a time, he let the steam moan through the open safety valve in order to check the piping at lower pressures. Then he closed the valve and shoveled more coal into the firebox, letting the pressure build. He checked the clutch system again to make sure that the drive shaft to the wheel was disengaged. He didn't need the land engine rolling off on its own.

While the steam pressure built, he continued to examine the steam lines and the heat distribution, wondering how he would be able to armor the land engine without cooking its operators.

But first he needed to make sure that the systems worked, before he worried about armor and weapons, both of which he was certain would be necessary. Then he had to decide whether the system needed to be reworked, and if so, how much.

With a sigh, he pulled the blocks from one wheel, then from the other.

'He's going to see if it runs!' squealed Elisabet.

Justen looked toward his sister, who covered her mouth and looked to their father.

'It is a momentous time,' she said in a low and serious voice.

Horas covered his mouth, but his eyes twinkled.

Justen slipped into the single seat that was in place, then engaged the clutch.

Clunnnkk!

The engineer winced at the stress on the reduction gears. He'd have to do something about that initial engagement, or ensure that he could feed steam to the turbine at lower rates, or he wouldn't have any gears left before long. Still, the land engine crept across the yard toward the lane.

Justen turned the steering tiller, and the land engine eased to the left, into the center of the narrow lane leading past the garden and the house and down to the main road.

Sssssss . . .

A fine jet of steam sprayed from a joint between the steam-return line and the condenser-radiator assembly. Justen shifted his concentration for a moment, but the leak did not appear to be growing. While his attention was on the leak, the engine had veered toward the house, and he corrected with the tiller, overdoing the change in direction so much that the engine lurched as the heavy wheel caught in softer soil on the edge of the lane.

Justen held his breath momentarily, but the front wheel found firmer ground and the engine straightened. Another problem: soft ground.

Should he consider widening the wheels? How much weight would that add? Could he avoid that?

The engine almost veered off the other side of the lane before Justen eased the tiller back in order to keep the machine on the packed surface of the lane.

Justen took a deep breath, realizing that he had better concentrate on directing the machine and worry about the engineering changes later.

At the end of the lane, he turned the engine onto the road and then throttled back so that it was barely moving while he turned it around to head back up the gentle slope of the lane to the smithy. His forehead was pouring sweat despite the summer breeze that blew past him.

Creaakkk . . .

Wincing at the stress on the iron-shod wheel, he eased the tiller, gauging whether the wheels would stay on the road. The left front tire gouged a track in the softer shoulder of the road and the land engine lurched again but stayed upright.

Sssssssss . . .

The joint leak was louder, and a second leak was bathing Justen in warm mist as he tried to line up the land engine on the lane to avoid running over the garden or hitting the house or getting mired in soft ground.

The soft ground bothered him because the armor would make the whole thing that much heavier. As it was, he wasn't even carrying the weight of a full load of coal or water.

The land engine lurched toward the garden, and Justen corrected, trying to keep his mind on steering and not on engineering, even while the hissing leaks and various creaks and stresses reminded him of too many engineering problems.

And he was going to travel hundreds of kays in it . . . when he couldn't even get the thing down the lane and back?

He sighed, then eased the tiller back again to avoid the softer ground.

By the time he had disengaged the clutch, eased in the converted wagon brake, bled off the steam, and blocked the wheels, his clothes were as soaked as though he'd stood in a summer rainstorm – dripping both from his own sweat and the leaking steam and water lines.

He looked at the water-coated framework and shook his head.

'It works. It really works!' Elisabet hugged him, then let go. 'You're soaked! Ugghhh.'

'Very impressive, son.' Horas looked at the land engine.

'But one of a kind, I think,' added Cirlin from the smith door.

'I'm not sure where to start in reworking it.' Justen slowly paced around the machine, seeing the other problems he hadn't had time to notice when he was driving: the leak in the waterline joint from the reservoir to the boiler, the need to reposition the steam-return line . . . He shook his head again. Why did he ever need a clutch? Why not just change the design so the throttle controlled the steam flow directly to the turbine?

'Looks to me like most of your problems are the kind that can be fixed,' added Cirlin. 'Doesn't the design work?'

Justen half-smiled. He'd been so absorbed in the little glitches, he'd forgotten that the land engine in fact worked.

'Yes . . . it actually does.'

'Has anyone else built one?' pursued Cirlin.

'Not that I know of.'

'I think you'd know.'

'It works, Justen,' affirmed Elisabet. Then she looked at his damp shirt and trousers. 'But you sure did get wet.'

Cirlin smiled. 'We can fix the little things. Remember . . . it works.'

Justen nodded, but his eyes flicked over the mass of iron and ordered oak and pine, thinking about all the improvements he should have considered earlier. His gaze halted on the area behind the boiler, and he realized that somehow he would have to add more space for coal.

'He's not here,' said Elisabet. 'He's already thinking about how to fix everything.'

'He wouldn't be Justen if he weren't,' Cirlin responded.

'He still ought to change into some dry clothes,' added Horas.

'I imagine he will . . . when he thinks about it.'

Justen reached out with his senses toward the condenser-radiator joint.

'That may be some time . . .'

There was so much to do, Justen reflected, and he really hadn't even gotten very far with the lenses, either.

129

At the sound of the horse entering the yard, Justen set down the model of the balloon and peered through the door, wondering if Ryltar had already sent someone after him. He took a deep

breath as he watched Altara swing out of the saddle and tie the
bay to the stone hitching post by the stable.

He walked out through the light rain. 'Greetings!'

Altara brushed her short hair back and shook the water off
her hand. 'I can see you've been busy. Got anywhere dry? I'm
on the way back from the Black Holding . . . again.'

'Let me just check something.' Justen walked back to the shed
and motioned for Altara to enter. 'What are you doing here?'

'Seeing what you're doing.' Altara glanced into the workroom
that had been a storage shed. 'Also, telling you that you had
better do it fairly soon. The so-honorable Counselor Ryltar has
begun to tell people that you are mad and that you should be
confined. I had to elaborate on your rest cure. And I did point
out that the iron de-ordering you had done, order-mad or not,
had saved us nearly a dozen golds since spring. Jenna and Claris
were impressed, but Ryltar just frowned and said that it showed
how dangerous you are.' The chief engineer laughed, off-key. 'Of
course, I don't see how they could hold you unless they shackled
you in cold iron. But that isn't the point.'

'No. It wouldn't be. I'd have to leave Recluce, which is what
he wants.' *Not that I don't want to anyway – just not until
I'm ready.* 'Has Gunnar told you what he found out about
Ryltar?'

'You look like the demons' hell. Worse than when you were
working night and day in Sarronnyn, and at least as driven.'
Altara shook her head. 'And, no, Gunnar hasn't said anything
about Ryltar.' She glanced toward the models on the bench.
'What are those?'

'Balloons. You put hot air in them and they rise. At least they
would if I could get the bags light enough.'

'Why can't you? But what good are they? You couldn't steer
one anyway, not like a ship.'

'Maybe I could put an engine in it with an air screw like a
ship's screw . . . but that would be a long time away. I can't
even get these to rise more than a few cubits.'

Altara waited.

'It's the fabric. Linen's too . . . It leaks too much unless I coat
it with wax, and it's too heavy then. Paper's too weak.' Justen
looked at the models on the bench. 'I'm trying to get some
silksheen from Naclos, but it hasn't arrived, and it may not.'

Altara frowned. 'I think it has. It must have. That was one of the things Jenna mentioned – that you had received a huge shipment of fancy cloth, and Ryltar said that showed how crazy you are. He wanted to know where you got the funds, because the cloth arrived with an invoice declaring it was prepaid.'

'Great. How do I get it without proving that I've gone crazy? And why didn't Hoslid let me know?'

'I think Ryltar prevailed upon him. His *Marshalle* – Hoslid's – was lost in the Western Ocean with a full cargo, and he borrowed heavily from Ryltar.'

Justen wiped his forehead. 'I just love getting such wonderful news. I still don't know how I can get the cloth if Hoslid thinks he'll be upsetting the Council by releasing it. Do I go in there and demand it?'

'You could. He'd have to give it to you.'

'And that would give Ryltar more fuel for his rumor-mongering, you think?'

'Probably.'

'You know what he's been up to?'

'I haven't the faintest idea.' Altara grinned wryly. 'But if you want to tell me, it can't be good.'

'We can't prove it, not with hard evidence, but he's gotten golds from Candar – a lot – for past services, and he's accepting smuggled gems from Hamor.'

'Fairhaven, you think? How could he?'

'He's never felt right to me.' Justen laughed bitterly. 'Honest corruption isn't quite chaotic. It feels different, and . . . without exile any more . . .'

'You really think he would have been exiled under the old system?'

'Probably not. Coins find a way around any system. Let's get you something to eat and drink. Can you stay tonight?' Justen set the models in their brackets and opened the door, looking at the increasingly heavy rain.

'I don't think I'd better. I can make Fallroth tonight, and that would get me back to Nylan by mid-morning.'

The two engineers hurried across the yard, dodging around the growing puddles and up onto the covered porch, where they scraped their boots and wiped them clean.

'You had an idea about my silksheen cloth?' Justen asked.

'Give me your authorization and I'll claim that we're testing the cloth for sails for the merchant fleet. Say that you ordered it because you could get it cheaper.'

'Ryltar will know that's not true.'

'So? He won't be able to claim it publicly. Besides, Hoslid couldn't refuse the Brotherhood, and Ryltar's at the Black Holding right now. That means four days before he finds out, and maybe another four before he could send any instructions.'

Justen nodded. 'Let's see what we've got here for you to eat.'

130

'Can I come? You put the second seat in.' Elisabet stood beside Justen as he removed one of the wheel blocks from the land engine.

High, thin clouds kept the midsummer day from being too oppressively hot, but Justen felt sweaty all over as he slowly walked around the craft, letting his senses roam over the piping, assemblies, and drive shafts.

The land engine still looked like a mass of struts and bars assembled around a small firebox, a boiler, and a steam engine, but many of the armor plates that would eventually cover the framework had been forged – some of them almost to parchment thinness. Justen did not intend to put any plating in place until the steam and drive systems worked perfectly, since repairs would require removal of the plating.

'No.'

'Why not?'

'I'm still not sure that things will work right, and I don't want to have to worry about you.'

'Justen, if nothing bad happened before, how could it happen now?'

'This time, we—'

'We? You mean I can come?'

'No. I meant that . . . oh, you know what I meant. You're just trying to take advantage of me when I'm thinking about other things.'

'It's the only time I can take advantage of you. Besides, Mother said you did a good job.'

'A good job isn't a safe job.' Justen reflected on his order-tipped arrows – definitely good engineering, but not safe for anyone involved. The same had been true of his efforts with cannon powder. He shook his head, wondering how he always seemed to get involved with destruction. Was it proof of what the ancient had said about too much order being no different from too much chaos?

He took a deep breath and opened the firebox to ease in another shovelful of coal. Above him, the steam valve began to whistle faintly, purging excess air from the system.

'Justen . . .'

'No. Once I *know* it's safe, then you can come.'

'Promise?'

'Promise. Now go back over by the house or into the smithy.'

'All right.' Elisabet walked across the yard and up the steps to the covered porch, brushing away a fly as she walked.

Whhheeee . . . Justen closed the steam-relief valve and walked around to the driver's seat, where he checked the tiller again to ensure that it moved freely and that the front wheels moved with it. Then he eased the throttle open, slowly, testing to see how the simplified direct steam feed worked.

The land engine rumbled forward slowly, the wider wheels offering more stability than those of the first trial an eight-day earlier.

Elisabet watched from the porch as Justen drove past, concentrating on keeping the land engine in the center of the lane.

At the end of the lane, he turned the tiller, steering the craft onto the road and away from Wandernaught itself. He studied the road ahead, but saw no horses or carts, not that he would expect any at midday.

Then he eased open the throttle and watched as the turbine began to whine and the wheels began to turn more quickly. The craft moved from the speed of a walk to a slow run to the quick trot of a horse.

Justen scanned the engine and the steam and water lines; everything remained tight. The road ahead was still clear and flat. He edged the throttle up farther, and the seat began to bounce him with each rough spot in the road.

After throttling back, he looked for a wide place in the road where he could turn. After turning, he opened the throttle again, slowing only when he neared the house.

He crept the land engine up the lane and into the yard, where he began to shut down the steam system.

'You were going so fast!' Elisabet stood less than a cubit from the machine as Justen climbed out and twisted open the steam-spill valve.

'I think it could go faster if I could put some springs under the driver's seat. It's hard to control it when you're being bounced around.'

'Faster? You'd have to gallop to go faster.'

'That's the idea.'

'It is?'

'You don't want horses . . .' Justen broke off. 'Never mind.' He studied the return lines and then let his senses drift across the drive-shaft connections; they were hotter than he would have liked. Did he need more grease on them?

'How did it go this time?' Cirlin inspected the land engine from the other side.

'The steam system was perfect. I'm still worried about the power train. It heats up too quickly, even with all the black iron.' Justen pulled at his chin, then wiped his forehead with his forearm.

'Mother! He was traveling almost as fast as a cantering horse.'

Cirlin raised her eyebrows. 'Oh?'

Elisabet nodded.

'Then, dear, I think we should keep that to ourselves. And please don't tell Silinna. I know what good friends you and she are, but—'

'Oh, she wouldn't tell.'

'Who told about the time you fell in the applesauce? When you didn't want Lyndner to know?'

'Mother!'

'Applesauce?' asked Justen innocently. 'Lyndner? Is that Shrezsan's little brother?'

'He's not exactly little any longer,' commented Cirlin dryly. 'But I don't think we should be gossiping to all Recluce about your land engine.'

'Probably not. I still haven't worked out the other half of what I need.'

'What is that?' asked Elisabet brightly. 'Is it the stuff with the balloons and the lenses?'

'That really shouldn't go outside the family, either, dear.'

'Oh, that I already knew. I wouldn't have thought about telling Silinna that. It's real wizardry, and you don't tell about that.'

Cirlin and Justen exchanged glances. Cirlin's lips quirked, and Justen shook his head.

'You're laughing at me – both of you!'

'No . . .' choked Justen. 'Just at the way you said that. I'm very glad you understand about wizardry. But the land engine's wizardry, too.'

'If you say so.' Elisabet's eyes were very round and purposefully innocent.

'Try that look on Lyndner,' suggested Justen.

'Justen! You're spoiling it.'

'Isn't that what big brothers are for?'

131

'Isn't it about time for you to turn in?' asked Gunnar, leaning back in the kitchen chair.

'I don't want to go to bed,' insisted Elisabet. Her lower lip trembled. 'I'm not some . . . some child.'

Horas adjusted the lamp, bringing a brighter glow to the kitchen table. 'Unlike some of you, I have trouble seeing in the dark.' He turned to Elisabet. 'I understand, Elisabet, but it is later than usual, and you are still a growing young girl.'

'I am a young woman, and I shouldn't have to be packed off to bed like a little girl.'

Gunnar's eyes closed. Justen frowned, but said nothing.

'It is late, dear,' added Cirlin.

'I'm not tired . . .' insisted Elisabet, trying to stifle a yawn. '. . . really . . . not . . .'

Justen forced his expression into one of concern and stood. 'You're sleepy. I can tell that. I'll walk down the hall with you.' He offered his arm to his sister.

'All right. I don't know why I'm so . . . sleepy . . .' Elisabet trudged beside her brother.

Once they were around the corner and almost to her room, Justen lifted the healing sleep-daze that Gunnar had dropped on Elisabet.

'That . . . Oh . . .' hissed Elisabet, struggling against Justen's grip on her arm.

Justen put his finger to her mouth. 'I know you're tired,' he said loudly. Then he added quietly, 'If you want to listen on the breeze, fine. Just keep it to yourself, and talk to me before you talk to anyone else. Especially to Silinna or Lyndner.'

'But, Justen . . . All right . . .'

Justen put his hand over her mouth.

'You'll feel better in the morning,' he added loudly, removing his hand.

Elisabet winked and lay down on her bed, offering a loud and counterfeit yawn, her eyes bright in the darkness. She blew Justen a kiss.

Justen walked quietly back to the kitchen, ignoring Gunnar's frown. 'She'll stay in bed. But I really don't like that, Gunnar. It's a form of force.'

'She would have argued all night.'

Justen shrugged. 'We did.'

'All right.'

'What did you want to talk about?' asked Cirlin. 'That you didn't want her to hear?'

Gunnar took a sip of redberry and cleared his throat. 'Ryltar already wants to send the marines after Justen, according to Altara. Jenna – she's the youngest Counselor – is holding him off, but he's working on old Claris. How soon before you can get your stuff together?' Gunnar turned to his brother.

'I need more time. I still haven't got that fabric from Naclos. Altara thought she could break it loose from Hoslid without letting Ryltar know, but I'll need time to get it stitched together. The land engine's ready except for the plating, and I've got a little oil stove that I can use for the balloon. And the lenses . . . grinding the fire-eyes takes a while. It's slow.' Justen shrugged. 'They should work, but I really don't know if they will. It's all theory.'

'You've proved rather adept at converting theory to practice.' Cirlin laughed softly.

'What else?' asked Gunnar.

'I need you, and we need a good marine to handle weapons. I think I know who, but you should talk to him.' Justen stood and walked to the cooler, extracting the pitcher of ale. He filled his mug.

'Who's that? And why me?'

'Martan. He's the one whose squad still uses the old armory.' Justen took a sip from the almost overflowing mug before continuing. 'Because you work in Nylan with Turmin a lot. If I go to Nylan, Ryltar will have three people following me.' The engineer slipped back into his chair and set the mug on the table in front of him. He reached toward one of the two remaining slices of berry bread, then thought better of it and put his arms on the table.

'Why would you trust Martan?'

'He's already asked to go, and he feels ordered and sound, and he's Hyntal's cousin. And we need a ship.'

'You're crazy! You think Hyntal would act as a transport for your crazy adventure?'

'Why not?' Justen smiled and sipped from the mug. 'If he's going to patrol the Gulf, why couldn't he drop us off?'

'The Council wouldn't let him,' Gunnar pointed out.

'That assumes they would know. Why would they have to know?' asked Justen.

The other three looked at him.

'Look,' he explained. 'The *Llyse* comes into port and picks up some odd equipment from the engineers and steams off. That happens sometimes anyway. Who would think about telling the Council?'

Cirlin shook her head. 'What about later?'

'If we don't spell it out, Hyntal can honestly claim that he thought we were representing the Brotherhood.'

'That's not exactly honest.'

'No, it's not. But I haven't figured out any truthful way to lie. So I'd rather not make any statements one way or the other. Just tell Hyntal we have some equipment that needs to be transported to Candar – some special equipment designed by one of the more inventive engineers. That much is true.'

'Sometimes the most obvious is the best.' Horas grinned.

Justen looked at Gunnar. 'You need to find out when Martan's squad is scheduled for duty on the *Llyse*. He'll know. Any time more than four eight-days from now ought to work . . . I hope.' He swallowed the rest of the ale in a single gulp.

'What about us? How can we help?' asked Cirlin.

'I'll need at least a hundred stone of coal, in small chunks, and a lot of preserved supplies. Then I'll need two copper poles, each about three cubits long. That's in case the fire-eyes don't work.'

Gunnar swallowed. 'That's dangerous, Justen.'

'Let's hope the fire-eyes work, then,' the younger brother answered with a brief smile. 'And I'll need to forge probably a gross of the order-tipped arrows.' A sharp jolt passed through his skull at the thought of the arrows, and he wondered if he could ever think of them without pain.

132

'There's a wagon, like the engineers' wagon, and it's coming into the yard,' announced Elisabet, sticking her head into the shed where Justen mumbled over the grindstone, trying to adjust the bracket and clamp he had designed to hold the gem in place.

'A wagon?' He did not look up.

'It has four wheels, and it's pulled by two horses, and a man sits on it and drives it,' offered Elisabet.

'Elisabet . . .' Justen set the clamp aside. He took a long look at his sister. 'Are you sure it's not Lyndner, come to carry you off?'

'Justen! That's not funny.'

Justen sighed and hurried after Elisabet, catching her in the yard. 'I'm sorry. But you were teasing me.'

'It's not the same. I don't tease you about Dayala . . . at least not anymore.' Elisabet sniffed.

'I won't tease you about Lyndner. Fair?'

'Fair.'

Creaakkk . . .

They both turned to watch the wagon. Warin gave a brief wave from the driver's seat, then concentrated on slowing and guiding the team up next to the stable.

Even after a few moments in the direct sun, Justen had begun to perspire, and he wiped his brow forehead on his sleeve. Then he walked over and slipped blocks under the right front wheel after Warin set the brake.

'I didn't expect you.'

'Altara sent me off with your cloth.' Warin pointed to three large bales in the wagon bed. 'She said for me to bring back some more de-ordered iron, if you have any more.' The balding engineer turned to Elisabet. 'Hello there.' He grinned. 'If it weren't for Estil, I just might consider moving right up here to Wandernaught.'

Elisabet blushed.

'Careful there, Warin, or I'll tell Estil.' Justen paused. 'There's a good load of iron in the bin. That's the least I can do for you . . . provided you keep admiring Elisabet from a safe distance.'

'Justen . . .' Elisabet was almost bright red.

'I think it's time to unload the wagon,' Justen said in a matter-of-fact tone. 'Elisabet? Can you take care of the horses while Warin and I move the silksheen to the shed and load the iron?'

'I can certainly handle the horses.' Elisabet tossed her head, and her blond hair fluffed in the light breeze.

Warin glanced at Justen and mouthed, 'She'll be a real handful.'

'She already is, if you haven't noticed,' Justen whispered back as he lowered the tailgate and reached for the wide, woven straps on the bale of cloth. He frowned, realizing that he had no thread or cording. He was always forgetting something, but perhaps he could get some from Basta in Wandernaught.

The two engineers hauled the first bale into the shed.

'What are you doing with all this cloth?' asked Warin as they returned to the wagon.

'Experimenting. Remember Lystrl's experiments with the hot-air balloons?'

'He could never get one to go higher than twenty or thirty cubits into the air.'

'I'm trying to figure out how to do better than that.' Justen reached for the straps on the second bale.

'For darkness' sake, why?' Warin grabbed the other set of straps.

'To destroy Fairhaven.'

Warin stumbled, and the bale almost wrenched out of Justen's hands before the older engineer caught his balance.

'You're serious.'

'Me? Order-mad Justen? Of course not.'

'You really are serious.'

They set the second bale beside the first.

Warin looked at Justen. 'I don't know which is worse – that you're seriously proposing this, or that I believe you might actually pull it off.'

'I'm not even sure about that myself,' laughed Justen. 'I just know that I have to try.'

'You've definitely got Ryltar worried, Altara says.' Warin turned to head back to the wagon.

'I think anything that's different upsets Counselor Ryltar.' Justen followed Warin out of the shed.

'I've got the first one stabled,' called Elisabet as she led the second horse toward the stable.

'Good.'

'Then I'll brush them both down. They're good horses.'

'Definitely a handful,' said Warin in a low voice.

'More than Estil?'

Warin smiled. 'Let's say that I'd be a lot safer with Estil, no matter what Altara thinks.'

'My little sister Elisabet? Dangerous?'

'No more so than her brothers.' Warin smiled faintly. 'All of you scare me a little.'

Justen frowned as he took hold of the last bale. 'I don't see why.'

'That's part of it. I like you, and I trust you, Justen, but you still scare me. You'll go off and change the world and then wonder why everyone's so upset. Altara told me about your black arrows and your matter-of-fact destruction of all the White cannon. And about how you walked the Stone Hills somehow.' Waring tugged on the bale, levering it toward the tailgate. 'And your brother turns a valley into a lake with wizardry, and you do him one better with engineering and rockets.' Warin took a deep breath. 'Let's get this in.'

They carried the last bale into the shed.

'The thing is,' Warin added, 'just like Dorrin, you're going to be a great person. But a lot of people die around great people, and as much as I like you, I really don't want to get too close.'

'I'm sorry.'

'That's not what I meant.' Warin waved off the words. 'I admire you, but I wouldn't go to Candar with you for all the iron in Recluce and all the gems in Hamor.'

'Stay for dinner?' asked Justen with a grin.

'Of course. I'll even stay for breakfast. Things are safe enough with your father around, and he's a good cook. Now, let's get Altara's de-ordered iron into the wagon.'

133

Carefully, Justen picked up the small silksheen balloon from the center of the workbench. The balloon skin of the second model measured nearly three cubits from top to bottom, but folded and deflated, Justen could lift it effortlessly. He glanced toward the carefully cut sections of silksheen lying in the flat rack he had built. Even with Elisabet's and Horas's help, the cutting and stitching and sealing were going slowly.

At the least, the models had proved that the idea worked – assuming that he could keep the basket and equipment light enough.

After setting the model carefully on the end of the bench, he centered the lens frame and remeasured with his calipers. The frame held the smaller of the two cut and polished fire-eyes and the lens that would focus the sun's light onto the polished and re-ordered gem. For his first experiment with the polished fire-eye, the beam from the gem would strike only a square of heavy iron less than two cubits below the gem.

Both the crystal lens and the gem were set in sliding and adjustable brackets, whose position would depend on where Justen wanted his 'organized chaos' to strike. He suspected that the brackets would have to be much farther apart when he actually used the balloon.

When he had finished measuring and locking the brackets in place, he lifted the square of heavy iron and carried it out into the yard, placing it on a square stone paving slab, a corner of it missing, that he had begged from the quarry.

Finally, after a quick glance to ensure that the cloudless summer sky had remained so, he brought out the frame and set it on the paving slab, too. Then he carefully centered the frame above the heavy square of one-span-thick iron plate, a chunk weighing more than a stone.

Elisabet, Cirlin, and Horas stood on the porch. Horas shifted his weight from one foot to the other, while Elisabet, looking more like the young woman she was becoming than the gawky girl she had been, gazed calmly toward Justen. The calm, feminine look vanished as Justen caught her eyes, to be replaced with a girlish grin.

Justen grinned back.

Cirlin's face was sober, as if she did not totally approve of Justen's experiments. That was not exactly surprising, Justen reflected. Since his return, he had indicated love for a druid, built two devices unsanctioned by the Council, and was planning worse.

Much worse, assuming that the experiment turned out the way he thought it would. Darkness knew what Gunnar would think.

His brother had indicated that he might show up . . . but with Gunnar, that could mean anything.

Justen turned the frame slightly, calculating the sun's position, and fiddled with the lens bracket. A point of light struck the fire-eye, and an even finer beam touched the iron.

Justen stepped back almost a dozen paces and concentrated, closing his eyes and weaving a little light into the lens, smoothing the flow onto and into the gem. The now-familiar shadow gathered around him and fell across the house.

Sssssssss . . .

The line of light from the gem became a line of fire that fell on the plate. Sparks fountained into the sky. Immediately, Justen relaxed his grasp on the light, and the shadows disappeared.

He took a deep breath and stood up.

'Is that all?' murmured Elisabet.

'For a moment.' Justen walked forward to inspect the plate. In the brief time he had concentrated the light, his light-sword had stabbed halfway through the heavy iron. The engineer frowned. Impressive as the beam from the gem had been in some ways, explosive powder was more effective.

He walked back almost to the porch. 'Don't look at the lens, please. It could hurt your eyes.'

'But we want to see,' protested his sister.

'Elisabet.' The name came from three voices almost simultaneously.

'All right,' conceded Elisabet. 'All right. I don't see why you're all so worried, but . . . all right.' With a flick of short blond hair, she turned to view the oak beside the road.

Justen wet his lips and took another deep breath before closing his eyes, stretching to gather a wider sweep of light, weaving, focusing, and sensing the growing flow of order like a river from the heavens, even as a darker force seemed to gather, welling from—

Sssttt . . . cruummppttt!

Justen felt himself being thrown against the stones of the porch foundation, the wind whipping past him with the force of a water-spout.

Thuddd . . .

He struggled to raise his arm, but the blackness smashed his thoughts from him.

'. . . *ugghhn* . . .'

Someone groaned, then groaned again. Justen realized he was the one groaning, and he forced his mouth closed.

. . . Justen . . . dearest . . .

Rain fell across his face, cold, dripping. He opened his eyes, but only bright sparks fluttered in front of his vision.

Justen . . . dearest. Think. Balance. Balance the forces . . .

Listening somehow to the faint thoughts of Dayala, he sought both the chaos and the order within himself, accepting both of them, and the bright flashes faded. He squinted.

Heavy clouds dropped rain and hail across the blackened space that had been grass.

Slowly, he levered himself upright.

'Demons . . .' Then he lurched toward the porch steps. 'Elisabet! Elisabet!'

His sister lay in a heap, crumpled against the furniture that had been swept onto the far side of the porch by the force of the power he had unleashed. Blood oozed down her face from a gash hidden by her hair. But his trembling fingers and senses revealed that despite cuts and bruises, she seemed unhurt and the pulse of order beat strongly in her veins.

On his knees, Justen scrambled toward the other slack forms. Horas seemed more stunned than physically injured. Justen turned toward his mother, sensing the pain and damage, and offered what order he could spare to Cirlin, whose breathing was labored and shallow.

The porch and the gray clouds beyond seemed to tilt. Justen tried to take a deep breath, but a line of pain shot up his side, and his chest seemed to contract. This time, he could not fight off the blackness that swallowed him.

134

Beltar swept into the lower room of the White tower, even before the clunk of the door against the chaos-whitened stone had finished echoing down the corridor. 'Eldiren! Eldiren!'

Eldiren looked up from the basin where he had dipped a corner of a towel to dampen it. He blotted the blood off one cheek with the dampened corner. 'Yes, mightiest of High Wizards?'

'Eldiren . . . do you want to go the way of Zerchas?'

'You'd only waste your power.' The slight White Wizard continued to blot away the blood. He laughed once. 'This business of exploding screeing glasses is getting to be a bother.' He straightened and looked at the High Wizard. 'No. I don't know exactly what happened, but it had the feeling of combined order and chaos.'

'That's what I thought. It came from Recluce.'

Eldiren inclined his head slightly and pressed the towel to the thin slash on his cheek. 'You know more than I, then.'

'I'd like you to try to find out what caused this . . . this abomination. It feels too much like that engineer you . . . "killed."'

'That killing may haunt me for some time, I fear.'

Beltar frowned. 'You still don't admit it, do you?'

'Admit what?'

'For having so little power, Eldiren, you're almost insufferable.'

'With so little power, mightiest of High Wizards, could I afford to be less?' Eldiren finally lifted the damp towel from his cheek. 'It would be nice to have a real healer around at times.'

'You . . .' Beltar finally closed his mouth. He walked over to the table on which broken glass lay in the rough semblance of a circle, then turned back to Eldiren. 'Use a goblet, or whatever, but find out what caused this . . . mess.'

'Of course. Your desire is always my command.' Eldiren bowed.

135

Gunnar and the healer, Gyris, looked down at Justen, stretched out on his bed. The lamp in the wall sconce flickered in the breeze blowing through the half-open window, but the early evening wind was light and too infrequent to cool the heat that had returned after the chill of the hail and the thunderstorm.

'Well . . .' grumbled Justen, too sore to wipe the dampness from his forehead.

'You have two cracked ribs, more bruises than you'll ever count, and you're probably lucky to be alive.' Gyris frowned. 'From the marks on your back, it looks like you were thrown against the wall. What happened?'

Justen started to shrug, but the twinges from his ribs stopped the gesture short. 'I don't know exactly. I was testing some lenses, and somehow that generated an explosion, or a storm, or something. I remember being thrown against the wall . . . and then crawling up the steps to find Elisabet and the others.'

'Very strange.' The dark-haired healer pursed her lips. 'I may talk to Turmin about this.'

'He was the one who suggested the work with lenses,' Justen offered. 'He said it was theoretical, but this isn't exactly a theoretical soreness.' He offered a faint smile.

'Once you get over the soreness, you can move around. But don't lift anything heavy, and stay away from smithing and hammering until the ribs knit. I suspect that you have more than enough order-sense to know when your ribs are healed.'

'Thank you,' said Justen.

'Thank you,' echoed Gunnar with a nod to the healer.

'I won't say it was a pleasure, Gunnar, but it was interesting to deal with . . .'

'Order-madness?' suggested Justen politely.

Gyris raised an eyebrow. 'You said that, not me. It has been interesting. But I prefer to avoid the interesting when possible.' She half-turned to Gunnar. 'Everyone else should be fine. Your mother has a badly bruised rib that almost feels like it was broken and healed.' Her eyes dropped back to Justen.

Justen smiled faintly. 'Don't look at me.'

'From what I've heard, I wouldn't put anything past you, Justen.' She picked up her pack and added, 'Try not to get into any more trouble.'

Gunnar took her arm for a moment, as if to lead her out.

'You, either, Gunnar.'

'Me?'

'The two of you.' Gyris frowned, then shook her head as she shouldered her pack and allowed Gunnar to escort her from the room.

Justen took a gentle, slow breath and waited for Gunnar to come back.

After Gunnar had seen Gyris to her mount and returned, he looked down at Justen. 'What in the demons' minds were you doing?'

'Working with order.'

'Darkness save us if you started to work with chaos!' Gunnar sighed. 'Exactly why are you doing this? And who will be the next innocent victims of your experiments?'

'No one.' Justen cleared his throat, gingerly and softly. 'I'm done with the experiments, at least with the dangerous ones. Now all I have to do is finish putting the balloon together and complete plating the land engine. I can probably start that in a few days.'

'With cracked ribs?'

'They'll heal fast.'

'You did heal Mother, didn't you? That's why you're in such bad shape.'

'What else was I supposed to do?'

Gunnar looked at the lamp and then gazed out the window into the growing darkness.

'Ryltar will be moving to have you confined – as soon as he finds out about this. You've just proved, you idiot, that you are not only order-mad, but dangerous to everyone around you!'

Justen stopped another shrug before he could complete it. 'Order-mad because I'm trying to figure out how to stop a threat that no one sees besides me?'

'We've lasted a long time with Fairhaven. Recluce won't blow away any time soon, unless you're the one who blows it away.' Gunnar frowned. 'Just what was this "experiment" anyway?'

'I was trying to order light and make it stronger.'

'You certainly made it stronger. But I don't understand the hail or the storm that appeared so quickly.'

'When the light gets ordered like that and creates heat . . . well, it doesn't really create heat. Remember the forge?'

'Oh, shit. So you made the air overhead really cold. That chilled out the water into hail and we got a thunderstorm. Now you're going to use your damned engineering to muck up the weather, too?' Gunnar slammed his hand into the wall.

'Not here. Not anymore.' Justen tried not to yawn, but the stifled yawn hurt all the same.

Tap . . .

'Is Justen going to be all right?' Elisabet peered into the room.

'He'll be fine,' snorted Gunnar. 'The rest of us may not survive his engineering, but he'll be just fine.'

Elisabet stepped just inside the doorway. 'What he did was really neat, Gunnar. You could see – I didn't look, Justen, I meant I saw with my senses – the rays of order coming from the fire-eye and hitting that iron plate, and it was like a huge storm building. I ducked and dragged Dad down, but Mom wasn't quick enough. She's lucky she wasn't hurt worse.'

'She was,' said Gunnar sourly. 'Justen healed her. That's why he's a mess.'

'So everyone's all right except Justen, and he will be. Why are you so upset?' Elisabet's fine eyebrows drew together for a moment.

'Because . . .'

'Is it because Justen's getting to be a good all-around wizard like you?'

'Elisabet, that's not fair to Gunnar.'

'All right.' She turned to face Gunnar. 'I'm not grown up yet, and no one really listens to me. But I think Justen's right. People here on Recluce just can't keep saying that what the Whites do doesn't matter because they can't hurt us. What happens when they get powerful enough so they can? Then how many people will be killed? Or won't it matter, because everyone who's alive now figures he'll be dead then?'

'It's not something that will happen soon,' Gunnar pointed out.

'Oh, you don't think Creslin should have changed the weather and made a refuge for order, then, because the Whites had killed only a few people?' Elisabet stared at Gunnar.

Justen grinned as he lay there.

'You've been listening to Justen again.'

'What if I have? If you won't go to Candar with him, I will. I can do everything he needs. Then you can sit at home and claim that whatever happens wasn't your fault. I hate you!' Elisabet glared at Gunnar.

'But . . .' Gunnar protested.

'Justen had to go to Candar before you'd think about it—'

'I never said I wasn't going with him. I did say that he was going to kill everyone around him if he weren't more careful.'

The door opened and shut with a dull thud. The three looked at their father.

'This has got to stop.' Horas delivered each word with the force of an ax. 'You three are arguing as if nothing happened today. Like schoolchildren. As if upsetting all of nature and blotting out the sun is just some . . . magister's learning tool. Justen almost killed all of us, and then himself.'

Gunnar looked at his brother. Justen tried to repress a grin, a grin he didn't quite understand.

'What are you grinning at? This isn't a game, son. You think I don't know, but you almost killed your mother, and then healed her before you thought she knew. That was dangerous, and it was dishonest. You have the right to risk your own life. You don't have the right to risk hers.'

'It seems that everyone has figured that out,' admitted Justen wryly. He tried to shift his weight, but his ribs twinged again.

'What happens when you kill someone outright?'

Justen took a deep breath. 'Just before you came in, Gunnar was telling me that I was going to kill everyone around me if I weren't more careful.'

'He's right. Just when are you going to stop this foolishness?'

'I'm done with the experiments. I was telling Gunnar and Elisabet that.'

'Now you're going to kill people for real?' Horas asked, exasperation in his voice.

'Stop sounding like Lydya in the old chronicles,' snapped Justen. 'Everyone says that life will be fine if I just forget this foolish obsession of mine. "Go on, Justen. Don't worry about anything. Recluce will be fine. Don't worry if the Whites conquer all of Candar. Don't worry if all trade with Recluce gets cut off. Everything will be fine."' Justen glared from his prone position. 'Well, it won't be fine. I'm sorry this happened. It won't happen again, because as soon as I can, I'm leaving.'

Horas's shoulders slumped. 'You can't keep doing this, Justen.'

The door opened again, and Cirlin stood there. 'It is rather difficult to get any rest with the four of you arguing about whether Candar and the world should be saved and if Gunnar or Elisabet should help Justen save it, and whether Justen meant to hurt us.' She turned to Horas. 'I know Justen didn't mean what happened.'

'Good intentions don't bring back dead people,' Horas said, an edge to his voice. 'Justen will go off and save the world, but I'd like him to leave our corner halfway intact.'

'That's the problem, and that's why Justen's right and you're wrong, Father,' Elisabet said.

Gunnar took a deep breath. Justen tried to hold back the insane grinning feeling he felt.

Elisabet turned to her mother, then to her father. 'I will go! And you can't stop me! You don't understand how important it is. You don't!'

'Elisabet . . .' Gunnar's voice was low. 'Justen and I and Martan will go, and as soon as we can.'

'You two . . .' sighed Horas. 'More death and destruction?'

'You act as if I have a choice,' said Justen slowly. 'I don't.'

'You have to blow up your family?' snapped Horas.

'No. I have to right the Balance . . . except that the ancients didn't exactly hand me a map.'

'You are going to save the world? And face who knows how many White Wizards, when you couldn't handle even a few in Sarronnyn?'

'I know more now.' Justen forced a smile. 'I think you saw that.'

'You'll destroy us all.'

'I don't have a choice.' Justen kept his voice even.

'But—'

'Horas,' said Cirlin evenly, 'if Justen doesn't have a choice, he doesn't have a choice. And if that's the way he feels, then we need to help him get to Candar as quickly as possible. Before we start a civil war here on Recluce.'

'That's ridiculous,' said Horas.

'Oh?' asked Cirlin. 'And what are we doing right now?' Her eyes swept the group.

A short silence filled the room.

'I think I can persuade Heldra and her daughter to help with the stitching on Justen's balloon,' added Cirlin.

Horas shifted his weight from one bare foot to the other.

'Father . . . I didn't mean it,' Elisabet pleaded. 'But Justen's right. I know he's right.'

'We'll see, daughter.' Horas looked at Justen. 'Heldra, unlike the rest of us, is not likely to stitch your fancy silksheen on faith.'

'I've still got some golds to pay them with.'

'That would definitely help.' Cirlin's eyes traversed the four. 'Now that we've settled that, can we get some sleep? Or some quiet?'

'Oh, Mother . . .' But Elisabet hugged Cirlin, very gently. Then she stepped toward her father. 'I'm sorry, Father.'

'It's all right.' Horas took a deep breath. 'Mostly.'

'I'm sorry, Father,' Justen added. 'I wasn't careful enough.'

Elisabet slipped her arms around Horas.

Gunnar gave a faint smile past her to Justen, and Justen nodded.

Cirlin shook her head. 'Such an amiable and agreeable group. So willing and eager to see each other's views.'

Horas coughed. 'Speaking of views . . . Since everyone's still up, and since no one is about to listen to my views—'

'Oh, Father,' said Elisabet, exasperation edging her tone.

'I'm going to put out cider and a perfectly good peach pie. Shouldn't go to waste, I say,' said Horas. His tone turned wry. 'After all, Justen might turn his lenses or something on it.'

'If you've got some ale,' said Justen, easing himself into a sitting position and ignoring the twinges in his ribs, 'I'll take you up on the pie.'

Gunnar gave a faint, exasperated headshake.

'I'd like that, too.' Elisabet led the way to the kitchen.

Horas stood aside, then gave Justen a long look and a sad headshake.

Justen swallowed, but struggled to his feet.

136

'I think the Council should consider an order for confinement of this . . . what's his name?' Ryltar glanced toward Claris.

'You can stop the act, Ryltar,' suggested Jenna, her eyes not meeting his, but drifting toward the light-splashed terrace beyond the Council Room. 'You know very well the engineer's name.'

'What is his name?' asked Claris, her voice deliberately sweet.

'Justen. You two make me sick with all your games, as if you'd never heard about . . .'

'Heard about what, Ryltar? That this Justen made money with some sharp trading? Or that he's apparently been a success as a trader while remaining highly ordered? Or is there something else we should know? Has he decided to compete with you on the Hamor routes?' Jenna turned her head and favored the wispy-haired counselor with a smile.

'The marines say that he's strangely accomplished with weapons,' added Ryltar.

'I believe your . . . cousin . . . noted that, even before this Justen went to Sarronnyn. Is there something else?' asked Claris.

'What does it take? The man's order-mad. I'm not talking about exile or execution. I just want him confined so that he doesn't hurt himself or anyone else.'

'I believe he is resting with his family in Wandernaught. His brother is a Weather Wizard who is directly under Turmin's supervision. This rest is a confinement of sorts, since he has been effectively removed from the engineering hall.'

'I would like to request that he be physically confined and thoroughly examined, not only by Turmin, but by several other mages in the Brotherhood.'

'Perhaps we should take that up at our next meeting,' suggested Jenna. 'It might help if you had some better reasons, also, Ryltar.'

'The next meeting is more than two eight-days from now.'

'As you have pointed out often, Ryltar,' added Claris, 'we do not have to act precipitously when we are not even sure something is yet a problem.'

'Fine. Next meeting.' Ryltar stood and lifted the thin leather case and walked out stiffly. The heavy door closed behind him with a thud.

'He's angry. I don't believe I've ever seen him that angry,' observed Claris.

'He's not telling us something, and I don't know why. It's almost as if he's afraid of this Justen.' Jenna brushed a strand of hair off her forehead and back over her ear. 'And he never answered my question about the Hamor trade. None of it makes sense.'

'If Ryltar's afraid, it might be well for us to fear it also, Jenna.' Claris stood and glanced toward the closed door. 'Ryltar is so cautious that he never wants to act. Now he does. What does that tell us?' She nodded politely. 'Good day.'

Jenna suppressed a frown as she stood also and answered. 'Good day.'

137

'Damned strange basket, if you ask me,' confessed Seldit, glancing at the oblong, waist-high woven basket standing in the middle of the cooper's workroom.

'Exactly what I need.' Justen smiled briefly, running his fingers across the triple-woven top ridge. 'You did this well.'

'Don't get much call for baskets this big, young fellow.'

'That's probably true. I owe you three for this?'

'We'd agreed on three . . .'

Justen caught the suggestion in the cooper's voice. 'But it took more time and effort than you thought it would?'

'Not a lot, but . . . Mallin had to help me some nights to get it ready.'

The engineer lifted his purse, opened it and set four golds on the bench. 'Here's four.'

'That's generous, Ser.'

'Not at all. You had it ready when I needed it, and that's important. I've got the wagon outside.'

'You'll take it now?'

Justen caught the undercurrent of – was it fear? – in the cooper's voice and answered as heartily as he could. 'Best strike while the iron's hot. Old smith saying, you know.' He replaced his purse and lifted the basket, light enough for him to heft alone, a good sign. 'If you would open the door?'

'Certainly, Master Justen.'

Justen carried the wicker basket through the open double doors and out into the street, where he eased it into the wagon bed, then lifted and latched the tailgate shut.

'Excellent work, Seldit!' the engineer exclaimed, loudly enough that Basta, standing in the doorway of his leather-and-dry-goods shop, turned to look toward the rotund cooper, whose shoulders slumped under the weight of the unasked praise. 'First rate!'

Justen added, trying to conceal a malicious grin as he untied the horses and climbed onto the wagon. While his ribs *seemed* healed, he did not want to attempt a vault.

'Thank you,' answered Seldit weakly. 'We try to please, Ser.'

Justen released the wagon brake and flicked the reins. The horses carried the near-empty wagon out of Wandernaught with easy steps. Thinking again about Seldit's reactions, the engineer frowned.

Shrezsan was working in the garden, her toddler nearby, and she waved briefly.

Justen returned the wave, still thinking about Seldit, and Ryltar. How much longer before Ryltar would push the Council into acting? He coughed to clear his throat, relieved that the cough didn't create even the slightest twinge in his ribs.

But why was Ryltar so concerned? The counselor didn't seem to be the type who really cared much about order, or even about tradition. The fact that he was involved with smugglers showed that his concern was with coin, not with higher considerations. Justen continued to mull the question as the team carried him back to the house.

He pulled on the reins slightly to slow the horses before they turned onto the lane and plodded up to the stable.

Elisabet waved from the orchard, then came running. Gunnar was waiting by the stable and slipped the wagon blocks in place as Justen set the brake and climbed down.

'Does anyone need the wagon?' asked Justen.

'Not that I know of.'

'No,' added Elisabet. 'Even the early apples aren't ready to go anywhere yet.'

'Then I'll put it away after I get this inside.' Justen lifted the basket over the tailgate. 'The balloon and the lens framework are finished. All I need to do is attach the brackets to this basket. After that, let's load the land engine and leave tonight.'

'I'd thought – Why?' asked Gunnar.

'Tonight? So soon?' asked Elisabet.

'Because someone is watching and thinks it will be later. Seldit really didn't want me to take the basket yet. He was obviously uneasy about it, even after I gave him an extra gold.'

'Free with your coin, aren't you?'

'I thought it was well invested to get the basket and get out.'

'Your coal bins aren't full. Dad and I can fill them while you and Mother do the brackets.' Gunnar paused. 'Is it a good idea to travel the High Road at night?'

'It might be better. I don't know how horses would take to the land engine.'

'There is that.'

'I can pack up some food to go with all the dried provisions stored in the chest,' added Horas, who had just walked past the stable from the eastern grove.

'We might have to wait a few days in Nylan for the *Llyse*,' added Gunnar.

'That's still better than being here. I could put the land engine in the engineering hall, I think, for the engineers to "study."'

Gunnar nodded. 'You're worried. A lot.'

'I think Ryltar's up to something, maybe a lot of somethings. And I don't understand why.'

'That might be,' said Horas, 'but you need to be thinking about loading and preparing to depart, if that's what you've got in mind.'

'Trust Father to be the practical one,' laughed Gunnar. 'Where do we start?'

'With the balloon. It goes in the inside compartments. I've packed some spare fabric, but I really don't want it ripped. The frame for the lenses is already broken down and inside the padded crate on the floor of the shed . . .' Justen began to detail what went where in the limited cargo space of the land engine.

'I never realized that you could be so well-organized,' Gunnar told his brother.

'I've thought about it for a while, and—'

'Tell me what I can bring out,' interrupted Elisabet.

'You can bring out all the supplies. Father knows where they are.' The engineer looked at the nearly cloudless late-afternoon sky. 'I need to get the land engine out. I don't think we'll need the canvases, though.'

'Canvases?' asked Cirlin as she walked down from the smithy.

'Those canvas covers you had Heldra make. They're to keep the rain or too much sun off us, but I don't think we'll need them on the way to Nylan.'

'No. There won't be any rain,' added Elisabet as she set off for the kitchen, scurrying after Horas.

Justen, Gunnar, and Cirlin wheeled the land engine out of the stable and into the yard.

'Take more than three people to move this once it's loaded.' Gunnar leaned against the side armor of the craft and wiped his forehead.

'Not on the road, but on soft ground.' Justen set the brake.

Elisabet returned from the kitchen with several waxed packages. 'Where do I put these?'

'Set them here.' Justen pointed to the seat beside the driver. 'I'll load them once they're all here. I know in which order they go inside the locker.'

Gunnar raised his eyebrows.

'I measured. What good's an engineer's training if he doesn't use it?'

'I think I'll get the balloon,' Gunnar answered.

'I'll help,' added Cirlin.

'Father wants to know if he can start dinner.' Elisabet looked at Justen.

'Yes. That would be just right.'

'Optimist,' muttered Gunnar.

Despite Gunnar's pessimism, the loading was complete just before Horas called out, 'Dinner.'

'I'll be right there. I'm going to get the firebox ready to light.' Justen whittled some shavings from a branch he had taken from the woodpile. Although he had some shavings in a box in the coal bin, they were to be saved for possible emergencies.

After setting the shavings and some chips and twigs in the firebox, he walked to the outside pump where he washed the coal dust and grime off his hands and face, then shook the water off his hands.

The others were at the table when he entered.

'Spiced lamb!' announced Elisabet. 'And berry bread, and pie.'

'That's for later, young woman,' said Horas.

'Pass the lamb, please,' asked Gunnar.

Justen extended the bread to his mother, and then to Elisabet, who promptly slathered her slab with cherry conserve. Justen set a slice on the edge of his plate and waited for the lamb, still wondering about Seldit and Ryltar.

'This is good,' said Gunnar. 'We're going to miss this kind of cooking.'

Justen took a bite of the bread.

'Why do you have to leave now? Why so soon?' asked Elisabet.

'Counselor Ryltar wants to lock me up because I'm order-mad,' mumbled Justen through a mouthful of hot bread.

'Finish eating before you talk,' suggested Horas.

'You don't know that for sure,' protested Gunnar.

'Sure enough.' Justen held up a hand and swallowed. 'I still don't understand why. All Ryltar seems interested in is trade and money.'

'If he's a trader,' suggested Horas. 'He wants to keep taxes low, because the levies fall on traders and businesses. If what you do starts a war between Fairhaven and Recluce, his taxes will go up and his profits will fall.'

'He wants to confine me because I *might* do something that leads to war?' Justen took a sip of ale from his mug and spooned more lamb onto his plate, reflecting that he wouldn't get cooking as good as his father's for a long time, if ever. He swallowed.

'Maybe he likes things the way they are,' suggested Cirlin. 'Traders don't like change.'

Justen frowned. 'He does handle smuggling.' He ate some of the lamb, enjoying the meat and mixed spices.

'It's not illegal here, just in places like Hamor and Candar,' added Gunnar.

'Maybe he doesn't want Justen to succeed,' suggested Elisabet.

'He doesn't even know what I'm doing.' *He can't, since I myself am still not exactly sure of what's going to happen.*

'Elisabet may be right,' said Gunnar. 'Let's say that you do something, anything, to unbalance things in Candar, anything that reduces the power of the Whites. The Whites control their trade absolutely, and they tax it heavily. They have to. That's how they support all those armies and levies.'

'So?'

'The Whites have always tried to reduce free trading. What advantage does Ryltar have over the other traders? He deals with smugglers. Now, smugglers can exist only if they provide things people can't get, or if they charge less for their services. If they don't pay the Whites' taxes.'

Horas nodded. 'So more White control means more coins in Ryltar's purse?'

'Is that enough to want to lock Justen up?'

'I don't know.' Justen shrugged. 'There has to be something else, but what it is . . .'

'Could anyone be that greedy?' mused Horas.

'I don't think you can underestimate greed,' answered Cirlin.

'I still think I could go.' Elisabet looked at Justen.

'Only when you're as good as Gunnar with the storms, or as good an engineer as Justen, dear,' responded Cirlin.

'That's not fair.'

The other four laughed gently.

'All right. Fair doesn't count, but I don't have to like it.'

Justen reached over and patted Elisabet's shoulder. 'Someday . . . someday . . . you too can go off into the world and do utterly idiotic deeds that could kill you.'

'. . . and fall in love with strange people in strange places that your family has never seen,' added Horas, a twinkle in his eye.

'. . . and build wondrous devices that throw your family through stone walls,' added Cirlin dryly.

'Promise?' asked Elisabet.

The older four laughed again, with less restraint.

By the time dinner was over, the sun had dropped behind the hills.

Justen and Gunnar carried their packs out to the land engine. There Justen checked the coal bins again, easing another shovelful of coal into them. Then he opened the firebox and used the striker to light the shavings and wood, adding a few chunks of coal to begin building up the fire. Once the edges of the coal had caught, he closed the door and left the scuttle by the firebox. He didn't want to use the coal from the bins until the land engine was actually on the road.

'Let's put the packs here.' He reached out and set his by the third seat, and reached back to get Gunnar's.

Then he used the small bellows to force the fire into a hotter flame, waiting to add more coal.

Sssssss . . . Justen reached above the back of the third seat, trying not to snag his sleeve on the wicker balloon basket, containing assorted supplies, in order to close the steam valve. The balloon fabric was folded and stored in one of the storage spaces under the black iron armor. Then he eased forward and climbed out of the land engine to stand beside the driver's seat with Gunnar.

In the early twilight, Cirlin, Horas, and Elisabet stood a pace or so back from the land engine.

'I still wish you'd let me go,' said Elisabet. 'One ride wasn't really enough.'

'Watching that one was bad enough,' mumbled Horas.

Elisabet turned toward her father. 'I wasn't in an any danger. Justen wouldn't even go fast.'

'Praise the darkness he didn't.'

Justen hugged Elisabet, then Cirlin and Horas. Gunnar did the same, beginning with Horas.

'We'd better get moving,' suggested Gunnar as he stepped back from hugging his sister.

'Be careful with that . . . thing,' warned Horas.

'It's no different from a Brotherhood ship, dear,' noted Cirlin.

'Ships are dangerous, too.'

Justen grinned as he caught the teasing tone in his father's voice. 'We'll be careful. As careful as we can be.'

'That's probably not careful enough.'

In the quiet, punctuated only by the gentle hiss of steam, Gunnar climbed into the seat beside the driver's seat, and Justen slipped into the driver's seat, wiggling the tiller. The third seat, raised and to the rear, was vacant.

Justen eased the throttle to begin the steam flow to the turbine.

Creakkkkk . . . The land engine rolled down the lane and toward the road. Behind them, Cirlin, Horas, and Elizabet waved. The brothers waved back through the twilight.

Neither Gunnar nor Justen spoke until they were on the road to Wandernaught.

'You know . . . some of the people are going to think that we're some sort of monster when we puff through town.' Gunnar pursed his lips.

Without taking his eyes from the road, Justen increased the steam flow to the pistons driving the shaft. 'They might, but not many people will be out, and we don't sound very different from a heavy wagon. The engine's not really noisy.'

'I don't know. This is bigger than most wagons.'

'Not if you consider that we don't have any horses up front. But we'll have to see.'

They rolled past Shrezsan's and Yousal's house, and Shrezsan's parents' house, and into Wandernaught. The main street was clear of horses and wagons. Upstairs lamps were lit in the quarters above the cooper's and above Basta's, and two lanterns flared outside The Broken Wheel.

Three men stood under the lanterns, two of them gesturing toward the larger figure, who lifted a truncheon.

'. . . off with ye! Not another word!'

'Our coin's good as any!'

'Light's piss! What the frig is that?' The middle figure turned and dashed toward the alley, away from the inn and the passing land engine.

The other two watched openmouthed as the machine rolled up the street and past the inn.

'It's something . . .'

'I know it's something! Looks like a wizard's nightmare.'

'Yousal said that wizard . . . Justen . . .'

The voices faded from Justen's hearing, straining as he was, as the land engine passed the post house. He turned the tiller, and the craft headed toward the High Road.

'You only scared the shit out of one in three,' said Gunnar, 'and they know it's you. How long before Ryltar finds out?'

'A day after we get to Nylan. Maybe two. We'll get there maybe two days ahead of the post.'

'How?' asked Gunnar warily.

'We're going straight through. Where could we stop?'

'You can't steer this thing that long.'

'I don't intend to.' Justen laughed. 'You're going to learn how.'

'Me?' gulped the Weather Wizard.

'You,' affirmed Justen.

138

Beltar took a deep swallow from the goblet and immediately refilled it. 'Here in the tower, you have to drink it quickly, before it sours.'

'The result of centuries of chaos, no doubt,' murmured Eldiren.

'No doubt.' The High Wizard set his goblet on the table and fingered the links from which the gold amulet hung across his white tunic. 'No doubt.' He picked up the goblet and took another deep swallow.

'Being High Wizard isn't as much fun as conquering places, is it?'

'No fun at all.' The High Wizard carefully set his goblet on the table again and glanced toward the half-open tower window. He wiped his forehead, for the stillness of the hangings revealed the lack of breeze on the hot, early fall day. 'Everyone hates you, and each one tiptoes around. No one says anything but "Yes, High Wizard. Yes, High Wizard."'

'Yes, High Wizard.'

'Eldiren! Just because I'm half-potted, it doesn't mean I can't think.'

'What would you have me say?'

'You could tell me what you found out about that wizard.'

'Which . . . wizard?'

'The one who exploded the screeing glasses. Twice . . . wasn't it?'

Eldiren's fingers brushed over the thin scar on his cheek. 'Ah . . . yes. That wizard.'

'You know full well it was that wizard.' Beltar reached for the wine bottle again.

'I don't know. He's hard to even find. The glass isn't clear, and it seems like there's a mix of order and chaos around him, but it's all ordered, except how can chaos be ordered?'

'Oh, frig you.' Beltar took another deep swallow from the goblet before refilling it and setting down the empty bottle with exaggerated care. 'You mean that we've got . . . a real, honest-to-darkness . . . Gray Wizard, the kind everyone says there can't be?'

Eldiren fingered his goblet, whose contents he had not touched. 'I couldn't say for sure. I think so.'

'Frig! I got "Yes, High Wizard" this and "Yes, High Wizard" that, and now I've got to worry about a demon-damned Gray Wizard who goes around exploding screeing glasses so no one can even find him?'

Eldiren stared at the table.

Beltar downed the remnants in his goblet and set the glass aside. 'You're not drinking. Let me have yours. You look at it too long and it'll turn sour. Like everything else round here.'

139

'Clever. Very clever.' Altara ran her fingertips across the parchment-thin black iron armor, backed with span-thickness black oak. 'But then, you've always been clever with applications, Justen. How, might I ask, did you get through the gate in this contraption?'

'He told the guards that he was delivering it to you,' said Gunnar, 'and that you would be angry if it didn't get there. When that didn't quite convince them, he pointed out that either the device was good, in which case, they couldn't stop him, or that it wasn't, in which case, the engineering hall was the best place for it. Then he told them that he was the order-mad engineer. Quite a performance.'

'I can bet.' Altara glanced from Gunnar to Justen.

'It really wasn't,' Justen protested. 'Besides, not very much of the land engine is original. I told them that, too – that it was just like a small ship. Most of the parts and assemblies are what we use on the ships, or small adaptations.'

'I recall that there was nothing terribly original about your black order-tipped arrows, either,' noted the chief engineer dryly. 'I'd be terrified to think what you might do if you really got original. Something like this is bad enough.'

Justen decided not to mention the balloon or the beam or ordered-light created from the polished and ordered fire-eyes.

Gunnar glanced at the hard-packed clay beside the rear loading door leading into the engineering hall.

'So, what am I supposed to do with this . . . device?' Altara offered a wry smile.

'I thought that you and the others might wish to examine it for a day or so before –' Justen broke off.

'Yes. Spare me the details, Justen.' Altara glanced toward the early morning sun, just above the Eastern Ocean. 'Do I understand that you want to hide this original needle in the haystack in the engineering hall for a day or so? Is that what you're really asking?'

'Yes, honored and knowledge-seeking Chief Engineer.'

'And in that way, you will doubtless ensure that every engineer alive knows what you have done and how to replicate it. So either your design will endure forever or the Council will decide to banish us all?'

'I think it highly unlikely that the Council will banish you all,' said Gunnar.

'Maybe not. Then again, it may not be that improbable. The honorable Counselor Ryltar has inquired about your health only a half-score times over the past several eight-days. He seems to want to ensure that your rest cure is . . . thorough.'

'I don't see it,' said Justen through a yawn.

'Who knows?' Altara looked at Justen. 'You look tired. How much sleep have you had?'

'Not much lately.'

'And what are you really up to? As if I didn't know.'

'You want me to tell you?' Justen forced a laugh. 'We're just trying to subvert the entire Brotherhood by showing how easy it is to build a land engine.' He tried not to wince at the stab of pain through his skull at this small lie.

Altara shook her head. 'You really can't keep this here long.'

'I know. But it is an engineering device. Two nights?'

'We'll see.' The chief engineer looked toward Gunnar. 'Can you keep him out of trouble? And get him some sleep?'

Gunnar shrugged.

'Are you going to sleep in Gunnar's room?' asked Altara, turning back to face Justen.

'Not at night. I have some provisions so that I can sleep in the land engine, or next to it.' Justen looked at the rear wheel.

'I'm not sure which is worse, admitting you to the Brotherhood quarters or to the engineering hall.' Altara laughed nervously.

'I'll stay away from the hall during the day,' offered Justen.

'Well, let's get this land wagon, land engine – whatever you call it – inside, before too many people see it.'

Justen released the brake and used the last of the steam to start the land engine rolling.

'Over there,' suggested Altara. 'We won't be using the big mill for a couple of eight-days.'

'Do you want me to explain it – the land engine – to anyone before we go get something to eat?' asked Justen.

'I'm sure you'll find a way before you leave—'

'Justen!' Warin walked past Altara and hugged the younger engineer. He paused. 'You shouldn't be back. You still look tired.'

'Maybe I shouldn't. Here's our project.' Justen grinned at Altara. 'A land engine. See . . . we took the small boiler . . .'

Behind them, Altara glanced at Gunnar. Both shook their head.

After Warin left, Gunnar grabbed Justen by the arm. 'I'm starving, and if you don't get out of here, Altara will throw both you and the land engine out.'

They slipped out the back door and down the alley toward the harbor.

'Why did you say you wanted to sleep in the hall with the land engine? That isn't going to be comfortable.' Gunnar looked at the shops ahead.

'I probably won't sleep.' Justen yawned. 'After we get something to eat at Houlart's, I'm going to sleep on the floor of your room.' He glanced toward the morning sun. 'Tonight and for the next few nights, I'm going to try to stay awake . . . or merely doze with some wards.'

'I doubt that wards will work well around so much iron. Maybe Martan could spare someone to help.' Gunnar yawned, too. 'Houlart's is around the next corner.'

'Good.' In turn, Justen yawned again.

Only two tables in the public room were occupied, and the brothers took a corner table, one from where Justen could study the entire room. As he sat down, he glanced at the doorway by the kitchen, where Houlart was speaking to a young woman. He strained to catch the words, but could catch only a few fragments.

'. . . Yersol . . . street opposite . . . engineer's back . . .'

He frowned. Where had he heard the name Yersol? Did it matter? It had something to do with Ryltar. He leaned toward Gunnar and whispered, 'You were right.'

'Huh?' Gunnar jerked fully alert.

'Never mind. I'll tell you later.'

'What'll it be, gents?' asked Houlart, standing by the table.

'Food, good hot food,' mumbled Gunnar.

Houlart smiled the professional smile of all innkeepers.

140

'Who's in port?'

'The *Yalmish*, and our *Viella*, and Slyak's bunch – I don't recall what the current name of his rig is.' Yersol set the mug of warm ale on the worktable between them.

'We need a little fire work. The *Yalmish* and Slyak's group ought to be enough.'

'Here? That's crazy.'

'We need to get rid of that thing in the engineers' hall. Besides, if the hall goes, the engineers won't get in the way for a while. I don't trust that Altara. She and Jenna are too close.' Ryltar shifted his weight on the cushion of the wooden armchair. His fingers toyed with the base of the black crystal goblet, still half full of ale.

'Why are you so worried about this engineer?'

'Don't you see? He almost won in Sarronnyn, and he's managed to get the demon-damned druids behind him. Now he's got this land engine that travels on roads like a steam ship does on water. But according to the engineers I know, it takes an engineer to run it.'

'The ones you pay to tell you what's going on?' Yersol took a last swallow of the ale, grimacing at the warm taste. 'No other trader could use it, and engineers don't trade.'

'This one does. He's got a deal going with the Naclans. Or the Naclans are using him. First it was lorken, and then that cloth that no one had except the Tyrant of Sarronnyn. Now he's got something that will cross Candar faster than the fastest ships.'

'He does?'

'Seldit watched him leave Wandernaught. He arrived here less than a full day later. The machine is up there in the engineering hall. Before long, they'll all be able to build one like it, and where does that leave us?'

'I told you, engineers don't trade, Ryltar.'

'You still don't see. What happens if he goes back to Candar?' Ryltar's fingers tightened on the base of the goblet.

'You're rid of him.' Yersol half-filled his mug.

Ryltar gave the younger trader a look of disgust. 'Would you think for once? Just once?'

'So I'm stupid. Would you explain what the problem is?'

Ryltar glared at Yersol before his expression softened. 'All right. Where do we make the most profit?'

'On the east-to-west Hamor trips.'

'Why?'

'You know –' Yersol paused, then continued. 'Because Hamor's bigger than Candar, and it's a long trip by land. Our ships are a lot faster than theirs, and we don't pay all their duties.'

'Do they have good roads?'

'Sure. But they're a bitch on wagons and pack animals.'

'And aren't there Order Wizards in Hamor?'

'Not many, but some.'

'If this engineer could run a land engine, could they?'

'Oh. Shit.'

'Now do you see? This damned land engine gets out, and we lose—'

'I'm slow, but I do get it.' Yersol frowned. 'But he wouldn't even think about this. You know that. Why would anyone think about taking a land engine to Hamor?'

'Look, Yersol. One thing I do know is that *nothing* in this world stays a secret, and the emperor of Hamor would do just about anything to stop us.'

'Yeah. I'll talk to Slyak. Have him talk to the *Yalmish*. It's going to cost probably double or triple.'

'It's worth it.'

'What if it doesn't work?'

'Even if it fails, the attempt will get Claris upset enough to get this Justen put away for a long time – for a permanent rest cure. She's almost there now.'

'I hope so.'

'It will work.' Ryltar nodded. 'It will.'

141

'Fire!'

At Gunnar's yell, Justen bolted upright out of his blankets and yanked on his boots even as he was trying to clear his head. Two nights of less-than-restful sleep, even with the naps he took in Gunnar's room, had left him sluggish.

A ruddy glow came from the front of the hall, accompanied by a faint crackling as flames seemed to race toward the back.

Justen glanced around. Martan and his two marines were dressed. 'Open the door,' yelled Justen. 'That one!' He pointed to the rear loading door, then threw his pack and blankets into the backseat of the land engine, even as he disengaged the brake and clutch and began to push, trying to rock the heavy machine forward.

Gunnar followed Justen's example, throwing his gear in the second seat and trying to push the engine toward the door that Martan and one of the marines had slid open.

Flames also licked up a rear corner of the building, and a dark-clad figure dashed away from the loading door.

'Someone . . . set . . . the fire . . .' grunted Gunnar, his shoulder almost touching Justen's. 'Threw oil . . . struck it . . .'

'Bastards,' grunted the marine pushing on the other wheel.

Martan joined them, and the land engine began to roll. Justen put one hand on the tiller to keep it lined up and headed toward the door.

Behind them, sounds of crackling and waves of heat rose. Flames also began to spread on the downhill side of the hall.

'Ugghhh . . .' The sides of the craft's armor scraped on a massive boiler section just inside the door, but Justen turned the tiller and the five pushed the land engine out through the rear loading door.

Nearly a dozen dark-clad figures stood a good thirty cubits beyond the door. Most of them bore staffs or weapons. One carried a torch.

'There's the demons' machine!'

'Destroy it!'

'No White evil in Nylan . . .'

Justen scrambled into the driver's seat and pulled on the brake lever to stop the land engine, then scrambled to the rear seat and the space beyond to open the firebox. He shoved some shavings and chips into place and lifted the striker.

'Get the demons!'

As the dark figures moved toward the land engine, Justen edged several small chunks of coal next to the wood and shavings and closed the firebox door, opening the draft vents.

Gunnar stood rooted just outside the hall, eyes closed.

The winds began to whine, to whistle, and the stars began to blink out as sudden clouds thickened.

'Send them back where they belong . . .'

From the road before the hall came the sound of more figures running.

'Get the steam pumps . . . cool it . . .'

'. . . take too long . . .'

'Weather Wizard . . . maybe rain.'

'Turmin . . . find him . . .'

The dark-clad group moved toward the land engine; less than twenty cubits separated them. Justen could sense the fear within the group, a fear that had slowed its advance, and he bent down and fanned the fire in the firebox, trying to build up steam pressure.

The crackling of timbers beginning to burn rose. So did the sound of the wind, and cold droplets began to pelt down.

A flash of lighting illuminated the back of the engineering hall and revealed the three marines . . . and Gunnar, who stood apparently oblivious to the commotion, trying to direct the storm onto the fire. As the rain increased in intensity, the intermittent hissing of steam began to replace the crackling of the flames.

'There, by the door!'

'Stop him. He's a weather mage!' screamed a short man in the front of the dark-clad group. The man beside him lifted a bow, the short type used generally by traders.

In the shadows behind the land engine, Martan raised his bow and nocked an arrow, then released it. The opposing bowman collapsed, a dark shaft driven through his chest.

Martan nocked another arrow.

'Marines!'

Gunnar shook his head, saw the dark-clad group, and concentrated again. Justen shoveled more coal into the firebox.

Cracckkk!

A thin, jagged lightning bolt smashed into the stone before the attackers, and a wave of hail rattled behind the flare of light. Justen blinked and shook his head, trying to clear his vision.

'Get the frig . . . out of here . . .'

'. . . not paid to . . . fight magic . . .'

'Run!'

The attackers scattered, leaving one body on the hail-strewn and wet stones.

Martan lowered his bow and glanced at Justen. 'Some trader wants you dead and your machine destroyed.'

Justen nodded, then saw Gunnar begin to totter. He vaulted out of the driver's seat and half-skidded, half-ran, toward his brother even as Gunnar stumbled into a sitting position.

Three engineers wheeled a hand pump to the rear corner of the building, and a thin stream of water played against the flames on the wood-framed windows.

The rain continued and the hissing subsided as the rain, and the finally operating steam pumps, poured water on the engineering hall.

Justen lugged the semiconscious Gunnar to the land engine and set him in the seat next to the driver's place.

Martan and the other two marines continued to survey the area around the back of the engineering hall. Finally, Martan asked, 'Justen do you know who's after you?'

'Ryltar, I think. But there's no way to prove it.'

Martan spat away from the land engine. 'Scum. Everyone on the docks whispers about it. No one wants to say anything. Bet those were sailors hired from his ships for some extra coins – or else they were some smuggler's bravos.'

Gunnar groaned and held his head.

'Everything's fine,' Justen reassured him.

'Fine? Head hurts . . . fire in the hall . . . arrows . . . and it's fine?'

Justen and Marten laughed.

'Fine? Some sense of humor you have. Ohhh . . .' Gunnar rubbed his forehead again.

As the rain continued to fall, Justen put up rain canvases over the seats, and the three marines climbed into the third seat. Justen stoked up the firebox and checked the steam pressure.

'The *Llyse* should be in this morning. Anyone up for a ride down to the pier?'

'Uh . . .'

'I won't make you ride,' Martan grinned at the other two marines, 'but it's probably safer than walking, or worrying about who's out there.'

'Yeah . . .' mumbled one marine.

'We can't get shot with an arrow, either,' added the other, a fresh-faced young woman.

'Ready?' asked Justen, his hand on the throttle.

The three marines looked at each other.

Justen released the brake and eased the throttle forward, and with an initial creak, the land engine headed out of the alley.

A look back as he turned onto the main road reassured Justen that the rain and the pumps had saved most of the building. Still, more than a score of engineers scurried around the steaming facade of the hall even as the rain continued to fall on the blackened roof timbers.

'Good thing most of the building's stone,' said Martan, following Justen's quick glance.

'They weren't after the building,' said Gunnar, still massaging his forehead.

'What were they after, then?'

'I could guess, but I really don't know.' Justen shook his head. Why was Ryltar after him? Was it just a question of coins?

A tall figure on the uphill side of the hall stood and watched. Justen waved to Altara before turning the tiller to guide the land engine down toward the harbor.

The machine puffed up onto the stones of the harbor causeway as a faint gray seeped out of the Eastern Ocean.

The command 'Cast off!' rang from the end ship on the short pier.

'Didn't want to stay around, I see,' said Martan as he watched two crewmen loosen and release lines from the bollards. Then the crewmen scrambled onto the black-hulled schooner, whose colors and lack of flag almost certainly announced her as a smuggler.

Justen turned the land engine onto the main pier.

'That's one of the ships Ryltar was dealing with,' said Gunnar.

'He knows every smuggler east of Hamor,' laughed the woman marine.

'Lurena?' Martan glanced down the pier.

'Yes, Ser?'

'Get the squad down here by full dawn and bring Jislik's kit and mine.'

'Yes, Ser.'

Justen brought the land engine to a stop to let Lurena out, then eased the engine out to the spot on the pier where the *Llyse* was supposed to dock.

'How are you going to get this on board?' asked Martan.

'Very carefully.' Justen laughed. 'With a heavy crane attached to the lifting posts.' He pointed to the heavy circular rings in front of the driver's seat and behind the third seat. 'All the

Mighty Ten have short cranes, and the land engine isn't as heavy as it looks.'

'Hyntal will love it.' Martan grinned.

'Why?' asked Gunnar.

'He hates the Whites, and anything that would upset them . . .'

'I hope so,' murmured Justen.

Gunnar raised his eyebrows, but said nothing. Martan leaned back in the third seat.

Even before dawn, the remaining ten marines had marched out to the end of the pier.

'Let's go, Jislik.' Martan smiled at Justen. 'This will be fun.'

'Fun?' muttered Gunnar from the seat beside Justen. 'Marines have a strange sense of humor.'

'That's why they're marines.'

'Form up!' snapped Martan as he stood on the pier before the land engine. 'This is a special engine that's going on the *Llyse*. Last night some smugglers tried to fire the engineering hall to destroy it. Your job is to make sure that no one – except members of the Council, if they should appear – gets close to this part of the pier until this engine is loaded on the *Llyse*. Is that clear?'

'What about the dockers, Ser?'

'Let them do their work, but keep them clear of this engine.'

'Yes, Ser!'

Justen leaned back in the driver's seat and let his eyes close.

'Justen?'

The engineer straightened with a jolt. 'Huh? What? Is the *Llyse* here?'

'No, but young Yersol is, and he doesn't look too happy. And I think Altara is walking up the pier.' Gunnar peered around. 'And Martan has that smile that says he's just waiting to turn his attack cats on Yersol.'

Justen yawned and struggled to clear his mind. He managed to brush his hair back and smooth his clothes, but his unshaven chin itched and his eyes felt like they contained half the sand of the western beaches. He climbed down and stood beside the land engine and waited for Yersol to speak. Altara had stopped a good twenty cubits behind the trader.

'I don't believe that this ... device ... should be leaving Recluce without the approval of the Council,' stated the young trader.

'Oh? Are you a member of the Council?' asked Justen.

'I am certain that Counselor Ryltar will be here shortly to ... reinforce that concern.'

'I'm sure he will be,' Justen admitted. 'I'm sure he will be. But there are a few problems with your statement.' He smiled faintly and waited, trying to keep his expression calm even while his heart had a disturbing tendency to pound. *What have I started? And why is everyone so upset over something as simple as the land engine?*

'I fail to see any problems,' announced Yersol.

'First, you are not a member of the Council. Second, Counselor Ryltar is only one of three, and he is not the senior member.'

Yersol swallowed.

Justen glanced out past the breakwater. Was there a puff of smoke heralding the *Llyse*? He hoped so, and hoped that they could get the engine on board. Still ... would Hyntal agree, and how long would the *Llyse* have to stay in port?

'We'll see, Justen. We'll see. You won't pull this off.' Yersol turned and marched back down the pier.

'He'll be back with Ryltar before long,' Gunnar prophesied.

'Not for a while. If Ryltar were around, he'd have already been here.'

Justen walked toward Altara, conscious that his legs felt like lead weights.

'Do you think you can get away with this, especially without getting Hyntal and Martan in trouble?' asked the chief engineer, her voice low.

'I don't know. But it has to be done.'

'Has to? Are you deciding the fate of the world, Justen?' Altara's eyes blazed.

Justen returned Altara's intent expression. Then he smiled faintly. 'Me? A junior and very order-mad engineer? How could I possibly do anything that would change the world?'

'You? You've made a frigging good start. The Brotherhood is about ready to close the gates and wall Nylan off from the rest of Recluce for the first time in three centuries. The only question is whether they turn the cannon and rockets of the Mighty Ten on all the smugglers first.' Altara lowered her voice. 'The only thing that hasn't come out is Ryltar's name, maybe because Yersol –' her hand gestured toward the end of the pier after the departing trader '– started talking really quickly about the problems of smugglers and Ryltar's efforts to keep them in line – and offering to pay for all the damage to the engineering hall.'

'None of that changes anything,' Justen responded quietly.

'And what about this? And what are you going to do with the *Llyse*? I can't believe you're just going to dump this in the Gulf or the Eastern Ocean.'

'Why not?'

'Justen.'

'I'm going to do what has to be done.' Justen's gray eyes – abruptly as black and as deep as the great forest – turned full on Altara.

The chief engineer stepped back involuntarily. 'You *are* dangerous. Ryltar was right about that.'

'All change is dangerous,' Justen affirmed.

Wheeee . . . The steam whistle on the *Llyse* announced the ship's entrance into the channel and called for dockers.

'Just about everyone around Dorrin died or suffered, Justen. Remember that. And Creslin was blind for most of his life. Are you up to that kind of sacrifice?'

'We'll have to see, won't we?' Justen swallowed. **Can I . . . ask . . . this . . .?**

The thin but clear response seemed to follow: **Can you not, dearest?**

He shook his head. *Am I imagining the answer? Or am I answering myself?*

'You're either great or truly order-mad, and I can't say which.' Altara offered a grim smile. 'Maybe it makes no difference. Do you mind if I stay?'

The marines drew up closer to the land engine as two dockers slowly walked from the port-master's office toward the end of the pier.

'No. I respect you, Altara, but I have to do what I feel must be done.'

'That is an interesting choice of words – "must be done."'

'Sometimes there aren't any really good choices.' Justen watched as the *Llyse* eased up to the pier.

The dockers avoided the land engine, and Justen could sens
the interest in it by the way the crew of the *Llyse* tended to paus
and glance toward it, or to stop opposite the craft for a momen

As the gangway dropped, Martan stepped up to Justen. '
might be better if I talked to Hyntal first, Ser.'

'You know him better than I do, Martan. Do what you can

'Thank you, Ser.'

Martan bounded up the gangway and seemed to fly up th
ladder to the bridge, where he touched the square-faced an
tanned captain on the shoulder. He pointed toward Justen an
gestured toward the land engine.

'Whatever he's saying,' observed Gunnar, 'he's certainl
enthusiastic.'

The interchange lasted longer than the time it took the cre
and dockers to finish securing the *Llyse*, but Martan nodde
toward the young engineer and the *Llyse*'s captain plodded dow
the gangway toward Justen, his face like stone.

Justen squared his shoulders.

'All right, young Justen,' began Hyntal. 'Martan's told m
you're trying to pull some stunt and that I'm supposed to agre
with it.'

'That's right.' Justen turned to the captain. 'I built this lan
engine, and I need to get it to Candar, preferably somewher
in Lydiar or Hydlen, near a great road. I intend to drive it t
Fairhaven and challenge the White Wizards.'

'I thought it might be something that daft.' Hyntal pulled a
his chin, his hand almost covering his mouth. 'My crew's du
land leave.'

Justen tried to avoid taking a deep breath.

'I see as how that causes you some concern. What am
supposed to do?'

'You have to do what you believe is right, Ser,' answered Juste
slowly. 'Just as I have to.'

'So . . .' mused the captain. 'You're a-worried about tim
aren't ye?' He frowned and looked at Justen. 'Has the Counc
forbidden this?'

'No, Ser. Not—'

'They haven't forbidden it, you're sure?' asked Hyntal with
slight smile.

'No, Ser.'

Hyntal gestured toward the land engine and Altara. 'Why is the chief engineer here?'

'She's worried. Someone tried to burn down the engineering hall last night in an attempt to destroy the land engine.'

'They did?' Hyntal walked across the stones toward Altara. 'Chief Engineer?'

'Yes, Captain.'

'It be true that someone tried to fire the engineering hall last night?'

'They did more than try. There is a great deal of damage.'

'Just to destroy this young fellow's device?'

'It would seem so.' Altara's voice was level.

'Has the Council made any statements on this device?'

'We are not aware of any.'

Hyntal nodded, then turned toward the *Llyse*. 'Belden! Run out the heavy crane. Get the colliers moving, and lay on the produce. We're pulling out at noon. Double leave on the return.'

'Aye, Captain.'

'If you will excuse me, Captain,' began Altara, winking at Justen before Hyntal turned back toward her, 'I need to return to convey the concerns of the Brotherhood to the Council, and to ask for immediate investigation of the fire. That may take some time. I leave Justen and his engine in your hands.'

'He'll be safe on board the *Llyse*. Aye, he will.' Hyntal nodded to the chief engineer, then turned to Justen. 'Get that toy ready for loading, young fellow. About time someone did something to those White devils. About time . . .'

Gunnar raised his eyebrows behind the captain's back. Justen shrugged at his brother. While he did not understand fully Hyntal's willingness to help him, especially given the trouble it would surely cause, he was not about to raise greater obstacles to his plan – even if the failure to be totally honest with Hyntal was giving him a splitting headache.

'Let's get all the loose gear out of the seats –' began Justen.

From behind him, Martan's voice called, 'Get your kits stowed as soon as Devor's squad is clear. Derra and Tynda – take the gangway.'

Justen trudged up the gangway with his pack and Gunnar's. Behind him, Gunnar carried a crate of loose spares that Justen had found no place to store.

By the time Justen had returned and readied the land engine for lifting, with the coal-bin covers in place, the crane was swinging out over the pier.

'How heavy is that thing?' asked the muscled officer running the crane.

'Right now, say a shade more than two hundred stone.'

'Wait a moment. I'll need to gear down and use the heavy links.'

The crane returned, more slowly, bearing huge iron links.

Would two of the big clamps fit within each lifting ring, wondered Justen as the operator lowered the harness that spread the links across a square iron frame.

Although the clamps made a snug fit, Justen and a crewman managed to bolt them in place.

'What is this thing?' asked the woman as she gave a last twist to the clamp nut.

'A steam land engine.'

'Wish I could see it in use.'

'If everything goes right, you will,' promised Justen, stepping away and holding his breath as the crane began to rise and the lifting rings took the entire weight of the machine.

When the iron-tired wheels touched the deck, Justen let out a sigh of relief. The crane operator grinned. 'Not as bad as a gun barrel. Better balance. Builder also made those lift rings big enough, and that helps.'

Justen smiled. At least he'd done something right recently. Then he looked at the ropes and chains and the deck rings and sighed, realizing that there was still more to be done.

After chaining the land engine securely to the deck, Justen and Gunnar followed one of the crew to the rear of the *Llyse*, where there was a small compartment with two short bunks and barely enough space to turn around in.

'Guest quarters,' announced the woman with a smile.

Gunnar cocked his head. Justen threw his pack on the lower bunk.

'I wanted that one,' said Gunnar.

'Fine.' Justen picked up his pack and lifted it onto the top one.

'The canvas should be ready for you now,' announced the woman.

'Canvas?' asked Justen.

'You don't want saltwater running all over your engine, do you?'

'No,' admitted Justen. He turned and followed her back to the deck, where three heavy, oil-canvas tarps lay beside the land engine.

After they finished with the tarps, and after the last of the coal and the last large basket of produce was being hoisted on board, a wispy-haired man marched down the pier toward the *Llyse*. Yersol followed behind Ryltar.

'Shit . . .' muttered Justen. He had just lashed the water-proofed canvases in place over the land engine, effectively disguising it from pier-side identification. 'Here comes Ryltar.' He yawned.

'Young fellow,' suggested Hyntal from behind the young engineer, 'best you go below. The less Ryltar sees, the less trouble he can make.'

Justen glanced at Gunnar, then eased behind the land engine and toward the ladder to the engine room. He stopped where he could watch without being seen.

'Best you come with me, Air Wizard,' ordered Hyntal.

Gunnar followed the captain across the deck and down the gangway to the pier.

'Counselor Ryltar,' said Hyntal, greeting the wispy-haired man at the end of the gangway. 'What brings you here?'

Ryltar glanced from Hyntal to Yersol and back, then at the squad of marines lined up along the railing of the *Llyse*. He cleared his throat. 'Ah . . . there seems to have been a fire at the engineering hall last night.'

'So I heard.' Hyntal nodded.

'Reports are that the engineers had built some . . . device. Some claim that this device embodies chaos magic.'

'We're safe from that here.' Hyntal gestured to the black ironplate of the *Llyse*. 'White magic wouldn't last an instant on my ship. No, Ser.'

Ryltar took another deep breath.

'It also seems that a young engineer – one Justen by name – may have been involved. The Council is concerned that he should not leave Recluce,' added Yersol smoothly.

Hyntal scratched his head. 'I have not seen any announce-ments from the Council, but seeing as the punishment for bringing chaos to us is banishment —' the captain grinned cheerfully '— should I see the young wretch, and should the Council let me know what to do officially, I'd be more than happy to put him ashore in terrible, chaotic Candar.'

'Ah . . .' Ryltar blotted his face with a large white handkerchief '. . . I think the Council would be displeased if such an "informal" exile occurred.'

'I believe the Council has repudiated exile, has it not?' asked Gunnar politely.

'Where is your brother, Mage?' snapped Yersol.

'I could not say precisely.' Gunnar shrugged. 'But I would be most interested in knowing what your position is with the Council, Yersol. Do you speak for it?'

Yersol flushed.

'I must apologize for my cousin's enthusiasm, Captain,' offered Ryltar, ignoring Gunnar, 'but it is a matter of importance that we find this device and the engineer Justen.'

'I don't believe I've seen anything from the Council on this, Counselor.' Hyntal looked blandly at Ryltar. 'If I do, of course I certainly will do everything within my poor powers.'

'Hyntal . . . I'll have your ship and you.'

'Counselor . . . I have always been most obedient to the will of the Council.' Hyntal inclined his head. 'And I will obey any orders issued by the full Council.'

Ryltar looked from Hyntal to Gunnar and to the *Llyse*, where the short crane was being dismantled and stowed and where faint smoke puffed from the funnel. 'Hyntal, I will have you and your ship, by darkness.'

The counselor turned and marched back down the pier.

'The madder he gets, the better I like it.' The captain scratched his head as he watched Ryltar almost run down the pier toward Nylan. 'Still, best we get underway before he beats Claris into signing something.'

'We're really going, Ser?' asked the heavily muscled Belden.

'Yes.' Hyntal nodded. 'I don't know what these young fellows are doing, and I don't know why. But anything that that stink-cat Ryltar is so worried about can't be all that bad.' He grinned. 'Besides, the last time that young scamp Justen went off to Candar, he and this fuzzy Air Wizard brother of his did more damage to the Whites than anyone else had done in a couple hundred years. None of my family's done much since my great-great-grandsire, and there's a chance to change that.' He gestured to the inshore bollard. 'Single up!'

Justen grinned briefly in his hiding place on the ladder leading to the engine room. Perhaps it was just as well that Hyntal had never forgotten his great-great-grandsire.

142

'What have you found?' asked Beltar.

'You've been drinking too much wine,' answered Eldiren.

'I'll thank you not to comment on my personal habits.'

'Of course, mightiest of mighty High Wizards.' Eldiren looked out from the top of the White tower to the south, toward the low hills that sheltered the great highway.

'Why I don't dispose of you . . .'

'Because you know you can, and because you need my honesty. No one else will dare to cross you. So you can't trust their judgment.'

Beltar coughed and cleared his throat. 'Someday . . .'

'But not now.'

'So exactly what did you discover, O Honest One?'

'The Gray Wizard is on one of their mighty black warships crossing the gulf. He has something on it that seems filled with order.'

'Where are they going?'

'Right now, I don't know exactly, but they'll probably land somewhere in eastern Candar – Renklaar, Lydiar, Perdya, maybe Tyrhavven. And I think the Gray Wizard just might be headed here.'

'Here? Fairhaven?'

'I'm only guessing, but if you wait until I know, or you know, it will be too late. One of the really ordered black buildings in Nylan was partly burned, and that ship carries a lot more

order than it should.' Eldiren's eyes dropped to the old center
of Fairhaven less than a kay away.

'Why does that mean he's coming here?' growled Beltar.

'I don't *know*, but this is the one who spent all that time in
Naclos. This is the one who blew all the screeing glasses. He's
on a Recluce warship with something that feels like an order
weapon. Isn't he the one who built all those demon-damned
black iron arrows? He's not exactly our friend, and he's no
running from us. So where else would he go?' Eldiren turned
from the vista to face the High Wizard.

'You're the diviner. You tell me. Don't ask me questions,'
snapped Beltar.

'Fine. He's coming here, and he has some plan to attack
Fairhaven. What are you going to do?'

'I told you not to ask me questions. Besides, what could one
ship do – even if by a miracle he transported the whole ship to
Fairhaven?'

'I don't think you'd want that. I suggest you convene the
Council.'

'Couldn't I just ignore these Blacks ... or Grays ... or
whatever they are? At least until I know what's going to
happen.'

'You've got one problem with that, Beltar. By the time you
know what is going to happen, it will be too late to call the
Council.' Eldiren waited.

'Are you sure?'

'Nothing is ever certain.'

'Thank you.' Beltar sneered.

'My pleasure.'

'Then perhaps we had better call in some of the powerful, even
Histen, but not all of them.'

'If you call for the Council, who will you leave out?'

Beltar shrugged. 'Fine. Call them all. But bring in the closest
Iron Guards – and that fellow from Recluce. Maybe he knows
some way to stop them.'

'As you wish. But do you want them in the city?'

'I'm not that dense. How about ... oh, find some place, like
the old southern barracks. You know what's necessary.'

Eldiren nodded.

'And you'd better be right, Eldiren, or I'll make you Derba's assistant. He'd fry you before breakfast.'

'Even you aren't that obtuse.'

'Try me.' Beltar turned away.

Eldiren took a long, slow breath.

143

'Before we call in Magister Turmin,' said Jenna, 'I would like to know why we are having this meeting. We were not scheduled to meet for more than another eight-day. And why was I required to ride almost two days to come to Nylan?' She glanced around the dimly lit room in the Brotherhood building.

'Based on what Ryltar has discovered, I fear we may be facing a great crisis,' Claris asserted.

'A crisis? From one engineer?' Jenna snorted.

'The engineering hall was torched. Thankfully, the damage was restricted.'

'Oh. This engineer torched his own guild's hall?'

'No. But someone was so worried about this device he has built that they tried to destroy it,' answered Claris.

'What is this device?' Jenna frowned.

'We know that it travels the roads under its own power.' Ryltar's face darkened. 'We also know that this Justen somehow enchanted Hyntal to take him and the device to some destination in Candar. We were hoping that Magister Turmin could tell us more.'

'You mean that Captain Hyntal refused to believe that you represented the full Council? I'm so, so sorry for you, Ryltar.'

'I think that once this crisis is resolved,' Ryltar added, 'we should also investigate the engineers.'

'They're thinking about investigating the Council,' responded Jenna.

'That can come later,' temporized Claris. 'Magister Turmin is waiting.'

'Fine. Call him in. Let's get this over with.' Jenna settled herself behind the round table.

Claris motioned to the black-clad marine by the door.

Turmin walked slowly into the room.

'Please be seated, Magister Turmin.'

'Thank you.' Turmin sat down and waited.

'Can you tell us why Justen and Gunnar boarded the *Llyse* and where they might be bound?'

'I was not aware until yesterday that something like that had occurred.'

'How did you find out?'

'Gunnar was supposed to meet me yesterday, but he did not appear. So I asked Chief Engineer Altara if she knew where he might be. She told me she had seen him board the *Llyse* before it left.'

'Magister Turmin, can you tell us where the *Llyse* is?' pursued Claris.

'I would presume that it is somewhere in the Gulf of Candar or on the Eastern Ocean. I'm not a part of the marines or the Brotherhood.' Turmin smiled faintly.

'We understand that the *Llyse* ported at Nylan briefly three days ago and that some sort of wagon built by Justen was hoisted on board. Do you have any thoughts about what that might be?' asked Claris.

Beside her, Ryltar masked a scowl.

Turmin frowned, finally asking, 'Do you have any idea—'

'We thought you might know,' Claris said firmly. 'At least since both Gunnar and Justen went aboard with whatever it was. And a marine by the name of Martan went with them.'

'I do not know exactly what Justen built, but earlier Gunnar had said that Justen was working on some sort of land wagon that used steam to propel it.'

'Is that possible? I thought steam engines required the order of water, like the ocean or very large lakes,' commented Jenna.

'For anyone but Justen, it would be impossible,' conceded Turmin. 'He could hold something like that together.'

Jenna and Claris exchanged glances before the older counselor spoke. 'What else is on the *Llyse*?'

'I don't know.'

'What else *might* be on the *Llyse*?' inquired Jenna.

Turmin took a deep breath. 'I don't know, but I suspect Justen has a device that he *believes* will destroy the power of Fairhaven.'

'Will it?'

Turmin shrugged. 'I hope not.'

'You hope it will *not* destroy the power of Fairhaven?'

'You see, counselors, matters are not simple.' The old mage wiped his forehead. 'In fact, they are very complicated. The Balance works. We know this. It means that if Justen's device destroys the power of Fairhaven, one of two things *must* happen. Either all those powers will find a single chaos focus . . .' Turmin shuddered '. . . and we all know what that means.'

The two women looked at each other again. Ryltar scowled.

'Or,' continued Turmin, 'he means to cancel their powers by simultaneously reducing both order and chaos. How he would do that, I do not know, but I suspect that is his goal.'

'But why is that a problem?'

'Because Recluce has built up a vast reservoir of order. If Justen drains it, I doubt that any of the Mighty Ten will retain their engines.'

'And you did not think of telling anyone?'

'I still do not see how it can be done.' Turmin shrugged. 'If I attempted to warn the Council of everything that *might* be possible or might happen—'

'That is your duty, is it not?' asked Ryltar.

'Counselor Ryltar, the world will end. When or how, I do not know. But it will end. Consider yourself informed.' Turmin stood. 'By your leave, Claris?'

The oldest counselor nodded. Ryltar flushed.

Jenna pursed her lips. 'We need to get all the Mighty Ten into port . . . if we can.'

144

'So the honorable Beltar has requested that all members of the
Council gather in Fairhaven to meet the challenge from Recluce?'
Histen snorted.

'Surely you are not going to refuse?' Renwek's hands fluttered.
'Beltar would not be pleased. He is rather powerful, you
know.'

The older White Wizard glanced from the antique battlement
to the harbor below. 'Yes, he is rather powerful, and it would
not be wise to refuse. But I have been ill, and it may take me
a bit longer to prepare, and my travels are most likely to be far
slower than normal.'

'You look hale and healthy to me, Histen, better than when
you left the amulet to young Beltar.'

'I have been ailing, Renwek, and while I will certainly heed
the High Wizard's call, my progress will doubtless be slow.
If you could see your way to assisting an ailing old wizard,
I would appreciate it. In either case, please convey, via the
wagon post, that we hear and obey as quickly as our ancient
bones will permit.' Histen looked down on the town of Lydiar
and the harbor, letting the sun warm him.

'Ah, yes. I do see that you may indeed need assistance,'
stammered Renwek.

Histen smiled in the sunlight.

145

Justen studied the river, wondering if Hyntal were not crazier than either he or Gunnar. But the old captain had been adamant. 'Lydiar's got a strong bunch of wizards – watch the Great Bay and everything that comes in. No one cares much about the Ohyde River, and Renklaar's a third-rate port. I'll bet we could get almost all the way to Hydolar and dump you on the old lower docks.'

'How do you know about the docks?' Justen had asked.

The old captain had just grinned. So had Martan. Justen wondered what else the captains of the Mighty Ten had been doing that neither he nor the Council knew of.

The engineer had done what he could. The waterproof canvases were off the land engine. The coal bins were topped off, and the reservoir was full. The firebox was ready to light. Only the chains were in place.

Of course, how they would ever leave Candar was another question. All Justen had told Gunnar and Martan was that he had enough golds for either a commercial or a smuggler's passage to return to Recluce. That was true enough, and it was also true enough that if his efforts worked, commercial passage would be on a sailing ship.

'Oh, how well we can learn to deceive with truth . . .' Justen glanced to the southern bank of the Ohyde River, where a small fishing boat angled toward the massive warship. He continued to watch, but the fishing boat did not change course and finally passed abreast of the *Llyse* less than a hundred cubits away. The fisherman waved, and Martan waved back from the side of the bridge.

Did the Council know that the Mighty Ten – or at least the *Llyse* – were traveling the larger rivers of Candar? Justen grinned. After his experience in Naclos, he was beginning not

516 L. E. MODESITT, JR.

to be too surprised at the unexpected.

'Oh, Dayala . . .' he half-murmured, half-thought.

You have . . . learned much. Be careful. . .

In planning to upset half the known world, I'm supposed to be careful? Justen's grin faded as he caught the serious expression on his brother's face.

'The lower piers are around the next bend,' Gunnar announced.

'It might be time for shields,' suggested Justen.

Pendak wiped the sweat off his forehead. 'There aren't any Whites near the pier. If I create shields, any White around will sense it and Hyntal will have the demon's time navigating.'

'You've had more experience at this than we have,' Justen conceded.

Pendak, Hyntal, and Martan nodded.

Gunnar paused, his perceptions far to the north, ensuring, Justen hoped, that no rain would come their way, at least not until the steam car was on the metaled road to Fairhaven.

'Damned fool idea,' grunted Hyntal.

Justen tried not to grin at the glint in the captain's eyes. Hyntal liked the idea of bringing the *Llyse* practically into the capital city of Hydlen.

'What are you calling that contraption?' asked Martan, pointing to the land engine on the deck below.

'Hadn't thought of a name.'

'Why not?'

'I've never named anything.'

'The "land engine" sounds like an unnamed ship.'

Gunnar's eyes flicked back and forth between the two.

'What would you suggest?' asked Justen.

'Call it the *Black Demon*. Aren't all the other demons White?'

'*Black Demon* . . . I like that.' Gunnar chuckled. .

So did Hyntal, who added, 'Then I can tell his mightiness, Counselor Ryltar, that the *Black Demon* was sent after the White ones.'

Justen watched as the *Llyse* headed toward a brownish point on the northern side of the river, just before what appeared to be a wide bend.

'Belden! Get the crane ready. Young fellow, you'd better have that thing ready to roll. Won't be long now. Those are the lower piers.'

Martan grinned. 'My people are ready.'

On the deck before the turret, the two squads of black-suited marines had formed.

Justen scrambled off the bridge and onto the deck below, where he touched his striker to the shavings and wood chips. While the wood and the first few chunks of coal caught, he began to loosen all the ties but two.

Martan began to stack the bundles of black iron arrows and the three cases of rockets on the small pallet next to the land engine.

'You don't have to go, Martan.'

'Wouldn't miss it for anything.'

'I would,' admitted Justen.

Martan looked at Justen slowly. 'You're not only brave, but crazy. I'm just crazy. Like all marines.' He returned to stacking the bundled arrows before straightening up and calling, 'Raid drill! Stations!'

The marines formed two rows on the shoreward side of the *Llyse*, the first row standing ready with bows. Behind them to the rear of the ship, two sets of iron shutters dropped open, revealing the rockets.

'Steerage way!' came the call from the bridge.

After that, Gunnar joined Justen beside the land engine, and the creak of the crane and the rattle of chains drowned out the captain's commands.

Justen watched as nearly a score of fishermen and others bolted from the pier that the *Llyse* approached. At least two of the fleeing figures wore the red-slashed uniforms of Hydlen guards. With that thought, Justen slipped back to the firebox and added more coal. They would need to have the land engine – the *Black Demon* – ready to roll when it touched the pier.

'What if he tilts it too much?' asked Gunnar.

'If he does, he'll break it and we won't be going anywhere.' Justen stepped forward as Belden lowered the harness.

He steadied himself as the *Llyse* lurched slightly.

Creeeakk . . . The heavy wooden pier squeaked as it resisted the weight of the warship.

Justen slipped the first clamp in place, then the second. Martan steered the third to him, but it took both of them to force the fourth in place. While they worked on attaching

the harness, two marines had helped Gunnar release the deck
chains.

Belden motioned Justen off the land engine, but the engineer
shook his head. Belden shrugged, and Justen hung on as the
crane lifted the *Demon* and him clear of the ship and swung
both of them onto the timbers of the pier.

Justen managed to release the forward clamps before Gunnar
had scrambled down to join him, and the two managed the
second set. Then Justen checked the brake and the steam lines,
and finally, the firebox, where he pushed the coal back into the
center and added another shovelful.

By the time Justen had finished his inspection, Gunnar
had stowed the loose gear. Then Martan and Gunnar began
unloading the small pallet of arrows and rockets.

Justen loosened the last clamp on the pallet and waved to
Belden. The officer and crane operator waved back, and the
heavy harness lifted. Justen ran to the edge of the pier.

'Captain!'

'Yes, Ser Wizard?' called Hyntal.

'Get back to Nylan as fast as you can and shut down . . . until
you find out how we fare.'

Hyntal nodded slowly. 'I'll keep it in mind.'

'Do it!' snapped Justen.

Hyntal tensed for a moment, then relaxed fractionally. He
waved stiffly.

Justen returned the wave and dashed back to the newly named
Black Demon, where Martan had already begun to rack the
rockets and arrows in easy reach. A froth of water spewed
across the edge of the pier as the *Llyse* backed around and
headed downriver – far faster than she had cruised upriver.

'He's moving fast,' commented Gunnar.

'Justen scared him. Scared me,' grunted Martan.

'He's scared me since about the time he was born,' said
Gunnar.

'I love you, too, Gunnar.' Justen checked the steam pressure,
then looked around. 'Everyone ready?'

'Hold a moment,' said Martan.

'There are three guards heading down from the higher road,'
added Gunnar.

'Didn't take them long,' said Martan.

'You haven't landed before, I imagine,' suggested Justen.

'That's true.'

The engineer released the brake and opened the throttle, letting the *Demon* ease forward across the slippery timbers to the packed clay of the road. 'Which way?'

'To the right. That goes to the old road around Hydolar,' said Gunnar.

'What about the guards?'

'There are guards on both ends of this stretch of road. Fewer on the right.'

'How many?'

'Just the three.'

Justen eased back the throttle when they reached the narrow spot in the road as it turned left and back up the hill to the old road. In the middle of the road stood the three guards as the *Demon* chugged up toward them. On the right side of the road was a deep ditch, on the left a decrepit stone wall.

'Devils!'

'Blacks . . .'

One guard, a thin man with a bushy mustache, hacked at the car, and his saber bounced from his hand. The second and heavier man jumped aside and watched without moving farther. The woman whipped an arrow from her quiver, but Martan was faster.

Both arrows missed, although Justen thought he felt the Hydlen guard's pass overhead. He eased up the pressure as the *Demon* bounced around a corner and past a hay wagon. The horse reared, and Justen glanced back momentarily to see the wagon flip sideways into the ditch.

'Watch the road!' Gunnar shoved the tiller, and Justen barely kept the land engine from landing in the same ditch.

Martan swallowed loudly. 'Shit . . .'

Justen overcorrected again, and the *Demon* almost piled into the low stone wall before he got it centered on the road. Below the wall ran a narrow creek that seemed almost dry.

'Justen . . . please, please concentrate on the road,' begged Gunnar.

Martan wiped his forehead.

The *Demon* chugged southward for a time as the road wound around the hills following the nearly dry creek bed. On the uphill side of the road were meadows and an occasional flock of sheep, and intermittent woodlots and scattered hovels. On the road behind them rose a plume of dry dust.

'Another cart ahead,' warned Gunnar.

'Can you put another shovel of coal in the firebox, Martan?' asked Justen.

'Yes, Ser. Just don't hit anything while the door's open.'

Justen concentrated on keeping the *Demon* headed straight and out of the deeper ruts until he heard the *clunk* of the firebox door.

'Done, Ser.'

'Thank you.'

Justen tried to steer the *Demon* as far to the left as he could to get around the cart and the swaybacked gray that pulled it. He resolutely kept his eyes on the road ahead. 'Tell me what that horse did.'

'He skittered sideways. That's all,' reported Martan.

In the third seat, behind the brothers, Martan checked the bows and the rows of iron-tipped shafts. Behind them were the rockets – the small ones, and only a score at that – with the two portable launchers, one mounted on the back of the coal bin, the other on a bracket between where Justen and Gunnar sat.

'Another shovel of coal?' asked Justen.

'Coming up.'

As the *Demon* rolled out of a wide curve and a straight stretch of hard-packed clay appeared ahead, Justen checked the engine once more, then opened the throttle. The land engine began to accelerate, the iron tires digging into the hard clay and the spring seats swaying more than ever. 'How far before we reach the main road to Fairhaven?'

'Even at the speed you're making, it should be mid-afternoon.' Gunnar pursed his lips. After a period where the only sounds were those of the land engine, the Weather Wizard spoke again. 'Could you explain in simple terms what you want to get done? I mean, just what is the point of all of this?'

'I told you. To balance order and chaos in Fairhaven.'

'How?' pursued Gunnar.

'I'm trying to force the White Wizards to band together, and then I'll try to hit them and Fairhaven with pure order.'

'That's what the balloon is for?'

Justen slowed the *Demon* as the road curved to the left and started downhill past a field of browning grain. Two men watched the land engine pass, their mouths full open.

'Surprised them!' laughed Martan.

'You keep on surprising people and every White Wizard in Candar will be after you.'

'They probably are already.' Justen let his senses run over the land engine, but so far, the engine continued to run smoothly, and even the drive shaft was not too hot.

'There are more troops ahead, at least a score of them,' warned Gunnar. 'They seem to know that you want to get on the Fairhaven road. They're waiting at the junction.'

'Is there any way around?'

'There's a farm road, but it doesn't go all the way, and it's got deep ruts.'

'Great. We need to put up the rest of the armor.' After throttling the *Demon* down to a stop and locking the brakes, Justen lifted the thin plate shutters into place, filling the grooves between the roof and the body of the car. He left only a space in front of his steering position, laying that plate sideways. Then he donned a thin iron cap with a flared nose guard, as did Martan.

'These slits are small,' complained Martan.

'Which ones?'

'You get used to the helmets. I meant the ones for the arrows. Too bad we couldn't have brought more rockets.'

'We're probably overloaded as it is.'

'It's already getting hot,' added Gunnar.

'So . . . bring in a little breeze. Given the mess we've already made, a little more weather work won't hurt.'

'That's easy for you to say.'

Justen began to throttle the *Demon* back up to speed. The land engine came around the last wide curve before the road pointed like an arrow toward the stone-paved highway north to Fairhaven. Justen could see the horse troopers ahead: a mounted squad comprised of two-score troops and one White Wizard, all under the crimson banner of Hydlen.

Justen throttled back, and his eyes flicked to the coal bin, calculating how much coal had been used. Perhaps they should take on some wood as well.

'Halt,' demanded the lead rider.

Justen slowed the steam car but did not stop. 'We are on our way to Fairhaven. Are not the roads open to all?'

'Not to those of the Black isle. Only to those who accept the beneficence of Fairhaven.'

'Stop . . .' whispered Gunnar.

'No. The car doesn't move well from a complete stop. We can outrun them.'

'The White Wizard's marshaling chaos!'

Justen sensed the accuracy of Gunnar's words, and he opened the throttle. The *Black Demon* roared forward.

The horsemen charged.

'Idiots!' snapped Martan. The marine lifted his bow.

Hsssttt! Fire washed over and around the oak ribs covered with the parchment-thin black iron plate.

'Go ahead.'

Martan released the first arrow, and one horse plunged into another.

'Damn! Worse than from a ship's deck.' Still, arrow after arrow poured from the armored slit before the raised third seat.

Justen centered the rocket launcher on the sense of chaos, tuning his own senses to the White Wizard, then pulled the striker trigger.

Psssst . . .

'Aeeiii . . .'

'Demons! Cursed . . .'

Flames and chaos flared across the rear of the Hydlen troops as Justen throttled the *Demon* to a higher speed and the black land engine rumbled forward and scattered the lancers.

Clunk . . .

Fire flared in front of Justen, and his eyes watered. The road blurred. 'Gunnar!'

'What?'

'Steer. Can't see . . .' Justen gasped, trying to squint to see the road in the sudden darkness.

'I've got it.'

Justen felt his brother's hands on the tiller and released his grip, trying to ease himself out of the driver's seat.

Even as he moved, he could hear a regular sound; *thump*

. . . *thump* . . . *thump* . . . He could feel Gunnar slowing the *Demon*.

'Don't slow down yet . . .' he mumbled. 'Get away from them.'

'I can't control this thing as well as you can, but we're not stopping, not until they're out of sight.'

'Good.'

'One idiot's still following,' said Martan.

Justen could sense the arrow being released, and then his fingers fumbled with the shaft that seemed to be stuck in the thin plate of his helmet.

'Missed!'

Another arrow followed the first.

'Shit! Got the horse, not bad, but he's reining up.'

The regular *thumping* continued, accompanied by a squeaking sound.

'What's that?' asked Gunnar.

'I don't know. I can't see. Can't get this demon arrow out, and I can't get the helmet off.'

'Hold still!' snapped Martan, leaning forward from the third seat.

Justen stopped moving.

'Uhhh . . . got it. Let's see that.'

Justen could feel the helmet coming off.

'Your helmet stopped most of it, but you're bleeding like a stuck hog. Head wounds do that. There's lots of blood in your eyes.'

As he fumbled out a cloth and blotted his face, Justen wanted to rub his aching forehead. 'Why does a cut hurt so much?'

'It's not just a cut. Part of it goes almost to the bone. That archer put a lot behind that. It's really more like a crossbow quarrel. It bent your helmet. You're going to have one big bruise.'

The *thumping* continued, and the squeaking increased.

Justen forced himself to concentrate on offering himself a touch of healing and re-ordering; some of the pain diminished and he began to see, although the images were somewhat blurred.

'What do you intend to do next time?' asked Gunnar. 'That was only a small group.'

'Next time, I think we let go with rockets sooner.'

'Good idea!' affirmed Martan.

'Now that you can see, can you tell me what the noise is?'

Justen shrugged gingerly and let his senses slide across the craft. The engine was sound, as was the drive shaft, but the noise came from the left front wheel, and the wheel wobbled as it turned.

'I can steer now. I need you to check to see if any of those troops are following.' Justen took the tiller.

Gunnar was silent for a time before answering. 'No. You killed the White Wizard, and they're just milling around.'

'Good. We need to replace the front wheel.'

'Already?'

'It was a freak thing.' Justen sighed. 'I think one of the crossbow bolts went through the bearing housing.'

'Bearing housing?'

'Never mind. We've got two spare wheels.' Justen throttled down the *Demon*. 'We need to unload them and the repair kit first.'

While the other two watched, the engineer unlashed the spare wheel, which Martan carried to the side of the stone-paved road. Then Justen turned to the storage lockers.

'How do you plan to replace this?' asked Gunnar. 'At least a quarter of the weight rests on that wheel.'

Justen rummaged in one of the lockers and pulled out a trapezoidal wedge and a square block. 'It would be a lot harder if the wheel had broken. But it hasn't.'

Martan nodded.

'When the wheel is on the flat part here, get me to stop. I'll set the brake and we'll block the other wheels.' Justen held up another heavy block of oak with a half-circle bored on one end. 'Then this goes under the axle, and we knock the other block out.'

'It looks like it will work,' admitted Gunnar.

With Martan in front of the *Demon* and Gunnar beside the block, Justen edged the craft toward the long wedge.

'Easy . . . easy. It's sliding.'

'Sliding?'

'The wheel just pushes it forward instead of riding up on it.'

'Shit . . .' mumbled Justen. 'It couldn't be that easy, of course. Let me back up and get it moving a little faster.'

The first time, Justen rolled up one side and down the other. The second time, he stopped on top but failed to set the brake quickly enough. The third time, the wedge spun because he hit it at angle. The fourth time, it worked.

'Now what?'

'This goes under the axle.'

'How?'

'Like this.' Justen inserted the half-circle under the axle shaft and took the heavy hammer, tapping it steadily until the weight of the axle rested on the block instead of on the trapezoid. He eased the trapezoid aside with gentle taps. Then he used the hammer and the wrench to loosen the lugs, and at last he slipped the wheel off.

He studied the bearings and nodded. 'See? Something smashed through here. I think that if I had to, I could fix this and make it work for a while.' He set the old wheel aside and picked up the replacement. With quick hammer strokes, he nudged it into place, then tightened the lugs.

'How are you going to get it off that axle block?' asked Martan.

Ducking under the land engine, Justen began tapping at the block, emerging with it in his hand shortly. 'It's angled . . . here.'

As Justen replaced the equipment in the locker and lashed the damaged wheel in place, Gunnar and Martan looked at each other.

Finally, Gunnar shrugged, 'Altara said he was weak on design.'

'That looked like it worked all right.'

Justen closed the locker and glanced at Martan. 'Can you add some coal to the firebox?'

'Yes, Ser.'

'Do you plan on stopping anywhere?' asked Gunnar.

'You hungry? The first package in the hamper there is lunch. You eat while I drive and then I'll eat. Martan can take his time.'

'Don't we have to sleep?'

'Yes . . . but not until we can find someplace a bit more distant

from people with crossbows and other assorted weapons.'
Justen grinned. 'Besides, we've hardly started.' He slipped into
the driver's seat, released the brake and opened the throttle.
'We're off.'

Gunnar groaned – loudly.

146

Beltar struggled with the mirror, trying to get the images to
focus. Even the breeze sweeping in from the tower window failed
to remove the heat from the room.

For an instant, the whitened dust of the metaled road appeared
before the white mist swirled back into place. The High Wizard
frowned and tried again.

This time the vision held, for a moment, of a black, wagonlike
object without horses, trailing smoke, that rolled along the road
from Hydolar toward Fairhaven. Even through the mirror, Beltar
could sense the amount of order forced into the horseless wagon.
He sighed and released the image, wiping his forehead.

'You see?' asked Jehan. 'It's like a miniature warship, and
nothing seems to stop it. Gorsuch brought two squads against
it.'

'And?'

'There are three, I think, in it. They have those fire rockets and
black iron arrows. Most of the troopers died. So did Gorsuch.'

'Why didn't they just pile stones on the road?'

'Stones are heavy, Beltar, and I doubt they had time. Besides,
do you want to be the High Wizard who blocked the roads? Also,
they haven't attacked anybody who hasn't attacked them first.'

'They don't look exactly peaceful.'

Jehan shrugged and waited.

'So why are they traveling toward Fairhaven?'

'I don't know, but you can tell how much order that machine
carries. It can't bode well for us.'

'So let them come. Let them bring their little land ship.'

'What will the world think if three wizards from Recluce take over the wizards' roads and deposit a huge chunk of order in Fairhaven? And what will the Council think?'

'Oh? Are you claiming that with one action, they nullify all the effort we've put into trying to isolate Recluce?'

'Some would see it that way.'

'Like Derba?'

'He certainly would.'

'Wouldn't it be better to ignore them, perhaps even to welcome them? Follow Cerryl's example . . . almost say that it doesn't bother us?'

Jehan coughed. 'For anyone but you – the wizard who has always relied on his power—'

'All right, all right. You've made that point enough. Let's just send the entire White lancers against this thing. Three Blacks couldn't fight through thousands.'

'I doubt they could. That's certainly true. Of course, we have only a few hundred White lancers nearby, and much of the Iron Guard is still in Suthya.'

'And?' asked Beltar. 'Your tone indicates that I have overlooked something.'

'What happens if the most powerful White Wizard in generations refuses to deal with a direct assault by a mere three Black Wizards and sends troops instead of showing up himself?'

'You're telling me that if I don't act like a wizard, the Council will be . . . upset?'

'So might the troops, although I could not say that with absolute certainty.'

'I do thank you.'

'It is always my pleasure.'

'How soon will those we called arrive?'

'Histen has pleaded ill health, saying that he will make haste but that his health restricts him, and Renwek is caring for him. Most of the others are here, or will be here before that . . . device arrives.'

'Histen . . . I'll have to deal with him yet.' Beltar glanced toward the unopened bottle of wine on the table.

'That is precisely what he fears, I am sure.'

'What about Derba?'

'Derba? He will smile until he can wrench the amulet from you, preferably taking your neck with it.'

'You are so cheerful, Jehan.'

'You asked, High Wizard.'

'So I did.' Beltar shook his head, and his eyes flicked back to the bottle of red wine.

147

The *Black Demon* had passed three single horsemen, one of them a White lancer who tried unsuccessfully to chase the land engine; several wagons, one loaded with cabbage; and a peddler with a mule.

As the late afternoon sun touched the rolling hills to the west of the old but solid stone road, two wagons and a line of horses stretched ahead.

'Now what?' asked Gunnar.

'We steam past,' said Justen. 'With the armor in place, of course.'

'But the White Wizards . . .'

'They already know. Speed is more important than secrecy.'

'How about partial secrecy?' suggested Gunnar.

'Shields so we're not visible to them?'

'Scare the darkness out of them,' laughed Martan.

'Can you do it?' asked Justen. 'Shields, I mean?'

'I think so. Can you steer?'

'If I slow down, but I'd have to anyway.' Justen paused. 'What if we get close, fire a rocket, and then vanish?'

'It might work, but they might just bunch up,' suggested Martan.

'Shields. No rocket,' decided Justen. He eased back the throttle as the perceived darkness of the light-shield fell across the *Demon*.

The land engine crept forward, heavy wheels rumbling faintly on the stone slabs of the road, the faint hiss of steam sounding almost like a summer breeze, and the muffled thudding of the engine like a giant heart.

Clink . . . clink . . .

'Firdil, do you hear something? Like a wagon?' The horseman's voice seemed to be almost beside Justen, although Justen could sense that the land engine was still behind the rider.

'. . . something . . . hissing like a snake. It smells hot . . . like brimstone.'

Clink . . . The horse edged toward the *Demon*.

Whheee . . . eeeee. The horse skittered sideways, as if burned by the contact with the land engine.

'What's with you?' the rider asked, yanking on the horse's reins.

'Mine's skittish, too,' answered the rider still in front of the land engine as she turned in the saddle. 'Maybe a demon's around. It's hot here. Look – look over at the fields there. It's hard to see them clearly.'

'Maybe it's because the sun's setting.'

'I don't like it.'

Wheee . . . The second horse jumped aside.

'Something big is breathing . . . right there. Don't you hear the grinding on the stone?'

'A demon?' The rider eased his horse off the road.

'What are you two doing?' yelled a voice from the wagon seat.

'There's a demon here!'

Justen eased up the throttle, and the *Demon* slid past the riders and alongside the wagon.

'A what?'

Justen kept his lips clamped, trying not to laugh even while the sweat rolled down his face. The last incident had shown that neither he nor the land engine were invulnerable, and he didn't really want any more arrows flying his way. Or swords. Or whatever.

'Demon!'

'Darkness! I hear it!' The teamster flicked the reins. *Clink . . . clink.* The two horses began to trot.

Justen pushed the throttle up, then pulsed the whistle.

Eee . . . eeeee . . .

The horse on the left veered toward the unseen land engine, and Justen eased the tiller. The left wheel rumbled on the graveled shoulder of the road. As the teamster saw the dust, he guided the team away from the 'demon,' and Justen steered the land engine back so that all its wheels were on the road again.

The teamster pulled his wagon to a halt, trying to calm the jittery horses. Then the lead wagon pulled over, and Justen and the *Demon* slipped by into the twilight.

As the *Demon* swung around the curve and out of sight of the traders, Gunnar dropped the shields. Justen pushed the throttle even higher before he wiped his sweating forehead.

'Whew . . .' mumbled Martan. 'Scared them.'

'Scared me,' confessed Justen. 'These roads aren't wide enough.'

'No road's wide enough for you,' Gunnar commented as the land engine continued northward and as the darkness grew.

'How can you see?' asked the marine.

'The road's clear enough.' Justen adjusted the tiller. 'I'm hoping we run across an empty way station somewhere ahead.'

'The last one had all those peddlers. They swallowed when we went past.' Martan shook his head.

'The way stations are usually about ten kays apart.' Justen peered into the darkness.

'How you can see anything . . . is that wizards' sight?'

'It runs in our family,' answered Gunnar absently. 'There's something ahead, like a hut, and I think it's empty. Anyway, I can't sense anything there. There's a small stream out of the hills, too.'

'How far?'

'About two wide curves.'

Justen concentrated on guiding the *Demon* along the seemingly thin strip of white stone.

'It's on the right up there.' Gunnar cleared his throat. 'Slow down. This doesn't feel right.'

Hsstttt . . .

A flare of light sprayed off the front armor of the *Demon*.

'Demons' light! Frigging wizards!'

Justen blinked, trying keep power to the wheels while dropping speed.

'Where's the frigging bow?' snapped Martan.

With one hand on the tiller, Justen throttled the *Demon* down to a crawl and tried to sense where the White Wizard stood in the darkness. Then his right hand left the throttle and groped for the rocket striker. He had only the one rocket in the front launcher. How many wizards were there?

'Two . . .' whispered Gunnar. 'One's behind the hut.'

'Great,' mumbled Martan. 'Two Black mages, two White Wizards, and I can't even see the White bastards.'

Justen took a deep breath. 'All right,' he whispered to Gunnar. 'After the rocket goes off, you take the tiller and slow this down.'

'Me?'

'Just do it,' hissed the engineer. **Oh, Dayala . . . hope this works . . .** His fingers flicked the striker.

Whhhsttt . . . As the rocket flared in the general direction of the wizard beside the hut, Justen slipped from the driver's seat and into the darkness, staggering as his feet hit the ground. He darted from the black iron of the *Demon* and toward the wavering white lines of the wizards' chaos.

Could he replicate the Balance struggles of the great forest? Did he have much choice?

He drew on the earth, on the mixture of Black and White within, and cast both toward the White Wizards, feeding in the hungers that seemed to come from both.

A huge white mountain cat padded toward Justen, but he let it come, instead raising a black cat, feeding the black cat to match the white cat. The white cat became a fountain of molten rock spilling toward Justen, and the grass beside the stone pavement began to burn.

Justen called upon the cold within the north and the Roof of the World, and a fountain of chilled ice and rock appeared beside the lava, which immediately formed a black crust and began to shrink.

Then he called upon the deep waters, and a fountain of ice-cold water burst from the earth, cascading over the hut and the two wizards.

Steam fountained where the water struck, and Justen turned the water into ice, and then back to water.

Oooooo . . .

Like a long whimper, the area around the hut was empty.

Justen sat down suddenly beside the stone serving as a step into the way station, absently noting the small fire and the two packs that seemed to shrivel into dust.

Wwhheee . . . eeeee . . .

'Those are horses,' said Martan, standing beside Justen.

The engineer had not even heard the marine approach. 'They had some wards I didn't know about. Kept them hidden.'

Martan scuffed the burned grass. 'What I saw was real, wasn't it?'

'Mostly.'

'This is serious business.'

'Yes,' added Gunnar, stepping out of the land engine after setting the brake. 'Everything Justen does, I think, is serious business.' He turned to his younger brother. 'What was that?'

'A trick from the great forest. The only way you can win is to accept both order and chaos within yourself. I didn't think any White could do that.' Justen wiped his still-sweating forehead.

'I don't think most Blacks could do that, either,' responded Gunnar. He glanced around the hut. 'I doubt anyone will bother us now. I also think that every White Wizard in Candar probably knows we're here.' He paused. 'Why couldn't you use that instead of that other . . . infernal thing?'

'It won't solve the problem.' Justen slowly stood, grasping the timber framing the way station's doorless opening to help him rise. 'These two weren't that strong, either.'

'Here . . .' Gunnar shoved a wedge of cheese and the end of a loaf of bread at Justen.

'Thanks.' Justen slowly chewed on first the bread and then the cheese as Gunnar brought in the pallets and some supplies.

Martan fed more sticks and a small log to the dying fire.

Even before Gunnar had carried in his second load, Justen had struggled to the hearth by the fire, where he soaked up warmth and tried to keep his knees from turning to water.

Martan knelt and looked sideways at Justen. 'That wizardry stuff takes it out of you.'

Justen nodded.

Martan rose and left the hut. When he returned, he offered Justen the small bucket of clear spring water.

'Thank you.' Justen took a deep swallow. His legs had stopped quivering, and he no longer felt as though he would fall over.

'I throttled it down and set the brake. What else?' asked Gunnar.

'Open the main release valve by the—'

'Oh . . . right.' Gunnar hurried back to the *Demon*.

Justen rose and followed, more slowly.

In the darkness, Gunnar turned to Justen. 'You didn't have to come.'

'The way things are going, we both had better check things.'

'Maybe.'

Justen threw the thin trap over the seats. 'This ought to keep anything from getting damp.'

'I don't feel any rain.'

'Let's get some food and rest.'

The two walked back into the way station and sat down on the stone floor. Gunnar spread cheese and bread on a square of cloth and then added some pearapples.

The three ate silently.

'We'll need more coal – or wood – or something,' Justen mumbled, his mouth full of cheese and bread.

'Can we buy it?' asked Martan. 'You said you had golds.'

'How? Do we steam up to the collier or the blacksmith wearing black and say, "Oh, I'd like to buy ten stone worth of coal or charcoal"?'

The marine laughed. 'How about stealing it honest-like?'

'Take it and leave coins?' Justen mused. That was certainly better than theft. 'Where's the nearest town? We can probably make only another twenty kays before we're running on coal dust. The *Demon* burns coal faster than I figured.'

'Well, we're traveling faster than I figured. When will we reach Fairhaven?' Gunnar asked.

'It's at least another half-day's travel, even with the *Demon*.'

Gunnar leaned back on the thin pallet he had unrolled and closed his eyes.

'Sleeping already?' asked Martan.

'No. He's riding the winds, trying to find a town.'

'You two . . . sometimes it's fine. Other times, I wonder what I got into,' admitted Martan.

'So do we.'

148

'Oh . . .' Justen awoke with a start as Martan touched his shoulder. He had slept deeply, perhaps too deeply. He had not even dreamed of Dayala, or of the White Wizards.

'If we're to get this coal . . .' said the marine softly.

'Yes.' Justen took a deep breath and stretched, trying to remove the stiffness from his back.

By the time he had pulled on his boots, splashed his face in the stream to try to wake up, and rolled up his pallet, Martan had repacked the land engine, and Justen had to move the pallets to get the buckets.

'I thought we were getting coal.'

'We need water, and we might as well refill the reservoir here.'

'With those dinky buckets? It'll take until well after dawn.'

'We need the water.'

Martan shrugged.

'Now?' groaned Gunnar.

'Now.'

'I'm hungry,' protested the Air Wizard.

'So am I. We can eat while we're traveling toward this place you say might have coal.' Justen carried the first bucket up from the stream behind the way station.

Splluuussh . . .

'Crap!' Gunnar stood ankle-deep in the stream. 'You and your water before breakfast.'

'Fill the bucket and pass it up, or carry it.'

The sky was noticeably gray by the time the land engine puffed northward.

'I told you it would take until dawn.'

Justen said nothing as he chewed on the still-moist bread packed by Horas.

'My boots will be wet all day.'

'Can't you use that wizardry of yours?' asked Martan.

'It works fine on clothes and me. If I use it on leather, it ruins it. The boots would fall apart.' Gunnar bit into a hunk of cheese.

'How far?' asked Justen.

'. . . nudder oo ays.'

'What?'

'I think he said two kays,' interpreted Martan.

After taking another wide curve, even Justen could sense the iron ore and the wrought iron piled next to the dark, hutlike home that stood beneath a small hill.

A packed and wide road led left off the main road and to the ironmongery. Justen turned the tiller, and the *Demon* followed the side road. To the east, the horizon was turning a paler gray.

'We need to hurry,' said Martan.

Awwooo . . . ooo . . . oo . . .

'There's a dog,' offered Gunnar.

'I hear,' said Justen. 'Can you put it to sleep?'

'Probably. Wait a moment.'

Justen eased back the throttle, and the *Demon* barely edged forward.

'Dawn's not that far off,' hissed Martan.

'He's sleeping now,' said Gunnar in a low voice. 'The coal is in a big pile between that shed and the house.'

'I'll drive right up beside it.'

All three held their breath as Justen eased the land engine across the yard and to the coal pile.

'Awful close to the house,' whispered Martan.

'Take your bow and watch it, then. I'm going to put golds by the door – I'll feel better about paying first – and then Gunnar and I will load the bins.'

'Be a moment 'fore I can get it strung.'

Justen set the brake and tried to walk quietly across the yard to the house. He eased four golds from his purse onto the flat log set beside the ironmonger's door. Then he walked back toward the coal.

'Stop right there, my fine thieves!' A stocky man stood barefoot on the stones outside the doorway of the house.

He carried a bow with an arrow, nocked and pointed a Gunnar.

'Should have put the ironmonger to sleep, too,' said Martan. His bow was trained on the man.

Justen sighed. 'We're not thieves.'

'Likely tale.'

'Since this has already turned into a mess, let me explain. I'm Justen. I'm one of those nasty Black engineers from Recluce. The man you have your arrow pointed at is my brother Gunnar. The fellow who has his bow aimed at you is Martan. He's a Black marine, and they don't usually miss.'

'I'm Thasgus, and I don't often miss, either.'

'If you will look beside the doorstep, or let me go get it, you will find that there are four golds laid there as advance payment for your coal. That's what we want.'

'Why are you running around in the dawn, then?'

Justen snorted. 'Since we landed in Hydolar, I've been shot at. My land engine has been attacked. Two White Wizards tried to destroy us last night. The last time I was in Candar I was chased practically across the continent by a pair of White Wizards.'

'Sounds like you're not exactly wanted here. Why did you bother coming back?'

'I'm not exactly popular anywhere right now. That's true. I came back because—' Justen shrugged, hoping he did not have to unbalance the order and chaos around him, although he was willing to do so '– I thought it might be interesting to meet the High Wizard in Fairhaven.'

'Mind if I have Dessa look by the step?' asked the stocky ironmonger.

'Go ahead.'

'Dessa! Look next to the step by the door. Tell me what's there.'

'You want me to look by the doorstep?'

'Yes, woman. Look by the step. And don't mind all the wizards in the yard.'

'Wizards in the yard? My, my . . .' A thin woman peered out the door. 'Well, there's a bone here. Looks to be chewed by Gutfull. And a bit of ribbon . . .'

'The other side, please?' asked Justen.

'Oh . . . here? There be four coins, Thasgus. Look to be gold. Wait a moment. My scissors are iron.'

Several faint *clinks* followed.

'They look gold, and they ring gold.'

'You lower that bow,' offered the ironmonger, 'and I'll lower mine. There's more of you, anyway.'

Justen nodded, and Martan lowered his bow slowly. So did the ironmonger.

'What kind of coal ye be needing?' Thasgus set the bow against the house. 'For four golds, you can have as much of the best as you can cart in that little wagon.'

'Could you throw in a little redberry and a mug of beer?' pleaded Justen.

Thasgus frowned. 'Who wants the beer?'

'I do.'

The ironmonger laughed. 'A Black Wizard who drinks beer?' Then his face clouded. 'Ye be sure you're a wizard?'

Justen drew the light around him, vanishing from the other's sight, then walked toward Thasgus, appearing less than three paces away. 'Satisfied?'

'Takes all kinds.' The stocky ironmonger shook his head. 'But those White Wizards will turn you into ashes, from what I hear tell. You fellows seem a little . . . nice . . . to do such a thing, even if you do have a funny way of doing business.'

'Don't judge the ore by its shine, Thasgus,' warned Dessa from the doorstep. She carried two pitchers.

'Yes, woman.' Thasgus glanced at Justen. 'You found the coal. Shovels are in the shed.'

'Thank you.'

'No thanks. You're paying for it.'

Martan nodded and smiled, but he kept the bow half ready.

149

'You take those curves too fast,' protested Gunnar. 'I can feel the wheels skidding sideways on the stone.'

'It's safer that way.' Justen laughed. 'It makes it harder for an archer to hit us.'

'What archer even knows we're on the road?' Gunnar paused. 'You know something? We haven't seen anyone on this road today. No one.'

'It's only a bit past dawn.'

'Early morning,' Martan put in.

'Fine. We still haven't seen anyone. I don't like it.'

'That's why it's better to move fast. They've probably warned everyone off the road. It will make it easier for us to get to Fairhaven. We're really not far away.'

'You're not going to just drive right into Fairhaven, are you?'

'Of course. We'll take the main road from the south and head straight for the great square, or whatever it's called.' Justen straightened the tiller and glanced to his right, then to his left. The road continued to wind between the low hills that presumably guarded the approach to Fairhaven.

'Justen, can't I get a serious answer?'

'I need a hill.'

'A hill?'

'A hill south of Fairhaven. A tall hill with a clear view of Fairhaven and the White Tower, and with a road that will take us partway up.'

'Just like that?' asked Gunnar. 'Am I supposed to create one?'

'No. Look for it.'

'While you're throwing me all over the land engine?'

Martan nodded from the third seat, his face slightly pale.

'Do what you can.' As the road straightened, Justen pushed the throttle forward. Behind him, Martan groaned almost inaudibly.

For another ten kays, Gunnar withdrew into himself and out of himself, and Martan hung on to the sides of the third seat.

'Around the next corner, there's a hill. It looks out on Fairhaven.'

Justen slowed the *Demon* as they rounded the corner and studied the hill. 'It's too far away.'

Gunnar sighed. 'We're getting close to Fairhaven.'

'Not as close as I need to be.'

'Great. Let me look again.'

A man and a donkey stared at the land engine from a side road. Justen waved brightly. The man's mouth dropped open.

'How about that one?'

'It's really not as high as I'd like.'

'What are you looking for? Maybe we should have brought a White Wizard like the great Jeslek to create what you need.'

'Gunnar, I'm worried, too.'

'There's a hill on the next curve. It's shorter, but it's mostly clear to Fairhaven, and you might be able to get this contraption to climb it if you really got moving. And it's the last real hill before Fairhaven. After it, there's one low ridge and then the city starts. This one is only a sheep meadow. The one below it has houses.'

'All right.'

'There's a lane there. It goes partway up.'

Justen eased the throttle farther forward.

Martan's fingers tightened around the iron-plated oak as the land engine swayed more violently. Behind them, road dust rose into a high plume.

More than five hundred cubits short of the hilltop, the wheels dug into soft ground and spun.

The half-score sheep had half-walked, half-trundled, toward the cottage downhill from where the land engine was stalled.

Justen sighed and set the brake. 'We'll have to carry the stuff up there.'

'With everyone watching?'

'You want to do it after they send troops?'

Justen climbed out of the *Demon* and stared at Fairhaven.

For a moment, the low, glittering white buildings to the north shimmered ... shifted ... and Justen felt as though he were standing on the edge of a deep abyss and that those buildings tilted into the depths. He swallowed. Fairhaven was even more unbalanced than Nylan – but different.

'Are you all right?' asked Martan.

'I'm fine.' Somehow, the marine's enthusiasm reminded him of Clerve. He swallowed again.

A man with a staff marched from the cottage uphill toward the *Demon* and the three from Recluce. Justen began to unfasten the wicker balloon basket.

'What business have you here?' The shepherd had a short brown beard, and he waved the staff at them.

Justen stepped forward, staying well beyond the range of the staff.

'I'm Justen, and I'm a Black – really a Gray – Wizard from Recluce. I'm setting things up to bring down Fairhaven and the White Wizards. Feel free to watch or to depart. One way or another, this won't last for more than a day.' He shrugged theatrically, appeared to disappear for a instant and then reappeared. He spun a coin toward the shephered, who let it fall. 'That's a gold. Call it rental for your meadow.'

The man scooped up the coin without a word and backed down the hill, glancing from the marine with the bow to the two wizards and back.

Justen smiled, then whistled as he finished unfastening the balloon basket and began to carry it up to the hilltop. The notes sounded leaden, even to himself.

'All of this?' asked Martan.

'Everything in the lockers that's not food or weapons. You bring what weapons you think we need, and Gunnar can bring the food.'

'Why are we carrying it all up to the top?' asked Gunnar.

'Because it's the highest point on the hill,' explained Justen between breaths. 'I'm out of shape.'

At the top, he set down the basket and started back downhill.

Gunnar shrugged and followed him.

It was still somewhat short of midday by the time Justen sat in the middle of a pile of equipment and a smaller pile of coal beside the small heating stove with the tubing to the balloon.

'Now what?' asked Gunnar.

Justen continued to fiddle with the single lens as the stove puffed hot air into the slowly inflating balloon. 'We put a shield – just the hint of one – around the balloon and then wait until they notice we're here.'

'What if they don't?' asked Martan.

'Oh, they will.' Justen grinned, glancing at the mid-morning sun well above the browning grass of the eastern hills. 'That's what these are for.' He nodded toward the curved mirror and the wide crystal lens. 'I intend to send a signal or two.'

'I was afraid of that.' Gunnar massaged the back of his neck. 'And after that?'

'I get the balloon and the lenses ready, and you and Martan build a rock shelter.'

'A shelter? I came to fight,' protested Martan.

'You'll fight, I'm sure,' Justen said gently, 'but not until after I take on the White Wizards. You need to protect Gunnar while he's ensuring that the skies stay cloudless. A wizard with his senses in the skies has no way to protect his body.'

'What about you?'

'I'll be up in the balloon basket. I should be safe from most weapons there.' Justen shrugged. 'But it can carry only one, anyway.'

The small heat stove continued to puff hot air into the silksheen.

150

The beam of light from the hilltop played across the White tower again. Beltar squinted. 'That damned engineer is giving me a headache.'

'That is clearly his intention.' Despite his calm words, Eldiren massaged his neck and forehead, his fingers lingering momentarily on the scar above his eyebrow.

'What's in that light? Light's supposed to be mostly chaotic.' Beltar walked toward the window, then turned back, his fingers playing with the amulet of office.

'It's ordered, somehow. That's part of the reason it's so bright.' Eldiren moistened his lips.

'I thought you said that the engineer was coming to Fairhaven.' Beltar paced back toward the window, glancing southward.

'I said I *thought* he was. He's close enough, isn't he? Do you want that light in the square out there?' Eldiren gestured toward the east window and the patch of green visible in the open oblong.

The light played across the tower again, and the screeing glass hummed faintly.

'Demon light! He's going to smash more screeing glasses. Isn't it time for the Council to convene?'

'You had me tell them mid-morning.'

'It is mid-morning.'

'Not quite,' observed Eldiren. 'Most of them are heading toward the Council chamber now. What will you have them do?'

'I think we need to move – behind adequate Iron Guard and lancers, of course – to the south of the city and bring our combined forces to bear on this . . . engineer.'

'Don't you think that is what he wants?'

'I don't really care what he wants. Just how much longer can we ignore him?'

'I could ignore him for a long time,' said Eldiren.

'I don't have that choice. I am, if you recall, the High Wizard, and all the members of the Council are going to have headaches, if they don't already. If we don't do something . . . today . . .'

'They may want you to do it alone,' suggested Eldiren. 'As you so rightly point out, you are the High Wizard.'

'Any Black who's strong enough to create that . . . is more than a match for any White.'

Eldiren smiled faintly, the smile giving a sardonic cast to his thin face.

'Stop smirking,' Beltar ordered. 'I admit it, and at least I do. You still claim you killed him. Some dead engineer!'

'At the very least, they'll insist you be the focus.'

'I know. I know.' Beltar took a deep breath and looked at the empty bottle of wine on the side table. He licked his lips, then stood abruptly. 'Call Jehan.'

'He's downstairs.' Eldiren eased from the straight-backed chair and walked to the tower door, leaving it ajar. His boots scuffed on the tower steps. 'Jehan . . .'

Beltar walked to the window on the south side of the room, his eyes taking in the flashes of light and the round object that seemed to burgeon from the top of the hill from where the light came. 'A sphere filled with hot air . . . what does he have in mind?' He shook his head, then turned as he heard two sets of boots trudging up the stairs.

The two wizards stepped into the High Wizard's quarters and stood, waiting.

'Jehan, after we finish here, I want you to find Marshall Kilera and have him assemble the Iron Guard – every one who's fit – and all the White lancers. We'll move out on the Blacks right after the meeting.'

'As you wish,' Jehan said without inflection. 'Is that what the White Council will decide?'

'That is what the Council will decide,' Beltar affirmed. 'Do they have much choice?'

'They could decide on another High Wizard,' suggested Eldiren.

'Ha! And they'd slaughter the thinnest pig in the yard, too. You really think that any of them want to go out and face those Blacks?'

'Well . . . they don't look especially overwhelming. Outside of that wagon and a handful of black iron rockets, what do they have?' Eldiren's voice was light, almost mocking.

'Just the confidence to challenge the mightiest wizards in the world,' Jehan observed. 'A bag filled with hot air, and more order than any one of us has ever seen in one place.'

'You two!' snapped Beltar. 'What do you mean?' He pointed at Jehan.

'This Black mage keeps doing the impossible. What is to stop him again?'

'We are. The entire White Council.'

As Beltar glared at Jehan, Eldiren lifted his eyebrows.

'You two,' repeated Beltar. He cleared his throat. 'Jehan – jus
go take my message to Marshall Kilera. I want him to ready
whatever forces he has to march as close to midday as possible
Then rejoin us. We'll be in the Council Room.'

Jehan nodded, then turned and hastened out the door and
down the steps.

Fingering the heavy amulet that hung from the chain around
his neck, Beltar inclined his head to Eldiren. 'What choice do
I have?'

'Not much. I think that you're stronger than the Black mage
but he clearly thinks he can win . . . somehow. And despite you
rumors that the Black Council was going to imprison him for
being order-mad, I don't think he is. I think they're scared o
him, and that bothers me.'

'It bothers me, too.' Beltar shrugged. 'But what am I supposed
to do?' He winced as another flash of ordered-light flicked
through the window.

Eldiren shivered.

'Am I supposed to walk up that hillside and say, "Please go
away"? Will that work?'

'No. And if you did that, Derba would have you in chains for
treachery, or you'd end up blasting half the Council into dust.
Eldiren laughed with a self-mocking note. 'I told you what would
happen if you got the amulet through sheer power.'

'You did, but that doesn't help now. Just what do you
suggest?'

'That you can accept?' Eldiren shrugged. 'Use more power
Back it with troops and hope that you don't end up destroy
ing us all. And don't turn your back on anyone until it's
over.'

'You're honest.'

'I'm not powerful. I don't have any choice.'

'Shall we go?' asked Beltar.

'I am at your command, High Wizard.'

'So you are.' The High Wizard straightened his tunic, let the
amulet drop to the end of the heavy gold links, and squared
his shoulders. He walked to the door, and Eldiren followed
The thud of their boots was the only sound as they descended
the stairs.

'You could give up the office of High Wizard,' suggested

ldiren as they entered the lower hall. 'Or try to talk to the Black.'

'Eldiren.' Beltar sighed in exasperation. 'If I gave up the mulet, I'd eventually get fried, just like Sterol did, because ey'll need someone to blame. Besides, that presumes that this lack will win, and that's far from certain. Last time, he ran om you. Survival isn't quite the same as triumphing.'

'Sometimes it's the same thing.'

'Then throw in your lot with Derba.' Beltar ignored the servant ho scuttled aside. He continued down the wide hallway to the ouncil Room without looking at Eldiren.

'You at least listen to honesty. He doesn't know what it is,' ldiren offered.

'Then you're trapped, just like me.'

'Worse. I have to depend on you.'

Beltar paused at the door to the chamber. 'Ready?'

'Of course.'

A low humming, comprised of multiple conversations, filled e room.

'. . . why doesn't our great High Wizard just take care of the opity Black himself? Why call the Council?'

'. . . same Black who destroyed half the armies in Sarronnyn . . .'

'. . . someone strong enough to worry the White Butcher? That a pity.'

'. . . pity us . . . you mean . . .'

Beltar stepped onto the dais, Eldiren at his shoulder, and e murmurs died away. He waited for a moment. 'I have alled the Council in order to deal with the insult posed by e Black mage.'

'You need the whole Council for that?' asked a voice from e group in the middle of the white-hung chamber.

Beltar shrugged. 'I think it's far better to use excessive force an to have wizards and troops picked off one by one, the way was in Sarronnyn. You might recall that we got nowhere there ntil we brought in more than a handful of White Wizards.'

Jehan eased in from the side entrance and stopped beside ldiren. As Beltar's eyes rested on him, Jehan nodded. Beltar niled.

'You are the greatest wizard ever, Beltar,' Derba began. 'That, least, is what one has been led to believe.' Derba offered a

smile that was not far from a smirk. 'Yet you're saying that i
will take all of us to deal with three mere Order Wizards from
Recluce?'

'You're supposed to be able to move mountains. Why can'
you just lift the mountains under them?' Inadvertently, afte
speaking, a heavyset wizard massaged his forehead looked awa
from the High Wizard.

Beltar sighed loudly. 'Just what will happen to all of Fairhave
if I call on chaos and raise mountains right here? What do yo
think, Flyrd?' His eyes fixed on the heavy wizard.

'You tell us,' suggested Derba.

The stone on which Derba stood vibrated, and the redheade
wizard lurched in place.

'Very pretty, Beltar.'

'I think what Beltar is trying to point out,' suggested Eldiren
'is that it might be rather dangerous. Raising mountains has
tendency to destroy the landscape and whatever else is nearby.

'Jeslek did it.' Derba crossed his arms and stared at Eldiren.

A pulse of light flicked through the window on the south sid
of the white-walled hall. Eldiren winced, while Jehan squinted
Several other wizards in the chamber shifted their weight.

'And we're still paying for it. Today there's only high deser
and thin grass on most of the so-called Little Easthorns,
continued Eldiren after a momentary pause. 'That scourge wa
nearly three centuries ago.'

'So . . .' Derba drew out the word. 'You're saying that if yo
use your mighty powers, they may be so mighty and you wil
have so little control over them that Fairhaven itself will b
destroyed?'

'I did not say that.' Beltar glared at Derba, and lines of flam
appeared around both wizards. 'The Order Wizard has shields
They seem strong. To break those shields will break everythin;
else around unless we can focus our powers directly on him
Also, you might remember that if we create great forces of chaos
we might just create another order-focus in him. Does anyon
remember what happened the last time chaos overbalanced orde
that much? Does anyone remember why Cerryl the Great—'

'You're invoking Cerryl?' asked Derba. 'I find that rathe
amusing.'

The flash of order-light flicked through the chamber again.

'Most powerful wizards,' called a voice from the group on the lower level, 'could we agree on a course of action? The rest of us are having some difficulty in dealing with the current disruption.'

'Yes, most exalted High Wizard,' said Derba. 'Exactly what do you plan?' His red hair glinted with what seemed the fire of chaos itself.

'We have two Iron Guard regiments and their Fifth mounted, plus the Eighth White lancers. Add maybe a hundred in detachments—'

'That's a great deal fewer than the two Black mages destroyed in Sarronnyn, is it not?' asked the heavyset Flyrd from near the back of the group.

'At that time, there were exactly two real White Wizards with our forces, opposed by several thousand Sarronnese, plus a dozen or more Black engineers and a detachment of Black marines, all supporting these Black mages. Here, they have themselves and one marine. That's scarcely an overwhelming force, friend Flyrd,' suggested Beltar.

Eldiren and Jehan exchanged a brief glance. Jehan rolled his eyes at the inconsistencies in Baltar's rebuttal.

'Might that just not signify extreme confidence? The rumors are that one of those Blacks is he who shattered every screeing glass in Candar.' Flyrd crossed his hands across his white robe and waited.

'The rumors also indicate,' countered Beltar, 'that he had to flee Recluce and that the Black Council was about to restrain him for being order-mad.' The High Wizard smiled. 'Any man who sets himself up to challenge an entire continent is somewhat unbalanced.'

'If he's mad, then, why don't you just handle it?' asked Derba, a broad smile playing across his face.

Beltar frowned, and white sparks rose around him, forcing Derba's shields back.

'I withdraw the question, powerful and mighty High Wizard.' Derba retreated, pursing his lips.

The white sparks dropped away from Derba, and Beltar smiled. 'Since we are agreed, and since this is best resolved as soon as possible – as suggested, let us depart.'

'Now?'

'What . . .'

Beltar smiled. 'I have already called up our forces and they are in readiness before their barracks on the south side of Fairhaven. Marshall Kilera awaits our arrival and support. I expect every member of the Council to be outside the hall and ready to go. *Now*.'

Derba wiped his damp forehead. Flyrd glanced nervously from Beltar to Derba and then to Eldiren before turning toward the rear of the chamber.

Beltar watched for a moment, then strode out, ignoring the murmurings that began to rise. Eldiren and Jehan followed.

'. . . notice that Histen just wasn't able to get here.'

'. . . Eldiren didn't look too happy.'

'Even Derba backed down . . .'

'. . . foolishness . . .'

'. . . be over in instants. Stupid Black . . .'

'So stupid. So stupid that he destroyed half our army in Sarronnyn.'

'. . . a choice? Who has a choice?'

The wizards began to move toward the waiting mounts and coaches.

151

The wind whispered across the browning hillside grasses, and Justen straightened from shoveling coal into the small stove, leaving the door ajar for a moment. He wiped the sweat from his forehead and took a deep breath, turning to the north.

There, in the center of the plain between the hills, the higher towers of Fairhaven glistened white, like fangs thrusting from the valley floor. The tallest tower – that of the High Wizard himself – pulsed with the shimmering white that carried the unseen reddish tinge of chaos beneath it. Between the orderly rows of buildings and avenues was the everpresent green of the short trees, the ines, the grass. White and green, green and white: Fairhaven, he jewel of Candar.

Justen shook his head. Did he really believe that he and Gunnar – and Martan – could take on the massed wizards who had built such a city?

You can . . . and you must . . .

He pursed his lips. Easy enough for Dayala and the Angels. They weren't the ones who were watching a small-sized army slowly march toward them. One army, accompanied by dozens of wizards – and good old Justen was intending to prevail with a bag of silksheen filled with hot air, a wicker basket, some rods, two fire-eyes, and the sun?

He laughed softly. His father had been right. He'd finally gotten himself in an impossible situation.

Justen, believe in the Balance . . . and yourself. You must!

Indeed I must . . .

I am with you, beloved . . . always with you . . .

He took a deep breath.

Above Justen, the balloon shivered in the breeze. On the hillside below, Gunnar and Martan carried black iron plate from the land engine toward the crude revetment of stone Justen had insisted they build. He could hope that the black iron and stone would protect them.

Clunk . . . The dull sound of metal against rock echoed across the hillside as the two men set the plate against the stones.

Justen took a deep breath, trying to relax, but the tightness in his guts persisted, as did the tension in his shoulders. He took a long look at Martan, young and proud and strong, and so willing to do great deeds. Justen sighed. Great deeds, indeed. Feeling more like a butcher about to be covered with blood, he swallowed and glanced back toward Fairhaven and the approaching White Wizards.

The line of White forces, while not nearly so impressive as those that had besieged Sarronnyn, stretched nearly a half-kay along the main road leading south. The White lancers leading the forces were no more than a kay from the point where the hillside road veered off the main road. Behind them rode the mounted Iron Guard, their crimson-trimmed banners fluttering in the light wind. Then came the Iron Guard foot. Behind them came the white banners of the wizards, with nearly a dozen of

the White Wizards mounted on white horses, followed by tw⟨
white-gold coaches flying gold-trimmed white banners. Over t⟨
oncoming soldiers and wizards hung a cloud of reddish-whi⟨
unseen except by mages, that promised power, chaos – an⟨
disaster to all who opposed the massed will it represented.

Justen shivered. Then he nodded and called, 'Martan! I nee⟨
to get up there!'

As the marine came trotting, Justen shoveled hot coals into t⟨
heat pan of the balloon. He checked the lines and disengaged t⟨
fire-cloth piping from the stove to the balloon. Gunnar walk⟨
up behind Martan.

'They're getting close enough. I should get the balloon u⟨
Justen glanced at the taut silksheen fabric and at the two lin⟨
holding it down, each line tied to a heavy stake. 'Martan?'

'Yes, Ser?'

'Once I get in the basket here, start letting the line go fro⟨
each stake. Hold on to just the one. The other should unwin⟨
by itself. Then make sure it's tied tight. After that, get back ⟨
your revetment and protect Gunnar. Like I told you, a wiza⟨
with his mind in the skies can't protect himself, and I'm countir⟨
on you.'

'Yes, Ser.' Martan nodded solemnly.

Justen frowned for a moment. 'How many rockets are left ⟨
the land engine?'

'Less than a score.'

'Use them first, while the Whites are still massed together an⟨
making a good target.'

'I'll do my best.'

Justen forced himself to meet the young, proud face. 'Than⟨
you.'

'Thank *you*. I wouldn't have missed this for anything.'

'I hope you feel that way when it's all over.' Justen turned t⟨
his brother, giving him a quick hug. 'Keep the skies as clear ⟨
you can. That's all I ask. All I need. And stay in that shelte⟨
We moved that armor plate for a reason.'

Martan and Gunnar exchanged glances before Gunnar's ey⟨
strayed to the crude rock barrier topped with two sheets of blac⟨
iron plate from the land engine.

'I mean it. You could go blind, or worse.'

A long drum-roll echoed up the hillside from the white-pave⟨

ad leading south out of Fairhaven. A second drum-roll fol-
wed. The standard-bearers dipped both the white banners and
imson-trimmed gray ones in response to the drum-rolls. The
r smelled like damp leaves, though the trees had barely begun
turn.

Justen climbed into the wicker basket, careful not to upset the
ns assembly or the brackets to which he would have to attach
once the balloon cleared the ground with room to spare.

Give me strength. Oh, Dayala . . . be with me.

I am with you . . . always . . .

The Gray Wizard, for he was a Gray Wizard, he knew, smiled.
his time, those warm thoughts were not just his imaginings. 'Let
e clamps go.'

Martan released one clamp, then the other, straining to keep
e line paying out at an even rate.

As the balloon rose, Justen grasped the sides of the basket,
des whose lightness, so laudable in his experiments, seemed
ore and more like fragility as the balloon rose. The cottage
the brown-grassed hillside below turned into a shed and then
to a doll-house – or so it seemed, even though the balloon was
ss than two hundred cubits above the hilltop.

Another roll rumbled from the drums. Justen lurched sideways
ghtly as he shifted his weight and the basket tilted.

'Oooo . . .' A line of fire burned his forehead, and the smell
singed hair filled his nostrils as he pulled his head away from
e small heating pan that had replaced the stove.

He took a deep breath and forced himself to rebalance order
d chaos in the burned patch of hair, and took another breath
relief as the pain faded and as the basket steadied.

Slowly, he lowered the bracket assembly over the side of the
sket and clamped it in place, so that the lenses reached out
deways. The light from the afternoon sun barely reached the
per lens.

Once more the drums rolled, and the lancers moved up to the
ne wall at the bottom of the hill. Justen continued to hang
er the side of the balloon basket, which had again begun to
ay, trying to adjust the brackets. Somehow, the adjustments
re harder to make when he was hanging from the basket than
en he was on the ground.

'Come on . . .'

The swaying increased as the balloon continued to rise.

Ummmphhh . . . The balloon gave a jolt as it reached the e~
of the tethers, and Justen grasped the sides of the basket w~
both hands. For a moment, his stomach seemed suspended, ~
he swallowed hard. Had Martan felt that way while traveling
the curves in the road?

Justen smiled a brief, wry grin and bent over again to adj~
the lens assembly. From the corner of his eye, he could see ~
White lancers and the Iron Guard nearing the bottom of the h~
After doing nothing for half the day, they had decided to m~
quickly. The white banners and the group of wizards remai~
in the same position farther back on the road. The new H~
Wizard?

Justen readjusted the brackets, but the light focus was ~
quite right, and he backed down the clamp a fraction o~
turn.

Hssstttt . . .

A firebolt flared toward the balloon, but seemed to fade ~
the side even before Justen had fully seen it.

Gunnar – it had to be Gunnar, shielding him while he work~
His eyes flickered down, but Gunnar was partly concealed by ~
armor. Martan still remained by the tether stakes.

'Martan!' he yelled. 'Light off those rockets to cover Gunn~
Hhhssttt . . .

The Weather Wizard deflected another firebolt.

'Crap!' muttered Justen, still trying to get the lens to focus ~
the fire-eye. He was going to get fried because he couldn't adj~
the settings while hanging upside down, and because the frigg~
Whites actually acted quickly, and because he was worried ab~
Gunnar and Martan, and they wouldn't have a chance if ~
didn't get his weapon working, and soon.

Hssstttt . . .

The balloon basket swayed again as Justen's boot slipp~
and he had to grab the basket with both hands to keep fr~
plunging out headfirst. He'd touched the bracket again a~
fuzzed the focus.

'Shit . . . shit . . . shit!'

He forced himself to be calm, and slowly he edged the cla~
a fraction of a turn.

Hssttt . . . *hssstttt* . . . *hhssttt* . . .

The last bolts were close enough for his face to feel as though
had been singed by a forge fire, close enough that he seemed
smell brimstone.
From the land engine came the whooshing of the rockets,
rowing downhill toward the mass of the White lancers.
Crummpt . . .
The first rocket sailed over the White positions and into the
eadow beyond, igniting browning grass into white smoke.
Crumptt . . .
The second plowed through the right flank of the lancers.
Whheeee . . . eeeee . . . eeee.
Ignoring the screaming horses, Justen adjusted the clamp
other fraction of a turn. The light hit the fire-eye at the right
gle, and the fire-eye was pointed, at least generally, toward
e White tower. A blade of light flared out from the assembly,
ding in mid-air.
Even as he realized that the brackets needed finer adjustment,
sten permitted himself the luxury of a tight smile.
Hssstttt . . .
Crummptt . . . Another rocket slammed into the stone before
e Iron Guard, spraying flame over a half-dozen foot soldiers.
ne ran forward and vaulted the stone wall and tried to roll the
e out on the ground. Instead, the fire grew into a long groove
the high grass, where a charred figure twitched, its screams
ing into moans, then into silence.
Hhssstttt! Another firebolt passed below the balloon.
Crummptt! Crumpptt! Two more rockets flew downhill into
e massed White center, leaving a blackened gap.
A quick roll of drums punctuated the air, and half of the White
ncers began to ride uphill.
Three rockets in succession turned the front line of the lancers
o a charred heap. The remaining riders split around the fallen
d continued toward the land engine.
Two of the next three rockets exploded into the turf before the
;ht wing of the lancers, raising smoke and dirt and slowing the
arge. The rocket aimed at the left wing brought down the lead
rse, but it did not break the momentum of the charge.
Gunnar deflected another pair of firebolts as Justen fiddled
th the brackets.
Cruumptt! Crumptt! Crumptt!

'Ohhhh . . .' In spite of himself, Justen glanced below, whe
Martan sprinted from the land engine toward the crude reve
ment, not even looking back at the tangled, twisted, and burn
mass of human and horse flesh created by the last rockets.

Hhsssttt!

Justen ducked involuntarily, although Gunnar's shields guid
the firebolt away from the balloon. He glanced below quickl
where Martan, despite Justen's orders, still stood in the open,
half-behind the stone-and-iron-plate revetment. The marine w
lofting black arrows downhill, where they exploded among t
remaining massed White lancers. As scattered shafts began
fly uphill, the marine released yet another black shaft befo
moving behind the barrier where Gunnar sat, eyes closed, ord
continuing to build around him.

Justen edged the bracket the slightest bit, and the light-bla
flared into the ground behind the High Wizard's coach.

The response was instantaneous, with firebolts flying towa
the balloon.

Hsssttt . . . hsssttt . . . hssttt.

The barrage of firebolts flew by the balloon basket, st
protected by Gunnar's shields. But the air grew warmer,
though the hottest days of summer were flying toward him.

Justen shook himself. 'Act, damn it!'

He took a deep breath, closed his eyes and concentrate
smoothing the flow and weaving the light into the collecti
lens. A web of shadow flickered around the balloon, and Just
could feel Gunnar withdraw his shields in order for Justen
gather the full power of the sunlight.

Darkness spread from the balloon, almost as sunlight wou
have radiated from a second sun. It seemed as though nig
had emerged from the balloon and fallen across the hillsic
then spread northward toward Fairhaven itself, glittering like
white gem between the browning green hills. The dark shadc
raced northward, its forward edge a knife-sharp line betwe
day and night.

Hhsssst . . . The firebolt seemed to drop away from the ballo
even without Gunnar's shields.

Below, looking like a doll behind his shelter, Martan loos
another string of arrows. Each arrow arced downhill, and ea
seemed to find a target, each shaft as inexorable as black dea

'ith every lancer transfixed by an arrow, there came a faint
ump as chaos and order met and exploded. The rhythm
ntinued, and Martan's hands and arms unleashed a steady
ream of dark shafts, flying so fast that they almost streaked
ke black lightning down upon the White lancers. The *crump,
ump, crump* of heads exploding as they struck echoed far into
e growing darkness. With each explosion came a faint point
: light in the twilight that had fallen around the hill.

Justen concentrated more intently, trying to block Martan
om his thoughts, trying to block out his concerns for Gunnar,
ying only to funnel more light into the lens and direct it to
e gem.

Sssssstt . . .

Like a sword of the ancient Angels, the blade of fire seared
e ground at the foot of the hill, cutting through the brown-
een turf, striking sparks, flinging molten rock like minia-
re firebolts as it tore through the stone wall beside the
ad. Small fires and plumes of smoke rose from scattered
oints in the field where the flaming rock droplets had fall-
.

Hsssttt!

The sun-blade dimmed as Gunnar's shields deflected the
ebolts, then flared back to brightness and slashed at an angle
rough a squad of lancers. Screams mixed with the hissing that
sembled the vent of a massive steam engine.

Where the light-blade had passed, white ashes swirled and
ifted snowlike, falling on the clay beside the road, on the
ass-hard melted stone of the road itself, and across the glassy
arts of the shoulder that had once been sand.

Horses reared, those that were left, screaming as they tried to
unge away from the rain of ash, and from the blackened heaps
at had been men and horses merely brushed by the light blade.
 the dimness, the white banners fluttered against the growing
ind from nowhere, their muffled crackling adding to the swell
 sound.

Hssstttt!

Justen winced as the heat of the firebolt seemed to blister
s face.

Another roll of drums sounded, and the crimson-trimmed gray
nners headed uphill toward the balloon – and toward Gunnar

and Martan. The Iron Guard horse trotted forward to lead th
next advance, and the foot began to quickstep.

Martan's arrows shifted to the gray-clad troops, but no longe
did the shafts explode and strew bodies. The Guards fell, but the
fell one at a time, and there were far fewer shafts than Guard
even as the marine's arms seemed to blur with their speed. Tha
blur stopped for a moment as Martan pulled an arrow from th
fleshy part of his shoulder and then, almost without losing hi
rhythm, released yet another black shaft, and another. But th
wave of gray troops surged uphill, ever nearer to Martan an
Gunnar.

Sssssttttt . . .

With his thoughts, Justen swung the beam across the line c
the White forces, trying to slow the advance. The blade playe
back across the hillside, cutting a blackened gash across the tur
flinging scattered bits of flaming debris out and away from th
line of sunfire.

'Aeeeeiiii . . .' Only a few cries rose from the Iron Guard.

Heavier gray smoke curled from the burning grass. The sme
of scorched turf and the odor of burned flesh – human an
animal – permeated the lower hillside. But the Iron Guard close
ranks, and the crimson-trimmed gray banners continued uphill

Hssstt!

Another firebolt flashed below the balloon; the wicker of th
basket crackled with the heat, and the balloon bounced.

Justen forced the sun-blade back toward the Iron Guard, bu
the line of fire crossed the road and the White lancers behin
the stone wall. The remnant of the lancers broke and curle
away. Horses foamed and screamed, some hurling riders ont
the road.

'Form up! Follow the Guard!'

Another drum-roll sounded, not quite in cadence, and th
remnants of two squads of lancers began to trot up the hillsid
road, almost as if following Justen's light-blade.

Higher on the hillside, nearer the land engine and the tethers c
the balloon, at least half of the Iron Guard – half foot, half hors
– continued to march, more slowly but steadily, uphill towar
Martan and Gunnar.

From the White Wizards on the road there swelled a growin
pressure: pure chaos, so deep that it was more red than white

Hhhsttt! Hhhssstt!
Hssstttt! Hssstttt!

From the host of fireballs flaring toward Justen, one slammed
past him and into the balloon. The basket rocked, and a faint
hissing began. Trying to maintain his concentration, Justen
grabbed the basket with one hand, but the light-sword from
the fire-eye slewed away from the White forces and across a
row of houses at the edge of Fairhaven.

One of the houses with a thatched roof exploded into flame, an
instant torch, and smoke poured skyward. Another structure's
tile roof cracked and splintered, sending hot masonry across
the street like red-hot arrows. A tall stone house slumped like
a fat wax candle caught in full summer sun, or a baker's oven,
oozing out in all directions, the molten stone creating a ring
of fire that caused nearby trees and garden plants to erupt
in flame.

The sounds of steaming vegetation, screaming people, and
panicked animals melded into a low roar that in turn merged
with the hissing of the light-sword itself.

Hhssstttt! Hssstttt!

The twin firebolts fell short, but Justen could sense the
growing mass of chaos building in the White Wizards.

Trying to hold back his horror at the results of the sun-blade,
Justen struggled to get his balance in the rocking balloon basket
and to swing the sun-blade back toward the Iron Guard, which
advanced inexorably toward Gunnar and Martan.

Martan continued to loose arrows, his right sleeve damp with
blood, and Gunnar struggled with the high and mighty winds,
trying to keep the sky clear for Justen.

Sssssttttt . . .

Justen wrenched the sun-blade back below him, playing it
across the advancing ranks of the Iron Guard, trying to ignore
the greasy smoke and the screams.

Still the Guard advanced, now no more than a hundred cubits
from where Martan stood and let fly his arrows.

Justen coughed, and the blade slewed wildly, flashing back
toward the horizon and slagging a corner of the traders' market
into molten white stone.

Again the White Wizards focused their will, and another
huge swell of chaos flared. Sensing the chaos, Justen slewed

the sun-blade across the firebolts. *Hhhsttt! Crummpptt!*

With the impact of chaos and order, the sky seemed
explode. Black stars and deep, blinding-white flares intersecte
flashing through each other and dwindling into nothingness
the wind built. The balloon bounced so wildly that Justen, ev
with both hands on the basket, was thrown against the coal p
and half over the side. The smell of singed hair again filled
nostrils.

The light-blade flared northward, and the park in the trade
square flashed into flame. Cinders and ashes spewed skywar
Even while Justen struggled upright and brought the blade ba
to bear on the Iron Guard, the trees in the traders' squa
burned like bright candles through the artificial twilight, ha
and ever-thickening smoke.

'That's it,' muttered Justen to himself. 'Meet chaos wi
order . . .'

He spit out blood and forced his thoughts back onto t
light-blade, focusing it on the front ranks of the Iron Guar
playing it back across infantry and troopers alike, ignoring t
white agony that welled from soldiers whose bodies explod
in steaming fury instants before they became piles of ash.

More chaos-fire flared around the balloon.

Hssssttt!! Hssstttt!

The balloon bounced again, but braced, Justen kept swingi
the blade across the Iron Guard, reduced now to less than a sco
of horsemen charging toward Martan and Gunnar.

Justen slammed the blade along a line between the two and t
Iron Guard, and still trying to hold on to the Balance betwe
chaos and order, stretched his light-gathering net to cover t
sky as far as he could reach. He needed to gather an ever-wid
sweep of light.

Below, Martan hacked an Iron Guard off his horse and th
mounted it, swinging a stolen sabre and charging the half-squa
of Guards remaining – as if to push or pull them away fro
Gunnar and Justen.

More firebolts flashed past Justen, and the hissing of t
balloon grew louder, a sound that Justen sensed more than f
since his ears were deafened by the shrieking of the light-bla
the roaring of the firebolts, and the rushing of the winds th
yanked the balloon to the ends of its tethers.

Below, the sabre flew from Martan's hands as one of the last three Iron Guards slashed from his blind side.

Almost sobbing as he mentally grabbed at the increased order-energy from his wider capture net, Justen threw the sun-blade at the three Iron Guards before Martan. Still weaving and focusing, Justen directed the growing flow of order that was like a river from the heavens, even as a darker force seemed to gather beside it, welling from the earth beneath.

Ignoring that dark force, Justen flung the wider light-blade back along the hillside, throwing bodies everywhere, burning through the turf and melting stone outcrops, trying to keep the Guards, those three remaining, from Gunnar and Martan, although he could no longer sense the marine, only Gunnar's will across the skies.

Then a long wave wrenched the earth beneath the valley, rolling from the hill and to the north. The undulating motion ran back through the tethers, rocking the balloon, but that rocking was muted because the tethers were slackening as the balloon had begun to sink.

To the north, the massive landquake rippled along the high-way, lifting the twenty-stone paving blocks and dropping some of them back into disjointed positions, others into cracked and shattered fragments.

Houses – those not already fused, charred, or exploded into fragments – heaved like boats in the surf as the solid ground around them turned into liquid and shook like jelly. One swell followed another, and timbered walls bent, and bent, and snapped apart like twigs. Stone and masonry walls shivered, and shivered, and sprayed outward in cascades of brick and stone.

Waves of white-red destruction, of lost and sundered souls, poured back toward Justen, and in desperation, he turned the light-knife on that misty white, slashing through it as if to shield himself, to shield Gunnar, even to shield distant Dayala.

The grinding sound of stonework collapsing and the distant, almost hissing, screams of survivors, of innocents dying under flame, stone, and churned earth, were all but lost behind the searing heat and boiling edge of the order-chaos blade that Justen turned back down across the handful of White lancers who had followed the Iron Guard uphill and had nearly reached a spot almost directly below the balloon.

Sssssstttt . . . No screams followed the wave of light. Only
blast of white pain rocked through Justen with the deaths so clos
below, and the slope on the Fairhaven side of the hill glistene
like glass. Lumps – like the remnants of the shepherd's hut
protruded from the shimmering surface.

Justen, nearly blind with the white agony, tried to rebalanc
his forces, to turn them and the order-chaos blade back towar
the remaining White Wizards.

Hhhsssttt . . .

With the continuing barrage of firebolts, most of them hel
at bay by Gunnar's efforts in pulsing order-shields and holdin
the clouds away, the balloon and basket bounced again. Th
hissing overhead grew louder, and the basket swayed, sinkin
even closer to the ground. Justen squinted, trying to concentrat
trying to remain ordered and calm even as the order-chaos blac
bounced around the chaos-shield of the High Wizard.

The blade shivered and slashed across the center of Fairhaver
somehow held together by a web of white. With the collision o
the light-blade and the white web, stonework melted. Ancier
trees exploded into flames before falling like charcoaled log
against rubble and melted stone. Stone avenues flowed lik
white-lava rivers.

Even in the balloon the air was hotter than midday in th
Stone Hills, filled with the odor of scorched vegetation, charre
flesh, and ash and cinders and more ash. Like an oven, th
valley baked in the light-blade-forged twilight, where thos
few buildings that remained became ovens that baked the
inhabitants.

The only sun in the sky was the light from the order-chao
knife wielded by Justen, and yet that light gave no cheer, on
heat and agony.

Another pulse of chaos flared into the sky and arced towar
Justen – a massive firebolt propelled by the will of desperat
White Wizards, held tightly by the High Wizard himself, whos
broad shoulders and sweating face seemed to fill Justen's min

Hsssstttt . . .

Again Justen wrestled the order-chaos blade and the energ
gathered from the skies of Candar back toward the High Wizar
focusing it not only on the shield, but around the shield. Anoth
land wave shivered the ground, rocking the balloon through th

ethers, and Justen was forced to grab onto the basket to avoid being pitched out.

The ground around the shielded wizards bubbled as though it boiled, and steam gouted up in pillars, even through the stones of the wizard-protected section of the road.

Another firebolt flared past Justen and into the balloon, burning through one cable holding the balloon to the basket. The balloon slewed wildly, and Justen tightened his grasp on the basket, trying still to force the order-chaos blade back upon the White Wizards.

Ssssttt . . .

The trees across the road and behind the wizards flared like black rockets before collapsing into charcoal, which in turn was covered by molten rock oozing down from the melted stone of the road.

Hsssttt!

Lashing back against the firebolts, Justen forced the order-chaos blade toward the White Wizards, where he again played against the High Wizard's shield.

'That's . . . it. Keep it centered . . .' he grunted, trying to force ordered-light squarely against the lines of focused chaos wielded by the High Wizard.

Ssssttt! Cruummppttt!

The ground seemed to buckle and explode simultaneously, spewing order and chaos into the skies and deep into the earth. Lines of dark fire and rays of flame heat arced across the glowering sky that abruptly flared sun-white in brilliance.

On the southwestern side of the White Wizards' shield, the light-blade gouged a pit so deep that what had been a raised stone road melted into a glass-lined pit.

Hhhssttt!

Justen mentally walked the order-chaos beam back toward the High Wizard. Yet that tight shield held . . . and held . . . even though it pulsed against the violence Justen directed against it, each pulse throwing Justen's light-sword back across the valley.

With each flash across the valley that had held the White City, more stonework slumped into waxlike heaps until the entire valley seemed to be in ashes – black, gray, and white – out of which reared shiny, once-molten stone, as though the

bones of the burned corpses showed through more clearly with
each pass of the fire-sword of the skies.

Hanging on to the wicker, Justen made a last effort to swing
the wildly spinning order-chaos light-sword back onto the shield
of the High Wizard.

Sssttt . . . crumppttt . . .

Against the buckling of order and the tide of white, against
the unseen ripping in the fabric of what was, against the white
and black knives that seemed to slash through him, Justen closed
his eyes and tried to picture himself as a lorken of Naclos, rooted
in the soil and order beneath Candar, drawing order from the
deep waters, from the iron in the rocks, and from all the growing
plants that had struggled against the nibbling of chaos.

The wind whipped past Justen with the force of a waterspout.
He felt himself being thrown against the basket of the balloon
and his fingers dug deeper into the fragile wicker as the balloon,
swinging wildly, ripped free of one of the tethers.

Almost unaware of his teeth biting through his tongue, Justen
curled the order-blade into a focus, attempting to lock the wizards within order, putting forth a massive effort to chaos-order
Balance the White Wizards forever.

'Aaeeaeeii . . .'

'Ooo . . . nooo . . .'

Even locked into himself, Justen could sense the twisting and
folding of order and chaos roll across the valley like the heat
from that second sun, dragging the remaining White Wizards –
those who had tried to unleash the full force of chaos against
Justen's order-chaos blade – down inside the shield they had
erected, down . . . down into some distant place where their
souls seemed to call as if from a deep well.

Deliberately, as if he and his thoughts were moving through
molasses, Justen twisted the massive forces of order held through
the fire-eye, twisted them like a key in a lock to seal the wizards
behind their own shield . . . forever!

Faces flashed before him: swarthy faces, fat faces, and a
haunted, thin face almost like that of an Angel, the eyes filled
with suffering. But he locked order around that chaos.

Justen, you must . . . must balance. Even Dayala's thought
were weak, fading away into smoke.

Crackk! The fire-eye exploded and filled the air with sudden but momentary silence, and weak sunlight replaced the darkness that had descended across the valley of Fairhaven. Clouds of ashes roiled over the valley, and cinders fell like rain.

A heavy roll of thunder rumbled from the high, dark clouds that began to cut off the remaining sunlight.

The balloon bounced wildly and swooped lower and lower, back toward the hill below in a series of pendulum-like swings, jerking to the end of the remaining tether and back.

Justen glanced toward the approaching ground. His eyes burned, blood ran from his mouth, and his arms and legs were bruised, leaden. What could he do? How? His senses seemed almost paralyzed, and he struggled to raise his arms, but the impact with the ground and the blackness that rose from it crashed into his thoughts, scattering them.

Around him, the land shuddered. Smoke rose into the sky and fell, and white knives seemed to slash his flesh from his bones . . . while drums rolled across the heavens and each drum-roll pulverized his already smashed bones.

Thrap . . . thrap . . .

. . . thrap . . . thrappp . . .

The heavy tapping increased, and cold blows struck Justen across his face. Slowly, he tried to swallow, despite his dry mouth and swollen and bloody tongue. Finally, he opened his eyes.

He lay against the limp silksheen fabric of the balloon, and hail interspersed with fat snowflakes was falling. Already, the hillside was blanketed in a thin layer of white.

Dayala . . .

The fragile thread of order remained, but so weakly that Justen could barely sense it as he struggled into a sitting position. His left leg throbbed, and white flashes of pain pulsed through his skull. His back and ribs ached each time he took a breath.

As he rolled onto his side to try to stand, his trembling hands slipped on a pile of hailstones that had collected next to the wreckage of the balloon.

Half-propping himself on the crushed wicker of the balloon basket, wicker half-coated with ice, he levered himself upright and began to struggle along the hillside. He half-walked, half-dragged, his injured leg, lacking the order-strength with which to repair the damage.

After less than a dozen steps, Justen stopped, his breath ragged as he saw the young face on the ground, partly hidden by the snow. Dark splotches ran across one cheek, almost touching the sightless eyes.

Martan sprawled beside the heap of charcoal that had been the stolen mount, his left side blackened, a charred arm flung across his chest, the rough blackness of his burns merging with the smooth black of his tunic, the tunic of which he had been so proud.

Justen's eyes watered. Another loyal person, another death.

Another Yonada, another Dyessa, another Clerve, another Krytella, even another Iron Guard. *Do the bodies just gather around me?*

He took a deep breath and continued dragging himself toward the heap of darkened rocks that were barely visible under the white coating of snow and hail, fearful of what he might find, but chaos and order-blind from the twisting of nature itself, unable to sense whether or not his brother lived.

Gunnar lay on the side of the hill, half inside, half out, of the rock-and-armor-plate shelter. Justen scrambled to the still form, then took another deep breath as he saw his brother's chest rise and fall, rise and fall. For a moment, he paused, his breath still ragged, his ribs aching with each gasping intake of air.

Dark clouds, darker than any Justen had ever seen, rolled across the sky. Even as he watched, lines of lightning forked and smashed into the churned and melted valley that had been Fairhaven the Mighty.

Despite the thickening snow, Justen could see that the White tower had melted like a wax candle in the hot sun. No structure stood in what had been the White City. Lines of white radiated from where he stood, lines where the light-sword had boiled away all vegetation and left the soil down to white rock.

Between those lashes of the second sun lay only ashes, ashes and melted lumps of stone, some of them white, some of them brown, but most of them blackened as if mixed with dark ashes before solidifying.

The snowflakes that fell past Justen were gray, and the mixture of ashes and snow and hail was gray, and his soul was gray.

He looked down at Gunnar, at his brother's chest rising and falling, rising and falling. Then he began the arduous trek back to the *Demon*, lying just at the edge of the glassy slag that had been a hillside meadow. Gunnar and he needed food, and blankets, and rest.

If someone found them, so be it.

Craccckk!

A long, jagged line of white slashed from the dark clouds, branching and twisting downward into the melted stone and collapsed masonry that had been the White City. The blaze of the lightning through the snow reminded Justen of just how unlikely it was that anyone would be searching for them at any time soon.

He laughed once, harshly. As if there were anyone who had survived, save he and Gunnar – and perhaps a dozen White Wizards locked in order-chaos beneath the abattoir that had been a proud city.

Justen took a step . . . and rested . . . and stepped . . . and rested. But he kept moving. Gunnar needed warmth. He did not look at the charred heap that had been Martan. Nor at the charred and molten destruction that had been the jewel of Candar.

He put one foot forward, then the other.

Gunnar . . . Dayala . . .

Gunnar . . . Dayala . . .

Justen kept moving . . . moving . . .

152

The four druids stood before the ancient, watching the sand shift and boil, watching as in places the outlines of the coasts changed.

The youngest druid wept silently, wracked with soundless sobs. In time, another held her as the sands continued to shift and boil, until the sand table showed the rebalancing of Candar and Recluce.

'Fairhaven is no more,' announced the ancient. 'The second sun of the Angels has been sheathed.'

'But . . . the cost?' asked Syodra.

'There is always a cost. None have paid the price in generations, and a price deferred is always greater. Most of the towers in eastern Candar have been toppled. Rivers have changed their paths. Half of the engineers' city has been swept into the Eastern Ocean.'

'And the steam-chaos engines no longer work,' added Frysa.

'They failed to listen to the songs,' added the sole male. 'Or to their souls.'

'It will take much time for the reservoir of order to rise to its past level – if the Blacks choose to follow that course. As they will in time, for little in wisdom passes from one generation to the next.' The ancient nodded to the others and then toward the youngest. 'You, and he, have done well.'

'Why . . . ?' Dayala swallowed. 'He felt . . . feels so much of the pain.'

'That is why you are tied.'

'But how can he return here . . . after what he has done?'

'Child, he will return to you. Trust the Balance.'

'Trust the Balance?' Dayala laughed, and the laugh was hard and brittle.

153

Neither Justen nor Gunnar had spoken more than monosyllables since pulling themselves from beneath their blankets and brushing away the damp snow.

Justen drank cold juice and chewed the last fragments of crust between bites of hard yellow cheese. His leg remained tender, but the order-chaos balance he had created with Dayala's help had held, and the leg had begun to knit.

'What did you do to the last Whites – the ones you didn't

burn with that horrible light-knife?' Gunnar took the jug from Justen, not meeting his eyes, and swallowed some of the juice.

'They're . . . trapped in chaos, inside order . . . somewhere under Fairhaven.' Justen shuddered. *Death . . . had they deserved that? Perhaps. But does anyone deserve to be locked in chaos within a block of order?* He still recalled one face, the one with the slight scar on the forehead and the look of a suffering angel. He had no illusions that all White Wizards were evil or, especially considering himself, that all Blacks – or Grays – were good.

'They're alive . . . still?'

'In a way.'

'Could they escape?'

'I don't know. Not physically.' Justen shuddered again. 'I don't know. I don't think so. They might possess . . . an unwary soul.'

Gunnar shivered and drew the blanket around himself, seated on still another blanket insulating him from the patch of browned grass where they sat amid slagged and frozen stone. The Weather Wizard fixed his eyes on a pile of hail yet covered with snow, although the morning sun had already melted much of the unseasonal covering, leaving the ground a whitish gray-and-brown blotchwork. The weather mage's eyes did not turn to his younger brother. 'You folded order and chaos together. No one's ever done that, not both black and white together but separate. That was true gray magic.' But he still did not look at Justen.

'That was what I learned in Naclos.' Justen finished the bread he had been eating.

'I can barely touch the winds.' Gunnar finally turned toward his brother. 'What exactly did you do?'

'Destroyed about half of the order and chaos in the world, maybe more. That's why those last explosions were so violent.'

'Justen. You knew that's what would happen, didn't you?'

'Yes.'

'And you didn't tell me? I don't like being deceived, even for the best of reasons, even by my own brother.' Gunnar swallowed.

'But . . .' Justen stopped as he felt the anger, and the rejection, from Gunnar. Hadn't he made it clear?

He looked back across the valley to where the corpse of

Fairhaven lay melted under the partial blanket of snow, melted like a wax model under a hot sun – melted so quickly. Under the glasslike melted structures, under the covering of ash, under the ruins that had disintegrated so swiftly that pockets of chaos were trapped in heat-ordered rubble, how many innocents had died? Had it been fair? And yet, what else could have been done?

The people of Fairhaven had accepted the rule of chaos. Did that make it right? Justen shook his head. Who had been there to protest when Sarron had been shaken into rubble? Or Berlitos burned into ashes? Or the outskirts of Armat boiled alive?

But his mouth still tasted like ashes.

And how long would it be before the destruction was erased, before the white scars that slashed through the soil and into the bones of the earth were covered over? How long before the screams stopped echoing from the rocks and the melted buildings? How long before the trees and plants grew straight and true?

'Justen?' asked Gunnar harshly.

'I thought you knew . . .'

'None of us knew, really knew, dear brother.' Gunnar slowly stood. 'If the rest of the world looks anything like this, it will be a long winter, and then some. Creslin had nothing on you. Blood followed both of you, but at least he used a blade. Oh, I forgot. You did, too. The most violent blade in history.'

'I . . .' Justen did not finish the sentence. What could he really say? Gunnar was right.

'Not even the demons of light or the Angels could have done better. I must give you that, Justen.' Gunnar fumbled with the pack Justen had brought the night before. 'There are so many lost souls screaming that I cannot stay here any longer. Not for one instant.' He slung the pack on his shoulders. 'If there are any ships left afloat, I'll find one in Lydiar. Good-bye, Justen.'

Justen struggled to his feet, his left leg stiff and weak, but Gunnar was already marching downhill, his back straight, his anger visible with each determined step.

The Gray Wizard took a deep breath, looked across the hillside at the iron land engine that would never run again in his lifetime, if ever. He began to gather the extra food, his own pack, and a staff. Somewhere, he suspected, he could buy or find a horse.

Gunnar would need help, the damned fool. Not all the White

Wizards had been in Fairhaven, and those left were likely to be
more than a little angry at anyone from Recluce. He laughed
brittly, despite the stabbing in his ribs. A little angry?

Then again, almost anyone from Recluce was likely to be
more than a little upset with one Justen. And with more than
a little reason. He licked his dry lips, abruptly remembering a
clear song sung on a warm night in Sarronynn. Poor Clerve. All
he'd wanted to do was to watch a real battle.

And Martan – all he'd wanted was a real battle, and some
glory. Some glory!

Justen looked up at the place where Martan still lay, half-
covered with snow, and then at the crude shelter Gunnar had
used. At least it would make a decent cairn. He could make good
cairns – that he could. And light-chaos knives, and ordered black
iron arrows.

Justen set the pack aside and trudged toward Martan's body.
All he could give the young marine now was a decent burial.
That was all. His eyes burned.

Later . . . later, he would follow Gunnar.

When he reached the clear young face, the wide, sightless eyes,
he bent down and swung Martan into his arms and trudged
toward the cairn-to-be. To the north, sunlight glinted off the
shimmering melted stone and off the stained, blotchy snow, each
as cold as death.

154

As the mountain pony plodded along, followed by the mule
with the two iron-copper bars and the supplies from the land
car, Justen continued to search out Gunnar. Gunnar, like Justen,
had clearly found a mount, assuming that the signs Justen had
been following were Gunnar's and that Gunnar had indeed been
heading for Lydiar.

Burying Martan and gathering his few personal items for his

family had taken a while, not that Justen begrudged that poor repayment. But during that time, Gunnar had gained a solid head start.

The Gray Wizard studied the rain-drenched countryside. Whatever else he and Gunnar had done, they had definitely called rain. The hillside meadows were drenched, and small rivulets poured down across the stone road. The catch basins nearly overflowed.

For once, Justen was glad of the solid workmanship of the White Wizards' stone road. The dirt roads would be mud after nearly three days of rain. Justen snorted. In his own way, he had also brought rain, not that Gunnar or any of the Black mages could have approved of his techniques.

The fast-moving clouds were higher now than they had been in the morning, and since midday, no rain had fallen. A break in the clouds foretold the possibility of sunlight later on.

Justen had just read the kaystone indicating that Hrisbarg, the small town said to provide the metal for the Iron Guard, was less than a dozen kays eastward when the air began to tingle.

His eyes followed the feeling to a low hill ahead, almost astride the road. A small stone house graced the summit, but the tingling came from lower on the hillside. Gunnar, calling storms even with his diminished powers? And a sense of chaos?

Justen nudged the chestnut ahead.

When he turned the next wide corner, just past a temporary waterfall that arched down beside the road, he could see the coach with the four lancers, and the single horse lying in the road.

Gunnar stood behind a gray boulder, partway up a hillside steep enough and wet enough to discourage the lancers . . . at least for a while.

Hhssttt . . .

A modest firebolt flared past the Weather Wizard.

Hssssttt . . .

Justen looked ahead. The White Wizards clearly blocked any passage on the road to Lydiar, and retreating did not seem attractive at the moment, not for Gunnar at least.

Hhhssttt . . . A line of reddened white, blinding and ugly, flowed from the White Wizard. Justen slammed an order-shield around himself and the mule, closing his eyes as the barrage of white fire-rain cascaded over the shields, and as the damp pine tree behind him flared into flame and collapsed into dust. He dismounted awkwardly, his left leg slowing him, and half-stumbled, half-ran, toward the mule.

Now . . . he recalled, the reason for creating the Brotherhood of Engineers had been the fact that in a world with less order, chaos was stronger on a one-on-one basis.

'So much power . . .' Even as he spoke, Justen fumbled with the long bundle on the mule, finally unstrapping the poles, hoping that the two he had would be enough.

Hhhssttt . . . The dark-haired engineer felt his order-shield shiver under the assault. He hoped he was helping Gunnar!

After he lifted the first iron pole with the heavy copper center, and the second, he began to scramble up the hillside. He needed to get uphill and in front of Gunnar – if he could.

Hhhsssttt . . .

The shock of holding off the firebolt flung him onto the rocky ground, and he could feel a slash across his cheek even as he gathered his feet under him and struggled uphill.

'. . . two of the Black bastards . . .'

An arrow flew past him, then another, as he dodged through the waist-high brush.

A gust of wind swept across the hillside, and the next arrow went wide, perhaps because of the sudden wind, or perhaps because he fell forward when his boot caught on a root.

He stumbled on until he reached a point that was almost above the coach. He plunged one of the iron poles into the soft ground and staggered on.

Hhhssttt . . .

The jolt of once more holding back the firebolt flung him forward, and his right hand came away from the sharp rocks bloody.

He managed another dozen steps before he took the second iron pole and jammed it into the ground, throwing his senses into the iron in the rocks far below, struggling, panting, trying to open a corridor of order from the iron below to the two iron poles on the hilltop.

Another firebolt whistled past him.

He took a deep breath and dropped his shields. Then he raised his hands as if to challenge the White Wizards on the road below. He waited, ducking as another arrow passed his shoulder.

Hhhhssstttttt!

The sky buckled with the power, and the trees on the distant hills shook as though a mighty wind had bent them, while the ashes of the vegetation around Justen swirled across the hillside.

Justen forced himself to leave his feeble shield down, instead channeling that massive bolt of energy toward the iron and copper poles, toward the channel that linked the poles to the heavy order of cold iron deep within the earth.

A cold, black bolt of order, a lightning bolt of nothingness, of darkness, flashed back from the two iron posts, even from the granite stones of the house on the hilltop above, and down toward the coach, guided by the channel Justen had opened.

Without thinking, Justen closed his eyes and covered his face.

Aaaaeeeee . . . The pain of the mental scream froze Justen in place, but only for an instant, until the blast hurled him into the ashes – and back into darkness.

He tried to climb from the darkness, but his fingers and feet seemed immobile, unable to lift him clear.

'Easy . . . easy, you idiot.' Suddenly, Gunnar was beside him. Water dropped on his face – tears. Gunnar's tears.

'I'm all right,' he mumbled, trying to get the taste of ashes from his mouth as he slowly sat up. Even the air smelled like damp ashes. *Does the entire world smell as though it has been burned?*

Gunnar held him for a moment. 'Are you sure? You look like fish bait.'

For a while, Justen leaned against his brother, conscious that the ground was warm under him, unpleasantly so. Finally, he sat up and looked around. Overhead, the sky was the darkness of a late winter afternoon, and heavy drops of rain had begun to fall, raising steam from both the hilltop above – where only two melted granite posts remained of the house that had stood there – and from the road where the coach had stopped. All that remained on the road was a raised lump of stone and metal resembling an irregular drop of melted wax.

'This place feels like chaos,' mumbled Gunnar.

'That's because it is. There's a lot of order and chaos locked up wrong in the rocks here.' Justen spit out ashes and used his damp sleeve to blot the blood off the slash in his hand. 'We probably ought to get moving. It's not really good to stay here long.'

'Is it good for you to stay anywhere long?' Gunnar forced a laugh as he helped his younger brother stand up.

They half-stumbled back down the road and around the curve. The pony and the mule had retreated but they remained in sight.

Justen sighed, hoping the animals didn't keep walking back to the west. He wasn't up to chasing them. For a moment, he looked over his shoulder, taking in again the melted granite stones, stones that looked like candles whitened and seared by a glassblower's pipe. Of the two iron poles there was no sign at all. He shivered. *What sort of force is it that can vaporize iron, even with the lower levels of order and chaos in the world? With what sort of power did the Naclans provide me?*

Yet what else could he have done? The Council had had no intention of stopping the White Wizards, and neither did the Naclans, except for the one called Justen.

'We need to get those horses,' reminded Gunnar.

'I know.' Justen turned. 'I know. But one's a pony and one's a mule.'

'I'm glad you followed me.'

'So am I.'

They trudged toward the animals, and the rain fell, and the steam rose off the rocks.

155

Altara bowed to the Council.

'Might we have your report, Chief Engineer?'

'I have submitted a written report, counselors. If I might summarize . . .'

'Please do.' Claris nodded for the engineer to continue.

'Whatever the nature of the . . . disruption in Candar—'

'The destruction of Fairhaven, I believe?' asked Ryltar.

'I understand that the . . . disruption had that effect. That does not include the destruction that apparently occurred all over Candar, or the tidal wave that destroyed nearly a third of old Nylan. All of those were, I believe, side effects. Even the destruction of Fairhaven was not the primary intent. Or at least not the major impact.'

The three counselors exchanged glances and then looked at Turmin, who sat at one end of the table.

'Go ahead,' ordered Claris. 'What was the primary intent?'

'To reduce the amount of free chaos in the world.'

'A laudable goal,' suggested Ryltar with only the slightest edge to his voice, 'except that it clearly had the opposite effect. That doesn't include the cost to us. The rather considerable cost, I might suggest.'

'No,' corrected Altara. 'The disruption effectively destroyed the massed power of chaos developed by the Whites, and according to Magister Turmin—' Altara nodded to the Black mage '—there is no chaos-focus or concentration remaining.'

'You mean that the disruption reduced the power of both order *and* chaos?' asked Jenna.

'Exactly,' interposed Turmin. 'Young Justen did what was thought to be impossible. He somehow concentrated disordered light into ordered light and focused it on chaos.'

'He did this alone?'

'Yes,' said Altara.

'That part he did alone,' said Turmin nearly simultaneously.

'Engineer, what does this mean for the Mighty Ten?'

Altara took a deep breath. 'We *might* be able to disorder what order remains in the black iron in all the ships. If Turmin is correct, we could build three much, much smaller ships – after we rebuild the engineering hall. It has suffered a great deal lately.' Altara glanced at Ryltar. 'Such smaller ships would be almost as fast, but we could not armor them heavily, and they would have to use a single gun. They would be effective against most ships on the oceans.'

'How?' protested Ryltar. 'The Hamorians have ships two hundred cubits or more—'

'Not any longer. No high-pressure steam boiler will operate without black iron – not now, and only small ones at that.' Altara lowered her eyes for a moment. 'Justen has destroyed most of the concentrated order in the world. Most black iron is not so strong as when it was forged. Even steel cannot contain chaos forces as effectively as before.'

'We could build it back, couldn't we?' asked Ryltar. 'Our trade . . . our traders . . .'

'It took more than three centuries of the efforts of the Black Brotherhood of Engineers to get from Dorrin's first small ship to the Mighty Ten.'

'There is another question, I submit,' suggested Turmin.

The counselors looked to the end of the table.

'Two, really. First, can Recluce afford to make such an investment again, now that the world knows that such an investment can be destroyed? Second, will anyone want us to do so once it becomes known that our power was based on actually creating more and more chaos in Candar?'

Altara nodded slowly.

'I see your point,' responded Jenna. 'Could we afford to tax our trade so heavily when most merchants and shippers will be sorely pressed to rebuild or reconfigure their ships without more taxes? That doesn't include the cost of rebuilding most of Nylan.'

Ryltar swallowed.

'Do you have anything else to add, Chief Engineer?'

'We will build one small ship that will work under the current order-chaos balance. That is all we can do without additional funds, and we doubt that more funds will be forthcoming. Nor do we wish to exceed the limits suggested by Magister Turmin. Not when we know the consequences.' Altara rose and stepped back. 'By your leave?'

'You may go.' Claris nodded brusquely. 'You also, Magister Turmin . . . and the clerks as well.'

When the chamber was empty, Claris turned to Ryltar. 'Ryltar? Weren't you the one who knew that this . . . Justen . . . was order-mad?'

The wispy-haired counselor frowned, but nodded.

'And yet you said and did nothing?' added Claris. 'And now
he has apparently decided to stay in Candar, where he canno
be touched?'

'We do not know that. And I did express some concern, you
will recall,' protested Ryltar.

'It does not matter,' pointed out Jenna. 'If he is that powerful
how could we touch him?'

'The way you acted let him destroy our warships and our
merchant fleet,' pursued Claris. 'Every ship berthed in Nylan
was either swept away or destroyed – as were those in Lydiar
Renklaar, and who knows how many other ports.'

'I did protest. And my office and warehouse were totally
destroyed.'

'Ryltar, most of your wealth is stored in Hamor, and tha
was where most of your ships are. So convenient.' Claris's eyes
were hard.

Jenna grinned, an expression less of glee than malice. 'Of al
of us, you had the most knowledge, and yet you kept asking
what we could do.'

'You seemed to support him.' Ryltar wiped his forehead. 'You
didn't listen to me.'

'Support him? If you, or anyone, were to review the records
you would see that both Jenna and I merely stated that we could
not act without knowledge. You had that knowledge, and you
kept it from the Council. Without the knowledge you had, your
protests were meaningless, and you hid that knowledge so tha
you alone would profit.'

'What are you getting at?'

'Your resignation, for the good of Recluce.'

'What?'

'It is likely to come out shortly that you kept this knowledge
from the Council – thereby preventing us from acting in a
timely fashion – in hopes of profiting from the information
you alone held,' suggested Claris calmly. 'You certainly would
have profited.'

'And,' added Jenna, 'you also ordered your ships out of Nylan
but did not tell Hoslid and the others of your actions. They los
ships. You lost only engines.'

Ryltar looked from one woman to the other. 'You're both
mad. You can't do this.'

'Mad?' Jenna laughed softly. 'No. And we can do this. In fact, unless you leave Recluce quickly, Ryltar, a number of very angry traders are going to be gathering at your door, and I don't think your excuses will carry much water.'

'Ryltar,' added Claris, 'being a counselor requires acting for the good of all Recluce. All too often, you found reasons why we should not act. Those reasons always benefited you. This time, we will follow your example and do nothing, except to tell the people what has happened.'

Ryltar wiped his forehead again.

'If you resign now,' suggested Jenna brightly, 'it might be a day or so before the official announcement is made. I suspect that with the powers of the White Wizards severely reduced, there might even be some opportunities in places like Sarronnyn and Suthya, where the Whites had not really consolidated their hold. You might find them more . . . congenial.'

Ryltar swallowed and looked from one set of bright eyes to the other. Finally, he swallowed again and reached for the pen before him.

156

Justen waited on the beach nearly a kay south of the main piers of Lydiar, watching the midday sun – the first in nearly an eight-day – play on the waters of the Great Bay.

Gunnar walked down from the road. 'The smugglers will take me into Land's End. They say that half of the port at Nylan is gone, washed out by the sea.' He shook his head. 'You don't do things by halves, Brother.'

'Some things can't be done partway.' Justen smiled sadly.

'You still believe that this is all a part of the Legend? Is the Legend even true?'

'Oh, the Legend's true enough. Remember, I did meet an Angel.'

'I think you overlooked mentioning that.'

'I have overlooked a few things,' admitted Justen. 'Still . . in the purest sense, the Naclans believe that everything is connected to everything else. That's why there are almost no edged implements of any sort in Naclos. Separation is a denial of reality, and even when necessary, it occasions pain. Order in the extreme is sterility and death, while chaos in the extreme is fire, anarchy, disruption . . . and death. In short,' Justen said glancing back at the calm waters of the bay, 'everyone was wrong, including me. And that's the reason for that obscure quote from that antique healer – Lydya, I think, was her name She told the Marshall of Westwind – she was Creslin's mother you'll recall—'

'I recall. Could you come to the point before my ship sails without me?'

'It won't. They need your coins. You also need to lighten up Gunnar. If you don't, I'll come back to Recluce. I might anyway In any case, I was going to tell you the obscure quote, the one about Dylyss and Ryessa creating the greatest good and the greatest evil Candar ever knew. No one really understood that. It wasn't the triumph of Fairhaven and Recluce, but the idea that order and chaos could be separated. It was good because it finally gave a voice to the need for order, but evil because it separated the two – and the Naclans were right. Look at all the pain that separation caused.'

'I think you helped there.'

Justen's eyes and senses finally found what he was seeking. He darted along the sand and reached under a bush. He picked up the moss-colored turtle and carried it back to Gunnar.

'Let it go . . .' suggested Gunnar.

'I will – in a moment.' Justen carried the turtle, withdrawn into its shell, to the rock Gunnar leaned against.

'Watch what I'm doing. Not with your eyes, but with your senses.'

'Is this some trick, younger brother?'

'Of sorts.' Justen forced a wry grin, even though his words were literally true. 'Just watch.' He cleared his mind of stray thoughts and began to adjust the flow of order around the small green turtle, trying to soothe the creature as he did so. 'Easy, little one . . . easy. Justen's not going to hurt you.'

Gunnar's eyes widened. 'How . . .'

'Just feel it . : .'

Gunnar continued to watch, his eyes wide.

'Do you have the pattern?'

'I think . . . yes . . .'

'Good.' Justen set the turtle on the sand, and after some time, its head and legs appeared and it scuttled into the bay.

'Wait a moment. Is that wise? Didn't you just make that turtle immortal?'

'Nothing's wise.' Justen laughed. 'Not in the long run, anyway. Besides, just because its system is ordered without chaos, that doesn't make it immortal. A ray or a shark could eat it before lunch. It's easier with water creatures like turtles, though.'

'Why did you show me that?'

Justen shrugged. 'You could do it to yourself, you know. Then you'd never grow old. You could still get killed, but your body wouldn't fall apart.'

'Where did you learn that?'

Justen's eyes clouded for a moment, recalling the glade, the stream, Dayala. He swallowed. 'In Naclos. From the druids.'

Gunnar looked out at the sea. 'It's no trick.'

'No . . . it's a curse, and it's my curse on you, older brother, my curse becuse I love you.' Justen turned and looked up into Gunnar's eyes. 'You won't be able to forget the skill, and you won't dare to let anyone know, or they'll demand you do it to everyone, or they'll exile you – if you're lucky. But it's true order. The true balance of order and chaos.'

Gunnar shivered. 'I could refuse to use it.'

Justen laughed. 'Perhaps you will, at least until your bones start to creak or your teeth start rotting. Toothaches are very painful.' He shrugged. 'Then you can reflect on the pain, knowing that you could cure it.' A dark ale would have helped, but instead, he licked his lips. His tongue still felt swollen.

Gunnar swallowed. 'And if I use this . . . skill . . . then in a few years, I'll have to leave Recluce.'

'Not necessarily. What if you – the great Gunnar – point out that living an orderly life prolongs life and health, and thus you prolong life for a few others.' Justen grinned. 'And by the way, dealing with chaos unravels the effect rather quickly.'

'How quickly?'

'Unless you rebuild the order image of your body within a few days, death is not far away. Something about the body knowing how old it really is.'

'You clearly have something in mind, dearest younger brother.'

'Of course.' Justen smiled faintly. 'This time, I thought it out beforehand. We destroyed a good chunk of the massed order and chaos. One of the problems was that no one understood that excessively massed order is just as bad as chaos, maybe worse. You are going to be the advocate of the Balance, including restoring a lot of the old customs that worked, like exile, and the use of herbs before applying order, and the responsibility of crafters for the orderliness of their apprentices . . .'

'Why would I do this for you?' snorted Gunnar.

'You won't. You'll do it for you. It's the only way you can stay on Recluce. Who knows? You might even last for a century or two if you work it right.'

'Then . . . no one who exhibits chaos tendencies will ever stay on Recluce again, no matter who,' declared Gunnar. 'That ought to include you, by rights.'

'What about your own child?' asked Justen, a glint in his eyes.

'I don't have one.'

'You will. What then? What if he questions? Or she? What if he or she is intrigued with the power of chaos, like Ryltar was? Will you send him or her to the chaos-tinged mess that we've made of Candar?'

'Yes.'

'Best you remember that, Brother, in the centuries that come.'

'Centuries?'

'Centuries,' confirmed Justen. 'I am frozen in order, like it or not, dear older brother, and you'll be the same, rather than rot from old age.'

'Sometimes, Justen, you're insufferable.' Gunnar fingered his pack.

'No, I'm just Gray. Very Gray.'

'And you'll follow me to look over my shoulder all the time? No thank you.'

'I'm staying here.'

'To be with your druid lady?'

'That . . . and to just wander around, fiddling enough to keep some sort of balance between chaos and order.' Justen wallowed. **Dayala, will I always be torn between repairing what I did . . . and you?**

'But . . . why?'

'Let's just say that I have to.' Justen grinned. 'Just like you have to shape up Recluce.'

'The druids?'

Justen walked down to where the water of the bay lapped up to the sand, letting his senses follow a struggling turtle seaward. 'I am one, in a way.' He turned. 'You need to catch a ship.'

'And you?'

'I have a long ride ahead. But there's time.'

The two brothers hugged a last time. Then one walked northward toward a black-hulled ship. The other climbed onto a mountain pony and rode southwest.

157

The silver-haired and green-eyed druid scooped the soil away and eased the black acorn into the hole, then replaced the soil.

She stood, smiled, and looked eastward, at the house behind her that would be grown larger by the time Justen arrived from the east. She, and he, would have time.

THE DEATH OF CHAOS

L.E. Modesitt, Jr.

The story of Lerris continues ...

Lerris has settled down as a carpenter in Kyphros, where his wife, Krystal, is the sub-commander of the autarch's military forces. His fellow apprentice from Recluce, Tamra, now travels with the Gray Wizard Justen.

But the world is in turmoil, and not only from friction between the island of Recluce and the continent of Candar. For now the distant Empire of Hamor has sent invading forces across the ocean, as they have twice in the historic past – and this time they mean to conquer the world. Gradually, but ever more deeply, Lerris is drawn back into action and forced to exercise and strengthen his magical powers to become the greatest wizard of all time – or see his world destroyed.

The Death of Chaos is an enthralling addition to the saga of Recluce.

THE SOPRANO
SORCERESS

Book One of The Spellsong Cycle

L. E. Modesitt, Jr.

Anna Marshall is a singer and music instructor at Iowa
State University who wishes she could be somewhere
else. The world in which she finds herself, however, is
not what she had in mind.

For on Erde, Anna Marshall is not just a professional
singer: on Erde, her ability makes her a powerful
sorceress. And this means that she immediately
becomes a target, not only of the political factions, who
fear the unknown, but also of the men of Erde, who
fear a woman with the power she possesses. Anna must
learn enough magic – and enough about Erde – to
protect herself before it's too late.

The Soprano Sorceress begins an epic new tale of sorcery,
song and political intrigue by one of the most exciting
storytellers in the fantasy genre.

THE BAKER'S BOY

The Book of Words: Volume I

J. V. Jones

The Book of Words is a thrilling new fantasy adventure
series, where the lethal conspiracies and deadly intrigues
of the mighty can be countered only by the power
of magic.

At vast Castle Harvell, where King Lesketh lies dying,
two fates collide. In her regal suite, young Melliandra,
the daughter of an influential lord, rebels against her
forced betrothal to the sinister Prince Kylock. In the
kitchens, an apprentice named Jack is terrified by
his sudden, uncontrolled power to work miracles.
Together they flee the castle, stalked by a sorcerer who
has connived for decades to control the crown,
committing supernatural murder to advance
his schemes.

Meanwhile, a young knight begins a quest, leaving
behind his home and family to seek out the treacherous
Isle of Larn, where lies a clue to his desperate search
for the truth.

And a wondrous epic of darkness and beauty begins.

'A deliciously intricate tale'
Katherine Kurtz

THE WHEEL OF TIME

Robert Jordan

The Wheel of Time turns and Ages come and go, leaving memories that become legend. Legend fades to myth, and even myth is long forgotten when the Age that gave it birth returns again. In the Third Age, an Age of Prophecy, the World and Time themselves hang in the balance. What was, what will be, and what is, may yet fall under the shadow.

THE WHEEL OF TIME SERIES

All available from Orbit

'With the Wheel of Time, Jordan has come to dominate the world Tolkien began to reveal'
The New York Times

'Epic in every sense'
Sunday Times

Orbit titles available by post:

☐ The Magic of Recluce	L. E. Modesitt, Jr.	£6.9
☐ The Towers of the Sunset	L. E. Modesitt, Jr.	£7.9
☐ The Magic Engineer	L. E. Modesitt, Jr.	£7.9
☐ The Death of Chaos	L. E. Modesitt, Jr.	£7.9
☐ Fall of Angels	L. E. Modesitt, Jr.	£7.9
☐ The Chaos Balance	L. E. Modesitt, Jr.	£7.9
☐ The White Order	L. E. Modesitt, Jr.	£7.9
☐ Colours of Chaos	L. E. Modesitt, Jr.	£7.9
☐ Magi'i of Cyador	L. E. Modesitt, Jr.	£7.9
☑ Scion of Cyador	L. E. Modesitt, Jr.	£7.9
☐ The Soprano Sorceress	L. E. Modesitt, Jr.	£6.9
☐ The Eye of the World	Robert Jordan	£6.9
☐ The Baker's Boy	J. V. Jones	£6.9

*The prices shown above are correct at time of going to press. However, the publishers reserve th
right to increase prices on covers from those previously advertised without prior notice.*

orbit

ORBIT BOOKS
Cash Sales Department, P.O. Box 11, Falmouth, Cornwall, TR10 9EN
Tel: +44 (0) 1326 569777, Fax: +44 (0) 1326 569555
Email: books@barni.avel.co.uk.

POST AND PACKING:
Payments can be made as follows: cheque, postal order (payable to Orbit Books)
or by credit cards. Do not send cash or currency.
U.K. Orders under £10   £1.50
U.K. Orders over £10   **FREE OF CHARGE**
E.E.C. & Overseas   25% of order value

Name (Block Letters) _____

Address _____

Post/zip code: _____

☐ Please keep me in touch with future Orbit publications

☐ I enclose my remittance £_____

☐ I wish to pay by Visa/Access/Mastercard/Eurocard

Card Expiry Date
